Exit Unicorns

Also by Cindy Brandner

Mermaid in a Bowl of Tears

Flights of Angels

Exit Unicorns

by

Cindy Brandner

Starry Night Press

ISBN-13: 978-0-9783570-2-3

This book is printed on acid free paper

Cover design by Stevie Blaue

This is a work of fiction. Names, characters, places, and incidents either are products
of the author's imagination or are used fictitiously. Any resemblance to actual
persons, living or dead, events or locales is entirely coincidental.

Printed and bound in the USA

Published in Canada by
Starry Night Press

Second Edition

Rev. 04/21/2012

For my Auntie Marlene

Contents

It's the smell of burning that I remember most clearly from that autumn. And the burning, the burning smelled like revolution.

I look back in age, in a stillness that grips and stultifies and think I saw even then shape of things to come. The design in the web that Fate in all her knowing wove.

I forget, in those months, at the end of a decade that became an emblem for change, that in the air about us there swirled a thousand possibilities attached to a million more.

Faith can move mountains they say, but they never tell you what price such faith can exact.

I believe, as perhaps I must, that there was only ever the one road to bring me to where I am today. I believe it and think that makes it true. But does it?

Part One

The Door Unlatched

Chapter One
The Pixillated Mick

Belfast, April 1968

A MOON, MILK-WHITE AS A DOVE'S TAIL, newly round as fresh churned butter, rose skimmingly on a furred black bed. This Jamie Kirkpatrick observed through eyes attached too dearly to a brain soaked and swollen from three days worth of scotch.

He was dead. Of this much he was certain. He was dead and someone was singing 'Ave Maria' in a tender voice that understood the childlike yearning of the music. Very nice, Jamie thought, so there was to be angels singing in heaven. A relief that, trite perhaps, but a relief nonetheless. He wasn't in hell and he supposed that was a good thing. He reconsidered his geography a moment later as the first orchestral wave of pain made its way through the layers of unconsciousness. Perhaps, he thought wincing, perhaps hell *was* singing angels.

An angel spoke. "The boy is drunk," it said.

An English angel? This *must* be Irish hell.

"If we don't bring him around soon he'll miss the funeral," said a rather more peevish tone.

Funeral? So he hadn't even been buried yet and that made this purgatory. He mentally demoted the speakers from cherubim and seraphim to outcast rebel angels. Neither heaven nor hell, *not* such a relief that.

There was a sound like a thousand nails on a chalkboard and then sunlight, turbo-charged, landed on his eyelids with a thump. Long filaments of pain plucked at blind nerves, the string section beginning its warm-up.

Powers of speech in abeyance, James Stuart Kirkpatrick the Third and it would seem, Final, settled for a weak wiggle of the fingers. No one noticed.

"Christ," said the first voice, "it smells like a three day old corpse in here, didn't anyone notice he was drinking?"

There was a short silence, embarrassed in its depth that spoke eloquently of how inappropriate the remark had been.

"Damned Irish," continued the first angel imperiously (definitely British origin that one) unimpeded by its faux-pas, "can't hold their liquor worth a fig."

"Let he," intoned a sepulchral voice that sounded, to Jamie, remarkably like his own, "who is lily-white gild the first stone, the corpse," there was a vinegary laugh that seemed to swoop about his face, "is not deaf."

God spoke then, voice of dry authority, words falling with spherical precision, like one ice cube upon the next, "Cast, dear boy is, I believe, the word you are looking for."

A sound of scythes, sparkling with sun, cutting through future words and thought, sliced through the room.

"You two may leave. I will get his Lordship up." The scurrying feet of dismissed angels and then a sigh, cleaving inebriation neatly down the middle and dropping it to either side of the bed.

"Can you open your eyes, Jamie?"

Jamie, in some instinctual wisdom, attempted one eye at a time. The left eye upon opening found the belt of Orion glittering above it, *Al Nilam, Al Nitak* and the small, tipping from the sky *Mintaka*—champagne gold, palest blue and delicate lichen green. He closed the eye and tried the right, above it hovered some fuzzy, wee being that was lit like milk over opals. His soul perhaps? He closed his eye again.

"I think not," he said through a vocal box that felt as though it were culturing penicillin.

"Damned barbaric Saxon custom, being sober at one's father's funeral. Nevertheless it is customary to be able to walk upright into the service, so up we go dear boy."

A whoosh of nausea, so vast and varied in its array that Jamie thought he might pass out from it (were he not already dead) swept over him.

"There you're sitting up and though you don't look very pretty, it is progress. Now tell me your name."

"James Stuart Kirkpatrick," Jamie croaked.

"Good and now mine," the voice coaxed.

"God," Jamie replied with certitude.

"My *name*, I said," the tone was quickly becoming exasperated, so much, Jamie thought, for eternal patience.

"Jehovah, Yahweh, Elohim," Jamie ventured meekly, hearing in the distance the firm click of pearly gates shutting.

"Well I suppose I've been called worse," the voice muttered, "alright, different tactic then, recite the Arabic alphabet to me."

God was Muslim. There were going to be an awful lot of irate Catholics in purgatory, he wouldn't be lonely at any rate.

He dutifully recited the alphabet; air swirling in bruising eddies about his fractured nerves. Rote memory failed and nausea prevailed just as he reached *eliph* and he halted abruptly to throw up in a champagne bucket that had been placed handily beneath his chin.

"Men," said a voice like honey melting through dark rum, "never know how to handle these things properly." Lutes of memory piped, drums of pain began their first thumping chorus in his head and Jamie began to consider that he might be really rather undead. There was death— yes—but not his own.

"I'll put him in the shower," the honeyed voice continued, "and you go down to the kitchen and see if you can't get hot coffee, a pint of scotch and some aspirin." Muslim or not, God was being bossed rather badly.

In no condition to protest, Jamie found himself submitting to hands whose ministrations were, if not tender, at least appealing. A shower of freezing cold water followed by hot then cold again. This pattern, repeated until he howled in protest, had its desired effect and he could, when opening his eyes, see the owner of the honey rum voice. There was a rather limited amount of sympathy in her face so he closed his eyes again.

Swirling champagne golds, palest fainting blues, mossy lichen greens settled and became the colors of his father's suite, the moon, no longer milk white, a gilded mirror. Moon, stars, God and angels fled in the wake of memory.

Like silk, like wine, like taffy or molten lead, depending on your perspective, Jamie was alternately poured, pushed and molded into an oyster gray suit. Washed, pomaded, buffed, gilded and spit forth from the half-shell like an errant pearl.

Coffee, blisteringly fragrant, was shoved under his nose, three white aspirin staring up at him like mutely blind mice.

"Velvet for the hammer blows," said Miss Honey Rum, her voice softened by several shades of grief.

"What's the scotch for?" he asked, nodding toward the bottle of amber-bitten poison she'd requested.

"Courage," she grimly uncapped the scotch, poured a generous three fingers into a glass and swallowed it smoothly down, "my own that is."

"Thanks Jessica," he said quietly, smiling at the one female of his own age he'd managed to keep as friend and nothing more nor less, since childhood. The enormity of the day began to press down rather heavily on his newly found sobriety. "How late am I?"

"No so very late," she said kindly, "but I thought you might like to know that President de Valera is waiting downstairs to make his condolences to you."

"What?" Jamie nearly choked on the mouthful of boiling coffee he'd been gingerly nudging towards his throat. Definitely undead.

"What indeed," God, in the form of his old Oxford literature professor and dearest friend, Jonathan Wexler, re-entered the room, a pearly gray overcoat draped over his arm. "His granddaughter Sile is with him and they'd like a minute of your time as he's not really well enough to attend the service."

Jamie rose carefully, giving his equilibrium time to sort out the dimensions of floor and ceiling.

"How long has he been waiting?" he asked, wanting to plug his ears and avoid the answer.

Jessica, fair and restrained in a black dress, consulted her watch. "About twenty minutes, which is—"

"About nineteen and a half minutes longer than he's used to waiting," John interjected, "so I propose we get downstairs."

Jamie nodded, numb and wordless. On the way down the stairs, he contemplated several methods of apology for his inebriated tardiness and rejected them all as inferior to merely falling facedown on the carpet and groveling at the man's feet. Which, when faced, in his father's study, with the man in the flesh, seemed quite inadequate as well.

Eamon de Valera, the stuff of Irish political legend, 'The Long Fellow', the man who had achieved mythic proportions akin to those of Old Testament prophets, sat, frail and sightless, in the study's harmonies of garnet and mahogany, a cup of tea balanced severely on his knee. The man who was Irish history for nearly all of the twentieth century, looked directly with blind eyes into Jamie's own and said, "Son, I am very sorry for your loss, your father was a fine man. He will be missed by many."

Sile de Valera composed and graceful in brown tweed, rose and shook Jamie's hand, "Forgive us for intruding here today but Grandfather was," she smiled ruefully, "adamant about making his condolences in person."

Jamie smiled, "Please don't apologize. I'm honored to have both of you in my home. It's I who should apologize for making you wait; I was only just informed—"

One long-fingered hand, the hand that had been fitted to the glove of its country, rose and put a halt to his words.

"No matter young man, no matter. Sit down will you? It makes me nervous when someone hovers above my head."

Jamie sat.

What followed was, in the light of Jamie's rather dazed and bemused recollection, a spot of warmth in a very black day. There were recollections of his father, a tangential discussion on the state of Irish literature in this year of 1968 and a dissection of the finer points of Anglo-Irish affairs. The entire episode, he would see in retrospect, had been designed to lift him up and away from his grief for a small space.

It was likely the only thing that got him through the rest of the day with any modicum of dignity. A funeral at best is a dismal affair, an Irish Catholic funeral, replete with incense, Latin intonations and the flutter and flurry of purple robes, was in terms of misery, at the apex of that particular quality.

At the graveside, things began to slide from bad to worse however. The omnipresent Irish rain had begun to fall and it seemed God was either spectacularly absent or possessed of a maudlin sense of humor.

Jamie knelt, kissed the polished mahogany of his father's coffin, felt the white-waxen scent of roses fill his senses and knew himself suddenly to be alone, without a guard between himself and his own mortality. He felt the fine mist of rain on his cheek and heard as though through a muffling veil one of the plump purple-robed pigeons of Christ mutter that a man who'd broken so openly with the church and whose death was at best questionable, ought not, perhaps, to have had such a sendoff.

Jamie, still kneeling, asked, quite politely all things considered, how many years one got in purgatory for the murder of a prince of the church?

It all looked likely to erupt into a less than reverent scene when a sudden silence descended and the empurpled pigeons scuttled to the far end of the grave. Turning his head, Jamie saw the long, tall figure that had so recently graced his father's study, stop just short of the grave, cane hitting the ground with a thump that reverberated under the feet of all assembled. Proud and rare as a blue heron, Eamon de Valera smiled at him quite mildly and said gently, "I believe your daddy was an admirer of John Donne, was he not?"

"He was at that," Jamie replied, suppressing an unseemly grin.

"Well then," said the backbone of the nation and began, without preamble, to recite:

> *Death be not proud, though some have called thee,*
> *Mighty and dreadful, for thou art not so;*

Moments later when he reached:

> *One short sleep past, we wake eternally,*
> *And death shall be no more: Death, thou wilt die!*

There was not a dry eye to be found. He stood beside Jamie like a stalwart relation as the mourners filed past, nodding and murmuring a word or two to their stunned and awed babble. When the representatives of God, faces plummier than their attire, made their way past, these men to whom all knees bent and all voices lowered, to whom reverence was mere sugar in the tea, to them he inclined his head slightly and said 'Gentlemen,' in a freezingly quiet voice.

"Thank you again," Jamie said to him later as the old man, leaning wearily on his cane, prepared to leave. "I can't tell you how much it would have meant to my father that you came here today."

"I came to bring you this," hands whose strength was still formidable grasped his own, hands that had bent and molded a nation for better or for worse for the greater part of one hundred years. Something small and compact was palmed into Jamie's grasp, "your father gave this to me, my wife Sinead and I enjoyed it immensely." Jamie gazed at the thin book resting in his hands and tears clouded his vision for the first time that day. When he looked up again there was a small smile on the face of the old man, "Your Daddy was very proud of you boy, don't disappoint him."

And then, without pomp or ceremony, the man who had inspired every human emotion in great quantities within the Irish, the man who'd been worshipped, scorned, deified and trampled into the mud and then risen to glory again, was gone. Jamie was never to see him again. But inside the defiantly slim book he held, was a loose sheaf of paper covered in a trembling, though still masterful pen. It was the opening of John Donne's *'Biathanatos'*. 'A Treatise on the Lawfulness of Suicide,' was the subheading and it was then Jamie realized how well the man had known his father and how far his grace had extended this day.

THE REST OF THE DAY QUICKLY LOST ANY SEMBLANCE OF DIGNITY. It might actually, Jamie thought grimly, be qualified as farce.

Upon returning to the house, 'Kirkpatrick's Folly,' as it was known in less polite quarters, there was heard a sound so unearthly and unholy that Jessica, not known for cowardice, refused to go in until John checked things over.

John was back only moments later, "Some misguided fool has gone and hired a professional keener if you can believe it. I've dispatched them," he said, "and paid them for their pains," he added in response to Jamie's enquiring look.

Later, around a lavish table of food laid for the wake, there was a narrowly averted international incident between a former French mistress of his father's and a not so former Yugoslavian one.

It was nine o'clock in the evening as the last of the crowd left, some still crying, others, having met hours earlier with the bottom of a bottle, hovering between recollecting every minute of their acquaintanceship with Jamie's father and passing out cold in the driveway. Jamie's primary emotion was relief.

He retired then, to his father's study, needing desperately the comfort of books, well-worn carpets and chairs and the last lingering scent of his father—pipe tobacco, dusty pages and the sharp overnote of lime from his aftershave. For Jamie it was the smell of comfort.

John, no longer looking nor sounding like a plausible God, Muslim or otherwise, sank into the vast reaches of an old Victorian armchair. Jessica, long American legs tucked up demurely sat on a velvet-covered loveseat. Both accepted, with sighs of exhaustion, the glasses of Connemara Mist he offered them. It was his own brand, made by his family for over three hundred years and was the beverage of choice for rich drunks the world over.

Through the south and west-facing windows, the evening sun poured flame. Jessica's slippery apricot hair turned red as rubies and John's neatly trimmed iron-grey coif seemed streaked with blood. They could see all of Belfast spread out below them, colored in the waning light in shades of brick and brimstone, of lavender and mint. Lights twinkled like jewels thrown from the hand of a careless sultan. And they perched above, minareted and mosqued, corbelled and fluted, blown-gold and husked against a cream-clotted sky. The study, sugar spun of iron and glass, sat at the far end of the house resembling nothing so much as a wrought-iron Victorian birdcage, safe from the vagaries of wind and rain, open to sky and light, to the moon and stars, though not, perhaps, to God.

They drank their first drink in comfortable silence, all tired and without the fortitude required for speech. All having been said, all having been done, Jamie thought he would quite like to redrink himself into a stupor.

Jamie had been born in this house on a cold, wet, windy Ides of March night. A snake had moved in the next day, the first snake, it was reputed, to be seen in Ireland since St. Patrick had banished them all in the Dark Ages. 'Cursed by God or blessed by the devil, depending on how you look at it,' had been his grandmother's unhelpful summation some months later when all manner of wildlife had taken up residence in the House of Kirkpatrick. Feathered and furred things, that twittered, hummed and crept between struts of plaster and marble at night. A nest of squirrels, grey and plump, that settled in the baby's wardrobe, a fawn that dropped grass and bluebells into his pram one sunny afternoon. It spooked the nanny, though to credit her, she didn't resign until the butterflies came. It was a hot, humid August afternoon and she'd gone to check on Jamie, having put him down for a nap some two hours earlier. Upon looking into the crib, she found a dozen butterflies, iridescent dust swirling in the air as the wings rose and fell with the deep rhythms of infant sleep. There, resting on his back in all the breathing colors of orange and blue, silver and green, purple and red. 'As if the lot of them were hypnotized,' she later told the sympathetic housekeeper. Nannies came and went, but the animals stayed, including the five-foot long coal black snake, which turned out to have milky-white sightless eyes.

Things began to grow that shouldn't have, wild things untended by the hand of man, clumps of blue forget-me-nots between the cracks in the house's masonry, meandering trails of buttercups across the immaculate green lawns, a white lilac tree that appeared outside his window that first spring and grew to a stunning twelve feet by the next spring. Pouring its blossoms with excess and abandon into his room where they rolled across the carpet like pearls toward an emperor.

Cursed by God or blessed by the devil? Who could say? Even his father, who could be quite prosaic when he chose to be, could not quite explain his son. How they'd lost him one terrible night when he was four and found him in the morning asleep and unharmed between the hooves of an unbroken horse. How a doe, two springs old perhaps, had followed him all one summer like an infatuated girl and how when they'd sent him away to school that year, sent him away from the animals and the ocean, she'd nearly died from it.

Away from the ocean, for they thought it would surely kill him, drawn as he was to it. In times of sorrow, he shot like an arrow, true and straight, to the water. He could manage a sailboat alone on the rough Atlantic seas by the time he was ten. And it was always alone that he wanted to sail. 'Not sad but not happy either, just less empty' he'd replied to his father's question of 'why?' His father had left it alone after that and Jamie continued, in sorrow and joy, to flee to the water's welcoming arms.

It was, on this night of his father's funeral, all he wanted. The forgiveness of water. Either cursed by God or blessed by the devil, it no longer mattered as the pain was the same.

He looked fondly into the faces of his two oldest and dearest friends and wished, desperately, that he was alone.

The doorbell rang as John, ignoring a stern look from Jessica, refilled their glasses.

Maggie, who was cook and counsel to the house of Kirkpatrick, poked her head in the door a moment later, "Sorry to disturb ye Jamie but there's a pack of gypsies at the backdoor says ye'll know they've only come to pay their respects." Maggie quirked her eyebrows as if she thought this last was of dubious likelihood.

"Aye, thank you Maggie, I'll deal with it," Jamie said, wearily rubbing the vertical crease between his eyebrows.

"Jamie, do you really think—" John began but ceased abruptly at the black look he received. Tinkers had always been welcome on Kirkpatrick land and given Kirkpatrick hospitality without stint. It had been so since time immemorial and if Jamie's look was anything to judge by, things weren't about to change now.

Kirkpatrick's Folly, known as such for its hodgepodge of Victorian, Georgian and Edwardian stylings, (the result of a disagreement between the husband and wife who'd built it) sat above Belfast like an albatross above a hot and shimmering sea. Long, narrow Georgian windows looked out over the city of steel and blood, a city built on ships and all they could carry. In the back of the house, the windows were Victorian octagons, half-moons, small wavy glassed portholes that looked over broad green lawns, lush gardens and the stone walkways that graced the last twenty acres left of what had originally been an estate of estimable size. It was, however, still large enough to take in a travel weary party of gypsies for a day or two. It was this Jamie intended to say before returning to his friends and his bottle of whiskey.

He was struck speechless however by the size of the group standing in utter quiet and stillness in his front garden. Three hundred Tinkers, Ireland's gypsies, stood, hats off, heads inclined, caravans parked in a sedate line down the curving length of the drive. The silence was so absolute, so heavy, that Jamie thought he might buckle under the sheer weight and expectation of it. Salvation came in a throaty voice; a voice filled with vodka and cigarettes, a voice that rumbled up warmly, a Russian wind from his childhood.

"Jemmy, my little boy, my baby," arms enfolded him; scent like black cinnamon on gardenias enveloped him.

"Yevgena," he said in relief, in gratitude. "You came."

Black eyes, like Adriatic plums, Levantine in their seduction, met the green of his own. "Of course I came, where else would I be but with you today? I am sorry to be late, it is not so easy being unofficial diplomat to this bunch," she indicated the crowd, still silent and watchful, arrayed behind her. "But I ask a friend to come in my absence. I think perhaps," Adriatic plums sparkled, "he was an appropriate substitute."

Jamie shook his head, a smile pricking at the corners of his mouth. "I'm not even going to ask how you know him."

Yevgena Vasiliovich, high queen to the gypsies, mother to every misfit and outcast in the world's population, representative of her people in the United Nations and still, at sixty-four, looking like a courtesan from the court of Ivan the Terrible, shook her head. Then smiled the slow smile that had seduced heads of state in boardrooms and, it was rumored, bedrooms as well.

"I wouldn't tell you anyway, even if you are the prettiest, most charming boy in the world. Now are we going to stand out here all night or are you going to let me in?"

Jamie nodded and turning back to the people, some of Europe's most poverty-stricken and proud, said, "Thank you for coming, my father would be honored, my home is your home tonight and you are welcome."

There were nods at this but it wasn't until Yevgena inclined her head at them that they began to move and talk.

Yevgena tucked her arm through his own. "I suppose you are keeping watch with that old terror from Oxford tonight are you?"

"I suppose I am," Jamie said as the 'old terror' came out into the entryway.

"Saints and bawds preserve us it's the Queen of the Gypsies herself come to visit," John said, a grudging affection tinting the dryness of his tone.

"The ancient mariner still lives I see," Yevgena retorted in turn and then, characteristically, grabbed John by the ears and treated him to an exuberant Russian kiss on each cheek.

Drawn by the scent of drama, Jessica appeared in the hall, cheeks whiskey-flushed, top two buttons of her sedate suit popped open, looking for all the world like a freshly tumbled dairy maid.

Exquisite ink black eyebrows arched over narrowed eyes, "Jemmy?" Yevgena demanded, laying a proprietary hand along his forearm.

"Don't you recognize my playmate?" Jamie asked causing Jessica's buttermilk skin to glow red.

Yevgena turned her head this way and that, narrowing her eyes even further, making Jessica twitch in discomfort under such intense scrutiny. A delighted smile dawned upon Levantine shores.

"Jessitchka?"

Jessica nodded and was swept up in the same fierce hug that Jamie had experienced only moments ago.

"Well," Yevgena held her at arm's length, "you have filled out most admirably. These two," she spoke to John, "spent a summer with me in California when they were only so high," she waved her hand at a height of about five feet, "such mischief makers they were. Still are I imagine," she gave Jamie an arch look. "Now," she flung off her red cloak, "will someone get me a drink?" She strode imperiously into the study, flicking back a wing of hair impatiently.

"Vodka," John, having followed her into the room, had Waterford decanter in hand and an evil twinkle in his eyes.

Yevgena held her hands up, "John my darling there are things you don't seem to remember so well, a Russian gypsy with a bottle of vodka is a disaster waiting to happen. I'll have some of that fog stuff you men swill."

"Mist," Jamie said.

"Fog, mist, is all bad weather; just don't put any ice in it."

Jamie brought her drink as specified and then excused himself for a moment while he made arrangements for the Tinkers' dinner.

Yevgena wasted no time in coming directly to the point.

"How is he, how is my Jemmy?" she asked, eyes gone opaque and piercing.

"Not so good," John said. "It was as you know rather unexpected, Jamie was in Paris on business. I think," he hesitated a moment, "I think his father was waiting for him to be away."

"My poor sweet James," Yevgena said, all of her sixty-four years echoing in her voice. John knew she meant the father, not the son, for both had been surrogate sons to her, though she was officially Jamie's godmother.

Yevgena Vasiliovich had been 'marked for reduction' some twenty-two years earlier in the Csillag internment camp and had been saved only by chance, the end of the war and the fleeing of the Nazis. The Csillag had merely been a way station for Auschwitz. Jewish by birth, gypsy by marriage she was doubly cursed under Hitler's regime. She and her family, a husband, three adolescent daughters and a pair of rosy brown twin boys had been rounded up and forced to march the fifty miles to the camp. Within a month, both her husband and daughters were dead of typhus and the boys had been transported to Auschwitz. She was never able to determine what happened to them, though the monstrous stories of Josef Mengele's private labs and his intense fascination with twins had never ceased to haunt her sleeping and waking hours. She herself had been transported to Auschwitz a month after the boys and had been due to go to the ovens when liberation occurred. She'd been too weak to walk out of the camp on her own accord and had thought to merely huddle in a corner and die, but as fate would have it, an Irish diplomat, there on a fact-finding mission for the UN, discovered her and carried her out. She spent several weeks in a British field hospital, her resurrector coming to see her as often as he could.

When she'd been released from hospital she'd nowhere to go, no family left, no home, no life. It was then that James Kirkpatrick the First, Jamie's grandfather, had offered her a job as a personal assistant. The title came to mean many things over the years and she had become an integral part of the Kirkpatrick family while not really meaning to. She was secretary, counsel, confidante, hostess and friend to her rescuer and after seeing how lonely a young man the second James Kirkpatrick was, she'd become a mother figure to him. Jamie, her Jemmy, had barely been more than a toddler at the time and she'd taken him to her heart with a fierceness that shocked and frightened her. Today she'd not actually been late for the funeral she just hadn't seen how she could bear to watch one son bury the other.

"He has been drinking?" she asked, looking directly at Jessica, knowing that John's views on drinking were somewhat more slanted.

"Yes," Jessica drew the word out reluctantly, "but only for the day and night before."

"We will let him have his way tonight but after that, *pffft*," Yevgena's long red fingernails sliced the air across her throat, "he is broke off."

"Cut off," John said on the rise of a yawn, "and who may I ask is going to wean him away from the bottle?"

"I have a plan, not to worry," Yevgena said in a tone that inspired alarm in her listeners. "Now let us join Jamie outside, is not good for him to brood about in this room, his father is too much here."

The sight that greeted them outside was rather startling to the Anglo-Saxon sensibilities of how a funeral day was to be spent. Fires were lit in pits, food was being cooked and distributed, spices skirled and scented the unseasonably warm air, children barefoot and laughing were running about and torches lit the night like great pulsating stars.

"Are you certain this is wise?" John asked, watching Jamie make a crown of ivy and crocus for a particularly grubby little girl.

"He will have his whole life to mourn his father, tonight though is a danger-ous time, tonight and for the next while. Jamie needs to look after someone, otherwise," Yevgena looked soberly through the thickening twilight, "he will be devoured by the pain. I saw it happen to his father, I won't allow it to happen to him."

"You could have brought him a puppy, three hundred gypsies is a little excessive even by your standards."

"Puppies he has," Yevgena retorted smoothly, "it is something else entirely that he needs."

John, feeling that to enquire further would be to implicate himself in later crimes, wandered off to better acquaint himself with Gypsy custom and drink.

Yevgena, followed by Jessica, made her way over to Jamie, stopping here and there to pat a baby, enquire as to the health of various people and to drop in her wake beads and baubles of such color and quantity as to cause a great squealing and delight amongst the children.

She stooped over Jamie, kissing him gently on the top of his head as he knelt in the grass surrounded by a group of giggling girls, pulling coins out of their ears and making a variety of accessories from the supplies in his garden.

"You need a haircut," she chided gently, pushing back the golden hair that hung in his eyes. "You also need a woman to look after you," she smiled at Jessica, "why don't you make an honest man of this boy?"

"When he makes a dishonest woman of me I'll be more than happy to," Jessica replied, only half in jest.

"Where is that wife of yours anyhow?" Yevgena asked sharply, bantering stripped from her words like blistered paint.

Jamie finished wrapping a length of cream and green ivy around a dark-eyed cherub's neck before answering.

"Yevgena you know full well where Colleen is and that she is not my wife anymore."

"Isn't she? Have you divorced yet? No, I didn't think so, her place is here not stuck up there in that home for dried up—"

"Yevgena," Jamie's voice was harsh, "don't."

"Alright, alright," Yevgena spread her fingers in pure Russian placation, "I only thought that—"

"Yevgena," the tone was icy.

Yevgena rolled her eyes and left him to his flowersmithing, pulling Jessica neatly to her side and leading her towards the cobbled stone paths that ran through the formal rose gardens.

"Are there any women for Jamie?"

Jessica, feeling rather harassed, answered diplomatically, "Not that I know of."

"He needs to move on with his life," Yevgena said firmly.

"He has done rather well all things considered." Jessica, bending down, feigned great interest in a freshly budding rose, trying to avoid the rather intent way Yevgena was considering her.

"He needs a woman; it's not healthy for him to pine after that half-dead girl who's shut herself off from the world."

"He's accepted Colleen's decision."

"How many times have you been married Jessitchka?" Yevgena was all sweetness.

"Four," said Jessica. *As you well know you old harridan*, thought Jessica.

"So," the word was as sibilant as the serpent, "four times it does not work, four times you think you are in love and then *pffft*, he turns out to be a swine. Sometimes," her voice lowered confidentially, "it is better to marry a friend and let the rest come and go as it will." She turned Jessica sharply around a corner, landing them on a small knoll where the festivities below were in plain view. "Jamie is very easy, as you Westerners say, to look upon is he not?"

It was true, Jessica thought, and there wasn't a woman alive who needed it pointed out to her. Even the sun seemed to bestow him with its last kiss of light, leaving him glittering while others moved about in darkness. Gold hair, merciless green eyes, lean and lithe as a cat, with a mind that could cut razors and occasionally did.

"I'd never want to lose him as a friend," Jessica said softly, barely realizing she'd spoken aloud. "Besides he's a dreadful tendency to match me up with his friends."

"Ah yes the Vietnamese photographer," Yevgena said.

"Canadian," Jessica amended politely, "he takes pictures in Vietnam."

"Well, war can be a very seductive mistress," Yevgena said, in what, Jessica thought, was intended to be comfort.

"Yevitsa," Jamie's voice rang out reprovingly from over a rosebush, "you're not telling her about your affair with Khrushchev are you?"

Yevgena made a face, "Mind your manners young man, that's Comrade Khrushchev to you."

"And darling Nikki to you," Jamie said with a grin.

Night had descended fully and the skies above bloomed with stars: gold and silver, yellow, blue and red, hot and scorching to the naked eye. The torches threw out long blazes of light, lending pools to the grass here and there, in and out of which small brown feet danced and shimmered. Someone took up a violin and the night air began to furl around the sad, bleeding notes of the mad Hungarian Liszt.

Yevgena, fondly stroking the hair of a man at least thirty years her junior had settled herself in a low slung garden chair, Jamie and Jessica to either side of her. She regaled them with tales of espionage and derring-do in the world of high politics that she claimed to merely dabble in.

"How did you fare at the conference?" Jamie asked, deflecting her attention from the potent liquid with which he was refilling his glass.

Yevgena sighed and ceased petting the man at her knee. She'd recently represented her people at a human rights conference held by Eastern Bloc countries, a group not notoriously famous for their interest in human rights in the first place.

"Could have been worse, I suppose," she said in that blackly prosaic Russian way of hers. "I have enough problems within the gypsy camp itself, the Hungarians think they are the only real gypsies as do the Romanians, though neither can clearly define for me what that actually means."

"But Yevitsa," Jamie chided gently, "you're Hungarian yourself."

"Only by marriage, though to be a Russian Jew is just as complicated and without definition these days. The conference wasn't going too badly once I got the Polish contingent off the booze," she looked pointedly at Jamie's half-drunk tumbler. "But then there was that terrible incident where four Roma were killed by a gas bomb. Someone had booby-trapped a sign that said 'Gypsies go home.' Which is difficult to do considering how hell-bent everyone is on ridding their countries of gypsies. After the news came in about the bomb it was a little hard to get everyone at the table to talk." She took a breath and then let it out all at once. "Germany was willing to pay reparation money from the war but it was to go towards building settlements. Try to explain that settlement and concentration camp are not so far apart in the gypsy mind and those grim Teutonic types go deaf. Besides Germany and the rest of the world would just as soon forget the gypsies that were exterminated, what are eighty thousand homeless riffraff compared to six million Jews." She drank broodingly from her glass, "Understand that I say this as a Jew. Jewish memory," she tapped her head, "is very long, maybe too long, I think sometimes. But gypsies," she gestured broadly towards the encampment, "gypsies act as if there is no memory at all. The world has forgotten too, there is no mention of us in the records and rarely in the history books that seem to be springing up like mushrooms. Perhaps it is our nature to forget though, all our tradition is oral and moving from place to place we shed our stories, change them, kaleidoscope them in and out to suit our purposes. Of course," the prosaic Russian was back, "illiteracy does not help."

She sighed and shifted her position, hair gleaming like polished obsidian in the firelight, strands of it falling and catching in the folds of her crimson scarf. Courtesan, queen and mother were tired.

"Perhaps is best what is easiest, to forget. Remembering only honors the dead; it does not bring them back. And so, you have more babies," she watched a pretty pair of boys scamper past, "and you build a future for them. Ah, Jemmy," she sat up abruptly and clapped her hands together, "I am too silly being sad, I am forgetting your present."

Jamie groaned. "Yevitsa, I would think after last time you'd give up on the gift giving."

Yevgena shrugged her shoulders expressively, "You give a man a camel one time and he never lets you forget it."

"You didn't really—" Jessica said, beginning to laugh.

"She did," Jamie said exasperatedly, "for my thirtieth birthday. Bertha the Camel, she of two humps and great spitting ability."

"Ah, but she came in very useful did she not?" Yevgena waved an index finger in his direction. She turned to Jessica. "He gave her to an Arab minister of trade in exchange for being allowed to export that poisonous Kilkenny Fog he makes."

John, looking very relaxed and happy, slid bonelessly onto the edges of their small group. "Talking about Bertha are you?" He grinned, "Dear God, don't tell me you've brought him another gift, Yevgena!"

"But of course I have," she leaned forward and pinched Jamie's cheek affectionately. "Would your Yevitsa forget your birthday?"

"I rather wish you would sometimes," Jamie said dryly.

"Well then what is it this time?" John rubbed his hands with relish.

Yevgena smiled slowly, gleefully, mischief abounding on Levantine shores now.

"I've brought you a girl," she said.

Chapter Two

Gypsy Girl

"IN THE OLD DAYS," YEVGENA SAID TO THE SHOCKED FACES AROUND HER, "there was a group of rather lovely young men of diverse talents, who, in return for food and gifts, would go about dispensing poetry, music and," her voice tilted towards a lower register, "love."

"The Pilgrims of Love," John said, amusement beginning to overtake shock.

"For lack of a better term," Jamie interjected acidly.

"Nevertheless," Yevgena continued undeterred, "history is there for us to improve and expand upon, so I've found a female pilgrim."

"Rings on her fingers and the requisite bells on her toes, I presume," Jamie said sarcasm liberally lacing his words.

"Quite a lovely set of each, actually," Yevgena said mildly. "I think perhaps it's time for you to quit hiding behind that glass and just finish off the bottle." Inky eyebrows arched and verdantly green eyes refused the challenge.

"One supposes you will have your own way regardless," Jamie said, the bite rather missing from his words, the bottle in hand.

"One supposes correctly," Yevgena's words, unlike Jamie's, had teeth.

A clap of hands, a word or two and a sudden hush like dropping snow covered the crowd. Then, like a Siberian rose rising from winter's blasted ground, rare and surprising, a girl emerged walking into the circle of fire. Smooth, slender, ivory-skinned and fine-boned with hair tumbling like bruise-black silk down bare and blameless skin, she was enough fuel to bank the smallest of flames. Exotic eastern winds, freshly sprung, tinkled the bells strung silver and delicate around her ankles.

Joints turned and shifted, became the support of elegant arabesques of arm and leg. Eyelashes, wondrously thick, hovered demurely over eyes. Hips and flank were swathed in a purple silk that flickered between opaque and transparent in the uncertain light.

"My, my," breathed John. "Are those ostrich feathers?" he indicated the upper body attire the girl held in front of herself, fluttering and furling in the breeze.

"Mm," Yevgena mumbled distractedly, watching with interest the interplay of firelight and lust on Jamie's face.

Jamie, robbed of speech again, was finding even rudimentary functions such as breathing quite difficult. Other things, of course, seemed to be in fully working order. A flicker of smooth hip there by the fire, and the smell of strawberries and amaranth, dizzying, overwhelming and dissipating into the night. Music began to flow, designed for the baser senses it was heavy, thrumming and sliding through veins, blossoming in blood, redolent with salt and musk.

Berry-stained feet moved in rhythm, hands, sweetly sealed about feathers, undulated carefully, rounded parts dipped and circled and eyes remained downcast, lashes thickly fanned against flushed cheeks. The air became laden with sighs of two variations.

"Imagine," John's voice was somewhat strangled, "all that and a command of Persian love sonnets."

"What?" Jessica asked, uncertain of what she was querying.

"Part of pilgrim lore, amongst other things those boys were never without an arsenal of Ottoman words of love. One never knows," Yevgena stretched, the picture of a Turkish odalisque in profile, "when these things may come in handy."

The music wound down and the girl disappeared, sighs gathered, collected and blew across the onlookers like an African sirocco.

She reappeared a moment later, ostrich feathers replaced by a length of crimson cloth. The music pulled hard from the strings, poured down from Spanish steppes, steeped potent in hot Cordovan suns. The dance was the dance of the Andalusian gypsies, the flamenco. Heel and toe moved in ancient and instinctive patterns. Hair whirled like silk around a tornado. She seemed all movement, skin and bone of a dissoluble piece. She seemed, Jessica thought in inexplicable despair, as if she were desire incarnate. The girl moved to the edge of her circle of fire and held out a hand to Jamie. Lashes tilted up and green eyes met their like.

"Dance with me," she said quietly, "if you can."

Gone beyond the space where madness and propriety were salient points Jamie, golden, reckless, rose in answer to her challenge and took her hand before anyone could think to stop him.

Despite the handicaps of inebriation, exhaustion and grief, Jamie *could* dance. He also knew, from a variety of experiences, how to hold a woman. Skin followed skin, blood beat in time and they whirled, spun, stamped and wooed there in the lost world of flame and body. Jamie was a spangled *djinn* in counterpoint to the girl's dark melody.

Jessica, feeling as though she had a shard of glass caught in her throat bid her goodnights to John and Yevgena who absently replied without once taking their mesmerized countenances off the dancing pair. She fled for the security and comfort of the room Jamie kept for her occasional visits, the music in pursuit. Her suite, as misfortune would have it, looked out over the gardens. Fire and shadow flickered on the walls and Jessica, drawn against her will, looked down into the scene below.

The music had taken a brief respite and she hoped Jamie had regained his senses enough to ask for it to be silenced. But then the lone, shattering note of a Celtic pipe began, wounding and strangling, killing ivy hidden within the couch of deceitful jasmine. The music of blood and winter and endless grief, purely, tragically Irish. Jamie, shirt half undone, leaned in exhaustion against the girl, pearls of sweat gleaming in his hair, eyes glittering in a way that spelled disaster. She saw his cheek move restlessly against the girl's, hands in a hard caress with the bones of her face. She could feel the words he spoke then, knew them as they slipped the breach of tongue and lip, "Take me to bed for god's sake," he said, "take me to bed now."

Jessica, closing the draperies, felt the beginnings of a crashing headache.

"GOD'S TEETH, IS THIS WHAT YOU HAD IN MIND?" John asked as Jamie, sparing a glance for no one took the girl by the hand and went into the house, shutting the door with firm intent behind them.

"John," said Yevgena, "Jamie is not a man that should be without the company of a woman for long, particularly not," she gave him a pointed look, "with his temperament. That silly girl he insisted on marrying has managed to tie him up so badly with guilt that I wouldn't be surprised if he hasn't taken a woman to his bed since the last time she deigned to allow him into hers. That being said there are more practical reasons. In the last ten years, he's lost three children, a wife and now a father. He's carried the weight of Kirkpatrick Industries since he left Oxford and now he'll have to decide whether to take up the political legacy his father's left behind. And there are things," she sighed deeply, "that even those of us who love him best don't understand about his life."

"I don't quite see how a half-naked gypsy girl fits into this picture," John said peevishly.

"Oh, I think you do John, besides there are reasons other than physical that she is here."

"Such as?"

"You old curmudgeon, try to remember all that poetry you used to believe in before you took such glee in dissecting it for children."

He gave her a look of utter mystification.

She leaned over and kissed him soundly on the forehead, "Destiny John, destiny. Now you old terror let's go get good and drunk."

John thought that was, perhaps, the best idea anyone had had all day.

"MY KINGDOM FOR A BUTTON," Jamie laughed in exasperation. He was trying without success, to locate a clue, however minute, on where to begin unwrapping his gift.

"Scissors," said the Gypsy Girl or Destiny if you preferred whose name was actually Pamela O'Flaherty.

He groaned with feeling. "Bottom floor, don't think I can negotiate the damned stairs again and I wouldn't know where to find them anyway."

"Pathetic," she said.

"It is," he agreed, pondering the feasibility of simply biting through the knot end.

They were in his room now, a room done in all the shades of the sea, from deepest murky green to silver-shot blue and the white of sun-bleached sky. The effect of it was a bit, he'd been told, like drowning.

"Well there's only one thing for it then," she said with equanimity.

"Yes?"

"Patience."

"Not my favorite virtue," he said, black hair slipping and sliding between his questing fingers.

"You keep searching," one fine-fingered ivory hand pulled her hair aside, "and I'll find a way to amuse you."

"Unless you're acrobatic by nature I don't quite see how to manage that," Jamie said doubtfully.

She cast a withering glance over one shoulder.

"Music then?" he suggested humbly.

"Left my harpsichord at home," she said blithely, "and my singing voice is likely to be less than conducive to," she paused delicately, "the mood."

"How are your Persian love sonnets?" He asked and she considered and then dismissed the idea that it was perhaps wrong to seduce a man so drunk.

"The mind is willing, but the memory is weak. However I've a head filled to the cusp with blue Elizabethan ditties."

"What an interesting education you must have had," he commented mildly, "perhaps you'd recite for me."

She accordingly cleared her throat, straightened her slim carriage and began:

> *Mine's the lance*
> *To start the dance*
> *Yours the lips*
> *For Cupid's pips.*

Blushing melon
Makes a felon,
Sheathe the blade
Sweetling maid.
Push asunder
Nature's thunder,
Maidenhead
Sweetly bled,
Honey mead
For the seed.
Turtledove,
Take my love.

"Blue indeed," Jamie said in admiration as she finished. "A-ha," he held aloft an unraveled end with triumph akin to the first man to set foot in the New World.

"What did they read to you as a child, precocious infant?" he asked as the unraveled end led into a labyrinth of tucks and folds.

"Everything I could get my hands on, my father used to say I ate books rather than read them. But my favorite—"

"Yes," Jamie prompted, hands carefully navigating frontal delicacies.

"Was *The Velveteen Rabbit.*"

"Might I ask why?"

"Because it's a very true story, isn't it?"

Confronted with an alarming amount of bare flesh, Jamie wondered if it was wrong to sleep with a girl who believed in stuffed bunnies springing to life.

"What I mean is," she warmed to her topic, "that you aren't real until someone loves you."

The crimson cloth, released at last, drifted then settled with a sigh around her hips.

The air became pregnant with the lack of touch.

"Is something the matter?" she turned around on the bed to face Jamie, who quickly cast his eyes heavenward.

"How old are you?" he asked.

"I'm legal," she said calmly, "if that's what you're worried about."

"I suppose that's a relief," he said a trifle grimly.

"Is it your father?" She laid a gentle hand on his forearm, "My father used to say that sex and death are natural companions."

"Your father," Jamie paused, "sounds eccentric."

She gave him a stern look, "He meant it was a way to deal with grief, the act itself is a reaffirmation of the living still to be done."

Jamie thought he'd never met such a terrifyingly pragmatic person.

"Shall we get on with the business at hand then?" In one lithe movement, she had swung a knee over his lap and settled herself quite comfortably.

"Um," said Jamie inanely, "you have very nice skin."

"Youth," she smiled and took one of his hands, "despite its various disadvantages has some rather nice compensations. Now do you think you could do something for me?"

"Cross deserts barefoot? Slay dragons? Cut out my soul and hand you the knife?" Due to the placement of his hand, he was feeling increasingly giddy.

She sighed. "Could you just, for a minute or two, be quiet?"

Jamie, not surprisingly, found that he could.

IN THE MORNING, UPON AWAKENING, JAMIE FELT LIKE A FLEECED LAMB—naked, against the laws of nature and left to die on a green hillside. Alone as well. It took him a moment or two to work out that last bit but then he spied the crimson scarf hanging off the bedpost and thought clarity was a quality he could manage without. Ignorance, for this morning, would do quite nicely.

He showered, shaved and putting on fresh clothes made his way downstairs.

John, Jessica and Yevgena were in the morning room eating croissants and drinking coffee, their morning chatter halting abruptly as he entered the bright, foliage-laden room. It was with relief well mixed with regret that he noted the absence of his nocturnal guest.

Yevgena, peacock brilliant in bright blue stretched up to kiss him on his nose. "Good morning, darling."

"Good morning," he replied, relief fleeing at the sight of the girl, cosily tucked in his best white terry robe, bowl in hand, appearing around a palm frond.

"Good morning," she said in a tone, he imagined that she reserved for cordial strangers.

"Pamela here," Yevgena steered him towards the privacy of the coffee urn, "has been telling me that you failed to deflower her last night."

Jamie looked at Yevgena in utter horror.

"Pardon me?" He sputtered, turning in quick succession white, red and an unbecoming bronzy-green.

"Oh," a breezy voice emerged at his left elbow, "it's alright you were quite willing but you said something about being too old to sleep with angels and then fell asleep."

"It seems our little pilgrim," Yevgena's face was grim, "has dispensed all things excepting love."

"I've lived this long with my virginity, I suppose," Pamela said gloomily, "I can manage a bit longer."

"A virgin," Jamie hissed somewhat louder than he'd intended, drawing the interested stares of Jessica and John.

"Yes," he received a cold glare from the girl, "it's not a disease you know."

"I did not know," Yevgena turned her hands up helplessly, "I have been, how do you say—hatblinked."

"Hoodwinked," John supplied cheerily as he bit into a melon.

"Don't play the Russian ingenue, you're a bit old for it," Jamie said fury icing his words black.

"Look," Pamela's head came up from the attack she'd launched on a bowl of cornflakes, "I'm sorry if I've caused problems here, I take sole responsibility for any upset."

"Very mature of you," Jessica said in a friendly manner exchanging a smile with her.

"Hungry?" Jamie asked sarcastically.

"Very," Pamela replied drinking milk straight from the bowl.

"Dear God," said Jamie in exasperation. Then seeing the faint blush as pale as the innards of a seashell that raced along her skin, he felt suddenly quite ashamed of himself. "No, it's I who should apologize, you are a guest in my home and I've treated you abominably. I'm sorry, please know that you're welcome to stay as long as the Tinkers are here."

A look passed between Yevgena and Pamela that made a rather unpleasant sensation take root in his stomach.

"What's going on?" he asked with as much calm as he could muster up.

"Well, you see, the Tinkers have already left, which is beside the point," Yevgena said rapidly, "because she's not a Tinker."

"Then who the hell is she?"

"Me, myself and I, as the man in the desert said." The voice was unperturbed, "or if you'd rather my name is Pamela O'Flaherty." A hand still lightly padded by youth extended itself and Jamie, head reeling, shook it. "Now if you don't mind I'd like some more breakfast and then I'll get my things and be gone."

"Like the wind," Jamie said, finding that his fury was quickly abating.

"Or through the back door," she said with a smile, "less romantic but more practical."

"There is still the issue of payment," Jamie smiled in return, "you did after all provide dancing."

"And would have provided love, had you been a more willing recipient."

Eyes, clear unwavering green, met his and he felt as if someone had stopped the hands of time with a light touch on the clock. "I was rather wondering," she said, "if instead of payment, well see the thing is..." she faltered, youthful bravado seeming to fail her for the first time.

"Yes," Jamie prodded.

"Well actually, I could really use a job."

"And what is it, exactly, you think you can do for me?" he asked in a tone of dry amusement.

"General dogsbody, Girl Friday, Saturday and Sunday, as well as a dab hand at poker."

"Admirable qualities certainly," he said, "and not without their place in the universe, but I'm afraid I don't see—"

"I could use a hand in the kitchen an' about the place," Maggie said, grunting as she set down a tray with sausages, soda bread, eggs and fried tomatoes on the sideboard. "I'm not," she said, treating Jamie to a gimlet glance, "so young as I once was."

"We're none of us getting any younger, Maggie," Liz Forbes, Jamie's secretary, light and lovely in pale yellow, entered the room, poured herself a coffee and smiling in a thoroughly professional manner said, "And I could use someone to run the occasional errand to the banks, post letters, type reports. There's certainly no lack of work to be done," she sighed in a melodic fashion and sat down with her coffee.

Jamie though young, was wise enough to know when he'd been outmaneuvered.

"I'd no idea I'd so overworked you ladies," he said pleasantly and then turned to the girl, eyeing him now with frank curiosity over the rim of her teacup. "I suppose that means, Miss O'Flaherty, that you're hired."

He then sat, helped himself to a healthy portion of everything on the tray and tried to ignore the look of smug satisfaction now shared by the three women who'd appointed themselves guardian fairies in his life long ago.

Moments later, absorbed in his sausage and vaguely disturbed by the bare foot that seemed to keep touching his in passing, he missed the wink, smile and nod that passed between his erstwhile fairies.

Flora, Fauna and Merriweather indeed.

Chapter Three
A Hundred Thousand Welcomes Home

AT ABOUT THE SAME TIME JAMIE KIRKPATRICK was having his grief compromised, Seamus McDowell was entering the doors of a public establishment. His ears were treated to the heartrending final notes of a Republican hymn of sorts called *'When Dawn Finds Her Way to Belfast'* offered up in the sweetest most melancholy tenor tones he'd ever had the distinct pleasure of hearing. His boy was home.

"Will ye be doin' us the honor of singin' another selection, Father?" a man called out, raising his half-empty glass in tribute to the priest's talent.

The 'priest', who stood atop Mr. O'Leary's well-worn bar, winked in Seamus' direction to ensure his compliance and said, with a note of genuine regret, "I'd love to oblige ye gentlemen as ye've been most kind but my pipes are a wee bit on the dry side an' I've just seen one of God's strayin' lambs an' must have a talk with him. So if ye'll excuse me perhaps I'll sing a song or two later when me equilibrium's been restored, if ye know what I'm sayin'."

"Another round for the Father," went up the cry and 'the Father' seating himself in the dark, shadowy corner table Seamus had indicated, found a frothing pitcher of warm, dark ale at his elbow. The priest thanked the serving girl with a wink and a barely discernible, but highly inappropriate, pat to her shapely backside.

"Found God an' the Pope in prison did ye, Father Riordan?" asked Seamus with a quirk of his sandy brows.

"Ah, it's all just a harmless bit of fun, they think I'm off for the seminary in the mornin', feelin' terrible sorry for me I imagine, this bein' my last night of freedom an' all."

"Yer first ye mean."

"Well first, last—a man certainly deserves a few free drops for either occasion, would ye not agree?" Casey Riordan asked with a boyish grin as he filled Seamus' glass to the rim.

"An' who am I, bein' a severely lapsed Catholic for more years than I care to count, to deny a soon-to-be-ordained priest of a few pints of the spirit?"

"Couldn't have said it better myself," replied Casey clinking his glass against Seamus' own upraised one.

"Ye look none the worse for yer wee holiday boyo."

"Aye, well could have been worse, no?" The words were uttered lightly enough but Seamus knew the full weight that lay behind them, none understood better than he the inevitability of the path this boy had chosen to follow.

"*Cead mile failte romhat abhaile,*" Seamus said. A hundred thousand welcomes home.

"Thank ye man, I know ye mean it." One broad hand wiped the foam off Casey's upper lip. "Christ it's good to be home, I knelt down an' kissed the ground straight off the boat train."

"That must have earned the queer looks."

"Now we've established that I'm home, what happens?"

Seamus had been dreading that very question for an entire month.

"Just how happy are ye to be home?" he asked, keeping his tone light.

"I'm not likin' the sound of this," Casey's eyes were dark over the top of his glass.

"We think it's best te send ye off before anyone knows yer back."

"Send me where?"

"The Middle East," Seamus' voice was barely above a whisper. In an establishment as notoriously republican as this one anyone who looked too comfortably Irish was likely to be a British agent, "there are some gentlemen there ye need to meet."

"Arms," Casey said, covering with a yawn.

"Amongst other things," Seamus raised his glass to an overly interested party.

"Can I at least sneak into Belfast an' see my brother?" The look on Casey's face was as close to pleading as the boy ever got.

"No," Seamus said regretfully, "we're puttin' ye on the plane in the mornin'. Dublin to Paris, Paris to Vienna an' onward connections."

"Christ," Casey's sigh was heartfelt. "Well then how is my little brother?"

"Didn't he write ye?"

"Three times a week an' twice on Sundays, the boy's more faithful than a nun. But knowin' Pat as I do I figured the bits that weren't borin' were fairytales. He's very careful about not worryin' me."

"Patrick's fine, doin' great in school an' only up to the usual things a man of his tender years is likely to be up to. He's fine." Seamus couldn't decide later whether he'd said the whole thing one beat too fast or one beat too slowly.

"What's he done?" Casey's voice, like the calm preceding the storm, was far too sweet.

"Nothin' really," Seamus glanced at Casey's face and decided the plain unvarnished truth was the only option. "He's joined the Young Socialists."

"Jaysus, Mary, Joseph an' the little green men, has he done his fockin' nut? I told the little bugger to keep his nose clean an' to the grindstone an' to keep well an' away from any extremist organizations."

Seamus wisely refrained from making comments about profoundly black kettles calling the pot names.

"The little bugger," Seamus said mildly, "is nineteen years old now an' not likely to appreciate big brother attemptin' to run his life." He lit a cigarette and offered Casey one. "We've kept an eye on him an' he's led a life a monk could be proud of an' ye've seen his grades, he made the honors list at Queen's last term. He's doin' all the things ye wanted him to, Casey, the boy needs to have some fun."

"Ye call marchin' around with that bunch of Marxist hooligans fun?"

"They're good kids from good homes an' there are many worse things he could be doin' other than marchin' for peace."

"I suppose," Casey sounded less than convinced. "Now Seamus," the boyo was all charm, they'd have to be careful of that, "I've only the one question left, where the hell was McDarmaid that day? He was supposed to be watchin' my back." There was no accusation in Casey's dark eyes, only a very plain question, 'what went wrong?'

And well he should ask, thought Seamus, for that day had been plotted down to the last second, nothing should have gone wrong and indeed nothing would have if McDarmaid had done as he was told, or if he'd kept his allegiances in the proper order.

"McDarmaid was talkin' to the London bobbies if ye must know."

"The sneakin', connivin', double-dealin'–" Casey's hand slammed down on the table's scarred surface.

"Lower yer voice man," Seamus hissed, "wouldn't want yer drink supply cut off now would ye? Just listen," he continued as Casey took a deep breath, in a valiant effort to rein in his anger. "McDarmaid had cause to regret his actions."

"Regret—the coward doesn't even know the meanin' of the word, wait 'til I get my hands on the sorry bastard!"

"That may prove difficult considerin' he's been lyin' in an unmarked grave for close on four years now."

"What?" Casey furrowed his black brows as if he were simply too thick to follow the conversation.

"Are ye deaf, man? I've just told ye he's dead."

"I heard—how an' when?"

"Ye want it spelled out, do ye? Well he's dead an' that's all that matters, yer revenge has been taken for ye. He knew the game he was playin' was a very dangerous one an' just what the penalties were for gettin' caught. Casey, ye can't be hangin' on to the personal angers, it'll chew up yer soul." The look he gave Casey went fathoms deep and both knew that Seamus was not speaking of the traitorous Willy McDarmaid.

"Ye've got to let it go man," Seamus said softly, "yer daddy knew what he was about that last day, a man such as himself doesn't make mistakes like that one."

It was a long, tense moment before Casey lifted his head, his eyes sparkling with anger or tears, Seamus could not be certain which.

"D'ye think I am so daft as to not know that? Don't ye see though that no matter which way ye turn the coin, it tells the same story? Those bastards up in Castlereagh killed him, oh he may have walked and talked and even once in a rare while laughed in that last year but they killed him as certain as if they'd put a gun to his head an' pulled the trigger. They took his soul an' all that was left was for him was to dispose of the body. Are ye askin' me to forget that, Seamus? Have ye forgotten yerself what they did to my daddy? Ye said ye loved him as a brother, does a brother turn a blind eye then?"

Seamus fought to control his own anger; this one was his father's son in looks and name only. Brian had been a quiet man, almost methodical in his speech and actions, taking the long view of things. Whereas his oldest son was a man of action, quick to anger and slow to forgiveness. Brian had never emanated the hair-trigger danger that Casey exuded from every pore.

"There are things ye don't understand, Casey an' won't unless ye manage to add a few years to yer life. Yer daddy wanted to go an' nothin' you or I could have done would have changed that. I loved yer da' better'n' my own brothers, God help me, an' when he took his own life, he took a part of me with him. But nothin', not anger, nor vengeance is goin' to bring him back. Don't ye remember what he taught ye of patience and faith?"

"Aye, well his faith did not help him much in the end, did it? I'm not a great believer in them that endures the most will get their reward in the end. The meek may inherit the earth but they're not fockin' likely to keep it long, now are they? I came to you six years ago, willin' if it should come to it, to give my life for what I believe in. I'll do whatever is asked of me Seamus, just please don't ask me to sit on my arse an' pray that God an' his wee angels will make it alright." Casey paused to draw a ragged breath, "'Cause he's not listened to any of the weepin' an' prayin' of the last eight hundred years has he?" He took a long draught of his ale and placing his empty glass on the table, resumed some of his customary sarcasm, "Or has God become a Republican whilst I was in the kip?"

"Might I disrupt yer sermon, 'Father' Riordan," Seamus said tersely, "to remind ye that I took ye in under oath an' that ye swore to work within the boundaries specified whether ye agreed with them or not. I took ye against yer Daddy's wishes, God help me, because I knew ye'd go an' get yer idiot self killed without someone to watch out for ye. Ye were a ragin' bitter boy then, Casey an' though I still see a child when I look at ye, yer not. Yer a man an' ye've had five years to cool yer temper an' I'm too old an' tired to play guardian angel to ye. So I'm askin' for a decision. Ye stand with us or against, there is no middle road, an' the one we travel is a damn lonely one. We march to a different drummer an' the price the drummer asks is sometimes higher than ye can ever imagine."

"My Daddy knew," Casey said quietly. "Where is it that I'm standin' Seamus? I've heard all the talk about the blurred peripheries of Republicanism, about workin' on the fringes, the one step for every generation but I don't believe in standin' on the sidelines of history while the British, the Prods an' all they represent run over us. Compromise was not my father's legacy, an' I'll be no less a man than he was."

"Oh, so ye'll follow that heroic path will ye? Will ye hold yer father's idols up high as well, for yer father did the same as they givin' his life over to this country."

"Tone, Pearse an' Collins were heroes of the Republic, my da' could have praised much worse," Casey replied heatedly.

"Oh an' a fine and glorious end they came to, wasn't it? Tone makin' a bungle of slittin' his own throat, Pearse facin' the firin' squad with the whole country jeerin' him, Collins shot down like a dog by his own friends an' yer granddad, oh aye have ye forgotten him?" he said to Casey's wary look. "Yer granddad who could have led this Godforsaken nation up out of the muck, shot in front of his own son, an' all yer uncles dead while scarcely out of their teens. And Brian, yer Daddy, who was never meant for that sort of life takin' up permanent residence in Milltown cemetery before he'd even caught sight of his fortieth birthday. It's a funny thing about heroes Casey, they're all dead."

"I'm not lookin' to be a hero, only a man, no more no less."

Seamus sighed, if the Irish were believed to be a stubborn lot then surely the Riordans were at the summit of that particular trait.

"Aye well, Casey in the end yer life is yer own an' ye'll do as ye like with it, just don't bring anyone else down with ye when ye go. Now I must be off, we've lingered too long as it is, ye don't want to be attractin' undue trouble."

He slid a package under the table, years of careful behavior making it seem as if he were merely scratching his knee. "Yer plane tickets an' all the rest of the information ye'll need to have a successful trip. We'll bring ye back to Belfast when I judge it's safe to do so. Until then," he lifted his glass which still held a swallow or two, "in the words of an illustrious former brother, that notorious man of letters Brendan Behan, "up the Republic an' fock the begrudgers!"

"In front of a priest now, shame on ye man!" The barmaid, who Seamus had not seen sidle up, scolded him hotly.

"Beggin' yer pardon, Father," Seamus was all contrition, "but I clean forgot meself."

"Let it be a lesson to ye on the evils of the drink," Casey replied with a face as straight as any dour old priest could have summoned up. And then as the barmaid once again took her leave, having deposited a bottle of Jameson's whiskey, 'compliments of the lads, Father,' Casey leaned towards Seamus, the irresistible twinkle in his eyes once again.

"Eh, Seamus what kind of odds would ye put on a certain priest gettin' himself defrocked tonight?"

"Found yer virginity in the kip as well did ye, Father?" was Seamus' caustic reply as he shrugged into his coat and with a final nod at Casey slipped out the door, ever the master of the quick disappearance.

As he began the walk home, he heard a rousing cheer go up and then the mournful opening notes of *The Foggy Dew*. He smiled, oh aye, his boy was home, he only wished he could be entirely certain that it was a good thing.

Chapter Four

Divine Circles

INSOFAR AS HISTORY WAS A MATTER OF INDIVIDUALS, a piece of history was sitting listening to what was quite possibly the most boring lecture he'd ever had the misfortune of hearing.

"If indeed History is, as it is claimed, a mere matter of starting points then the dichotomy of the Irish people, even in the assignment of dates, becomes very apparent..."

'Irish history, you pompous ass,' thought Pat Riordan while drawing a series of naked women down the border of his paper, 'has never been a mere matter of starting points. Irish history,' he stuck his tongue between his teeth concentrating on a particularly round curve of buttock, 'has always been a matter of circles.' Dante-esque circles that is, Hell, Purgatory and, he glanced down two rows to where the new addition to Modern Irish History sat, occasionally Paradise.

He continued to draw the same woman, one-quarter profile, three-quarter profile, lying on a bed in a tussle of pillows and blanket. Pat, tongue clenched firmly between teeth, raced with soft charcoal to catch the light as it shone on the head of his unknowing muse. He was listening, with half an ear, to the lecture.

"...from the time of the Norman invasions...agrarian revolt...Battle of the Boyne...Protestant ascendancy...uneducated peasant population, ill-prepared..." The words drifted in and out of Pat's hearing. History was mere bedtime fodder in the home in which he'd grown up. He'd known the basics of Irish history from the time of his fifth birthday, understood the tenets of the American constitution by ten and could argue philosophy, religion, literature, poetry and all the semantics thereof at twelve. He knew entire portions of Thomas Paine's *The Rights of Man*, off by heart. Robert Emmett's speech from the dock went without saying; many a young Irishman and woman had been inspired to take up the fiery cross of revolution by the famous last words of the patriot martyr.

'Let no man dare, when I am dead, to charge me with dishonor; let no man

attaint my memory by believing that I could have engaged in any cause but that of my country's liberty and independence...' These were words of inspiration certainly, but hardly practical to live by. When it came to revolution and its likely outcome, Pat Riordan, born into endless generations of Republicanism, was of a more prosaic frame of mind.

He brushed a dark curl out of his eyes and dug a piece of white chalk out of his pocket to highlight the shadow in his drawing. He'd have to get his hair cut before Casey got home, which should be any time in the next month or so. Long hair, holey-knee pants and the Young Socialists, there was only so much, Pat knew, that his brother could be expected to accept. So, he pulled his ponytail tighter, the hair would have to be sacrificed.

"...with the post-war collapse of agricultural prices," the professor was saying and Pat, chalk tilted at an angle, allowed the man's voice to waver along the surface of his ear until two phrases caught his attention, *'agrarian aggressors... Ribbonism... Karen Riordan...'* 'Kieran, you silly bastard, the name is Kieran and he'd roll over in his grave if he heard you calling him a Ribbonist.' He continued on rolling the chalk between his fingers to loosen some of its particles and then realized with a terrible chill up his spine that the class had gone preternaturally silent and some forty pairs of eyes, including the apoplectic looking professor, were now staring at him. He realized in an instant what had happened and wholeheartedly wished the floor would open up and drop him into hell.

"Something you'd like to share with the class, Mr. Riordan?" The Professor said in that maddeningly smart-ass way teachers seemed to pick up with their diplomas.

Pat, not the boldest of souls in public situations, was about to stammer an unintelligible reply but then his muse turned her head and offered him a look of sympathy that shifted the parameters of his world. He answered her smile and from reserves he wasn't aware of possessing, found courage.

"Kieran," he said, "the man's name was Kieran and he was never a proponent of Ribbonism," he said with an assurance he did not feel.

"Relative of yours was he, Mr. Riordan?" the teacher said with a smirking smile.

"My great-great grandfather actually," Pat said anger giving him firmer ground to stand upon.

"Perhaps then you'd like to enlighten us as to history as it *actually* happened." The professor, smiling creamily, was certain he'd refuse, Pat saw. The teacher, however, hadn't counted on the rather intense pair of green eyes that were gazing up at him with great interest. *'Seize the day'*, he told himself, *'or it will seize you.'*

"Ribbonism was a generic term covering a variety of small insurrections; it was a general term to cover a movement that never really came out from the dark of night and the shadows of hiding. It was well over by my—by Kieran's time. Ireland by the mid-1800's was leaving its agrarian roots behind and moving into the industrial age. Kieran believed in some of the same concepts but not necessarily in the methods. The industries based on large-scale agriculture, such as linen and brewing, were the industries that prospered but the day of the peasant farmer was over. Ribbonism was like the old Catholic priests in its call to go back to the land, to revert to some golden era that had never existed in Ireland in the first place, Kieran was the sort of man who looked forward not back. He supported the purveyors of change but never saw himself as a devout follower of anyone. He believed that a man should stand alone rather than compromise his beliefs."

"And what exactly were those beliefs?" the professor, eyebrows arched, was intently polishing his glasses.

"He believed in a system, a world if ye will where a man is not judged by the cut of his clothes or the color of his skin nor the size of his wallet. A world where truth is not to be feared, he believed," Pat took a deep breath and looked directly into the eyes of his Muse, "that all men should live free and that freedom is worth any price."

"Bravo," his Muse said, green eyes sparkling. Pat felt suddenly that, like the mythical hero Diarmuid, he could leap entire forests in a single bound.

"Commendable," the professor was readjusting his glasses to the bridge of his beaky nose, "but words are cheap at half the price, action is what costs."

"Well," said Pat, recklessness still thrumming sweetly in his veins, "perhaps if ye'd read further ye'd know that my great-great-granddaddy was a Fenian an' was hung by the English for staging an uprising an' after they hung him they had him drawn an' quartered, then stuck his head on a pike as a warning to the rest of the croppies not to get anymore ideas. The history of Ireland has been the history of my family."

"Surely you don't mean to suggest that in a land of three million people your family constitutes the entire story of a nation, do you, Mr. Riordan?"

"No, of course not," Pat said feeling angry that the man had picked one point out of what he'd said and deliberately misunderstood it. "Look, you can read every book an' text on Irish history that was and ever will be written an' still not get the slightest feeling for it. There are five things ye need to know before you approach Irish history with any real depth of understanding." He held up four charcoal dusted fingers and one chalk-laden thumb. "First of all ye need to remember that ye are dealing with people, living, breathing, sleeping, eating, laughing, weeping human beings," he took a breath and attempted to unfurl his tongue, which in any seizure of emotion, his neighborhood and its linguistics took firm hold of. "In Irish history an' I suppose in any land's history ye cannot discount the human beings that bled an' died on the stage of time. Second, an inability to see that the present is merely our past repeatin' itself with many of the same results an' as few solutions. Third, that hatred, while a great motivator, tends to get in the way of any genuine progress an' fourth, an' this one is perhaps the truest of the lot, we are prepared to take defeat after defeat but we will never accept losing on a permanent basis. We don't understand the concept. Lastly," he looked out over the class meeting every eye in turn, "ye need to understand that we are our own greatest enemies, that the Irish have killed the Irish and trodden on their fellow man, have incited hatred merely to maintain a sense of superiority over their neighbor. To the British we are one problem, an' likely an insignificant one at that, to us they are THE problem an' in that perception alone lies the reason we cannot bring an end to hundreds of years of rage an' bloodshed."

His Muse, green eyes clear and undiluted with admiration, began to clap and was soon followed by the rest of the class. Pat, face red, dark curls slipping out of their bondage acknowledged their tribute with a curt nod.

"You make an impressive orator, Mr. Riordan," the professor said dryly, "I'm certain your Fenian ancestors would be proud. Now class, if I might beg a moment of your attention, tonight you will be assigned to read pages 300-450 in your text." There was an assortment of groans and the sound of books sliding into bags amid the general shuffle and babble of a dismissed class. Pat, gathering up his own things realized, to his infinite horror, that his drawings were no longer in the clutch of books and paper. He looked under his chair and on the floor surrounding it, feeling increasingly desperate as several square feet of ground did not yield up the nude studies.

"Looking for this?" asked a lilting voice.

Pat, thinking that his own personal circle in life seemed to be, at present, hell, looked slowly up and met the amused countenance of his muse. She handed him his drawings and he reluctantly took them.

"You've a strong, bold hand," she said, "for drawing that is," she added as Pat, feeling like he was on fire, turned a beetroot red.

"Aye, well, thank you," he muttered, wishing she would go away and leave him to drown in mortification alone.

"You've a talent there," she said sincerely.

"Ah, it's only a bit of a hobby."

"Have you ever seen Michelangelo's sketches?" she asked.

Pat shook his head.

"Well I have and these remind me of them, same raw, unleashed talent. Though," her eyes had a wicked twinkle to them, "it seems you may have a greater love of the female form than did Michelangelo. Oh, by the way," she leaned close enough that he could smell her scent, vanilla and strawberries, "I've got a birthmark on my left hip, I thought you might want to add it in for authenticity." With that final thought, she left him standing openmouthed, books and drawing instruments puddling around his feet.

"Mr. Riordan you'll be tardy for your next class," said the professor in his best uptight teacher voice. "Thinking up more revolutionary rhetoric are you?" he asked as Pat still stood unmoving. Blinking like a stunned owl, Pat turned and said in a soft voice,

"No sir, I was just wondering if maybe the circles of Hell and Paradise don't sometimes overlap."

"Of course they do, Mr. Riordan," the professor, laying out his books for the next class, looked over the top of his spectacles, "that's what we call Earth."

Perhaps, thought Pat, at last gathering up his papers, pens and charcoal, perhaps the man wasn't totally hopeless after all.

PAT HAD MEANT IT WHEN HE SAID THE HISTORY OF IRELAND was the history of his family. He was not bragging, for the Lord above knew that in Ireland to have your past generations mirror the events of its nation was not a happy situation. His statement was simple and unexaggerated; the fortunes of the Riordans had paralleled those of Ireland. Which is to say, in no small manner, that neither had ever known peace, nor much prosperity or happiness. It was also to say that both had seen more than their share of bloodshed, sectarian violence and longing for an unattainable dream, something that over the years had taken on the ethereal form of normality, a life of simplicity and small happinesses. However, in all truth, neither the nation nor the family understood what dreams had to be discarded and sometimes crushed to attain these things. In either case, neither was willing to find out.

There had been a tradition of a rising in every generation since the days of Theobald Wolfe Tone and his tragically failed uprising of 1798. Irish history tended to remember the men who failed gloriously with greater fondness than the men who actually won some sort of advancement. The Riordans too had their tradition of a rising in each generation and as a result, not a man of them had seen his fiftieth birthday, some falling a few decades short even of that.

The story of Ireland was a tale as old as mankind itself. A story of resistance in the face of insurmountable odds, of a refusal to put one's neck under the master's boot willingly. The boot in this case being the stiff-legged and unwieldy one of British imperialism.

The trouble of Ireland fit quite nicely into an old Vietnamese proverb in that Ireland was '*too close to England and too far from Heaven.*' Some would say that the problems all started when King John thrust his tri-leopard banner into Irish shores, for after that the successive English monarchies, Tudors, Stuarts, Old King Billy et al, considered Ireland as an English island just off their west coast. It was in this frame of mind that James I of England 'planted' colonies of English and Presbyterian Scots in six of the northern counties, cutting a nation in two irrevocably. The blood from that cut would still be running freely some three hundred years later.

Catholic farmers were pushed off their land and the Protestant landlords with large holdings were forbidden by law to give them tenancy, the landlords with smaller holdings were permitted to grant them tenancy but were taxed at a higher rate for the sin of doing so.

The list of Thou-Shalt-Nots for the Catholics were formally disguised as penal laws.

Thou Shalt Not own land.

Thou Shalt Not Vote.

Thou Shalt Not be educated within Ireland nor without.

Thou Shalt Not hold public office, nor work in the civil service, nor own a weapon, nor earn more than one-third the value of your own crops. Nor be a doctor, a lawyer, a merchant nor a professional of any sort.

The Catholic religion was for the most part banned, illegal and the practice of it subject to severe punishment. Seminaries to train new priests were outlawed and foreign-trained priests forbidden entrance into Ireland.

There was one Thou Shalt and it managed to be the bitterest of the lot, a law that demanded Catholics pay tithe into Protestant coffers. The commandment that remained unwritten was no less forceful for its lack of ink and it was firmly etched within the Catholic consciousness, thou shalt not live as a human being nor aspire to the lofty notion of being one and this we will not let you forget. Ever.

The dour Lowlander Scots who settled in Northern Ireland were a God-fearing, hardworking, suspicious minded breed who saw the 'Old Irish' as a feckless, lazy, yet dangerous foe. Even the Pope, far away in Rome, was as suspect as if his middle name was Beelzebub and he sprouted horns under his hat.

Where the Riordans fit into this history was also, as anything inherently Irish must be, a point up for debate. However, the first one to breeze into history with any aplomb was the organizer of the Defenders, a rural underground group who would eventually forge strong links with a group of young Protestant idealists called the United Irishmen, led eventually by the unfortunate Wolfe Tone.

It was Wolfe Tone who led the Rebellion of 1798 that set into action events which were to forever alter the course of Irish history. The Rebellion failed miserably from the perspective of the peasants but for the British it was a bit of a triumph. It proved what they had believed all along—that the Irish were a feckless, upstart bunch of hooligans who were not to be trusted. It was this mentality that brought into being the Act of Union of 1800 which was passed by the use of force, threats and bribery, an Act that forced the Irish Parliament to amalgamate with the British one, rendering them voiceless in an assembly of some 650 strong. The Irish Parliament had consisted of the Protestant Ascendancy, leaving the three million Catholics of the time without representation.

One fallout of the Act of Union was that political power shifted from Dublin to London and so did many of the titled landholders. Irish landholdings were exploited in an effort to maintain lavish lifestyles, while in Ireland the people who tilled the land faced starvation, disease and death.

In an effort to maximize yields from small landholdings, potatoes as an easy and hardy crop became heavily relied upon, which led to the disastrous famine of the 1840's. The famine would kill one million and send another million fleeing to America, though they would often die on the disease ridden ships and never see the shores where they'd sought sanctuary. Ireland would lose nearly half of her population and would forever change the face of America.

Cathal Riordan, father of Kieran, chose to stay. He watched his brothers leave and knew that he would never see them again. Then he set himself the task of surviving and keeping his family alive. It was, even for so strong and determined a man, a daunting task. It meant eating grass and stealing fish from the landlord's pond. It meant hunting in the night and learning to ride the wind as if he'd been born to it. It meant watching your friends and neighbors die because you could not spare them a morsel. It meant holding the only baby girl ever known to have been born to the Riordan line and knowing that there was not enough food for her mother to nurse her, it meant building a wee coffin with your two hands and putting your own flesh and blood under the ground. It meant losing faith in God and church and man. It meant having your home seized by English troops, razed to the ground and burnt, just so you couldn't drag through the ashes for your meager belongings.

It meant watching your oldest boy die in agony from the 'bloody flux', blood pouring from his body and being unable to help him. It meant not making love to your wife for fear of pregnancy and finally because you were too weak to even consider the idea. It meant selling every scrap of clothing, bedding, leaving only the cloth on your back, which was louse-ridden and filthy. It meant finally putting your only remaining boy on a famine ship and praying to a God you no longer believed in that he would make it to America alive. It meant watching your wife die from a combination of starvation and heartbreak and then stumbling drunk with grief and pain along roads where entire families lay in ditches, dying of the black fever, typhus. It meant walking for endless days and nights, never stopping, gone beyond the limits of degradation, humiliation, pain and affliction into the no man's land of madness. Not knowing where you were, lost, alone and crazed, falling to your knees and then onto your face only to discover that you'd made your way to the ocean and would likely die because you were too weak to lift your face from a mere four inches of saltwater.

Cathal did survive, was pulled out of the water by a grizzled old fisherman and taken to Inisheer, the southernmost island of the Arans. Cathal came from a long line of men who preferred to keep their feet firmly planted on land but from necessity, he learned to navigate the frail wickerwork curragh, the traditional Irish boat, on the rough and unpredictable north Atlantic waters. Fish and seaweed became the staples of his diet and he would swear to his dying day that he could still taste the both of them.

Healing comes even to those who don't want it and so it came to Cathal. In 1852 he remarried, a quiet dark island girl who gave him three sons within the space of five years.

From the seeds of famine sprung the sapling of the Irish Republican Brotherhood, an oath-bound secret society whose object was revolution. Its tentacles reached across the ocean by the following year and Clann na Gael was established on American shores. Thus began the long relationship of support from the United States for Ireland's fight for freedom.

In 1866, twenty years after his father put him on a famine ship, Kieran Riordan came home. He brought with him an American wife and a ten-year-old son, Daniel. A year later, he and his father would be hung for their part in an unsuccessful uprising. The British hung, flogged, jailed and transported the leaders thus adding more names to the very long roll of Irish martyrs.

Kieran's wife decided to stay in Ireland and raise her son. Daniel would grow up in an Ireland that saw the likes of Charles Stuart Parnell, the Protestant lawyer who became the leader of the Irish Parliament and devoted much of his life to the issue of Home Rule, giving the Irish the right to rule their own destiny. It was as close as Ireland would ever come to complete independence. Parnell was ruined by a divorce scandal and died only a year later. His cause would be taken up by others but never with the same fervor or charisma. Home Rule would be tabled, put aside, shunted about and never seriously considered by the British Parliament. Its ghost would hang about firing more generations, leading them to insurrection and defeat.

The Unionists, descendants of the Lowlander Scots, had no interest in Home Rule, 'Home Rule is Rome rule' went a popular slogan of the day and the Unionists led by Edward Carson and Andrew Bonar Law wished to remain firmly wrapped in the Union Jack. They would play the 'Orange Card' and appealing to the most primitive fears and hatreds would stir the cauldron for another generation of sectarian strife and hatred.

Daniel Riordan became a leader of sorts, helping Parnell to tie the disparate limbs of politics and force, the marriage of these two bedfellows forged another link in the chain that would eventually lead to the formation of the Irish Republican Army.

Daniel, never comfortable in the city, settled in Connemara, home to an ancient and lonely landscape. It suited him well. He raised four sons, the youngest of whom was Pat and Casey's grandfather, Brendan. The Riordan household became the hub of the surrounding countryside, a place where wisdom was dispensed in equal measure with food, drink and respite. If two men had a quarrel over a piece of land, a horse, a cow or even a woman they would take their dispute to Daniel who could be trusted to make a fair judgment. Strays of all sorts made their way to the Riordan door, dogs, cats, children, men on the run, women in despair, all certain to receive a welcome and a place to lay their head for as long as need be. Though a blacksmith by trade, Daniel ran a small but productive farm. He'd a way, people said, of coaxing the best from the soil, of making the cows produce more milk and the chickens more eggs. It was true that despite the raising of four big, hearty boys with appetites to match, there was never a better table than the Riordans for good, honest fare.

Daniel, despite a happy home and full belly, never forgot the past. He had, as a boy of eleven, watched his father and grandfather hang and vowed he would honor their memory. Kieran and Cathal had come late to Republicanism, but Daniel was born to it. It became in his time the religion of the Riordans. By no means an orator, still Daniel had a quiet strength that made him a natural leader, a magnet to which people were drawn and, once drawn, became disciples. Under his guidance, people banded together to push for reform, to defend their rights, to take back what had been stolen and nearly destroyed in the Irish soul. Though not a proponent of force as a means of change, Daniel nevertheless believed its use justified when necessary. Land reforms slow to come finally resulted in the buying out of landlords in the later years of the nineteenth century and a return to the Irish owning their own land.

However, for every reason to hope, there was an equal and opposite reason to despair. Nineteen twelve saw the signing of a covenant by 470,000 Unionists, loyal to the British crown, swearing an oath never to accept Home Rule and to prevent the implication of it by force if necessary. One hundred thousand men joined the Ulster Volunteer Force, an organization that would come to be feared for more than its numbers. Three hundred tons of rifles and ammunition were landed for their use in April 1914 while the British Army stood idly by, allowing a sectarian group to arm themselves. The Unionists had no reason to fear. Home Rule, though put into effect by law, was rendered impotent by its suspension until the Great War should end.

Daniel, far away from the world in which the illusions of politics were practiced, saw the ruse for what it was. The action had, in effect, done little other than to pacify the Unionists, who seemed blinded by the sight of the Union Jack into believing that the British saw them as equals and peers of the realm. Perhaps in British eyes they were not as Irish as the Catholics but they were still incontrovertibly Irish and thus somewhat less than human, though handy to use as a trump card during election times.

Daniel could feel change coming. In answer to the formation and arming of the UVF an Irish volunteer corps was formed. They were banned from arming themselves by the same government who'd sat idly by and allowed the UVF to bring in 300 tons of illegal arms. Shortly after, there would be a split in the Irish corps over the issue of conscription, and the largest section would go to war, fighting and dying in British uniforms, believing they were fighting for freedom and justice for nations without voice. They were, to a certain extent, cannon fodder for the British generals, much as the Canadian and Anzac troops would be.

Those who refused conscription became the Irish Volunteers and they, along with the small force of the Irish Citizen's Army, would change Irish history forever. England's difficulty being Ireland's opportunity, it seemed the time to take a stand.

During the Easter week of 1916, a group of idealists, poets, teachers and socialists stood on the stairs of the General Post Office in Dublin and proclaimed the Republic of Ireland. Daniel's son Brendan was amongst their numbers.

They fought valiantly for Irish sovereignty, to declare Ireland for the Irish, in the name of dead generations and ones yet to come, they fought for a cause which five decades later still had not come to fruition. They were outnumbered twenty to one but managed to hold out for a week before admitting defeat.

Sixteen of the Rising's leaders were executed, some so badly wounded from the fighting that they had to be propped up in chairs to be shot. Suspects, innocent or guilty, were rounded up and jailed in British prisons. Brendan Riordan, twenty-six years of age, was one of these. While he sat without trial in a British prison, his father was shot through the head twice and killed. It wasn't known who the shooter was, but beside Daniel's lifeless body was left the message, 'Fenian lie down.' Brendan, unable to attend his father's funeral, vowed from his prison cell to never lie down. He was released three months later because of a great tidal wave of public anger, from both the Irish and American sides of the Atlantic, directed towards the governments of England and the United States. The Irish immigrants were an important electoral body to a president trying to win support to go to war. The prisoners, for reasons having little to do with justice, were released. By force of charm and family legacy Brendan, without actually intending to, gathered about him a group of young insurgents and became their unofficial leader.

Brendan went to Derry, a northern city that was a hotbed of sectarian strife. Catholics there lived under the some of the worst discrimination in Ireland, consigned to ghettoes called the 'Bogside.'

The remnants of the Rising's leadership formed the Irish Parliament, 'Dail Eireann' in 1919, with Sinn Fein as its ruling party. The elected President, a gentleman with an ungainly figure and an even unlikelier name, Eamon de

Valera, was absent from the Dail's first sitting as he was locked up in prison, a rather inauspicious beginning for a man who would rule, on and off, for much of the century. In fact, on that twenty-first day of January many people were absent. The Unionist party, though invited, didn't even bother to refuse, they simply didn't come. When the roll of Sinn Fein representatives itself was called the words *'fe glas ag gallaibh'*, 'jailed by the foreigner', were called out thirty-six times. *'Ar dibirt ag gallaibh'*, 'deported by the foreigner' was another oft-used phrase that day. In fact, there were only twenty-eight deputies present out of the one hundred and four names called.

De Valera was not to rule for long that first time. The Irish Volunteers and the Irish Republican Brotherhood melded at this point to become the IRA. Michael Collins, a man of no small brilliance, was the commanding officer of the army at this time and he and his colleagues brought the British to the table to hammer out a treaty. The Irish got less than they hoped for but it was enough to cause Collins, never a pushover, to accept the terms of a limited form of government for the twenty-six southern counties with full recognition of the existing powers and privileges of the British-Loyalist government in the north. Collins saw it as the first step in a long and bloody process. His friend and rival, Eamon de Valera saw it as nothing less than treason and resigned as president of the Republic. Those who followed him became the Anti-Treaty faction, those who stayed with Collins, Pro-Treaty. Ireland went to war with herself. In the end the seven hundred who died, the hatreds that were inflamed and the divisiveness that would taint Irish politics for decades served little purpose. Ireland remained partitioned.

Brendan, after much soul-searching, found himself fighting under Michael Collins. It was here he would learn many of the skills that he would need in the years to come. He would see prison twice more in his lifetime, would survive beatings and floggings and hunger strike and tear his own soul apart in trying to separate his political ideals from the course of armed struggle he had chosen to follow. He would die from four bullets to the chest and be laid to rest beside the three sons who were killed before him. Brian, his oldest, alive only by the fortune of not being home when masked armed strangers killed his brothers, was a quiet man, not given to fighting nor a great many words. Brendan, a family friend had once said, had been born with his hand fitted to the shape of a gun; he hadn't liked violence but had understood it in the context of its Irish marriage with politics. Brian neither liked nor understood it. His republicanism tended to be of the mythical, rather than practical sort. Romanticism though fled in the face of imprisonment without trial or real accusation. Brian was jailed on trumped up charges, a privilege the government granted itself under the Emergency Powers Act of 1939, allowing it to intern Irish citizens it suspected of crime, real or imagined. Such an imprisonment could not be challenged in the courts as the Act was not subject to the court's power.

He was jailed, they told him, for crimes against the Republic and they produced signed statements saying he'd been seen in the area where a bomb had killed four people. Brian had not even heard of the incident much less been present at its execution. To secure his confession he was, over the course of two weeks, beaten, half-starved, denied access to a toilet, beaten some more, chained to his bed post, allowed to sleep only in twenty minute snatches then seized by the hair and awakened by his face slamming into the bedpost. He was certain after the first week that he'd sustained brain damage and would, indeed, walk with a limp for the rest of his life. Four weeks after his initial arrest he was released without reason or explanation. He went home to his mother who nursed him back to health and when he was well enough to get about on his own he went to Belfast. Within a week, he had joined the IRA. It had been easy for him; his father's name still carried enough weight within the Army to ease his initiation.

He never moved to the forefront of the army, he took his orders from other men and carried them out quietly and obediently. He was, as it turned out, rather expert at explosives, a job that required a still hand and a steel mind. He managed both. He was particularly effective during the Border campaigns of the fifties.

The Fifties were a decade which saw a great reduction in the violence that had defined the Forties. Many within the Republican movement favored passive resistance as an alternative to armed struggle. Wearied and disillusioned by bloodshed and death, the generation that had seen the IRA through the forties began to fade into the background, the new generation stepping forward, many merely seeking excitement without being aware of the consequences of their actions. There was sporadic activity within the ranks of the movement, some of so little consequence that it seemed, even days later that the incidents were mere rumor and never really happened at all.

Within this rather loose framework, Brian managed to find a niche for himself. He revived, on a smaller scale, the Republican newspaper his father had founded some thirty years earlier and poured what little time and money he could find into it. He'd been taught Gaelic as a child and now taught his own sons, born in 1944 and 1949, to speak it as well. His boys were the core of his life and when their mother left, shortly after Pat's second birthday, none of them, it could be said, was sorry to see the back end of her. Brian raised them to be self-sufficient, to cook and clean and mend and should the occasion eventually arise to not be too big of burden for a woman. He told them stories, pretty silver spun fancies when they were small, grand tales of rebellion as they got older, always at a safe remove in the mists of ancient Ireland. He gave them the sky on long summer nights when they went to the west coast to fish. In another life he might have been an astronomer or a poet or perhaps even both, one thing leading quite naturally to the other. Instead, he worked his weeks at a brewery and nights he built weaponry for a revolution whose coming he feared. His weekends and evenings belonged to his boys.

They were good boys, Casey a little wild at times though not getting up to any mischief that a normal boy wouldn't. With Pat there were no complaints, he was too quiet at times and too hard on himself, but all in all they gave Brian no sleepless nights. It was other things that did that. Casey, by ten, started doing odd jobs after school and on weekends, delivering groceries and then when he was a little older he did cleanup at the brewery after hours, which led to driving forklift in the warehouse and then driving van when he was of an age to get his license, delivering crates of Connemara Mist to the four corners of the country. School didn't hold his interest but Brian was determined he would see it through. Pat was of a more academic bent and excelled particularly in literature and history. He too took on odd jobs and among the three of them, they managed to avoid the poverty and unemployment that plagued their corner of the world. They weren't rich and never would be but as long as they 'had the sky and a bit of something to eat,' as Brian was wont to say, it was enough.

Enough until Pat came home from delivering papers one day, black with bruises, blood running from cuts. A gang of Protestant boys had cornered him in a blind alleyway just off a road he'd unwisely taken as a shortcut. Brian, cleaning wounds and checking him over for broken bones had been grateful he'd only been beaten up and nothing more. Casey took a dimmer view of things. Always protective of his little brother he was enraged at what he saw as Brian's lack of concern. Brian had to physically restrain him from leaving the house, afraid of what might happen to him if he let him out the door.

"Goddamnit Da'," Casey had sworn at his father for the first time, "how can ye sit here an' do nothin' after what's been done to him? How can ye?"

"Casey," his father had said sternly, "sit down an' behave as if ye've the grain of sense God gave ye. Now look," he'd continued as Casey unwillingly sat, "what earthly good can it do to rampage up an' down the streets lookin' for a bunch of boys we've not the slightest notion of? We don't know what they look like or who they are an' runnin' about knockin' all their heads in isn't goin' to help yer brother."

"So we sit an' do nothin'?" Casey, never still at the best of times, had leapt up from his chair. "Why do we live this way Daddy? It's like we're hidin' from somethin', it's like we're supposed to pretend that we don't know where ye go after we're in bed. It's like ye expect us to deny our own birthright."

Brian had gone very still and white. "An' just what might that be Casey?" he'd asked, voice deceptively calm.

"To live as free men an' if not that then to fight for freedom every day.

Like yer father did," Casey said, flushed with anger.

"An' to die like my Daddy did?" Brian asked, voice still light but the syllables flattened out in a way that, had Casey known his father's anger, would have warned him to cease and desist.

"Aye, if one must. It's better than to live afraid."

"Better to die like a dog in the street, with only the one son left to mourn ye? That's better, is it? I didn't think our life here together was so terrible but apparently," Brian gave his son a look that made Casey's knees wobble ever-so-slightly, "I was mistaken."

"Daddy, ye know I mean no disrespect," Casey began in a conciliatory tone but was cut off by Brian's black look.

"No I'm afraid boy that I don't know that. Ye hint that I'm hidin' in a corner like some cowerin' child but ye think I'm so daft that I won't notice the insult. No, boy," he said firmly as Casey began to protest, "ye'll let me say what I must in my own home. I loved my daddy, loved him like he was the whole damn world when I was a little boy, he seemed to fill up the sky he was that big, he'd that much presence an' power. He carried the burdens of an entire nation on his back for most of his life an' yet he'd time to read to us an' play with us an' spend days where we felt we were the only thing of any importance in his life. But I was his oldest son," Brian's voice lowered and softened, "an' I saw the nights when he could not sleep an' he felt cornered, when he couldn't reconcile who he was with what he believed, until he got so weary that he didn't know what he believed anymore. I saw the man who sacrificed things an' people in his life but never was able to leave them behind. Yer granddad never knew peace a moment of his life. He gave everything he had, sacrificed things he never told anyone about an' for what? Is Ireland free? Are we the inhabitants of an undivided peaceful nation?"

"No," Casey replied in a chastened voice.

"No, we are not," Brian agreed, "an' so Casey tell me— for what did I stand in the street with my father's blood on me? So that I could raise another generation to go out an' make war? For no better reason than anger? I want you an' yer little brother to be safe an' to grow to see yer own sons grow an' prosper, I do not want to raise another generation of men who die before their sons are out of nappies. An' yet," Brian looked sad and old in the dim twilight that entered their kitchen, "an' yet when I look at ye boy I'll be damned if I don't see the shade of my Daddy on yer face an' in yer limbs."

"Then what," Casey asked quietly, "are yer nights about, Da'?"

Brian had taken a long moment to reply and when he did the words were those of a defeated man, "Because, an' may I burn in hell for this, I cannot help bein' my father's son."

"An' I cannot help bein' mine," Casey said.

Brian had watched his eldest carefully after that, knowing that the boy was biding his time and waiting for his moment. Knowing too that when all was said and done he could not choose Casey's road for him. He had a motor running in him, the boy did, a motor that would roar into life when he found what he was looking for and Brian was afraid that he knew, too exactly, what that thing would be.

Brian had worries of his own at this point. The Irish Republican Army had begun on their Border Campaign by then, a series of skirmishes that would never amount to a war but would disrupt the surrounding countryside, causing destruction and death. Beginning in December of 1956, it would run through to February of 1962 and would cost the British government one million pounds in outright damage and ten million pounds in increased police and military patrols. Six Royal Ulster Constabulary would lose their lives and eleven Republicans would forfeit theirs as well. In the South, there was an additional 400,000 pounds per annum in increased patrols and the money needed to re-open the Curragh internment camp. Belfast, with too many Catholics in a very vulnerable and tenuous position, was not included in the war. Brian was grateful for this as it kept Casey away from the action that the boy seemed only too eager to take part in. However, with his ties to the South still strong, Brian was called on in his capacity as weapons expert and tactical guide several times. He'd not much faith in the campaign itself, seeing too clearly the disorganization, the blunders and near farcical cock-ups that seemed to take place in far too many instances. It was one such blunder that would lead to his downfall.

It started as a favor for Seamus, who insisted that there had been too many injuries and aborted attempts at bombing customs huts, by reason of a young and inexperienced weapons contingent. Brian could get in and out, trigger the explosion and there would be no loss of life, merely property damage. Brian had done as he was asked and the next day he and another fellow, dressed as Dominican priests, had crossed the border without difficulty and found shelter in a nearby village. There they spent a good part of the day in agony as there was a man in the next house dying and they fully expected to be called on to administer last rites. The gig was given up, not by a lack of Latin, but rather by the need for nicotine. Brian's young partner had gone to a local shop and requested a brand of cigarettes only sold north of the border. It was enough to tip off the local constabulary, who swooped up and arrested them within minutes.

The next two months found Brian living within the confines of the Curragh internment camp. As such things went it was not so terrible a place to be, the food was plentiful, there was tea to be had and the prisoners were encouraged to take exercise. There were four huts with approximately ten men to a hut, each with its own OC and chain of command. Brian, rather reluctantly, became the OC of his own, with the job of keeping up the morale of his fellow inmates and preventing the in-fighting which was becoming a problem within the ranks of the IRA.

Escape was a thought which haunted his waking and sleeping hours. There were certain logistics to be worked out which would require some careful planning. There were five sets of fences surrounding the camp, two sets between the camp and a six-foot deep, eight-foot wide trench which was booby-trapped with flares and tripwires. Then if one was lucky enough to surmount these obstacles there were three more sets of fences, four elevated sentry posts at each corner of the camp, manned by armed guards with the added luxury of strolling guards patrolling the perimeter of the fences, a revolver in one hand and an ammonia grenade in the other. Brian, if not exactly cheered by the odds against him, was not entirely dismayed by them either.

The opportunity for escape or rather the means of it, came to him one day while he was shampooing his hair in the shower. A clean man by nature, Brian knew he would raise no eyebrows by requesting a shower each day. The window in the shower had two not altogether sturdy bars, which when wiggled and prised gave way rather easily. Two showers later, a squeaky-clean Brian had his out. He requested his shower in the evening and given permission, went in, turned on the water full blast and shot out the window.

Wire cutters, acquired through a lengthy and tortuous negotiation with a nineteen year old internee who doubled on the outside as a metalworker, facilitated his way through the first two fences. It was when he was very carefully navigating the intricacies of the trench that he realized he was not alone. Pete Kelly, he of the wire cutters, was directly behind him, bellydown in the mud, ready to take the trip across the trench.

"What the fock d'ye suppose you are doin'?" Brian had hissed, infuriated at the gall of the boy.

Pete Kelly had smiled the feckless smile of nineteen and replied, "I would suppose I am escapin'."

Brian had little choice then but to take the boy with him, it was either that or abandon the plan altogether. He was to regret the choice he made for the rest of his life. Brian cleared the trench safely but Pete, made overconfident by clearing the first two fences, tripped a wire and sent up a flare. Within minutes the perimeter was a hail of bullets drenched in ammonia fumes. The wire cutters were lost in the ensuing panic and Brian, dragging an injured Pete behind him, had to tackle the last three coils of fencing with his bare hands.

The miracle of it all being that they made it, aided by dumb luck and the not altogether enthusiastic efforts of the guards who could have at any moment shot the both of them stone dead. Instead Peter, blinded by the ammonia, was shot in the leg and able with Brian's help to more or less run when they cleared the last fence.

They made it to a byre some six miles down the road, where Pete, now gushing blood from his leg and unable still to see through streaming eyes, collapsed and could go no further. He urged Brian to go on 'as there was no use the both of them being captured, an' perhaps he could slow the bastards up a bit.' Brian, being who he was, stayed. He tied off Pete's leg as best he could, fearing an artery had been struck and then put the boy flat on the floor following this position himself. The police were most likely to let loose a barrage from chest or waist height, they'd not escape capture but they would escape death by lying low.

The ear-splitting fire of bullets came a half hour later and Brian laying silent on the floor, waited it out. Afterwards there was a bit of chatter, a shout or two and then the sound of trucks pulling away into the night. Brian, astonished, waited a full fifteen minutes knowing snipers could be waiting outside to pick them off like wounded geese.

Outside he checked the area thoroughly and realized there was no one lying in wait. He went back in to retrieve Pete and saw that unlike himself Pete had not been bound by unnatural luck that night, a bullet ricocheting off a beam in the byre had struck him neatly in the temple, leaving only a small trickle of blood in its wake. Pete was dead. Brian, mindful that luck was likely to run dry at any moment, said a brief prayer over the boy's cooling body and fled into the night. Two days later, he was back in Belfast, never quite understanding what had transpired that night in the byre.

It was for him the end of the fighting and the end of all things signifying it in his life. He chose to live the rest of his life quietly, in what peace could be bought or bartered for in the realm of souls. It was to be brief. In early 1961, four men entered his house in the wee hours and dragged him off to an unidentified house somewhere north of Belfast. He would never tell another living soul what happened in the five days they kept him and he would never be a whole man again. A year later, he would die from a blast of gelignite handled improperly. Accident, was what his oldest son would tell the youngest and Pat, for Casey's own comfort, would pretend to believe it. Pat knew though that his father had gotten out of the business of bombs some time earlier and had not gone back. But for Casey, who was his last blood link on earth, Pat would and could pretend.

In Brian's will there was enough money and a request that they take it and go to America. Casey would not go and Pat could not be persuaded to leave without his brother.

Casey, against every wish his father had ever had for him, joined the ranks of an IRA that once the Border Campaigns fizzled to an end, was almost entirely defunct. It seemed that all signs pointed to the end of the IRA. In a sense, this would prove to be the truth; the IRA as it had existed in its previous decades and incarnations was over but from its ashes would rise the deadly military force of the Provisional IRA.

Acting with permission of a tiny cell group and the force of his own grief and rage, Casey set off a bomb in a London tube station. No one was hurt but the damage was estimated to be near 50,000 pounds. Nineteen years of age and unrepentant in the face of judge and sentence, he landed himself five years in the British penal system, not the pleasantest of places for anyone, less so for an Irish Republican militant.

Pat, fourteen and very much alone in the world, was taken in by an old lady who, from time to time, looked after boys in trouble, boys on the run, or in Pat's case a boy with nowhere to turn. Pat stayed until he was eighteen and then in anticipation of his brother coming home, took up residence in a Catholic housing estate, one that trembled on the brink of the Shankill Road, the dividing line between Protestant and Catholic settlements in Belfast.

On the day that Pat explained Irish history to his class, his brother had awakened for the first time in five years on Irish soil, had bid a polite goodbye to the girl in his bed, bathed, dressed and gotten on a plane for the Middle East and had begun by that simple act a ripple in the very fabric of their lives, a ripple that would continue to grow and build until it became a tidal force. Twenty-four, clean-shaven, hair freshly cut, he appeared nothing more than a handsome, extremely charming young man to the air hostess he flirted with for much of the flight. In some ways, that's exactly what he was.

Chapter Five

Little Miss Lolita

"Humbert Humbert," said Jamie, "is not a role I ever particularly fancied playing."

Yevgena, buckling her suitcase, took a moment to reply, "Jemmy, at nineteen she hardly qualifies as Lolita and you are not a likely candidate for dirty old man either."

A triangle of green peeked out at her from under a white-sleeved elbow. "Then why do I feel like one?"

"That," said Yevgena sliding into a leather coat, "is a matter between you and your conscience. I," she glanced at her watch, "have a plane to catch."

"Are you certain you don't want me to take you to the airport?" Jamie asked for the tenth time.

Yevgena, sighing as only a Russian can, replied for the tenth time, "Jemmy I am perfectly content to have Liam drive me as the dear man always does. Quit trying to escape that poor girl. It was you, after all, who gave her a job and, without anyone else's coercion, offered her shelter under your roof."

Jamie, lying prone on a cream-silk couch, let out a sigh that in its length managed to convey injury and desolation in equal parts. This invited nothing more from Yevgena than a roll of her eyes. He sat, his sigh quite earnest now and rubbed the crease in his forehead.

"Head still aching?" Yevgena asked, eyes surveying him in detail.

"No, strangely enough it stopped aching when your little friend appeared on the scene."

"And hasn't since?" Yevgena asked, patting powder down the slim line of her nose and then snapping her tortoiseshell compact shut.

"And hasn't since," Jamie agreed grudgingly. "I do wish," he continued, voice rather too convincingly light, "that the child would see fit to tell us where she's from and how she came to be here."

"All I know is I found her in the gypsy camp dancing for her dinner and she seemed a suitable distraction," Yevgena said mildly, "besides she's told you the same story she told me. I think it's her way of saying that we should mind our own business."

"Yes, well I'd rather not have some rabid pack of brothers descending on my head when they find out she's living here."

"I think you'll find, Jamie, that there are no brothers or any other relations to bother you. Call it a hunch," she added as Jamie looked at her sharply.

"I think the more relevant question," Jamie mused, "is to ask why she would lie about her origins, what purpose could it possibly serve?" He rose to take Yevgena's bags and escort her to the car.

"Jemmy, perhaps for now, let her have her little mystery. If someone comes looking for her then the mystery is solved, if no one does," Yevgena shrugged, "then she is safe here for the moment."

Jamie walked Yevgena to the car where the mist of a cool morning still hung in the air, gelling and rolling off the black-barked oaks and dripping off the scarlet berries of the rowans.

Yevgena pressed her knuckles into his jawline, smoothing out the muscles the way she had when he was a child. "You will be alright my darling boy?" Jamie nodded, knowing it was half-statement, half-question and that he wouldn't be able to give her an adequate answer just yet.

"Don't worry about me," he said in his best blarney tone, "I'll be busy, it's not like you haven't left me with my hands full."

"Worrying about you is a full-time job," Yevgena said as she slid neatly into the car. Jamie shut her door and smiled down at her open window, mouthing the words 'I'll be fine,' as the car slid down the drive and out of sight.

JAMIE KIRKPATRICK HAD BEEN THE ONLY SON OF A LONELY FATHER. While not actually an occupation, it was a role that occupied most facets of his life—valiant son unable to save unhappy father. It wasn't anyone's fault, not Jamie's, not his dead mother's and not even, it would seem, his father.

Jamie had tried, from a very early age, to make happiness, to giftwrap and present it to his father on birthdays, Christmases and every bloody day that rose and set before and after. Approval, every child's dream, every child's nemesis, seemed the surest way. It had, even now as he looked thirty-two full in the face, never ceased to be an avenue of fruitless endeavor. The best grades in school, the bloodiest injuries in sports, the dreams a father and son could share and build. None of it had done. His father, kind and loving, had been somehow absent, a shade that had never quite managed to be fully born. And now having put the barrel of a gun in his mouth, he was fully absent. It wasn't, as everyone seemed to be certain, Jamie's grief that was likely to destroy him, it was his anger. A man's life was his own to do with as he wished, to take or to give as he so chose, but his father might have told him first, might have warned him ten years ago before he, Jamie, ruined his own life. His father, who had looked at him once with bitterness in his face and gall in his mouth, "such devotion to duty Jamie, you should have been a Jesuit after all, you'd do them proud." The irony of that as his father had pushed Jamie's shoulder to the wheel.

If only he'd said, 'Laddie, I think at some point I'll end all this," then Jamie could have thanked him and not wasted ten years of life trying to keep the pieces together for a man who didn't want the picture completed. His father had chosen to lie down in guilt, but had through the force of filial love commanded his son to keep walking, to take the burden and face the mountain. Jamie, twenty-two, freshly graduated from the English department at Oxford, dizzy with dreams and expectation, had turned his back on all those things he was too young to even know he desired and shouldering his father's burdens walked, if not willingly, at least open-eyed into the fire.

Twenty-two and head of an international export business that he didn't want. He had however, decided that if he was to do it, he would do it right. The Kirkpatricks had made linen and whiskey for three hundred years, each the best in its class, each a symbol of status and savoir faire the world over. Linen and whiskey could be made cheaper in all parts of the world, but none made it better. The linen with a thread count so high it felt like silk on the skin, the whiskey a painstaking process of separately malting forty-two small batches of whiskey to be combined into the special blend that comprised Connemara Mist. It was aged in oak barrels to give it its distinctive mellow taste.

Jamie's father had kept a somewhat steady hand on the tiller, kept the sales even, the bank balance neither falling nor climbing for the years he'd run the companies. Jamie though, sensing in the postwar economy a new world market for the taking, had gone out of his way to sell Irish. The Romantic Ireland, the Ireland of Yeats, Synge and Joyce, the soft green pastures uncut by highway or high-rise, the wide empty sugar sand beaches and the dear little cottages furled in peat smoke. The long-legged, jittery racehorses, the Georgian gentility of green and gold Dublin, the pewter mist folding into purple mountains that seemed the stuff of fairies and leprechauns. When you bought Kirkpatrick linens or Kirkpatrick whiskey you were buying a piece of what your ancestors had left behind, you were buying a dream. A dream Jamie knew, that was wrapped in shamrocks and tied up with dollar bills, a dream that bore little resemblance to the truth.

The reality of rural Ireland was one of dying villages, rundown shops and men who often clung to bachelorhood well past the point of being any earthly use to a woman. It was a land of old men and women, a land that time had forgotten. A land that saw 40,000 of her people emigrate each year, never to return. The cities were often worse, elegant ruins became rundown housing for the poor with inadequate plumbing, heating or space. Diseases that other western nations had obliterated still rode, like spectral horses, through the streets of Irish cities.

Jamie, with a certain amount of longing for the land that time forgot, knew what Ireland really needed, what the Irish needed were jobs. Jobs that meant they could stay in their own country, raise their children on Irish soil, send them to school for free, get proper medical attention and have a little left over to hope with, to dream with. So he, in place of his own dreams became the seller of dreams. Selling Ireland to the rest of the world to buy it back for her own people. It was, some days, almost enough to make him forget what he'd left behind.

The Seller of Dreams. He'd been called worse. Paddy, Mick, Bogtrotter and several variations on that theme. Colleen used to call him 'you beautiful mick bastard,' in affection and frustration. Colleen had been the one thing he'd done for himself, the one time he'd put what he wanted before the needs of his father.

He'd known Colleen from the time she was eight and he was ten. He'd wandered off from his father one day, waiting for him to finish a conversation with a man and found himself, several harrowing hours later, in a mean and lean part of Belfast he'd never encountered before. It had been Colleen, small and sprightly, a silver-eyed elf who'd found him and taken him home to her mother like a stray puppy.

'An' what have we here Colleen?' Mary MacGregor had asked, work-reddened hands on hips.

'Jamie,' Colleen had said as if, very simply, she'd known him the entirety of her life.

'Well young man, ye look hungry, sit yer backside down on that chair an' we'll feed ye.' Jamie had nodded gratefully and taken the appointed chair. Moments later a steaming bowl of stew was placed under his nose alongside a plate of fresh bread. He ate like one half-starved, Colleen across from him tucking into her own bowl of stew. Her mother looking on now and then as she busied herself about the stove. Colleen smiling encouragingly through the steam above her bowl. He'd never felt so comfortable or welcome in his life, not even in his own home. He'd almost wished that his father would not find him, at least not for a little while.

Of course, his dad did find him but it wasn't until the evening, long after he'd decided he'd marry Colleen when he grew up and live in the rundown little flat forever. Eventually he did marry her but, as was inevitable, he took her to live in his world and he was to always think perhaps that was where he'd been very, very wrong.

Colleen Colleen Colleen, eyes gray as the moon, a smile to light the world and his, his for the asking, his for the taking. Perhaps God never meant for people to have that which their heart desired the most, perhaps that, right there, was the ultimate sin. For it seemed to Jamie that if He let you have it He damn well found a way to take it back.

They grew up together, the two of them, Jamie spending what time could be stolen, bought and borrowed under the fond eyes of Mary MacGregor and her middle daughter. Seven kids and Colleen was number four, three above and three below her. 'Nondescript,' was the word she'd tossed at him when he'd asked her how she felt about her position in the family. 'The only thing special about me Jamie was that I found you,' she told him later still when life had seen fit to break her heart for the third time in seven years. 'Three strikes and you're out, isn't that what they say in American baseball?' she'd said to him over closed suitcases, closed doors, closed chapters and then she'd taken herself away, for good and for always and gave herself to a man she'd never be able to see or to touch and therefore would never hurt her.

He still couldn't really absorb it; Colleen had been his, not God's. His in a way that she could never belong to God. He couldn't even close his eyes without seeing her like golden webbing on the back of his eyelids, half-reclining on their bed, sweetly unselfconscious, because there was nothing to hide from Jamie, 'come here you beautiful mick bastard,' curling her fingers in invitation and he, young, so young, eager, in love, mad with it, unbelieving that this woman, this pale moon and water creature would allow him the liberties she did. Divine heat, so power-ful that it felt sacred, religious, frightening even at times. He'd been in a state of grace for that short space, pure and without sin, or so he'd thought. There, within the sacristy of sheets, limbs and skin, he had believed love inviolable. A lucky bas-tard, for once. It was the way he tried, strenuously, to remember Colleen. Other pictures interfered, Colleen lying still and diamond white, death's hieroglyphs traced fine and swirling upon her face, pools of blue-black blood laying silent beneath her upturned hands, a self-crucifixion gone awry. That had been the day she'd discovered she was pregnant with Stuart.

'I cannot do this again, Jamie,' she said simply, calmly, when the doctors had brought her around and informed Jamie of his impending fatherhood.

Third time lucky, he'd told himself with enough grim determination to almost believe it. Three strikes and you're out, he should have listened to Colleen, for she'd the wisdom of blighted motherhood on her side. Unlucky bastards, he and his three sons, unlucky bastards all.

'I cannot do this anymore,' she said again, after Stuart. 'I have seen too many little blue coffins and I cannot hope anymore. I may, just may be able to stay sane if I leave now, but if I stay I will surely go mad.' So, he'd let her go, thinking that sanity was highly overrated. His own sanity seemed determined to stay as hard as he tried to drink it away, work it away, fuck it away. His own holy, or unholy as it were, trinity. Drinking, working, fucking. Drinking at night until he could find oblivion in a scant few hours of sleep, working until he thought his

brain would crack in half, company doubling its profits, then trebling and him not giving a damn about any of it. Pissing the money away on booze and women. There were plenty of women, he was beautiful, rich and wild, a combination that raised blood pressures and lowered knickers. He'd actually bought a deserted Pacific island for one woman on a weekend he'd no memory of. Fucking to Oblivion, the required journey for the only destination he longed for. Yevgena had been wrong, there'd been a lot of women, just none that he'd allowed under his skin. He did all the permutations, fucking, screwing, shagging, banging and any other crude metaphor one could think of for the Black Act, the Dirty Deed, the Sheet Shimmy, the Horizontal Hoochie-Koochie, he just didn't make love anymore. A night for each of them, never more than once, no matter how sweet and suppliant, no matter the tears and recriminations, no matter the pounding, thrusting, slick, sweating white goddamn heat of it. Nomatternomatternomatter.

Paddling so hard and wondering why he didn't just let himself drown, people had pissed away their lives on less pain, less heartbreak, less black sucking fear. Other people had, why not him? Why oh why not? Because it would be letting down the team, the one comprised of the raging son and the sad, mad dad. As if his father was breathing his breath, standing on his feet, circulating his cursed blood. Well the sad, mad dad had really let the team down this time. At the time of his father's death, some echo of self-preservation had kept Jamie from the ocean.

Jamie knew Yevgena had a sharp eye, always had, for the obvious and the not so obvious, he knew why she'd brought this girl, this lick of flame, this heat and need and God-awful fragility and set her down like a sacrifice on his doorstep. He knew and had been utterly suckered by it anyway, just as Yevgena had known he would be. This girl who seemed to have been born yesterday, because he knew that there was no farm in Nova Scotia, no rundown little farmhouse with old, silent parents and a dog with a black patch over one eye. Oh yes, such a place probably existed but not for her. No cold, lonely, misted up northern patch of earth had grown her. It just didn't happen that way. All that fine, white skin and perfumed hair, all that length of leg and wit of mind hadn't been fired and brought forth upon a harsh, barren bit of rock. She was lying, but, he'd credit her, she did it like a trooper.

'Tried for years and then when she's fifty she gets pregnant and there I was, nine months later,' she'd said, smiling and popping the last bit of a jam sandwich in her mouth. Her appetite was voracious, as if she was afraid she'd never see food again, as if in the very recent past it had been a limited resource and she'd come to know hunger rather too well. Liar, liar, beautiful liar.

Odd, she was the first woman to stir desire, to make it break like a sickness in his veins and she was the first he had turned down. He'd wanted to make love, with all the elements there, mind, body, soul but drunkenness, for once, had prevailed. He'd slept, there beside her and had been sober when he awoke and had no desire to remedy the fact. It worried him, that.

Insanity, that was her game he supposed, the sort of insanity that youth insulates itself with, known in less cynical circles as innocence.

She'd learn, everyone did, he'd been severely infected with innocence himself once. She'd learn that there was an eleventh commandment that negated the previous ten. Hope Is the Only Sin.

FOUR WEEKS AFTER PAMELA O'FLAHERTY had taken shelter under his roof, Jamie, for a variety of reasons, found himself sorely in need of a drink. However, for quite possibly the first time in its history, the House of Kirkpatrick was without refreshment of the alcoholic sort. He searched each floor, including the cellar, where there was nothing more potent than wine to be found and even resorted to crawling on the floor looking under furniture and fixtures. The result of which being himself, standing in the middle of the study floor, cobwebs tangled artistically through the gold of his hair, utter fury flushing his face.

"What do you mean you got rid of it all?" he said, thinking with lover like longing of the twelve cases of Connemara Mist that only this morning had graced his cellar.

Pamela, head bent over her recently begun studies, took a moment before looking up. There was, Jamie noticed, very little in the way of repentance in her face.

"I took the tops off and poured it down the sink, believe me it took up a lot of my day and Maggie is still complaining about the stink of it in her kitchen. "D'you know the Latin word for drunk?" she asked, brow furrowed over her books again.

"*Ebrius*," he replied automatically, almost missing the insult. "Now look," he said trying to keep his voice steady, "you've no right to go rooting through my things and disposing of my belongings. If you are to go on living here we'll have to set up some basic rules."

She closed her books with deliberate precision and looked him directly in the eye. "Do you suppose," she said tartly, "that the Romans had a term for piss-artist?"

"I—what—pardon me?" Jamie spluttered.

She sat back, quite relaxed and waved a hand around indicating the study. "I thought, seeing as you've such a taste for dead poets and dead languages that you'd be more comfortable if you could hide behind dusty words."

"More comfortable with what?" Jamie was feeling flustered and more in need of the absent drink by the minute.

"Your title, the name of your occupation. A man who practices law is a lawyer, one who teaches is a teacher, one who drinks, seemingly as his life's work, is a piss-artist, at least that's what they call it where I come from."

"And just where exactly is that ?" Jamie asked, voice like splintering glass.

"I've told you," she said hastily, "Nova Scotia."

"Well it's quite an education you got down on the farm isn't it? Latin, Greek, philosophy, psychology, classics, all that and," his hands shot out lightning fast and grabbed her own, "you managed to keep such pretty white hands. How did you do it?"

"Goat's milk," she said smiling, fingers curling up over her palms, "it does wonders for the complexion." She pulled her hands smoothly out of the grip of his own, "It's supposed to be a real tonic for the nerves as well, you might," she picked up her books and made to leave the room, "try it for your own, you seem to be shaking rather badly."

Jamie, left cursing ten ways from Sunday, picked up a Waterford vase and hurled all twenty pounds of it at the fireplace. It made a glorious smash, though it wasn't as satisfying as he'd hoped it would be. He sank into his father's chair and finding no comfort there wished he didn't need a drink quite so damn badly.

THE 'DOLLAR-A-DANCE' GIRL FROM MULLIGAN'S STEW AND BREW on 42nd Street in New York had never actually seen a goat much less bathed in its milk. The milk she drank, served up by Hugh Mulligan himself, came in pint mugs and always held the aftertaste of stale beer. The cows who produced it grazed some two hundred miles to the south of where she lived in a seedy, one room walk-up. There were only four months separating her from that life, four months and a lifetime of dreaming. It was indeed, she thought wearily flopping down on her bed, a bloody long, long way to Tipperary, or the settlement one hundred seventy-five miles (as the Irish crow flew) to the northeast of it, more commonly known as Belfast.

She had spent three years dancing with old men, fat men, ugly men, smelly men and men of every sort other than decent. She'd crossed an ocean, traveled down dark, deserted country roads, been fondled, rubbed and propositioned by every down-on-his-luck, seedy wastrel on either side of the Atlantic, all this so that she could come here and discover that Jamie Kirkpatrick had no memory whatsoever of her. It was, regardless of the rosy light one tried to shine on it, less than flattering.

She had given him as many memory cues as she could without completely abandoning her pride. Last night she'd even tried the poem he'd written for her when she was eleven years old, she'd managed quite skillfully to work it into the conversation, only to have him say, 'It's merely a variation on a fifteenth century French poem and not," he'd raised his eyes from the book he was reading, "a very good one."

She'd only just managed to choke back the words, 'Well you should know as you bloody wrote it' and he mistaking her look for insulted injury had hurriedly backpedaled, "Well it's not so bad. Here though," he'd risen and fetched a blue cloth-bound book from the overflowing shelves, "this is the original," he opened the book and smoothed the page down, "humble, charming and syntactically tight. Three syllables per line, never more, with the emphasis always falling on the middle syllable, listen:"

> *Ma mignonne*
> *Je vous donne*
> *Le bon jour;*
> *Le sejour*
> *C'est prison.*
> *Guerison*
> *Recouvrez...*

Chills chased down her spine as the French fell off his tongue like Parisian snow, soft, sooty and not altogether wholesome. This close she could smell the individual notes that made up his particular scent, limes and sandalwood with an undernote of something very comforting, freshly baked bread or newly mown wheat fields or...

"So you see simple and yet really rather clever," Jamie, having reverted to English, was looking at her oddly.

"Um yes, rather," she said jumping slightly in her seat.

"Are you feeling alright?" he asked, looking absurdly paternal in spectacles and cardigan.

"Fine," she assured him, trying to tame what felt like a horribly overeager smile.

"Mmphm," he turned back to the book, "now your fellow while catching the gist of the poem, has his syllables all over the place, and seems to have thrown structure out the window with the bathwater. Could you just recite it for me again?" He'd taken out a pen and a piece of paper, and with black ink poised expectantly over the muted sand of the paper waited for her to begin:

> *My sweet girl,*
> *Head aswirl,*
> *I come to wish*
> *A good day.*
> *The bed's constraint*
> *Your blush does taint*
> *Your constitution*
> *Please recover,*

So that I may
Cease to hover
Near thy chamber door.
Sweetmeats
To treat
Thy languor.
Indulge thy whim
Because of him,
Who says it must
Be so.
For if not
My dimpled nymph,
I fear to see
An elfin sylph,
In thy plenteous stead.

"See," Jamie said pen still stroking across the page, "the syllables run the gamut from two to six, the emphasis is uncertain and the control non-existent. Still," he smiled indulgently, "it's a nice gesture. Though I must say there's something a bit Humbert Humbertish about both of the poems, original and secondhand, it's as if he can almost imagine himself licking the back of her knees or something. Rather inappropriate, though perhaps we're mistaking the age of the addressee."

"I was twelve," she said stiffly, wishing to God and his impish angels that she'd never mentioned the poem. "And I had a broken ankle, so my *friend*," she allowed the word to fall under the weight of emphasis, "made up stories and poems to amuse me."

"Kind of him," Jamie said jotting notes down the side of the poem, "but still," he looked sharply over the top of the gold-rimmed, half-spectacles, "but still you were only-"

"Twelve," she supplied rather testily.

"Hmm," had been his only reply, then he'd sat down and begun playing with the poem, shuffling words, syllables, languages, mumbling to himself, lost in a world of ink and paper where words were master and slave to one's pen. He'd not even noticed when she left the room.

Tonight had been a disaster. She shouldn't have thrown his whiskey out but the truth was he did drink too much, a rather disturbing amount. At least then he didn't ask too many questions. Questions, she saw quite suddenly, she'd no desire to answer.

She undressed and changed in the tiny bathroom across the hall, cleaned her teeth and after offering up a half-hearted thanks to God for the day, slid between the worn linen sheets, with their lovely scrolling 'K', just in time to hear a knock on her door.

"Yes," she called out in a muffled tone as she discovered that her hair was wrapped around the buttons that adorned the pillowslip.

Jamie's head popped around the door. "Just thought I'd check if you're alright, need more blankets, anything of the sort?"

"No," she said sharply as the pillow, with the aid of her fingers, wound ever closer to her head.

"Actually," he stepped all the way into the room, "I came up to apologize, perhaps I'm not used to such blatant honesty, but that doesn't excuse my own behavior. You're right, I drink far too much and I plan to rectify that, though I may," he smiled like a small boy, "need some help."

"Certainly," she said, tears stinging her eyes as the pressure on her scalp became more pronounced.

"Are you quite alright?" he asked, peering through the dim light at her.

"Fine, well actually my hair's wrapped around this damn button," she gave it a yank, "ouch."

"Here." He sat on the bed and with sure, deft fingers unwound her hair, strand by strand, from the offending button.

"I thought," he said, "that if we talked in the evenings, played cards, games, it would distract me. And perhaps you could help me finish off some of my father's work. He was translating some old Irish folk tales when he—when he—"

"Died," she supplied for him.

"There you are," he said releasing the last hair from the button and handing the pillow back around to her. "Funny old pillows, aren't they, all buttons and lace, they were my mother's. They still smell like her," his voice drifted down to a breath.

"Old roses," she said.

"Pardon me?"

"She must have smelled sweet and old-fashioned, like old roses," she shivered and wondered if she'd imagined the ribbon of touch down the length of her hair, so light, like snow falling on a moth's wing. "I'd love to help with your father's stories," she said softly, "though I'm hopeless at Gaelic."

"I'll teach you," he said and moved with haste off the bed and towards the door. "Good night."

"Good night," she replied to the closing door, wondering if she'd offended him somehow.

It took a long time to fall asleep after that, though she was content enough to watch the stars and the moon, a chaste quarter, scroll by as if they rode the wheel of a child's wind-up toy. Later, much later, she dreamed.

Twelve must have been a number cursed by the ancients she'd decided. Not just the number but the entire bloody age. Neither child nor woman, but lost in that hinterland of 'girl', though everyone still treated her as a child. A child to whom nothing could be told. There must be an unwritten commandment somewhere about not talking to your children as though they were actually possessed of a brain because something in her twelve-year-old world was seriously awry. Stuck for the summer on the Vineyard, away from her friends and father, the two pillars that upheld her world. Generally she loved the island, loved her horse and dogs and the complete freedom that being away from the city provided. But this summer an ugly bug had gotten under her skin and she was determined to be miserable. Her father, only coming down on weekends, was utterly distracted and not at all like himself.

Her only company was Rose, the woman, neither young nor old, that her father had brought over from Ireland to care for her when she was a baby and her mother had run away. Actually run away from the hospital and left her behind in a glass bassinet.

Rose was not much of a conversationalist, though the things she did say generally had a lot of color to them. 'May the angels of heaven fly up yer nose and the divils of hell fly out yer arse,' was Pamela's favorite. That was Rose's idea of a benediction. Another good thing about Rose was her expectations. They were very low. Bathing was required only once a week, shoes were lost in the first few days and never found, food was to be eaten when the hunger struck you and dinner was often comprised of berries one found on one's explorations.

This summer however, exploring had lost some of its charm and Rose was buried nose-deep in the ravaging romances that women with names like Beryl and Josephine wrote. Pamela had taken to spending long days out in the hayloft, eating apples stolen from the orchard on the neighboring farm, apples so wild that they tasted like the first apple from the first tree. Pamela, apples piled high, read anything and everything she could find. Bailey, her good-natured, rotund little mare took to stamping her feet every time Pamela walked past. It did the horse little good. Pamela wanted a real horse this summer, a real bad horse, truth be told. She began to cast longing glances at Nemesis, her father's big black stallion. He had a miserable disposition but he could run like a bat out of hell. At least that's what Shorty, her father's jockey, said. She could understand the horse though; she knew what it was to have that itchy, restless, got-to-run-or-I'll-die feeling.

It was a Tuesday and raining when she succumbed to temptation, she'd been in the hayloft all morning reading an old copy of 'Pilgrim's Progress' and thinking that while virtue might be its own reward it also made for damned irritating characters. She wished she'd brought the Byron down to the barn, but reading Byron made her feel funny, if she really just let her thoughts go and allowed the words to rock her (she could think of no more apt analogy) then she got this strange, melty, icky feeling, which was not altogether unpleasant and therefore that much more disturbing.

Nemesis was whickering and chuntering about in his stall, wanting, she knew, to be out running until there was no thought or words or strange feelings, just clear perfect feeling, sky above, pure earth below. She couldn't stand it any longer and swung down out of the loft, bits of hay floating airily in her wake. Nemesis rolled his eyes prettily at her approach, he was a friend and he trusted her, at least enough to give him apples and lumps of sugar and for the occasional nose rub.

Today though, the gate opened before him and nose rubs and wild apples became the least of his concerns, he could smell freedom and it had an intoxication like absolutely nothing else. He barely noticed when the girl swung up on his back, her weight would not slow him down. After the first mile of sand and oat grass, when the thunder really began to pull up into his legs and he was stretched out fully feeling the thrum and burn of every muscle, he forgot her completely.

Forgot her even as he covered mile after mile of even, sandy beach and the rain began to come down like hard, stinging needles, even though her knees dug into his bare back like burrs and she rode horizontal to his rippling mane. Forgot her even when he saw a snake, twisting its slow, sweet way across his path. He reared in mindless, frothing terror and did not even notice the weight that tumbled and fell end over end over end off his back and onto the sand or how when he reared back again something more substantial than a twig snapped under his hoof.

She never was to remember much later, except for a moment of mind-numbing pain and then a blessed blackness that came down like a stone on her head. When she awoke, it was to see an angel above her, or at least what seemed like an angel to her dazed, eleven-year-old eyes. Then the angel spoke and didn't seem very holy after that.

"What the hell did you think you were doing just then? You could have killed a damn fine horse and yourself into the bargain, insane child."

"Ow," she said and promptly passed out again.

The next time she'd awakened, it was on a bed, a cloud of blue and white ivy crisscrossing and twining above her. Her ankle felt like it was on fire and all the demons of hell were ramming pins into it. When she tried to sit up and have a look at it her head swam in nauseating loops and she fell back again, then swiftly twisted over the side of the bed and threw up on a very fancy looking carpet.

She started to cry, an entire summer of bored sophistication crumbling in the face of pain, a strange house and vomiting on a silk rug.

"It's alright, I should have had a bucket there, it's likely the fright and the doctor gave you a shot for the pain, I take it it's not helping." The angel hove into view, golden and no longer glowering. The angel sat.

"Who are you?" she managed to croak in a miserable attempt at bravado.

The angel smiled. "James Kirkpatrick at your service, but you may call me Jamie. And you," he raised his golden eyebrows a smidge, "must be the little O'Flaherty girl, I've seen you out stealing mine host's apples this summer."

"Mmphm," she said not wanting to talk about her thievery.

"I've called your home and Rose said she would call your father. The doctor said it would be best not to move you tonight, you've done a real beauty of a job on your ankle."

"Where am I?" she managed to croak before passing out for the third time that day.

It was the afternoon of the next day before she learned that she'd been moved to the hospital and that she would be staying there for the next week. One week became two, as it turned out she was allergic to morphine. Then her ankle didn't mend as it should have and had to be re-set after it had begun knitting together. It was, altogether, a nightmarish few weeks. The pain had sunk her in a black pool for the first week, a pool she only sporadically emerged from before sinking right down again. Her father, haggard with worry, had come and gone, staying until he could not leave his business unattended in New York any longer. Jamie had stayed and stayed. Holding her hand through the worst of it, when she'd emerged from her peaceful black hole and the pain had made her scream. Lulling her to sleep with story after story after story, myth, legend and anything embroidered with enough romance and adventure to distract a girl's mind. There was one about the Queen of the Fairies being turned into a bejeweled dragonfly that had particularly caught her fancy.

Playing Monopoly and cards with her and then finally teaching her the intricacies of chess to pull her mind away from the dull, throbbing ache in her ankle and leg that made her irritable and angry.

He brought her books, chocolate, fresh fruit, anything to brighten up her days. One day he'd come bearing a particularly thick tome and when she'd asked what it was about he'd said, 'it's about the depths of misery a man can sink to and the heights he can rise to in his soul and I promise you that when we've finished the last page you will be out of this place.' They took turns reading aloud and the words became a magic spell for her, an incantation that took away the pain and the misery. Years later the first lines, paragraphs, pages would still be firmly limned in her memory.

'In the year 1815 Monseigneur Charles-Francois-Bienvenu Myriel was Bishop of Digne. He was then about seventy-five, having held the bishopric since 1806. Although it has no direct bearing on the tale we have to tell...' she had begun that afternoon and eight days later when Jamie read the words that closed the book, the doctor had come into the room and politely waited for the tale to be done before telling her she was going home.

Home to Rose, which suddenly seemed unappealing, home to boredom and loneliness again, home to her father who came only on weekends, flying in late, late Friday night and leaving early Monday morning. Not his old, fun-loving self. Worried and tired and thin.

Home was not the same place however. Her plain little summer room had been transformed with new paint, a beautiful Star-of-David quilt that smelled of *apples and bayberry, a walnut shelf filled with books of every sort and description and a delicate perfect cut-crystal angel that hung in the window and refracted the morning sun into a hundred rainbows.*

Rose was more attentive, insisting on three regular meals a day and baths at least every second day. Her father came down for two solid weeks and actually had a tan and put some weight on before he headed back. Jamie continued to visit and was mutually adored by Rose, her father and herself.

When at last she could move beyond the confines of porch and the masses of morning glory that adorned it, it was Jamie who took her for walks on the beach, offering his arm should she need it. Jamie who insisted very strongly that she had to get up on a horse again before the fear became a permanent part of her. It was Jamie who took her to her first party; it was Jamie who was the first man to dance with her.

It was an open-air party with summer food, corn, clams, beer, women in pale cottons, yellows, pinks, whites. Fireworks breaking the thick, velvet blue sky with shards and spangles of light. The air heavy with salt, wild roses and end of summer nostalgia. It was the beginning of the Sixties, there was a beautiful, charismatic president in office, Vietnam was a world away and America was still gold. The light of that seemed part and substance of the very atmosphere itself. She had sat on the ground and listened to the music and sunk her bare feet in the sand, feeling it sift and swirl through her toes like the touch of dreams, fine and clinging. She watched Jamie, for it seemed half the island knew him. The butcher, the baker, the candlestick maker and every female under the age of sixty and maybe a few bold ones that were over. They drifted, brushed and sighed around him like so many web spun butterflies, young ones, lush little eighteen year old nymphets, with sugar floss hair and lips painted bubblegum pink. Bodies at their peak point of nubile perfection. Young mothers, still pretty, with bruised yearning eyes, middle-aged women on the prowl, silken and clawed like jungle cats and old ones who flirted with him like he was a beloved but distant relation. Pamela could not articulate these things but she felt them and knew herself to be only a child in the face of all of it. A child with a foot on either side of dividing earth, neither innocent nor assured, neither infant nor adult. The mirror, like a divining stone, told its own tale. The tale of the awkward duckling, too long of leg and lean of line, who would, when one least expected it, become a swan. But divining stones take discerning eyes and what she saw in the mirror was a gangly, pre-adolescent with braces, bruises and an unruly cloud of hair.

It was enough to watch Jamie—almost. Enough to see him dance and laugh and even, after some coercion, play the fiddle like one possessed. Enough to watch him single out the people who hung back from the fray, who found the shadows their natural companions, and draw them like fearful moths into the warmth of his light. Enough, almost. To accept with a smile the plate of tiny blue crabs and to feign delight in the small glass of beer he brought her. To dance with rough-hewn, silent island boys who would rather be gone into the salt and mist and water of their native land than be holding a miserable half-Irish, half-American not-quite child nor woman in their arms. Enough, almost.

Magic came at the waning minutes of the last hour, when someone played 'Waltzing Matilda,' softly, sweetly, bow coddling the strings to draw out the most melancholy, aching notes and Jamie, taking her hand and pulling her from her self-imposed exile on the outskirts of the firelight had taught her how to waltz. Precise, gliding steps, one sliding effortlessly into the next. Dancing there on the edge of the water, where the salt and spume licked at their ankles and tiny water creatures scrabbled about their toes. Letting her feel the pattern, the count of it in her waist and arms. His eyes holding hers, making her feel that this moment was theirs alone, forever. Making, she would later realize, a child who'd had a wreck of a summer feel special. And at the end, when he'd spun her softly out, he'd conjured up an orchid from behind her ear and laid it in her hands, then kissed her forehead and bowed. She'd fallen in love with him, had been halfway there anyhow, the crystal angel had begun it and the dance had sealed it.

He'd taken her home, dropped a kiss on her head and left her there on the porch, alone with the smell of dying, bleeding gold honeysuckle clinging to the air like a lover. Too much she didn't understand and not enough language to put it into words. Someday, she'd vowed to herself, someday I will know what to do, what to say and then I will make magic for him. Jamie was gone in the morning and she didn't hear from him again, though he'd left the copy of 'Les Miserables,' behind for her, inscribed with the words 'To island summers, broken ankles and youth that is far too fleeting.' And then from Wordsworth, he had borrowed the lines, 'Bliss was it in that dawn to be alive, but to be young was very heaven.'

She'd pondered, analyzed and deconstructed brick by brick those words over the years but could never quite make of them what she wanted. What was left of her youth was hardly bliss and came nowhere near approaching heaven. Her father was still worried, still drawn, still tired and only seemed to get more so as time went on. Staff got smaller, so did houses, horses were sold and finally, though he'd hung onto it for as long as he could, the island house went to a family from California. She didn't care by that point, she couldn't be on the island anymore; the island had become Jamie for her. Other people had their bibles—Matthew, Mark, Luke and John, but she had the gospel of James, Stuart, Kirkpatrick.

Her father died when she was sixteen, Rose had passed away the previous spring of lung cancer and that left herself and the dog. With no money. Her father, once a tough thirteen year old that had disembarked off a ship from Ireland and fought his way up in the New York business world, had died broke. Hit by a car in the street. She'd been numbed by the news, furious at her father's carelessness and so awash in grief that she hadn't considered the full ramifications of her situation. Sixteen and alone made her a ward of the state. Vulnerable and by this time beautiful enough to make middle aged men sing to her in the street made her open to all sorts of problems. So she took her clothes, her face and what little chutzpah she could summon up and went to Hugh Mulligan. He gave her a job and one room over the bar. It was enough at the time. She danced with customers at night and learned to defend herself firmly but in such a way that no one got belligerent. Days she taught dance to senior citizens and bored society matrons. Her partner was a Spanish boy named Carlos and together they made a pretty enough sight for people to sign up for several sessions.

What time she had to herself was spent finishing her schooling, not in any formal manner but with books taken out by the armload from the New York Public Library.

Birthdays and Christmases were spent alone, though Carlos brought her a cake on her eighteenth birthday and offered to relieve her of her virginity. She'd refused and he'd shrugged and said she didn't know what she was missing.

Every penny she saved, eating the least amount of food, taking the produce that stores generally threw out. Accepting the occasional greasy fry-up from Hugh Mulligan. Never wavering from her goal. To get to Ireland and find Jamie. She only hoped it wasn't too difficult or that he hadn't left years ago, because if he had she'd no idea where to find him. She didn't know if he was rich or poor, married or single, with or without children. She only knew that she had to find out for herself. Shortly before her nineteenth birthday in the spring of 1968, she'd paid her way and caught the plane to Ireland.

The angel had begun it, the dance had sealed it. She would find Jamie and know her fate when she saw it in his eyes.

Chapter Six

A Variety of Boys

"DID YOU KNOW THAT A MALE ELEPHANT'S PENIS weighs sixty pounds?" Pamela asked sliding her bare-naked and impossibly perfect bottom across a sheet of blue silk.

"Would you quit twitching," Pat said for what seemed, to both artist and model, the thousandth time that hour, "and put down the copy of 'National Geographic', as I don't want it in the picture."

"You're too literal," she retorted flinging the magazine down and resuming her pose. She was seated in one-quarter profile, facing away from Pat, head turned just enough to present him with the shadow of her features. A half-naked Psyche catching Cupid's eye for the first time.

"Do not move, I'm working on the fabric now and the folds are just perfect," Pat said focusing, in a way that wasn't particularly flattering, on a ripple of material two inches below her left breast. Whatever had possessed her to think being an artist's model was the height of exoticism had fled in the all too present realities of cramp, chill and unmitigated boredom. Pat was working on the sketches for a surreal variation on Frederic Leighton's famous milk-breasted Psyche. The results thus far, in Pamela's view, did little for a woman's ego.

"Are ye comin' to hear Dev Murphy sing with the rest of us?" Pat asked, stopping briefly to exchange a dull pencil for a sharp one, "There's a rumor runnin' about that Jack Stuart may be there an' read from his latest work."

Pamela rolled her eyes, if she had learned one thing since coming to Ireland; it was that Jack Stuart, famed Republican poet, much like God, was always rumored to be everywhere and never did show his face.

"It's more likely that Christ will descend on a cloud and hand out revisions for the Sermon on the Mount."

"Blasphemer," Pat muttered, completely intent now on a milky fold over her ribs.

"Against Christ or Jack Stuart? Both seem to have equal standing in this country."

Pat gave her a quick, black look. "Not everyone subscribes to that point of view."

"I know, Republicans tend to place him a little closer to God's right hand than Christ and those of the Orange persuasion lump him in with a dark gentleman who resides much further south."

"If ye'd read his work before passin' judgment—"

"I have," Pamela said and leaned over to dig in a bag, producing a small black bound, gilt lettered book, "and I liked it." The cloth fell off her shoulder as she handed the book to Pat, who glared and set his pencil down with a thump. Just then with no warning a head, sublime with short black curls and dark sparkling eyes, popped around the corner. "Lucy I'm home," it sang and then taking in the situation before it, blinked twice and grinning in a most irreverent manner looked at Pat and said, "Lucy, you got some 'splainin to do."

"Pamela," said Pat grinning just as irreverently back, "meet my brother, Casey."

"MILK? SUGAR?" ASKED PAT'S BROTHER, holding a pitcher and bowl of the respective items in either hand.

"Neither, thank you," Pamela said, eyeing the door with great longing.

"As it suits ye," he said easily and helped himself to a generous portion of both. "Ah that's grand. I haven't had a decent cup of tea in five years."

"Been abroad have you?" Pamela asked inanely, wishing she'd the courage to look down and see if her shirt was right side out and the buttons done up properly.

He cleared his throat and gave Pat an odd look. Pat in turn shook his head almost imperceptibly. "In a manner of speakin' I suppose ye could say that."

There was some joke she was missing here and she devoutly wished she'd not let their innate hospitality coerce her into staying for tea.

They could not stop grinning at each other like two very silly Cheshire cats. Brothers obviously, unmistakably in size and color but at this close proximity one could not help but see the differences. Casey was bigger, hewn from harder rock than his brother, it showed in his face, he was granite to Pat's mica. Limbs, from years or experience, were tighter, harder. Pat still retained some of the loose-jointedness of boyhood, his face still dreamed, his brother's did not.

Casey turned, dark eyes friendly yet guarded and she realized she'd been staring and he'd felt the stamp of her eyes on his face.

"Welcome home," she said, the words slipping from her mouth before she even heard them in her head.

"Thank ye," he held her gaze until she, completely flustered, jumped up from the table and announced in a voice that seemed too loud and foreign to her own ears that she really must be going.

"I'll see ye tomorrow then," Pat said helping her on with her coat and looping her bag over her shoulder.

"Nice to have met ye," his brother's voice was polite but nothing more.

She walked all the way home, too hot to be confined to a bus, pausing halfway up the tree-lined drive of Jamie's house to watch in wonderment the moon sitting like a Christmas angel on top of a cypress, a silver crayon cutout against the pale evening sky. Without warning, it looped upside down and she had to step back to avoid falling. She blinked trying to fend dizziness off and put one hot hand to her forehead. She'd best go straight to bed as she seemed to be developing a raging fever.

"WELL," SAID CASEY RIORDAN TO HIS LITTLE BROTHER.

"Well," said his little brother back.

Casey let out a long, shaky breath and grabbed his brother in a ferocious hug. "Goddamn it's good to see ye, Pat." He held him for as long as comfort would allow, closed his eyes and breathed in. It was strange to hold a man in your arms when you'd been expecting a skinny kid who always smelled of dirt and sunshine even when it had rained for weeks. This entity smelled of wood and charcoal, of water and something sweet. It was in this sweetness he found a vestige of the little boy he'd left behind, not knowing it was the scent of a man falling in love. He would regret the oversight later but by then it would be too late.

'My brother,' he thought in his heart, though aloud all he said was, "When did ye cut the hair off?"

"Two days ago," Pat said laughing, "I must have felt ye crossin' the water."

"Look at ye," Casey brushed the pad of one thumb down his brother's face, smoothing the eyebrow, touching the bone below the eye. It was a gesture so replete with tenderness that Pat turned away, uncomfortable. "When did ye go an' grow up Paddyboy?" he asked reverting to his brother's childhood nickname.

"Five years will be a long time," Pat said eyes turned down and away from Casey's searching gaze as he collected cups and spoons off the table. "In more ways than one."

"Aye, it will be," Casey rejoined quietly and helped his brother clear away the table. "Are ye goin' te tell me about the girl?"

"Her name is Pamela." Pat said stiffly.

"Alright then, Pamela."

"I've known her for a couple of months," Pat said taking two apples from the counter and throwing one to Casey who caught it neatly in his open palm. "She's at Queens an' we have a class together."

"Two months an' she's naked in the kitchen? Yer obviously not as shy as ye used to be."

"She agreed to pose for me; it's a project I'm workin' on for art class. We're friends," Pat said defensively.

"Aye an' then what?" Casey asked folding his arms.

"An' then nothin'. Look ye can't come back here an' play big brother like ye were only gone out to get the milk. Ye've been gone five years an' a boy will grow into a man whether there's bars in front of his face or not."

Casey nodded, feeling quite weary, the adrenaline rush of being home flooding away and leaving him awkward and feeling too large and cumbersome here in the neat little kitchen that belonged to his brother.

"I expect ye'll be angry at me Patrick an' ye've a right to it but can we leave it for another day? It's only that," he pressed his fingers into the hollows at the top of his nose, shocked that he could still feel tears after all this time, "I'm a wee bit tired."

"Aye, we can leave it."

"Thanks," Casey said, wanting suddenly to be behind a closed and locked door, away from eyes that had always seen too much. It was terrifying not to have eight steel doors, barred and locked, between you and the world. It made him feel tired and much younger than his brother.

"Yer room is ready; it's the one on the right at the top of the stairs."

Casey nodded, vocal chords knotting around his throat, desperate to escape the too bright light of the kitchen. It seemed to sear right into his brain, it was that strong. Only later would he realize it had only been the last of the sun coming in through the window.

Discipline, the one thing that had ensured his survival for so long, demanded that he unpack and wash up before succumbing to fatigue. Rituals, small and insignificant, had stood between him and despair while he lived a life apart.

When he finally lay down and closed his eyes, it was his daddy's face that came to mind and it broke his breath just to see him there. He'd expected him somehow, not in a logical way, but just the ghost of him in Pat's face. His brother was his own man now, though, and not a remnant of the father Casey could not think of without anger and bottomless pain.

Tired as he was, sleep would not come, so he lay awake watching night claim the sky through his window. Blue, pale to deep, then indigo and finally black. He got up hours later and hung a blanket over the window; it would serve as bars for now until he felt ready to wake to a sunrise. Freedom, it seemed, would have its own price.

DISCRETION, THOUGHT THE REVEREND LUCIEN BROUGHTON, was indeed the better part of valor and the power of dominance was often in the display rather than the fact. Destruction of a country, a race, a people, a way of life was often in the details. These things he held to firmly, they were his credo, one might even say, his religion.

A delicate minx of a man, blue of eye, flaxen of hair, he sat now in the supremely upright position men who are uncomfortable with their small stature will aspire to. Outside the window to his left lay the grounds of Stormont, ostensibly the government building of Northern Ireland, beneath the veneer of gray respectability a Protestant palace for a Protestant state. The road of history in Northern Ireland ran through Stormont, the road of progress stopped abruptly at its doors.

As a denizen of Malone Road drawing rooms and country houses, Lucien Broughton felt himself British by birth, British by destiny. If you needed it, the proof was in the Queen's head which adorned the stamp, the red pillar boxes that graced the roadsides and the weather which was as cold, gray and invariably dour as any proper British morning could be hoped to be. It was, in his opinion, unfortunate that the rest of Ireland insisted on hanging on to, or off, the bottom of the six states of Ulster.

Fanaticism could not be gleaned by the perusal of his parts, was not even betrayed by a telltale gleam in the eye. He was smooth, unruffled, lucent as a new moon and untrustworthy as a fox in a hencoop.

Mick Bigsby, exhausted civil servant, sometime advisor to a variety of politicians and at present feeling very much like a chicken, sat at a desk, papers scattered in weary abundance, under the calm, dissecting gaze of Reverend Lucien Broughton.

What he knew of the Reverend was little; a self-taught fundamentalist who'd acquired his doctorate honorarily from the Wilbur Walker College of Christianity in faraway Louisiana. An orator of impressive talent, his voice had been known to shake the walls of many an Orange lodge with the thunder of his rhetoric. Fear of the trampling Roman Catholic hordes was the rock upon which he preached and a solid rock it was found to be even at this late date in history.

What he felt of the Reverend Broughton was fear—pure, unmitigated, skin-crawling fear. The thing he couldn't quite put a finger on was why he was here in his, Mick Bigsby's office, on this early spring day as a faint mist of green was lacing the trees outside.

"I was given to understand," began Lucien Broughton, placing one well-manicured hand over the other, "that you were the gentleman to whom I should speak to about a matter which has come to my concern."

"Yes," Mick said, wondering what on earth this man could possibly want his help for.

"I want to acquire James Kirkpatrick's seat in the House."

"I'm afraid I don't understand," said Mick who was afraid he really did understand.

Lucien wore a look of saintly patience, "His death," he paused for effect, "has left a seat open in Parliament, I believe. I was given to understand that an election would be called shortly as it cannot be left vacant." He spoke slowly and precisely as if to an immigrant just learning the profundities of the English language.

"Well, yes, but it is hoped by his constituents that his son will fill the gap, left as you say by his," Mick gritted his teeth, "death."

"Correct me if I'm wrong but seats in Parliament are not a matter of inheritance."

"Well, of course not, but Jamie, the younger Lord Kirkpatrick I mean to say," Mick took a deep breath and attempted to sort out his verbs and nouns, "would be a favorite to win."

"Are you suggesting," Lucien blinked twice precisely, "a mock election or had you just planned to hand over the district to this man merely because he is the son of a popular father?"

Mick put a firm tamp on his temper and answered calmly. "Of course not, it's only that, and you'll forgive my saying this, but that district contains an overwhelming Catholic majority and even the Protestant contingent has been very happy with what Lord Kirkpatrick managed to do for them. Housing has been improved and is given out according to numbers and need, the streets have been cleaned up, crime is down and unemployment rates are lower than in any other district in Belfast and the environs have been brought into accordance with the strictest of health codes."

Lucien smiled, the chilliest smile Mick had ever seen and said, "I've no doubt that Lord Kirkpatrick did an admirable job, however I don't see how that bears on his son being a shoe-in for the position. Nor had I heard that he was stepping up, as the Americans say, to the plate."

"May I be honest with you Mr. Broughton?" Mick asked, lacing his hands together and feeling as if he were breathing ice in, so frigid had the room become.

"It's Reverend Broughton," Lucien replied and though there was calm on his tongue there was no warmth in his aspect, "and honesty is always welcome, one indeed finds it refreshing, water to a fire if you will."

"Indeed," Mick echoed and took a sip of water that seemingly lodged frozen in his throat. It took a most undignified coughing fit to clear it and he emerged watery-eyed and red-faced from it moments later.

"More water?" Lucien asked, hand solicitously poised over Mick's water glass.

"No thank you," Mick replied hastily, jerking the water glass towards him and slopping its contents on several important documents in the process.

"I make you uncomfortable Mr. Bigsby," Lucien said, polished hands once again rejoined on his lap. "Do not deny it, I have that effect on many people. It is my burden to bear and as burdens go a very small one." His face assumed a beatific air and Mick mused that even St. Francis of Assisi could not have projected such an aura of triumph over torture.

"Reverend Broughton," Mick said firmly, "if I may be honest I will tell you that a man such as yourself has very little chance, a snowball's in hell really, of being elected to parliament in a Catholic district. Perhaps if you looked elsewhere, several terms will be up shortly—"

"It's this district I'm interested in Mr. Bigsby."

"I don't understand why you've come to me," Mick said, wishing he'd never laid eyes on the man.

"To submit my name, of course."

"I see, well, there are channels you will have to go through, Reverend Broughton, formalities to be observed etc..."

"Giving you time to warn the remaining Lord Kirkpatrick that he'd best stop grieving and get in the arena?"

Mick wondered uneasily if the man was reading his mind.

"No of course not," he said and had to admit that the words sounded false even to his own ears.

"You don't approve of my entering the race, do you?" Lucien smoothed one faultless eyebrow with a delicate finger.

"I don't agree with your tactics Reverend Broughton," Mick said feeling the ball of ice reforming in his throat, "I've always thought the pulpit should be reserved for religion not politics. But it is a free country and you may do as you wish."

"You are wrong Mr. Bigsby," the Reverend Broughton rose from his seat in one unmarred movement, "it's not a free country, but perhaps someday with the right leadership it might be."

"It's your choice," Mick said hoarsely, straining to not succumb to coughing until the man was gone.

"Indeed, Mr. Bigsby, indeed it is." Lucien performed his chilly smile again and Jack could feel frost spread through his throat and down into his lungs. "Good day Mr. Bigsby."

Mick nodded tersely at the man and then as the door closed behind him gave in to the coughing that felt as if it would tear his lungs apart. Later that night he would be admitted to the hospital, coughing blood and diagnosed with a severe case of pneumonia. By the time he returned to his desk six weeks later, Lucien Broughton would be officially standing as the candidate for West Belfast. Unopposed.

"YOU ARE NOT GETTING YOUR MOUTH AROUND IT," Jamie said patiently, as Pamela feeling like an inarticulate lummox, bit her lips in an effort to put some feeling back into them. "Move your chin forward with the last sound," he made a noise that sounded like the shushing of the tide sliding in over sand, "it's a very soft language if you'll allow it to be."

"Yeuch," Pamela said thumping back in her chair in frustration well mixed with equal parts of exhaustion.

"Perhaps," Jamie said with the air of an overtaxed diplomat, "that's enough for tonight."

The Gaelic lessons, now grinding into their second week, were not a raving success. Jamie was a patient teacher, Pamela, at first a willing student, became increasingly angry and frustrated as it became apparent that linguistics was not her natural gift. She felt by the end of every evening as if her mouth were filled with thick, cold porridge. Helping him to translate his father's unfinished work was at best a flimsy excuse for staying under his roof, it was, however, the only excuse she had. Unless one counted the endless number of errands, tasks and odd jobs Maggie, Liz and Jamie seemed to conjure up each day. Jamie's contributions to her job list seemed the work of an inventive sadist. Today's inventory had included: mucking out the stables before lunch, typing up a thirty page report on the last meeting of the European Linen Guild and, then, for the icing on the cake, beheading, gutting and cleaning the dozen trout Jamie had caught during a morning's fish with some duke or other. She reeked of a heady combination of manure and fish guts, her fingers were stiff and sore and she was completely exhausted and uninterested in the complexities of the Goidelic branch of language. She yawned lavishly, barely managing to summon up the energy to cover her mouth.

Jamie, rubbing the crease in his forehead, always a sign she'd come to learn, of weariness, turned and gave her a quick, bright smile.

"Come on let's go for a walk, clear the spiderwebs from our brains."

"Now?" she said stupidly, looking out the windows which, braced by darkness, threw back their reflections and gave no glimpse of the external world.

"Now," he replied firmly.

Thus, she found herself clad in a thick sweater Jamie had dug out for her, picking her way along the headlands that ran beside the Irish sea for some miles. Jamie navigated the rocky terrain as if he'd learned his first steps on a high wire. High wire being an apt description, she thought, trying to not calculate the hundreds of feet that plunged at a ninety degree angle into the water below. It was in just such a calculation, watching the rocks below, rather than the ones beneath her feet, that she lost her footing and with barely a millisecond for a sharp scream, saw the moon-limned sea arc dizzily upwards and closed her eyes in anticipation of a quick, brutal death.

"You have," Jamie said with a firm hand on her shoulder, "to watch where you're stepping up here."

"Brilliant advice," she muttered, eyes closed now in embarrassment rather than fear, "wish I'd thought of it."

"Take my hand," Jamie said patiently. Opening her eyes she did as she was bid, surprised at the warm, dry strength of his hand, long and fine-boned as it was. After another twenty minutes of hard climbing they emerged on a plateau at the summit of the headlands where it seemed the whole world was made of moon-blazed sea. The water swam with light, silver and dancing, gilt and perfect. Standing there on the plateau, earth slipping away on either side, one step from falling and falling endlessly into water, and above only sky, a fragile film between them and the universe that ran, ever and always, away from man, stars fleeing grasping hands and pleading hearts.

"Dear God," Pamela breathed in wonderment.

"Seems possible here," Jamie said dryly, spreading his coat on the damp rock and indicating that she should sit beside him. She sat and he pulled a thermos of hot chocolate out of a bag, poured two cups and handed her one. She clasped its warmth gratefully, unable to drag her eyes away from the sight before her.

"I used to come here when I was a boy and imagine what the Irish chieftains felt when they saw English ships coming, if they knew what it would mean or even felt the whisper of what was to come. They managed to evade the Romans by a simple trick of geography and I have to wonder if we wouldn't have done better in the end if the Romans had been able to make it here."

"Why?"

"Because we would have learned Roman ways, come to hand and heel the way the Saxons once did. We wouldn't have been so different when change did come, we wouldn't," he closed his eyes as if quite suddenly the spectacle of sea and sky were too much, "have been so bloody, inalterably, hopelessly Irish."

"Being Irish isn't any sin," she said lightly, wanting to pull him back from that dark place he seemed to journey to on a regular schedule.

"Isn't it?" He turned and faced her and her breath quite suddenly hurt in her lungs and stomach. He was all gold, in every varying shade and spectrum, in heady darkness and blinding, all consuming light. Gold from bronze to sunlight, from first morning to last blink of day. Gold in his heart and head and hands. A fallen angel cursed by light.

"Who are you?" he asked softly, eyes pinning her carefully, like a butterfly to a clean, unlined page.

"No one special," she said and turned her head away with as much effort as it would have taken to tear skin from bone.

"That seems as likely as unicorns on the moon," he said, voice still speculative.

"Unicorns on the moon?"

"Aye, it's what my Daddy used to tell me when a thing was impossible. When I'd ask about God or my mother coming back or any of the thousand other questions a child will ask. He'd say, 'That's as likely, Jamie, as unicorns on the moon.' The problem was that I believed in unicorns and God and mothers who could come back from the far side of the moon. It was my father's fault in a strange way; he fed me so full of fairy stories and enchantment when I was a child that I believed all sorts of things."

"If he was anything like you I'd believe him too," she said before she could stop to measure the wisdom of her words. "Tell me what he told you."

"Well it all started because I was afraid of the moon when I was small. I'd this notion that it could come down and get right in my window at night and I'd just get lost or swallowed up in that light. So my father told me it was a world like our own, only the skies were the color of apricots in the day and plums at night. There weren't any people, just unicorns, which of course explained why they weren't to be found on our own planet anymore. See the dark body there?" He brought his arm into alignment with the path of her eyes and she nodded. "That's Mare Tranquilliatis."

"The Sea of Tranquility," she said watching the great blue shadow that crossed the face of the moon.

"It was where the unicorns drank and held meetings, where they swam and gazed out at that blue green orb that always rode their horizon and wondered if such a place could harbor creatures of their own ilk. They were ruled by a triumvirate of benevolent creatures, ancient bearded unicorns who went by the names of," he laughed, "Copernicus, Kepler and Galileo. I can't begin to tell you how disappointed I was when I found out they were mere humans and that there were no seas on the moon, that it seemed most likely there was never any water there at all."

"They were perfect names for unicorns," she said, "all of them dreamers and your father as well it would seem. He gave you magic, that's a pretty wonderful gift for a child."

Jamie nodded as a small cloud scudded with velvet feet across the moon and left him in shadow for a moment. "I only wish he'd kept enough magic for himself, just enough to stay alive."

"Perhaps a sea is a sea even without water, Jamie," she said causing him to regard her intently once more. "Are creatures that live in our imagination any less real than a man who lives on the other side of the planet or down the street that you will never know?"

"A philosopher in our midst and one who believes in magic to boot," Jamie said looking at her as if she were a riddle, one he didn't quite know how to begin untangling.

"Kepler once said that we don't question why the birds sing, we presume they were created for the very purpose of singing and so we shouldn't ask why the human mind puzzles over the heavens, why we spend a lifetime asking *why*, even though we know there's no answer. It's what we were created for, to ask why to all the questions that have no answers. So perhaps we shouldn't question unicorns on the moon, perhaps we should just believe in them."

Silence held them for long moments after that, a silence that was not fraught with strangeness, nor expectation, nor the need to say vacant words merely to fill space. Pamela wasn't certain how it had happened or when but she was comfortable in his presence now.

"When you have the moon, you can't have the stars," she said thinking aloud.

"Hm?" Jamie inquired, reverie disturbed.

"I was only thinking that when the moon is at its brightest you can't see the stars as well so for all intents and purposes when you have the moon you can't have the stars and vice versa."

"It's quite an interesting mind you possess, Miss O'Flaherty," Jamie said putting the lid back on the thermos of hot chocolate and draining the dregs of his cup. "Do you suppose you'll ever tell me the truth about how you acquired it?"

"It's simply a part of me," she said lightly.

"The story you told me about Nova Scotia and ancient parents, it's just a story isn't it? It's no more real than unicorns on the moon, is it?"

She looked up at him and found with his eyes on her, there on his lonely hilltop where he'd dreamed as a boy, she could not lie, nor was she quite ready to tell the truth. "No it isn't," she replied quietly.

Creeping back with much more care over the rocks, hand firmly held in Jamie's once again, she found the nerve to ask a question that had been bothering her for days.

"Why won't you take your father's seat in Parliament?" she asked and regretted it instantly for he dropped her hand, her few simple words having shattered the fragile bond they'd begun to build on the hilltop.

"Why would you ask that?" His eyes were hard and unflinching in the light, wind blowing strands of gold across his forehead.

"Only because everyone else seems to be asking it," she said, the words sounding halt and lame to her own ears.

"Such as?"

She swallowed, intimidated by the look on his face. "Such as your friend, the one who came the other day, the one who looked quite ill."

"Eavesdropping were you?" Jamie's voice was pure acid.

"No, he told me the situation as he was leaving, said I should try to talk some sense into you because he'd no luck in doing so."

"I see," he said tersely, "well I apologize then, but he shouldn't have told you. It's all just wasted effort because I'm not going to take it."

"Why not?" she asked daring to look him directly in the eye.

He gave a short bark of laughter. "Did no one ever tell you that it's not polite to ask all of the questions all of the time?"

"No."

"Alright then the truth of the matter is I don't have the head for the job. I'd take every problem and injustice home with me and if I couldn't right it would eat me up. I know I cannot do it, it's very simple really, I just wish people would believe it."

"Having the head for the job isn't what matters, it's having the heart for it," she said softly.

"Oh Pamela, what am I to do with such an innocent? Perhaps dear girl I don't have the heart either."

"I believe that you do."

"That sweetheart," he said sadly, "*is* about as likely as unicorns on the moon."

'*No Jamie*', she thought as they resumed their course along the rim of the sea, slowly tracking inland until the lights of home became apparent, until there was no excuse for her to continue holding his hand, '*you falling in love with me, that's about as likely as unicorns on the moon.*'

When Pat's brother answered the door, Pamela had to squelch the desire to turn and run. He unnerved her in a way few had in the course of her young life, unnerved her and made her feel as if she were perpetually naked, both physically and mentally.

"Is Pat here?" she asked, trying to avoid his eyes and finding herself staring at his buttons.

"No, he ran out of here on some emergency for the Young Communists," he smiled lazily, "I take it yer not on the security council."

"Obviously not," she said stiffly, wondering why she could never think of anything witty or even halfway intelligible to say to this man. It annoyed her deeply.

"Could you please tell him I was by?"

"Yes'm, I will," he said grinning, which only annoyed her further. She walked swiftly towards the gate, knowing, in a way that both infuriated and pleased her, that he was watching her do so.

"Pamela, stop will ye!" he caught up with her on the narrow laneway, shoving his arms into a coat and halting in front of her. "I got a job today an' I thought I'd go have a meal an' celebrate, would ye care to join me?"

'No thank you, most kind of you to offer but I have plans this evening already,' was one variation on the theme playing in her head. What actually came out of her mouth was, "I'd like that."

Thus she found herself, one rainy half hour later, seated at a grubby table in a fish and chip shop, which existed under the rather lofty name of 'Finnegan's Wake'.

"Best fish in Belfast, I'll guarantee," he'd said and unlike his brother had not felt the need to apologize for the seedy ambiance of the place.

It was, indeed, very good fish and he was very good company. With a tongue as glib and silver as his brother's but without Pat's innate humility, Casey was a consummate teller of tales, able to infuse tragedy and comedy into the space of one small sentence. He was also discomfortingly direct. A game, Pamela mused after a particularly brutal set of questions dealing with his brother that two could play.

"What was prison like?" she asked, and had felt some small flicker of triumph when it stopped him cold. The small flicker was abruptly smothered by a trickle of fear though as he narrowed his eyes and with a smile that had nothing to do with humor asked, "What is it that ye want to know?"

She would have done well, she thought fiddling nervously with her water glass, to remember who it was she'd sat down with. *'Bring a long spoon when ye sup wid the devil,'* Rose used to say. It hadn't made a great deal of sense at the time, but it was beginning to now.

"Oh, I don't know," she did her best to assume an airy tone, which came out with a wobble and squeak. "What were your days like?"

He considered her carefully, dark eyes boring hard into her own. "Up at dawn to bathe an' dance, high tea at three an' bridge on Thursday evenings," he said coolly.

"I was serious," she said stung by his sarcasm.

"It's not," he took a softer tone, "a story one necessarily wants to share with a pretty girl."

She blushed and he raised his eyebrows over the top of his cracked coffee cup.

"It could have been worse," he set his cup down gently, as if it were made of eggshells. "I'm a big man aye; it went much worse on the small ones, if ye'll take my meanin'."

"Being beaten you mean?" she leaned onto the table meeting his eyes without fear for the first time. Curiosity, she was to acknowledge later, was inevitably her downfall.

He cleared his throat and looked down where one broad hand was splayed across the laminated surface of the table. "Aye, amongst other things. Being beaten is hardly the worst thing that can happen to a man."

He had lashes like a girl, soft, thick and long. It was oddly poignant against the strong, almost brutal lines of his face. She had to resist the impulse to reach over and brush the pad of her thumb across his eyelids.

"Then tell me something else," she said, "something you can share with a girl."

"Well," he looked out the window where the gray drizzly mist was fast dissipating into a black drizzly mist, "it seems most of my memories are prison now, as if my life before wasn't quite real or doesn't count for much anymore. Does that make sense to ye?" His eyes came up and met hers then looked swiftly away, but she'd read vulnerability there in that one flash instant.

"It does," she said steadily.

He considered his coffee cup with great care. "The first day out was a strange one, I was certain everyone could read where I'd been on my face an' by my clothes an' even in the way I walked. I was like an alien seein' the wonders of this world for the first time. I hadn't felt the rain or the sun in any real, proper way for six years. It's as if when ye are contained within those walls even the air an' light is not free, 'tis as if it loses some of its substance an' purity by comin' over those barriers an' down onto the concrete ground. So, perhaps ye can understand that I was a bit giddy, near drunk-like on the freedom, but scared as well. Even misery is a comfort if it's what ye are used to an' we human bein's are entirely creatures of what is rather than what might be. 'Tis only in dreams that we believe in what might be." He smiled shyly and she saw clearly what he must have been like before and that the boy was still there even if he could not, at present, acknowledge him.

"Anyway, my first thought was I wanted a decent meal. Nothin' with potatoes either. Ye'd think even an Englishman could cook somethin' so simple as a potato properly but the ones we got in prison were boiled to glue an' scorched so they tasted like ashes in a man's mouth. We ate them every day, mornin', noon an' night an' the taste of them became like bile in my throat. Other men dreamed of iron bars an' women but me I dreamed of those damned potatoes. An Irishman's curse maybe," he smiled ruefully, "an' I was determined to never eat another one. So I found a restaurant, a little French place with the sidewalk tables, because on that first day I didn't want to be inside not even to eat nor sleep. An' I ordered myself a meal with a nice piece of meat an' some vegetables an' when the waiter comes he puts down the plate an says, 'zee chef apologisees but ve have no rice so he bakes you a potato instead.' Well I tell ye I laughed so hard I thought I'd pass out from it. I'm certain they thought I'd gone right off my nut."

"Was it a good potato?" she asked smiling with him.

"Likely it was," he said eyes traveling her face from forehead to eyebrow, to eye and nose, to linger on cheekbone and lips and come to rest in her eyes again.

"And the rest of the meal?" she asked tapping her fork on the table and going to great pains to avoid his frank, open gaze.

"'Twas strange," he said an undercurrent of regret in his voice, "I felt as if people were watchin' my every move, it was like I couldn't do the simplest things properly, like chew an' handle my cutlery. I was sure every move I made fairly shouted, 'this man has been a convicted felon for five years now and an Irish one at that.' But ye see it was all in my mind for someone, be it guard or other prisoner, had been watchin' every move I made for five years, an' seein' somethin' suspicious in all of it. A man couldn't take a piss without someone thinkin' he was tryin' to hide somethin' up his backside—" he stopped abruptly, "I'm sorry, I'm not used to bein' in the company of a woman an' my mouth is still a bit rough."

"I've heard worse," she said lightly.

"Anyhow it was a waste of the bit of money I had for the food, fine as it was, tasted like sawdust in my mouth. I ate it all anyway because it seemed as if I'd been hungry for five years an' never able to stop that gnawin' feelin' in my gut, though logically I knew it had little to do with hunger."

"And where did you sleep that night?"

"Cardboard city. Ye'll not have heard of it?" he asked in response to her quizzical look. "It's where all failed Irishmen sleep in London. Under the Charing Cross bridge in cardboard boxes, too afraid to stay an' yet more afraid to go home an' admit they've failed at whatever thing called them away from Irish shores in the first place. A bunch of homeless, luckless Micks. I felt more comfortable there than I had since I left my own home. I shared a bottle of Powers whiskey with an old man from Cork, who'd been livin' under that damn bridge for twelve years. I said he could come home with me, that I could manage his passage over an' didn't he long to see Irish shores again? Well he looks at me for a long time without speakin' like I am ten kinds of fool an' then says, 'do ye not know boyo that an Irishman who leaves Ireland can never go home again?' An' I, havin' the courage of whiskey in my veins says he's an old liar an' doesn't the boat train leave every blessed day for those exact shores? An' he gives me a look, this old drunk without even the grace of his own teeth in his head, as if to say I'm a very stupid Mick indeed an' says 'I suppose youth is an excuse for ignorance an' for not knowin' there are several kinds of leavin' an' some that ye can never go back on.' I suppose it's true," he shook his head, "though I don't entirely want to believe it. I'd like to think there's a way home for all of us, including myself."

"But now you are home and everything is new. It's a chance to start fresh."

He swallowed the last of his coffee and grimaced, " 'Tis a very American attitude if I may say so."

"You may, if you explain what you mean by that."

"Well it's only that ye are an optimistic bunch, perhaps that comes from bein' such a young nation, though yer lessons have been bitter they've not been so many as Ireland's. The name of this establishment for instance, 'Finnegan's Wake' 'tis typical of this land that we would cultivate the greatest writer of the twentieth century an' then ban the majority of the man's work an' turn around an' use his fame to sell things to anyone who isn't Irish. Or that we don't teach our own history in our schools, but present Irish history only in the context of how it relates to the history of the British Empire an' that's as the thorn in the great side of imperialism. Or that we've been stripped of our native tongue an' to actually be able to speak it with any fluency has become something of a specialization. We can be a bloody backwards lot."

"I wasn't talking about nations I was talking about you, your own life and fate."

He gave her a strange look, weary and a bit bitter. "My life an' my country's life are one an' the same."

"And where does your brother fit into that picture?" she asked quietly.

"Ye pull no punches do ye? Pat is my little brother an' someone I will protect with my own life if necessary."

"He's not so very little."

He waited until their coffee cups were refilled before responding. "That's a fact I'm well aware of. In my head, I knew he was nineteen years old and likely to be all the things that come with the age, but in my heart he was still fourteen an' grievin' our Daddy's death, he was still someone who needed his big brother to look out for him. I suppose that if he had been I'd have been able to keep my promise to my Da'. But he's not a child as much as I might wish it."

"No he isn't," she agreed.

Casey paid the check then, giving her an amused glance when she suggested she pay half, and they walked out into the rain, where streetlights, orange and grim, were the only stars visible.

"I think maybe I resent my brother a bit," Casey said out of the corner of his mouth, the other side occupied with lighting a cigarette, "I can't believe how well he's done without me. Makes me feel a bit obsolete, I mean," he said to her raised eyebrows, "here I come home expectin' this gawky teenager with spots an' no social graces an' I find this tall man who's runnin' dissident organizations an' has a gift for drawin' none of us ever suspected an' is entertainin' naked women in the kitchen."

"The light," she said, grateful for the dark that hid her furious blush, "was best in there."

"That," she could feel his grin without having to see it, "I will tell ye, threw me for the hell of a loop."

"It was entirely innocent."

"I don't know if there's anything entirely innocent about drawin' naked women, but it's certainly a pleasant way to make a livin'."

There was really no appropriate way to respond to that so Pamela wisely refrained from doing so.

"Where are we walking to?" she asked some time later after they'd passed several nameless buildings and faceless streets.

Casey stopped and looked around. "I'm sorry," he said, "I'm so fond of wanderin' now that I've got no walls stoppin' me that I forget most people have a destination in mind when they're out. I'm not certain of where we are, though if ye give me a minute I'll sort it out. Where is it that yer headin'?"

"Up there." She pointed at Jamie's house on the hill, distant enough to seem a fairy castle, twinkling with light, mythical and impossible to reach from the cramped dank laneway they stood in.

"Christ," he let out a long, low whistle. "That's where ye live?"

"In a manner of speaking, yes," she replied, wishing for some reason she couldn't yet define that she'd not told him.

"Ye'd need a map to get from here to there."

"It's not so difficult, you take the Shankill up as far as—"

"That's not what I mean an' I think ye know it," he said his tone softer by far than the words.

"I can't really help where I live."

"Can't ye?" he asked and then lightning fast smiled and lightened the atmosphere by several degrees. "I've talked yer ear off an' been so rude my Da' would be ashamed he'd raised me an' ye've not said a word about yerself."

"I told you where I live."

"Aye an' that only deepens the mystery doesn't it? Everyone in Belfast knows who lives there an' I imagine he's not yer uncle."

"He's my friend, the best one I've ever had," she said quietly, a thread of anger running beneath the surface of her words.

"I imagine he is," Casey said and there was no judgment in his voice. "Shall I walk ye home?"

"No, it isn't necessary, I know the way perfectly well."

"The question was only for politeness sake, I wasn't actually askin'," Casey said firmly, "I'd like to think I'm not the sort of man who'd let a wee girl walk home alone in the dark."

"Wee girl," she said indignantly.

"Aye, my brother may not be so little as ye say but you," he glanced over his shoulder, "are."

He set off at an easy pace though she had to half run to keep up with his long strides. "You have to take the street on your left up here," she said breathlessly, trying to stay abreast of him.

He glanced sideways at her, dark eyes amused, "I know the way."

"Bloody bastard," she whispered stopping in the middle of the street to catch her breath.

He halted, giving her a minute to catch up. "I'll say this ye may be a Yank but ye've the tongue of an Irishwoman in yer head."

This time she didn't bother to whisper.

YOU COULDN'T TELL A WOMAN ABOUT PRISON, they were too fine for it. At least this one was. And it seemed as much as there were nights you'd like to unburden yourself and stop living with the nightmares, you couldn't tell your brother either. Your brother who saw you as some living embodiment of the struggle. How to put into words anyway what you'd seen, done and been in the last five years? It was, for the most part, beyond words. How every day was a fight for your life, in a way that even people who lived in war zones could not understand. How you had to battle to keep your mind, soul and body from being torn apart.

When he really thought about it, which he tried not to do, he knew he didn't want to tell anyone. The beatings, the questioning that went on for hours, questions that both you and your interrogator knew there were no answers for. Answers were not the point, blood and pain were. Body searches, rectal exams that so humiliated a man that he would weep later in his cell. He'd learned the hard way to separate his mind from what was being done to his body. He'd gotten fairly good at it. They'd left him little choice in the matter however. If the mind wasn't hard and honed to the consistency of steel, the bastards knew it and they would use it to take you down, they would use it to kill you. And that was just the screws.

What the prisoners could do was something else entirely. They knew you in a way the screws could not. They could take a man's mind and bend it hard, bend it until there was no hope for survival, until the outside world seemed of no more consequence than a child's storybook. They had tried especially hard with him, 'the little fucking terrorist', they'd called him. 'We'll show you real terror you Paddy bastard.' And they had. He'd only been a boy when he went in, a boy who'd made a tragic mistake but he was a man now. It wasn't the method he'd have chosen but it had been most effective.

He missed his Daddy, missed him purely and without anything to break the fall of grief. He hadn't wanted to be the grownup one, hadn't wanted to look into his brother's face and know he was responsible for a life other than his own. So he'd fixed it, blown up a train station and gone to jail, telling himself it was for a higher cause. It was just fear though. It hadn't always been that way.

He remembered believing in life, the way you believe in God or fire. When his father told him about the stars and how they were great roiling fires in the sky, it had made sense to him, he'd never pictured them cold and aloof like diamonds the way so many children did. Made sense that God's light would be fire—vast, consuming fire burning itself out over billions of years in the center of infinity or nothingness, which regardless of your optimism or pessimism, was the same thing. He couldn't reach back to find the place where he'd stopped believing in, well pretty much anything. Some places you could not revisit if you wanted to keep going, if you wanted to make it through another day with any semblance of normality still within reach of your fingertips. You just couldn't. You went through the motions, he was hardly unique in this respect and he knew it, everyone did it in their own way. Living, the way he'd believed he would when he was young and foolish, was too frightening, a freefall into the unknown. Knowing with his primitive brain that he might never hit bottom or that if he did he'd die from the impact, both literally and figuratively.

He was seven when his father had given him the one piece of advice essential to survival. It had been a night from one of those long ago autumns and they'd stood outside and his Da' had pointed to the sky and said 'that and this' he swung his hand down and pointed to the ground, 'is sometimes all ye'll have boy an' it will have to be enough.' At seven he hadn't understood, his father's words, stark and ungentle, had merely made him uneasy. Now he understood and though it had served him well over the last few years, it still made him shiver in the primal regions of his body. Night was when infinity was present and infinity seemed too vast to contain something as simplistic as heaven. So he picked one star, Orion's lucida, the warrior's shoulder which must bear the brunt of war. Red Betelgeuse, forever away, visible from earth only because of its spectacular vastness, four hundred million miles across, swallowing planets and entire galaxies with the appetite of a star who feels death's imminence shadowing it across time and space. His father had been right, sometimes it was all he had, the same sky and earth as his brother, the knowledge that man is made to be broken and even stars die.

Chapter Seven
He Who Hesitates

THE WEEKLY MEETING OF THE YOUNG SOCIALISTS had started out at seven thirty PM in a somewhat orderly fashion, by eight o'clock they were swiftly sliding into chaos, by eight-thirty it was outright pandemonium, as groups large and small fought over vague theories and definitions.

"In America they didn't analyze it, they just got out and marched," shouted one red-headed, gap-toothed miss over the fray.

"Ye'll never get the Irish to march," said a bespectacled intellectual, who bore an uncanny, and one could only presume purposeful, resemblance to the young Lenin.

"We're Irish aren't we?" Pat Riordan said and though his voice was low, he might well have shouted for a sudden silence descended upon the rabble.

"We've not the numbers that we need here," said Mr. Lenin, determined as always to be the pessimism to the group's overabundant optimism.

"We need to mobilize the masses, rouse the community—"

"Have you taken a look around you? People are apathetic, we've lived under the yoke of British oppression for almost a millenium and we seem to like the feel of the bit because we're getting very little response from the community."

"If ye want a crowd in Ireland, forbid a crowd," Pat said patiently.

"Ye crafty, wee devil," said a girl with long toffee-colored hair and eyes that didn't so much shine as flame. "That's bloody brilliant."

"Thanks Bernadette," Pat said blushing slightly.

"Alright then," the girl named Bernadette said in an authoritative voice, "we leak word of what we're plannin', we make certain it reaches the right ears an' then we get ready to march."

"Do ye really think that non-violent protest is goin' to make anyone sit up an' take notice?"

"Do ye suggest we take machine guns with us?" the redheaded girl's tongue was all vinegar.

"The fundament of non-violent protest is violence," Pat said, "ye challenge the system in place, ye provoke them to violence an' thus show them for a corrupt, morally bankrupt institution. The only problem we have here is that the Unionist system has always run on open obvious violence an' suppression, it will hardly undermine their credibility if they act in exactly the manner we can count on them actin'. However it's not so much Irish institution we're concerned with, it's the rest of the world."

"Aye Pat, go on," Bernadette encouraged.

"Well to the Unionists we will only be provin' the opinion they've held of us since birth that we are a bunch of reckless, ill-educated, riotous, tattered an' not to be trusted Celts. They know they are better housed, better educated, more readily employed, richer, sweeter an' more deservin' of their slice of the pie. They hardly need us to point it out to them; they know it an' believe it's their God-given right. The rest of the world an' their television cameras doesn't know it though. Violence plays to the television viewer, be it in Britain or in America, like nothin' else. The riots in the streets of America have proven that beyond a shadow of a doubt."

"So do we send graven invitations to the world's press? People are hardly aware that Ireland exists anymore other than some mythic, sheep-dotted green island their ancestors fled from," protested Mr. Lenin.

"We start small, we build up an' the world will come to us."

There was a space of silence as people digested this astonishing bit of strategy.

Mr. Lenin rubbed his nose thoughtfully, innate cynicism taking a short respite. "I suppose it makes sense in a dangerous sort of a way." He looked at Pat, the beginning of a light in his eyes, "Do ye really believe they'll come to us?"

"I know they will," Pat said firmly.

"Damn if I don't believe it when ye say it," Mr. Lenin smiled revealing a pleasantly homely face with his teeth.

"If I know one thing it's that for every move on our part there will be a backlash from the Protestant community an' we had best be prepared for the consequences."

"So we're agreed, we start with a series of small marches an' build interest an' then plan a large one for further down the road when we've built some momentum." The girl named Bernadette shoved a wing of toffee hair impatiently behind one ear. "Pat we'll need ye on the planning committee for this, yer input would be invaluable."

"Aye, count me in," Pat replied not looking up from the paper where he was drawing the girl in question with flames flowing down her back instead of candy-colored hair.

"It's a very good likeness," Pamela said from the vicinity of his shoulder, blowing a ripple of her own hair out of her face. Silent throughout the meeting she had listened carefully to the Tower of Babel cacophony of ideas, theories, arguments and pure idealism that was both the strength and the downfall of the Young Socialist movement. If the energy in the room could have been harnessed, the entire world would be changed. She watched the side of Pat's face as he drew Bernadette as a fire-headed Medusa, lost in the swoop and slide of pencil and thought he was a puzzling mix. Idealistic enough to make even a confirmed cynic believe all things were possible, he also had the figurative underbelly of a dogmatic cleric, seeing the reality even when he didn't want to. It was an uneasy brew and she wondered which side would eventually out; she was rooting for the starry-eyed believer but knew life rarely left such gifts untouched.

An hour later, they stood on the table of land that began the long sweeping plateau of the Kirkpatrick estate. Mist was coming in off the sea in gossamer fragments, the sky above still clear and thick with stars.

"It's a different world up here," Pat breathed, shoving his hands into his pockets, a certain sign of discomfiture.

"Not so different as you might think," Pamela said in a somewhat dejected tone causing Pat to eye her shrewdly.

"Will you come in then?" she asked as Pat stood feet firmly planted in the ground.

He shook his head. "No there are some places even a fool like myself is wise enough not to tread."

"What is that supposed to mean?" Pamela halted halfway through the footgate that was hidden between two giant cypresses.

"Nothin'," he said far too hastily.

"No tell me, do people think there's something to be afraid of up here? Because there isn't you know."

"There have always been stories about this house," Pat said, looking through the gloom of the cypresses to where lights bloomed and spilled from their separate windows. "That it's haunted an' the people who live under its roof are fated never to be happy."

"Superstitious nonsense," Pamela said sharply, disturbed by the hollow undertone in Pat's words.

"Maybe, but where there's smoke there's bound to be some spark of fire."

"Are you actually afraid of something, Pat Riordan?"

"What if I am?"

"Because it's silly, a childhood fairytale told by people jealous of what and who the Kirkpatricks are." She moved out of the sheltering warmth of the trees and challenged him directly. "I thought you had more sense and courage than to believe stupid tales."

"Scared I might be, jealous I'm not," Pat retorted angrily.

"Then prove it, come and beard the lion in his den. The study lights are on so he's home."

"Fine, I will," Pat said with more conviction than he felt.

Though he'd seen pictures of the house in magazines and newsprint photos of the man himself, there had been something one-dimensional about the former and grainy and unrevealing about the latter. He wasn't prepared for the reality though he made a good show of nonchalance. A façade he maintained until Pamela, without so much as a knock, led him into the study.

Before him lay the riches of Babylon, books stacked and piled, books spilling and straying, books lined up like little soldiers, spine against gleaming spine. Bound in leather, bound in cloth, printed on the finest vellum paper pressed hard and mated with ink. Dante, Cicero, Virgil, Pope, Keats, Byron, Yeats, the very names enough to make the head swim. Words from the four corners of the earth: Arabic, French, Chinese, Russian and lesser dialects from forgotten lands. Latin, Greek, Egyptian—languages so dust-bound they survived only in the liturgy of ancient churches, words written on the shredded and pressed reeds of the warm and silted waters of the Nile. History, linguistics, poetry, mathematics, philosophy, religion, commerce, revolutionary tracts and dissertations. Volumes of such antiquity they could not normally be found outside of a museum.

"You might," he was startled by a quiet voice that held nothing of Belfast in it, "introduce your friend."

"Pat, this is Jamie Kirkpatrick, Jamie this is Pat Riordan."

"Hello Pat," said the voice and rounded the desk from which it had emerged.

So here was the prince of the castle, made king now by his father's untimely death. He looked the part. As though God had been fully absorbed in the making of him and had thought his creation out to the finest detail. Pat wondered uneasily if it was strange to think a man beautiful and yet there seemed no fit substitute to describe this man.

It stood to reason, all things considered, that he would hate him on sight. But he didn't, not from the first moment Jamie extended his hand and welcomed him into his home. His sincerity was apparent, his warmth and ease not a matter of trickery, though Pat felt certain that he was capable of feigning these things should the situation warrant it.

"Perhaps you'd care for a drink; we generally have something round about this time of night."

"That would be nice," Pat found himself saying.

Tea came some moments later in a silver pot surrounded by glass cups set in silver-filigreed bases. A plate of oatmeal cookies was placed before him, fragrant with butter and spices, his tea poured and left at his elbow.

"Pamela tells me you are quite the speaker, had half of Queens ready to riot," Jamie smiled, taking the mockery from his words while helping himself to two cookies and a slice of lemon for his tea.

"Hardly," Pat blushed, inwardly cursing himself for it. "It's only that my tongue gets ahead of my brain at times an' I hardly know what I'm saying in the moment nor afterwards."

"Never underestimate the power of words," Jamie said indicating the books around him, "people who do are always sorry in the end."

Pat, taking a sip of tea, glanced over to where Pamela sat perched on the arm of Jamie's chair, like a fond daughter or affectionate wife. She looked decidedly smug. Jamie seemed unaware or at least very comfortable with her nearness and continued on chatting with Pat about history and literature, peppering the conversation with questions about what Pat was taking at the university, what his future goals were and what, (Pat realized several days later) his intentions towards the girl seated on the arm of Jamie's chair were. It was all done so subtly, so warmly, so graciously that Pat did not see that he was being grilled rather mercilessly, and could not remember later whether any of his answers had been in the least coherent.

When he left, and he was chagrined to realize he'd stayed several hours, he found he'd been thoroughly bedazzled by the man he'd been determined to hate. Jamie had clinched the entire evening and brought it neatly into his own palm when he'd told Pat he was more than welcome to borrow any books as he might find of interest on his shelves.

"I couldn't possibly," Pat said, mouth watering at the very thought.

"You can read, can't you? Pamela tells me you love books and I trust you'll return them when you are done, so I rather think you can if you like."

"Th- thank you," Pat had managed to stutter out before leaving the scented air and warm confines of the home of His Grace the Lord of Ballywick and Tragheda, James Kirkpatrick the Fourth.

He hadn't wanted to like the man, but he thought grudgingly, as he passed through the cypress portals and left Kirkpatrick land, he bloody well did.

IN EVERY COUNTRY WITH A REBEL PAST OR A REBEL FUTURE there are similar rooms for similar men with different faces—cramped, dark, dirty rooms. Cold with damp, cold with snow, cold with pain. The only real warmth coming from the internal fuel of idealism, the belief that their moment in history has come. In Russia there will be a bottle of vodka on the table, a dog-eared copy of '*The State and Revolution*', tattered slogans adorning the walls from last season, last year, last century. In Beirut, qahveh, lemons and the Koran will grace the table, a fine scree of sand under the bed. In El Salvador a picture of Che beside a statue of the bleeding Christ, priests who disrobe in order to serve God more clearly, martyrs who die in foreign lands fighting for lost causes. They will travel everywhere in search of a hope, a prayer. Men with delicate amber faces working the kitchens of white hotels in cold, chattering cities. Tall straight-backed ebony princes trudging through the snow and indifference of the northern hemisphere's great bloody swathe of industry. Cities built on the backs of their ancestry, cities where they must now beg, borrow, steal time and money, where the past is prologue and prologue past.

In Belfast there is tea, tepid and scummy, a bottle of Powers whiskey half drunk in a doorless cupboard, a nicotine stained copy of the Proclamation of 1916 lining a drawer in a desk rarely used. Paint peeling walls, a cot without sheets for men on the run, men who sleep briefly during the brightest hours of day and flee at night with messages, with guns, with the hope of a nation in their hands. Men on intimate terms with fear, exhaustion, dirt, a rebel Celt version of the White Rabbit, running, running, forever madly running, with the vision of a cell in the not too distant future. Not a job for the easily disillusioned or the romantic of heart, not a job for a human being.

Hope skips a generation and returns in the form of a strong back and even stronger mind, idealism stripped down to a bare bone and left in a corner of the soul for the knacker's cart. The men vary and there will be the odd woman thrown in but for the most part, they will be working-class, raised on bleakness, poor diets, piety and fear of the other. There will be a few from the upper classes, well educated, maybe bored, maybe afflicted with true idealism, waiting to be crushed by the great slow grind of social change.

The question, regardless of country, will always be the same—how to inspire hope, naked and raw, in the minds, hearts and bellies of the general population? How to pull a people up off their knees and remind them as they clutch their rosaries and plaster saints that God helps only those who help themselves. Blood, their own and that of The Other will often be the answer, the only answer that demands certain attention.

Casey Riordan knew such rooms. He knew that hope sometimes was as simple as washing the cups, keeping the tea hot, the whiskey bottle full, the walls painted and a warm blanket on the bed. Taking the proclamation, the ghostly ideals out, shaking off the dust and pinning it back on the wall where it can be seen. As simple as being ready, regardless of the mindless fear, to bleed and die for a thought, a breath of words spoken generations ago. As simple as a lit candle in a dark window, even if the comfort of light was only for yourself and your memories.

He sat down on the edge of the freshly blanketed bed, eyeing the new white paint, the clean cups, the re-hinged cupboard, the polished desk with satisfaction. He looked then into the clear heart of the candle flame and whispered to the night and its ghosts.

"I'm home, Daddy."

IT WAS A LOVELY SPRING DAY, the air tart as an old whore's tongue, the apple blossoms beginning to throb red on their undersides and the sun slanting at a newly sharpened angle. Devlin Murphy was to play that evening at the county fair and Casey, still somewhat drunk on the nectar of freedom, suggested a day of it.

They set out early, the three of them, a modest lunch and a hot thermos of tea carefully packed, sweaters and coats flung carelessly over shoulders that were soon too warm to abide them.

The uneasiness between the brothers had vanished and they returned to old habits, taking turns at being bait to the other's good-natured teasing. They put Pamela swiftly and tactfully at ease. She had a feeling it was a natural game with them, making strangers feel welcome and inclusive to all their jokes and boldly flung comments.

The fair was set in a long field, rolling over small hills and knobbles of land like a green velvet blanket. It was crowded, overflowing and funneling with streams of people, people fond of fun but rarely fortunate enough to have an unfettered hour of it. The sun, taking part in the festivities lasted the whole day through, imparting a blessing on the children, parents and animals that wove through its rays. The countryside and its gifts were on full display: lacemakers, whiskey runners, wool blankets dipped in berry juice to stain them red, round ruddy cows, corkscrew lambs just past the wobbly legs stage and horses. Ah horses, the great love of Ireland. Dappled and silver, roan and black, legs so fine they seemed made of blown glass, high proud heads adorned with plaited and ribboned manes. Pamela, leaning over a paddock gate, closed her eyes and took a breath of heaven. Casey, an Irishman to the bone in most respects, was in this one, most assuredly not.

"I cannot look," he said, turning swiftly pale as Pamela bent her head to allow a big, evil looking stallion to nuzzle her neck. Pat, neither terrified of nor a supplicant to the mysteries of equine love, merely smiled and kept a safe distance from the large, bared teeth of the stallion who was now nosing, in a bold way, down the front of Pamela's shirt.

"Give me an apple," she said to Casey who with a grim look fished one out and closing his eyes took the required step and a half to drop it in her hand and then jumped quickly back. She raised her eyebrows at Pat as the horse blew out a great gust of air and settled to chewing the apple with an air of content.

"Horse bit him in the arse when he was four," Pat said, "an' he's never gotten past it."

"Thanks for sharin' that bit of information, Pat," Casey said daring to open his eyes and shoot a filthy look in his brother's direction.

"Big ugly stallion was it?"

"No," Pat ignored his brother's glare, "'twas a Shetland pony, a half-grown filly."

"It had," Casey shouldered the lunch sack with injured dignity, "very large teeth."

"I'm certain it did," Pamela said straightfaced and then meeting Pat's eyes broke with him into helpless laughter. Casey, eyeing them both darkly, turned on his heel and strode off, away from the smell of horses.

They caught up with him near the shore, where the tide had left all sorts of creatures in its wake—small scuttling crabs, fronds of kelp, tiny gelatinous beings that caught and refracted the sunlight into prisms and miniature rainbows.

"We're sorry," Pamela said breathlessly.

"We are," Pat chorused and they both started to giggle again.

"Ye can both go to hell, the two of ye," Casey said and then face slowly cracking began to laugh too. Laughed and laughed until he had to sit down in the wet, rocky sand, tears leaking from the corners of his eyes.

"I still don't think it's funny," he said and this put them all into fresh gales of mirth. "It's just," he finished a moment later, "so damn good to laugh."

Later when they'd all grasped some fickle straw of sobriety they set off down the beach, abandoning socks and shoes, running in great looping arcs around each other and then back again, opening their arms wide to the wind and the taste of freedom. Pamela, tying her hair over one shoulder to keep it away from her eyes, sprinted down the beach ahead of them.

Initially the boys gave chase, but soon it became sport between the two of them. Brother against brother, shoulder to shoulder, pushing, jostling, vying for the lead, sand flying silver beneath their feet, sweat breaking clean upon skin under sunlight. Legs of similar length flew, feeling the sweet, shuddering burn of long muscle and sinew stretched to extremes. Rocks loomed ahead, black and glistening, slick with salt spray. They fought for toeholds, fingerholds, air. Feet, used to the confinement of shoes, blossomed with bruises. Mind played subservient to body, agility and stamina becoming the only qualities of worth.

Casey pulled ahead ever so slightly, veered sharply to the left and chose sheer lunacy over nimbleness of limb. Before them stretched a quarter mile of massive boulders, sharp upthrust rock and myriad small, glinting razor edges. Casey had chosen instead the sheer face of the cliff, opalescent blacks, grays and whites in the clear spring light. Pat, knowing that he who hesitates never wins the race, veered in turn and hit the cliff face right behind his brother. It was an impossible climb, handholds consisting of sand-encrusted quarter inches, purely vertical from base to nape. Ten feet up muscles were screaming for mercy, fingers numb with tension, lungs seared and burning. Twenty feet up reason was abandoned without regret.

Casey moved gently, feeling the wall like it was the body of a woman to be explored with leisure and the luxuriant presence of every sense. The meager handholds held, bore his weight which he'd centered into the heart of the rock and then crumbled in his absence. Pat had to find his own path and grimly did so as sweat stung his eyes and nose and his legs began to cramp in long rippling seizures. He spared a swift glance down the beach through a fug of rose red pain and saw Pamela picking her way gracefully through the last of the rock. He turned his attention back to the cliff face and, body strung like wire across a minefield, followed in his brother's wake.

There was a sharp, short scream from ahead causing Pat to lose his tenuous handhold and drop down the sheer face, landing painfully on his rear end in a mound of sand-skiffed kelp. Casey, face now pointed towards the sound, never flinched, ten feet along the face of glittering rock and he'd cleared the worst of the stone below, fifteen feet and there was sand beneath him. At which point he pushed himself out from the cliff face and dropped lightly to the ground, legs moving across the wet wrack before his feet had even made certain contact. Pat lost sight of him instantly and it was another panic-stricken, scratching, scraping, bloody five minutes of it before he caught a glimpse of him again. When he did, his first emotion was confusion, for Pamela was turned into his brother's chest, Casey's arm protectively across her back, the other hand stroking her hair in a comforting motion. An emotion, bred in his chest, cut with the finest edge through his heart as he surmounted the last rock and ran the final length of green and silver ground.

The cause of the scream was instantly apparent and the sight of it some thirty yards down the beach took the words from his throat. At first glance from high up and far away it had seemed no more than a gleaming half-submerged rock. Closer though he could see that it was too smooth by far, too smooth and shaped for movement not fixation. A thing of eons but soft with life, sleek with speed and silence.

"Christ, how do ye suppose it got there?" Pat managed as Pamela's white, stricken face emerged from his brother's shirt front.

"They beach themselves, it happens," his brother replied shortly. "Come on we'll have to see if it's still alive."

That it was not alive became swiftly apparent as they shortened the distance between themselves and its carcass. The smell was ripe and splitting to the nose, catching with the rot of seaweed in their throats. Casey nevertheless put a hand gently over the blowhole, pulling back the muscular flap which had closed in death, to see if there was even the slightest hissing exhalation. There was not.

"Been here a few days," Casey said hand gliding down the back that shone blue and black in the sun. "An old male, suffocated from the weight of his own body, works beautifully in the sea but they're their own worst enemy when they land."

"How can you tell?" Pamela asked, still pale but looking with interest over the dorsal fin, the cream coated tail flukes, the yellow tinged underbelly.

"Size. He's near to thirty feet long, only the really old males get that big. A lot of them beached here during the last war; scientists figured it was the submarines did it, mixed up the whales' internal sonar or something an' threw them off their natural routes."

"*Orcinus orca,*" Pat said softly.

Casey's head came up and he smiled, a fine, white smile of memory shared.

"Class mammalia," he answered.

"Order cetacea," Pat rejoined.

"Family delphinidae," they chorused together.

Pamela looked from one brother to the other, eyebrows arched in delicate lines of soot.

"'Tis a game," Pat explained, sensing her unspoken question, "that our Daddy used to play with us when we were small. He said if we understood the hierarchy of things an' the connections we'd have a greater appreciation of life an' the world we live it in. How all things are connected an' work in various ways together. He'd name an animal an' we'd see who could name the class, order, family, genus an' species first an' whoever won would get a toffee. It worked well until Casey started demandin' cigarettes an' whiskey as his due."

"Here," Casey said and took Pamela's hand, placing it on the silken underside where the flipper, limp in the air-laden atmosphere, joined to the force of body. "Ye'll never feel its like again."

"It's softer than a baby's skin," she whispered and heedless of smell stepped in closer, caressing the flipper with her own hand where it curled with a fragile sigh across and over her arm. "It feels like an enormous hand," she breathed as if afraid that she would wake the great leviathan from its deep blue slumber.

"That's because their flipper bones are very similar to our own finger bones. 'Tis believed that they once lived on land many millions of years ago an' that we are more closely related to them than we could have suspected."

"We have to put it back in the water somehow," she said turning tear-bright eyes on the two of them.

"D'ye have any idea of the weight of the thing? It's likely near to three tonnes. Nothin' short of God's hand coming down an' scoopin' it away is goin' to move it back into the water."

"We could at least," Pat said softly, "put a piece of its heart back into the water, a creature should rest where its heart lives an' for a whale that's the sea. We can't move it but we can move the part of it that beat an' felt an' sustained its life."

Casey regarded him for a long moment, as if he were weighing and measuring the insanity of the suggestion or the plausibility of it.

"Yer right," he said finally, "I suppose it's the least we can do."

"We'll have to take it out a ways," Pat regarded the sea, a heavy green, with trepidation.

"Aye, we'll manage." Casey leaned down then and pulled his pant leg up in one quick yank. Beneath the cloth, next to his skin nestled a knife, innocuous enough in its mother of pearl casing, but transforming into a wicked-winged butterfly with one smooth flick of his wrist.

"Why are ye carryin' a knife?" Pat asked through gritted teeth.

"Habit," was the terse reply.

Because the whale had beached on its side, it made a near to impossible task slightly less impossible. The skin, generally tough and oily, was dried by days in the sun and more susceptible to the knife. There was a small cracking noise as Casey split it and then there was a good eight inches of blubber to breach. It leaked an oily, heavy smell that lingered hard in the nostrils. He cut in a long arcing strip just beneath where he'd gauged the ribcage's end, hands slicked with whale oil and then, as he hit the hard shoal of bone, a black ooze of blood.

"Jaysus Christ," he yelled, leaping back before the worst of it pooled in the sand. "Pat come help me will ye, this was yer godforsaken romantic notion."

"Yer goin' to have to cut a triangle in the flesh or we'll never get to the heart," Pat said and then took the knife and with the precision of a surgeon, cut a perfect triangle beneath the massive ribcage. It took an hour to reach the organ cavity by which time both brothers were soaked with an aromatic variety of oil, blood and sweat.

"It's there," Casey said at long last, arm completely disappearing up into the cut. Pat in turn felt and shook his head.

"That's the liver, go left."

"Is the liver not a life sustaining organ?" Casey said irritably, the original romance of the idea buried in the ruination of his shirt, pants and scent.

"It has," Pat's face was grim, his arm submerged up to the shoulder, "to be the heart."

And the heart it was, though it took another fifteen minutes and a great deal of dexterity on Pat's part to emerge with a three inch width of it, jagged and torn in his hand. He looked purely pagan, bloody tissue held aloft, face spattered with blood and oil. It might have been a thousand years ago and he painted with the viscera of his enemy, part of the barbarian horde that terrorized Europe. The words that came from his lips completely incongruous with the portrait he presented. "Will I take it in then?"

"I'll come with ye," Casey said pulling his shirt off over his head.

"No, I'll do it," Pamela stepped forward, "It was me that wanted him back in the ocean."

The brothers looked at her in twin consternation, brows furrowed in disapproval so identical that she had to smother a laugh.

"Ye have no bathing suit," Casey said as if indeed that settled the entire matter right there.

"Nor have you," she said pointedly. "Besides there's no one else about and it's not as if the two of you haven't seen all I own before." So saying she stepped, in one easy movement, out of her dress. Two throats cleared in unison, two dark sets of eyes appealed the heavens for rescue and found a cheerfully blue sky with no salvation written in its blameless hue.

"Right then," Casey said tightly, face still carefully averted, "let's get this done."

The boys ran into the sea as if the pair of them were on fire, Pamela close on their heels.

The Irish Sea was not by any means a hospitable body of water and un-inclined to treat intruders gently. The cold knocked the wind out of a body immediately, the current had a savage pull to it and even the strongest of swimmers was advised to go gently. Pat and Casey cut through the icy green waves cleanly, Pamela, used to warmer waters, struggled to keep up, extremities at first tingling and then disturbingly numb. Her throat and lungs burned with the chill, breath forming just above the surface of the water. The boys had struck out in a diagonal, northeast line, swimming straight and true as if they were possessed of internal compasses, while she cut a wavering and exhausted line behind them. Close to, the water was black, not green, black and unholy as the waters of hell itself.

Casey and Pat had stopped ahead of her some ways, treading water, though they appeared from a distance to catch and ride the cusp of the small, choppy, white-crested waves like sprites.

"Are ye alright?" Casey called when she'd struggled some distance further.

"Fine," she shouted back gamely only to take in a mouthful of freezing saltwater. By the time she finished sputtering and wiping the salt out of her eyes Casey was beside her.

"I think we'd best head back for shore," he said and struck out at an easy pace that she could match without difficulty. When they were close to shore she turned back to find that Pat was only an indistinct blur on the horizon.

"How far will he go?" she asked through chattering teeth as they crawled out of the water.

"As far as the limits of his strength will take him."

"That's crazy, he could drown out there." She found a warm patch of sand and proceeded to wring the water from her hair.

"It's his nature; it'll be the only way that he feels he's done the whale any honor."

"And if he doesn't know the limits of his strength?"

"I'll go get him," Casey said easily, casting her a sidelong glance as he toweled off with his ruined shirt. "Do ye not feel any shame?" His voice was curious not condemning, as if he found her puzzling.

"If you are referring to my lack of clothes, no I don't. Do you?"

"No, but I figure that's normal for a man. I've never known a woman or girl who didn't make a big fuss over it. The Church an' their mams tell them to keep hidden from the time they are wee an' they never seem to shake the impulse to do so."

"I didn't have a mother and church was a once a year occasion for Christmas; there was never anything to make me feel ashamed."

"Well that's good, though I'll not say as I don't find it damned disconcertin'." He smiled a sweet, wide grin that made her blush. She'd never been as aware of the physical proximity of another human being as she was of this man. His heighth and breadth, the deep lines that furrowed his knuckles, the fine hairs on his arms. How the crisp edge of his rolled up cuffs so white against the flesh of his forearm actually made her weak and dizzy. The way everything he did had a sharp edge to it, a physicality that was deeply erotic, as if he would waste neither word, nor movement, nor emotion. An intelligence tempering the brutality that would be his wont if not carefully and firmly channeled. He could hardly have been more different from Jamie on the surface, Jamie who was her ideal, precious and held tight against disillusion. Therefore it stood to reason that she should not find this man so damnably attractive and yet, oh and yet...

She closed her eyes, salt-rimed lashes pressing down against flushed cheeks and reached for her dress which was placed gently in her hand. So he knew then and was likely embarrassed by that which she could not keep secret.

"Pat's turned back. I'm just goin' down the shore a ways to be certain I can keep a clear eye on him."

She nodded, not trusting herself to actual speech.

She managed the rest of the day fairly well. Pat came back to shore, exhausted and blue from cold and when he'd warmed sufficiently, they ate their lunch while Casey went out of his way to be charming. Her past considered, it was a form of behavior she found somewhat humiliating, it had been done as a salve over naked feeling before. She understood the play in all its acts now, and didn't particularly want a part.

DEVLIN MURPHY HAD THE FACE OF A DISSIPATED CHOIRBOY and the voice of a gelded angel. Over the years, his throat, having seen a river of whiskey and the smoke of thousands of tobacco fires, had begun to slip from a pure gold registry into the cooler tones of silver, mellowed and sweetened by the earthier base notes of bronze. Regardless of its place on the chart of precious metals though it was a voice heaven sent that sat in the base of its listener's spine and spread tendrils of ether into the blood and cells and bone.

He had at one time been an actual choirboy, possessed of cherubic curls, melting blue eyes and a voice that was surely meant for Gabriel. Beautiful enough in his youth to make priests, who still recalled the echoes of the flesh, pray for long hours on very hard floors. He was famous for a variety of reasons; a homegrown boy from the meanest part of Belfast, he had made it his primary occupation in life to record through music the entire history of the Republican movement. Among the favorites were a ballad about the Rising called *'The Best of Intentions'*, a long narrative song sung in two parts about the slaying of Michael Collins called *'The Mouth of Flowers'* and *'The Lord of Cork'* a lament for Terence MacSwiney who'd died on hunger strike whilst serving as the mayor of Cork. He was internationally known, internationally loved and still chose to make his home in Belfast. It was this last that made him most beloved to his Irish audience.

Pamela, having been deprived of said dulcet tones all her life, was completely entranced. Devlin, a notorious womanizer with a nose for beauty, had spotted her by the end of his third song and proceeded, to the dismay of her escorts, to sing her a song ripe with double entendres. As he slithered his way into the ending of the tune, he espied something or someone of equal interest to her it seemed for his gaze, tenderly drunk, had lit on an aspect near her own and sobered swiftly.

The next song, launched rapidly and with no remnant of the sozzled bard, was an onslaught. Irish pipes, Irish fiddle played to the farthest reaches of their keeper's talents, lit the air with fire and rebellion, recalling every uprising, every wrong, every drop of blood shed on Irish ground. It was a call to arms. At the apex of the music that shot and sundered the night, Devlin Murphy, former choirboy and defiler of priestly dreams, rose and tipping back a headful of lusty yellow curls howled into the night. It pierced the air, took aim at the stars, drowned the pipes, washed away the fiddle and sat sharp and primitive in the marrow of all who heard it.

"Now some of yez will have heard the tale I am about to tell before an' some of yez will not," Devlin's voice had taken on an incantatory swing, his eyes fixing them to the ground with the force of hammered quartzite. "'Tis the tale of a black eyed boy," his voice had lowered to a whisper, his eyes narrowed, one nicotine stained finger sweeping across his audience, "an' the love he one time lost."

"Christ have mercy," Casey's groan was heartfelt, "he's seen us."

"What's going on?" Pamela whispered to Pat who sat scrunched against her right-hand side.

"'The Black Eyed Boy' is a poem—"

"Callin' it a poem is flattery," Casey interjected.

"Written," Pat continued unperturbed, "by Devlin's grandda'—"

"A man of absolutely no talent," Casey supplied.

"In honor of *our* granddad Brendan, who—"

"Was not so much honored as entirely humiliated by this particular bit of music."

"Nevertheless it was a well-intentioned piece of work even if Devlin's grandda', whose name was also Devlin by the way, was a bit left of center."

"Left of center?" Casey snorted, causing the people ahead of them to turn round and glare at him. "The man was stark ravin' mad, thought he was the king's own musician in the court of Finn MacCool. Ran naked down the lanes with nothin' but ribbons in his hair half his life."

"Don't exaggerate; he only did that on Sundays for religious reasons."

"So now runnin' about in the altogether with roses an' lace in yer hair is an accepted Christian practice?" Casey said bitingly.

"Why did he write a poem about your grandfather?" Pamela hastily asked.

"He thought," Casey drew his eyebrows together for emphasis, "that grandda' *was* Finn MacCool."

"Hush, the song is startin'," Pat said as the musical lead up began its winding down into words. The pipes and fiddle had hushed to a soft moan when Devlin's voice hissed like a rush of velvet into the atmosphere:

> *A black-eyed boy*
> *Came he down*
> *From Carrickmore*
> *And Callagmaghtown.*
> *The way was dark*
> *The night uncertain*
> *When God's finger*
> *Drew nigh the curtain,*
> *Revealed He fire*
> *Through that door,*
> *And the moon sat shivering*
> *On a foreign shore,*
> *Aye, the moon sat shivering*
> *On a foreign shore...*

The song wound on through a tale of war, defeat, love found and love lost, the tale of a black-eyed boy who near to died for the love of a redheaded girl. By the end of it, Pat's jaw was slack and Casey's face a stark white.

"What in the name of Christ was that?" he asked no one in particular as the song ended in an eruption of clapping and cheering.

"I have no idea, it sure an' hell wasn't his grandda's version though," Pat said, "that one began with '*there was a boy named Finny MacCool*' an' suffice it to say the rest is not fit for a lady's ears."

"Ye'll perhaps have noticed," Devlin began, putting out his hands to still the applause, "that my wee song has been re-vamped somewhat an' given a more serious tone, an' though," he smiled with cream coddling charm, "I'd like to take credit for the revisions I must bestow credit where credit is due, this new an' may I say masterful version was compliments of our great poet, the last revolutionary to wield a pen, Mr. Jack Stuart. Many of yez will have no doubt heard the rumor that Jack was to be here tonight," he paused as the expected gasp rose from the audience, "an' though I am loathe to disappoint such a fine bunch as yerselves, I must sadly an' with regret announce that Jack was detained in Paris an' could not be here." There was a great deflation of lungs and stomachs as disappointment sat down heavy on the shoulders of all assembled. To have been a part of history, to have been the first people to know whom Jack Stuart actually was, to have that hope dangled in one's face and snatched back just as fast, well it was perhaps more indignity than even Devlin Murphy could cure. There were mutters and murmurs as Devlin inclined his head to one side and held up a hand once more.

"Now I know ye all are sore disappointed but tonight, to my own surprise as well as yer own, I've discovered that we've the descendant of the real, original black-eyed boy here in the audience."

"Shit," said Casey and Pat in perfect and profane unison as a murmur of curiosity rippled across the crowd.

"Our country," Devlin said once again commanding the audience's attention, "is standin' on the fissure between the grievances of the past an' the promise of a new future. A *bright*," he twisted the word sharply, "future, bright with neon signs an' shiny new cars, bright with regular paychecks an' a garage attached to a three bedroom in the suburbs, bright with the light of television screens. So bright in fact that we'll be hypnotized, they're bettin', by all the things we can purchase with our regular little paychecks. So bright that we'll not be able to look away from the promise of prosperity to the past, to that which lays just over our shoulders. They are certain we'll forget what our ancestors fought an' died for, that we won't care why five years out of a young man's life can be taken away from him as this young man's was, Casey stand up."

Casey muttering curses that encompassed the names of half the population of the New Testament, slowly got to his feet. The audience turned and eyed him in complete silence. "For the last five years this boy has been incarcerated in Parkhurst Prison, on British soil, by British law and judgment a terrorist. This boy," Devlin strode out into the crowd with measured steps, "whose father died in service to this country, whose grandfather was the man who almost brought the British to their knees during the civil war, this boy has already had to give them five years of his life merely for the bein' the wrong race in the wrong country at the wrong time.'

'But we," he smiled cannily, "why should we care about these things, these wrongs, we with our full bellies an' electrical lightin', with our four door cars an' entertainment to be had for the price of twistin' a knob. The past is after all the past an' everyone, ourselves included, tells us that that's where it should lie, in the past," Devlin's voice had become deceptively soothing, hot gravy being poured over an otherwise unpalatable meal, "There's only one problem with sleeping dogs, though, people, they leave their throat exposed for the wolf to come an' tear out. An' we know who the wolf is, don't we? We have always known the wolf even when he paraded in the dress of a lamb. We have known," he shook his head sadly, "an' yet we have opened the door an' given him our throat again an' again." Devlin sighed, a melodic outpouring of air that seemed to encompass the pain of every Irish existence. Casey, looking extremely uncomfortable, shifted from one foot to the other, the very picture of glowering misery. "We've been told by the deal-makers in their German made automobiles that this is ground zero, starting here, starting now Ireland can begin again, she can put her hands in the pot an' take her share of the booty this time an' all its gadgets an' baubles has to offer. But I ask at what price, that of her soul? Is that a fair price for a car, a house, a holiday in Spain? Is it? So the question becomes, do we surrender to a new sort of oppression, is servitude more bearable if it comes wrapped in tinsel an' ribbon? Do we," Devlin's eyes, narrowed and hard, pinned each person in turn, "give them our throats once again? This young man," he seized Casey's elbow and thrust him forward, "says no an' so do I. What say you my brothers an' sisters, what say you?" He allowed a long moment to lapse and then in an altogether more genial tone said, "I'll be takin' a break for now, avail yerself of the refreshments as I certainly intend to."

"What the hell," Casey muttered as the usual hot-eyed groupies began to cluster and move towards Devlin with intent, "was that for?"

Devlin smiled smoothly, a shark's smile for the girls advancing on him. "Ye smell like ye've been swimmin' in a vat of herring, shall we go an' have a drink?"

"Aye," Casey sighed, "I suppose we might as well, just let me fetch my brother an' my—" he halted suddenly.

"An' yer what?" Devlin cocked an eyebrow at him.

"My brother's friend."

"Pat's doin' rather nicely for himself these days," Devlin smiled knowingly at Casey.

For a man who decried the ravages of modern comfort so stirringly Devlin had a very comfortable, very large trailer. And the very finest of whiskey, which he told them to help themselves to while he 'signed a few autographs, kissed a few lips an' dealt with his public.'

"You know him?" Pamela asked from the depths of an orange velveteen couch.

"In a manner of speakin', our da' used to see his older sister at one time," Casey said nonchalantly, peering through the bead-fringed curtain to what looked to be a bed of mammoth proportions in the back end of the trailer.

"Saw her quite frequently, she was our mother," Pat said, voice tight, whiskey Casey had poured lying untouched before him.

"*That man*," Pamela coughed around the harsh fumes of her drink, "*is your uncle?*"

"Aye," Casey drew the syllable out with great reluctance, "that he is."

"We shouldn't have come here tonight," Pat said angrily, "we were just askin' for trouble, ye know the sort of company Devlin keeps, ye knew this might happen."

"Aye, I knew," Casey replied mildly, meeting his brother's stare unblinkingly, "as did you."

"Why are we here?" The air around Pat was charged with tension.

"To hear one of Ireland's finest musicians sing, don't read anything else into it." Casey's tone was still mild but the look in his eyes was not.

"Ye let him use ye out there an' now yer in here drinkin' his whiskey as if not a thing was amiss in the world." Pat stood, white-faced, body one long fuse of anger.

"The appearance of a thing," Casey said coolly, "is not necessarily the truth of it."

"Ye bloody bastard," Pat whispered face incredulous, his hands curling into fists, "why the hell did ye even come back, if this is what ye had in mind?"

"Sit down Pat an' calm yerself."

"I don't take orders from ye anymore big brother," Pat spit the final two words out as if he could no longer bear the taste of them in his mouth. "An' make no mistake if ye an' Devlin are cookin' some mad scheme up between the two of ye I want no part in it, no part at all do ye understand?" With that, he flung open the door and strode out into the night, slamming the door so hard behind him that the entire trailer shook.

"I'm sorry ye had to hear that." Casey drove his hands through his short curls, rubbing his scalp until his hair stood on end like an electrocuted hedgehog.

"It's alright," Pamela said, "I haven't got the slightest idea what's going on. And," she added as Casey parted his lips to speak, "I think for now I'd like to keep it that way."

"As ye like," Casey said sounding relieved. "Would ye care for another drink?"

Pamela, who felt like butter left to melt in the sun, said she would. Casey grabbed the bottle and came to sit beside her, still smelling distinctly fishy. He refilled her glass and his own generously and placed the bottle back on the table.

"How is it," he asked quietly, "that I've spent days in yer company now an' I've never yet heard ye speak of where yer from or of yer family?"

"I don't have a family, not anymore at least," she said, "and I'm not from anywhere in particular, though right now I suppose I could say I'm from Belfast."

She let her head fall back into the cushions and turned it to the side, only to find disconcertingly, that Casey had done the same and was a scant few inches away from her. She could smell his scent, the one that underlay the reek of whale oil and blood and found it warm and comforting. As if right now it was safe not to lie.

"I was born in County Clare, spent my summers there as a child occasionally but for the most part I grew up in New York. I don't know my mother, my father's dead and my grandparents were gone long before I was born. So there's only me," she giggled, feeling like a legless puddle, "you see."

"I see," he reached out a hand and ran a thumb softly along the line of her jaw, "that you are very drunk."

"Am I? I thought I was only very," she hiccoughed, "tired."

"Aye well," his dark eyes were swimming in and out of focus, "a nap wouldn't be amiss I'm thinkin'. I'll take ye home after Devlin gets back."

"Oh, I couldn't possibly sleep in front of," her eyelids seemed to be closing of their own accord, each the weight of a large and immovable stone, "a stranger," she said blearily, vaguely aware of a hand brushing her hair back from her forehead.

"Hush, ye could do with a sleep."

It seemed, though the words came from far away, very sensible advice, so she, very sensibly, took it.

HE HAD WATCHED DEVLIN MURPHY'S LITTLE PERFORMANCE and wanted, for a moment, to throttle the nervy bastard there on the spot. However it would have been a disastrous move on his part and he had after all enjoyed the spectacle somewhat. *'Must announce sadly an' with regret that Jack has been detained in Paris,'* he'd enjoyed that bit, the bugger had balls he'd grant him that.

Raising his face to the night sky, eyes the tint and hue of half-lived stars, Jack Stuart wondered what the people would have thought if they'd known he'd stood in their midst all night. And reflected as he turned his feet homeward that it wasn't something he could afford to find out.

"SHUSH," CASEY SAID TO HIS UNCLE, who having been sufficiently adored was back and ready for a drink. "She's asleep."

"I can see that," Devlin said, "Pat's girlfriend eh?" He raised an eyebrow at the salt-encrusted curls and flushed cheeks, like those of a child, that lay across Casey's lap.

"She fell over," Casey said by way of explanation, "pure exhausted."

"Mmphm," was Devlin's only reply. He disappeared into the back of the trailer only to re-emerge moments later, heady with expensive aftershave and appearing every inch the unrepentant lecher in a gray cashmere sweater and Italian silk pants to match. Casey let out a long, low whistle.

"Hot date?"

"Aye, ye could say so. I'll not be needin' my trailer tonight so yer welcome to the use of it."

"We need to talk," Casey said, face suddenly serious.

Devlin cast a nervous eye to the window and down across Pamela.

"How deeply asleep is she, d'ye suppose?"

"Very deep, she'll neither hear nor remember." Casey placed a protective hand on the side of her head, fingers cupped over the ear.

"Alright then," Devlin swung a chair about and sat down splay-legged. "My message is short an' not likely to make much sense even to us much less someone out of the loop. We've a new contact," his face had cleared, sobered and narrowed with the message he relayed, "an' I don't know who he is or what he does, the codename is *aingeal liath*, an' if ye need to contact him yer to go to Finnegan's Wake an' leave a message with our Jim Pat."

"The Blue Angel?" Casey scratched the crown of his head doubtfully. "Someone has to know who the hell the man is."

"Aye, well I suppose we'll find out in due time, but for now the man is more shrouded in secrecy than the virgin birth."

"How are we to be certain he's not an agent then?"

"I've been assured that's not the case."

"By who?"

"Listen boyo, the word I'm gettin' from up head the line is that your re-emergence in Belfast society is not an entirely welcome event. Stop pushin' an ye'd be advised to walk softly an' carry a big stick as the man said."

"Are ye warnin' or threatnin'?" Casey's face had gone hard, a mask pulled down as quickly as it took to say the words.

"I am yer mother's brother an' I don't take blood lightly an' that my little man *should* be taken as threat." Quartzite clashed with obsidian and neither blinked.

"I apologize," Casey finally said, "I've learned to live on the defense an' it'll not be a habit easily broke."

"It's not like ye'll want to break it at all now, ye'll need all yer wits about ye. Rumor has it," Devlin took a swallow of whiskey, "that ye haven't reported in with GHQ."

"No," Casey looked down to where his fingers stroked in a measured tempo across ivory bone, "I haven't."

"Well the Riordans have always been mad to a man, but that's purely suicidal boy."

"Times are changin' Devlin, ye can feel it in the ground ye walk on right through the soles of yer feet. The time for the Dublin boys is well past, they'll argue on into the next century an' never notice opportunity tryin' to bang down the door."

Devlin shook his head slowly the low light picking out the strands of silver that threaded his choirboy curls and making him seem, for once, his age.

"Oh Jesus boy ye are mad, aren't ye? Christ that yer Daddy should see this, he'd be rollin' over in his grave."

Casey's face was tight and pale, eyes bruised by the late hour. "Ye leave my daddy out of this, these times are different."

"Don't ye think that every goddamn generation thinks its own time is different? It never is though Casey, not here leastwise, not in Ireland. Here the past just keeps returnin' an' takin' a bit more blood with it each time."

"How can ye say that?" Casey's voice was softly pained. "How can ye give a speech like ye did outside an' not believe in anything Devlin?"

Devlin stood, reaching for his coat, a smooth charcoal number that brought out the dove color in his irises. "Because if there's one thing I understand in this world, laddy, it's how to hold an audience." His face fell a little, "An' that it's best not to expect miracles much less believe in them." He took a deep breath, reassuming the guise of playboy to the western world. "Well I'd best not keep the lady waitin' any longer. Al will drive the two of ye back to Belfast in the mornin' unless it's urgent that she get back tonight?"

"No, we can stay til mornin'."

"No strict Catholic daddy waitin' at home for her?"

"No, she's not a soul in the world to call her own," Casey said softly.

"Now I wouldn't say that's entirely true, would ye?" Devlin gave his nephew a long, questioning look. When he got no response he merely sighed and said, "Change yer shirt would ye? Ye smell like a dolphin pissed on ye, there's clothes in the closet that'll fit."

"Thanks."

Devlin paused in the doorway, torn between the promises of the longest pair of legs he'd seen outside of a racetrack and the pull of duty he felt toward his sister's son.

"Is there anything that ye need?" he asked, looking back at Casey who was already half-asleep.

"No, not a thing in the world," the boy smiled bemusedly.

"Right then, well ye know where I am should the need arise."

"I know."

Devlin closed the door quietly behind him, thinking, with no little worry, that his nephew looked like a man who had, if not everything he needed, then at least all he wanted laying right in his lap.

Chapter Eight
An Invitation to Dance

ORNING CAME AND WITH IT A HANGOVER in all the pretty shades of green. From celery to sludge, Pamela could feel it pushing with a sickly weight into her head and stomach. It was a wonder that two glasses of whiskey could do so much damage.

When she opened her eyes the light was still a soft blue, coronaed with subtle hints of rosy sunlight. She was wrapped snugly in a quilt that was dizzying with the residue of aftershave. She had obviously been put to bed at some point. Rolling over and feeling as if the world rolled with her, she had through the beaded curtain, a clear and disturbing view of Casey, bare-chested and shaving in the tiny mirror, morning light touching him here and there, gentling his darkness. The tenderness of the scene caught her in the throat and made her close her eyes once again.

She ventured sitting a moment later, one hand going to her head and the other swiftly to her mouth, the former withdrawing in revulsion as it encountered a snarled mass of salty, knotted curls.

"Urggh," was the longest speech she could manage.

"Feelin' rough?" Casey inquired politely, head poking through the amethyst and amber beads, looking inhumanly rested and refreshed.

"Let's just say I feel a real kinship to the worm in the bottom of a tequila bottle right now." She moved her tongue experimentally and found that it felt like a piece of furniture that hadn't been dusted in years.

"Here drink this," Casey put a glass of water in her hand, "should have made ye drink it last night but ye were dead to the world."

She took a sip and curled her lip in disgust, it tasted like a dirty sock. She could feel it trickle down her esophagus and as soon as it reached her stomach, she bolted for the door. Moments later she was back, face pink and stomach settled.

"Better?" Casey asked, voice muffled as he pulled a thin, cream-colored sweater over his head.

"Better," she replied awkwardly, aware suddenly of her rumpled and stained dress, her snaggle-toothed hair and the smell of seaweed, perspiration and just the faintest lacing of vomit.

"Well good mornin' then," he ran a hand across his close-cropped hair and managed to make it look perfectly groomed. Irritation, like a determined flea, began to nit at her.

"Something wrong?" she asked testily, uncomfortable under his frank gaze.

"No, nothin's wrong, why do ye ask?" He put a kettle of water on to boil, turning the blue flame up high.

"It's only that you look at me as if I'd a wart on my nose or something," she shoved a hand through her hair self-consciously and encountered a foreign object that felt distinctly slimy.

"No warts," he said smiling and stepping over gently disengaged a long strand of something from her hair that had once lived in the ocean. He tossed it out the door and turning back to her, no longer smiling said, "I do stare I know, it's only," he gave her a direct look and she read there a vulnerability that she'd not thought him capable of, "I was in prison for a long time, an' a man will get to imaginin' all the things he's missin', women bein' one of them. An' in yer mind ye see them as goddesses, as everything good an' beautiful about the world outside yer bars. Ye know that it's not true, that's there's as much small-souledness amongst women as there is in that prison but then ye come out an' see that even the plainest of women is enough to make ye lose yer senses. Slowly ye begin to adjust an' women start to just look like everyday people. But I came home see, an' there was a real, live goddess sittin' in the kitchen an' I'm afraid ye'll have to forgive me the stares because I don't see me bein' able to do much about it."

She opened her mouth and closed it again. Lacking any intelligible reply, she wanted to flee from his presence and his eyes. The way he looked at her, dear God in heaven, it was something else altogether, a thing completely out of her range of experience. As if he saw everything, the secrets and lies, the thorns in the roses and none of it mattered a whit. With grace, he saved her from response.

"One of Devlin's lady friends left some clothes behind, I laid them out on the bed for ye, they're clean an' it's my suspicion she'll not be back for them."

"Thanks," she muttered and scuttled thankfully behind the beads, hearing the click of the door closing as Casey went outside.

Devlin's friend had been, it would seem, of the hippie variety. There was a blouse of exquisitely fine cotton that looked as if it had belonged to a color-blind Russian peasant with exotic tastes. The skirt was more of the same. However, it was clean and smelled sweetly of distilled gardenias. It was an improvement of sorts. She found a brush and dragged it through her hair, braided it and after washing as best she could in cramped quarters found herself feeling slightly more human.

She emerged from the trailer to find the sun warming the fields, a faint mist sighing up from the ground. Casey stood, mug of tea in hand, sun painting him in shades of spice, cinnamon and nutmeg, clove and cayenne, warm to the eye and undoubtedly warm to the touch.

"I can wake Al an' get him to take us back to Belfast, if that doesn't offend yer proletarian senses too much," Casey said without turning around.

"This girl," she said, "can take the train like any self-respecting communist."

"Alright then, Comrade," he said with a grin, "we'd best head back."

He returned his tea mug to the trailer, locked the door and returned with a leather, bead fringed coat that he settled about her shoulders. The lazy, cloying smell of marijuana rose from its folds.

"It's Devlin's," he said, "I'll return it when I see him next. It's chilly out this morning."

They set off, wending their way through the tents and sleeping bags of Devlin's faithful, still slumbering, dreaming of their choirboy god and his angelic voice.

They crested the first hill, sun warmer now, gilding grass and cows, lambs and leaves alike in the still morning. Below lay the town, toy-like, only beginning to awake.

"I've a friend," Casey said, "name's Kevin an' he's gettin' married in a couple of weeks. I'd every intention of goin' solo but I've been wonderin' if perhaps ye'd like to come with me?"

He looked so like a little boy, eager and embarrassed at the same time, that she had to stifle a laugh.

She looked at him for a long moment, knowing with every thread of her pulse and every fiber of her being that he was dangerous. With this knowledge weighed and considered, she gave her answer.

"I'd love to," she said.

Chapter Nine

The Games People Play

"Care for a scrum?" Pat asked Casey lightly on Sunday afternoon. Far too lightly, Casey would later think. But his radar was not working as it normally would so he, thinking some raw physical endeavor would be good, agreed.

This was how he found himself playing the back half of the field at St. Dominic's, the local highschool. Thoroughly winded, caked with mud and considering the possibility that his brother had set up this entire afternoon's delight simply to murder him in the sight of several witnesses.

At the first break, someone threw him a bottle of water and he took the opportunity to assess the damage. Two ribs, likely cracked, bottom lip split and bleeding like a stuck pig, a bruise on one shin coming out in an amazing array of colors all hovering in the black range and a ringing in his right ear that wasn't going away any time soon.

"Break's over," Pat said cheerily, jogging past him and slapping him hard enough on the back to wind him for several seconds.

"Scrum my arse, this is all out war," Casey muttered to himself, taking the field once again, only now with a pronounced limp.

Friendly neighborhood scrimmages, with an even number of boys on each side or odd man sitting out, were never, considering the neighborhood and the nature of the male beast, very friendly. It wasn't uncommon to go home bleeding or to the hospital to be splinted. Quarrels and disagreements often found their settling on the local green. However to have your brother captain the opposing team and then declare all out war, not on the ball, but on your own physical well-being was an entirely new slant on the concept of fratricide.

Five minutes into the second half Casey found himself with the ball. Speeding upfield, he spied a clear opening ten yards directly in front of him. He charged for it, bulling his way through, shedding attackers as easily as autumn leaves falling from a tree. Twenty yards from the goal line and it was his, he could smell the point, fifteen and the way still clear, ten and he put a burst of speed on, confidence surging, five and his brother, smiling murderously, stepped in the finish the job he'd started. Pat took him out at the knees, causing him to sail gloriously through the air, coming down headfirst with a crunch that could be heard on the sidelines.

Casey, when he dared to move and had determined that he hadn't actually passed out cold from the pain of impact, saw several constellations waver into view and blink out just as swiftly. Pat's face hovered above his own, a smile like warm caramel laced with arsenic upon his mouth.

"Fockin' had enough yet?" Casey asked through teeth gritty with turf.

"Not quite," said Pat, still smiling his sticky smile, "have you?"

"Try me," Casey hissed, fury flushing the pain out of his body. Each took the field again, the ball no longer even a peripheral objective for either.

Pat was rough-handed the ball only seconds later, caught it on its wobble and ran as if Satan himself pursued, which in a manner of speaking, he did. Casey nailed him halfway up towards the goal. He caught him with a tackle in the stomach that would have given a smaller, less determined man, internal bleeding. The ball flew sideways though neither brother noticed. They were pulled apart swiftly and the game, such as it was, continued.

Pat played as if his life depended on it after that. For every goal Casey managed to eke out, he tore out two. His jersey, already a disreputable muddy green, was ripped all down one side, a cut above one knee leaked a steady trickle of bright blood, and his hair was plastered to his head with sweat and fury. The other boys on the field, fearing for their own survival, played half-heartedly. The spectacle of the Riordan boys, trying to play each other to the death had become fascinating enough to step aside and let the two have at it.

Casey had a kick on him that was like a lightning bolt cleaving the ball in half. Pat on the other hand, possessed a magnetic iron grip once the ball was in his grasp that was impossible to break. Their skills, though opposite, were well-matched and the game could very well have gone on into the night. Considering the stubbornness inherent to both it might have, had Casey not leaped on Pat in a hip-crunching tackle that took them down to the ground so hard and fast that neither was quite certain which limbs were his own and which his brother's.

Pat, facedown in the mud, managed to gasp out, "Dirty whorin' bastard."

"Mouthy upstart pup," Casey replied in kind, grunting savagely as he tried to disentangle his legs from Pat's.

"Filthy back-stabbin' son of a bitch." Pat struggled to get out from under his brother's weight.

"Fockin' little red commie." Casey put a forearm hard across Pat's back.

"Judas," Pat hissed and then let his body go slack into the mud.

"You win," Casey said wearily and rolled off his brother, "are ye satisfied?"

Pat muttered a string of obscenities into the dirt.

"Wouldn't Daddy be impressed with how our vocabularies have expanded,"

Casey said, spitting blood out of his mouth.

Pat gave a small choking sound.

"Christ, was that a laugh I heard? I'd thought yer sense of humor had abandoned ye entirely."

"If it had," Pat said pushing himself over onto his back, "ye'd be dead right now."

"That," Casey put a ginger finger to a vicious cut over his eyebrow, "I believe."

Their teammates, having kept a safe distance, now hove into view.

"Are ye ladies done with yer nap then?"

"Aye," Pat replied, "we're finished here."

"Are we?" Casey asked quietly.

"For now," Pat replied in kind.

"Right then, next Sunday same time lads."

There was a chorus of ayes and one by one, they slowly drifted off into the gathering dusk, towards the lights that were turning on here and there scattering darkness in their path.

Casey and Pat lay for a long time in the grass, joints beginning to reassert themselves, bruises throbbing and blood drying in itchy patches.

"I'm sorry, Pat," Casey said simply, quietly.

"I know ye are," Pat replied, "though ye make it damn hard to believe when ye pull stunts like ye did Friday night."

"The speech was Devlin's; I think he got carried off by his own grandiosity."

"Wouldn't be the first time."

"D'ye think he'd be ashamed of me?"

Pat turned his head sideways and looked at his brother, "Devlin?"

"No."

"Daddy?"

"Aye."

"He loved ye Casey, he always forgave us our mistakes, he'd of forgiven this as well."

"I did it for all the wrong reasons, I did it because I was angry at him an' scared of havin' to be the man. I can't bring the last five years back Patrick but ye have to believe that if I could I would."

"Then don't go back." Pat's voice was barely above a whisper, as if he were afraid that if he said the words too loudly, his brother would be certain to refuse him.

"I'm not goin' back in the way that ye think, Pat."

"That's what frightens me."

They were both silent for awhile after that, knowing that if they proceeded down that path they'd end up in another fight and neither had the strength for it at present.

"I hope he has stars wherever he is," Pat said, offering a simple truce.

"An' a big damn telescope," Casey added.

"It was an astronomer," Pat sat up and put his arms around his drawn up knees, "that made me realize how angry I was at the two of ye."

"How so?" Casey asked.

"When that man in California discovered quasars in '63. I was so excited an' I ran into the backyard where Daddy used to sit with his tea after dinner to tell him. I was standin' in the alley before it hit me that it wasn't my yard an' there was no daddy to tell things to anymore."

"An' no brother."

"No, no brother," Pat agreed.

"Quasars, eh?" Casey chuckled, "Takes a damn object a billion light years away to get yer attention."

"Daddy would have loved that. Think of it, out there as far as we can see are these ancient lights, light that has taken a billion an' a half years to reach our eyes an' we are witnessing the birth of the universe by looking so far back in time that our minds cannot even comprehend the vastness of it. When they were closer, can ye imagine, the sky must have seemed like it was on fire."

"An' not a soul here to witness it," Casey reached across the small divide between him and his brother and took Pat's hand, remembering how small it had once been, how it had been engulfed in his own as they crossed streets and walked to school. He felt the breadth of it and the strength and knew with a sadness that shook him to his core that he could no longer protect his brother. Not from life, not from love, not from himself.

"Are ye still my brother, Pat?" he asked and could not keep the tremble of doubt from his question.

There was a quiet that stretched far and deep before Pat's words travelled back to him, soft and firm, *"Pari passu."*

Casey sighed, "Ye know I could never get my head around those Latin phrases the way Daddy an' yerself could."

"Side by side, my brother, side by side."

When at long last they felt the need to leave the damp, cold couch of ground and begin the long limping trip home Pat turned to Casey, eyes fathoms deep and said, "Brother or no, if ye break her heart, Casey I will kill ye."

Casey nodded, "I think ye would at that. For now though can we just get home?"

"Aye, let's go home," Pat said and for one moment, it seemed very possible that they might both get there and find, for a time, some measure of peace.

"Is he dead?"

"No, he's not dead but he'll not be runnin' round the ring again anytime soon, or I miss my guess." The answer came from the mouth of Dannyboy Kilmorgan, a fighter of legendary reputation, who had almost thirty years previous gone out a winner and spent his time since running Belfast's most popular gym. Sixty-five if he was a day and used to the inescapable brutality as well as the delicate finesse of his sport, still he'd never seen such precise and emotionless violence as he'd witnessed this day. And from such an unlikely source, though perhaps not so unlikely, he thought uneasily as he watched the source of the violence, still bouncing lightly on the balls of his feet as if electrically charged, not a glimmer of sweat on the man after five ugly rounds.

Danny's gym was famous for being neutral ground. If you came through his doors you came to box, you left your grudges, whether personal or political outside and if you were foolish enough not to you'd soon join them—outside on the pavement. Today, for the first time, Danny wished he'd turned a man away purely on appearance. For the Reverend Lucien Broughton sent a chill right to the marrow of Danny's old, unromantic bones. Killer instinct was a term bandied about a lot in the gym and generally was meant as a compliment conferred upon a lad who had both the talent and the drive to go the distance. Today it had assumed a completely different meaning.

He'd been very doubtful at the Reverend's appearance, thought the man was too small and finely built, very little muscle was apparent under his phosphorescent white skin, his bones as delicate as those of a young girl. Appearances had never been quite so deceiving. He'd put Gillybear Reese in the ring with him, so called because of his girth and sweet-natured face. Gilly'd wear him out and only rough him up enough to make him realize boxing was perhaps not his natural vocation. After the first round, Gilly was exhausted and had received two uppercuts to his jaw that had knocked him to the canvas. At the end of the second round he'd a great deal of blood to rinse out along with the spit. By the third round Gilly was no longer playing but could not manage to get around the Reverend's light-bodied dance. Lucien was fast, accurate and had a steely-eyed strength behind his blows that was deadly. By the fourth round, fighters were drifting away from their exercises and own sparring matches to witness the massacre. The fifth round was a travesty that Danny had been grateful to see end. Gilly, who possessed the unassailable head of a mule, was out cold on the canvas and the Reverend Broughton was still high and tight on his feet.

Lucien took in the glares and furtive angry glances he received with a cool smile. "A man," he said as he climbed nimbly from the ring, "should be prepared to fight if he gets in the ring. I am prepared." Danny had been tempted to put the gloves on then and there and teach the Reverend a thing or two, but had refrained. He was happy to see the back end of the man when he re-emerged from the locker room, impeccable in white linen and gray flannel and took his leave of them.

Later when it was determined Gilly had sustained no permanent damage and Danny had retired to his office to sort out his bookwork, his co-manager Tiny Brown, a wee dark nut of a man, had entered waving a sheaf of paper.

"Did ye see this? The nerve of the bastard after knockin' Gilly cold."

"Did I see what?" Danny took the sheaf of papers and felt a ball of ice begin to form in his intestines as he looked them over.

"He's runnin' for this district? That's crazy, the like of him won't get elected here, nine tenths of the neighborhood is Catholic."

"Aye, but who's to run against 'im?" Tiny asked practically.

Danny pursed scarred lips and frowned down at the flawless picture of the Reverend in front of him, underlined in bold letters by the improbable tag line, "A Vote For Lucien Broughton is a vote for your conscience."

"He'll win by default," Tiny said craftily.

"Quit hintin' about Tiny, just say it, someone is goin' to have to go an' give the boy on the hill a talkin' to."

"Aye," Tiny agreed, a small smile adding to the numberless creases in his face.

"An' I suppose," Dannyboy Kilmorgan, never one to turn from a fight, sighed from the depths of his flattened knuckles, "it'll be me makin' the trip up."

"I suppose 'twill," Tiny said with satisfaction.

"A MR. KILMORGAN IN THE KITCHEN TO SEE YE," Maggie said to Jamie, one rainy afternoon later, with a face on her a prune would have had difficulty imitating.

Jamie, knowing Dannyboy wouldn't leave the confines of the comfortable kitchen, the only room in the house he claimed where he didn't feel like he ought to be bowing and scraping, followed Maggie's stiff back down the hall and into the warm kitchen fragrant with the smell of lemon poppyseed cake baking in the oven and a pot of Earl Grey steeping on the sideboard.

"His Grace Lord Kirkpatrick will see ye now, Mr. Kilmorgan," Maggie said with sweet hostility.

"Mr. Kilmorgan?" Jamie lifted his eyebrows at Dannyboy, no stranger to the kitchen of the Kirkpatrick home over the last twenty-two years.

"Aye, she gave up callin' me Dannyboy when I asked fer salt on my food last Christmas."

Maggie did not even deign to look over her shoulder, though the carrots she was slicing got an audible and protracted thumping from the knife.

"Seasoning is an insult to the chef's abilities," Jamie said, trying not to laugh.

"D'ye suppose a man might have hope of a wee slice of that cake," Dannyboy said in a wheedling tone, winking at Jamie.

"That would depend," Maggie said, knife continuing its vigorous dance, "on precisely where ye'd like it."

"I always did say that'd be yer cookin' that would get me to bed in the end," Dannyboy said.

"Ye've high aspirations in this life for such a battered old specimen," Maggie retorted, spilling the abused carrots into a simmering pot of broth on the ancient Aga.

Dannyboy eyed Maggie's squat stature and ample backside appreciatively, "A mite more wide than high, I daresay."

"Dream on old man," Maggie said equably and then as Jamie shook with suppressed laughter, "an' if either of ye laugh ye'll feel the sharp side of this knife along with yer cake."

"There's somethin' I've come to discuss with ye," Dannyboy, never one to waste nor mince words, came directly to the point, shoving a piece of paper across the table at Jamie, who looked it over with no change of expression and handed it back.

"Yes, I've seen it."

Dannyboy sighed; this was exactly the reaction he'd been fearing. How far he could push any advantage he might have from this point was debatable. Not very far he'd guess from the obstinacy, refined as it might be by the boy's practiced concealment that had settled quickly on Jamie's face.

"D'ye know what it will mean to the people in that neighborhood?"

"Why," Jamie asked revealing a small frustration, "does everyone seem determined to act as though he and I are the only options in this game?"

"Because if ye were thinkin' clearly, ye'd see that ye are."

"Dannyboy come on, it's a strong community with solid political ties. Can you honestly tell me there isn't a Nationalist candidate who could stand against this man?"

"It doesn't matter," Danny insisted stubbornly, "I've a feelin' that if this man wants to win he will, regardless of the tactics he'll have to use to pull the vote his way. Christ, boy this is Ulster, ye know the candidates are rarely the result of a fair vote."

"If you're so certain of that why come to me?"

"Because ye could beat him, there's no question of support, they loved yer daddy—"

"Exactly," Jamie said quietly, "my father, not me."

"An' to be blunt, yer rich an' pretty enough to get past the Protestant voters."

Jamie smiled, not entirely amused by the assessment, but taking it, as he did most things, in the spirit it was intended.

"Flattery, in this case Dannyboy, isn't going to get you what you want."

The soft soap having failed Dannyboy thought he'd best get straight to the hard tactics. "Ye used to be a fighter. What happened to that boy who wasn't goin' to be done down by any mealy-mouthed dirty streetfighter."

"That was boxing," Jamie said, "which is not a metaphor for life, even if no one in that gym of yours realizes it."

"Don't be throwin' yer high-minded words at me." Dannyboy said with a look that had, in the past, reduced two hundred pound brutes to jelly. "Boxing *is* life. An' life, in spite of the flowers an' poetry, is a fight from the first minute to the last. Now will ye put the gloves on an' get in the ring or will ye hide behind yer books an' words an' be a coward," Dannyboy drove the flat of one meaty fist onto the table in an effort to drive home his point. This earned him a sharp cuff across the ear from Maggie as she'd just set the tea down and he, in his desperation, had sent boiling liquid in ten directions across the table.

Jamie, sopping up the fragrant liquid with a tea towel, was saved from answering. Dannyboy saw from his silence that he would have to resort to his final plan of attack, all out, no holds barred, pleading. It wasn't a position he'd often found himself in and wasn't one he'd cared for on the few occasions the necessity had arisen. He was rescued from contemplation of it by the entrance into the kitchen of a girl. Dannyboy, who was fond of saying of himself, that he was tough as 'chewed leather left to dry in the desert' felt weak and dizzy as though some huge fist had driven him in the solar plexus.

"Got your coriander, and the thyme and even a clutch of bergamot," the girl said, putting a damp bag onto Maggie's immaculate counter, "but I couldn't find so much as a twig of aroo-goo-lah," she laughed and turned his way, "I have trouble getting my mouth around some words." Dannyboy, still searching for his breath, thought there were many better uses for such a mouth than pronouncing long, foreign words. He immediately felt like a lecherous old man and turned to distract himself with the tea. In doing so, he caught a glimpse of Jamie's face, naked with a yearning that made Dannyboy feel as if he'd stumbled drunk into the sacred inner chamber of a temple. The emotion stayed there until the girl turned and faced Jamie, who blinked and swiftly resumed his polite façade.

"Are you going to introduce me to your guest?"

"Of course," Jamie said, "how remiss of me. Pamela O'Flaherty, this is Dannyboy Kilmorgan, the greatest Irish fighter who ever graced the ropes. Dannyboy, Pamela O'Flaherty, my—" he paused, face still pale, "houseguest."

"In perpetuity," she said with a light mockery, "at least that's what he's afraid of."

"I have," Jamie said, "no such fears at all." His smile, though genuine, seemed much more akin to pain than joy.

Dannyboy had taught Jamie boxing from the time he was ten years old right up until he went away to Oxford and to England, a move Danny had been disapproving of. In those years he'd come to respect the slim, golden-haired boy who had never, though baited, teased and taunted, for his face, his brain and his wealth, let anyone get the best of him. He'd even become a good boxer, skilled with his fists, quick with his feet and always leaving his opponent with his dignity intact. A gracious winner, an able opponent he was finally and, Dannyboy had to admit, satisfyingly well-matched. Perhaps even, he thought as he saw the girl meet Jamie's eyes in a strange look, outclassed, outflanked and with luck, outmaneuvered. He quite suddenly saw an angle that hadn't occurred to him before, an angle that until the last two minutes would have been dismissed as a complete impossibility. Dannyboy smiled and sat back in his chair to enjoy the fresh tea Maggie had brewed. Life, like boxing, occasionally presented a man with a clear field and well-defined options.

PAMELA HAD PICKED DREAMILY AT HER DINNER and then vivisected her lemon poppyseed cake into twelve equal pieces as if she sought the answer to a riddle within its air laden interior.

"An' me havin' won three firsts wid this cake an' she doesn't even try a bite," Maggie said clearing away the dishes with an aggrieved air.

"I wouldn't take it too personally, Maggie, she fell asleep beside her plate a couple of minutes later," Jamie said, sipping contemplatively at a California wine he'd been sent in the hope that he would market it throughout Europe under the auspices of Kirkpatrick Distilleries.

"Well I suppose the child did drag in at such an unholy hour, lookin' as if she'd been dragged twice backwards through the knothole."

"When did she get back?" Jamie asked, sniffing the wine and classifying its topnotes as flowery but not overtly so.

"Round noon, went straight upstairs an' showered then came down to see what I needed for the meals an' set back out."

"Pat bring her home?" Jamie asked lightly.

"No, 'twas his brother," Maggie carefully stacked the translucent white china, smattered with tiny shamrocks, on a tea tray.

"His brother?"

"Aye, he walked her right to the door, bit bigger than Pat, bit more in the way of a man an' less boy than his brother. Friendly sort, dark an' bold-lookin' if ye like the type," Maggie, hefting her tea tray with a filmy smile, appeared as if she liked the type rather well.

"Did he mention his name?" Jamie asked sharply enough to cut her reverie in half.

"Aye, said it was Casey—Casey Riordan. Ye'd do well to keep an eye out for our girl, the young one didn't worry me but this one means business."

"Means business," Jamie echoed to Maggie's back as she headed back to the kitchen to wash china, "what sort of business?"

Maggie turned her short bulk in the doorway of the dining room, "the sort of business men generally have with women," she said dryly.

"That's preposterous, she's still a child," Jamie said with a laugh that was distinctly lacking in humor.

"Aye well, I suppose that would depend on the viewpoint yer bent on takin'." Maggie said and waddled off to her kitchen.

Jamie, taking his last sip of wine thought that it tasted suddenly quite bitter.

'NEVER HEARD YE SPEAK OF WHERE YER FROM OR YER FAMILY.'

'That story you told me about Nova Scotia and ancient parents, it's just a story isn't it?'

Geography was simple; you could name a place, stick a pin in a map and say 'this is where I'm from.' But it was just a lie as well, it didn't take into account the various environments, the thousands that could exist in a single square mile. It didn't explain the curve of light in the morning, the sound of birds, the walls of your home, the voices that you heard as you fell asleep and the ones you did not.

So begin at the beginning. The beginning is always a woman, whether she is known or not, a woman who has held the structure of your bones and flesh within the cage of her own for nine months and for that fact alone she is mother. Not mama, or mommy or the endearments that will come naturally to a child's lips but mother for reasons of pure genetics.

Her own mother was a bit of a fairytale, told by her father, glossed over with his forgiving tongue and rose-colored memory.

Arielle Vincente was a certified Southern belle, from the wounded heart of the Deep South. Bourbon with a mixer of swamp water ran in her veins rather than blood. Black-haired, violet-eyed with the skin of a hothouse flower, she was occasionally mistaken for Elizabeth Taylor by strangers in the street. No money but breeding aplenty which in the South was more important, even in the bleak years following World War Two.

Arielle Vincente walked as though she were doing so horizontally rather than vertically. In fact, as her Aunt Dick had been wont to say, Arielle managed to imbue each and every movement as though she were committing it 'buck-nekkid on a mink rug'.

Arielle had been spoiled, that was certainly no secret, and in a family as eccentric as the Vincentes, so little a sin was hardly worth a mention. Why, when on her third birthday she'd been given a strand of pearls and had promptly bit them to see if they were real, the family had only laughed. Avariciousness after all was not uncommon amongst the Vincentes.

Arielle had been forgiven everything in advance of her sojourn on earth because, quite simply, she was terribly, exquisitely, frighteningly beautiful. Personality, said Aunt Dick, wasn't crucial when you looked the way Arielle did.

She could smell money, all the Vincentes could, but Arielle had a nose like a bloodhound on her. Thomas, Pamela's father, said she must have scented him on the wind like a ripe piece of fruit, fuzzy, sweet and just dying to be plucked. Thomas, a hardheaded tough Irishman who'd fought his way from an immigrant ship with two dollars in his pocket to being counted among the top five hundred wealthiest people in America, was little more than putty in her hands.

'She had the Fall of Man stamped all over her...I'd never seen anybody who looked like she did.' Her father, two glasses into the whiskey bottle would tell her the same story and show her the same pictures of a woman who was no more familiar than a movie star was. 'But some women just aren't made to be mothers,' he'd say to the bottom of his glass.

It was a hard lesson to learn. That the simple biological ability to procreate did not necessitate a maternal heart. That whispering the word 'mama' like a prayer into the night didn't get you an answer, the word just faded into the blackness like all the others. She'd come to accept it on an intellectual level as time went on. That contrary to what men thought and the Bible said, women weren't born to have babies and love men, maybe some were but a whole hell of a lot weren't. Which accounted for the anger and sadness that seemed to hang about most women like a gray, sour miasma. Still she'd been sad, known anger and despair towards the woman who'd given birth to her. Not that there weren't several women who tried out as replacement. They could smell money too, though, and even when she was small, she knew this wasn't a promising quality in a potential mother. Her dad was attractive in his own right and she figured they were just as thrilled about his thick, black hair, hazel eyes and raw Irish good looks as they were about his money. She just didn't quite see how she fit into the picture.

Once, not long before he'd died, her father had said to her that a man ought to know better than to try to capture something so beautiful as her mother had been, because that kind of beauty is always going to break someone's heart. She started picturing her mother as a moth after that, one of the pale, pale green ones that looked like a leaf until you got up real close and saw it quiver. When you were foolish enough to put one in the cup of your hands, just because you wanted to feel that beauty for a second, it would flap and flap, getting more and more frantic until your hands were full of its wing powder that her father had said were actually tiny hairs and then the moth couldn't fly anymore. And if a moth couldn't fly, it might as well be dead.

Maybe she'd inherited that need to capture that which shouldn't be touched from her father along with her height and squared off nails. Because it was how she was starting to feel about Jamie, that if she were to reach out and touch she would destroy whatever fragile balance it was he maintained for himself. It wasn't warmth she felt there only a brilliant shattering pain that glittered for the world and cut him to shreds inside. When she reached out her hands, she wanted heat, not something that dried the breath in her lungs and cut a valley through her chest. When Casey had looked at her that morning in the trailer she'd felt fire, but when he'd touched her the night before—just the rough side of a thumb on her chin—she'd felt warmth and had liked the feel a lot.

Chapter Ten
Under My Skin

There were times when all the troubles in the world paled in comparison to finding the right dress. It was just this Pamela said to Maggie, having hunted in futility and now wilting hope that she would find anything to wear to the wedding of Casey's friend. Maggie had nodded, taking a break from washing crystal and lighting a cigarette, ran an assessing eye over Pamela and muttered something to herself.

"Ye must like this boy a great deal," she said, a wicked light twinkling in her brown eyes.

"Not so very much," Pamela said hotly and unconvincingly.

"Well not to worry, I think I might have just what yer lookin' fer."

Doubting this very much, Pamela was pleasantly surprised when, after the remnants of lunch were cleared away, Maggie had dragged her off upstairs to one of the guestrooms and leaving her standing in the middle of the echoing room came back with a dress that was beyond any expectations. Even those of a girl wanting very much to look like a woman.

"Tisn't a color any woman could wear, but I thought those eyes of yers could stand up to it."

It was somewhere between green and silver, silk, a color that shifted and slid and beckoned and called without making a sound. The waist was nipped in, the skirt full, falling to mid-calf. Held up by two velvet straps, it exposed a shocking amount of skin. If not by the decade's standards then by the standards of the Roman Catholic Church she'd look like a woman, who if not already fallen, was certainly looking to take a headlong tumble. It was, without question, perfect.

"Wherever did you get it?" she asked the admiring Maggie, as she cast a flirty look over one bare shoulder into the mirror.

"Was her ladyship's, she'd clothes like nothin' I'd ever seen before an' when she was done with 'em she'd let us have our pick an' the rest were to go to charity. She was so slim though, 'twas a rare woman who could squeeze into her leavins'. This dress though I couldn't bear to part with. I thought of it as soon as ye said—what are ye doin'?"

"Taking it off," Pamela said firmly, "I'll not wear someone else's clothes."

Maggie raised her eyebrows in a way that told Pamela she knew it wasn't the secondhandedness of the dress but rather who had worn it first.

"It's not as if the woman's dead or anythin'," Maggie said practically, "an' Lord knows where she is now she's no need of fancy frocks."

Two days later, after a relentless hunt through shops she couldn't afford and ones she didn't want to, she was forced to admit there wasn't a dress in Belfast that could hold a candle to that simple, elegant dress that had once belonged to Jamie Kirkpatrick's wife.

Which was how, after some sly coercing on Maggie's part, she found herself standing in the kitchen with Casey staring speechlessly at her.

"Well," she said in desperation after two minutes under the assault of his relentless gaze.

"Ye look like an angel," he said simply and offered her his arm.

It was a lovely day for a wedding, the sun bright, the blue sky glorious, the smell of orange blossom ambrosial, the bridesmaids radiant butterflies in their pale yellow dresses. The boys uncomfortably handsome in their suits. Pamela had never been to a wedding before and found she quite like the unabashed sentimentalism and celebration of love.

Arriving on Casey's arm she attracted quite a bit of attention. Most of the stares were friendly, curious, half-shy wondering who this girl with Casey was, a man they'd grown up with and were seeing for the first time in five years. There was one discordant note amongst the lilting glances though and it came in the form of a girl, who, though a bit hard around the eyes was undoubtedly beautiful. The kind of girl who ought to have left Ireland at the first shot and gone to bloom in more worldly climes. This one hadn't left and it showed in the narrowness of eye and clench of mouth. Her eyes made no secret of their interest in Casey and the glare she periodically bestowed on Pamela felt like a scarlet brand on her forehead. Casey, on the other hand, seemed blithely unaware of the focused attention and though friendly to all, didn't spare too many glances for anyone but Pamela.

When finally after the ceremony was complete, the pictures of the happy couple taken, the light dinner eaten and the first ramshackle notes of the band sounded—'cousins of the bride ye understand' Casey informed her—she worked up sufficient courage to inquire as to the identity of the hard-eyed miss, Casey replied with a laconic, 'dated her if ye could call it that before I went away.' A satisfactory answer it wasn't but it quieted her curiosity for the moment and in the enjoyment of the evening, she almost forgot the girl and her disturbing glare. She was danced off her feet by every male, young and old, eligible and otherwise but found herself in Casey's arms every time the music slowed to a beat designed for intimacy. She almost wished there was a nun about with a ruler who would push them apart for decency's sake. Casey, as was to be expected, considering the nature of the day and that it was his first social occasion since returning home was plied with drinks and was sweetly drunk by the midpoint of the evening.

The band, near to the end of their second set, in a rather startling display of talent, launched into a silky, peach-hot rendition of '*La Vie en Rose*'.

> *Hold me close and hold me fast,*

Casey sang in her ear, voice in melting honey contrast to the trumpet's throaty chuckle and the piano's sliding glissandos. His hands traveled the smooth, bare skin of her back and tangled in her hair.

> *Give your heart and soul to me*
> *And life will always be,*
> *La vie en rose.*

He was little more than whispering now, his lips on her ear and she was just about to tilt her head back and offer her mouth in replacement when a voice rang out.

"Did ye lose yer voice over there in England, or will ye sing for us tonight, Casey Riordan?"

Casey, raising his face from its blissful perusal, shook his head ruefully. But then the bride called out, "Come on Casey man, ye can't refuse the bride, sing for us, just one."

Casey disengaged from their embrace and Pamela could feel the regret of his skin as it lost contact with her own. A whiskey, pressed on him by hands that pushed him towards the band, made him less reticent about the whole thing and after looking behind and saying something to the band, he sang an old Irish favorite. His voice was a surprise. It had a purity on the higher notes, a clarity like bells that only true Celtic voices ever possessed and a whiskied huskiness on the lower ones that made more than one girl in the crowded hall wear a loose, dreamy look. The next song, demanded by the increasingly rowdy crowd, was meant expressly for her and Casey looking with direct intent left no doubt of that in anyone's mind. Someone had lit and handed him a cigarette so that his eyes met hers through the sifting blue smoke that hung on the close air. He was perfectly still through the lazy, swinging first notes and then with a loose-jointed click of his fingers he slid very comfortably into the opening words of a tried and true Sinatra favorite.

> *I've got you under my skin,*

He sang, with just the right amount of gin in the honey of his throat. Several interested heads turned to stare openly at her. She found however that as much as she might have liked to she could not break the gaze Casey's eyes held her locked tight in.

> *I've got you deep in the heart of me,*
> *So deep you're a part of me,*

He crooned on, taking a drag on his cigarette in a lovely parody of Old Blue Eyes. She barely heard the words after that, aware only of his eyes and their heat, the way his tone and look left absolutely no doubt as to his intentions or feelings.

> *But why should I try to resist, when I know so well...*

The words wove their spell and she would remember it forever, the first time she knew herself to be a desired woman, desired beyond sense and reason, desired beyond breath and need.

> *I would sacrifice anything, come what may*
> *For the sake of holding you near...*

It was only later that she would understand just how deliberately he had chosen the song and she would cry for all the things youth only senses but does not, blindly, understand. He was hers for that moment and that moment only, but it was a magic that would taste sweet even when she was too old to remember the touch of a young man's hands. By the next song, he belonged to the entire room again and the moment had slipped irretrievably into the white room of memory.

He sang a few more ballads, sentimental favorites—'One For My Baby', 'I'll Be Seeing You,' hazy, three am, my-baby-left-me-cryin'-in-my-booze songs. His voice handled it well, ambling, throaty, sexy songs. But then the tempo changed and the mood in the room shifted, tensed and heightened with some expectation she couldn't understand and the music, as was inevitable she would later see, entered the hinterland of Republican paean. Music of the defeated, the rising up, the spiritual *sturm und drang* of a nation too long and well acquainted with the taste of losing. Songs of bards, poets, writers, lemmings and warriors, which all somehow in Ireland managed to amount to one profession.

"Sing *The Bold Fenian Men*, a female voice said, from somewhere far to the right of the hall. Casey, taking a drink, looked in the direction of the shadows on that side of the room, his face suddenly wary and sober.

"Ach no, my throat is near wore through, I need a stiffer drink than this," he said holding a glass of water aloft.

"Sing it, Casey. Get the man a drink so's he can sing," a different voice, less strident, more drunk.

"Aye, sing it man," more voices joining the chorus, voices lacking in lightness, the mood in the room cooling so rapidly that Pamela could feel a distinct chill creep up her backbone.

"What's the matter man? Have ye forgotten the songs yer daddy sang ye to sleep with or can ye only remember the words te *God Save the Queen,* now?"

Pamela turned towards the voice but she didn't need to see the speaker to know it was the hard-eyed girl, trying to provoke something ugly that had been simmering just under the surface of the crowd.

She saw Casey hesitate, knew that for some reason he would rather walk wordless out of the hall than sing the song, but that it would be tantamount to suicide for him to do so. Particularly now that the friendly inebriation had turned to hostile drunkenness.

He closed his eyes for a moment and then started in low and clear on the old and dear anthem of rebellion.

> *As down by the glenside, I met an old woman,*
> *A plucking young nettles, she ne'er saw me coming,*
> *I listened awhile to the song she was humming,*

His voice rose, strong and fine, a cool wind blowing away confusion, his eyes still closed to the room.

> *Glory, O Glory, O, to the bold Fenian Men.*
> *As I passed on my way, God be praised that I met her,*
> *Be life long or short, sure I'll never forget her,*
> *We may have great men, but we'll never have greater,*
> *Glory, O Glory, O, to the Bold Fenian Men!*

The voice of the crowd surged in roaring on the last line, but still Casey did not open his eyes, his words swept on over their heads, a single note of purity, a thousand years of blood and pride and insurrection there in one man's song.

> *Some died in the glenside, some died midst the stranger,*
> *And wise men have said that their cause was a failure,*

Beads of sweat broke out on his forehead and the chords in his neck stood out like thickly woven wire.

> *But they loved dear old Ireland, and never feared danger.*

His eyes snapped open as if he'd been jolted from reverie and he stared above the crowd at some point that was beyond the room and the walls and even the breezes and the night sky and the stars that shone outside. He stared back over dead loved ones, to ghosts that would not rest and blood that would not wash away no matter how strong the water and he paused for a moment, several seconds that stretched across the silence and brought everyone under his power and then he spoke the words softly—

Glory, O Glory, O, to the Bold Fenian Men!

The crowd roared their approval and she saw that he'd been put to a test and had passed it though some uneasy currents drifted and eddied about the edges of the room. She saw him exchange looks with someone far behind her and nod almost imperceptibly. A moment later Pat stood at her elbow.

"Casey wants me to take ye home," he said simply to her questioning gaze.

"Casey can take me home himself," she replied calmly, waiting for Pat to shrug and say 'please yerself.' But instead of performing to suit, he shook his head stubbornly, his dark eyes troubled. "No he wants me to take ye home an' he means it."

"Alright," she said and Pat was to wonder later why he didn't notice that she was too agreeable by half, "but give me a moment, I've got to visit the little girl's room in the worst way." She stood and slipped past him before he could protest and headed with what seemed convincing haste to the washing up room. She did have need of the facilities and was just patting down her face with cold water, wondering how she could give Pat the slip when she sensed someone hovering rather menacingly close to her.

She opened her eyes, blinking away the sting of falling droplets of water and saw blurrily the outline and angled contours of Casey's previous girlfriend in front of her.

The girl wasted no time on introductory chatter and got rather swiftly and bluntly to the point. "D'ye have any idea of the sort of people yer feckin' wid?"

"Pardon me?" Pamela asked, taking a step back only to make hard, jolting contact with the tiled wall behind her.

"Pardon me," the girl added a high whine to her mimicry, "ye heard me an' don't fergit it. Ye can tell yer boyfriend," she smiled suggestively, making the entire evening seem tawdry and begrimed, "tell him that when a man is gone too long, people look to others fer the things they need, ye tell him he's not the big man he thinks he is in these parts anymore, ye tell him to watch his back, ye tell him Cassandra says so."

"Tell him yourself," Pamela said angrily and pushed past the girl, grabbing hold of the door only to find herself yanked back sharply by a long taloned hand in her hair. She was shoved brutally into the door making it impossible to open and escape. "He was mine ye know, before he went to prison, ye don't seem the type to hold his fancy long. Yer a girl an' his sort needs a woman who knows her business," her hiss left very little doubt as to what that particular 'business' might be. Pamela wrenched her head hard, bruising her neck and leaving the other girl with a clutch of silky, black hair. She faced the girl squarely, fury dancing in uneven rhythm through her blood, racing and pumping recklessly.

"Well, he doesn't want you now, does he?" She opened the door and stepped directly into a knot of females chatting and laughing, waiting their turn for the necessity of a mirror, all falling silent as she walked through their midst, face burning white.

"Don't mind Cassandra," said a blonde near the end of the line, "she's always a right bitch an' she's jealous as hell tonight."

Pamela walked past, searching for Casey and failing to locate him tried to find Pat's comforting face in the sea of people. She could see neither of the brothers and was pushed towards the doors by a wave of men in great haste to exit into the night. There was no singing anymore, the music was silenced, various members of the band seemingly eager to take the air as well.

It was a beautiful night, full of stars and sweet perfect breezes that still held a lingering hint of orange blossom, a night for romance, for lovers but not for the scene Pamela found laid out before her. At the far side of the area the hall sat in, beyond the cars and the reach of lights, where the darkness seemed to swallow even sound, stood Casey surrounded by a semicircle of four men. Something in their stance told Pamela their intentions were not friendly, that whatever had begun inside with the song was going to be finished tonight.

Pat emerged silently at her side, an unfinished curse dying on his lips as he saw his brother outnumbered four to one. He grabbed her arm in a hard clench as she started forward.

"Don't," he said, "this fight is his, ye'll only make it worse if ye interfere."

"What the hell is going on, Pat?" she asked, her voice sounding shrill with anxiety to her own ears.

"It's a challenge to his authority, he's been gone a long time, an' there are people who aren't thrilled with his bein' back."

"I don't understand, Pat."

His eyes met hers and he sighed, "There are things that will need an explanation before the night is over, but not here an' not now."

The sound of rustling taffeta passed them and the bride, face grim, walked determinedly over to the huddled group.

"Not at my goddamn weddin' ye don't," they heard her say, "ye take it out of here, Casey is a guest an' he's welcome to stay until the night is done, the rest of ye are not."

At first, it seemed as if the four men were deaf to the bride's words but a moment later amidst rumbles of protest they disappeared into the night.

Casey rejoined Pamela and his brother, face dark and closed to inquiries.

"I told ye to take her home," he said to Pat, voice like splinters of steel.

"Aye I'll take her now," Pat replied as if he'd failed to comply with a set of marching orders from the supreme commander.

Pamela stepped forward. "I would appreciate it if you would remember that I'm present and no more deaf than your average woman."

"I apologize," Casey turned face softening as if he only now remembered her presence. He stepped closer, the angle of his shoulder blocking out Pat's face. He took her hands, cold with anxiety, into his own.

"I'm sorry the evenin's turned out this way, but it's unavoidable. Pat will take ye home an' I'll come see ye tomorrow if that's alright." His hands moved to her face, hard with grace over the fretwork of bones and he leaned in and kissed her, the sting of whiskey burning into her lips. It seemed in its depth and gentleness, more promise, less a fond end to a not entirely unpleasant evening.

He took Pat aside then, muttering terse words that amounted, she had a nasty feeling, to orders to keep her firmly under lock and key for the remainder of the night.

Headlights played across the brothers as someone swung a car around and in the brief illumination, she saw Pat reach in under his jacket and pass over an object, an object that while not so large was obviously of a considerable heft. Her knees turned to water, even her inexperienced eye knew a gun when it saw one.

"No," she heard Casey say forcibly and put the gun back in his brother's hand.

"Are ye daft, man?" Pat asked in obvious frustration, "They'll be armed to the teeth an' yer goin' to walk in there with nothin' but yer two fists should somethin' happen?"

"How far," Casey's tone ladled out patience and weariness in equal servings, "do ye think I'd get with that thing on me? I have to show good faith. 'Tis the only way to stop this thing from becomin' a bloodbath. Now put the damn thing away."

"Good faith," Pat's voice, carried up on a slight breeze, was full of incredulity. "Is challengin' yer authority in front of a couple hundred people at a weddin' their idea of good faith? They don't recognize yer right to yer own existence."

"An' why should they, Pat? I'm the intruder now, I'm the unknown quantity."

"Jesus, Casey," Pat's hands dropped to his side the gun still cradled in his palm, "I don't know what to do anymore."

"Let him go," her voice was quiet but carried with the force of conviction to the two, who turned and looked at her surprise written plainly across their faces. "Come on Pat, take me home and let him be on his way."

"Aye," Pat moved across the ground to her side. "Go with care my brother," he said softly over his shoulder.

The answer came back gently, the speaker already walking into the night, his path turned away from them.

"*An comnaidh, mo ban neach,*" he said, "*an comnaidh.*"

"What did he say?" Pamela asked as Pat started the car, a rattletrap Citroen borrowed for the day.

Pat didn't reply at first and she watched his face in the dim light of car's interior, his smile sad.

"It's something my daddy used to say to me when I was small and in need of reassurance. He'd say 'always my white one, always'."

"What does that mean?" She asked, mystified by the ties that bound the men in this family.

"It means," Pat found her hand in the darkness and gave it a squeeze, "that Casey will look after us an' we're not to worry."

"Easier said than done," she mumbled, feeling nonetheless a relief at the words, as if indeed by their mere utterance Casey had made things right.

Relief was less palpable hours later, when having convinced Pat that she should accompany him to his home and wait out the night with him, she lay on the boys' couch, shivering despite the night's mugginess. Trying with little success to unmuddle the various nuances and happenings of the day. She gave up on sleep and found Pat in the kitchen, still dressed in his suit, a cold cup of tea untouched between his hands.

"Worried?" She sat down across from him.

"Aye," he sighed.

"Don't you think maybe you should tell me what's going on, Pat?"

"I think, all things considered, my brother should tell ye himself. It's not my place now."

"I know why he was in prison, Pat."

"What?"

"He told me himself on the train back to Belfast that morning. He thought I should know before—" she hesitated, not wanting to hurt him.

"Before the two of ye fell any further." Pat supplied, staring into his hands as if within them lay worlds only he had ever imagined could exist.

"Tell me how it will have gone tonight?" she asked.

He gave her a hard look then capitulated with a nervous rub of his hands.

"They'll have waited for him; someone would have stayed behind to make certain he didn't run. Which," Pat shook his head, "if they knew my brother at all they'd know he's not capable of running, though God knows it'd be better at times if he was."

"And then?" she prodded, impatient with opinionated digressions.

"They'd of blindfolded him an' taken him in a car or van, most like, to wherever it is they keep their rathole. They'd have driven around a bit to disorient him first, make certain he doesn't know where he's goin' an' would never be able to find his way back. He'll be told in no uncertain terms that he's not welcome in Belfast anymore and that the territory has been taken over, thank you very much, by a pack of jackals that are not fit for my brother to wipe his feet on. An' then if he's lucky they'll stick him back in that same van an' ride him around for a bit before dumpin' him out on the street."

"Will they hurt him?" she asked, lips numb with the fear the question caused.

"They may rough him up a bit just to be sure that the message was received clearly, but they don't understand that compared to what he's faced every day of the last five years, 'twill be nothin' to him, except perhaps fuel to the fire he's been carryin' since Daddy died."

"You miss your father a lot, don't you?"

"Aye, don't ye miss yer own daddy?"

"Not in the way you and Casey miss yours. I was alone even before my father died."

"We were a good family the three of us, we were tight an' it seemed as if nothin' could ever touch that. But I was wrong about that. This business," he raised his head, eyes translucent with fatigue and worry, a muscle contracting the corner of his mouth into a grimace, "this business of my brother's, it was my Daddy's too ye understand an' he died for it an' so did his daddy before him. My Daddy didn't have the heart for it an' neither do I. Casey's different, he's harder in the things that matter an' more levelheaded when the crisis comes."

It was she who reached across and took his hand this time, cradling it between the cold comfort of her own. "I like you just fine, Patrick Riordan and I'm sure your Daddy would have too."

"Aye but it's my brother yer fallin' in love with," Pat said and as much as she wanted to close her ears to it she could not miss the note of bitterness in his voice.

"I'm sorry, Pat," she said aware of the futility of the words even as she spoke them.

"Don't be," he said wryly, "it seems none of us can help who we are or," he added taking his hand away from hers, "who we love. Besides," he smiled, "I'm not certain I'd want to be in direct competition with Jamie Kirkpatrick, that would take a braver man than me."

She was struck speechless by his words and could think of no denial that wouldn't sound false or be too late in coming. Pat rolled his neck about on his shoulders, the bones popping back into place with several loud clicks and taking a deep breath, looked at the clock.

"He should have been back by now?"

"Aye, he should have, it's been hours."

"Pat, you shouldn't be here standing guard, I've nowhere to go and I promise to stay put. Do you have any idea where to find him?"

"Not exactly, but—" Pat hesitated and she knew she'd have to push her advantage now before he decided it was madness and did instead as his brother had told him.

"But?" she prodded.

"I may know someone who can tell me or at least will have a better idea than myself."

"Then you should go, you'd never forgive yourself if something was to happen to him..." she let the sentence linger and hang. Pat gave her a very black look that told her he knew exactly what she was up to but that she'd had her intended effect nevertheless.

"Alright," he said and the word came out with great reluctance, "but ye have to promise, it'll be my hide if yer not here when he gets back."

"I promise," she said solemnly and very nearly meant it.

He gave her one last mistrustful look then, taking only a moment to grab his coat, he was gone.

She allowed a full five minutes to elapse before setting out herself, worried lest Pat having seen her designs too clearly, was waiting to catch her. Apparently though, his anxiety over his brother had taken the upper hand and he was nowhere to be seen.

Morning was still a full two hours away, though the sky was beginning to wear a heavy, tired face that bespoke of the last fragments of night rather than its fully dark heart.

It was dawn when she arrived at her destination and despite the indecency of the hour, she was not surprised to see lights peering out dimly from behind heavy draperies. Jamie, as she had suspected he would be, was awake.

She took a steadying breath for courage and slipped up the back way between the rose gardens and statues that were powdered a sooty gray in the dim light. She made for the soft glow that shone from the study windows and realized her mistake almost as soon as she stepped forward.

The curtains were opened slightly enough to see, enough to see and to sit with a thump on a stone bench, quite fortunately situated behind a screen of thick, uncompromising ivy. Enough to realize that she had unwittingly followed Pat to his destination.

'I may know someone who can tell me or at least will have a better idea...'

The words echoed strangely in her head. Pat could not possibly have meant Jamie, could he? And yet what other reason could there be for him to be sitting, head tilted back over the cushions of the sofa in utter exhaustion, or perhaps, complete relaxation, watching Jamie, who was on the phone, from under his half-shut eyelids.

From her vantage point she could see Jamie quite clearly, sitting at his desk, phone cradled on his shoulder, talking rapidly, while he wrote something on the blotter paper below his hand. Rimless spectacles perched on the end of his nose; he looked preternaturally alert for such an ungodly hour. He hung the telephone up sharply and still jotting down words, said something that made Pat sit up and lean forward so rapidly that he overbalanced and almost fell onto the carpet.

Jamie rose then, laid his spectacles down on the desk and rubbed the bridge of his nose. She could feel the pain behind his eyes as he did it. Then he approached the long glass doors, pausing to look up at the morning sky as it fired in the east, before twisting the knobs and opening the interior to the first breezes of the day. She was lost for a moment watching him in such a simple unstudied act, his beauty caught like light trapped in water, inescapable and undeniable. In the time it took to blink, she realized that he'd left the study and not crossed back over the floor to his desk as she had expected him to.

Instead he stood in front of her before she'd even time to decide which avenue provided the cleanest escape.

"It seems to be my morning for visitors," he said dryly, "may I ask what errand of urgency has brought you scurrying up to the castle doors or do I need to?"

"I was just on my way in," she said mustering up a dignity she didn't feel.

"Indeed," Jamie looked pointedly at his watch, "at five am on a Sunday morning?"

"Had to come home sometime," she said feebly, trying to dart past him.

His arm shot out with one of those catlike movements she'd yet to become accustomed to and halted her. "I think you'll join your compatriot in the study."

"I really ought to change first," she said uncomfortably aware suddenly of whose clothes she wore.

His gaze took all of her in and his eyes elongated slightly, "Where did you get this?" he asked, anger written plainly across his words for all their calmness.

"I- Maggie said that- I... I'm sorry," she trailed off awkwardly.

"No I imagine it was something she'd left behind, it looks very well on you." He gave her a strange look, "Colleen would have hated such pretty clothes going to waste. Now if you'd like to follow me inside."

"I'd rather go up to change first," she said wincing at the look that flashed out of the green eyes at her, realizing what she would rather or rather not do was of very little bearing at this particular moment.

She followed him through the study doors, studiously avoiding Pat's eyes until the last moment when she'd no choice but to meet his gaze, as Jamie directed her to sit beside him on the sofa. Pat, far from the exhausted boy he'd seemed when she'd glimpsed him earlier, was glaring daggers at her. She swallowed and attempted a watery smile of conspiratorship on him. It had no effect so she made herself as small as possible in the corner of the couch, upholstery buttons pushing into her back like hard little fists.

"What the hell are ye doin' here?" Pat hissed as Jamie sat behind his desk again, looking like some x-rated version of the classic Oxford don.

"I might ask you the same," she retorted primly.

"I believe," Jamie said eyeing them like they were two recalcitrant children, "that Casey will be the one asking the questions and the two of you will be doing the answering."

"We were worried," Pamela protested feebly.

"We were," Pat agreed for lack of anything more convincing to say.

"It's not me you need to get your excuses in order for. You," he looked specifically at Pamela, " would do to keep as well shot of Casey's doings as possible. Though I don't know the gentleman terribly well," he looked at Pat, green eyes withering in the glare of the early sun, "it seems that your brother is not altogether incapable of looking after himself and that he is also quite used to rough company."

"Aye, I suppose that's true," Pat said miserably, appearing for all the world like a six–year-old who'd had his hands rapped with a ruler.

"And you," Jamie turned the green gaze on Pamela once again, "have you quite taken leave of your senses running about the city in the middle of the night, a city you're not as yet over familiar with, looking like an extra in a French wedding farce?"

A small and not very brave clearing of the throat was the best she could summon up in response.

"Now that being said, can I interest the pair of you in joining me for breakfast?"

"No. Yes," said Pamela and Pat in imperfect unison.

"Right then," Jamie stood ignoring the vagaries of their various wishes, "come to the kitchen, Pat. I believe Pamela will join us after she changes into something less formal."

When, ten minutes later, Pamela joined them in the kitchen they were quite comfortably chatting, coffee perking fragrantly in the background. The kitchen shone in the light, its windows facing south and east over the city, that from this distance glowed with an aquatic haze as sun pushed fingers through the morning mist.

Jamie was cracking eggs into a bowl and whipping them with a sure and deft hand. Pat was gainfully employed in chopping tomatoes and mushrooms.

Jamie cocked an eyebrow at her, "Sit, we'll be done here in a moment."

True to his word, an omelet with neatly sliced toast and a cup of hot coffee was placed before her in moments. After providing Pat with the same he sat down with an apparently much heartier appetite than either Pat or Pamela could summon up.

"The condemned are condemned whether their stomach is full or empty," he commented mildly as they pushed food listlessly about their plates. Pat, seeing this for the bit of advice that it was, dug into his food and finished it all off, going to the length of accepting a second helping of toast. Pamela on the other hand found even the soft, buttery eggs would not get past the lump of fear in her throat.

"Ready then?" Jamie asked, having finished off his second cup of coffee and eaten his breakfast with deliberate leisure.

"I've a car," Pat said, patting his pockets for the keys and then patting again with rather more haste.

"Looking for these?" Jamie asked, dangling the desired object in front of their faces.

"When—how?" Pat stuttered, brow furrowing in confusion.

"Sleight of hand, easy as pie," Jamie said with a smile that bordered on a grin. "Mm, no I think not," he continued as Pat took a swipe at the keys. "I believe my instructions were to deliver you home personally, as Casey couldn't get you himself because 'that little bugger has swanned off with the keys.' It's not a direct quote you understand," Jamie said with mock seriousness, "but it's as close as I could come without using profanity."

"I can drive myself," Pat said stiffly.

"I'm certain you're quite capable," Jamie replied equably, "but as I promised your brother that I'd deliver you myself, to prevent any possible escape, I'd just as soon you didn't belabor the point.

There seemed very little to say to that, the result of which being the two of them finding themselves firmly ensconced in Jamie's dark green Bentley. In reply to Pamela's suggestion that she stay behind Jamie had said as though he were talking to someone very dim, "I'm not certain how large of a fool I seem to you, dear girl. but I suggest you don't try to test the limits of it this morning."

"My brother, where'd ye find him?" Pat finally found the nerve to ask.

"Called your home number," Jamie said, overtaking a large delivery van with breathtaking swiftness.

"Oh God," Pat said, expressing Pamela's thoughts to the letter. "But I thought—it sounded as if—Oh God," he finished rather weakly.

"Indeed," Jamie turned a cheery look on Pamela, "Pat here is under the illusion, flattering as it is," he paused to concentrate on shooting the beginnings of a stop light, "that I am a man who knows people, who know things."

Pamela shot a murderous glare over her shoulder at Pat, who was huddled in pure misery in the back seat.

"He'll kill me," Pat said after a few more moments of calmly maniacal driving on Jamie's part. "He'll be furious that I've involved an outsider in his business."

"I don't think he has actual murder in mind, though, " Jamie slowed and stopped for an old man crossing the street at midpoint, "I am of the opinion you may wish yourself dead a few times before he's done with you."

"Damn you," Pamela muttered under her breath, forgetting that Jamie seemed to have the radar acuity of a bat.

"Pardon me?" he inquired politely.

"You heard me," she said, the stresses of the night breaking into anger, "you're enjoying this and it's not a bit funny."

"I think you will find, Pamela," he said and there was no humor in his words, only an anger that had hovered, she realized, under the amusement all morning. "That if you are going to act as a child you will be treated accordingly."

She bit back tears that welled without warning in her eyes, wondering where all the fond teasing he'd bestowed on Pat had gone.

They were there then, crumbling walkway, red door and fading paint stark and unlovely in the morning light.

The car barely had time to halt before Casey, face black as thunder, emerged in the doorway.

Jamie did not so much as open his door but Casey came around to his open window and gruffly said "thank you for looking after him," before hauling Pat out unceremoniously by the collar and dragging him towards the house. For Pamela there was a hard look and nothing more.

Jamie took her home in a silence so tight and relentless she had to press her lips against her teeth to prevent herself from yelling.

"Come sit down for a minute," Jamie said after they'd entered the house, which was still and warm with a haze of Sunday morning content. She followed his lead rather miserably to the kitchen, refused the warmed over coffee he offered and placed her hands, folded in front of her, on the table.

"You have bought yourself a summer in Scotland young lady," Jamie said grimly.

"What?" she asked, wondering if she'd heard him right.

"As it would appear that you've neither kith nor kin, someone has to look out for you. I find, rather against my own better judgment that the task has fallen to me. I've been extremely poor at it thus far and intend to rectify my ways. I think that two months away from Belfast and those boys is advisable at this point."

"You can't make me go," she said aware that she sounded like a petulant teenager and not caring a wit.

"Oh," he smiled and raised his eyebrows, "don't make me prove that I can. You work for me, you have chosen to live this space of your life under my roof, and it's time one of us took some responsibility for those things. You've shown a complete and utter recklessness in regard to your own well-being so I *will*," he underscored the word, "be taking responsibility for it." He sat down facing her and asked with some urgency, "Do you have any idea what you're getting into here? Do you know who those boys are?"

"Yes," she said, teeth clenched around her tongue in an effort to not cry.

"Pamela," his voice was softer, though no less urgent, "do you know what it will mean if you fall in love with him?" He gave her a long, questioning look. "Or is it too late for such a warning?"

She shook her head sadly, knowledge breaking hard on the shores of consciousness, a realization of the untimeliness of life's messier events dawning. "No—yes—maybe, I don't know Jamie. A few weeks ago I'd have said no," she turned her hands palms up in a gesture of complete helplessness, "but now I just don't know."

He turned as white as if she'd struck him across the face and pushed back from the table. "I see," he said as if he didn't see anything at all. "You will still be coming to Scotland. Two months should give you enough time to make an informed decision."

"What do you mean?" she asked uneasily but he merely walked past her out of the kitchen.

He returned a moment later, arms loaded with books. "Here," he said, placing the volumes one by one in front of her, "books on Republicanism, on the Brotherhood, statistics, numbers and specific incidents. Tomes and tomes analyzing, dissecting and studying a perfectly hopeless cause. When you've done with that, I'll take you to meet some real people who've lost everything because of some goddamned airy-fairy notion that they could buy freedom with their lives. There are generally speaking two roads that every one of these people end up on, the one to prison or the one to the grave. Your friend understands those choices; he's already had a fair taste of the one and may be well started on the second. You, however, are coming from a more naïve standpoint and I don't intend to be responsible for you going down one of those paths without understanding the signs. So like it or not, you will be coming to Scotland."

She nodded meekly.

It was, even from the perspective of a rose-colored glass wearing, dyed-in-the-wool optimist, an exceedingly miserable day. Jamie didn't speak to her but closed himself up in his study, emerging in the early afternoon to inform her that she should pack as they would be leaving in the morning.

She accordingly packed and then descended to the main floor to tell him she would be going to see Pat and wasn't requesting permission but rather telling him.

He gave her the keys to his car and told her she would be home by eleven or face the consequences. Altogether, it was not a pleasant exchange.

Pat's house was as quiet as Jamie's, but not quite so fraught with tension. Pat, cleaning up the remains of his dinner, gave her his day in a nutshell.

It seemed that the day had been one of long quiets and chilling politeness. Casey had invited Pat to explain himself in a deceptively amiable tone. Which Pat had done in a faltering, stumbling and finally lame and insufficient way. At which point Casey pointed out in a rather blistering manner that he 'didn't believe his brother was quite that daft though the preceding hours couldn't prove it.'

Never once, in the long afternoon that followed did he raise his voice, though it seemed to Pat that it went through every possible modulation in the lower range. Pat, for variety, provided the occasional mumble of protest, an apology that may have seemed less than apologetic to its listener and began to feel the faintest flicker of rebellion against these fraternal constrictions. He made the mistake of articulating these finer feelings and watched as his brother smiled, stood and walked calmly into small front room and threw a thirty pound crystal lamp to the floor. Upon venturing into said room he found his brother, still in the fit of blazing calm, sweeping up the remains of the lamp. Pat wisely said no more and retreated to the kitchen where he began to make dinner.

Casey then announced that he would be going to fetch the car and could he trust Pat not to start a revolution in his absence? Whereupon he left the building and Pat breathed his first comfortable breath of the day. Which brought her entirely up to speed Pat said and with yet another mumbled apology, fell asleep, head on the table by his half-eaten dinner.

Pamela, finding the house too still and knowing Casey's haunts, climbed with the aid of a ladder, a drainpipe and a fence onto the roof. From there she watched the sun, bleary through a hot day's smog, settle in a coiling, shimmering heap on the horizon. It was thus employed that Casey found her.

"It's a nice evenin'," he said quietly, not wanting to disturb the dreamy look on her face, nor the stillness of her body.

"It is," she agreed.

They sat for some time, the silence companionable, not strained as he had expected. Casey, not a man given easily to fear, had found himself of late, afraid. It was this girl he knew, this girl and what she made him feel, things he had promised himself he would not allow into his life. He had never wanted to cloud the issue of his responsibilities, didn't feel that a man who took up revolution as his occupation had any right to enmesh a family in those bloody threads. He had taken precautions, never allowed things to grow past the point where he was taking more than comfort in a woman's body and company. But he could be forgiven, he supposed, for not anticipating this. Who could have predicted that when he came home his brother, his shy, once wordless brother, would know such a girl? This girl, who seemed made of every dream a young man, locked away from the world, could conjure up.

The vulnerability, the fragility, the tongue, the wit, the mind, the body, the face, all seemingly of a piece to make a man, even a strong one, entirely lose his senses. And he *was* lost. He was aware, as an intelligent man will be, of his weaknesses as well as his strengths and knew just what he was able to withstand.

He took her hand, uncertain of whether she would withdraw. He compared it against his own dark, rough ones and marveled at the differences between them, even in small ways. Her skin, in the dying crimson of the sun, was luminous, washed through with shade upon shade of red.

"I apologize if I seemed angry before," he said.

"It was stupid of us," she replied, "though it was only out of concern. You frightened Pat. You set him a certain example but expect him to live by different rules than you do. It doesn't seem entirely fair."

"There's not so much that has been fair about my brother's life," Casey said, laying her hand gently on the tiled roof. "I need to keep him safe, I promised my Da' a long time ago that I would an' I'll not fail him a second time, especially not because Pat takes a notion that I need rescuin'. It's fortunate for the both of ye that ye went to Jamie, though for what reason I can't quite fathom. Still, my brother knows better than to go tell a stranger our business. In the world we live in, such things can get ye killed."

"Your Daddy left you an awfully big burden," she said sidestepping the issue of Jamie.

"Pat's my family, all that's left, I don't consider his well-bein' a burden."

"Still, you were terribly young."

Casey leaned back on his elbows, eyes closed, the soft, silted evening breeze ruffling his hair.

"Aye, I was young an' stupid. Daddy was about two weeks dead when I broke the promise I made him an' was carted off to prison and left my brother alone. Da' was always careful of Pat, said he was made of poetry an' that sort of material didn't wear well in the world. Pat didn't talk much as a child, Daddy had him looked at by specialists here an' in Dublin, 'cause we weren't even certain he could talk. But then when he did he could tell stories that'd take ye to another time an' place. I think sometimes that's where he belonged, to a gentler time an' place. I wonder if we don't have guardian angels an' they're not so much more competent that human bein's an' maybe times they set ye down when they're not supposed to."

"He's stronger than you give him credit for," she said fingers brushing the side of his cheek, releasing an errant curl that the wind had tangled in his lashes.

"Aye, I suppose he is," he smiled, his one dimple slicing and curving like an ivory new moon in the dark of his whiskers. The smile disappeared as quickly as it had come, clapped out like a candle flame.

"Pat says yer off to Scotland for the summer."

"I am."

"Ye can run if ye feel the necessity, but this thing between us—it won't go away, it'll follow ye there an' it'll be here when ye come back."

He took her chin in gently firm fingers and turned her face toward his own. She could smell the smoke of cigarettes there like a blue-black mist, a more earthy undertone ribboning in and out underneath. It was the smell, the singular scent of it more than anything that made her cry. When, she wondered, had the mere smell of his fingers become so tangled up in all the things she couldn't sort out enough to understand with any clarity.

"Runnin' away with him won't help either," Casey said softly, "he won't let ye love him, darlin', but I think," he paused, the pressure there in the fingers again, forcing her to meet his eyes, "I think yer beginnin' to care enough for me to make the pain of that bearable."

He kissed her, carefully at first, then with more demand. Last night's kiss had been a promise that he would return safe, that he would keep things on an even keel. Tonight's kiss asked that she make the same promise.

They watched the stars for a time, those bright enough to pierce the city's phosphorescent glow and when at last exhaustion and Pamela's curfew bid them off the roof, she spoke the words she'd given him silently on the roof.

"I will come back."

Chapter Eleven
To Hell or Connacht

Having fasted five days and nights in order to draw closer to the presence of his Lord, Lucien Broughton was in body and soul as white and empty as the scourged innards of a wentletrap shell. He believed he had at last received an answer to the question he'd posed God some days earlier.

With an answer in hand, a man could proceed to action, clearly, brilliantly and expediently. Rising up off his knees and ignoring the blood that began to leak through the scabs, he surveyed himself in a full length mirror. He looked well for his deprivation, incandescent, as though he burned from inside with a pure, scorching light, which indeed he did.

Naked, he took stock. Skin without flaw, a white so unearthly that at certain angles there seemed a silver tint to him. He despised messiness in other people, did not allow it in himself and could not understand why anyone else should. Not a ripple of muscle, a bump of bone, a wavelet of tendon displayed itself through the gilt covering of his skin. It was to his advantage this; it caused people to misread him, to underestimate his power.

This age he lived in was messy, violent and filled with contradiction, all of which displeased him. But things could be changed to suit, shifted to fit, broken in order to achieve alignment. It was only a matter of having a skilled hand upon the rudder and a firm mind behind it. Lucien knew he had these things in abundance. God had intended that it should be so, he had intended that his son, his pale and perfect son, be a man of destiny. God was the mind, Lucien the vessel.

Still naked, he walked to the window, surveying the city around him. Grander cities there were, larger cities, shinier cities even, but this one was his. Of a size and temperament to make the task of seizing hold the reins and guiding it to a better future, so much the easier.

He breathed deeply, taking in the air of evening, the colors as they lay lambent and molten, layer upon lacquered layer in bronze, gold, crimson and purple. July was only around the corner. In Ireland, summer was the season of rage and July its burning epicenter. The Marching Season was upon them in all its slashing orange, drumgutted glory. He himself was to lead a crowd of thousands, to finish on the lawns of Stormont with a ringing oratory no one would ever forget.

There had been rumors, suggested by the foolish, that perhaps it was time to stop the parades. That such aggressive and open hostility only stirred the sectarian pot, adding more poison to the bubbling, heaving, ready to boil over mess that was Northern Ireland. But it was a Protestant statelet with a Protestant government and no Unionist government in their right mind was going to cancel the event that was a two and a half century old reassurance of their superiority. It would be insanity and political suicide all in one move. In times of trouble, people needed reassurance, dressing in their father's sash and beating the drum gave them this. And there really was no more effective method of polarization to separate the two communities that in other times and seasons had come dangerously close to melding.

Lucien eyed the sun as it sank well into its evening descent. Time to dress. To don the vestments of his calling. He'd a meeting with the B-Sots, as he called them, or 'Benevolent Sisters of Temperance' a name, which he thought, had a rather profane popish smack to it and then he was to offer prayer and verse at the Orange Lodge, Chapter 46 later in the evening.

Lucien smiled, a pleasant smile, which brought a glow to his pale blue eyes and made old women sigh. Even for a Man of Destiny things couldn't be moving any closer to schedule.

He took a last look over the city, raising his eyes to encompass the outlying hills and the smile, well practiced, faded quickly from his face. For on the hill, reflecting all the colors of sunset, refracting and winking like an obscene jewel was the house of James Kirkpatrick.

Perhaps there was, after all, one fly in the ointment.

A WEEK AFTER PAMELA'S DEPARTURE FOR SCOTLAND Casey was fired from his job. He'd finished his shift that day and was looking forward to a pint with a few fellow workers when he was called over to the shift foreman's office.

"Kevin said ye wanted to see me," he said, ducking under the low doorframe.

"Aye," the man sighed and turned from the blueprints he had rolled out across his desk. He needn't have said a word. Casey could read what he had to say all too clearly from the discomfort in the man's face. He'd be damned if he'd spare the bastard the misery of it though.

"It seems, Casey," the foreman twitched papers and pens about in front of him, "it seems that we will have to let you go," he cleared his throat nervously and Casey suddenly saw that the man was afraid, "for the present time."

"I'm fired then," Casey said mildly.

"Well, not technically, no—" the man was actually sweating.

"Just to clear things a bit," Casey said slowly as if he were talking to a dimwitted child, "when I get up in the morning I will not be coming here an' come next Friday there'll be no pay for me an' yet somehow I'm not technically," he drew the word out like sticky toffee, "fired."

The foreman swallowed nervously once or twice. "It's a possibility that we'll need you back in the autumn."

"Bullshit," Casey said wearily, seeing the game very clearly for what it was. "Who is it needs a job then, boss' nephew, his wife's cousin, his auntie's bingo partner?"

"This isn't about nepotism," the foreman said testily, pen drumming a nervous beat on the table.

"Really? Then what have I done to lose my job? Have I been late, slacked off, taken long breaks?"

"No," the foreman agreed hastily.

"Then what is it?"

The man took a long, shaky breath and spent several seconds studying the nub of his pen. Casey sat down.

"I'll not leave until I've had an honest answer. There are boys with less seniority out there, so I'd like to know why it's me specifically that's bein' given the sack."

"There've been rumors..." the foreman said eyes still firmly fixed to the desk.

"Rumors about what? Ye knew I had a prison record when ye hired me, I made no bones about that," Casey said, willing the man to look up and meet his eyes. He did a moment later.

"It's not the past we're concerned with, it's the present company that yer keepin' that has tongues waggin'. We keep no truck with those sort of dealins' around here."

"I see," Casey said rising stiffly, feeling older and heavier than he had only moments ago. "I wasn't aware that my weekends an' evenins' were of any concern to the company."

"'Tis when yer activities could get the place blown up."

"I don't bring my politics to work."

"The sort of politics ye practice have a way of followin' a man wherever he goes."

"Do they?" Casey asked, moving towards the open door. Knowing that once it was behind his back it was closed for good and all. It was a hard lesson to learn about doors for every one you walked through represented an ending. There would be no job in the autumn, or any other season for that matter.

Outside, his pals, the five token Catholics of the three hundred man-work force, stood together. Desperation as much as comradeship had drawn them to one another.

"Will we still be havin' that pint then?" asked Kevin Doherty, father of three blue-eyed girls and possessor of a new mortgage away from the neighborhood. A man who wore the tight look of one fleeing from something that cannot be escaped.

"Aye," Casey smiled, flipping his jacket over his shoulder, "it's on me lads."

NOT ONE TO BE DAUNTED BY THE PROSPECTS OF UNEMPLOYMENT, Casey, the Monday after his dismissal took to the streets in search of another job. After a week of solid, unequivocal rejection, it seemed that something temporary might be in order. Window washing presented itself as an option that would leave his afternoons open for a variety of activities. However, three days into the endeavor, having yet to wash a window, the only real opportunity for wages that had presented itself came from a lonely widow and had little to do with the state of her windows. He received a similar offer from an older gentleman when he took up house painting, an enterprise that netted him two jobs that were, in the end, just enough to pay for his brushes, paint and ladder.

He began to spend more time at home than was good for the condition of his soul and to clean with an obsessiveness that bordered on the unhealthy. Pat, on one of his rare appearances, caught him cleaning the washroom grout with an old toothbrush for the second time in one week and voiced the opinion that perhaps he needed to find an alternative activity to occupy his time.

"'Tis easy for ye to say," Casey said scratching at the tip of his nose with one rubber-gloved hand, "yer not stuck in this damn place day after day."

"Nor are you," Pat pointed out, "ye've been unemployed before an' managed to find something to do, this is no different."

"In fact," Casey said ignoring altogether Pat's last statement, "yer never here. Ye breeze in, grab a bath an' fresh clothes an' breeze back out." His eyes narrowed suspiciously, "Just where do ye spend all yer time?"

"In Oriental massage parlors, where do ye think?" Pat retorted acerbically and left his brother to his grout.

Casey caught up to him in the kitchen. "Will ye be around for dinner? I've made stew and dumplins', the little ones with apple that ye like."

"Jesus Christ," Pat said on an explosion of breath.

"What?" Casey asked, all innocence, wooden spoon in hand.

"Would ye listen to yerself? Yer like some nittin' broody hen."

"What are ye tryin' to say?" Casey slapped the spoon down.

"I'm not tryin', I'm bloody well sayin' it! Christ Casey, I'm beginnin' to feel like the flea that couldn't get rid of the dog."

"Well thank you very much," Casey said peevishly, picking up the milk

Pat had poured and left on the counter and wiping the ring of condensation under it.

Pat sighed and rubbed his neck, leaving a smudge of ink in the wake of his fingers. "Listen, I've got to go down to Tom's tonight. We're to finish up the pamphlets an' then we've got to leaflet an area of about five square miles."

"For what?" Casey said, tone lightly disinterested.

"We're picketin' the Housing Trust in the morning. Five houses have gone to Protestant families with one or no children an' they've been bumped over Catholics who had larger families an' greater need."

"Such is the way of our world," Casey said laconically.

"So we should just let it stay so?" Pat asked, grabbing an apple and some bread and stuffing it in his pockets.

"No, I'm just sayin' I'm not certain it'll lead anywhere all this protestin' and pamphletin'."

"People can respond to things other than the sound of a gun," Pat said quietly.

"D'ye think I don't know that?" There was a transparency in Casey's words, a desperation that made Pat halt for a moment, even though he was already late.

"Tom's uncle has offered us a few weeks work peat cuttin' out west. Why don't ye come?"

"Can the revolution survive yer absence so long?"

"It'll manage," Pat said, fighting not to rise to his brother's bait.

"An' what about Declan, doesn't he need yer stout slingin' skills over the next bit?" For Pat had taken a part-time job as a bartender at Declan O'Ryans, a comfortable if not trendy establishment known for its good food and showcasing of local talent.

"He always closes down for a few days durin' the height of marchin' season an' he decided to close for three weeks an' make a holiday of it, he's taken the wife an' kids to Greece."

"Oh," Casey said, turning and giving the stew a dejected stir.

"Come, why don't ye?" Pat infused the smallest bit of wheedling into his request.

"Out west, eh?" Casey said and leaning against the counter faced his brother once again. "Is it to be 'to hell or Connacht' for me then?"

"It's beginnin' to look that way," Pat said smiling.

"Aye well, perhaps I'll try Connacht. I've been to hell an' didn't find the temperature to my likin'. Now go on, ye can't leave the revolution in Tom Kelly's hands for too long, he's like to lose it in the first five minutes."

Casey sat after Pat left, ate three bites of the stew he'd ladled out for himself and then pushed the bowl away with a heavy sigh. It was no good pretending. He didn't want to eat, cared little for sleep and was about as settled as a dog with an arseful of porcupine quills. He could have pointed to any number of reasons and likely even convinced himself of their validity. The stagnation in the Republican rank and file, the fact that his brother seemed like the whirl-wind at the center of some exciting event while he felt awkward, alone and an outsider in his own community. While it was true that in their neighbor-hood almost every household held a Nationalist sympathy or a Republican under the bed there were still those who walked past him in the street without a word. People he'd known since childhood, mothers who'd fed him bread warm from the oven. One old lady had actually spit at his feet the other day. Sometimes he wondered if he'd be able to leave prison behind. There were still moments when he thought he could smell the place on his skin, feel the grit of it under his nails and the darkness of it in his heart. All the hot water in the world wasn't going to get rid of that. But when he'd held Pamela in his arms the other night, when he'd touched her face and kissed her, he'd felt a lightness inside, he'd felt clean, as if he held no taint from his past, no weariness that did not belong in a body so young. She'd felt like salvation, a fine and good thing that he could protect and care for, a beauty that would save him from himself.

He stood, took his bowl to the sink and faced himself in the merciless reflection of window and dark night.

'To hell or Connacht then," he whispered to himself and found it difficult to smile.

IN MAY OF 1968, A GREAT CONCRETE AND STEEL EDIFICE was erected in West Belfast. It was the first of its sort there, though unfortunately it wasn't to be the last. It was called by the rather uninspired name of Divis Flats and it would rip the heart out of a neighborhood, opening vital arteries that would bleed despair and disillusionment for decades. It was also monumentally, undeniably ugly.

The architects of the monstrosity hailed it as an opportunity for a new community, a time for the society of West Belfast to recast itself around the advantages of modern living, stating that having 'a bird's eye view' would give the people who were fortunate enough to live there a 'new and more meaningful social relationship between communities.' The architects, of course, did not have to live there. There had been nothing wrong with the community of the old West Belfast, the housing had been rundown and needed replacing, but as far as the ties that bound one house to the next and one street to another, even the most stringent social planner would have been hard put to find a stronger, more densely woven population. People knew their neighbors and moreover, quite often liked them. They knew who was about to be born and who was about to die, whose father had fought in the war and whose had not. Whose paycheck was blued on the dogs or the drink, whose arthritis flared up in the winter, whose nerves were being lost on kids and bills, who was falling in love and who was falling out. They needed new homes, warm, clean, properly plumbed, well-built homes, what they did not need was a government imposed eyesore about which they were given neither choice nor vote.

It was typical and they were used to it. The older generation had seen it in myriad ways; aspirations had come to ashes before and would again. There was no trial and error as far as the government was concerned there was only the trial of error upon error. The bottom line was the largest number of housing units for the least amount of money and to hell with a sense of community or security. The government had taken it upon themselves to make decisions for a section of the population they had no connection to, no understanding of and no fondness for. It was the way of things in Northern Ireland and had been for as long as anyone cared to remember.

The young, mercifully or unmercifully, have no memory. And the youth of Northern Ireland were no different from their counterparts around the globe; they saw discrimination and sought to right it. They were, however, different from their predecessors in that they were the first generation of Catholics to have access to higher education and a hope at something more than a marriage with too many mouths to feed and the occasional flutter at the track to look forward to.

To them, life had to be more than a mill that sucked you in and ground you down, spitting you out the other end soulless and hopeless. Life just had to be more than that.

Pat, standing in the street and eyeing the block of concrete, felt as if he were shouldering a good deal of the weight of it. Over the last few weeks, he'd heard his father's voice in his head a lot. 'Don't expect life to be fair an', Paddy, for God's sake, don't ever give all yer love to just one thing.'

It had seemed simple enough advice at the time and he'd followed it as best as he was able and he'd certainly never expected life to be fair. The result of which was he was in love with a girl his brother had boldly taken from under his nose, a girl who apparently didn't understand Catholic guilt, at least not the debilitating Irish form of it. He was up to his neck in a movement founded on hope and youthful illusion and he *had* found another love and her name was freedom. It was true that he hadn't gotten the girl. But he knew he had found something, his father's way, his brother's way were not for him, there were other avenues and he thought perhaps he'd found his.

Community activism didn't quite have the romance of televised protest but Pat found it more to his liking. He was good at organizing small groups, at listening to individuals, at ladling out hot soup along with sound advice.

It was democracy on a small scale but even peaceful revolutions had, he surmised, to begin somewhere. Stuffing envelopes, writing and distributing pamphlets, teaching people that they'd a right to expect better than the miserable conditions imposed upon them by a cold-shouldered government, making thermoses of hot tea and chocolate to survive long days of illegal squatting in untenanted homes formed the backbone he knew of the larger protest. It made him happy, it gave him, if not the blaze that resided in his brother's belly, then at least a warm glow that was less likely to damage himself and those he cared for.

There was no money for a base camp, not even a hole in the wall but Declan let them use the pub after hours and a small backroom during business hours. The pamphlets Pat composed at home on a typewriter that had mysteriously appeared on his doorstep one day. He'd a fair idea where or rather from whom it had come. His little group had no official name, no anagram for the history books and he'd no idea where they were going or what they might achieve.

For now, it was enough.

A SLIM CRESCENT OF MOON LAY ON ITS BACK IN A DRIFT OF CLOUD, floating effortlessly across the sky. Its colors—gold, silver, pewter and powdered white were appreciated from the vantage point of a small but snug craft, drifting itself on a rippling plate of silver.

"Pass the milk over, would ye?" Casey said into the warm night air.

"Pass it over yerself," came the reply, "it's been up by yer head for the last hour."

"So it has," Casey said companionably, after a long and satisfying draught on the thick-lipped bottle. "Where'd ye get it?"

"Nicked it off Old Misery's doorstep," Pat replied easily.

"That's thievery, I tell ye this summer in the wilds has brought out traits in ye that are shockin'."

"He only leaves it to sour anyway. Eight bottles of milk like clockwork, week in, week out an' he leaves them to sour on the porch. I'm only puttin' it to the use it was intended for. Besides he still owes us for the peat, tight old bugger."

"So we're takin' our payment out in milk, are we?"

"It would seem so," Pat said and shifted slightly in the boat, an action that caused it to rock precipitously for a moment before it settled back to its gentle, meandering drift.

"D'ye think," Casey paused for a protracted yawn, "the fish are sleepin'?"

"I'm so tired that a sturgeon could bite an' I'd not take notice." Pat gave his rod, tied with an elaborate set of knots to the side of the boat, an unenthusiastic wiggle.

"I've muscles I wasn't aware of possessin' before this summer. Christ even my arse hurts," Casey complained around a mouthful of brown bread.

"Mmphm," was Pat's only reply, indicating that he'd neither the strength nor intellectual fortitude for articulate speech.

It was near to the end of July. The tiny white flowers called *cean-a-bahns* that had covered the bog in May were long gone, the sun seemed to stand overhead all day and the night, Casey could have sworn, was no longer than those found in the high summer of the Arctic.

Turf cutting was an old and honorable profession and, though most people cut and stored their own haul for the winter, those with the means would often have it done by others. And one could hardly blame them, for it was backbreaking work, with only the promise of a fragrant winter fire as reward.

After the first week, though, Casey's back had ceased to complain and he'd begun to turn gypsy brown in the warm summer light. He'd even begun to enjoy some aspects of turf cutting. There was, after all, a certain tranquility and sense of comradeship to be had, one man working in unison with another out on the isolated bogs.

Casey and Pat paired up and took turns at being bar man and barrow man. Casey cut the bars, each a spadeful in depth and heaved the sod up onto the bank where Pat, as barrow man, loaded it into the barrow and took it off to higher and drier ground. At the end of the day, they would then build grogans, small stacks of turf that were made of four sods stood upright with one sod balanced across the top. There they were left for the sun to dry them. Closer to the end of the summer, when the turf had dried, they would bag it and transfer it off the bog where a tractor would take it down to the barn of the big house. They took smaller orders on the side, such as for Mr. Trotter, on whom they had bestowed the name 'Old Misery' early on in the season.

Pat seemed unfazed by the sheer physical strenuousness of the work and, other than having a propensity to sleep immediately upon sitting, showed no ill effects. As if, Casey had thought that first week, stifling a desire to smack his brother alongside the head with the pitchfork, as if the act of pouring stout and bicycling up to the Causeway on weekends was enough to keep him in fighting form.

If there was one immediately apparent benefit to such hard physical labor, it had to be that a man had neither the time nor energy to think or dream. Even if occasionally, unbidden, a certain green-eyed girl tended to slip into one's nocturnal musings.

Casey trailed one hand over the side of the boat; even the water was warm at this late hour.

"Can I ask ye a question?" he said, half hoping that Pat was actually asleep.

"Since when do ye ask if ye can ask a question?"

"Well it's only that it's of a rather personal nature," Casey cleared his throat wishing he'd not opened his mouth.

"That's hardly stopped ye in the past."

"Well it's—I—have ye ever made love to a woman?"

A long silence issued forth from the opposite end of the boat. "Well I'm not a virgin if that's what yer askin'," was the dry reply just when Casey was getting desperate enough to change the subject.

"I'm not talkin' about sex," he said quietly, "I meant have ye ever *made love* to a woman?"

"I've tended to take Daddy's advice in that area," Pat said and propped his head up on an overturned basket. "Ye know, keep yer pants zippered when ye can, don't sleep with a Catholic girl if ye can avoid it. Protestants are less guilty an' more honest about sex and fer God's sake," Casey joined in on the well imprinted lesson, "don't marry a girl just because ye'd the good fortune to get into her knickers." They laughed, the sound of it echoing off into the night, spreading warm and happy over the mountains.

"Sound advice if not terribly romantic," Pat said, tearing off small chunks of bread and scattering them over the surface of the water. "But to answer yer question, no I've not. Have you?"

"No. I'd sex before prison, but it came in the form of quantity, not quality."

"So why are ye askin' then?"

"It's only, " Casey sat up and flung a pebble into the still surface of the lake, watching the ripples undulate, spread and eventually shimmer into nothingness before answering, "I imagine it'll be a great deal different, won't it?"

"I imagine it will," Pat replied softly, "if it's the right girl an' the right time."

"An' how do ye know that, if it's the right time I mean?"

Pat shrugged, his shoulders rising up above his ears and tipping his cap over into the water. He watched it float for a moment and then retrieved it as it began to sink. "Ye'll just know."

Casey snorted, "That's the answer people give when there is no bloody answer to be had."

Pat sat up, propping his elbows on his knees, fists cupped beneath his chin. "If ye have somethin' to ask Paddyboy, ask it."

"Why do ye presume I've a question to ask?"

"I've known ye since ye were born, slept in the same damn bed for years, watched ye when ye were sad an' when ye were happy. I know when ye've a question yer not certain ye should ask."

"How was it for ye in prison? I mean did anyone try—no," Pat shook his head, "I shouldn't be askin' ye these things."

"Why not?" Casey asked, flicking a match against the side of the boat and putting it to the end of a cigarette.

"Because I can't know what it was like for ye in there an' what ye may have had to do just to survive. It's maybe somethin' ye'll not want to talk of."

"I managed fine in prison, no one raped me, Pat. They did everything else that came to mind, but no one raped me."

Pat let out a long breath of pent-up air. "It's been botherin' me, ye know. What might have been done to ye an' I knew there were many things ye could bear but some that ye couldn't. It used to keep me awake at night, wonderin' if ye could sleep comfortable or if ye always had to have one eye open. If ye could do anything without fear on yer back."

"Fear," Casey said softly, staring out over the water away from Pat, "is yer best friend in prison an' it's only a damn fool who ever forgets that. I forgot once an' then I never forgot again."

He picked a flat stone from a small hoard he kept in his pocket, a leftover habit from childhood, and flung it in one sharp, hard movement. They watched it skip across the water, arcing and diving. Hanging in the air and catching silver light against its wet body, it seemed almost a living thing, something that might cry out to the night and the wind and the sky if it but had the choice. It sank on the downsweep of the fifth arc, the air currents closing over its silent descent and leaving no remark upon the dark water.

"I'm alright, Patrick," Casey said and took up the milk bottle again, cleansing it with several long-throated swallows.

"Ye don't have to protect me, Casey. I'm not yer tongue-tied little brother anymore ye know."

"I know," Casey nodded at a point just past his brother's shoulder. "It looks like ye've got a bite on yer line."

Pat gave his line a mild glance and then turned to the side, the rod, consisting of fishing line knotted around a stout but pliable wand of willow was bent in half, and the boat was beginning to drag slightly under the effort.

Pat shifted his weight over to the other side and taking the rod halfway up, pulled hard against it. It gave an inch above the water, encountered resistance from below and sank back again.

"Got Moby Dick on the line, do ye?"

"Something like," Pat grunted, shifting his body further round still and trying to brace his feet against the lip of the boat, levered his upper body against the pull of the rod. "Ye could do something other than sit there," he said through gritted teeth.

"We'll sink with the two of us in the one end," Casey said sensibly.

Pat muttered something decidedly filthy under his breath and hauled back on the line until his body was nearly parallel to the water and only inches above it. Casey, seeing that, with or without his help, they were likely to capsize, decided that he'd best go down trying. He shimmied his body out full-length, balanced across the seats on his stomach and put the strength of one large hand to the assistance of his brother.

"We'll have to try in unison," Pat grunted, taking a second to draw breath.

"Right," Casey grunted back and then they counted to three and strained, heaved and cursed and felt sweat begin to bead on their faces. All to no avail.

The rod, bowed over in a high and tight arch, was at the limit of its give.

"One more try an' then we cut it loose?" Casey suggested, not wanting to even guess what might be giving such a monumental struggle on the other end of the line.

Pat made an affirmative noise. Casey nudged himself over until he was on his side, affording his arms more leverage. Pat counted out, "One, two, three," and they gave an almighty heave. At the very limits of the pull, the line gave all at once heaving the boat over at a harsh tip and sending the boys and other various contents out in a cascade of rushing, hissing air.

Plastered and spluttering they came up in time to witness the boat being pulled at an alarming clip across the frothing water.

"Christ on earth, what sort of fish can that be?"

"I don't," Pat replied, spitting out water, "think we should be askin' God."

"What about the boat?" Casey asked as Pat looked toward shore.

"Ye intend to chase it down?" Pat asked and didn't wait for an answer before launching forward toward land.

Casey cast one last glance over his shoulder at the swiftly disappearing boat and decided some things were fated to be lost. He set out for shore close on his brother's kicking heels.

In any event, they needn't have worried about catching the boat, for it caught them. Unawares. Casey, looking up in an effort to gauge the distance to the shore, sensed it behind him and turned, getting a glimpse of blinding white and a hard blow to his shoulder as the boat shot past like a large and unwieldy arrow headed straight up the path of his brother's back.

He yelled but the speed of the thing was such that it was upon Pat before he'd even closed his throat around the sound. He swam towards the boat, arms slicing the water with a burning speed, closing his mind to the thought of what brute force must lay below.

He stopped by the boat, which was now ominously still, no sign of Pat anywhere. He dove under the water near the prow, thinking Pat had been knocked unconscious. He couldn't see a damned thing; the darkness was palpable and heavy in his face, coming down with the weight of a stone on his lungs. He sensed movement in front of him and pushed toward it. In seconds he was enveloped in a churn of water. Whether it was made by man or beast he could not tell. Trying to infuse calm down the length of his arms, he groped in the inky blackness. Something of a sliminess, heretofore unknown to his experience, slid like a bolt through his hands. There was only a sense of great size and a revulsion that made him want to fly in the opposite direction as swiftly as possible.

He pushed up, gulped air and dove again trying to calculate how long his brother had been without air. When did brain damage begin? After four minutes and before twenty? There was less frenzy in the water now and the thought of why that might be panicked him. He located the side of the boat, sought with numbing fingers the line and, after what seemed very long minutes, found it. It was strung tight and he followed its length down through the water, down and further still down and found Pat at the end of it.

He hung motionless in the water, frighteningly still. Casey found his chest, put a forearm under Pat's arms and pushed for heaven. They stopped just short of it. He could feel the water lighten, knew they were only inches from where oxygen diffused its particles and could give them resurrection.

He dove, got under his brother's body and shoved upwards hoping to give Pat a split second even of air. But something pulled with greater force in the opposite direction. Something that sought darkness with a craving equal to his for light. He grabbed for Pat's ankle, found his knife and lungs aching pushed himself away from the light. He felt down Pat's right leg, which was, now that he felt it, straining unnaturally for a man who was unconscious.

The line was wrapped hard, biting into Pat's ankle and then feeding down sharply into the water. Casey slashed at it, the pressure of the water taking the force from the knife's blade. Short of gravity, it needed slack to loop itself in but Casey pulling on the line couldn't supply any. *'Please God, please, please, please,'* he chanted furiously in his mind.

He knew he'd have to pause soon for a breath, but that Pat could hardly spare another second without a breath of his own. He sawed at the line again and felt it snap just as something whooshed past him and broke the surface.

He reached up to grab his brother and his fingers met cold, black water and nothing else. He scissored his legs and shot above the surface, gasping for air and looking frantically about at the same time. Pat was nowhere to be found. He dove again and again and again, clawing the water with increasing desperation. He found nothing. He tried for some last shred of calm and abandoned the idea swiftly. This panic was purely instinctual, born of dread and certainty, that at some point, he'd been bound to do this, to fail his brother in the ultimate and most final of ways.

Breaking the surface, he could feel a weighted numbness settling into his limbs and knew he didn't have much more time himself before the water would claim him as well. Tipping his head back and dragging a cutting breath into his lungs, he saw above him, clearly delineated in the night sky, the blue-white fire of Vega. Vega of Lyra, the star of high and eternal summer. It had been his father's star. *'Sometimes it will be all ye have an' it will have to be enough'.*

"Oh God, Daddy no not like this, not now," he cried with what power was left in his bruised throat. His voice fled into the night, dissipating quickly on the warm air. There was no way it could have reached to heaven, but perhaps an unbeliever's voice never could. Perhaps all the prayers by those less than pure in faith and heart merely sank under the weight of their own disbelief.

He would try one last time and if he could not save his brother, he would not bother to save himself. Some mistakes a man can only live with once.

He dove again and brushed full length down the side of that preternatural whiteness he had glimpsed before. Something was shoved against him and it took his panicked mind a moment to realize it was his brother, placed, it almost seemed, directly into his arms. He began to struggle towards the surface with him and felt something brush the back of his legs before applying pressure and shooting he and Pat out of the water with amazing speed.

There was no time for terror. He flipped over onto his back, pulling Pat up onto his chest and kicking for shore. A curious calm descended into him, spread its quietude into every last cell and allowed him to function to the limits of his body rather than flailing about and wasting precious time.

'Sometimes it will be all ye have an' it will have to be enough.'

'Just let him be alive Daddy and it will be enough, just let him be alive,' he silently prayed.

They made shore, Casey's strength so drained that he couldn't stand and had to crawl onto the pebbled beach pulling his brother by the collar with one hand. He bent over Pat, searching for signs of life and finding by the moon's cold light, none. He pinched Pat's nose and sent his breath into his brother, trying to close from his mind the last time he'd done this. How helpless and tiny Pat had been then, a baby who simply forgot to breathe. Common enough, but in Pat it had gone on long after the time when the brain should have seen breathing as an involuntary function. Pat had been three and Casey seven and it had been Casey who turning against him in their shared bed had felt the unnatural stillness. Had leaned over him and seen morning's light strong against the delicate and purling blue of his brother's face. He had given Pat breath then and it had been enough to save him, he only hoped it was now.

'Borrowed breath, stole from death.' An old child's rhyme came unwanted into his head. How many times could you cheat death and not have to somehow ante up the balance?

He blew again, counting carefully between puffs, putting his ear to Pat's lips and hoping against hope for some small flutter of breath. There was none.

"Don't do this to me, Patrick. Don't you dare goddamn do this," he gritted his teeth and took a deep breath, forcing it as hard as he dared into his brother's lungs. There was still no response. He compressed Pat's chest, hoping to force water out of his lungs and turned his own head to the side, towards the water, to listen for anything, even the smallest gurgle to give him hope.

Staring directly at him, with what appeared to be head and shoulders above water, was a being of such terrifying whiteness that he knew it had never before been blessed by light. It was of a distance that he could not distinguish singular features but it appeared almost human, long strands of kelp-like hair plastered to its neck. He could have sworn it was looking directly at him but it did not seem to have eyes, at least not of a sort familiar to those who live above ground. There was a strong and undeniable sense of being stared at however, of one species meeting another whose kind was long gone from the planet.

"Thank you," Casey whispered, afraid to startle it, worried that the breaking of silence might provoke it to some action. It had been this creature, this strange being of lightless water, who had saved his brother's life, who had pushed them both with fearsome strength towards that thing it did not understand.

Its head tilted back on the heavy neck, face bathed in lunar radiance, a thing of gleaming, glowing white. The mountains and water surrounding it gentle gradations of winnowed blue. Sound issued forth from it, sound so small and forlorn, a strange and exquisite cry of loneliness that made every hair on Casey's body stand quivering. The cry of the last of its kind, stranded here out of time and season.

Beneath him, half-forgotten, Pat coughed, lurched to the side and vomited a stream of water. Casey made certain he could breathe before glancing swiftly back at the dark, bottomless lake. There was no sign of the creature, not so much as a ripple on the water to betray its return to the place of profound darkness it had emerged from.

"What was that howlin'?" Pat asked, still coughing, though he'd managed to struggle up to his knees.

"Just a lost soul," Casey said softly, knowing there was no way to speak of what he'd seen, no words to describe a creature that should not exist during this tick of the earth's clock. A white creature of impenetrable solitude who had risked its life for a glimpse of the moon. Who had wanted to feel, just once, the blessing of light upon its face. However many thousands of years separated its kind from his own he could understand that. How you could risk shattering your own soul just to feel the wash of moonlight on your skin.

"Are ye alright?" Pat asked, upright now and looking quizzically into his face.

"Fine," he said faintly. Meeting his brother's eyes, Casey knew Pat had seen it too and that neither of them would ever speak of it to the other.

"Where shall we camp for the night?" Pat, shivering in his soaked clothes, had returned to the realm of practicality.

A small cloud sifted across the face of the moon, a bit of out-flung ether, enough to cast a shadow. Casey shivered in turn and felt superstition, primal and unsheathed, settle on his bones.

"As far from the water as we can get," he replied.

Chapter Twelve
Altar Boys and Angels

What advantages were possessed by an occupied, as distinct from an unoccupied bed?' James Joyce had asked it first, Jamie pondered it now. Joyce had answered— '*the removal of nocturnal solitude, the superior quality of human (mature female) to inhuman (hot water jar) calefaction, the stimulation of matutinal contact, the economy of mangling done on the premises...*' and so forth. Practical reasons certainly and not without their own homely romance but not entirely applicable to a man silly enough to bring a nineteen year old, rather forward thinking, much too attractive girl away for the summer in some misguided notion that he was saving her from herself. Saving her for himself might have been more accurate, though Jamie, with some days of summer still facing him, didn't want to look too closely at his motives.

At home, in the sprawling interior of Kirkpatrick's Folly, he had not thought of what close proximity might mean. What living in a three bedroom, low-beamed snug of a cottage might actually be like. The result of which was they spent a great deal of time out-of-doors.

The cottage, for it couldn't actually be properly considered a house, was flung down by a harsh hand in the hollow of two long, sloping hills, which bore a close resemblance to an old woman's sagging breasts. It was situated on a long, narrow ribbon of farmland, complete with cows, sheep and a small dairy. A working farm where he'd spent his summers as a boy, learning the value of working with one's own hands. As the years progressed, he'd spent less time here, though he always tried for at least a few weeks in the summer. Hard work cleared his head, enough of it and he wasn't able to think at all. He'd found refuge in that state before, he wondered if that's what he sought now. If so, it wasn't helping a great deal. Sleep seemed not the only appetite whetted by the clear air and long, sunny days.

Their days had acquired a rhythm that hugged the land and animals. Up at dawn with the cows, followed by a breakfast they took turns making. Out again to work in the garden, both flower and vegetable. Jamie, who had understood the soil and its moods from a very young age, found in Pamela an avid student of horticulture. He taught her what plants were hardy, which fragile, which flourished in shade and which in sun. He gave her the Latin names, showed her what was poison in large amounts and healing in small. How to coax and encourage the haughty plants, when to behead the roses and when to leave them to die on the stem.

Lunch then and a few free hours in the afternoon, during which time he conducted what business he could from this remote corner of the world, made decisions at his kitchen table that would affect hundreds of lives, and tried not to think about how much he needed a drink.

Pamela spent her afternoons walking around the lake that sat in a bowl at the lowest point of the property, horseback riding, or pretending to read the Republican literature he'd given her while actually idly daydreaming in the hammock.

He watched her now as she ambled and skipped along the shore of the lake. Montmorency (a stray dog who'd shown up on the first night and refused to leave since) following in her wake, a bright-brindled, lollop-eared, sun-stippled gadfly. He was quite possibly the ugliest dog God had ever seen fit to set onto the earth and Pamela loved him to spoiled distraction. The affection was returned in unstinting full measure, doubled and trebled with the tongue lolling abandon only canines could manage, causing Jamie to wonder if dogs didn't have it all sewn up in a way humans could never aspire to.

Sitting at the table, papers ruffled by a slight breeze that came in the open door, he closed his eyes, felt the elements as they touched her singly, the sand soft-sucking at her toes, the pop and snap of shell-souled creatures. Delicate, luminous, exposed to shrivelling air. And what of air, air that sought with unfeeling digits declivities hot and healing and played wimple-fingered through swirls of silken hair. And light, solar light laying skeins of distilled sunflower down forearm and flank, kissing here, blinding there.

'*Behold the handmaid of the moon.*' Moon or sun, did it matter? She had become for him a coruscation of flame, beauty that stood on the razor edge of terror, light that he could only just bear.

He opened his eyes and saw her turn, wave at him and continue on her way. Oh yes, light. *Angel, if I had the courage to reach out my hand, would you have the sense to see that it does not grasp but only warns you, turns you away? That my currents would drown you even as they pushed you far from me? For I am afraid here on my hill, in my exile..*

'*Touch me. Soft eyes. Soft, soft, soft hand. I am lonely here. O, touch me soon, now... I am quiet here alone. Sad too. Touch, touch me...*' Joyce again, bloody man had understood too much about ineluctable human yearning. About the dreams of the cripple.

And what did she dream? He knew too well. Her dreams were written plain, lay swimming in heavy-lidded eyes and indolent limbs. She dreamed her dark-eyed boy, the one who brought fire in his hands and flood with his heart.

And what of his own role? There was, in this play, no part for the paternal. He had tried to father that which no longer needed nor wanted to be fathered. He'd been a reluctant actor at best. No, it was greed that had brought him here, greed for the things he'd seen in her eyes, the flush in her cheek, the pretty cravings that played across her consciousness and showed themselves plain in her movement and expression. Yet he could not quite bring himself to return her to Belfast, to what waited there for her, to the loneliness that would again be his companion when she was gone.

He returned with a sigh to the papers before him. Three of the huge mechanical looms needed replacing at the linen mill. Four of his best men at the distillery were nearing retirement and he'd no one of equivalent skill to replace them and a middle-aged woman, Penny McGee, mother of five children, had been hurt badly and would require the setting up of a compensatory package and would likely not be returning to work any time in the near future. These things were small matters, dealt with easily. Retirement funds were generous and Jamie's grandfather had long ago set the custom of the gift of a trip to any destination a man might wish upon retirement. The Kirkpatrick tradition held that you looked after your workers and they would look after you, a theory that had stood the test of time and benefited all over the years.

He rubbed the crease in his forehead and idly flipped the pages of *The Irish Times*. Generally, he tried to avoid news from home during his weeks here, it was time out of time and he needed no reminder of what troubles lay at home. The same troubles for hundreds of years, technologically updated, dressed in different clothes, but wrapped in the same despair, futility and frustration they had always come bound in. But this summer, between the lines of ink, he could smell smoke. The north was beginning to smolder, threatening to ignite and torch them all in the process. It was, as such matters were, only a matter of time.

In Derry, small tongues of flame were already beginning to lick at the tinder of age-old hates. Pretty Derry, with its famous walls, winding river and green fields, its very name a point of divisiveness. Londonderry to the Protestants, Derry to the Catholics, who wanted no reminder in their city of the bastion of imperialism across the sea. Men had been beaten, and badly, for using the wrong name in the wrong pub.

Derry was an obvious flashpoint. The last stronghold of the Protestant, the place where they had beat back the Catholics three hundred years before and not let them forget it since. Derry where the Apprentice Day March was strutted along the walls to anthems of bigotry and pennies were thrown down into the slums of the Bogside. It had always puzzled Jamie this, that men who lived in relative harmony despite religious and political differences all year could turn into beasts of an entirely different nature during one mad week each summer.

Lucien Broughton had been present at both the marches in Derry and Belfast. Jamie had to admit the man knew his business, knew where he had to establish a foothold. The speech he'd given on the lawns of Stormont was still being talked about a week later. His rhetoric had been carefully honed, filled with small tidbits for the subconscious. There had been nothing overtly hateful, even the *Times* had taken a hopeful slant on it. This worried Jamie more than if the man had been blatantly vile; there was something that smelled very bad about the whole situation. There was a picture of the Reverend, arms spread like an avenging angel, face wearing the look of a mad, medieval saint. Jamie felt a small ticking fear begin to turn over right then in his heart. As much as he did not want to be some inadequate replacement for the hope his father had given a community, he wondered if perhaps he'd made a dreadful and irrevocable mistake by refusing to enter the fight against Lucien Broughton.

"Jamie."

He started, scattering papers onto the floor, where a few caught the faint summer breeze and drifted dreamily out the door.

"Yes," he said more sharply than he'd intended, feeling like a child who's been caught out with its hand in the cookie jar.

"It's a lovely day," she said, leaning into the doorframe, tanned and slightly flushed from the sun, hair in an untidy ponytail, long legs bare and dusty.

"It is," Jamie agreed carefully.

"It's only that—well I thought a picnic would be nice. We haven't had a picnic all summer."

"We haven't?" Jamie said incredulously.

"No," she said almost shy, a long ringlet of loose hair blowing across her throat and causing Jamie to swallow hard.

"Well then we must fix that now, today, in fact this very minute," he stood, thinking it was quite possible he was about to take complete leave of his senses.

"I'll pack the food if you get the horses," she said, and Jamie, knowing her idea of a good meal was an extra spoonful of peanut butter on her bread, was tempted to say no. There was such an eagerness in her face though that he merely nodded and headed out to the stable to get the horses.

HE HAD DETERMINED, SOME SHORT TIME AGO, that a man of his years and experience ought to be able to draw and keep the invisible line between propriety and the seduction of a teenage girl. No matter how aggravating and bewitching said girl was.

It was rather easy to be noble, Jamie reflected wryly, when the object of your indecent lust was not in view and an infinitely more delicate matter when her lovely denim-bottomed self was only feet away adjusting the stirrups on her saddle. Looking altogether too alluring in her thin cotton shirt, the color of late summer delphiniums, her hair a slovenly mess of curls that served to make her look like a hungover nymph the night after a particularly decadent bacchanal.

They rode in silence, the air heavy with thoughts unspoken but sensed nevertheless. Past a gurgling brown brook, through a field dark with dying heather, into a pine wood where the smell of sap, flushed out with the heat, was sticky and ripe on the air.

Pamela, cantering slightly behind and away from Jamie, found herself in an altogether unwelcome flux of emotion. There were only a few weeks left to the summer and then they would be back in Belfast and she would have to make a choice. To stay under this man's roof, to be wrapped in the warmth and headiness of his governance or to keep the silent promise she had made to Casey with a single kiss. She could not keep a foot in each world, not with the earth threatening to crack apart beneath her. She could not continue to pretend that she was in any way the equal of this man who rode beside her with effortless grace.

His was a terrible beauty, an aching, tearing thing that was best left alone. She could not stay, even if her dreams, pale in the light of reality had been tempered by respect and care. Even if—she gave a weak smile as Jamie turned, gilt eyebrows lifted, green eyes soft—even if the man could have her very soul if he but asked. For he would not ask, of that much she was certain.

"Penny for your thoughts," Jamie's voice intruded on her musings causing her to flinch guiltily and flush. "Though perhaps they're worth more. To judge by the look on your face I ought to have offered a hundred pound or so." The knowing grin on his face hit a nerve and made her retort more stingingly than she'd intended.

"Perhaps your Lordship there's not enough money in all your overflowing coffers to make me spill my private thoughts." So saying she flashed him a look of icy disdain and spurred her horse to gallop.

Racing full tilt without a care for her safety was the only way it seemed she could outrun all the yearning in her soul. If only she could always go far enough, fast enough to obliterate the hold he had over her.

She didn't see the tree until it was too late to veer away, the young whip-like ends of its arcing branches catching her full across the face, blinding her and completely unnerving the horse who threw her instantly.

Jamie was upon her in seconds. "Pamela are you alright? Blink if you can't speak."

He felt the length of her body with light, deft hands. "Nothing's broken."

"I—I," she stuttered, trying vainly to draw breath, feeling as if a very large fist had mashed her kidneys.

"I think you've knocked the wind from yourself." Jamie helped her into a sitting position then rubbed her back in great broad circles until she at last drew in a shaky breath.

"There now, there's a girl, are you hurt anywhere else?"

"No," she replied with what dignity could be salvaged in her current position, "and please don't address me as if I were one of your great bloody, broody mares."

Jamie's relief quickly turned to anger.

"What the hell were you doing, spurring him on like that? You could have broken his leg and your own bloody neck in the bargain." He looked at her in exasperation as she gingerly clutched her ribs with one hand and bit the back of her other to refrain from laughing.

"Women," was Jamie's final and inadequate pronouncement as he got to his feet and scanned the horizon for the horse.

"He'll go to the pond; he drinks like he's a camel about to cross the desert. We'll find him there. Besides it's a lovely spot for a picnic," she cast a glance at the basket his obedient gray mare carried. "Please don't be angry, Jamie."

"Come on then," he said in as short a tone as he knew how to manage.

She wanted to scream at him, to ask why his memory held no echo. That she had laughed because they had, so precisely, been here before. Instead, she mutely took his hand up into the saddle.

The pond sat in the middle of a glade of pine, a still body of water, murky brown and edged with grass bent over and wilted from the heat. The air, strong with resin, was still and heavy.

Jamie helped Pamela down from the horse, found a shady spot to tether it just as her own horse, aptly named Lickety-Split, ambled into the clearing, reins dangling, blowing drops of water off his lips and looking supremely pleased with himself. Jamie unsaddled him and tethered him near his own horse.

When he turned back, a blanket had been spread upon the burned grass, food laid out that was in quality and form, rather alarming. Item by item his consternation grew as each toothsome delicacy was revealed in all its aphrodisiacal glory. Oysters, gray, chill and raw, figs melting in their own sugar, strawberries with a complement of Devonshire cream and a bottle of Chateau du Papillon Blanc 1954 (a very good year, though hardly the picnicker's choice). The food of seduction, not subtle and somehow all the more effective for it. And in the midst of it, Lolita, bare feet limned with dirt, nose dusted with freckles, a strawberry tucked in her cheek along with a flush that told him she was frightened of her own audacity.

"What, no peanut butter and jelly?" he asked lightly, finding a seat on the grass beyond the blanket.

"No, I thought a picnic called for something a bit grander." Still flushed and uncertain, she poured two glasses of wine near to overflowing and handed him one.

"Tell me about her, Jamie," she said quite suddenly, nibbling on a fig in a manner as to make him believe that her virtue, such as it was, had better make a run for its life.

"About whom?" he asked, quite used by now, to her abrupt turn-abouts in conversation.

"The woman who taught you the art of love."

The opening gambit, a bold move, designed to knock distracting pawns off the board with one sweep. Jamie decided to play.

"What makes you think I know anything about the art of love?" he asked, reclining on his elbows, a look of curious amusement on his face.

"Even a girl of twelve knows the difference between a man who simply loves a series of different women in his life and a man who adores the entirety of female kind and knows—yes knows," she stated, emphatically ignoring his grin, "how to really love a woman. And that would indicate to me—" she paused to take a swallow of her champagne, blissfully unaware that near to five hundred francs of bubbles had just slid down her slender throat, "that a woman taught you the finer points. Oh, the instinct was there from birth, I've no doubt, but only a woman could have brought it into full flower."

"Indeed," replied Jamie, feeling rather like a petunia must with a brimming water can poised above its wide open head.

"Yes," she replied, warming to her subject and Jamie noted with a twinge of alarm, filling her glass for the second time. "You see, my father, who I might add, attracted women in only slightly smaller droves than yourself, told me that for a man to truly love a woman, love her as she needs to be loved, must be loved in order that she not wither away on the stem before her prime. For her to blossom fully," (all these metaphorical flowers, Jamie mused, were making him feel a bit like a bee who'd overdone it on the nectar) "she must have a man who knows how to respond innately to her cues without needing to be given point for point instructions." This last given added emphasis by the tossing back the remains of her second (or was it third?) flute of Chateau du Papillon Blanc, 1954. She was beginning to sport a perilously reckless glint in her eyes.

If he'd the sense of a tiny, wee gopher, Jamie reflected later, he would have taken his pieces, one by one, without hurting or alarming her, off the board and made it clear he could not be a partner to this game. A woman was truly one of the great luxuries, the necessities a man simply could not do without. And a woman such as this one, fine and rare, eloquent and bold, was rather like having a case of the very best scotch set in front of an alcoholic with the three day shakes. Surely though her question was harmless, she had asked and he struck into obliging by a combination of the sun's fist, alcohol and a lurking weakness, would answer. Anything would be easier than watching her toss back champagne and oysters, with one sinuous toss of shiny black curls, as if she'd been fed them in her crib.

"Her name was Clothilde and she was thirty-one and I was eighteen."

"A-ha, a Frenchwoman, the best of teachers."

"Your father's sage wisdom again?" Jamie commented with a light sarcasm.

She nodded, taking the time to finish her delicate munching on a whisper-thin slice of toast burdened with paté. "He said that every woman should have an Irishman at least once, and every man, a Frenchwoman—a ripe one, I believe were his exact words."

"Have?" Jamie inquired.

"In the biblical sense of course," she said sweetly.

"Of course," he echoed rather stupidly, wondering if somehow the alcohol she was drinking was affecting him.

"Please continue," she prompted, as if he were the rather slow schoolboy he presently felt himself to be.

"As I said, her name was Clothilde and she was a lady in the grandest sense of the word, the French sense if you will—"

"Ah, I see it, four impossibly perfect Chanel suits in sensible colors, black of course for lunch meetings, Mainbocher for days in the country, Dior for evenings out and very special occasions. But nevair ze frippery of say a St. Laurent, no—no St. Laurent is ze stuff of dreams, not hard-line serious couture. She knew the perfect wines, her Brie was always just the right temperature, her servants knew their place and she had a collection of lingerie that would give a harem the night sweats."

He had best, Jamie thought with some alarm, hide what little was left of the champagne. He was slightly amazed by her assessment of Clothilde, she'd come very close and indeed her servants had known their place. Unlike, it would seem, his own employees.

"She was a Madame, not some inconsequential mademoiselle."

"A married woman, Jamie? My respect for you grows immeasurably."

He eyed her with mock sternness, "One more interruption and I'll not give you another word of my lurid tale."

"I shall be a paragon of silence, pray go on." She made a creditable attempt at seriousness, spoiling the gesture by lying down on her front, hands propped into fists under her chin. The Queen flashing the Bishop a naughty bit of leg, he supposed. He sighed and resumed his story.

"Her husband died in his eighties, most honorably acquitting himself to the end, dying in a manner entirely befitting a French gentleman of his means and advanced years. Meaning of course that he died in his mistress' arms."

"Was she very beautiful—Clothilde I mean?" Picking the crown off a strawberry, Pamela had apparently forgotten her recent vow of silence.

"In a refined manner, like purest Meissen china, looks very fragile but in reality is tougher than hell." Memory, rather than distraction, bore him along on his tale now. "Her hair was very pale, ash-blonde I suppose you'd call it but her eyes were dark, so dark there seemed hardly any separation between pupil and iris. She did wear Chanel and Dior and, just for your note, she thought St. Laurent was a genius. She had that certain something, a grace of carriage, a presence, a bit like Grace Kelly after she became the Princess of Monaco."

His mind, aided by the champagne, was drifting back along the current of recollection, to that summer in the south of France. Clothilde de Rengac had been a friend of the family, her father having done business with two generations of the Kirkpatricks. As a child he'd admired her from afar, she was quiet, not easy to know and he suspected later, stifled by rank and religion. As he'd grown, his admiration had become more frank. She had never, for all her formality, condescended to him. His opinions she listened to with interest, finding them of worth, never dismissing him as a child. They'd spent hours discussing poetry, music, authors and philosophy as well as lighter topics.

Jamie had been at her wedding, watched her drift, hauntingly pale and drawn, down the aisle to join her life with that of a sixty-year-old minister of the French cabinet and had seen her, in that centuries old act, grow immeasurably ancient. She had become what so many women before her had been, a chattel, a bit of goods sold to the highest bidder. Clothilde had, as those in her circle were wont to say, married very well. In Jamie's opinion, it was the poorest match he'd ever seen made.

'Exchanges, James,' she'd told him some time later, 'marriage in my world and no doubt many others, is about exchanges. I have something Henri wants, and in return he has something my family is desperate for." The somethings as it turned out were her family name, one of the oldest and bluest in France, which came with all the rarefied privilege and respect that Henri so craved. In exchange, Clothilde's family had access to his numerous and very lucrative business contacts. Clothilde however, was not quite as valuable as Henri had first estimated, for after five years of marriage and numerous consultations with a variety of specialists it was concluded that Clothilde was unable to conceive, she was, in that cruelest of summations, barren.

'Ah James,' she'd said as they lolled about one lazy summer afternoon in Provence, first editions of Byron, Shelley and Jamie's omnipresent Yeats scattered in the grass about them. 'Have you not heard the words, 'when I was a child I spake as a child, I thought as a child but now I am a man and have put the things of childhood away?' Love is the thought, the wish of a child. I have learned slowly and yes painfully to put away the wishes and dreams of a child. But I never thought, not once, to be denied the joy, the absolute right to see those dreams in the faces of my children, no I did not. Bitterness is a very bad thing James; try never to drink from its cup, for the taste can become appealing in a perverse fashion. Just a few sips are enough to make an addict."

He had kissed her for the first time that day, hardly knowing how long he'd wanted to. She had let him, let him kiss her with all the pain and passion his tender young heart had felt, but after she had shook her head sadly and said 'no James, as much as we might desire it, some things are simply not possible.'

That had not been her opinion the following summer, his eighteenth. He was spending an idle month of it in France, free from the teachings of Jesuits, headed for Oxford in the autumn. Caught between an ending and a beginning, he was in a poor humor, he'd never liked those lapses in time, they made him feel quite lost. He attended a dinner with her and Henri, to which Henri saw fit to invite his mistress. Clothilde, all things considered, had been perfectly composed, gracious to all who sought her company, though Jamie had noticed she was a shade or two paler than was usual. She made the excuse of a headache to their hostess early in the evening, and left without so much as a glance in Henri's direction.

"Jamie will you take me home please," was all she said, but he had noticed her use of the more familiar form of his name and wondered at it. She'd taken his arm in what he perceived as tightly controlled rage and smiling politely, left the house. He was not, as it turned out, completely off the mark in his assumption, only mistaken about the precise nature of her anger.

"Jealous?" she had scoffed in reply to his question. "Oh my naïve boy, that is absurd. Of course I know of his mistresses, that is hardly shocking, in fact I approve of it wholeheartedly, it saves me a great deal of unpleasant business, does it not? No Jamie, it is the humiliation—that he should flaunt her so publicly, so flagrantly in front of our friends, in front of the President, *mon dieu*, it is unthinkable that he should be so—so stupid, so disregarding of the proprieties. Dignity is precious little, but it is what I have in this marriage." She had turned away then, but Jamie had seen some unnameable quantity in her face that he hoped never to see again.

She came to his room that night, once again composed, dressed in a white silk peignoir, seeming no more than the girl he'd first known her to be. She'd stood silent as Jamie hastened to cover himself with the Kirkpatrick linens she had his bed freshly made with each morning. Then she'd come towards him slowly, sitting on the edge of his bed with the dignity of a born princess, sadly fragile in the light of a summer moon.

"Would you make love to me Jamie, just this once, make me feel like the woman I have never had the privilege of being. If I thought you would find this task distasteful I would not ask, but the desire in your eyes mirrors the desire I have kept hidden."

Jamie, with a knowledge older than his eighteen years, knew she did not want words, could not indeed have borne them. She wanted no declarations of love, no messy *scandale* from which to extricate herself, so Jamie gave his heart in silence, for no matter the cost to himself he would never cause her a moment of pain.

And so he made love to her gently at first, then with a wildness of heart he'd been unaware of possessing. Clothilde stayed with him all that night, leaving only when dawn streaked into view. Returning, he knew, to her rooms before the household staff arose. Henri might have reneged on the delicate deal of their marriage but Clothilde de Rengac had not been raised for such unseemly behavior.

Their affair continued throughout that summer, Jamie learning bit by bit the subtleties and nuances, the thousand shades of gray that lay at the foundation of every woman.

There were only two instances in Clothilde's life when her rigidly set mask slipped, one was when she made love with Jamie, and the other was to come years later, in a manner he had not wished to see.

It seemed hardly more than yesterday and yet a lifetime away. The last time he'd made love to Clothilde, out in the country, away from suspicious eyes, she had discarded his clothes along with her own. She'd drunk him in with unabashed pleasure, knowing it was the last day, the final time, basking herself in the pained adoration that shone from his own eyes.

She had cried a little, afterwards, clinging to him in a manner so foreign to her sharply controlled nature, that he knew it came from depths she could scarcely acknowledge.

It was the way he remembered her. Face flushed with love, the heavy branches of an apple tree dappling her face in sunshine and shadow, her hair, fine as a child's spread about her face like watered rays of light. She had grasped his face between her hands and stared at him with a fierceness that made her seem angry.

"Whatever happens Jamie, don't let them sell you, don't be just another part of their ludicrous business dealings. You are too fine for that, keep that sweet soul of yours—swear to me James that you won't let them do that to you, swear to me." Jamie had in his innocence sworn, never knowing for one minute what terrible little tricks life could play upon one.

The next day he flew back to Ireland to prepare for his sojourn at Oxford as five generations of Kirkpatricks had done before him.

His path would not cross Clothilde's again for some years, though he always sent her a breathtaking arrangement of flowers on her birthday and a polite note at Christmas.

Then one wintry day in Paris, where he was conducting a lengthy round of negotiations for the purchase of two Belgian linen mills, he saw a slender figure in a deep gray coat alighting from the back of a silver Daimler. Her ash-blonde hair was a little paler but still not a strand of it out of place.

Henri had died a year earlier and Jamie had sent the proper condolences, though he'd felt congratulations were more in order. Clothilde would finally have her freedom and at forty-two a woman, such as she was, was only coming into her vintage years.

He'd coaxed her into dinner that night and it was then she brought up the past they'd so carefully skirted all afternoon.

"So James you too have grown a little older, perhaps a little wiser. Ah, *mon dieu*, is that a touch of the cynic I see in your eyes? Well, James, that is what comes of breaking promises. Do not give me that puzzled look, acting is not one of your talents. You made me a promise once, not such a long time ago. But you broke it, didn't you? You let them have what was most precious in you for their own ends."

"Life only gives you so many choices," he'd said quietly, eyes turned away from Clothilde's all-seeing dark ones.

"Don't lie to me James, it ill suits your nature. It was an exchange, you gave your dreams to save your father's soul, one of you was cheated though and it wasn't your father."

Jamie made no reply, for Clothilde expected none. He had no argument to make in his defense. She knew as well as he the reasons he'd let go of the deepest desires of his heart, that his father, to whom he'd given love and loyalty without measure all his days, had used the very fineness of his son's character against him in the end.

It wasn't until after they had returned to her beautiful apartment, overlooking the Seine, for after-dinner cognac, that Jamie saw how tired she appeared, how drawn and old.

"Are you ill?" he'd asked bluntly, not knowing how to broach such an unbroachable subject.

"Ill, Jamie what a weak word that is, no I am not ill. I have cancer, some would classify that as ill, but I can reassure you there are many, many worlds between those two words."

He did not need to ask the next question, for it was answered by the quiet desperation that every pore and fiber of her being spoke of. Clothilde would not have her vintage years, would never be granted freedom in this life. She had been given away to an uncaring, thoughtless man years ago and now some unseen force had seen fit to give her over to a disease that in its monstrous, mindless gluttony would clutch and claw at every cell in her body, until it took the very last breath from her. Clothilde, aged forty-two, would never know another moment of freedom in her life.

She would live another eighteen months. Brutal, agonizing months. It would be Jamie who stood by her through the worst of it. He who lived this double life—a wife, pregnant for the second time and terrified, at home and an ex-lover dying in Paris. Flying back and forth, exhausted, fleeing grief in two countries. He who held Clothilde's hand when she wept with pure terror and held her head on the days when her stomach refused to hold so much as a cup of weak tea.

Jamie who buried his second son while Clothilde took a few more steps towards her own grave. Who watched his wife spiral into a depression so severe he feared for her life. It was he who held Clothilde at the end as she hovered somewhere between the agony of the final stage of cancer and the oblivion of drugs. Jamie, who against doctor's orders took her from the sterile confines of the hospital and drove her to her beloved Provence, praying the whole way that she would make it through those last few miles. And so, it was he who held her tightly, like father to child, as she watched the last rites of the world she knew, the rise and fall of the summer moon, the burning fire of a red-gold sun in the dewdrop hours. Jamie who heard her last words.

"Jamie, the colors of my life have been dark, but for one summer I had a rainbow. Thank you, my love, for that season." She'd held his hand tightly, crying a little as the pain came in waves, rhythmic and unceasing. "I will take care of your babies for you, I promise. Remember, in the beginning and in the end there are only dreams."

He had, only minutes later, closed her eyes against a glorious summer morning. Relieved in some small measure that her pain was over and hopeful, in a place very far down, that his baby sons would no longer be alone. Through Clothilde he'd made reparations to the mother who had died so similarly, took care as the man what he could not as the boy.

One year later, there was another son, a wee fiery-headed scrap of a man who was born before his time but unlike his brothers before him, born breathing. Stuart Gordon Kirkpatrick survived only three weeks and when Jamie laid his third son to rest in a little blue velvet-lined casket he closed the door on hope and happiness and saw his wife do the same. Neither spoke of children again, it was a silent agreement. Another death would finish them both. Colleen took refuge in God, had the marriage annulled by taking Holy Orders and went away to live with the Blessed Sisters of Mercy.

In a world that had once seemed so limitless with possibility, so wide open with an unending array of adventure, that had seemed so damn—golden, the lights for Jamie, once an incurable optimist, had dimmed considerably.

"OH JAMIE, I'M SO SORRY, I'd no idea—about your babies—I—"

Jamie came round sharply and suddenly to the realization that he had revealed far more than he'd intended to and that Pamela had tear tracks streaming down her face.

"Sweetheart I'm sorry, I never meant to go on like that. God knows I've been drunk and foolish many a time but I've never babbled on like this."

She disregarded his protest. "Your sons, all three, it seems too cruel to be true. How can you believe in God after He took so much from you?"

"Because I'm a good Catholic boy at heart," he said bitterly and then meeting her eyes gave in to the truth. "I'd nothing else left to believe in and there were plenty of dark nights when I cursed him aloud, but if there's one thing I've learned in this life it's that you've got to believe in something, small or big, or you'll completely lose your hold on living. My sons are with God. So you see if I didn't believe in Him I'd have gone insane."

"Do you still love your wife?"

The very air stilled around the question, as if the heat itself had an ear and waited for his answer.

"I will always love Colleen, but in a different manner now than when we were husband and wife. We grieved our sons together, we will always be bound through them and perhaps being their mother, having carried them under her heart, she may have suffered more than I."

What he did not add was that Colleen had refused to see Stuart, had turned her face to the hospital wall and said she could not bear to know his face, when it would only be gone from her. He, father of first Michael, then Alexander and finally Stuart had dressed them in christening gowns, wrapping their still wee forms in shrouds of baby Irish lace. In awe, even through his pain, of the perfect peacefulness of their faces. He alone sat by Stuart's incubator day and night, willing him to live until the nurses begged him to rest before he himself needed a bed in the hospital. He'd been alone when Stuart ceased his struggle; his paltry three weeks having been a valiant fight, as though from the first he'd felt the angels waiting. Near the end, Stuart had opened his eyes, eyes soft and green as springtime and looked, Jamie would swear to his dying day, directly into his father's eyes.

"He's askin' yer permission to go," a kind nurse had told him. "I've seen it before, they're wise these ones, moren' if they'd lived a hundred years, it's time ye held yer son, Mr. Kirkpatrick. Send him to the angels in yer arms, surely there's no way he'd rather go."

It was the first time he'd held a son living in his arms. He'd been nervous, scared of doing something wrong, of causing him harm or pain. But then Stuart had been placed next to his heart, his head fitting just so into the crook of Jamie's elbow and he'd let the tears fall as he kissed the tiny wee feet, each toe a thing of wonderment and the silky soft head with its fine fuzz of red curls, as delicate as a spider's web with the first glow of dawn upon it. And he said the words that broke his heart forever and took away some part of his wholeness as a man.

"It's alright, wee man, I can see you're tired. You've put up a fight worthy of ten warriors, no one could ever expect more. You sleep now love, Daddy's here and he just wants you to have your peace." He sang to Stuart then, a low and ancient lullaby that spoke of green hills far away, of moonbeam boats that glided through the milky way of dreams and adventures that his son would never know. Stuart Kirkpatrick died that way, secure in his father's arms, with the warmth of his father's voice in his ears.

The German poet Rainer Maria Rilke had once said that man's pain had yet to outlive the garden but Jamie had stopped believing in the garden, had come to see flowers as merely flowers, not a metaphor for some unquenched longing. Here today though, with the heat like a spreading fist gloved in kid leather, he felt a flicker of doubt.

"Is it enough?" she was asking, moving with the one question, her queen out into an extremely vulnerable position.

"Is what enough?"

"This life you lead of books and papers and good manners, is it enough for you?"

"It has to be," he replied gently, knowing that in light of what she was asking it was an inadequate, foolish response.

"Why?" With one word she had opened the board, leaving it clear for his attack, his move. But rather than playing king, he opted for knight errant. He formed the words, lined them neatly up behind his throat, ready to spill them in a steady and mannered flow. But she with the insanity of innocence, bounded on heedless of the realities.

"I'd give you everything," she said, trembling, sun stroking her hair to indigo, hazing her lines. "My heart and soul and everything that goes with it, we could have babies, as many as you wanted, sons and daughters, a house filled with them." She clung to his hand, her own two shaking violently and freezing cold.

There was after all it seemed, an agony he had not experienced and it was this.

He allowed himself a small portion of weakness and with his free hand brushed her face softly, stroking away the tears that had begun to spill. Dear God in heaven but the child meant it, believed it could be.

"It is not possible," he said, "I carry the genes that killed my sons. I am a blight that forecloses the chance of a harvest."

"But—" she began and he, the scent of strawberries ripe and red in his senses, struck out her words.

"I cannot love you and you must not love me," he said gently, firmly and yet unequivocally.

She leaned forward and kissed him. Simply and softly, honey mixed with the thorns of her mouth, the smell of dust and sun and the taste of something sweetly, verdantly green on her tongue.

She felt to him as fragile a dream as the Elysian fields, all the pleasures of

Paradise and none of the pain. Here was water to slake his thirst, here a salve to pull the fever from his bones. She kissed as though it were innate to her, as if she had always known kissing his particular mouth.

Long ago, for reasons of sanity or insanity, he'd sought Reason with its fine and careful lines, its rules and evenly spaced stairs, its well-insulated walls and tightly sealed roof. Passion, with its unbounded field and dark wood was rejected as too dangerous, as limitless, unwalled, unroofed and unstable. To taste was to know addiction with one draught, to be unable, ever, to quit oneself of the flavor and need. To discover, perhaps, that there was a God, to kiss his face and find it angry.

There was, however, nothing of anger to be found here. She felt, in his arms, as natural and essential as air and light. All silken youth, she took his very breath and twisted it, laced it with pain and laughter and gave it back to him filled with life. The taste of it in his mouth was terrifying. Still he followed her to the ground in a natural progression, as water will always find earth.

Her blouse was open to the waist, fragile folds of it falling away like petals from a bruised flower. Her flesh swelled and warmed under his hand, breath tightening and muscles quivering. Ready for him, denying him nothing. Seeking to place all the comfort her body could offer within his grasp. He bowed his head with a reverence he'd never known before, resting his face for a moment in the lovely valley created by her young, high breasts.

He took a deep breath, his senses drowning, struggling to surface. Spring-time and youth in all its bitter green. The dew of dawn bright mornings stirring the dull roots of pain. Grief, long dammed, broke through desire in horrible, choking waves.

She made no exclamations, expressed no surprise, merely cradled him to her breast and made soft, soothing noises, as if she were the mother his had not known how to be. How long he lay there he never knew. How long does it take a man's soul to fall in upon itself, to break and shatter into innumerable pieces and begin the first tentative steps toward re-birth?

As the ebb and flow of exhaustion at last calmed the wrenching pull of his grief he noted somewhat fuzzily that evening had begun its encroach, damping the trees and water with shadow. Small birds, liveried in feathered blue, twittered down towards sleep. He pulled himself with great reluctance from the sticky warmth of Pamela's embrace, covering her gently with the crumpled delphiniums of her blouse. The fracture of parting was physically painful, every cell protesting. He knew his grief had imbedded her within him as a sexual joining would not have done. Blood of my blood and cursed by it, he thought bleakly.

"Jamie?"

He could have wept anew at the unspoken questions that one utterance contained. He forced himself to look up, to see her, to meet the hope that burned hotly in her face.

"I cannot," was all he said, knowing full well he'd go to the grave seeing her stricken look.

"I see," she said with a calm finality, as if indeed she'd always suspected it would come to this between them. She did her buttons up, smoothed the delicate material, unconsciously raveling that which had become so swiftly unraveled between them. Pulling the threads of her torn dignity about her protectively.

"I cannot play moth to your star, Jamie," she said finally, a shadow of something akin to pity in her eyes. "You can't continue to hold me in your hands if you refuse to hold me in your heart."

"Does that mean you won't be coming back to Belfast?"

"In a manner of speaking."

"I suppose it's my turn to see," he said the words costing him far more than he'd anticipated, "you'd best take care, the kind of fire your Casey will take you into will burn a moth until it can't even recognize itself."

The face that turned to him in the dusk was pale but composed.

"It's a very cold world, makes a fire appealing, wouldn't you say?"

She went to her horse, swung up lightly, a flicker of heat in the waning sun. "I'm sorry, Jamie."

"Don't be."

The horse tossed its head, cantering sideways, impatient to be gone from this garden. "Sorry," she continued without contrition, "that you are so afraid of living again, a quick death my father used to say is infinitely preferable to one that takes a lifetime."

The horse took the reins then, and, in a glimmer, they were gone, girl and beast melted away like myth, like life.

And that, he supposed, was checkmate. Or from the Arabic, *shah-matte*, meaning 'the king is dead.'

> *And the heavens reject not:*
> *The desire of the moth for the star,*
> *Of the night for the morrow,*
> *The devotion to something afar*
> *From the sphere of our sorrow.*

Only Shelley could answer Shelley:

> *I can give not what men call love.*

FROM THE GREEK 'KATHOLICOS' MEANING UNIVERSAL *and 'kyriakon' meaning* *'belonging to the Lord' and 'ekklesia' meaning 'assembly' came the Church, the*

Holy Mother Church founded upon the rock of Peter, Her hem wetted by the receding tides of paganism. Bound on earth by Christ's gathering of his disciples in His last days, bound in Heaven by Divine Law. The formation of given over to a simple fisherman, who was to become the shepherd and feed the sheep of the Son of God, the Son of Man.

Peter, keeper of the keys of heaven, denier of Christ, walker on water, a doubter and defender of the first order, a member of the elite circle who walked with Christ on earth. And saw Him shoulder to shoulder with Moses and Elijah after his death. Crucified and buried in Rome, the city that was to become the epicenter of the world's largest religious community on earth. The first Bishop of Rome, the pope.

Grounded in the theology of Paul—madman, zealot, wandering missionary, tentmaker, lover of Timothy, scourged and jailed repeatedly, crushed in the crux of Judaism and Christianity. A Jew for the Jews, a Christian for the Christians, all things to all men in order to be their savior. Speaking in the tongue of men and angels, he preserved the faith through desolation, frustration and personal darkness. He was the writer of some of the tenderest and most passionate love letters in the history of humanity, words written to his flock, his children, known for all time as the Epistles of Paul.

Rival of Peter, he would meet his end in Rome, beheaded and hoping with his last breath to be reunited with his Christ on the road beyond the grave.

The Church was proclaimed as the presence of the Body of Christ on earth. Christ's own humanity would allow all of mankind to be taken fully into the heart and mystery of redemption. All part of The Plan, one no human, struggling in darkness and childlike naïveté could fully understand, for to be taken into the heart of God, to see His face, was to surely die.

Small pockets of Christianity began to establish themselves across Asia Minor, the seeds of faith scattered along the trade routes, the coasts, rivers and roads of the Empire's far-flung interests. From Jerusalem to Damascus, southward, following the scent of spices and sand, into Arabia. Across the burning wastes of Syria into the imperial splendor of ancient Egypt. Across the Adriatic over the Alps men followed the cross and brought the word of the Son of God to all who would hear. To Spain and Gaul and to an island on the edge of oblivion called Britain.

The old religions still existed but their flames were dying low. Judaism, decimated by persecution, taxes and a series of revolts in which Jews sought to recover their homeland and their freedom, gathered about Her huddled and frightened masses, their numbers sadly diminished and poured what fire was left into the pens and scrolls of old men.

In Egypt, they still worshipped their pantheon of sacred creatures. But by the end of the fourth century Isis, Osiris, Ra and the rest would be spirits of memory, not divinity and terrible deeds.

Christianity was the first equal opportunity religion. It cared not for a man's class, nation, nor the circumstance of his birth. All men were inheritors of Christ's salvation. To the downtrodden, the cripple, the maimed, the bereaved it was a promise of a better world, beyond the one that had shown them little more than squalid misery. All men were equal in Christ's eyes, all men capable of holding God within.

With ritual and spectacle, borrowing from pagan rites, Jewish ethics and the metaphysics and philosophy of the Greeks the church gave poetry where before there had only been prose, color to bleakness, light to darkness.

Jesus the Jewish man was abandoned. In his place was created the risen Christ, the god divorced from Judaism and made palatable even to the mouths of anti-Semites. The separation of the cloth of Christianity from the fabric of Judaism was done by a succession of tailors, some infinitely skilled, others who understood little more than hacking and tearing. Paul, Christ's own disciple, made the first cut, many others would follow until the Christian would scorn the idea that Judaism was his rightful mother. Centuries later under the hand of pale-faced fanatics, named Cromwell and Luther, Christianity would move back again toward the aesthetics and stricture of Jewish law and call itself Protestantism.

The fervor and ardency of early Christianity was based in large part on the certainty of Christ's return. The spirit must be made pure and quickly so that it might dwell in Paradise with its maker. Centuries though, ticked over, faded and were gone, a tracery of breath in a universe of fog and still the Prince did not return to the castle. Even the millennium, numbered by the event of his birth, could not lure him back to earth.

In the meantime, though it took three centuries to happen, Rome the Great Whore of Babylon, the Mother who took from the cradle of Greece the infant of Western civilization and nurtured it to young adulthood, was dying. But with her last breath, she gave her maternal blood to the Church, leaving it what strength she might. It was a generous legacy.

In the Church, Caesar and Christ blended and became one, the fiery passion of the Jewish intellect, the love and vision of one solitary man combined with the law and order, discipline and unity of the Roman Empire. Christ died to save all mankind, Rome, to give life to the Church. It was a case of the old making way for the brash newcomer. Birth and death would remain the two great mysteries of the Church and of humankind itself.

The Church would always maintain Rome as its seat, building upon the three pillars of sacrament, mediation and communion, but its supplicants and true believers would take all roads leading from Rome, dispersing upon the winds and taking God with them to every corner and every human being they crossed along the way. Warriors who would both wound and heal as they traveled the rocky road to the Holy City, Jerusalem. Fevered blackbirds from Spain and Portugal who would fly across the water to the New World, under the banner of 'Ad majorem dei Gloriem.' Anything and all for the greater glory of God. Many would give their lives; some would even give their souls trying to convert a race of people who did not want a white God, descending from a white Paradise.

In Ireland it was less Caesar, more Christ. Before Patrick, he who banished snakes and brought God, the Irish had a highly developed society. Nonetheless history, written in part by Rome, would remember them as barbarians, savage Celts, naked and hairy, having barely crawled from the cave. They had an alphabet, extensive literature, poetry and legend, passed down in the oral tradition round fires under star-strained skies. Their art took form in the molds of clay, bronze and gold. They worshipped nature, the sun, stars and moon and populated their land with countless fairies, demons and pointy-eared elves. Their priests were white-robed druids who ruled through magic and controlled the movement of sun and moon, rain and fire, using wands and wheels. They foretold the future, counseled kings, educated the young, formulated law, studied astronomy and faded into extinction with the coming of the other priests, the black-robed ones who would hold sway over the hearts and minds of the Irish for centuries to come.

Perhaps it was inevitable, being bound by water on all sides, to believe that heaven lay across its fluid surface, in the mists. A land where there was nothing of harshness, nothing of pain or treachery, but only music and fairness. The Avalon of the Celts.

But then Patrick came and brought with him a soul divided from nature and the pure longing for another world and a man whose absence seemed the root of all human sorrow. Born in England of a Roman citizen he was christened Patricius, moderately educated, but nevertheless so well versed in his Bible that he could quote it in its entirety. Captured at sixteen by Irish raiders and taken to Ireland, he was to spend the next six years as a pig herder. It was there in the lonely hills that he found God in all His consuming glory. He was devoted, rising each day at dawn to pray in snow, rain or hail, finding in the discomfort some echo of his master's voice.

He escaped to the sea, was picked up by sailors and taken to Gaul. He worked his way back to England and his parents and stayed with them for a few years. But Ireland was in his blood, she called across the sea to him, she came to him in dreams and he knew his return was inevitable. He studied for the priesthood, was ordained and when the Bishop of Ireland, a man by the name of Palladius, died, Patrick was made Bishop and took up the ecclesiastical sword for the church.

A pagan still sat on the throne of Ireland and though Patrick failed to convert him, he was granted permission to establish his mission.

Over the next thirty years of his sojourn in Ireland he would be credited with many miracles, giving sight to the blind, hearing to the deaf, cleansing lepers, casting out demons, raising the dead, but perhaps the real miracle was the conversion of an entire nation from paganism to Christianity. Patrick, former slave and a man who had always been a misfit in the Roman world, brought Christ to Ireland and put Ireland into Christ. Separating the Church from Rome and all the sociopolitical baggage that came with that august city-state. In Ireland the

Church would gain a new face and become irrevocably Irish, giving a sly wink to held over pagan festivities, keeping custom with May Day and All Hallow's Eve but casting away the harsher elements, the ritual sacrifice, the bonds of slavery, the swords of battle.

British Christianity did not recognize the Irish as Christian because they were not Roman. The British believed that the terms Christianity and Roman were one and the same. If you weren't one you couldn't possibly be the other. Patrick's cry to heaven may have been the first Irish cry to God for the implacability of the British heart but it certainly wouldn't be the last.

'Can it be that they do not believe that we have received one baptism or that we have one God and Father? Is it a shameful thing in their eyes that we have been born in Ireland?' The answer may well have been yes, both then and fifteen centuries later.

Even the British could not alter Patrick's legacy to the Irish and Irish Catholicism would always retain some traces of paganism and be, at its heart, inherently Irish. Patrick, for his own part, established monasteries and nunneries, ordained priests, built churches and left his children well-guarded spiritually from the older order and religion, which had begun its death throes when Patrick first alit on the shores of the island. He died in 461 AD , an Irishman on Irish soil.

Two offshoots of Patrick's legacy were literacy and the formation of the Church in Ireland around the central hub of monasteries. Monks, seeking non-violent martyrdom, would seek out a remote spot beyond the pale of tribal boundaries. There in huts of daub and wattle, shaped like beehives, they sought solitude, shared only with the Lord. But martyrs inevitably attract their like and soon small communities of beehive abodes would spring up around these men, forming communities, which in turn threw out their own tendrils of succor attracting even more people. These monasteries would often become centers of learning and one of these would even become a university of sorts, attracting students from all parts of Ireland, Britain and Europe.

Never literary snobs, the monks filled their libraries with every book that came to hand. All of Christian doctrine devoured and copied, they did not shirk from the delights of Greek and Latin pagan literature. Words were of value merely for being words, no language too far above or below their interest to be of merit. Much of the literature that survived the dark ages that were devouring Europe was owed to the long, candlelit nights of patient Irish monks, copying millions of words and giving all of humanity a priceless gift.

There would be saints to follow Patrick, Columcille who would go to war over a book and be exiled from the land he loved for taking up arms. He would suffer the same fate as millions of his countrymen would centuries later, banished to another land, fated to die on foreign soil and never to cease dreaming of Ireland. Brigid, well believed to be the saint most influential after Patrick. A rebellious noblewoman, cast away from her family for her love of the poor and afflicted, she was to rule as High Abbess over a double monastery, an institution that admitted and housed novitiates of both genders. She was the center of her own city, a city of supreme beauty and countless wonders, where the treasure of kings was guarded well and numberless crowds came to festivals, came to watch, came to worship, came for safety and sanctuary.

In the meantime, continental Europe had fallen into a darkness it would not emerge from for centuries. In the first decade of the fifth century, a horde of barbarians crossed the frozen Rhine and broke what had once seemed unbreakable, the line of Roman defense and the backbone of the Empire. Rome fell under the onslaught of illiterate barbarians, crumbling into the dustpile of history, while Christianity clung to life on barren rocks in the Atlantic Ocean. The Germanic hordes, who, in seeking Rome destroyed it, warmed their hands over the blaze of libraries, burning thousands of years of history without a qualm, unable to read, they neither understood nor cared for the power of books.

Scholars of all description and denominations fled to Ireland, a land out beyond the recollection of the Empire, a green and quiet oasis in a world gone mad. Bone-thin Egyptian aesthetics carrying Coptic script, cloth-bound Armenians with the gleam of fanaticism in their eyes, olive-skinned Syrians still smelling of sand and the scorch of desert sun, all fleeing the wrath of hairy, smelly barbarians who would usher in the Middle Ages, a time of illiterates ruling illiterates, when Christianity would be narrowed down to something hard and mean that Christ had certainly never intended.

Ireland at peace, housed the monks who copied the books that were left in the world, they living in their bee-loud glade were the last literary culture as the Roman eagle vanished from the skies and human memory. Only one thing stood between Ireland and Europe and that was England. Columcille, leaving Ireland, crossed that divide. Following him were monks who wandered Europe trading books, small pockets of light in a continent of darkness. Most of them would never see the shores of their mother country again. With them went the institution of the Irish monastery, the seeds of which would begin to spring up all over Europe. 'They changed their skies but not their souls.' And saved civilization as we know it.

But as was inevitable the world found them out and the Vikings found them sleeping the sleep of those too long used to peace. The tall red men came in off Northern seas to pillage, rape, torture and destroy all that lay in their path. For some three hundred years, fires would blaze across Ireland burning monasteries and the communities they were the center of, again and again.

There would never really be peace again for Ireland, for not far behind the Vikings came the Normans. And though the Normans became as it was said 'more Irish than the Irish themselves' those who followed would not show the same inclination to blend in with the local culture. The Elizabethans would come and plunder the forests in an attempt to flush out the natives who had already learned that they could not meet the British on their ground and trust them and so took *to the forests and fought them guerrilla style. The British would also contemplate the complete annihilation of the Irish people but would save that task for Cromwell who would come a century later and almost achieve the task of genocide. It was Cromwell who would pass law forbidding Catholics to own land anywhere but in the westernmost and least fertile portion of Ireland, known as Connacht.*

Ireland had been held by the British since 1171 under the excuse that the island could be used by France or Spain as a base of attacks, but it had never really been conquered and, as the British would learn to their own sorrow, the Irish never would be conquered. This knowledge, however, did not stop the British from trying. Elizabeth I saw a Catholic Ireland as a dire threat to Protestant England and to that end ordered an enforcement of Protestantism throughout the island. Mass was outlawed, monasteries closed down, priests survived only by going into hiding, able to administer to a scant few. Irish society, deprived of its moral underpinning, descended into chaos. Murder, rape and theft abounded. The Irish leaders appealed to the Pope for help and he in turn sent an Irish blackbird, a devoted and courageous man, a Jesuit, home. His name was David Wolfe and he, in establishing forbidden missions and secretly bringing in other Jesuits to administer to the people, gave the people back some glimmer of hope.

Under Elizabeth's iron fist, the Irish, never a people to take no for an answer, continued to rise again and again, fighting recklessly and bravely. Elizabeth would respond with massacres in which men, women and children were all put to the sword. Famine left some counties almost entirely bereft of their native people. Peace, bought with blood and souls, came in the form of desolation. The seeds of it scattered with a bountiful hand by the English would sow a hatred so entrenched that it would divide Ireland from England forever.

After Cromwell and his pogroms came the Penal Laws, denuding Catholics of the most basic of human rights. The light of Ireland began to seek warmer shores, she would lose her great minds to countries that could feed and nurture them. Swift, Burke, Goldsmith, Sheridan, all of one nation, divided and sundered before God.

Catholic resistance to English rule, borne of dread desperation, was sporadic and ineffectual. The leaders of uprisings inevitably found their end on the scaffold, many barely past boyhood, still with the flush of youth on their cheek.

Still the Irish, spirits indomitable, managed to survive, occasionally to flourish. The famines, however, took a final and wretched care of that. As one million died, another million and a half fled and by 1914 that number would swell as another four million emigrated and spread over the face of the earth.

In the wake of the famines, the Catholic Church rose from the ashes and took firm hold of what was left of the Irish people. The Church was always involved in national events, backing the Protestant lawyer, Charles Stewart Parnell in his campaign for Home Rule and destroying him just as ably when it was revealed he was having an affair with a married woman.

After the failure of the 1916 Rising, Ireland was divided, north and south, Ulster and Free State. Because the Free State was so overwhelmingly Catholic, the newly formed government decided to build much of its policy around Catholic teaching. As a result, in 1925, divorce was outlawed and in 1930 a censorship board was established. Eamon de Valera, the newly crowned head of state, drafted a new constitution that relied heavily on Catholic moral and social teaching. It was tyranny of a subtle sort, ensuring the continued exile of the twentieth century's greatest writer, James Joyce and forcing an unnatural piety on the Irish people. And yet the nation, decimated with war and famine, crippled by the loss of so many of her children, would manage to give the world, in the twentieth century, the eternal lights of William Butler Yeats, George Bernard Shaw, Samuel Beckett, John Millington Synge, Sean O'Casey and Brendan Behan, the angry young man with a pub-installed typewriter under one hand and a drink in the other. Words, not religion, would be the savior of the Irish people.

The Irish survived and so, clinging with the slenderest of threads at times, did the Catholic Church, until it came to seem at times that the one term was interchangeable with the other. Irish and Catholic, Christ and Caesar hand in glove, presiding over a nation too small to bear the weight of Rome comfortably, too firelit to linger long in its shadow.

*J*AMIE HAD BEEN BORN INTO A *C*ATHOLIC FAMILY *who adored the Church in theory and abandoned it in principle. Rites of passage were held to, however, and he had known the perfume of chrism upon his forehead as a baby and as a young boy. He had been mesmerized by the scent and smoke of the thurible, sweetly numbed by the call and response of the antiphonal songs. Caught in the webbing of memorized, rhythmic prayers. Made safe by a burning candle under the benign gaze of a blue-robed Mary at night. Secure in the arms of such an ancient mother, who knew her children in a way no young offshoot ever could.*

The Kirkpatrick household of his childhood had been one of long silences broken by bouts of parties, social evenings, great throngs of artists, writers, actors and activists sprawled about on beds, couches, carpets, smoking, eating, drinking, laughing and singing into the wee hours. A quiet child, Jamie had watched through banisters and from around corners, smelling the perfumes of tobacco, whiskey and more exotic, less definable substances. Had seen his mother whirl at the center of it all like some bright, burning avian-hearted creature, who would singe if you touched her. She had been all motion, forever going out the door or coming in with a horde of bohemians, a rabble of dispossessed who alternately spoiled and ignored the small son of the woman they adored. Caught up in causes, the more hopeless the better it seemed, in the life of the mind, in the extension of the soul into artistry, Jamie's mother had been unable to stop running. She seemed afraid that if she were ever to stop some horrible, unnamed thing would catch and consume her alive. Perhaps she'd been right, though, for when she was thirty-two and Jamie only ten, the unnamed thing became a known quantity, cancer. The quietness had descended audibly then, memories clustering and becoming more real than the woman who'd clung to life still in the bed down the hall.

He could smell the sickness in her and it had, at his tender age, frightened him. It was the smell of decay and fear, of some monstrous thing completely out of control and Jamie had been terrified of catching it, of awakening one morning and feeling that horrible, growing, leeching thing sliding and slipping through him, surviving on his oxygen, destroying his life and its own through greed. So he, in some ways his mother's son, had run. And found Colleen MacGregor and been given unstintingly her family and a safe place to hide.

The MacGregors were stalwart Catholics and Jamie, mercilessly scrubbed and polished with Colleen's two brothers, was taken to church each and every Sunday. It was a refuge, a place of comforting mystery. Where someone could lay their hands upon your head and give you the gift of the secrets of the universe. He went into it fully, without hesitation, giving himself over with the passion his childhood had not allowed otherwise. Felt the strange rapture of the Eucharist when the bread was placed in his mouth, heard the whisper 'this is my body' and accompanying the wine, 'this is my blood' with a shiver rooted in his spine. Had confessed his sins in the misery of certainty that he was stained forever black and been physically relieved to know the Church always took her children back to her bosom, forgave, if not necessarily, forgot. Found comfort in the jet beads of the rosary clicking over, an unending cycle of man's plaintive cry to heaven.

He'd watched as his mother was given Last Rites, had held her hand and prayed silently along with the priest's audible words. Had felt life pull slowly away, like the tide going out from the shore and finally retreating altogether.

In the years that followed he'd lost himself in the Church, been tutored by Jesuits ablaze with their faith. He'd even considered Holy Orders himself, had wanted to burn alive in the crucible of ecstasy and agony that love of God seemed to promise. Had found himself one night, in a fit of adolescent passion, clinging to the gates of a monastery, certain he'd found his destiny and aware on a level he couldn't acknowledge that he did not possess the key nor the character to open those gates. Still, in the ignorance of youth, he'd pursued the star. His mentor, a gentle man named Father Lawrence Loyola O'Donnell, had told him to pray carefully, to fast and to receive an honest answer from God, even if it wasn't the one he wanted.

He had done that, prayed from early morning until shadows of evening had crept across the chapel he knelt in and the flames of the candles seemed to stretch into a grotesque thinness. Had waited in the silence for God to answer, had searched the faces of the gaudy saints, John of God with his mad eyes, Christopher, figment of religious myth, Mother Mary with her blank face and Christ with the omnipresent streams of blood coating his pale body. Nausea, thick and cloying rose in him, bile tasting like hot, salted blood tinged the back of his throat and tongue, he'd run from the church, desperate for fresh air and anything to escape the pain that had risen and clenched like a vise around the breadth of his head. He'd thrown up outside, retching in the grass until the muscles in his throat and around his ribs felt torn and burning.

Father Lawrence had found him there and brought him cool water to drink and a cloth to wipe his face with. And told him gently, kindly that whatever destiny awaited him, it was not to be found within the walls of the Church. The Church was not, Father Lawrence had said, a place to hide from whatever it was about the world that scared you.

He had truly listened in the chapel, had stilled his heart and mind and cells and synapses to a whisper and had listened with every straining, yearning bit of humanity that was in him. Yes, he had prayed as well, carefully at first, softly, so as not to alarm God nor himself and then finally into a silence so terrifying it had made him dizzy with ardor. As the silence lengthened with the shadows, ardor became panic.

'Why this yearning, why? How did molecules come to this, be they stardust or not? Be more,' he had prayed, 'be more than what I am, what earthly gods I serve, be more than the sum of my memories, hopes and fears. Be more than the sum of all that is. Remain the infinite mystery if you must, but BE MORE than the equation of simple human yearning. Sweet Jesus BE MORE.

Where, where was the mercy in loving that which was mortal, that which broke, for without the more there was no mercy, no sense, neither rhyme nor reason.

And yet where was the mercy in not loving that which was mortal? For a flame could burn in its moment even if seconds later there was only smoke to know it by.

'What Lord,' he'd cried silently, 'what of pain and terror and loneliness?' But if MORE than it would also be the more of difficult things, the unsightly, the unseemly, the lowly of heart and mind.

He wondered after if he had asked too much, or if to not ask these things was faith. There had been no still, small voice in the darkness, no gentle finger skimming his face. Was it so very much to want that whisper at the gate, to hear the leaves rustle and know the sound of God's music in their dance? To want that simple voice in the night that Julian of Norwich had once heard, the one that gave no absolutes but neither took them away.

'This I am. I am what you love. I am what you enjoy. I am what you serve. I am what you long for. I am what you desire. I am what you intend. I am all that is.'

He had learned that day in the chapel that to search for God was to break your heart again and again and again. To accept that healing would not come in this life.

He'd gone to ground after that, a fox searching for the hole that would make him safe. Tried for comfort in words, as he'd always done and found even the masters of pen and wit had no answers, only plaintive cries, swallowed on the universal wind as surely as his own.

Now years later, after the loss of children, wife, father, he no longer searched, *for he was afraid that someday he might actually find an answer and would be unable to bear it. Rilke had been right, the pain had not outworn the garden, because the garden was built not to care, to encompass infinity and as much pain as man was capable of.*

And now this girl, holding out hope in her hand, believing he'd the courage to take it. All angels are terrible, but this one was not fruit, she was flower, easily bruised, felled and blighted by winter's frost. He could not partake of the blossom without destroying it. As much as it appalled him, he would have to open the cup of his hands and let the wind take her where it would. Even if it was to the heart of the fire.

He supposed, in the end that he was, indeed, still a good Catholic boy.

IN THE MORNING, THEY PLAYED A COMEDY OF MANNERS, all politeness, walking in measured circles around each other. There were a number of things that had to be done in order to make the place ready for another long absence. Pamela disappeared down to the village for the better part of the afternoon, coming back and finding him in the garden, shearing the heads off of the roses, knowing he'd not be back in the fall to do it.

She was, despite the heat of the day, pale and shaking with cold. He paused in his beheading, a chill radiating from the tip of his spine through the sweat his labors had produced.

"What is it?" he asked, knowing somehow that it had nothing to do with the events of the previous day.

She shook her head, mutely handing him a rolled up paper from underneath her arm. He took it and knew with every fiber of his being that he didn't want to see what it said, that somehow the smoke he'd been smelling all summer was about to burst into a conflagration he wouldn't be able to direct or control. He opened it.

Before him was a sight he'd become all too used to over the preceding months. A picture of the beatific Reverend Lucien Broughton, managing to gleam even from the grain of newsprint. It was, unusually though, a small picture, a posed headshot. It was the photo opposite that stilled his heart for a beat and when it resumed beating, it was in a jagged and painful rhythm. There stood his father, in one of the last photos taken, face turned away from the camera though not far enough to disguise the terrible melancholy that resided there. A picture he'd taken himself on the last Christmas they'd had together, two sad and lonely men trying to pretend holidays meant a thing to them anymore. He didn't need to read the headlines, he already had a very good idea what they said, but of course he did.

'Questionable Death? Coroner's Office to Re-Open Investigation into the Death

of Wealthy Businessman and Politician James Kirkpatrick III.'

'Something about the whole situation seemed a bit funny from the start,' says the Reverend Lucien Broughton, currently seeking to become member of Parliament in the district the deceased James Kirkpatrick had represented from April of 1962 until his untimely death in early March of this year. 'It seems as if the public was never given an adequate explanation for his death, a man relatively young and in good health, tragic yes, but, accidental, well that remains to be seen,' continued the Reverend Broughton. 'He was a much loved public figure and I feel that the people of his district and this city deserve an honest answer to what actually happened.'

Questions about the death of James Kirkpatrick have been swirling since his death in a hunting accident; however his son, now Lord Kirkpatrick, assured the press and media that it was nothing more than an accident. Strange, perhaps, for a man whose skill with a gun was impressive but not entirely out of the range of possibility. Now, however, disturbing facts are coming to light that cast doubt on the story...'

Jamie, body cold and rigid, scanned the rest of the story and saw that it gave details of his father's life, medical and psychological history, relationships and then went on to chronicle his own woes. He felt a cold trickle begin to build into a hard ball of ice in his stomach. There were things in this article, half-hints and insinuations, which alluded to particulars no one outside of himself and his father could possibly have known about. Unless someone had done a lot of homework, had set out to lay a trap, had rifled his papers, fine-tooth combed their business dealings for the last three decades and searched his home. Someone who had bided their time until it was beyond his powers of damage control.

"Dear Christ," he breathed out, head reeling, pruning shears slipping to the ground and rolling away into the soil.

"That's not all, you'd best look at page three," Pamela said miserably.

He flipped the page over, wondering what grimy detail they hadn't thoroughly exhumed and examined on page one. His question was answered in a black and white, 3X5 picture. Taken on the night of his father's funeral it showed he and Pamela by the fire, at the precise moment he'd leaned against her in exhaustion and despair. The pose, however, indicated anything but despair.

'Mistress of the Castle?' read the caption. The accompanying article made no pretense at being respectable and proceeded in five paragraphs to dissect his love life, his marriage, Colleen's defection to a nunnery and speculated with outright lewdness about the whys and wherefores of the girl who'd taken up residence in his home. Including a bit on what was snidely referred to as the 'summer love nest in Scotland'.

Fury and fear jostled for primacy in his head. The words themselves were bad enough, censure, ruination, defamation... and the list went on of the damages the tone of the article could and, he admitted, would wreak. But there was something else, a feeling sliding blackly under the words themselves that told him much more than business dealings and standing in the community were at stake. A fool, he knew, should have seen some of this coming. You couldn't take a young, beautiful girl under your roof and expect people not to speculate and outright accuse you of a wide variety of perversities. There had been bound to be whispers about his father's death as well, gunshots to the head caused supposition and suspicion by their very nature.

But the pictures—who on earth had taken one of Pamela and himself that night? And the other one of his father gave him real cause for worry as it had been in his desk, a private moment of memory, a melancholy father caught on film by an equally melancholy son. Someone had been through his home, had spied on him with malevolent intent for some months now it would seem. The question that begged to be answered was who? He thought, with a chill, dropping sensation in his stomach, that he might know the why all too well.

"What do we do?" Pamela, still pale but less visibly shaken, was looking at him with questioning eyes.

He took a moment before answering, but when at last he spoke his voice was calm and firm, "We go back to Belfast, find out who's behind this and then dig in for a long and ugly fight."

It was, at least, a place to start.

Chapter Thirteen

Journey Without a Map

"Take a break Casey, there's someone out back waitin' to see ye."

Casey, putting down a trayload of freshly cleaned glasses, nodded, paused behind the bar to get his cigarettes and with only a mild curiosity as to the identity of his guest headed out to the back of Declan O'Ryan's pub.

The early evening light was bright in comparison to the dimly lit interior of the pub and he took a moment to adjust, sliding a cigarette out of the pack and lighting it by feel alone.

"Hello," he heard a quiet voice say, a voice he'd spent all summer remembering and forgetting.

"Oh, it's you," he said gruffly, eyes adjusting and taking in the sight in front of him.

"Yes, it's me," Pamela said, voice in response to his own, less soft. "Pat told me I could find you here."

"Come to say goodbye an' fare thee well, have ye? Could have saved yerself the expense of bus money, the papers pretty much said it for ye." He sat on an empty milk crate, eyeing her dispassionately through a haze of smoke.

"No," she said warily, "I came to see you, I promised I would."

"Aye well," he took a long pull on his cigarette, the next words coming out in a slipstream of blue, "ye've kept yer promise, so ye can go back to the other side of the tracks with a clear conscience. Ye'll have to excuse me I've inventory to do." He stood grinding his cigarette out and disposing of the butt in a slimy looking bucket.

"Do you believe everything you read?" she asked as he turned his back to her and reached for the door handle.

He stopped, gripping the handle tightly wishing he could just open it and be done with her. Christ he needed this conversation like he needed a hole in the head. Another hole in the head he revised, as he turned to face her once more.

"Fools generally believe what they want to, whatever's most handy to their own wants an' needs," he said coolly, "an' I am no fool."

"I never thought you were, though, I'm wondering," her brows drew into two delicate lines, "if I'm going to have to amend that opinion."

He stepped towards her, all the confusion of the last week coalescing itself into a tidy knot of anger. "What is that supposed to mean?"

"That if you allowed a bunch of half-baked suppositions and filthy innuendoes change your mind about me then perhaps you are a fool and not worth the fare it took to get me down here. What exactly did you learn from those stories that you didn't already know?"

Throwing accusation into the fray didn't help Casey's anger. "Ye come here accusin' me? Yer the talk of the town, you an' yer gentleman friend on the hill. Ye told me ye came to this country because of childhood memories but ye came here for him, didn't ye? He's yer memories."

She met his fury squarely, "Yes, I came here for him, because of him."

"I knew it," he said, shaking his head. "Well then I don't see that there's anymore to say."

"No," she said her voice suddenly sad, "perhaps there isn't after all."

"Well then," he said awkwardly, "I'm busy as ye can see, I'd best get back in."

"Yes, I'm busy myself," she smiled, a bright, slivered fake smile, "I have to find a new place to live and I've only got started."

He was at the entry, had the knob turned when she spoke her last words and he leaned his head against the door and closed his eyes.

"So that's it, is it? Ye had yer summer with him, threw yerself at his head and got turned down stone cold. Am I gettin' the picture clearly here?"

"Yes," she said in a tight voice.

"An' so now ye thought ye'd come an' I'd welcome ye with open arms." There was a resounding silence behind him. "Aye well isn't that rich? Ye'd think I was no more than a dog on his doorstep for ye to kick or kiss dependin' on yer whim," he turned back to her, knowing his emotions were there for her to see plainly but not caring, "an' ye know the saddest bit is that like that dog I'm happy to see ye, I'm grateful for whatever ye throw my way. I'm willin' to take the scraps off someone else's plate an' make a meal of it." He rubbed a hand over his face, bristles of his whiskers rasping against the palm. "This is what I'm reduced to an' I can't say I care much for the feel of it."

"I came because of him, I'm still here because of you," she said quietly, pale beneath the tan that dusted her skin gold in the fading light.

Casey let out a long and frustrated exhalation of breath, "Christ, girl what the hell do ye expect me to say to that?"

"I don't expect you to say or do anything," she responded, "only believe me when I say that I'm sorry if I've hurt you but I had to know where I stood with him."

"Is that meant to comfort me?" he asked, sarcasm heaped neatly over each syllable.

"No."

"Well I'll give ye top marks for honesty," he gave a low laugh, "but not for much else."

"Fair enough."

He shook his head, nonplussed by this girl. Her honesty took him off guard, left him open to all sorts of confusion and doubt. Just her presence here was enough to give him all the signs he needed, to tell him the truth that was written on this particular page of his life. Pinwheeling senses, jellied knees, cascades of stars, difficulty breathing and a complete and utter lack of logic presiding in his brain.

"I really must get back to work," he said, the words difficult and forced, feeling hard and stripping to his throat.

She nodded, not turning away, not walking off into the evening air the way she was supposed to.

"Alright," he said in defeat, "I've got to make a short trip this Saturday, it's a trip I meant to make alone, but if ye'd like to come, I think I can manage the company." It was he knew, a less than gracious offer, but the rest of his suffering senses had made him angry.

"That would be grand," she said, tipping forward on her toes and kissing him on the corner of his mouth.

He watched her walk off, mindlessly mesmerized by her thoroughly female undulations. He'd an uneasy feeling that she hadn't had the slightest doubt of the outcome of their meeting.

CONNEMARA SAT BY THE SEA. An ancient, misted landscape, marked, pitted, scored and scarred, an old woman settling down hard on her bones.

Long ago, the Riordans had originated in Connemara and still to a certain extent claimed it as their ancestral home. It was a land suited to such men, wilder, less pastoral, harder and less forgiving than the rest of Ireland, a land that refused to be tamed or give much comfort to the inhabitants thereof. The first of the Riordans, it was said, emerged from the sea onto rock and swore he'd never put a foot in water again. Legend surely, repeated with a smile and a bit of drama, from one generation to the next, but oddly enough not a man of them had any fondness for the sea. Living on an island one learned to deal with it, to understand it well enough that it couldn't take one's life easily, to use it for practical reasons and harbor no romance whatsoever about it in one's soul. It was neither friend nor foe merely a great implacable fact that must be regarded with respect and a certain amount of fear. The sea was like a woman, a tricky business, never quite understood but respected for its vagaries. Rock on the other hand, which was what the vast majority of Connemara consisted of, could be depended upon, would change only minimally through countless seasons of rain and sun, it was something a man could stake his life upon. And so the Riordans had, though perhaps they had loved the land too much. At first in a very literal sense, for they ploughed it, cultivated it, brought forth food and sustenance from a barren wasteland. Of late in an interpretation that was purely figurative. The land on both counts had betrayed them, taken their lives with as little emotion as the sea would have.

Casey's pilgrimage here today was a personal one, an homage to ancestors and a long postponed apology to a father he'd never had a chance to say goodbye to. It was a trip he'd been avoiding since he'd come home, but had decided on this first Saturday in September that the time to face his ghosts was long overdue.

The day, somewhat like his mood, had been one of sporadic showers, heavy oppressive cloud and now on the brink of evening had sprung out in glorious sunshine, soft cross-hatched clouds in watery pinks, lavenders and melting yellows, painting the sky. Light, mellowed by the pull of night, danced tender-footed on leaves, was caught in the clasp of water and mating became strings of diamond. It was enchanting, if somewhat soggy.

"You might," said an annoyed and exhausted voice behind him, "have told me we'd be jumping fences and pulling through haystacks all day, at least I could've dressed for it."

"Now how was I to know ye'd turn up lookin' like ice cream on Sunday," Casey gave a mild look over his shoulder.

Of the verbal sort there was no reply, but a pebble, deliberately sharp, pinged off the back of his head seconds later.

"Ouch, what the hell was that for?"

"For inviting me," she answered, looking a little less forlorn than she had a moment previous. She was, like the naiads, inappropriately clad and soaking wet.

"Where are we?" She halted beside him, shivering.

"Don't exactly know," he replied bemusedly, taking his coat off and settling it around her shoulders without even looking sideways.

"You don't know?" her tone was incredulous. "You've made me march about in grass up to my backside all day, sit through a deluge of rain buried in suspicious smelling hay and you don't know where we are?"

"I will when we get there," he answered and set off once again after studying the rock formations in the distance.

"If you won't tell me where, can't you at least tell me why we're going and what we're going to do when we get there?" she asked, grumpily keeping pace with him.

"Who, why, when, where, what, yer full of questions aren't ye? Have ye ever considered there aren't answers for everything an' that some things must be taken on faith?"

"Are you asking me to trust you?" She irritably brushed a piece of hay out of the neck of her dress.

"Have I given ye any reason not to?"

"Point taken."

They walked on some further way as the sky abandoned its grasp on the day and a soft, subtle shading began to occur, casting shy phantoms before it.

Just when she thought she might have to throw herself into a hedgerow for a rest, Casey suggested that they stop while he regained his bearings.

"How can you get yourself righted if you've no idea where we are?"

"It's a feelin' I'm lookin' for more than an actual landmark, though there ought to be a twisted oak an' a stream..." he trailed off, peering distractedly through the gloom.

"We've been walking in great bloody circles all day and you're looking for a tree with a hump in its back? Are all Irishmen mad or is it you in particular?"

"Me in particular most like, why do ye ask?"

"It's only that we've passed a tree like that twice," she said wearily, shucking off her shoes and standing first with one bare foot and then the other in the wet grass.

"We passed it twice an' ye didn't say anything?"

"I didn't, if you'll recall, have any idea what we were looking for."

"Where was it?"

"Ten minutes back that way," she gestured, a tired elliptical motion that indicated both sky and sea but not land.

"Where?" he asked more patiently.

She sighed and taking her shoes in one hand set forth across the field they stood in, towards the thickening skin of night to where clouds curdled in blackened piles over the sea.

"There," she said as they crested the top of a hill. Below them lay a small valley, a precipitous gouge in the land, as though a giant with a sharp hand had scooped out a handful of earth and flung it away. In the last of the light, a tree could be seen at its lowest point, a narrow stream hissing past its roots. The tree was indeed hunchbacked, gnarled and knotted to such a degree that it seemed it had been lifted whole from Eden and transplanted here. Or Eden itself, an Eden of stars and Samarkand, of dark voices and wily serpents, of comforting apples. Of eastern fruit easily bruised, the apricots that last but a moment in a season.

"That's the one," Casey whispered and taking her hand firmly in his own, began the climb down into the valley. They picked their way through rock, slid with frightening velocity down a thirty-foot drift of loose shale, waded through a patch of bramble bushes and came out cursing on the brink of the stream.

"Where are we?"

"We're on my great-granddaddy's land," Casey replied.

"How can you be certain?" she asked looking about as if she expected the ghosts of ten dead generations to come piping across the fields.

"The tree looks right, but I know one way to be sure."

Up close, the tree was even more formidable. Leafless and stony, it seemed an iron fist of earth erupting from the ground, weathering eternity. Casey took his hand away and dropped to his knees at the tree's roots and began to scrabble in the dirt.

"What is it, Casey?" she peered over his shoulder, unable to discern much of anything.

"It's our rock," he whispered and though he faced away, she could hear the tears that stood at the gateway of his words. She knelt down beside him and saw clearly what his hands, dripping with earth, had revealed. A long, thin wedge of slate, obsidian in the night, clear as a mirror under the moon, inscribed with the only tangible legacy Casey's family had left behind.

She read the names aloud in a reverent whisper as Casey's fingers blindly traced them.

"Cathal, Kieran, Daniel, Brendan—" and as Casey softly trembling ran his fingers across the terrible blank spot, "Brian," she whispered.

"Aye," Casey said, "Daddy. The son always comes and carves the name of his father here, so that our family wouldn't merely pass away into legends that can hardly be believed. I meant to come here after he died but I just couldn't, I was too angry. I thought putting letters to stone would make it real, that my Daddy would be no more than a name on a rock, just another dead Riordan when there were already so many of us." He took a hard breath and when he spoke again, his voice was darkly gritted with the pain, skinned over with a fragile translucence, that his father had caused him by losing his life. "But then after all dead is dead and there's only so long one can deny it." His head dropped down into his soil smeared hands and though she heard no sound, she saw clearly the tears that fell and shone on the names of all the men that had left him a history that would surely engrave his name here one day, carved with an inevitability that marked him out for violence and death the moment he was conceived. She shivered, a tremor running fine and electric along her bones, the weight of years landing on her suffocatingly. History, Jamie had said in an unguarded moment, could kill a man more certainly than a well-placed bullet. She understood now what he'd meant and could bear it no longer. She ran back, unseeing, the way they had come, feeling water spray coldly up her side when she stumbled into the stream, the cold didn't matter, nothing mattered but getting out of this place. She reached the bottom of the hill and was about to plunge upwards, uncaring of sharp, piercing rocks and long, brutal falls when Casey caught her from behind and pinned her roughly in his arms.

"Jaysus, will ye stop!" he took a ragged gasp, "Did ye not hear me yellin' for ye to stop?" He fought to catch his breath, never lessening the iron grip he held on her.

"Let me go," she spat out, "I can't breathe."

He loosened his hold a little and she twisted violently in a vain attempt to get away.

"Damn it," his voice rose in anger, "are ye crazy, woman? Ye'll break yer damn leg an' then we'll be in a fix, not to mention we're trespassin' on someone's land here. I've no wish to have Pat out here chisellin' me own name in stone because some farmer shot me for an intruder."

"I thought you said it was Riordan land."

"It was, a long time ago. The Riordans haven't owned so much as a pot to piss in much less land for close to fifty years now. Please," his tone softened, "if I let ye go will ye stand for a minute and tell me what scared ye so bad back there?"

"You," she said, voice exhausted, "you scared me, it's as if you can see your own name there, already written into legend while you go off in a puff of smoke. How could you leave Pat alone? If you die there's only himself to sacrifice and don't think he's beyond it."

"Is Pat the only one I'd be leaving behind?" His breath stirred the downy curls at the base of her neck.

"Does it matter? You'd leave us both behind anyway; you'll do what you must. Men always do, don't they?" she said bitterly, ceasing to struggle.

He turned her gently but firmly in his arms, so there was no chance of her bolting and forced her eyes to meet his own.

"And what is it ye know of men, darlin'?" Casey asked, his eyes so dark, so fathomless, reflecting the pale beginning moonlight and revealing nothing to her.

"Enough," she said defensively.

"Aye," he said, bending and softly touching his lips to her own, "perhaps ye do at that."

She melted to it, yielding against all instincts except for the very oldest one of all.

His lips were warm and sweet. 'I will take care,' they seemed to say. She did not want hesitation though, she wanted something irrevocable, something they could not return from, a place where she was far, far away from the no man's land she'd existed in all summer.

She took his hand and placed it on her breast, he groaned low in his throat and tried to pull it away, she kept it firmly there.

"Darlin' I can't—ye musn't," and then on a shaky exhalation, "Lord, girl do ye know what yer doin' to me?"

She tipped her head back into moonlight and met his eyes squarely, "I know," she said softly. "It's what I want. Take me back there."

"Back where?" he looked truly confused for a moment.

"Back there to your rock. Tonight I want you to choose the living. I want you to see there are choices that won't end with you nothing more than a name carved in rock."

He closed his eyes, struggled within himself for a moment and nodded, "Alright."

He led her back by the hand, her heart pounding so hard it hurt.

He helped her with her clothes, face dark with hunger there under the moon, in a primordial garden. She helped him with his and he stood naked, silver then black then silver again as clouds chased the moon and never quite caught it. She was shaking with nerves and buried her face in his chest when he put his arms around her.

"I don't quite know my way," she said, a small giggle rising toward her throat, "I think I need a map."

He chuckled, "I can point ye in the right direction." He let out a laugh that was half gasp, "Though I can see yer not one to wait for explicit instruction."

"Don't laugh," she rubbed her cheek against his shoulder, smelling the heat of the soft skin where muscle met joint and separated limb from body.

"I'm sorry," he whispered and took her face in his hands, thumbs stroking the quivers out of her jaw. She closed her eyes and allowed her skin to feel him, giving her four other senses rein. Her fingers traveled sightless, muscle here, scar there, hair coarse and fine, the cool translucency of eyelids and the feathery brush of lashes.

He took her hands in his own, lacing their fingers together and kissed the back of each of hers. "I want ye to be certain of what yer doin' here," he said, voice slightly hoarse, "because it'll not look the same to ye in daylight. It never does."

"I'm certain, Casey," she whispered, "are you?"

He gazed down at her for a long moment, the fine hair on his arms gilded silver, his skin washed with a frail light. "I've been certain since the moment I first saw ye, I've only been waitin' for ye to come to the same conclusion."

It was simple then to fall, fall into empires forgotten with the grace of lilies dropping. To feel a hand so fine on her skin, like the skirling of spectral leaves from trees long dead, to touch and sense his blood thrum beneath the skin and know her own pulsed only a breath away. To not be certain where one ended and the other began. Skin, slicked and salted, tasting like blood to the tongue.

His lovemaking had a grace and tenderness she knew would not be found in a smaller man. It was as if he was afraid to break or bend her and yet could not stop himself from doing just that.

The pain was small, a little sputter of fire deep inside, overwhelmed by a heavier, harder tide that pulled and bore her above the pain, even as it touched the fringes of it.

She breathed him, in that moment he became essential to her. It seemed as if she had known this before and could live no longer without it. The sand-fine rub of his chest hair on the finer still skin of her breasts, the line of his backbone, a rope of large pearls strung by sheaths of long and glittering muscle. Blood to bone and back again, the grass and rock beneath seemingly created for the purpose of questing, writhing bodies. Graceful and graceless, laughter and tears that he took away with his lips and winged kisses. To know him as a lover was to know him finally as a man.

And what he asked was everything, with broken breath and silent occupation, everything and all. The prize, lotus-wreathed and redolent with musked promise, was the beginning of love.

'Will you, can you, are you able?' These things said with each thrust, with breath so hard it condensed and gelled and rolled like shattered stone down between their bodies. Over hard, over soft, unstrung and scattered across the ground, nascent and whole with a blue-white light. Fallen from heaven and made of the stuff of stars.

LATER, HOURS OR MINUTES, NEITHER KNEW NOR PARTICULARLY CARED which, the sky began to lose the stars and there was a faint pulse in the air and ground which said the clock, even for lovers, would begin to turn again.

Casey lay full length on his stomach, eyes heavy-lidded with exhaustion and intimacy. Pamela, propped on one elbow, traced looping nonsensical patterns on his back.

"They hurt you very badly." It was a statement but one of the sort that required answer.

"Aye,' he said sleepily, "but I'm still alive so the bastards didn't get what they wanted."

"Who did it?" she asked, fingers splayed and moving in circles across the flesh of his back, flesh knotted, milled and ground, then fleshed again into long, runnelling grooves, luminescent and finely grained as a baby's skin in the faint light.

"Don't know exactly, screws or fellow inmates, was just a group that took me from behind one night an' decided to carve a warning into my back. Opened me up an' poured acid into the cuts. I couldn't even scream for the pain was so bad it seemed to just paralyze my throat."

"I'm surprised you didn't die," she said in horror.

"I wanted to, I truly did but I eventually healed in more ways than one an' I must say in view of the last hour or two I'm glad I did."

She pressed her lips, wet with tears, into the grooves, following the path, smooth as silk, that a knife had once taken. He groaned aloud as if the action were causing him fresh agony.

Certain things in life are irrevocable and we know them in the moment. The subconscious sees them, snatches them up and knows it's too late, though we foolishly think we can take them back as if love can be restored to the giver by patching over the hole it was ripped from. The heart, much as it may dumbly beat on, knows this. Love is irrevocable, it cannot be taken back. Stars may fall from the sky, men may walk on the moon and toast may burn in the morning but love will always exist in the moment it is given. Irrevocably. So memory takes what it can, washes it softly and makes a gift of first mornings under blue-bled skies, of warm September suns and the first knowledge of physical love. Memory makes it sweet for youth, for girls confused by love that can't be contained to one person and boys who lost childhood under the cut of knives and concrete walls.

Memory is irrevocable as well, we may misplace it, refuse to answer its summons or just plain lose it but, somewhere, within cell and neural pathways, it abides forever, hidden but alive, existing always in the place in which it was formed. Forever and irrevocable, irrevocably forever.

"Are you going to carve your father's name then?"

Casey rolled over and sat up reaching for his shirt, "No," he shook his head and she wished for a moment she could take his thoughts, his fears into her own head and keep him safe from them. "I think it's time to break with tradition."

Rising from the crush of grass, scars wet with tears and kisses, Casey Riordan looked at his first love, his only love and said, "Will ye come home with me?"

And she, too drunk on a sky that has to lose stars every morning to consider consequences, gathered her clothing, took his hand and said, "Yes."

To Jamie's surprise Pamela was sitting in the library on Monday morning, dressed smartly in a gray twinset and skirt to match, hair skimmed back in an uncompromising knot. She was hard at work already, Gaelic dictionary at the top of the desk, a stack of opened and sorted correspondence to her right, two cups and a pot of tea on a tray to her left.

She acknowledged his entry with a small, polite smile and a slight rise of her brow.

"I wasn't certain I'd see you today or tomorrow for that matter," Jamie said, sitting opposite her.

She poured him a cup of tea and handed him the top sheaf of papers off the stack of letters.

"There's lemon in the tea already. I've marked the most important letters with red ink, the less urgent with blue and all the invitations are here." She pointed to a separate stack of heavy paper in shades of cream, pale blue and marbled gray. "You've two urgent phone messages from a steel mill in Pittsburgh, Franc from the Luxembourg mill needs an answer on this month's shipments to Japan, Ronan called from the Antrim distillery and says he had to sack someone and the union is rumpussing over it and," she smiled at his dumbfounded look, "Mr. Kilmorgan wants to know if yer arse isn't mightily sore from straddling the goddamned fence for so long, his words not my own. If you don't mind, I'll deal with the less important correspondence and have you sign off on it before I send it out. Meanwhile," she glanced down at her watch, "you have a meeting with your bankers at ten o'clock this morning, an appointment to get your hair trimmed just after lunch and I've mapped out your afternoon activities and calendared the month of September which, as you'll see, is extremely busy." She pushed an open book across the table at him, neatly lined, blocked and lettered in a sensible shade of black.

"As a friend of mine used to say it looks as though the cat has absconded with your tongue," she said amusedly while topping up the tea he'd barely touched and handing him the cup along with a stack of phone messages.

"Where's Liz?" he asked weakly.

"Family emergency, she flew out to Edinburgh this morning, she's left you a letter," she handed a sheet of his own stationary to him, filled with Liz's neat squared off hand. "She'll call you tonight. When she's back, which won't likely be for a few weeks, she's mentioned that she'd like to cut down on her workload. She is sixty-three you know and her daughter's been asking her to come for an extended visit for quite some time. She'll talk to you when she returns, in the mean time you'll have to make do with me."

He endeavored to make eye contact with her, only to receive a quizzical and slightly annoyed, "Yes?"

"It's just, I thought," he took a deep breath, feeling stupidly adolescent, "that you might not want to be here after what happened in Scotland. You disappeared as soon as we got back and I haven't heard from you since."

"You hired me to work, Jamie and, I must say it's been a bit of a farce on both our parts thus far. If I'm going to stay as your employee, then it's time I actually did a job. I'm entirely dreadful at Gaelic, though I can manage the rougher translations for you if you don't mind polishing up the entrails so to speak. This though, organizing your day from home, keeping track of calls and appointments I can manage quite well. As to what happened, well you were only being honest, weren't you? I can, if it makes you more comfortable, endeavor to blush and dimple as you enter the room and sigh audibly when you leave it. I can even," she smiled wickedly, "throw in a thwarted seduction every month or so just to keep the peace."

"Have you found a place to live then, so soon?"

For the first time that morning, her composure seemed to slip slightly. "I have."

"May I ask where? I will after all need an address to send the checks to won't I?" He strove to keep the sarcasm from his voice and failed completely.

"I'm staying with Casey and Pat for now, they've a spare room."

"Do they?" he retorted sharply, "Perhaps Pamela you should have actually read those books I gave you this summer."

She smoothed a sheet of paper and took a careful breath before replying.

"I'd like to stay on working here Jamie, I think I can actually be of help to you, but once I walk down that hill at night and through those pretty gates, my business is my own. If that seems unreasonable to you, I'll find another job elsewhere and you can wash your hands of me entirely. You aren't responsible for me Jamie, I don't need taking care of."

"Don't you? I'd say that your choice in roommates says the opposite."

"Jamie," she said simply, professionalism stripped from her voice, some echo of the vulnerable girl he'd rejected showing herself for the first time that morning, "I can't do this with you."

"It's only," he shook his head and sighed, "I've gotten into the habit of taking care of you, of having you about in the evenings. I've, as the saying goes, grown accustomed to your face."

"I'll miss you too, Jamie," she said softly and then smiling brightly resumed her mask of professionalism. "You really had best get back to Ronan, he sounded just a bit desperate and if you don't face up to Dannyboy he'll be on your doorstep by this evening, once again his words. I," she stood up, smoothing her skirt with hands that betrayed only the slightest trembling, "have to order some stationery from the printers and go over the plans for your dinner party with Maggie."

"Dinner party?" he echoed, feeling somewhat bruised by her brisk tone.

"Yes, you're having a dinner party on the fifteenth of October for the Duke of Dungarvon, at which, after lulling him into complacency with good food and even better whiskey you'll broach the subject of the deplorable working conditions of his factories in Belfast and Derry."

"I will? And just where might his Belfast factory be?"

"In your father's old riding, as you well know. Lucien Broughton will be invited as well."

"What?" Jamie shot forward in his chair, causing his tea to slop over the rim of the cup.

"There's an old Chinese proverb that goes something to the effect that you must fight the enemy on ground of your own making, or as my father once said 'before sticking the bastard over the fire you should lightly butter him on all sides.'"

"You want me to have that viper in my own home?"

"We've dug in as far as we can on an exposed hill; it's time to start fighting. It's time as well don't you think, to get off that fence Jamie before someone gets permanently damaged."

"Perhaps," he said, taking in the tone of her voice and the paleness of her aspect, "it is."

Part Two

The Skein Unwound

Chapter Fourteen

A Whiff of Revolution

IN THE SPRING OF 1968, IT SEEMED AS IF THE WHOLE WORLD was on the march, on fire, ablaze with ideals and bright, burning hope. There were student riots in Paris protesting Vietnam, the incandescent, leaping promise of the Prague Spring, the pouring flame-ridden speeches on American campuses, in American streets against a war that was cutting open the great mother heart of America and spilling her blood across the people, seeping irrevocably into her soil. But Paris ended, the students went home and the pale light of the Prague spring was squelched by Soviet tanks and guns, and America witnessed the end of the decade two years before the calendar would admit to it. The swift and merciless deaths of Martin Luther King and Bobby Kennedy saw to that, as did Tet and the escalation of troops into Vietnam and the realization that some wars were never meant to be won.

The Irish were late to catch the fever, out of time and mind as they were. But being Irish burned all the harder to catch up. It was the opening act in an unconventional war. War was never the aim of the students who began the revolt, who marched through the streets regardless of bans and opposition and outright hostility, stones had been thrown before and would be again, it was only the unfortunate that died. The ideals and demands were as old as the human longing for justice and seemingly as out of reach; freedom of speech and assembly, an end to the gerrymandering of political districts, an end to discrimination and one vote for every one man. Simple enough, seemingly. Feet may be quick to march but as a wise man once noted the march of the human mind can be damnably slow. The Irish, stubborn regardless of caste, class or religion took hard to their own sides of the fence and were not, regardless of the passion and fervor of youth, to be pulled willingly down the road to democracy. The older generation scratched their heads, long comfortable in misery or ignorance now, they'd lost their need to rock the boat. Rocking the boat got you drowned, plain and simple. Unionists out and out accused the emergent civil rights movement of merely being Republican foot soldiers in camouflage. The government dismissed them as rabble-rousers, agitators seeking their fifteen minutes of fame. The students with the wisdom of youth ignored all imprecations and sallied forth under ban, under the blow of rock and baton, coming up repeatedly against the hard, ugly face of hatred. They were the flame that would be put to the tinder of sectarianism and old hatreds, caught in the headiness of that year, of that dying, burning decade, they did not see that regardless of who sets the fire all who touch it will be burned and bear the scars for it.

Pat Riordan, as sweetened by the wind of optimism as any other nineteen year old with a pure heart is bound to be, found himself smack-dab in the middle of the new movement. He'd come back early from his country summer, intending to settle into his studies, continue his job at the pub and do what he could on a grass-roots level for the advancement of democracy in his own community. And found himself swept into the tides of history by the events of one autumn afternoon.

It was a march in Derry to protest the discrimination that had long divided the city by the river. Derry had always been recognized as second only to Belfast in political importance. It was a town in which a Nationalist majority was denied control of local government by a flagrant re-alignment of electoral boundaries. Not a single new house had been built since 1966 within the city boundaries. Over a thousand houses in Derry were occupied by more than one family and in some cases seven or eight families were huddled in homes that had originally been single dwellings. The Unionist body that controlled the city's council refused to extend its borders in fear that they would no longer be able to control the vote if political lines were expanded. Over 1,500 families were on the local wait list for housing and almost all of them were Catholic. Derry was a city filled with grievances and old hatreds and as such an obvious sight for a march.

The organizers of the march had chosen a particularly inflammatory route, over sacred Orange marching ground, feeling that change never came without provocation. The numbers attending were smaller than hoped, as the lure of an at home football match proved too much for many well-intentioned hearts. Some four hundred eventually formed up in Duke Street, the starting point, were treated to five minutes worth of speeches from the march organizers and turning about to begin the march ran into simultaneous police baton charges from either end of the street. Pandemonium and panic ensued, men, women and children cudgeled to the ground with equal impunity. Pat, stopping to help a small girl who was wandering about alone, found himself firmly thwacked across the back of the head with a baton. Scrambling to his feet and grabbing up the little girl before he could think twice about it, he tucked her face into the protection of his neck and shoulder and ran in the direction that seemed the least dangerous. Chaos blossomed redly behind, the marchers were knocking each other down in their panic to flee, the police, mad with bloodlust were wreaking vengeance for uncommitted crimes and all of it, Pat saw as he dodged yet another upraised stick, was being captured on film by a man on the edge of the crowd.

Scenes flashed before his eyes that he would only have time to realize later. A young girl being dragged by two policemen, half-dazed, shirt rucked up around her shoulders; a middle-aged man in a suit being struck repeatedly in the groin with a baton; and a boy near his own age, reeling and dizzy, blood coagulating and trickling down his face, struggling to get to his feet only to be struck savagely at the base of his neck by a police shield. Pat, holding the little girl, who'd gone very silent, as tightly as he dared, headed for the bridge at the top of the street, beyond the bottleneck of the frantic crowd.

He made it through the gauntlet of sticks and stones, still clutching the little girl, bruised and winded and about to make a dash for it across the bridge when a huge cascade of water caught him full in the face and threw him back several feet. He stumbled backward, caught his heel on a loose stone and fell down hard with the little girl still clinging for dear life to him.

"You okay?" he heard as he fought to catch his breath and shaking his head to clear the dizziness, he peered up at the speaker.

"So ye do have a tongue," he said. The little girl sat on his stomach, dripping with water, smiling a toothless smile. She looked about six.

"We got to run," she said, with what seemed great sense for a six-year-old. She hopped nimbly off to the side and waited for him to regain his feet. When he did so, she grabbed his hand and said, "this way." For lack of a better plan Pat did as he was told. They ran away from the crowd and away from the city, ran far enough, she with such sprightly speed, that Pat thought he might not be able to keep pace after awhile. She stopped just as abruptly by a tree in a vacant lot. "My Sylvie said to come here if there was trouble, my Sylvie will find us here."

"Sylvie?" he gasped out, leaning against the tree and smelling the bitter-soap smell of an old hawthorn.

"Aye, my Sylvie," the child said and sat, tidying the folds of her blue cotton dress as if she were about to take tea with the Queen. "I'm hungry, d'ye have anything to eat?" she asked with the equanimity of a child whose stomach takes precedence over horrors of every variety.

He patted his pockets down and found a soggy, half-melted chocolate bar that he handed over to her.

She ate it quickly and neatly, licking the last vestiges of it off the silver wrapper and smiling her gapped and gummy smile at him when she was well and truly finished. "D'ye have anything else to eat?"

"No, no I don't. I'm sorry about that, if I'd known I was goin' to be on the run with ye today I'd have filled my pockets."

"Hmmphm," she said and cast a famished eye over her surroundings as if she expected something to fall from the sky.

"What's yer name?" Pat asked.

"Sarah," she said, searching the pockets of her dress for a crumb and sighing when they produced nothing.

"Were ye with yer mammy an' daddy?"

"No," she chewed briskly on her index finger, a digit that looked as if it was thus abused on a regular basis.

Pat sighed. "Who did ye come here with then?"

"My Sylvie. Are ye sure ye've nothin' to eat?"

"You can search my pockets yerself," he said in exasperation. "Now who is Sylvie?"

"My sister," she said, voice muffled as she attempted to stick her entire face in his coat pocket. "It smells like chewin' gum in yer pocket," she said accusingly, "do ye have some chewin' gum?"

"No, it's all gone," he said firmly. "Now how did you get separated from your sister? We have to find a way to get you back to her; she's very worried I'm sure."

"She got smacked an' then I fell down an' there was all these legs about an' I couldn't see—"

"Legs?"

"Legs," she nodded emphatically, "an' my Sylvie she said if we was to get supperated then I was to come an' wait for her here an' she'd come find me. My mam told Sylvie she wasn't allowed to go today, that there'd be trouble, my Sylvie's goin' to catch some trouble, she is." This last said with a nod that sent her blonde hair flying. She was cute, if a little ragged and dirty around the edges. Pat sat down beside her; he'd just have to wait for this Sylvie to show up. Unless of course she was too badly hurt. If she didn't show up, he was uncertain what to do. He couldn't take this child to the police station, judging from the day's events, that was the last place to be.

In any event, he didn't have to worry about it, for after a protracted game of 'I Spy' and a game of makeshift hopscotch, the rules of which were so convoluted that he was declared out of bounds every five seconds, Sylvie appeared. She ran across the lot, eyed him suspiciously and swept her small sister up with words of both relief and scolding.

Despite the fact that she had all her teeth and had yet to demand food, she seemed a larger version of her sister. Fine blonde hair, dark brown eyes and a splash of freckles across her nose. She was a tiny thing, no more than five feet likely and maybe seven stone soaking wet.

"Hello," he said stepping forward and smashing his head into a low hanging branch. "I'm Pat Riordan," he managed to gasp as he bent over clutching his head in agony.

"Sylvie Larkin," a small, rough brown paw extended itself under his nose.

"Thank you for looking after my sister."

"Christ on earth," he muttered as the numbness began to wear off and the pain tore in needling ripples across his head, "yer welcome."

He felt a light hand touch his head, pull his hair aside, "Ye've cut yerself an' yer bleedin', ye'd best come back with Sarah an' me an' I'll bandage it for ye."

"It's kind of ye but I really should get back." He straightened himself slowly and met the calm yet somehow stern gaze of Sylvie Larkin.

"Get back where?" she asked, "It's still a battlefield back there an' it's shapin' up to last a bit more. Come on, don't stand on yer manners while yer bleedin' to death."

With Sarah clutching his hand and chatting a mile a minute, Pat followed the slim form of Sylvie Larkin to her home.

It was a small house, squeezed between a butcher's shop and a rundown storefront that advertised shoe-repair and beeswax soap amongst its services. Pat, left to sit in the front room while Sylvie bustled off to get antiseptic and tape for his head, surveyed the threadbare yet homey surroundings. Everything was clean, well polished and had obviously seen many years of use. Sarah was perched opposite him, a smudge of chocolate licking the tip of her nose and a ragged tear in her blue dress.

"Are ye married?" she asked, swinging her legs back and forth in a cheery manner.

"No, I'm not," Pat said.

"Sylvie's not married either, mam says she never will be if she doesn't stop havin' so many ideas in her head. I've got too many ideas too, but it's alright 'cause I don't want to get married. Mam's married an' it doesn't do her no good anyhow, daddy lives in England an' we never see him. Would you like to get married?"

"Sarah, leave off the poor man an' go clean yerself up," Sylvie, coming back into the room with a pan of hot water under one arm and a fishing tackle box under the other, cast a stern glance at her sister. "An' leave yer dress on my bed, I'll mend an' wash it tonight."

"Sorry," she flashed a shy smile at Pat as Sarah scampered off, "she thinks everyone's business is hers for the askin' an' ours hers to share."

"Curiosity's a good thing," Pat responded, then clutched the arms of the chair he sat in as Sylvie applied a hot cloth to the top of his head.

"It'll get her in trouble one of these days," Sylvie said and opening the tackle box took out antiseptic and applying it liberally to the cloth, put it back on Pat's head.

"Were ye in the march?" Pat asked, trying to distract himself from the unholy stinging that was sending shivers through his scalp.

"Nooo...well I suppose yes I was, though I didn't entirely intend to be. Mam had told me I wasn't to be anywhere near it an' I'd promised I wouldn't go, but then I just had to see."

"See what?"

"History in the makin', I wanted to be there an' not just read about it in the newspaper or hear someone else's comments about it that hadn't been there themselves. I didn't expect it to turn into a free for all with the police, though in this neighborhood I suppose I ought to know better."

"Have ye always lived in Derry then?" Pat asked as a deft and light hand swabbed the cut on his head.

"Born here, probably die here." She sighed, "They say in the papers that right now all roads lead to Derry but I just wish I could find the road leadin' out. Where are you from?"

"Just up from Belfast for the day," he said as she leaned over him to inspect her work and he smelled the old-fashioned scents of lemon verbena and lilacs.

"You smell nice," he blurted out, made awkward by her proximity.

"Thank you," she said simply and patting his hair into place stepped away and closed her box up with a snap.

"Ye don't need stitches though it looks like a near thing, it's a narrow cut an' ye'll have to keep it clean. Do ye have someone at home that can do it for ye?"

"Aye."

"Good, are ye hungry? I need to fix dinner for Sarah an' I an' ye look as though ye could use a bite."

"I shouldn't impose, ye've been very kind, but I really ought to get back out there an' see what the damage is an' if I can't locate a way home."

"I think goin' back up near the bridge is a very bad idea, ye may not have noticed on the way in but they're puttin' up barricades around the neighborhood, that's not a good sign, there's like to be plenty of trouble tonight."

Pat rose and went to the front window, parting the lace curtains carefully and angling his head to peer up the street. In the distance he could see dim figures running, hear the echo of shouts and a drifting haze on the air that looked like smoke. The girl was right, larger trouble was brewing.

"Come an' sit, I'll make ye some eggs an' toast an' then if ye've a mind to go out there into that at least it'll be on a full stomach."

"Okay," he nodded and followed her to the small kitchen, where she began to take down bowls and plates, eggs and milk.

"Can I help ye with anything?"

"No, sit down an' rest, a blow to the head like that is nothing to mess about with."

She took out a loaf of bread and sliced it neatly so that it fell away in perfect, narrow slices. She then cracked a half dozen eggs into a bowl, added a little milk and set to beating them up to a froth.

"Does yer father work in England?"

"Aye, an' it's not so bad as Sarah made it sound, he works there, he lost his job after Darin was born, that's my little brother, an' he couldn't find another to save his own life. So he went over to England, he's relatives there an' found a job. He sends as much of his pay home as he can."

"Why don't ye join him there?"

"Mam refuses to leave the Bogside, she grew up here an' she says she's not leavin' it til they cart her out feet first. Couldn't see herself livin' in England she says."

Pat watched as she poured the eggs into a hot skillet, smoking with bacon fat.

"An' how about you? Could ye see yerself livin' elsewhere?"

Sylvie glanced over her shoulder at him, one eyebrow quirked.

"Oh could I, I dream about it all the time."

"An' when ye dream where are ye?"

"Oh, I don't know that it's a specific place, it's dreams after all, but it's always warm in my dreams an' there's sand an' flowers an' a lot of water. Really blue water."

"I dream about California," he said quietly. He'd never said it before, hadn't felt an urge to share, but now in this instant he'd wanted to tell someone.

"Want to be in the pictures, do ye?" she asked and lifted the skillet to dole the eggs out onto chipped china plates.

"No," he replied though he knew her comment had only been teasing. "It just seems a grand place, don't ye think? Right on the ocean but with mountains an' huge trees an' enough fog at times to make even an' Irishman feel comfortable. An' ye could be anything an' do anything an' no one would care who your family was or what religion ye came from."

"I imagine even people in California have troubles," Sylvie said practically, setting down eggs and toast in front of him.

"Aye well," he said feeling foolish that he'd shared this much with a complete stranger, "it's only a silly dream."

"I don't think it's very silly at all," Sylvie said with a look of seriousness on her face. She smiled then, a quick, bright smile that wasted nothing and lit her face up like a candle. "Sarah," she yelled, "yer supper's ready."

Sarah bounded down the stairs, freshly washed, hair brushed to a soft gold, clad in a well-mended pink nightie. Sylvie said grace in a low and even voice and after a cluster of murmured amens everyone set to eating.

"The eggs are very good," Pat said, hungrier than he'd realized, he'd polished off his plate while the two girls were scarce halfway through their own. Sylvie took his plate and going to the stove, wordlessly refilled it and returned it to the table.

"Thank you," Pat said.

"Well I imagine it takes a bit more to fill ye up than a bit of eggs an' toast, what with yer size but I didn't get out to the shops yesterday so it's what was left in the cupboards."

"Don't ye think my Sylvie is pretty?" Sarah asked, bored with all the adult politeness.

Sylvie turned a black look on her sister and snatched up Sarah's plate as well as her own, though neither of them was done eating.

"She is," Pat nodded at Sarah, meeting her merry brown eyes in a smile of complicity. "She's a lovely name too."

"It's French," Sarah said, accepting the piece of toast Pat handed her off his own plate and pausing to liberally load it with jam. "Our Granny was French."

"Sarah," Sylvie said, "it's bedtime for you. I want those addition sums done before you go to sleep an' ye know Mam likes ye to read a chapter of the bible."

"The bible," Sarah leaned confidentially across the table, "is wretched borin', 'cept now I'm on the Psalms an' that's not so bad. Specially the bits about kissin'."

"Sarah Anne Larkin," Sylvie said in such a tone that Sarah jumped up and hastily licking jam from her fingers, fled up the stairs.

"She's very bright," Pat said, picking up plates and glasses and carrying them to the sink.

"Too bright for her own good likely, it's a hard contrast between her and our little brother, he's four an' completely deaf. Mam's gone over to London for a few days, Da' managed to get an appointment with a specialist an' he's to look over Darin. We're hopin' there's somethin' can be done for him."

She had filled the sink with hot, soapy water and was briskly washing the dishes. Pat grabbed a tea towel and set to drying them.

"My mam'd have fits if she saw a man doin' dishes in her kitchen, she says it's the only place she's queen an' she'll not a have a man muckin' about in it."

"She'd really have fits in our house then, there was nothin' but men all our growin' years."

"Did your mother die?" Sylvie asked pausing to look at him as she pushed a strand of hair out of her eyes with a soapy finger.

"No, just left."

"I'm sorry."

"It was a long time ago, but thank ye all the same."

Just then there was a strange *woofing* boom outside, causing the tea cups to rattle in the cupboard. Pat knew the noise for what it was and shoved Sylvie down to the floor, dropping himself beside her.

"Bomb?" Sylvie asked, face ashen.

Pat nodded, keeping low to the ground and beginning to crawl towards the small entryway. "Petrol bomb. Go check yer sister," he said tersely. He listened for a moment at the door and then standing, opened it narrowly and stepped out into the street. Twilight was falling, edging the events outside with a surreal softening light. At the head of the street, he could see a knot of people, the dissolving silhouette of flame throwing darkness down upon their heads and onto the paving stones.

"What's goin' on?" he asked a winded lad, who was slouched against a wall.

"Barricades are goin' up, bastards chased us down into the Bogside an' everyone's afraid if there's no defenses they'll start bustin' up the whole damn neighborhood."

"An' the bomb?" Pat asked.

"Don't know," the boy shook his head, "they had to expect it would get ugly after today." He looked up at Pat, eyes narrowing suspiciously, "Were ye out for the march?"

"Aye, got doused with the water cannon an' batoned across the head."

"Me as well," the boy turned up two hands whose palms were scored and scraped, then tapped his face where a glorious bruise was coming out in shades that ranged from ocher to ebony. "Bastard caught me right across the cheekbone, thought he'd smashed it, it's still throbbin' like a bugger mind. It's not as bad as it might be though, there's a regular battle goin' on up in Little James Street an' police attackin' people in Williams Street."

Pat nodded, hearing over the crackle of fire the screams that reverberated in the distance. It was hard to say if they were those of fear or fury. He began to walk, hardly knowing where his feet were leading him, only aware that he had to outrun the pounding in his own head. His very blood seemed to demand something, movement, forward motion, a reaction to the action being taken on these streets, in this neighborhood where oppression had been the norm for far too long. If a man was down on his knees long enough, he learned to walk on them. He'd be damned if he'd get used to it. He was running before he knew it, stopping only to grab a tattered tricolor from its resting place above the door of a pub, his legs pumping faster and faster until he had the giddy sense of being close to out of control, of almost flying.

The air that streamed past him and caught the white, green and gold of the flag, smelled of fire and a heady freedom. It smelled to Pat in the dark autumn night like the beginning of something new, like a thousand possibilities attached to a million more, like a whiff of revolution. And the scent of it alone, borne on the night, seemed worth dying for.

He saw fire in front of him, felt stones whistle past his head and knew he was approaching a barrier in more ways than one. Did he have the courage to go past it?

What did courage demand? What did the blood of dead ancestors call for in a moment like this? And before he knew it, he was past. Behind him someone screamed "Get back ye daft bastard, they'll kill ye!"

Behind him a torrent of stones were let free and then a whistle that told him a bottle had been launched. Ahead of him, shoulder to shoulder, glittering like malevolent beetles in their shiny new government supplied helmets, black clubs gleaming, were the police. Paid to protect their own and no other.

The bottle landed in front of them just before he did, exploding in a vicious spray of glass and leaping, roaring flames. Several of the police were distracted and he used the opportunity to slip past, climbing the base of the hill that ran up to the old, walled city.

It became a bit like a deadly game of rugby after that, with Pat holding the most desired ball in existence. He feinted, dodged, caught a harsh blow to the head and felt the blunt end of a club across the back of his knees. He kept running though, eyes on the wall ahead. Counting down the distance as the ground dissolved beneath his feet, the rhythm of his childhood drumming in his head. *'Ten for the Papist, nine for the Prod, eight go to hell and seven get to God...'* . A club raked the side of his head, leaving a swathe of fiery pain in its wake, *'Six for the Lady, Five for the Queen,'* a hand grasped at his ankle, biting the flesh through to bone and then tore off, a hot trail of blood trickled down his foot. *'Four for the orange, three for the green, Two for the fountain,'* he made the wall, felt the impact of stone against his chest and drove the tricolor into a crack in the wall. And yelled *'one for the fire'* just as the first club caught him full in the back of the head and an expanding halo of light exploded before his eyes. Then all was blissfully black.

"...WAS ALWAYS A STUBBORN LITTLE BUGGER YE KNOW.."

"...already had a head injury, fixed it up as best I could but..."

"Aye, well he's the Riordan skull, take more than a couple dozen clubs to break it. Are ye awake then Sleepin' Beauty?"

"Water," Pat croaked around a pain that seemed to fill the entire room it was so weighty.

"Here, no don't sit up for god's sake yer like to pass out for another twelve hours, I'll tilt the bed up, there ye go. Yer right eye's swollen shut an' the left isn't much better, can ye see anything at all?"

Pat slit the eye with exceeding caution, the small flutter occasioning several needlelike ripples of red-wired pain to scuttle across his eyelid and then trot briskly down his cheekbone. "Ow," he said succinctly.

"That's an understatement," Casey muttered grimly, sticking a straw between Pat's teeth.

"How'd ye get here?" Pat asked after taking several long sips off the straw.

"Yer friend here, Miss Larkin, got ye to the hospital an' then had the graciousness to call me. Though ye'd not be a hard man to locate today."

"What?" Pat asked, the dull throb of his head, teeth and face pinching the coherence from every second word.

"Open that eye wider my bonnie boy an' take a look at today's headlines."

Pat felt the smooth weight of newsprint being laid on his lap. He opened his eye as wide as he could and blinked to focus. Under the banner of the *Irish Independent* was his picture.

"Large as life an' twice as cute," Casey said wryly.

The headline in bold black read 'The Fires of Revolution'. The camera had caught him at the exact moment he'd thrust the flag into the wall, gloriously backlit by a sheet of flame.

"Yer on the front of the Times an' the Examiner as well," Casey said tossing two more papers onto the bed. "An' rumor has it the New York Times ran the photo on page three."

"The New York Times," Pat echoed, struggling to absorb what he was hearing and seeing.

"Aye, yer the darlin' boy from the Ardoyne today, likely the RUC is wishin' they'd finished ye off well an' truly last night."

Pat looked up from the paper to meet the gaze of Sylvie Larkin, dark and tense.

"It seems I owe ye thanks again. How'd ye find me?"

"Followed ye," she said, looking away from him to the floor. "Only a small ways at first but once ye started runnin' I had a bad feelin' an when I saw ye grab the flag I knew ye were goin' to do somethin' crazy."

"Where's Sarah?"

"I imagine that's meant for me to change the subject," Sylvie said, raising her brow, "she's with our neighbor an' can talk of little other than yerself. Yer in real trouble now, she's determined to marry ye."

Pat smiled and then promptly winced at the pain it caused. "Thank you," he said, "for everything."

"It wasn't much of anything," she said shaking her head, a flush of pale pink smattering itself amongst the freckles on her cheeks. "Twas nothin' compared to what you did."

"Aye, it's hard to match all out stupidity on such a monumental level," Casey said lightly but Pat saw the worry in his face and the hollows beneath his eyes.

"An' how'd ye know who to call?" he asked, the neatness of the situation raising several questions in his mind.

"There was a wee bit of paper in yer inside pocket that said if ye were found in trouble yer brother was to be called."

"Was there?" Pat asked, casting a dark, albeit slitted, look in his brother's direction.

Casey was saved from answering by the sound of a scuffle outside the door, several raised voices and the strident tone of a head nurse whose patience was severely taxed.

Pat saw Casey and Sylvie's eyes meet in an odd look across his bed.

"What's goin' on then?"

"That'll be the papers," Sylvie said with a rueful look, "they've been waitin' for ye to wake up since ye were brought in."

"There's a lady from one of the English dailies," Casey said, "an' her mind seems as sharp as her pen. I'd talk to her first if I were you."

"An English reporter?" Pat queried doubtfully.

"Aye," Casey grinned, "fame'll be that way, all sorts of strange things can happen. Yer public is waitin' boy, do I let them in?"

Pat swallowed and met the dark and steady gaze of Sylvie Larkin. She smiled and nodded almost imperceptibly.

"Let them in," he said.

Chapter Fifteen
Guess Who's Coming to Dinner?

IT WASN'T ENTIRELY SURPRISING that a man who found the comforts of whiskey so sublime would, of all his interests, find his deepest pleasure within the walls of the family distillery. Jamie had to admit that making whiskey, the delicacies, the slow painstaking process, the unhurried atmosphere of it all gave him a deep sense of peace and well-being. It was unfortunate for him that he rarely had the time to spend there.

'Connemara Mist' came in a variety of elixirs. From a light, delicate single malt, to the long sweet-noted finish of the sixteen-year-old distillery reserve.

When Jamie had been fourteen his father had put him to work in the summers in the distillery, a four hundred year old site on the slow-moving and aptly named River Sweet. He'd worked in all areas of the distillery, learning each stage of the process. The hot and heady fumes in the malting process as sprouted barley was dried in anthracite fueled kilns, the great open kettles of the brewhouse where the barley was boiled down to its fermentable sugars, the dance of sugar and yeast that resulted in the beginnings of alcohol, the low wines of first distillation, the soft-hearted feint of the second and the final mind-glazing spirit of the third. This third distillation was eighty percent alcohol. At each stage, he learned how to separate the less desirable elements from the desired, to achieve the level of quality and taste the Kirkpatrick distillery was famous for worldwide.

The huge warehouse where the casks were stored and matured was his favorite area though, dry and cool with a sweet vanilla-nut scent in the air, dimly lit by the brown and gold of the bourbon-seasoned barrels. Barrels baptized by the harsher American whiskey to leach out the stronger tannins and oak extracts, leaving the wood nicely mellowed and sweetened for the aging of its Irish cousin. The famous names on reserve casks had given him a thrill as a teenager—writers, actors, politicians who understood that the Kirkpatrick name gave their table a certain distinction or just liked to indulge in the finest whiskey made.

He strolled the aisles, deep and cool on this late October afternoon and

wished he could hide amongst the barrels for just a while longer. It was however, a two hour drive back to Belfast and then he'd have to dress for dinner
and prepare himself for what was likely to be one of the most unpleasant
evenings he'd spent in recent memory.

"Alexander," he nodded and smiled at his Master Distiller who was assessing a cask of the ten-year malt.

"Have a taste, James?"

He stopped and accepted the glass Alexander held out to him, noted its
clarity and pure gold reflection, took a taste and let it linger on his tongue
giving the palate a chance to secure the various flavors. It felt like silk in his
mouth, its warmth expanding to fill out into notes of heather and honey,
with an undernote of chocolate and a slightly dry finish. Perfection.

"I'd say it's ready, what do you think?"

"Absolutely," Alexander nodded, his nose drinking in the heady fumes
with the look of a man who knows he may very well have the best job on
the planet. "Lena was through here a minute ago, said if I saw ye to let ye
know that ye'd a call from home."

"Thank you," he returned the glass to Alex and with a sigh turned towards
the offices high up in the warehouse that looked out over the casks.

Once inside he dialed the numbers for home and waited while it rang
four times, he was just about to replace the receiver when a breathless and
somewhat annoyed female voice answered.

"You left a message," he said, trying to sound placatory.

"I did."

"Talk to me then.

"If—" there was undue stress placed on the word, "you leave right now,
you will find you just have time to get home and change for dinner, otherwise
you'll have to swap clothes in the mudroom with my assistance."

"I'm leaving now," Jamie said, smiling at Lena who'd entered the office
with a swathe of paper and was now standing and listening most intently to
his conversation.

"Anything I need to sign?" Jamie asked a moment later when he'd gotten
off the phone.

"Nothing," Lena smirked, "that can't wait until tomorrow. It sounds as if
you are needed rather urgently at home."

"Good," he replied, heading for the door with reluctant speed, only to turn
back at the top of the stairs, "call my florist would you Lena, have them send
round a bouquet of stargazer lilies to my house would you?"

"Of course Mr. Kirkpatrick and to whom shall the flowers be sent?"

"Herself," Jamie said with a smile.

"Herself?" Lena gave him a puzzled look, as if he'd taken leave and dropped
his senses on the floor in front of her.

"Yes, she'll know who they're for. Have a nice evening Lena, take yourself and Bob out to dinner why don't you? If you go to Johnny Fortescue's I'll arrange to have it put on my account."

"Well thank you sir," Lena said somewhat flustered.

Leaving the building, Jamie found himself whistling.

THE SCENE AT HOME WAS ONE OF SEVERELY RUFFLED CALM. The kitchen being the apparent center of the hurricane. Maggie was cursing into a pan of burned pastry, Montmorency was running around with what appeared to be the shank of a cow in his mouth, and Pamela was speaking in severely sweet tones into the phone while spooning a dripping green mess into the garbage. She smiled at him as if the entire scene were normal. Her attempt at having the whole show neatly in hand was rather spoiled by her appearance though. Her hair having been stuffed hastily into a ponytail at some point was either hanging in her face or sticking out at angles from her head. Her white sweater, immaculate when she'd arrived in the morning, had a long greenish streak of some indefinable food substance on it and her face was flushed red with fury.

"The florist sent round carnations if you can believe it!" She said banging the phone down with considerable vigor. "Carnations for a dinner party, they're funeral flowers for god's sake. The butcher delivered mutton instead of beef and so when the beef finally did come it went into the oven far too late and won't possibly be ready on time, the apple tart burned on the bottom because the bake-oven chose today of all days to stop working and—and—," she sat down on a kitchen chair, Montmorency running in wagging, panting circles around her denim clad calves. "And it's all going to be a bloody disaster, isn't it? I should have listened to you and never attempted this in the first place. At least, though, if the undercooked meat kills them we'll have flowers handy for the wake." She gave a ragged laugh that was half exasperation and half frustrated tears.

Jamie wordlessly poured her a glass of wine from one of the decanted bottles and handed it to her.

"Drink it all and then go upstairs and have a bath. You've got an hour before we need to be dressed and downstairs. What's left to do Maggie and I can sort out between the two of us. I make a champion crème caramel, don't I, Maggie?"

"Ye do," Maggie replied.

"But I'm not staying to dinner," she blew a stray lock of hair out of her face, looking warily at him over her wineglass.

Jamie smiled sweetly, "Oh yes you are, this party was your idea and seeing as your guest list leaves something to be desired I think you should join me in the festivities. Go on," he pointed out of the kitchen, "and have a soak, you look as though you deserve it."

An hour later there was a crème caramel glistering on the counter, Jamie was freshly showered, shaved and attired in a pair of gray Italian silk trousers, a crisp white shirt and a jacket to match the pants. It was rather more casual than dinner party attire generally called for, but it had been laid out on his bed and he surmised that it was all part of some grandly laid scheme.

He met Pamela coming down the hallway and stopped for a moment to admire the transformation she'd undergone. For a girl who'd no intention of staying to dinner, she'd obviously brought along all the accoutrements that femininity required for just such an evening. Her dress was a floating, ethereal thing of autumnal browns with just a hint of red setting fire to the green of her eyes. Clipped on one shoulder toga fashion, it left the other bare and vulnerable. Her hair was up, parted and twisted down the sides of her face and tied low on her neck. Helen, he mused and just as likely to start a war here at Kirkpatrick's Folly as the original had been in Troy.

"You look lovely," he said, offering her his arm at the top of the stairs.

"Thank you for the lilies," she said and took the arm, "how'd you know? They're my favorite flower."

"Educated guess."

They parted at the dining room doors just as the bell rang.

"Ready to enter the lion's den?" she asked, taking a shaky breath as footsteps sounded along the hall.

"Only question is," Jamie said quietly, "are we the lions or the Christians?"

"I imagine," she murmured as the Duke and his toothy wife came into view, "we're a little of both."

DINNER WAS, IF NOT ENTIRELY DIGESTIBLE, CERTAINLY NOT DULL.

Jamie, educated by Jesuits, was well-schooled in the art of dissembling. The entire table, with the possible and noteworthy exception of the fair Reverend, was charmed, disarmed and thoroughly under his spell before the second spate of wine had been served. He flirted lightly with the women and skillfully wove banter and business talk, into a tapestry all the more confusing for its variety of threads, with the men. He professed great interest and displayed detailed knowledge of the art of deep sea fishing, (the Duke's grand passion) then proceeded to flatter, cajole and flagrantly butter the beaming Duke up. Women blushed, men guffawed and all professed to not knowing when they'd had a better time. Lucien Broughton, seated three seats down to Jamie's right, remained stoic and apparently impervious to the caducean rod of Jamie's charm. Pamela, seated rather purposefully next to him, could get no sense of his thoughts nor feelings. He ate rather spartanly, refused the wine and later the whiskey and still later the brandy. He answered any question directed at him, was polite and to the point and then returned to a pale contemplation of the rest of the assemblage.

She herself tried to engage him in small conversation, only to have him answer in words of three syllables or less, apparently untouched by the scent or sight of young female flesh.

After dessert, the talk inevitably turned to politics, for every man in the room was connected by strings fine or corded to the machinations of government as practiced in Northern Ireland.

The Duke, face jolly and well shaded by the array of alcohol he'd consumed, had leaned over and looking down the table two places said,

"What's this I hear Reverend about you throwing your hat in the political ring?"

"It's true," Lucien replied, carefully placing his folded napkin on the table beside his untouched tea.

"What would your father think of that, eh Jamie?" the Duke turned to his host, unaware that the whole table had stilled, chatter dying the length of the room like dominoes clocked into silence with one swift stroke.

Pamela, breath stopped in her throat, watched Jamie's face for a reaction. There was little to be seen. He sat relaxed, a glass of wine held in his left hand, light refracting through it to cast a puzzle piece shadow of fragmented gold glitter onto his face.

"I imagine," he drawled in a tone that held a rapier slice in its edges, "he'd hate it."

"What," the Duke asked, slightly sobered, "d'you have to say to that Reverend Broughton?"

"I imagine," Lucien replied, his voice through lack of intonation, matching the cut of Jamie's own, "Mr. Kirkpatrick is right. But perhaps I'm permitted to ask a question of my own?"

Jamie nodded.

"Not having known the gentleman it's perhaps presumptuous of me to say, but it strikes me that as much as your father would have hated my entering the race, he'd have hated you not entering into the fray even more."

"As my father is dead what he would or would not like seems to be rather irrelevant."

"Do you not believe in the eternal soul, Lord Kirkpatrick?" Lucien asked quietly, his voice, pale and measured, casting gauntlets before it. "Or does your faith deny heaven to those who leave this earth in an untimely manner?"

"We leave it to God to damn souls rather than taking such responsibility upon ourselves," Jamie said easily.

"How convenient," Reverend Broughton replied, never once taking his colorless eyes off of Jamie's face.

"Well human judgment and error can be a damned inconvenient and ill-informed vice at times Reverend, or have you not found it to be so yourself?"

"Error at least requires action."

"Touché," Jamie said and rose gracefully from the table, "perhaps all of you would like to join me in the drawing room for drinks?"

"Of course," the Duke said with forced joviality and Pamela began to feel rather warmly towards him.

In the drawing room with the guests scattered about in plush furniture and the tinkle of Mozart's *Rondo alla Turca* in the background, the talk turned to real estate, of the new money flushing through the streets of Dublin, the reawakening of the slumbering city on the banks of the tidal Liffey, coming up from the dreaming Georgian days of the last century to find men in mohair suits with harsh accents in her streets. And to witness the death of the old days and perhaps the death even of a nation, brought in chains forged by men who cared only for money. An Ireland of golf courses and resorts, tacky souvenirs and self-mocking patriotism, a Celtic theme park for foreign consumption. So all those who had gone away could come back generations later and shed a tear for the old country.

"Gentlemen, you speak as if we here in the North had concerns in the Republic," Lucien said, "when our fortunes are untouched by their own."

"Reverend Broughton," the Duke said coolly, "my family seat is in Cork and has been for seven generations. For many of those generations Ireland was one nation and, God willing, will be again."

At this astonishing pronouncement, Mozart's moonbeam notes paused and fluttered into the opening of Handel's Water Music.

"I didn't know you held such nationalistic notions, Your Grace," Lucien said and one had to listen very closely to hear the contempt in the words. "However, the facts are that Northern Ireland is part of the Empire, the British Empire and as such marches under a different standard."

"D'you think England gives a damn about Northern Ireland?" Jamie's voice sliced like a seared knife through butter. "Everyone else has shed the bonds of empire and gladly so, even Britain knows when a dead horse has been flogged. Northern Ireland is just the crazed relative in the attic that's too embarrassing to parade even for eccentric company. The sun has not only set, Reverend Broughton, it's sunk beyond retrieval and memory. England has used us when it was politically expedient to do so, but she has too many of her own problems at present to care a great deal about a bunch of fanatically loyal Irishmen and, make no mistake Reverend Broughton, to the English you are an Irishman regardless of what flag you fly and what colors you paint your curbstones every July."

"In view of the fact that one million people in Ulster are of the Loyalist persuasion that may be a somewhat unfortunate view of things."

"Regardless of religion, Reverend," Jamie said mildly, "everyone in Northern Ireland needs to start looking forward rather than back."

"And does looking forward mean looking South?"

"It means looking in all directions that the compass points, to Europe, to America and yes, to the Republic."

"Well said, James," the Duke said, accepting with a wink and a smile Pamela's offer to refill his brandy snifter. "This global market notion wafting around in Parliament has its merits. Ireland will need to heal her wounds in order to be fit enough to compete on a world level."

"Change for the sake of rich man's banter? You'd have a hard time selling that notion to your average voter in the streets."

"It's only the orthodox who are afraid of change, Reverend," Jamie said mildly.

"And it's only the radicals who embrace change without questioning its long-term consequences."

"At least," Jamie replied, pausing to put more ice in his drink, "embracing requires action."

"As you said yourself, Lord Kirkpatrick, touché. Tell me though, are you willing then to embrace a new Ireland of jerrybuilt houses and glass monstrosities, of people—poor people—living in stacked-up housing on the fringes of this new moneyed society?"

"Have a care for the poor, Reverend and how you use them as a figure of speech. If you take my father's old seat in Parliament these people will be your concern, all flesh and blood, all with lives and hopes, fears and dreams. How do you propose to de-marginalize the poor, bearing well in mind, of course, that the vast majority of them are Catholic? Will you bring the Catholic ghetto inside the walled bastion of old line Protestantism? Will you sit down to tea in the Ardoyne? Will you break bread with the priests and kiss the ring of the Cardinals? Be wary in your use of the poor, if you make promises, they'll watch to see that you keep them." All this was said lightly, almost blithely as if he were discussing the mating habits of butterflies or some other contrary creature.

Across the room though, looking through the soft evening light, a flurry of sprightly violin notes reaching their apex around her ears, Pamela watched and listened and heard the discordant notes in his speech. The strain of the evening was beginning, however faintly, to show. And knew if she had sensed it so had the Reverend.

As apparently, for all his bluff and hearty posturing, had the Duke for he carefully turned the tables.

"James tells me you've a few opinions about my factories that you'd like to share, Miss O'Flaherty."

Pamela swallowed and shooting a glare in Jamie's general direction said, "Did he?"

"He did," the Duke replied dryly but with an encouraging smile. "Perhaps you'll be so kind as to come and sit by Edyth and I and tell me what these opinions are."

After pouring herself a tumbler of whiskey for courage she sat near the Duke which put her in range of Jamie and the Reverend. She marshaled her thoughts and avoided the amused green of Jamie's gaze.

"Perhaps first you'll tell me what's wrong with my factories."

She took a deep breath and smoothing the brown fabric across her knees with a sweaty palm plunged in headfirst.

"Well to begin with they're antiquated, the machinery dates back to the last century. The safety record is abominable; there's been seven serious life-altering injuries in the last year alone. You're in violation of at least sixteen different city ordinances that I can think of and the pay scale isn't even seventy percent of the European average for similar industry. Benefits are close to non-existent, and the take-home pay is only enough to exist on, not enough," she turned and met Jamie's eyes, he nodded in encouragement and she faced the Duke again, "to dream on," she finished in a rush of breath.

The Duke eyed her for a moment, a hard light in his eyes. "You've done your homework, I can admire that but what exactly do you know of these people that work for me, Miss O'Flaherty? Or are they statistics on a sheet to you?"

"I think I could relax better Your Grace if you'd call me Pamela."

"Then I think it would be best if you left off with the 'your grace' bit my dear."

"Deal," she smiled shakily. "I live in the Ardoyne. It's only recently become my neighborhood but some things don't take an entire lifetime to understand. There's a surfeit of hope wherever there's a lack of employment, surely anyone can see that. Still, people shouldn't have to feel fortunate to have any job, regardless of the meager pay and medieval working conditions."

The Duke raised his eyebrows.

"Alright," she acquiesced, "I'll take back the medieval, but really you need to go into those factories, talk to the workers, see them as people with families, with needs and wants. With faces."

"You've taken a socialist under your wing here, Jamie," the Duke said but the words were spoken warmly and his wife patted his knee approvingly.

"I've been called worse," Pamela said.

"Will you come with me then, if I go meet the people as you suggest, will you come along as a liaison? A link between neighborhoods so to speak, between the red bricks of Knockdean Park and the ones of Shankill Road."

"I would, but I am as much of an outsider as yourself Your—"

"Percy my dear," the Duke's wife said warmly, "his given name is Percy and it's not used often enough."

"Percy," Pamela amended. "I know someone who does belong to the neighborhood, who understands the lay of the land, someone that the people would trust. If he went with you it would be taken as a show of good faith."

"Who is this person?"

"His name is Pat Riordan," she said and took a nervous gulp of her whiskey.

"A name," the Duke said dryly, "I've heard once or twice of late." He eyed her shrewdly, "And if it's not too impertinent may I ask how you are acquainted with this man?"

"I share a home with him and his brother."

"I see," the Duke said and she could see he was taking her measure, weighing her words and the reasons he had to listen to her advice. It was possible that he'd disapprove of her bringing Pat into the situation.

"Right then, young lady you've presented your case and I've listened. But that's all just words isn't it? You bring this young man," he gave a wry smile, "to my offices on Monday morning first thing and we'll see what there is to be done."

"Thank you," she said.

The Duke turned then to speak to the man on his right who worked with the Trades and Commissions Bureau. His wife patted Pamela's hand, "You did a good job there dear; he really listened to you. Most brave, all things considered." She shot a stern look over Pamela's head at Jamie.

"Riordan is a name," the Reverend cleared his throat, "rather famous in Republican circles, isn't it?"

"It's a common enough name," Jamie said lightly, saving her the expense of answering.

"It's only that someone in the public light has to be careful how far out into the fringe elements they venture, wouldn't you agree, Lord Kirkpatrick?"

"One should always be careful when they stray out of their own element and when they do would be wise to remember they may not understand the rules by which this other world is ruled. Being on the road doesn't necessarily mean you know where it leads."

"You're being rather cryptic, even for you, James," the Duke said his attention turned back to the two men.

"Oh not at all," Lucien said a benevolent smile on his lips, "Lord Kirkpatrick puts me in mind of an old Chinese tale wherein the Emperor is tricked into believing he's merely visiting a friendly home when really he's being borne across the ocean toward the enemy. A stratagem I believe it's called, a military maneuver designed to obscure the true purpose or design of something. Am I right, Lord Kirkpatrick?"

The pale eyes met and locked with the hectically green ones.

"Smoke and mirrors, Reverend Broughton, so much in this world is smoke and mirrors," Jamie said prolonging his stare until the Reverend blinked.

"Indeed," Lucien murmured, "the appearance of a thing is rarely ever the true nature of the thing at all, is it? As you say, Lord Kirkpatrick, smoke and mirrors. And on that note, I believe I must take my leave of you. I thank you for a most pleasant and enlightening evening."

"I hope you didn't take offense to any of our differing opinions," Jamie said, all polite charm.

"Certainly not, I always enjoy matching wits with someone of similar intelligence. Again thank you for your hospitality, no you needn't walk me to the door, I know the way. You must attend to your other guests."

"Indeed I must," Jamie rose, all fluid grace and control. Pamela hoped she was alone in noticing the faint sheen of sweat on his forehead. The sparring had gone on too long; the façade was maintaining itself on borrowed time as it was.

The Duke, casting a quick eye over Jamie himself, announced in loud tones that he too must take his leave as the hour was reaching unholy climes. Following suit, as indeed the Duke had intended they should, the rest of the company departed with effusive thanks and murmured invitations to their own homes.

Pamela retrieved the Duke and his wife's coats herself, taking the opportunity to thank them for their time and consideration in listening.

The Duke paused in the doorway, as his Bentley slid smoothly round on the graveled drive. "Knew a chap named O'Flaherty, damned good businessman, American, well transplanted Irishman actually, any relation to you?"

"No, I'm afraid not, it's a common enough name, isn't it?"

"I suppose," he met her eyes in understanding, "you look rather a lot like him, funny world isn't it?"

"It is that."

Closing the door behind the Duke, she leaned against it in relief, exhaustion running into her full tilt.

"Well," she said sensing Jamie's presence behind her, "who won that round the Christians or the lions?"

"I'm afraid it was overall a bit of a draw, though we may have to award him the opening gambit." His voice was grim.

"What's wrong Jamie?" she turned seeking his face in the shadows.

"He's been here before and the worrisome thing is he wanted me to know it."

She strained the evening's conversations back and forth in her mind, "Are you certain?"

"Oh yes, I'm certain. He made a comment about the scent of white lilacs and how heady they'd been in the spring. It was out of context and very pointed. He was here in the spring, or someone who works for him was and he wanted to be certain that I knew it. The question of course is why?"

"Too many questions and not enough answers. Are you alright, Jamie?" For he had slumped without warning against the wall.

"Fine, too much wine and not enough water I'm afraid."

"Are you drunk?" she asked, guiding him up toward the stairs.

"There's no need to insult my dear," he replied, "twelve drams of whiskey, four firkins of ale and a vat of wine only lend a mellow sweetness to my spirit."

"You *are* drunk," she said opening the door to his bedroom and standing aside so he could enter unimpeded.

"I can hear all the hallowed generations of Kirkpatricks whirligigging in their Hebridean graves at the thought," he sighed extravagantly, and flopped with a certain elegance onto his bed, managing to kick his shoes off in the process.

"It's only that you don't look well," she said.

"Please you'll make me blush flinging all these compliments around."

"Can I do anything for you before I leave?"

"Stir up the fire, tie me down in silk pajamas, blush, dimple and perhaps throw in a seduction just for old time's sake, all or any of the above and in whatever order you prefer."

"Chivalrous of you." She moved about the room lightly, smooring the fire, opening the window a crack, setting a glass of cool water where Jamie could reach it. Then stopped at the foot of the bed, eyes watering, "What on earth is that smell?" She wrinkled her nose in disgust at the strangely acrid smell that had, without warning, filled the room.

"The sweet scent of cows in hell," Jamie murmured, head bright as a new penny against the shadow of his pillows.

"What?"

"I think you'll find that you've thrown my shoe into the fire," he said.

"Oh heavens so I have," she looked in consternation at the merrily crackling shoe. "Well the shoe's a loss I'm afraid," she said peering into the fire, "is there anything else you need?"

> *"Here with a Loaf of Bread beneath the Bough,*
> *A Flask of Wine, a Book of Verse-and Thou*
> *Beside me singing in the Wilderness...*
> *And Wilderness is Paradise enow."*

Jamie said lightly.

"Not I presume," she said tartly, "from the works of the venerated and prolific Jack Stuart?"

"My dear girl you disappoint, any Pilgrim worth her salt should recognize the honeyed vowels and consonants of that venerable Arabic bede, Omar

Khayyam."

"Persian poetry," she said and had the memory to blush.

"And now if you don't mind I think I'll go to sleep. Won't your knight be impatient at the gate?"

"I suppose he will," she said, hesitating only slightly before heading for the door.

It closed with a quiet click behind her and Jamie opened his eyes and gave the door a look that the perceptive observer would have apprehended as longing, pure and undiluted.

Then with the smell of burned leather still clinging to the air, he closed his eyes and wished for sleep.

IN THE MIDDLING HOURS OF THE NIGHT, when the moon's light was impeded by a milk-splot of cirrus cloud, the Duke, feeling an acute craving for his cook's fried chicken, eased his girth from under his wife's limp arm and made his way downstairs.

Having secured the chicken and a glass of port to accompany it he headed to his study. The door, freshly oiled that morning, slid to with ease and shut with an equivalent and pleasing silence.

"You do choose the most unappealing hours for these assignations my boy. You might have at least lit the fire," he grumbled, setting the chicken and port down on his desk.

> *"Then let us meet as oft we've done,*
> *Beneath the influence of the sun,*
> *Or, if at midnight I must meet you*
> *Within your mansion let me greet you,"*

said a voice cheerfully from the corner of the study.

The Duke struck match to paper, watched it kindle and placed a couple of peat bricks on top when it was well caught. He rubbed his hands over the blaze and turned to contemplate his nocturnal guest.

"Lords and lambs a-leaping boy, how many goats went to the guillotine for that confection?"

"Fret not over them, like all good little Muslim goats they went willingly and with Allah's name on their lips."

Swathed in luxuriant black from head to toe, looking like some dandeli-on-headed Kashmiri prince or very well-heeled White Russian boyar, head wreathed artfully in spinning blue smoke, emerald clad fingers poised around a black cigarette, lay the supine and ankle-crossed form of His Lord of Bal-lywick and Tragheda, James Kirkpatrick.

"Slipped the charms of your soubrette so soon have you?"

"She's far too sensible for French perversions Percy, besides she seems much more interested in dressing rather than undressing me."

"Pity," Percy replied, filling another glass with port and handing it over to his guest.

"No thanks," a smoke-spiraling hand waved it away, "I've drinked enough drops tonight."

"Pigsticks you have," the Duke snorted, "you didn't drink even one drop of alcohol tonight, though I imagine your bladder's seen enough apple cider to last it a goodly while."

"What does a man have to do these days," feverish leaf-green eyes met his own through a haze of burning French tobacco, "to maintain the appearance of debauchery?"

"Those bloody-minded Jesuits have a lot to answer for boy," the Duke growled, "I can't discern between artifice and art with you anymore, did they feed you evasion with your oats?"

"I am merely the glimmer in the gimlet's eye, the quivering aspen in airy cage, the shining, if you will, from shook foil."

"Speak native boy, but as long as we're tossing about glimmering gimlets, where do things stand with the government?"

"Well," Jamie drawled, bemused momentarily by the construction of an airy plume of smoke, "it would seem we find ourselves caught between two rather famous Greek rocks."

"The devil and the deep blue sea, is it?"

"Something like," Jamie swung his legs around neatly and sat up, black cashmere stippled with diamond points of dew. "The Unionists are looking to shove their own man out of the tent and possibly use anyone within party ranks whose ideas are too radical as the lever to do it."

"Mmphmm," the Duke mused and offered Jamie a leg of chicken, which was politely refused. "The Piranha Theory is it?"

"A little blood in the tank attracts every cannibal in the bunch," Jamie agreed.

"And you get rid of all your undesirables in one fell swoop and then it's business as usual. Could be to our advantage boy."

"Could be," Jamie rubbed the back of his neck with one hand and tossed the remains of his cigarette into the fire. "But at least O'Neill was approachable on a few fronts, if we end up with someone like Faulkner or Chichester-Clark in power, we'll be firmly wedged between those aforementioned rocks."

"Orange to the bone those two."

"O'Neill has a plan, however, that he intends to present in the next few weeks. Derry has forced his hand. However it consists of simple reforms, would have seemed like revolution two years ago but now it's too little, too late I fear. Really, it's hardly more than a promise to listen to the Catholic complaint. But no one is willing to talk to deaf ears anymore. Stormont doesn't seem to understand the politics are in the streets now and not in the marbled corridors."

"And what do we hear from London?"

Jamie grimaced, "Ireland is not on their agenda at present. I've made a few inquiries, discreet and otherwise and when I wove all the whispers together it basically came down to a rather large shout of 'we're not getting sucked into the Irish bog.'"

The Duke took a swig of port and wiped his fingers with a linen napkin.

"And so you think Derry was merely the opening shot in a larger battle?"

"Derry opened the ground up a crack and the Nationalists are seeing light for the first time in decades they aren't going to allow anyone to snuff it out."

"And our more radical friends?"

"Quiet, too quiet really," Jamie idly toyed with a crystal ballerina he'd picked up, "it's never a good sign when an underground organization isn't making the slightest peep of protest."

"Larger things on their collective mind, perhaps?" The Duke tried to catch Jamie's eyes and failed. "What's bothering you, Jamie?"

Jamie carefully replaced the little crystal dancer on her table before answering. "Percy surely you recognized the name of the young man Pamela is bringing to you."

"Yes, I did see the papers after that debacle. Is he our worry?"

"No, he's only getting his political feet wet and is for all his background and neighborhood a bit of an innocent. It's his brother."

"Inheritor of the family legacy is he?"

"It would seem so."

"And you're worried about her? I take it it's the brother she shares a mattress with and not the pretty poster boy for the nationalist left?"

"I think he's planning to split the army."

"What?" The Duke leaned forward, as if he couldn't believe his own words. "That's insanity."

"I don't suppose he sees it in quite that light. The army has stagnated, it needs change, schism is change. Dublin doesn't understand Belfast and vice versa. He's a man of action, not words. All the speeches and marches may only be a precursor of what they've always been in this country."

"Prologue to the gun and requiem to any real change." The Duke eyed his guest shrewdly, "How'd you come across this tidbit? Surely she's not spying for you?"

"No, she's not." Jamie smiled deprecatingly, "I hear things, acuity of a bat, my curse and not your problem."

"Christ you are slippery," the Duke said admiringly, "raised by Gypsies and Jesuits what else can one expect though? Tell me are you so intent on protecting her that you'd allow her to spy on yourself?"

"No," Jamie shook his head wearily, "it's not her. I'm not quite so blinded by her charms as to not consider that as a possibility, but no Percy, I've not let the viper in through an open door."

"You do know who she is though, don't you?"

"My memory, despite occasionally bearing a resemblance to Swiss cheese, does have its solid spaces. Yes," Jamie said softly, "I do know who she is."

"And yet you let her think you don't remember, not terribly flattering to her," the Duke said, regarding him with an eye that, despite the late hour, was sharp and shrewd.

"I imagine if and when she's ready to tell me she will, and if not perhaps there are reasons it's better she doesn't." His words were said with a polite finality, indicating that this topic, by his measure, was exhausted.

"And so we come to the real viper. What did you make of your dinner guest?"

"He's playing his hand very close to his chest."

"But?"

"But nothing, I can't make head nor tail of his animosity towards me."

"And who is in whose little orange pocket?"

"I don't think the Reverend takes well to confined spaces."

"So he's the puppetmaster?"

"And so skilled at it that not a one knows when he's pulling the strings."

"He's a real danger Jamie; you need to take care for yourself."

"I am," Jamie said thinly, looking suddenly to the Duke's acute gaze like a prince caught within the fired walls of his own castle.

"You shouldn't have chased her away Jamie, she's good for you."

"Have we come so soon to the fatherly advice portion of the program?"

"Your tongue doesn't fool me the way it does most, James. You always did like to create difficulty where there wasn't any though. Do you really think you can keep her safe at arm's length?"

"Safe from myself at least," Jamie rose, an elegant blackbound courtier, face impassive.

"One night in her bed boy would do you more good than a year's worth of those pills you take, or are you taking them?"

"I'm not in any danger of being locked up in a hospital," Jamie said eliciting a stern look from the Duke. "I take them with my oats and evasion in the morning and my whiskey at night."

"You're impossible."

"I do my best." Jamie smiled, a flash of white amidst the gold and green of his countenance.

"So, in summation, we are wedged rather tightly between the green of Scylla and the orange of Charybdis, with little room to breathe and even less to maneuver."

Jamie turned, firelight laying stars down the length of his lashes, slender costly form limned in dying embers. "Oh Percy, there's always a backdoor if you know where to look, and I," he winked and reached for the window latch, "do."

A breath of frosted air, a light displacement of currents and the tempest, with holy goats swirling, was gone.

The Duke sighed and returned to his chicken.

Chapter Sixteen
Under Ben Bulben

IT WAS A SATURDAY, EARLY WINTER BESTOWING ITS FIRST LINGERING KISS hard on the trees and fields, when Casey woke Pamela in the dark hours in a manner enjoyed by both, then told her, as she snuggled back into the blankets, that it was time to get up.

"Go away," she said, pulling the blankets up over her head, "it can't be more than five o'clock."

"Come on," he threw the blankets back, "there's someone I'm takin' ye to meet today."

"At this unholy hour," she said, swinging her legs over the bed, irritated at his alertness regardless where the hands of the clock were pointing.

"Aye it's a bit of a drive, an' then it's a matter of finding him as well."

"Who," she paused to yawn and stretch, "are you taking me to see? And where did you get a car?"

"Borrowed the car off Devlin an' as for who I'm takin' ye to see ye'll see when we get there," was his unenlightening response.

They took the Antrim Coast Road, partnered on one side by green fields swiftly browning and on the other by a gunmetal gray sea, surging with bearded breakers over rocks, reflecting the pale sky imperfectly. They had breakfast in a small seaside village, a postcard painting silent in the dying of the year. Lobster pots lay like abandoned toys in the rocky harbor, the smell of fish and salt blending with the scent of frying eggs and sausage.

After breakfast, they cut across country, through Ballymena, outskirting some towns, past Omagh, through Enniskillen, veering upcountry along Lough Erne, through Ballyshannon, down the high streets of tiny, depressed towns with poetic names forgotten moments later. She fell asleep in the early afternoon and was only awakened by the car coming to a soft halt some time later.

"Where are we?" she asked groggily, peering through blurred eyes at what appeared to be miles of sand and endless ocean.

"Donegal Bay," Casey said, smiling softly as he smoothed her hair away from her face. "Come on," he said and slid easily out of the car, tilting his face into the wind as he stood.

"Daddy used to bring us here occasionally, to blow the city stink off he said."

"I'm sorry he's gone," she said, sliding naturally under the shelter of his arm, warming herself against his side. "I would have liked to have known him."

Casey didn't answer at once but kissed the top of her head and rubbed his cheek in her hair. "He would have liked to have known ye as well, Jewel. He'd likely have warned ye off me as quick as he met ye."

"I wouldn't have listened, not even to him."

Casey sighed, wrapping both arms around her, "Christ ye scare me when ye talk like that. I'm so afraid of hurtin' ye an' yet I'd rather die than do so."

"I'm sorry if I've hurt you," she said, laying her ear against his chest and listening to the rhythmic thumping.

"I'd be lying if I said ye hadn't, when ye went away in the summer I thought it likely ye'd never come back or if ye did it would be with himself. An' the worst bit was I couldn't have blamed ye a bit. The scales were weighted heavily in his favor."

"He was just a childhood dream, this light that got me through a lot of dark days. But I never factored in that he was a man, not some prince in a fairytale who was going to rescue me. This here, you and me, it's real and it's what I want."

"I can't help but feel that I stole you away. It's as if I stepped into a story where I had no part an' grabbed the princess before the prince had time to make up his mind."

"You didn't steal me I came of my own accord."

He looked down to where their hands were clasped, raised one of hers to his mouth and kissed it gently. "I cannot offer ye much, an' ye know there are many reasons why ye should leave an' not so many to stay."

"You are more than enough, Casey," she said and kissed the hand that held her own. "Now who is this mysterious person you've brought me to meet?"

"It's my godfather but I'll not be sure of his whereabouts until later this evening. He's a man of some mystery but there are things about him that can be counted on with dead certainty."

"Such as?"

"He'll be tippin' his elbow at Davy O'Brien's pub by seven o'clock, if it were summer the time'd be somewhat more flexible but as it's not he'll be there on the dot of seven."

"Your godfather? I'm not certain I'm prepared for that after meeting your uncle."

"Devlin an' Dezzy are worlds apart, ye've naught to worry about." He squeezed her shoulders reassuringly. "In the meantime there's something I want to show ye."

"Is there indeed?" she said raising her eyebrows and smiling.

"Ye've a dirty mind," he grinned, "don't ever lose it. However much the idea appeals though we're on a public strand an' there's many windows overlookin' it. I've no desire to have my hind-end on display for half the town."

"Pity," she sighed, "it's such a nice hind end."

"Come on with ye woman before ye have us both in the clink for indecency."

They headed north along the strand, whippets of foam rushing at their heels. Clambered up black rock, slick and rank with seaweed to emerge on a barren headland buffeted by autumn winds off the Atlantic.

"This way," Casey said and led her along a dirt road that ran parallel to the cliff's edge. It ran for a goodly length and then abruptly petered out into a barbed wire fence. Several black-faced sheep peered curiously through the wire at them.

"That's a new addition," Casey stopped and stared at the fence. "There used to be a path down to the second strand through here," he shrugged, "I suppose we'll have to take the shortcut."

"The shortcut?" Pamela eyed the narrow footpath that hugged precipitously close to the edge of the cliff with some trepidation.

"Aye, wind's strong enough to keep us upright," Casey said and set off along the path, with an apparent lack of worry.

The cliff edge was positively battered, with the wind whipping in at an increasingly alarming rate, Pamela could hardly see for hair blowing across her face and into her eyes. She followed nevertheless in Casey's sure footsteps. Until they came to a deep gouge in the cliff head, a round hole whose maw ended some one hundred feet below in a throat of churning, freezing water.

"What now?" she said not relishing the thought of the walk back nor the walk forward.

"Fairy well," he said mystifyingly.

"Fairy well?"

"Aye it's what these holes are called, as a person could drop through them straight into another world."

"Yes, it's called the grave," she retorted, "only the Irish would call a suicidal opening in the earth a fairy well. We'll have to turn back, there's no way to skirt it."

"No need to skirt it," he said and without so much as a running start, he leaped it in one easy, fluid jump. On the other side he held out his hands, nodding reassuringly to her.

"Are you insane?" she yelled straining to be heard over the wind.

"Completely," he yelled back, "now jump."

She eyed the hole, measured it at around four feet across and knew there was no way on earth she could clear it.

She met Casey's encouraging look across the abyss and shook her head. "I can't," she said gripped suddenly by a paralyzing fear.

"Ye can, Jewel, just trust me, I'd never let ye fall."

It seemed suddenly, standing here in freezing cold wind, a deathly whirlpool swirling beneath her feet, that the leap he was asking her to make was one of faith and that to walk from the brink now would be to irreparably damage the fragile fabric of what they were weaving together.

She uttered a silent, terse prayer that consisted mostly of the words 'please' and 'God' and jumped. Beneath her, a horrible yawn of nothingness opened and the sense of falling a horrible distance to that child's nightmare place of no bottom and then, as promised, he caught her.

She balled his shirt front into her fists, sinking her face gratefully into his scent, letting go of a pent up exhalation.

"There's nothing to fear," he said, "I said I wouldn't let ye fall an' I never will."

She nodded, wondering if the tears prickling her eyes and nose were those of relief or worry.

"I don't understand you," she said shakily, "you hate horses, avoid the ocean and yet you think nothing of leaping out into space with nothing to catch you." And then, quite unexpectedly she burst into noisy sobs, muffled by the wind and Casey's proximity.

"Shh, darlin' it's alright, yer safe."

"But are you, Casey?" she asked, hands still crushing the cloth of his shirt.

"As safe as any man who leaves his bed every mornin' and ventures out into this world. There are no guarantees in this life for any of us; we can only live the days as they come, moment by moment."

She tilted her head back, tears drying as the wind flew against them.

Casey cradled one large hand against her cheek, sheltering her face.

"I feel safe when I hold ye, I'm safe in the night when ye take me inside an' the world just goes away, that's as safe as I've ever known life to be. I can't imagine askin' God to do any better than that."

"I don't see that God has much to do with what happens in our bed."

"Oh darlin'," Casey smiled, "God has everything to do with that."

He kissed the last of the tears from her face, the salt absorbing into his own skin, the liquid evaporating to the elements and mutual warmth.

"Come on," he pulled her up and away from the fairy well, her legs still shaking with fear, "it's goin' to rain somethin' fearful or I miss my guess. We'd best find shelter quick-like."

The wind had picked up considerably, the grass blowing horizontal to the ground and a great black mass of cloud scudding ominously in from the western sky. Below on the wide arcing beach with its coral- colored sand she saw the splintered remains of an old boat, washed up without passengers, half-drowned and tossed on lichen covered rocks, waiting for the next tide to regain some vestige of its former buoyancy. Caught between worlds, a thing of neither water nor land. She felt a pang of sympathy for it as she always had for things neither alive nor dead but only caught, defenseless, upon the edge of two separately spinning planes.

"This way," Casey said some moments later. At first it appeared that they hung over yet another of the deadly holes that seemed to fester the cliff head. But leaning down as the first large drops of rain hit them, she saw that though the ground did indeed give way to the sea, there was a set of stairs, carved by some fickle whim of nature into the rock. Steep, and at present slick with spray, nevertheless they looked navigable. Casey's black curls had already disappeared beneath the grass and skeletal remains of sea pinks that hung round about the rim's opening.

It was a treacherous climb, Pamela had to stop several times to take a breath and assure herself of her footing. Casey stayed only a few feet below her, guiding her by a light touch on her ankles to the next foothold. By the time they made bottom her feet ached as did the back of her calves and thighs. They were both sunk into sand over their feet and even now the ocean was rushing towards them, breaking hard against the shoreline rocks and flurrying onwards.

"This way," Casey pointed behind her and she turned to find an opening in the cliff. He had to turn sideways to slide through and even she had to hunch over, tilting her shoulders at an awkward angle.

She felt his hand touch her arm to guide her into a darkness so complete that it felt like veiling encasing her skin.

"Another few feet," she heard him mutter to himself as if he wasn't quite certain about the distance. Her entire body was prickling with the lack of light, small catpaws of panic dancing down her spine. In the heavy atmosphere, she could feel Casey disappear from in front of her as though he'd dropped soundlessly into a fissure in the earth. But just as quickly his hands reached back to guide her into the opening.

She stumbled onto her feet, it was still impossible to see but there was a sense of a vast space around them. The air was dry and surprisingly warm. She felt the tension begin to leak out of her spine.

"Stay there," she heard Casey say from somewhere to her left and then there was the sense only of noiseless steps and an echo of breath on stone.

"What are you doing?" she asked, the impact of the whole darkness sitting in the notes of her voice, making it small and tinny and echoing it back a hundred reedy ways.

"Findin' light," he said, two words that splintered and divided again and again, against stone, so that it seemed he surrounded her on all sides.

She didn't ask what he meant by this as the sound of her own voice, endlessly refracted, spooked her. A moment later there was a soft hiss, followed by the eruption of a halo of light in the darkness. It moved through the still and became, one by one, several pinpoints of light, tiny warm stars in the night of the cave.

"How—" she began halting as the word came back to her in twenty ghostly syllables.

"Candles," Casey said, "seems as if no one has discovered this place since I last was here."

"How long has it been?"

"Not so very long," he hunkered down to the floor, seeming in the half-light to be searching for something, "but it might as well be lifetimes. I've never brought anyone here before, even Pat an' Daddy didn't know about it."

"Thank you," she whispered and the whisper rippled in, lapped upon itself in concentric circles until it disappeared with a misty sigh in the middle of the cave.

"Ah, there—come here, Jewel," he said, beckoning with one hand the other having found what it sought. She knelt down beside him, the stone completely smooth beneath her legs. "Give me yer hand," he commanded and she did as bid. He guided her fingers into several small grooves in the stone, rippled with irregularities, not at all like the unblemished surface above. She shivered, an indescribable chill emanating up her arm from the grooved rock.

"What is it?"

"Footprint," Casey said and lowered the candle he held until her hand gleamed against the black rock.

Eight fissures divided the rock, eight precise tears that mimicked the shape of her own hand, though shorter by a good two inches in each case and with an additional three digits beyond her thumb.

"It looks like a hand," she said part of her wanting to snatch her own fingers away and part of her wanting to absorb all the time that resided in the rock.

"That's exactly what it became, though there was a long time between what you see there and your own hand." He swung the candle back, opening the darkness a swatch at a time. "See."

Behind her stretched a trail of footprints, the same eight fingered foot, four tracks to a set as though the creature had walked in a very measured step, indicating it would seem a body too heavy for its appendages.

"It would have been one of the first walkers, maybe even as old as the Devonian age, when the world was populated by hordes of fish an' not so much else. It could have left these tracks because the ground was swampy, still half-submerged in water. But this creature, whatever it was, was making the first tentative steps toward land. Maybe for food, maybe for shelter, or maybe like me he wasn't so overfond of water."

"How long ago?"

"Three hundred an' fifty, maybe four hundred million years, give or take hundreds of thousands either way. I'm no scientist, but I read about an eight fingered fish they found in Greenland back in the twenties an' this seems to fit with that."

"You never told anyone?"

He shook his head, face half-sheltered by the dark, the other side flickering in the uncertain candlelight. "No, y'know what would have come of that, masses of scientists, newspaper an' magazine people, an' then bunches of tourists coming to stare at these impressions in rock. They'd have had to tear the cliff apart to make it more accessible an' so on an' so forth. I couldn't be responsible for that, couldn't do that to Harry."

"Harry?" she raised her eyebrows.

"Aye," he responded somewhat sheepishly, "it's what I called him. He felt like a friend somehow, as if his echo were left to reassure, here in his footprints. When I die I want to be left with some dignity an' peace, I'd not want people staring at my remains an' takin' pictures of them. I think maybe he would have appreciated the same consideration."

"But these are just his footprints."

"Aye, maybe that's all they seem to you an' I, but they are all that remains of what may have been the first inkling of what was to come. Just the fact that he chose to crawl out of the water one day opened up a whole new world of possibilities. He stumped out of the mire an' millions an' millions of years later Michelangelo painted the ceiling of the Sistine Chapel an' Galileo pointed a stick of glass at the sky an' opened up the universe. I think maybe we owe this eight-fingered ancestor a little privacy for those things."

"You're a poet, Casey Riordan," she said and closing her eyes took a lungful of dry, warm air, pressing her palm into the impression left in rock by a creature that had walked this way on a hot day hundreds of millions of years before. Her mind's eye fleshed him out, the short heavy limbs, the ponderous body made for water, the sleepy eyes colored a deep and heavy amber. Harry indeed. A slow thinking creature drunk on steam and vegetation and yet one day he had made the move from the sweet ballet of the waterworld to the gravity pressed environment of land. And worlds later Michelangelo had painted his heart and soul onto the ceiling of a crumbling church. This creature deserved his peace and then some.

"Why did you bring me here?" she asked softly.

"I'm not talented with words," he replied, "but I wanted to show ye something that I'd never shown anyone an' give ye a part of myself I never thought I'd share. So that ye'd know that I trust ye as I've never trusted anyone else in this world."

"But there was always Pat and your father."

"Aye, but it's instinctive to trust yer parents an' Pat is Pat, he can't help bein' honest, it's like breathin' for him. An' ye'll forgive me for sayin' so but it's different between a man and a woman. There's more at stake." He lowered his head, watching candle wax drip and congeal on the stone. "I've known a lot of rough characters in my life. From the time I was born, I've been surrounded by people who had to be strong everyday just to survive. They had to be hard in mind an' in heart to get from one year to the next. An' ye've seen my back, I've known hatred, come to understand it well an' promised myself I'd never be vulnerable to it again. But I'd no idea that love could make ye ten times more open to destruction. I've had men beat me until I was certain there was only a minute or two left between me an' the grave an' yet the fists an' the knives never hurt the way it does when I think of losin' ye."

"You aren't going to lose me, Casey." She took her hand from the hollowed and ancient fossil fingers and stroked it across his head, sweet with warmth, trembling with life. Another thing to thank the nameless creature for. For if the pattern of the hand had not been laid down there would have been no need for the overlarge and unwieldy head of the human species. From whence flowed an unstoppable flood of creativity, imagination and emotion. Emotion, both blinder and builder, destructor and creator, soaring to death-defying heights and descending to slime-ridden pits. Anger, angst, beauty, despair, melancholy, joy, faith, hope and of course, love. In the beginning and in the end it was what the trial and tribulation of the human journey came back to, circling round the center sometimes for a lifetime. Love, both the simplest and hardest answer to all questions.

"I love you Casey, the rest you'll just have to take on trust."

He reached through the half-light, fingers fumbling with a primitive urgency and she, breath caught in her throat, reached back, closing the divide. Grasping, cleaving, arching and aching as the small gasps and cries of lovemaking arced through the air and multiplied against stone, flew back in the form of a thousand soft-winged caressing sounds, rocking the stuff of cell and synapse into a heady addictive mindlessness. And then after, in the dark, with only the pale flicker of wasting candles for stars, a warm satiation like drowning in amber without a care for dying.

"Ye know what I said about bein' vulnerable in love," Casey said, fingers tracing a delicate and wavy line down the center of her belly.

"Mm," she mumbled sleepily, smoothing hair damp with exertion away from his forehead.

"Well ye could kill me now an' get no fight from me."

"Darkness makes you say the sweetest things," she said, sarcasm marred by a luxuriant yawn.

"It'd be the kindest way to go I'm thinkin', leavin' this earth with stars whirlin' in yer head." He propped himself up on one elbow and leaning over kissed her softly on the navel, causing her to shiver along her entire length.

"Before, you called me Jewel, why?" she asked as his whiskered cheek blindly traveled the length of her skin, leaving a faintly pleasant burn in its wake.

"Did I?" he asked. "Hmphmm, that's odd I don't remember sayin' it. I suppose it's how I think of ye though, somethin' fine an' rare an' perfect."

"Do you then?" She caught one of his hard-skinned hands in her own and put the tips of his fingers to her lips.

His eyes in the dark were deep and soft, a wellspring of sweet oblivion she could have lost herself in forever.

"Aye, I do. My Da' took Pat an' I to Dublin one time, he'd business to attend to, an' so he gave the two of us some pocket money with strict instructions on where to meet him an' what streets we weren't to venture down. We were happy though just to wander an' contemplate what to spend our riches on. I must have been about eleven I suppose. Anyhow, we ended up in front of this jewelry store an' there was a stone in the window that was like nothin' I'd ever seen. 'Twas a star sapphire an' it was so blue. I'd never seen a blue like that before not in the sky, nor the ocean. I'd the feelin' that I could just fall into it an' never stop fallin' an' in the center there'd be a whole universe, galaxies an' galaxies of stars unendin'. It fair took my breath away, made me dizzy. That's how I felt the first time I saw ye, breathless an' reelin' like I'd been hit hard between the eyes. Well the shop owner came out an' told us to shoo, that he didn't need riffraff hangin' about scarin' off the customers. An' I asked him bold as brass what the price of the thing was an' he laughed in my face. I was so angry I just stood there an' repeated myself, indignant like, 'how much will ye want for the blue stone?' I must have seemed a prize eejit. An' the man looks me straight in the eye, with so much contempt on his face that I could feel it shrinkin' me right into the pavement an' says, 'Such a thing is not for the likes of you boy an' ye'd do well to remember it.' An' then he turned his back on us an' walked inside. I never forgot what it felt like though to be told I'd no right to touch somethin' so fine, that the likes of me was to be denied such beautiful sights. An' when I met ye, I thought the same, 'don't even think it boyo,' I said to myself, 'a woman as fine as her is not for the likes of yerself.' But still I couldn't help myself an' you, ye never looked at me with contempt, not even at the first."

"Why would I?" she asked softly, running one finger featherlight down the bridge of his nose and over his lips, "When it's the same for me. When you look at me and there's that certain expression on your face and I want to escape your eyes and yet I want to stay within their gaze forever at the same time. And I can't breathe or think properly and sometimes I wonder if I ever will again."

"There are times," one hand glided with the grace of water up her side, "that thinkin' properly is vastly overrated. Would ye not agree?"

"I—would," she gasped as he moved over her and the darkness lapped softly at their skins like the brush of velvet. She could feel his lips at her neck and then their slow exploration downward, the soft outrush of air as he moved, the silken brush of his hair against her breasts, her stomach, her thighs.

"Casey," she said in alarm, "what do you think you're doing?"

"Well," he said against the supremely sensitive skin of her inner thigh, "I don't know that I can recall the exact name, but I can assure ye that if I do the job right ye won't be thinkin' any thoughts, proper or otherwise."

"YE'D BEST," CASEY SAID DROWSILY SOME TIME LATER, "catch a wink or two darlin'." He settled with a happy sigh beside her, nose nuzzling her neck. "I'm in no condition at present to face the likes of Desmond O'Neill an' I'll warrant yer not as well."

"He sounds a little fearsome," she said, wanting at present to do nothing more than stay in the cave for the foreseeable future.

"He's not so bad, but I'll need all my wits about me when I see him." His voice drifted near the end of his words, subsiding into the sonorous rumble of deep sleep breathing. He'd the talent of waking and sleeping on a dime, as if he'd never had the time nor patience for the drifting white minutes or hours that hovered between the two states.

She envied him that and yet loved these moments best of all, when he slept and she could watch him, unobserved, quiet, without the sweet agitation of his conscious presence. Could kiss him gently on nose and forehead and let her eyes linger on his lines and know with a fearless certainty, that regardless of what had brought her here in the first place she had, albeit unwittingly, found her way home.

Later, while he still slept and the candles burned down to stubs, she retraced the floor with her hands, fitting her own once again into that of the ancient creature. Even if love was only the product of centuries of feverish longing, the development of minds that could not cope with their own abilities, the longing for something here on earth that could not be guaranteed in heaven, even if only that, they still had a lot to be grateful for. Even if it all came down to an aberrant fish with an inexplicable whim to call land his home. Even if.

Feeling along the bumpy inroads of rudimentary and crude finger she closed her eyes and whispered,

"Rest in peace, Harry."

BY A QUARTER PAST SEVEN THEY STOOD OUTSIDE THE DOORS of Davy O'Brien's, a hole in the wall establishment painted in the colors of Irish defiance, white, gold and green.

"Well," Casey said taking a deep breath for the third time in as many minutes, "well then." He cracked his neck nervously and, rather unnecessarily, kept checking the time on his wristwatch.

"Are you scared of him?" Pamela asked, starting to feel as if his nervousness was virulently contagious.

"Christ yes," Casey said, not even attempting a show of bravado.

"You said he wasn't near as bad as Devlin."

"I said," Casey took another gulp of air, "he was entirely different than Devlin. I don't think I was ever foolhardy enough to suggest he wasn't more intimidating."

"We could go," she said hopefully.

"No, temptin' I'll admit but it'd be only delaying the inevitable."

"Then let's get it over with," she said and grabbed the door handle with a determination she didn't feel stepping over the threshold of Davy O'Brien's, pulling a reluctant Casey in behind her.

Silence, complete and terrible, greeted their arrival. Through a miasma of cigarette smoke and the smell of spilled Guinness, at least twenty pairs of hard, unblinking eyes surveyed them. Pamela stepped back, trodding on Casey's toes, an action that caused him to exclaim in pain and broke the tension.

"Johnny," Casey said, nodding to the barman, who nodded in return.

"It'll be nice to see ye home," he said in a soft voice that matched his pale hair and skin. "Dez'll be holdin' court in his usual spot. I'll bring yer drink back there." He nodded at Pamela, eyes shifting back instantly to the pint he'd already started pulling.

"Right then," Casey muttered grimly, guiding Pamela behind him with a hand that shook just slightly.

Davy O'Brien's had seen better days, but even in its hour of glory hadn't been noted for its decor or ambiance. The walls, originally painted cream, were stained a dirty yellow from nicotine, the bar was a ghastly red, the stools split and shaky, the tables missing an occasional leg and the floor, laden with tobacco spit and spilt alcohol of varying brands, was plain poured concrete, which in light of its adornments, Pamela thought stepping daintily over a stream of snuff, was probably for the best.

In the far back there was a dartboard, a picture of the Holy Family next to one of John Kennedy and a green, white and orange banner that saggily proclaimed, 'Ireland for the Irish—Brits Out!'

Under this triumphant statement sat a table full of men, whose heads turned as one at the approach of the two strangers. Unvarnished men, lacking any sort of polish, craggy of face and body. And to a man, their faces were filled with a wary hostility.

Casey stopped short and Pamela bumped into him from behind. There was a protracted silence as if they were all indulged in some kind of combat where the loser would have to break the silence.

"Stubborn as always," she heard a soft voice say, "Prodigal son returning, I presume."

She peered over Casey's shoulder on tiptoe. Sitting, back closest to the wall, was a man neither big nor small, neither fair nor dark, neither old nor young. He'd sandy hair, ruddy skin, sagging a bit by the jowls and glasses of a thickness and heft as to make him look like an owl. The godfather, she presumed, the Desmond O'Neill that made Casey shake with fear. He didn't look intimidating, but as his soft-spoken words reached out she could, all the same, feel the authority they were spoken with.

"Aye, it's me Desmond," Casey said with a humility in his voice that made her blink in surprise.

"Did ye leave yer manners in England? Or does the girl plan to hide behind yer back all evening?"

Casey pulled a reluctant Pamela around to face the full scrutiny of Desmond O'Neill's myopic gaze. It was not a pleasant experience.

"Desmond this is Pamela O'Flaherty, Pamela my godfather Desmond O'Neill."

He nodded and she resisted the urge to step forward and shake his hand. He would disapprove, she suspected, of such a forward move in a girl.

"Kevin, give over the seat to the lady," Desmond said without once taking his eyes off of Pamela. She meekly took the seat as he indicated she should, but only after Casey forcibly removed her hand from his own and gave her a small push towards the table. Desmond had seated her next to himself. He smelled surprisingly of a light aftershave, tangy with lemon.

Casey had been left standing, quite deliberately it seemed. His face was tight, his eyes locked with Desmond's though there was no hostility in the mutual stare. Only a reassessment she suspected, a cartography, of the land and the years that lay between them.

"If ye'll excuse us," Desmond said cordially to Pamela as he stood and then turned to the displaced Kevin, "get the lady a drink, a beer shandy—'tis the only lady's drink they serve here," he added apologetically to her, giving a nod that seemed like an abbreviated courtly bow. He was, regardless of the surroundings, a man of some refinement it would seem. "Casey," he swept past him towards the door, "if ye'll be so kind as to come outside with me."

Casey let out a sigh that seemed made entirely of relief, said "Of course," and followed the tweed-coated form of Desmond O'Neill out of the pub.

The man named Kevin returned to the table, set the beer shandy down in front of Pamela and then leaned against the wall with his own drink.

"Wouldn't you like to sit?" Pamela asked, pointing at the chair Desmond had vacated.

Kevin smiled sweetly and said, "No tanks, not wurt de risk to me life. No one sits in Dez's chair, 'cept the chief hisself."

"Will they be long?" she asked, feeling increasingly uncomfortable as the men at the table cast furtive glances at her and said nothing to each other.

"Only as long as it takes," was the cryptic reply supplied by a man across from her, who ventured a timid smile as he spoke. She returned the smile and he flushed scarlet and tipped his head quickly to stare into his drink.

"Will ye be familiar wid de works of Mr. William B. Yeats?" Pamela turned to her right where the question had issued from and found a pair of bright blue eyes regarding her from over a snowy white mustache and beard.

"Not as much as I'd like," she said politely.

"D'ye know the inscription on his headstone then?"

"Aw, Barry don't start on the poor girl, ye know Des doesn't like it when ye do this. It gets Smoke all agitated."

Pamela took in the man's curt shake of the head and by a process of eliminating the two speakers and Kevin, decided Smoke must be the gray-haired man directly opposite her. He seemed more likely at present to pass out in his drink than to succumb to the vapors of agitation.

"Pardon me then, Miss, but I asked did ye know the inscription on his headstone?"

"Um, well not word for word but I'm familiar with the gist."

The white mustached man snorted, as if to say one couldn't expect better from foreigners.

She took a sip of her drink and deciding anything was better than the silence said—

> *"Cast a cold eye on life, on death*
> *Horseman pass by."*

"Ah, ye do know it then," said Barry with some satisfaction. "Johnny," he waved at the barman, " 'nother shandy for the lady."

"No, really I'm fine," Pamela protested only three swallows into her first drink and notified by the gurgle in her stomach that she should have had the good sense to eat before coming here.

"Barry cleans off the headstone once a week wid a wee feather duster," said a man in a plaid shirt, two chairs around from her "an' when it rains he thinks it's Yeats cryin' his thanks to 'im."

"Ye ought to have more pride in him yerself. The greatest poet of the age," Barry thumped a walking stick into the floor for emphasis, "nay the greatest poet ever in the history of this planet buried not a half hour from here an' ye don't know even a line of his poetry."

"Sure an' I do," said Plaid Shirt with a wink in Pamela's direction—

"There was a young lady from Dingle
Who slid on her bottom down a shingle,
She rubbed it with lotion,
She—"

"There is a lady present," said Barry, waggling his walking stick in a threatening manner. "Did ye know," he continued pleasantly in Pamela's ear, "that Yeats died in Paris an' the dirty Frenchies buried him there as if he were their own?"

"Really?" she said with what she hoped was polite interest. "Casey and Mr. O'Neill have been gone a long time."

"That," said Plaid Shirt, "is a good sign, means Dez is actually speakin' to him between the blows."

"The blows," she echoed faintly.

"Aye, 'tis why he called the boy outside."

She made to rise out of her seat but Barry detained her with a gentle hand on her arm.

" 'Tis between the two of them lass, the boy came to sort it out with Dez an' ye'd best leave them to do it properly."

"Oh," she said stupidly and sat back down.

"Anyhow to continue, once the Irish heard Yeats had been buried in France there was a great kerfuffle as ye might well imagine there would be, what with them tryin' to steal the greatest poet of all time an' pretend he was theirs—"

"It was war time an' it was bury the bastard or let him rot," supplied Plaid Shirt for which he received an impolitic look.

"So the Irish got together a contingent of men an' went to Paris to collect Yeats, but once they got there all was confusion what with the Irish speakin' the Irish and the French speakin' the French—"

"An' to make a long story short they dug up the bones an' brought the poor bastard home." Plaid Shirt finished, earning him the rubber-tipped end of a walking stick waving wildly in his face.

"Ye take care of the damn graveyard, ye ought to have more pride in the place," Barry was fairly spitting with rage, an action impeded by the clacking of his false teeth.

"I take care of the Catholic side an' they don't even supply me with a mower so I don't tend to get emotional over the grave of a dead Prod who'd a fancy way with words. Besides, the fact they don't know to this damned day if they got the right poor bastard. Ye could be dustin' the grave of some French peasant. Who the hell knows what happened to Yeats."

"That's an ugly lie," Barry got to his feet shaking with rage, "take it back or I'll shove it down yer throat with me stick."

At this point the comatose Smoke raised his head, a strange gleam in eyes that were a startling silver gray, one thin fist rose off the table and slammed down hard enough to make the drinks jump, "Where de feck is Yeats?" he yelled and then leaned across the table halting only inches from Pamela's face. "Do ye be after knowin' lassie where de bones of dat poor bastard is?"

She shook her head and Smoke settled with a sigh and hung his head over his drink once again. "Dey should of buried de man in a bee-loud glade, den he would have rested easy."

"On the Lake Isle of Innisfree," Pamela supplied gently.

Smoke looked up and smiled and she saw that once he'd been a nice-looking man, though time had more than done her work on his battered face. " 'Twould be a good rest in such a place as dat wid de sound of de lake lappin'."

"And nine bean rows in the garden," she said smiling.

Smoke reached across the table and patted her hand with his own gnarled and twisted one, stained yellow with tobacco and brown with the fields. "Yer a good girl lass a good girl an' sure the prettiest I've ever seen." With that, he returned to the contemplation of his drink and said not another word.

Plaid Shirt and Barry were surveying her with a sort of stunned bemusement.

"Is something the matter?" she asked wondering if she'd committed some breach of etiquette.

"Knowed Smoke me whole life an' I never heard him string moren' five words togedder at a shot," said Plaid Shirt. " 'Tis a bit like a mute burstin' into song te hear him talk that much."

Just then Desmond, followed by Casey, re-entered the premises.

Casey held up a hand reassuringly and mouthed the words, "I'm alright." He pulled a chair up and waited until Desmond sat before sitting himself.

"All's right now, Dez?" asked Kevin, still nursing his ale against the wall.

Desmond looked at Casey, a fond look, "All's right lad?"

"Aye," Casey nodded, "all's right, Dez."

"An' how's the boy?" Dez asked.

"He's fine an' I thank ye for keepin' an eye upon him while I could not."

"I'd never let a son of Brian's go hungry, though he's a stubborn wee eejit at times. He'd not take money nor help of any sort."

"He's his own mind, our Pat does, an' I respect that." Casey reached over during the conversation, took Pamela's hand and squeezed it. She took stock of his face and saw no bruises nor any swelling and decided the men must have been mistaken about Desmond's intention in taking him outside.

Conversation continued at the table, swelling and buzzing. Male talk of crops and boats, livestock and times long past that wouldn't come again. Politics were avoided assiduously. Pamela settled back in her chair in a sweet shandy-induced haze, letting the swing and flow of the conversation lull her. Through all of it, even when the tone and current of things bordered on the argumentative, Smoke remained silent staring into his drink as if it contained endless wonders, as perhaps it did.

It was near to midnight when Casey made his apologies and said they really must be gone.

"Ye'll take a room at the hotel," Desmond said and then as Casey began to protest, "surely yer not so much of a brute as to drag this poor lass back across country in the wee hours, are ye? Ye'll take a room."

"We'll take a room," Casey agreed.

"Tell Siobhan to give ye the best in the house, it's empty this time of year."

"We will."

They began to move away from the table, acknowledging good-byes, Pamela almost stumbling over her own feet in exhaustion when Smoke suddenly reached out and clutched Casey's shirt sleeve. He turned his head, hazy eyes shot through with a strange light.

"Ye'll be certain she's taken care of boy."

"Aye Smoke, I will," Casey said and patted the old man's hand.

"Even if it's not by yerself, ye'll be certain?"

Casey paused for a moment and Pamela shivered at the intensity in Smoke's gaze, it seemed to understand things, to see beyond the present atmosphere.

"I will be certain." Casey said in a tone more fitting for a blood oath than the appeasement of a half-senile old man.

Outside the night was chill, frost puckering on the grass, pub windows steamed solid so that the feeling of having stepped into a strange netherworld was total.

"What did he mean by that?" Pamela asked, shandy glow having disappeared with Smoke's words.

"Ah, only what he said. Some say Smoke has the sight an' that's why he drinks so much an' speaks only rarely. He's not right in the head, hasn't been since his wife died, they'd only been married the one year an' were expectin' their first baby an' one day he was in the field, ploughin' with a tractor an' she'd come out to see him, bringin' him his lunch or some such. Well the tractor'd got bogged down an' he was reversin' it, layin' hard on the pedal an' the tractor shot out suddenly, ran her right down, killed her an the babe. 'Tis likely why he told me to be certain ye were cared for."

"Life isn't fair," she said.

"No it isn't but somehow on a night like tonight, with every star in the sky as clear as glass it all seems worth it. The good an' the bad."

"Is everything alright now Casey, with Desmond?"

"Aye, it's fine."

"The men seemed to think he'd taken you out to beat you."

"Well they'd know Dez's ways as well as any, been drinkin' with the man everyday for the last thirty years or more."

"But there's not a mark on you."

"Jewel, there are places ye can beat a man that don't show on his face."

"But—do you mean to say—"

Casey grimaced, "Ye may not have noticed darlin' but my stride's not so easy. Desmond said as I'd acted like a fool child I'd have to take my punishment as such as well."

"He spanked you?"

"Aye, with a boat oar, made me bend over an' grip the rim of that wee bridge a ways back an' took his sweet bloody time about it. The man knows the anticipation is ten times the agony of the actual paddlin'."

"That you let him is what surprises me."

"There's a certain respect that exists between Desmond an' I. I broke that respect a thousand times over when I set the bomb, for him 'twas as if I'd spit in his face an' followed it with a slap. I had to humble myself in order to make it up to him. A bruised arse is a small price to pay to be back in good standin' with the man. We're just up here on the right."

She turned when they reached the hotel, a small but comfortable looking establishment and looked back down the road. The town sloped away from them towards the sea, pretty in the dark, the eggshell pinks, yellows and blues of its blistered and fading paint softened by night's gentle arm.

She turned then into the arm of her own lover, following him into the lobby, no more than a sitting room really. But it had a fire of glowing embers and a warmth they were grateful for. A woman roused herself sleepily from an armchair in front of the fire, her head a tousled mass of graying curls.

"Will ye be after lodgin'?" she said yawning and crossing a cardigan over her flannel clad bosom.

"Finest room ye've got, an' nothin' less will do, Mrs. O'Neill."

She peered at them and then a smile broke her sleepy features. "Casey Riordan ye wee eejit is it
yerself?"

" 'Tis."

"Have ye not a hug for yer Auntie Siobhan, then?"

"I do." He engulfed her in a massive hug, swinging her off her feet and setting her down breathless and laughing.

She patted her hair and shook her head at the same time. "An' who's the girleen?"

He drew Pamela forward and introduced her. She shook the woman's hand, just barely suppressing a yawn. "Ye look all done in child. I'll put a fire in number six an' it'll be snug in no time. The sheets are pressed an' there's a lovely heavy quilt on the bed. An' how many rooms will ye be needin'?"

"Just the one," Casey said firmly.

There was a distinctly uncomfortable silence and Pamela was grateful for the dim light as it hid the scarlet hue of her face.

"Mmphm," Siobhan made a disapproving sound and then sighed. "Ye've seen Dez then?" she asked Casey as she stirred up the fire with a poker and added another turf log to it. "Here ye wee eejit, take some of these," she stacked his arms with peat logs, "an' follow me upstairs."

"I have been to see Dez," Casey said, "an' before ye ask, we've settled our business."

"I knew ye must have if ye dared to show yer face here. Well I thank Jaysus above for it, he'll be more bearable to live with now. He's been miserable these last six years I tell ye, it right ruined Christmas for him too." She paused near the top of the staircase to catch her breath.

"Are ye still takin' the heart medication?" Casey asked, easily transferring the load of towels she'd carried upstairs from her arms on to the top of the peat he was carrying.

"I see yer still as meddlin' as ye ever were," she gave him an exasperated look and continued up the stairs.

The room was on the left hand side, its windows looking out over the town and beyond to the sea, a great shushing void in the night. And far, far in the distance was the hulked over form of Ben Bulben, casting its moonlit shadows upon the grave of the poet of the age or perhaps that of a nameless Frenchman.

Casey set a fire in the grate and within minutes, the chill was gone from the room. Siobhan yawning, said she was for bed and would see them in the morning. She kissed Casey on the forehead, the way a mother who'd seen him only yesterday might have done and patted Pamela companionably on the shoulder. "Sleep ye tight, child," she said and then looking at Casey added, " We've missed ye boy," and went out the door.

They undressed and clambered under the great quilt that covered the bed, sighing with pleasure at the warmth of the sheets that Siobhan had slid towel-covered bricks in between.

"Ah, now there's somethin' more like it," Casey said with a happy sigh, curling his body to hers in a manner that had become habit for the two of them.

Despite the events of the day and her previous exhaustion she found sleep didn't come quickly and lay quiet, Casey's hand warm in the curve of her hip, his breath coming deeper and deeper on her shoulder. They'd left the curtains open and it was one of those winter nights where the sky was clear as water in a bowl and it seemed as if she might stick her hand in it, carefully, each finger in turn and watch the ripples pour out into the universe, to the very edges of time itself.

"Maybe that's why Harry came out of the water," she said quietly not wanting to disturb Casey if he was asleep.

"Aye," he murmured only half conscious, "why's that?"

"To see the stars more clearly. Maybe he wanted to reach out and touch them and for that he needed a hand."

A small creature, trundling out of water, feeling for the first time the true weight of his body, the crush of gravity on flesh, great gold eyes rolling back in his head, toward night to the twinkling lights in the heady darkness above and beyond him. Perhaps he'd felt the first longing for that which was unknowable, unreachable, a faint whisper in the night of need for something that could not be defined and even less touched.

"He should have kept his snout in the mud," Casey said, lips brushing the back of her neck, "created a damn lot of trouble, reachin' for stars, the rest of us have kept tryin' but we're no closer to touchin' them, are we?"

"I think maybe it's only the reaching that really matters, what would we do with a handful of stardust anyhow?" She watched blue Rigel blink on the lip of the window ledge and closing her eyes, made a wish in the form of wordless prayer. She was distracted from higher thought though by the feel of a large, callused hand sliding the length of her thigh and dipping round with obvious intent.

"I thought you were asleep," she said on a sharp intake of breath.

"Not entirely," came the answer, the owner of the voice sounding much more alert than he had a moment before.

"I'd have thought you were too stiff," she rolled back as his body tipped over her own, in the beginning language of two bodies well suited to each other.

"I'd say stiffness was a necessary element to the operation at hand," Casey nudged her knees apart to prove his point.

"You know," she nipped at his neck, an action that had caused him, in the past, no end of sweet distress, "what I mean."

"Ahhh," it was half word, half groan as his body found the sanctuary of her own, "ye'd be referring to the back end as opposed to—sweet Jaysus do ye know what that does to me?"

"As opposed to?" she prodded.

"As opposed to the front—stop that... on second thought don't stop—end."

"You could...mm...injure yourself though."

Casey snorted and threw the quilt back with one arm, "Well Jewel, if I do it'll be in a good cause. Now if ye can't think of a better use for yer tongue, can ye at least have the grace to keep it—ahhh that's nice that is—silent?"

After that, conversation ceased and desisted for quite some time.

Chapter Seventeen

The Water Under the Bridge

WHEN APPROACHED WITH THE NOTION THAT HIS BROTHER was about to embark on yet another civil rights march, with the bruises and contusions of the previous one still in recent memory, Casey ventured the thought that Pat might very well have gone stark raving mad.

"If yer completely intent on killin' yerself in this manner, there isn't much I can do to stop ye. Ye've no need for anyone's permission but if ye want my approval an' support I'm not inclined to give it. It'll be a bloodbath, the police won't protect ye an' the Paisleyites are gonna see to it that ye pay for yer cheek. It's sheer madness."

Three days into it Pat was inclined to agree with his brother's less than charitable summation of the event. Things had started out mildly enough, some twenty-five of them gathered at City Hall on New Year's morning, under the blankly haughty gaze of Queen Victoria, stamping chilled hands and feet, full of youthful fire and an uncompromising zeal to remember their goals and stick to a program of non-violence. To break beyond the boundaries of religious hatreds and show that they marched for the rights of all oppressed be they Catholic or Protestant. Their objectives were clear, simple and to the point—one man—one job, one family—one house, one man—one vote and a repeal of medieval repressive laws. In the three days it had taken to get from Belfast to Claudy, however, it had lost some of its straight edges and clear-eyed values. The lot of them had been kicked, punched, cursed, called a variety of inventive invectives plus all the old standbys: teague, taig, Fenian bastard and so forth. They'd been detoured off the original route three times, 'for their own safety' the police had sternly said, only to be led like lambs to the slaughter straight into an ambush. Everyone was exhausted and jittery from the tension. And today was likely to be the worst day of all. Today they were headed for the gates of Derry but first they had to cross Burntollet Bridge, where trouble, on a larger scale than what they'd thus far experienced, was expected. To further complicate matters, Pamela had decided to come with him and he'd felt a compulsion to keep an eye out for her. He'd also, since the

Derry march, become, rather unwillingly, a sort of unofficial spokesperson for the civil rights movement.

On this last morning he stood, clutching a mug of lukewarm tea, wishing for something stronger to clear his head and tried to gather his thoughts into a stream of coherency. Pamela, yawning, sat cross-legged on the ground, rolling her own cup of tea between her hands trying to get the last of its warmth. In front of them the morning's initial speaker was just wrapping up his pep talk for the day and Michael Farrell, generally acknowledged as one of the organizers and leaders, was giving Pat the nod to get on deck. Pat sighed, felt Pamela give his leg a nudge of reassurance and stepped forward.

He surveyed the higgledy-piggledy crowd in front of him, rumpled clothes, sleep-sticky faces, uncombed hair and an overall air of stubborn resilience that he was rather proud to be a part of. Since his one mad moment in Derry, they had come to see him as some sort of fire-eating nationalist, who would do what he had to for the cause and damn the consequences. That image bore no resemblance to the boy in the mirror but this morning these people needed a little inspiration, someone to galvanize them and spur them on for the last fifteen miles. He cleared his throat, took a last swill of tea and began.

"We've come sixty miles in these last three days and if ye see it as a journey of the soul as well as the feet, then I'd have to say we've come much farther. We cannot turn back now. There are people in this country who may not know us, who may not like us merely because they think they know what we are all about but we are marching for them, we are putting one foot ahead of the next for them, for our neighbors, our friends, and for those who would swear to be our enemies.

'We don't ask much, only for basic human rights. The right to have a roof over yer head, food on yer table, and to have yer vote count for something at the ballot box. We ask that laws that go against every aspect of democracy, laws which revile the democratic process be abolished. We ask that men not be imprisoned unjustly, tried unfairly, brought before kangaroo courts that are merely the shadow puppets for a police run state.

'They tell us this march is irresponsible and misguided, that we should just be grateful for the opportunities we have, the things our generous government provides. Grateful for rundown council housing, grateful to live in an environment that breeds disease and despair, grateful for education that does not meet the poorest standards, grateful for non-existent jobs and homes and dreams that they've made us believe we don't have a right to reach for. Well, I for one don't intend to say thank you to the man who stands on my hope and grinds my dreams under his heel. They may subjugate our bodies, beat our minds with bloody rhetoric but no man owns my soul and no man in a fifty-guinea suit owns yers either.

"Today we wash our hands with the blood of our ancestors, with the blood of every oppressed man who ever stood and said 'no.' We walk in the footsteps of those chained, beaten, flogged and killed for merely uttering the word 'no.'

"It is said that man is the only beast that laughs and weeps; for he is the only animal that is struck by the difference between what things are and what they ought to be. Here today we know how things ought to be, we can see the future, it may be a distant light but we can see it."

He paused for breath as the morning air rippled past his face, chill with the season and thought he felt, in passing, the warmth of his father's hand upon his head.

"We all know what we may face today and that, regardless of provocation, we must hold firm to our policy of non-violence, it must be shown, in all our actions, how committed we are to these beliefs. They may stone us, beat us, rain down verbal fire upon our heads but today," his gaze swept over the ragged crowd and he felt again the reassuring pressure of his father's hand, "today we will be like Dr. Martin Luther King and we," he reached into the air, reaching for the hand of a ghost, though the crowd roaring its approval took it as a thrust of empowerment, "we will fear no man."

A rousing cheer greeted the end of his speech and smiling he nodded to the crowd, feeling a strange surge of emotion from them, a thing that gave to him and pulled from him at the same time.

The first leg of the morning's march was relatively quiet. There was the occasional shout of 'say yer rosaries now while ye've still the chance,' from hostile onlookers, the usual name-calling and kids scampering about wildly waving Union Jacks.

"Fine an' future upstanding lodge members," Pat said to Pamela who walked to his right, closer in to the body of the marchers. "I have to say all this police presence makes me nervous," he continued, only too aware that the police had come today in full battle dress, well-equipped for a riot.

"There's a bad feel in the air," Pamela looked crossly at a child who scampered past merrily singing, 'Up to our knees in Fenian blood.'

"There's always a bad feel in the air when there's people like this about, ignore them, we'll be in Derry for afternoon tea," Pat said with a reassurance he did not feel.

The River Faughan lay seven miles out of Derry. To its left was a low-lying field, on the right the ground rose sharply and was obscured from sight by a ragged hedge. It was towards this hedge the police motioned the marchers, to protect them from any flying stones.

"Christ, we can't see damn thing now," Pat mumbled, looking warily up into the snarled branches. Along the high ground strolled a squad of police in ordinary dress, parallel but slightly in advance of the marchers.

"Why aren't they decked out like their compatriots?" Pamela asked over the nervous babble that had begun to percolate in their ranks.

"Don't know but I don't think it's good," he shivered as a flutter of unease passed its fingers up his spine.

The next field was well-hedged and provided only strange, rippling glances of police strolling along, occasionally talking to men who seemed to be idly standing about in the fields. Seen through the lacework of gray branches and glossed leaves it lent a slow-motion, sinister feel to the atmosphere which was quickly tensing. Between the leaves and branches they could see more men, not police anymore, men armed with clubs and cudgels, their gait as easy as if they were out for a Sunday after-church ramble.

The junction of the next two fields was a gully overgrown with bramble and gorse, surrounded by tall trees. From these trees a young girl emerged, silver winter light pale-fingering her brown hair against the shadow of the trees. A chilly smile turned her lips up at the corners, she couldn't have been more than fourteen. She raised her hand up from the shadows, the glitter of a large stone clutched against her small palm. A spasm of rage contorted her face and she flung the stone straight into the marchers.

"Incoming," Pat yelled as warning to those behind them who couldn't see what was happening. But the girl's hand had unleashed more than her one stone, for it appeared that she had been the signal to those on the high ground. All around the marchers fell a hard, unflinching rain of stones, bricks and bottles. Pat heard a scream behind him and turned to see a girl drop to the ground, blood streaming from a gash in her forehead. Stunned and blinking she was pulled out from amidst the marchers by the police and towed toward one of their vehicles.

What Pat could now make out on the high ground chilled him to the core, close to two hundred people milled about, all heavily armed, chatting amiably with the police, white-banded special constabulary amongst their ranks. Ducking his head every few seconds to avoid the rocks, screws, bolts, nails and bottles that rained down with impunity, he saw men and a few women as well armed with crowbars, iron bars, lead piping, cudgels, and some elaborately spiked and gleaming instruments of punishment. A small body of marchers broke panicking through the hedge, seeking safety in the open field. The police herded them quickly back to danger in the open road and it was then Pat saw what was happening and knew the worst was still to come.

"Dear God, the police are here for them."

"What?" Pamela shouted back, her coat pulled up taut over her head, providing a fragile shelter from the missiles pouring down on them.

"The police up there on the bank are here to be certain we don't retaliate against them."

"No," Pamela said faintly, turning away from him toward the field. An industrial bolt missed her head by a half inch.

"Come on," Pat said grimly and pulled her to his side, affording her what little protection his body could give her.

Ahead of them the field tapered to an end in a small laneway that was heavily treed. The lane met the main road at a sharp angle, providing a convenient bottleneck. The police flanked the marchers front and left, leaving their right flank completely exposed and fully open to the head of the laneway.

Pat cursed to himself, he was willing to bet they were being delivered like a tidy package into the hands of a bloodthirsty mob. Delivered by the very men who were supposed to protect them. There was nowhere to go but forward though, so the march pressed on, bleeding and bruised. The fallen culled from their midst by stone-faced policemen.

The first ranks of marchers had barely come abreast of the laneway when from its dark tunnel burst what looked to Pat to be about sixty men armed to the teeth with a dazzling array of homemade weapons.

The police put up a slight show of resistance and then melted like sieved butter through the ranks of armed furies. Some few marchers managed to get past the armed cordon. Pat and Pamela were near the front but not as it turned out near enough, for they along with the main body of the marchers were as effectively cut off as if they were cattle fed into a funnel.

From the left, on a path hidden by the sharp turn of the main road, stood another phalanx of angry men, shored up by piles of stone, brought there specially for the occasion. The entire road was descending into chaos. Pat grabbed Pamela's hand hard,

"We're going to have to break for it, into the field."

They both bent double, running as best as a slow crouch would allow, unable to dodge the sticks and stones any longer, such was their profusion. A man dashed up from the lefthandside of the road and smacked Pat across the head with what appeared to be a broken off chair leg, then not satisfied he raised his arm and whacked Pamela solidly across the back. She let out a small 'oof' of surprise, stumbling to stay on her feet as Pat pulled her harder towards the field. Around them, people screamed, were cudgeled to the ground, beat about the head, shouted and cursed at.

Marchers dazed and injured staggered to their feet, limping towards the bridge, only to be forced off the road and into the fields where yet another armed contingent awaited just this eventuality. Out of the corner of his eye Pat saw a man on his knees being cudgeled about the face and head.

"Say you're sorry," his attacker screamed, spittle flying from his furious lips.

"Sorry," the man said, hands held up to try and catch the blows.

"I don't believe you" his attacker replied and set about quite happily beating the man again.

The two of them stumbled onward, dodging clubs and rocks. Just ahead of them a photographer raced, turning back and forth in a strange dance, his black eye on the world clicking and whirring in rhythm with his steps.

To their left, in an open expanse of field, an old woman was clubbed down with three sharp blows and then finished neatly with a broadside to the face from a flagpole on the end of which the Union Jack fluttered gaily in the breeze.

"We better help her," Pamela said and before Pat could stop her, she'd slipped his grasp and ran towards the prone woman. Pat cursed and ran after her.

The old woman lay facedown, gray hair streaked gruesomely with blood. Pamela knelt beside her in the long grass.

"We'll get you help," she said patting the woman's outstretched hand. Pat saw the five men approach from out of a ditch before she did. And he reached her just in time to find the three of them neatly surrounded by five club-wielding brutes, smiles on their overheated faces.

"Well, what have we got here?"

"Please, we need to get her to an ambulance," Pamela said turning her face up towards them. "She needs help now."

"Ah where's the pope then when ye need him, go ask him for help, Fenian bitch," the man raised his arm, extending the stick in his hand to full length where a nail glittered evilly at the end of it. Pat stepped forward to shield her and caught the full brunt of it in his arm, he felt the nail rip a good two inches down before it was torn out.

He heard a sharp scream and saw Pamela being dragged by one arm and her hair towards the river. Three of the men had taken her while the other two stayed behind, clubs slapping their hands, a look of anticipation in their eyes. He knew he'd never seen such concentrated hatred before.

He stood for a long moment, eyes locked with their own, feeling the breath wash in and out of his lungs and then feinted to the left and as they lunged shot through to their right running for the river. The bank was awash with armed attackers throwing people into the river and forcibly clubbing them back into it when they tried to crawl out. He couldn't spot Pamela in the melee and panicked, his mind churning with all the ugly possibilities. He scanned the bank and the water where people were wading in a panic for the far side. His heart skipped a beat, halted for a terrible split second as he saw a black-haired girl facedown in the water and then resumed beating a second later as a man pulled her out. It wasn't Pamela. The photographer from moments before was hip deep in the river, trying to keep his camera above water, his precious pictures safe while a man slogged behind him repeatedly hitting at the photographer's arm with a lead pipe.

And then he saw her, fifteen yards upriver from the photographer, kneeling in the river, hair streaming and eddying on the river. He started to run and then crashed to his knees as a stunning blow caught him hard in the kidneys. His attackers having knocked him to the ground were happy to deliver a couple of blows to his head before they moved on. Rising up on his knees and fighting back a wave of nausea from the pain, he desperately searched the river again and saw Pamela struggling to get up on the bank. And saw the man on the bank who waited, spiked stick in hand for her. He yelled and then cursed his stupidity, for hearing his voice she'd raised her head and gave the stick-wielding thug the opportunity he'd been waiting for. The nail caught her right below the cheekbone, sinking deep in the hollow until it made contact with her upper jaw. Even from a distance he could see the surprise in her face, the shock and her first instinct to tear away from the offending object. Blood sprayed as the nail tore out and then streamed brightly down her face.

He made the water's edge seconds later, the look on his face enough to make the attacker seek meeker pastures and flee back towards the bridge with great haste. He checked both banks of the river and seeing they were still thronged with swinging clubs he grabbed Pamela by the shoulders and pushed her upriver through the current.

"How's yer face?" he asked tightly in her ear as he glanced behind him to be certain no one was following.

"It hurts," she said in a small voice, the hand that clutched the side of her face streaked with drying and fresh blood. "Where are the police?"

"Standin' on the road talkin' to the stone-throwin' bastards."

"Oh God," she said hollowly, "how can this be happening?"

"It's Ireland," Pat said bitterly, "how could it not?"

They had to wade a good half-mile by Pat's estimate before they reached a comparatively safe spot.

Pat made her sit and then hunkered down in front of her, "Yer goin' to have to let me look at yer face."

She nodded but didn't move her hand away from her face. He took her fingers gently and pried them away from her skin. They came away with a sticky, sucking pop, a fresh well of blood appearing in their absence. With all the blood it was hard for him to tell what the damage was, though it didn't look good. There was a deep open gash following under the cheekbone and blood was beginning to run out of the corner of her mouth from the cut inside.

"How bad is it?"

He shook his head, forcing a smile onto his face, "Not so bad, couple stitches an' it'll be fine."

"You're not a good liar, Pat," she said and made a grimace that he realized with a shock was meant to be a smile. "I suppose I got the better end of it. They spent a good minute trying to decide whether they should throw me in the river or rape me. All things being equal I'm glad they decided on the first option. Are you okay?"

"I'm okay." He looked around eyeing the pale winter light. "We'd best get back on the road, find ye an ambulance. What the hell is that?" For from the sodden ball of her coat she had pulled a square black object.

"Exactly what it looks like," she said, and checked the camera over for damage.

"Yes but how'd ye get it?"

"The photographer threw it to me, I guess he thought I'd have a better chance of keeping the pictures safe than he would."

"But I saw him with his camera only minutes ago."

"I think he must have had two, one to decoy and the other with the actual goods in it."

"An' which do you have?"

"Won't know until the film's developed will we, there's extra rolls taped to the bottom too." She looked the camera over with an air of excitement that disturbed Pat.

"That thing is only goin' to invite all sorts of trouble, ye'll never get it past the police when we find ye an ambulance."

She rose to her feet, clothes soaked and icy, a look of grim determination on her face.

"I'll not go in one of those damn police tenders, not after what they did. I'll walk. There's only seven miles left to Derry, let's go."

It was a shattered and bleeding lot that staggered into Derry while their opposition seemingly had jumped in their cars, taken time for tea and refreshments, only to show up in force on the streets leading into the town. Faces, now unhappily familiar appeared on the escarpments of Spencer Road on the outer fringes of Derry, stones rained down and police, amiable faced and compliant, allowed the attackers to have their fun.

Once again, Union Jacks danced at the front of the marchers, leading the way into the town with old Orange songs that gloried in the spilling of Catholic blood. And then, after seventy-five miles of road paid for with blood and broken bones the marchers were denied entrance within the walls of the town on the grounds that it was too inflammatory.

"Sacred an' hallowed Orange ground is more like it," Pat muttered, as the weary mass of marchers was shunted down yet another re-route. "They're lettin' those bastards up inside the walls though ye'll note. Leaves them in an optimum position to keep droppin' rocks on our heads with the police neatly lined up to protect them against us of all things."

"Four days ago I'd have thought you were cynical," Pamela said bleakly, a bruise spreading out from her cheek in deep and heavy shades.

Ahead of them loomed the Guildhall and the streets were now lined with crowds of friendly, cheering faces. Pat searched them wearily without even knowing what he was looking for until he saw the fine blonde hair, the freckled nose and the smile that burst out from the mass of faces at him. She was waving wildly and he grinning back was swept past her and onto the Guildhall Square.

Michael Farrell, injured on the road into Derry, was hastily brought in from the hospital to speak to the weary crowd and the people of Derry. He summarized the events of the march, reiterating the goals and intents of the People's Democracy. He was followed by other speakers of the PD and then he nodded at Pat, a questioning look on his face. Pat nodded in return and winding his way through the crowd, took the speaker's platform.

"Well I suppose if nothin' else," he began, "we've shown them that these Fenians have no intention of lyin' down." A triumphant roar greeted his words. He held his hands up, "All jokin' aside though, it's been a difficult few days, an' some of us are lyin' in the hospital as a result. But we stuck to the promises we made ourselves, we marched for the rights of our own people an' people who likely would have been more than happy to see us dead today. We can be proud of ourselves an' of all the people who supported us. Now I for one could use a hot meal an' a soft bed."

He rejoined the crowd amidst tremendous cheering, people patting him on the back and clasping his hands. His eyes glanced past them all, flickering here for a moment, there for a second until at last his eyes lit on a small, light intense person, who smelled, even in the melee and crush of bodies, of lemon verbena and lilacs.

"Hello," he said feeling suddenly shy.

"Hello yerself," she said, "I've come to offer ye that hot meal an' soft bed if ye've a mind for it."

"That'd be grand, but I've got to get Pamela to a hospital first."

"Pamela?" she said, an embarrassed look flashing across her fine features.

"Aye, she's my brother's girlfriend."

"Oh," she flushed self-consciously, "she's welcome to come as well."

Just then Pamela came up, squeezing through the massed crowd, blood-streaked rag pressed to her bruised cheek.

Riots and small scuffles were already breaking out in the streets as Sylvie led them down and away from the Guildhall.

"There's small first-aid clinics bein' set up in the houses, or we could get ye to the hospital though ye might wait a while for someone to attend to ye. Are ye in a great deal of pain then?" she asked, brown eyes sympathetic but not pitying as she surveyed the mess on the left hand side of Pamela's face.

"Do I need a lot of stitches?" Pamela asked, giving Pat a level look.

"Aye, ye'll need a fair few an' a good cleanin'."

"Is there anyone at the clinics qualified to sew up my face?"

"I know just the place to take ye," Sylvie said firmly and led the way out of the crowd and away from the developing trouble.

The place turned out to be the front room of a small two-up, two-down in the Bogside.

"Is Father Jim here?" Sylvie asked a harried looking woman who was putting rags on to boil in the kitchen.

"Aye he's out back takin' a minute."

"I'll be back," Sylvie said and true to her word returned a moment later with a rangy, dog-collared man in tow.

"I'm Father Jim," he said and went directly to Pamela. "Let's see what we've got here, girl."

"You're American," Pamela said and winced as the crusted fabric was pulled away from her face.

"You as well," Father Jim said and nodded to Sylvie, who swiftly disappeared into the kitchen. She returned with a bowl of steaming cloths and a tray with alcohol, sterilized instruments and swabs on it. Pamela blanched when she saw the array of wickedly sharp needles.

"It's alright," Father Jim said reassuringly, "I've got to clean the tear up before I can assess the damage, but I've got Novocain to numb your face." He turned and donned a pair of surgical gloves, "I was a medic in Vietnam, I've patched up worse than this and seen them come away with only a little scar. Now you'll need to sit down, maybe your friend there," he gave Pat a cursory glance, "can help to hold your head still."

Pamela sat in a kitchen chair that seemed provided for the purpose and Father Jim pulled a stool up near her, angling himself so the maximum amount of light hit her face directly. "Are you ready?"

She swallowed, took a shaky breath and nodded.

"Alright," Father Jim soaked a sterile cloth with alcohol, "this is going to hurt like holy hell."

Pat took her head between his hands and realized he was shaking. Pamela's right hand came up and covered his own, "Today we fear no man, right? Not," she gave a wary glance at Father Jim as the cloth approached her cheek, "even him," she finished and promptly passed out.

Chapter Eighteen
Peace Be Unto You

PAMELA FELT LIKE SIFTED SMOKE. Fine, airy and able, like the angels, to dance lightly upon the head of a pin. The small part of her brain that was recovering from the shot of Novocain and the painkillers that Father Jim had given her, told her she wasn't actually invisible or invincible but she quashed the thought swiftly and continued on her way.

She hadn't actually intended to lie to Sylvie, she really had been going out for a breath of air but then she'd seen an altercation occurring down the street and light-footed, the drugs drowning out danger signals, had followed the sounds of rage and fear. The camera had still been around her neck and so when she'd seen a group of thugs beating an old man she'd begun to shoot the pictures. They had been so caught up in their savagery they hadn't even noticed her which, unfortunately, only added to the aura of invincibility she felt snugly cloaked in.

Now however confusion was beginning to set in just the slightest bit. She wasn't entirely certain she *could* actually find her way back. Everything looked the same. Red brick on the left and red brick on the right and cobbled pavement under her feet. Quite suddenly she wished Casey were there to protect her, to guide her by the hand out of this maze of narrow, winding streets, with buildings that seemed to loom ominously over her head.

From a distance, she heard singing, a vaguely familiar melody that she couldn't place and the jolting sound of breaking glass. The voices approached and she, still confused, sidled towards it. As the words of the song became audible she recognized the song as one she'd heard the flag-waving children singing. Pat had told her it was called 'Derry's Walls'.

> *...For blood did flow in crimson streams,*
> *On many a winter's night.*
> *They knew the Lord was on their side,*
> *To help them in their fight.*

The voices paused for a moment and there was the sound again of glass shattering and falling out onto the street and then they happily resumed.

> *...At last, at last with one broadside*
> *Kind heaven sent them aid...*

Pamela turned a corner, stepping up into the shelter of a shop entryway and crouching, peered down the street, the scene before her freezing her blood cold. A group of about twenty policemen, swinging riot clubs, were the singers. On the apex of every verse, one would step from formation, raise his blackthorn stick and smash a window out. They were only about twelve yards away from her, coming around the twisting close. It was too late to run, they'd see her certainly if she stepped out into the street, but if she stayed here in this dingy entryway, clutched in close to the filthy brick, she might escape notice. They'd taken up a new tune with a somewhat jauntier beat, the leader twirling his club in the air like an orchestral baton:

> *A rope, a rope*
> *Tae hang the pope*
> *A pennyworth of cheese*
> *Tae choke him...*

She managed to shoot off the last two frames on the film as the men gleefully shouted the end of the ditty. She leaned back into the brick, breathing rapidly, swimming in adrenaline, fumbling as she removed the finished roll and fought to control her fingers enough to insert the new one and wind it onto its spool. When the camera was securely locked into place a strange silence had descended onto the street. Holding her breath she peeked around the corner and saw to her horror that a small man, his back hunched discernibly on one side, was coming up the street. He'd a bag of groceries under one arm and his gait was extremely awkward by virtue of one leg being a good four inches shorter than the other. The police were grouped loosely, like a pack of milling wolves, waiting leisurely for the prey to present itself.

The little man walked with his head down in a manner that suggested it was the habit of a lifetime, a necessity demanded by his crooked body. He was only about twelve yards off from the police when the unnatural silence seemed to finally impress itself upon his senses. He looked up blinking, eyes aslant in a soft, dreamy face. From her hiding place, heart thumping painfully, Pamela thought he looked like a tiny owl forced to look straight into the noonday sun, dazed and uncomprehending.

" 'Tis a bad day to be about on the streets Paddy," said one of the idling policemen, blackthorn stick swirling in a delicate eddy from the base of his palm.

"M'name is Timmy, not Paddy, 'tis Timmy ye know."

Pamela felt her heart crash into the pit of her stomach. The man had the bright, innocent voice of the mentally handicapped, of one eternally trapped in childhood. He had no intimation of danger, no instinct to warn him, no shred of self-preservation.

"Timmy, is it? Were ye named fer the monster who fathered ye?"

Timmy shied away a bit, the grocery bag knocking against his side. "No, mam named me for the saint she did, ye know. Named me for him, didn't she? Grace, mercy an' peace to follow him all of his days an' mine as well. Grace, mercy an' peace from God our Father an' Jesus Christ our Lord. Born on a Saint's Day I was, an' named so." He was doing an agitated little dance now, the words rolling off his tongue faster and faster, setting up a chain of freneticism in his body by their well-worn recitation. "Timothy made miracles ye know, he did then. An' mam says I pray hard enough to him an' someday he'll make me whole then won't he, won't he then?" He nodded vigorously, seeking approval from the men who ringed him now entirely, evenly spaced and cutting him off from any salvation. "I've got to go home now, I'm bringin' Mam her tea, I am, tea an' milk an' the papers she likes them every evening, six on the dot Timmy she says, we'll have the tea then won't we Timmy an' she'll read me the paper. Mam doesn't like me to be late, so excuse me then, excuse me then please." He shuffled his feet in a small circle in a vain effort to sidestep the men in his path. "Grace an' peace be unto you," he said rocking his upper body back and forth in agitation, "Grace an' peace be unto you an' excuse me then please. Got to be home before dark then, home before dark or mam'll be scared. She will then won't she, won't she," his free hand had begun a frenzied jig up and down the side of his body, like Rachmaninoff caught in the last frenzied notes of a piano crescendo.

"A genuine freak," said one policeman, his bright blond hair catching the dim light in the streets. "A freak an'a Fenian, two words meanin' the same thing, what's that called? I said, what's that called freak?" The man lifted his club and stuck it hard in the bent curve of Timmy's neck.

Timmy shook his head frantically, the hand fluttering in the dark of the street like a damaged butterfly. Pamela swallowed hard, clicked the flash of the camera on by feel alone and stepping into the street called out loudly. "Two different words meaning the same thing are a synonym you dumb bastard." Then she lifted the camera, shot off three frames, the flash illuminating the street like explosions of lightning. And then she ran as she had never run before in her life. Ran blind and without a mental map, with absolutely no idea of where she was going or how this might all end. Only knowing she had to get those men away from that poor, frantic broken boy in the street.

She could hear them behind her instantly, knew they were young and strong and able-bodied and even though she was fleet of foot that it was only a matter of time before they caught her and then there'd be hell of a kind she couldn't quite imagine to pay. The streets were dark, cobblestones slick with damp, one winding into the next as she took bends willynilly, scraping her elbow on a brick corner, thumping her shoulder hard on a post, trying frantically to discern in the unfamiliar blurred terrain a place to hide, a hole to bolt through, a white rabbit miracle to shoot her from this world to the next. Then she saw it at the top of the steeply curving street she was running up, a back laneway that shot sharply right off the street. She spared one last frantic glance behind then slid hard into the turn and ran for the shadows. She hid in the overhang of a doorway, heard the thumping of her pursuers feet go past the head of the lane and waited until all was silent before venturing out.

The lane was pitch-black, a narrow ribbon between close-set buildings, ending in a solid brick wall, the only light a dim glow reflecting off the wet pavement at its top end. She looked up, squinting in the dark, trying to gauge the height of the wall and judge if she could scale it in the blackness when a voice slid through the dark at her back.

"You left something behind."

She froze, recognizing the voice of the blond policeman, hearing now in the thickening silence the sound of his stick swirling the air.

"Turn around," he ordered and she turned slowly, hands out and palms up. A brilliant flash of light cut into her eyes and it took her a second to realize he was shining a flashlight directly into them.

"You forgot your film," he said pleasantly and she heard the sickening sound of it unspooling and dropping delicately in an exposed pool at her feet. "Nasty dressing on your face," he continued in the same chillingly polite voice, "did our bold laddies give you need for it up by Burntollet Bridge? Did they? It's impolite not to answer questions when you're asked them," he said and caught her unawares with a sharp slap of his club to her face. She could feel the stitches burst under their bandaging and a warm swell of blood soak them. The light blazed in her eyes again, "My mother always said Fenians bled green with gangrene, but you seem to bleed red. Curious, isn't it?" The club poked at the waistband of her jeans, "My mother also said Catholic girls were impure, dirty creatures that a boy shouldn't sully himself with, but I've always preferred to decide these things for myself."

"An' I've always been curious to see if soulless bastards such as yerself bleed at all," said a mild voice in the darkness. The light suddenly flew into the air, turning end over end accompanied by the sound of flesh hitting a solid brick wall. "Grab that flashlight would ye, Jewel an' see if ye can't find the bastard's handcuffs."

"Here," she said breathlessly a minute later, shining the flashlight onto the policeman only to see that he was shoved ruthlessly against the wall, Casey's forearm like an iron bar against the back of his neck. Against the man's neck sparked a glint of razor thin steel, from which a tiny purl of tremoring blood began to collect and fall.

Casey cuffed the man's unresisting hands behind his back and then stepped away, flashlight still trained on his eyes, blinding him as effectively as the absolute darkness would have.

"Get his identification," Casey said sharply. She stepped forward and took it out of the man's coat pocket gingerly. She shone the light on the laminated surface of the small card.

"Constable Bernard McKoughpsie," Casey said out loud, "Now there's a name I'm committin' to memory an' I," he paused ominously, "have a memory like an elephant. D'ye have a family constable, a wife who's alone at night an' wains sleepin' tight in their beds? Do ye?"

"What's your name you coward?" The man managed to gurgle out between lips mashed against brick.

"Ye want my name, do ye?" Casey whispered, a soft hiss in the darkness, "I'll do ye one better Constable, here's my signature." There was a sharp cry from the man against the wall, "It's yers to keep, a little something to remind ye next time ye pick on a helpless man an' a bit of a girl. An' before ye sleep at night remember that I, unlike the people ye took such pleasure in beatin' today, have no compunctions about the sanctity of life, leastwise not the life of scum such as yerself." He added something guttural in Gaelic and then spit at the man's feet.

"Come on, Jewel," Pamela felt the reassurance of his big hand grasping her own, "let's get the hell out of here."

They fled into the dark, the street black and silent though further down she thought she caught flashes of fire and the sound of people screaming. They ran for what seemed miles, ran until their legs felt like rubber and the winter night sat at its apex. And everywhere they ran they saw fire, broken glass, people knocked into the pavement, people standing stunned in the street.

"What—what's happened?" Pamela fought to catch her breath and Casey led her down a back lane, slowing and finally stopping in a patch of darkness, the sounds of devastation and madness distant.

"The police have gone crazy, they're determined to show the upstart Catholics just who the boss in this city really is, just in case today gave them any ideas." He was bent over, chest heaving, "What the hell did ye think ye were doin' back there? Ye nearly got us both killed."

"I couldn't leave that poor man alone in the street Casey, they would have beat him badly."

"Oh, I understand the motivation, Jewel," he breathed out shakily, "but they'd of done worse to ye if they'd caught ye. What if I hadn't been there?"

"How'd you know?" she asked, leaning against the wall as the fear took her directly in the knees.

"Had a bad feelin' about this whole venture but I woke up this morning with knots in my stomach an' figured I'd best come up and see the situation firsthand an' then drag the two of ye home. Found Pat at Sylvie's house an' she said ye'd stepped out for a breath an' not come back. Pat and I divided up the streets an' thank Christ I spotted ye when I did. I was waitin' for the police to go by before I let ye know I was about but then they started bullyin' that poor man an' I knew I'd have to step in if it actually came to blows but then ye leaped into the street an' all hell broke loose. It was no easy task keepin' ye in sight after that without be spotted by the bastards myself."

He stepped towards her touching her wounded cheek gently his hand coming away bloody. "That bastard, I'm sorry I wasn't there to prevent this from happening."

She shook her head wordlessly, a painful knot spreading in her chest and he wrapped his arms around her, stroking her hair with a shaking hand.

"Won't he follow us. Casey?"

"Not anytime soon, I handcuffed him to a pipe. Took all the presence of mind I had not to slit his throat then an' there. We'd best get out of Derry as soon as possible, though we'll have to find ye medical attention first."

"Oh Casey," she shivered against him, the events of the day beginning to catch up with her. "I was so afraid without you."

"And I without you," he whispered back.

A half hour later they crept through the back patch of yard at Sylvie Larkin's home. Pat opened the door to them his face white and tense.

"Oh thank God," he breathed when he saw Pamela and then as he took in her battered face, "what happened?"

"A story," Casey said tersely, "best left for later. Right now we've got to get her a doctor."

"That I believe," Father Jim ducked under the lintel of the kitchen doorway, "would be my summons. Sit down," he said to Pamela and then "Sylvie you know the routine, alcohol, needles, suturing thread.

"Are ye a doctor?" Casey asked, eyeing the tall, rawboned man suspiciously.

"Medic," Father Jim said shortly. "Came over here to visit family and relax if you can believe it," he peeled the soaked bandage away from Pamela's face, peering critically at his ruined handiwork. "Alright, Pamela let's freeze you up and try this again. I ran into Pat as he was searching for you and came here to see if I could help in any way, I suppose it's fortunate I did."

"The police have gone mad," Sylvie said laying Father Jim's tray down beside him and then moving to fill and boil the kettle, "They were stoning my neighbor right in the street an' screamin for all us Fenians to come out an' get what they ought to have given us fifty years ago. Some of them looked as if they'd been drinkin'. An' Mrs. Tuttle from up the street said they stormed into Wellworth's an' just started batoning all the customers an' smashin' the glass out of the counters."

"When the law makers are the law breakers, there is no law," Pat said quietly, watching with a strained countenance as Father Jim filled a hypodermic syringe with Novocain and began to apply it in measured amounts to the area surrounding the wound. "I'm sorry Casey," Pat said softly, "I didn't look out for her the way I should have. This is all my fault."

"We'll discuss it later," Casey said gruffly and sat down, taking Pamela's hand in his own, murmuring things to her only she and possibly Father Jim could hear.

"How badly will I scar?" Pamela said it low, so Pat would not hear.

Father Jim, who had learned the hard way in Vietnam to differentiate between those who wanted the truth and those who wanted a version they could live with, gave her a hard look and sighed seeing she was of the former school.

"Not so terrible as you're imagining but it will be noticeable. I'll make it as thin and straight as I can, but I can't completely erase the damage."

"Just do the best you can," she said and closed her eyes as Father Jim began picking the torn stitches out of her cheek.

That night Derry became a storm of devastation. The police rampaged through poor Catholic neighborhoods, indiscriminately beating men and women, smashing windows and howling abuse at the various inhabitants, swearing to make the roads run red with blood, to rape the women and torture the men. They did what they could to make good on the promise. In the days that followed there would be story upon story of outrage after outrage.

Prime Minister Terence O'Neill responded in the wake of the violence with a long speech which in essence blamed the marchers for all they got and gave a passing slap on the wrist to the men who'd attacked them. In Northern Ireland it was business as usual. A case of the downtrodden finding a neck lower than their own to step upon. The Catholics, the Fenian other had been shown again who ruled, whose blood had been spilled for Ulster and the Union Jack, who owned the government and the streets and the people. And that, as far as the Unionist government was concerned, should have made an end to it.

Of course, it was only the beginning.

Chapter Nineteen

Lace Curtains

THE BOSTON IRISH WERE A RACE UNTO THEMSELVES.

In the beginning, Boston was the least Irish of cities and had someone in the know been around to advise the hopeful immigrants, they would have told them that Boston was the last place in the Americas for an Irishman to settle. Boston's roots were sunk deep in the earth of Puritanism. Puritans, regardless of leaving Mother England under the lash of religious persecution were, nevertheless, Englishmen, with the English love for law, order, refinement and liberty. England's coin of humanitarianism had always been tarnished on the underside, however, by an equal love of subjecting other nations and cultures to their imperialist agenda. Regardless of the colonists' streak of independence, there still existed a cultural bridge between the Old World and the New that the first Americans took great pride in, a bridge built of a common language and literature, of constitutional rights and taxation based on representational government. A bridge shored up by old stereotypes and prejudices. The English and the Irish had been at war in one sense or another for five hundred years and the colonists seemed only too happy to continue the old war on new soil. The New England colonies were founded on the principle that no man be deprived of life, liberty or property save through due process of law. No man, it seemed, except the Negroes and the Irish.

The first Irish to immigrate to the New World were Protestants, in the main, from Ulster. An estimated 200,000 to 250,000 during the Colonial years. These first immigrants, unlike the mass of Catholics who would follow later, tended to scatter upon the shore, to Pennsylvania, New York, Maryland, Virginia, the Carolinas, Georgia and the less populated areas of New England. As early as 1753 history records police being called into the Boston harbor where an angry mob of people were trying to prevent the Irish immigrants from coming ashore. Boston was already acquiring a reputation for its hard-nosed Congregational biases, for feeling that people of different background and culture were lesser, unclean and most certainly unwelcome. Fleeing their homeland because of high rents, disastrous harvests, food shortages and ballooning prices, the Irish, despite their Protestant faith, faced a hostile and sometimes violent reception from the New England colonists. Nonetheless, as was the usual case, the worst of the animosity would be saved for the Catholics who would come in starving, sickened droves when the Famine drove them from their homeland.

The Catholics, despite virulent persecution and oppression from both the English and the Protestants to the North, were more reluctant to depart from Ireland. Tied to the land by social conditions, they were, by circumstance, more rural, less literate, and bound to clan and parish. The harsh poverty of their lives meant that, often, familiar faces and the land you were born to were the only continuity life offered.

However, there were tragedies even the Irish could not endure. When the Rebellion of 1789 failed, Protestant troops were unleashed to suppress any sign of insurrection in whatever way was deemed fit. Men, women and children were flogged, beaten, hung and murdered for so slight an infraction as wearing the green ribbon of the Revolution. The Act of Union was the final blow however; despairing of ever gaining independence for their country, the Irish began to emigrate to shores where hope might again be resurrected.

It wasn't until the Famine, though, that the Irish Catholics began to set across the ocean in vast numbers. Two years of failed crops, winters of freezing rain, icy gales, no wood to burn, no crust of bread to eat and the drama of seeing tens of thousands of their countrymen die in the fields and roads, convinced many of the Irish that in Ireland there was no future, only a past that threatened to happen again and again.

But, if the Irish had expected a warm welcome and open arms from the Americans, they were to be sadly disappointed. In Yankee dominated Boston, the reception was even chillier. The Brahmin class of Boston, who held in their white-gloved hands the reins of education, culture and civic duty, had the undiluted Anglo-Saxon abhorrence of Roman Catholicism and an inbred contempt of all things Irish. It was fine for the Irish to starve and die as long as they did it quietly and on their own shores.

Faced with hostile natives and a system they could never hope to penetrate, the Irish tended to congregate together, knowing there was safety in numbers. The waterfront of Boston soon became crowded with congested tenements riddled with unsanitary conditions, several families often sharing a claustrophobically small space, ill-lit, unheated and rife with the specter of disease. Men could only get temporary work and often the women would become the breadwinners, hiring out as domestics to the elite of Boston who didn't mind the Irish scrubbing their floors so long as they never thought of walking across them.

Editorials of the time castigated the new immigrants as 'filthy and wretched,' 'evil foreign born paupers,' 'idle, thriftless, poor, intemperate and barbaric'.

They were also accused of making the city of Boston into 'a moral cesspool', setting their children out to beg and thieve and of importing 'their vile propensities and habits from across the water.'

In an alien country, faced with rejection and isolation, with a people who saw their culture as wrong and coarse, the Irish closed ranks and became a world unto themselves. They understood lost causes, insurmountable odds, battles that were lost before the first shot was fired and the failure of every hope they'd ever cherished in their own land. They never, though, understood how to lie down and stop the struggle. If their race was fated, so be it. If God had turned his cheek and abandoned them, well He'd done so before and they'd survived. They would bend, but as a people they would never break. It was this backbone they brought to America and to Boston. Eventually their spirit would out. As would their numbers.

In the five years between 1850 and 1855, the Irish accounted for half of the total increase in Massachusetts population. In a state and a city jacketed and ruled by Puritan ethics even the old Yankee core had to distastefully admit the Irish were becoming a body to reckon with. And a community with the numbers also had the likelihood of evolving into a solid political bloc, whose votes were likely to all swing in the same direction. Slowly the Irish began to see that the United States was not just a refuge to bide time in before the return to the 'old country' and that despite harassment, libel and ostracism, their voices, if their cry was loud enough, would be heard in this strange new land.

The city of Boston was divided up into electoral districts called wards. By 1876, there were twenty-five wards in the city and, with the migration of the Irish into the suburbs and outer neighborhoods, they began to wield a mighty political club. Each ward had its own boss. These ward bosses were the recognized center of power in their neighborhood. The ward boss was the big man on the streets, the purveyor of favors, loans and empathy. He was the man who would look after his own and their interests; who knew the intricacies of his district's streets and back lanes. He understood that the needs of the immigrant poor were basic and held to three tenets: food, clothing and shelter. If he could provide these things, he would have the people's undying loyalty—particularly at election time. Though being ward boss was a means to political power and personal advancement, most Irish ward bosses didn't abuse their power. It was a way to give their own people, friends, family and neighbors what they needed, to provide a helping hand that spared the Irish the humiliation of begging at the austere Yankee knee. The Irish ward bosses practiced human politics as opposed to the rational politics of the world of corporations and bureaucracy, which often viewed the individual as irrelevant to the larger political machine.

Politics were the one battlefield that the Irish saw they could win on, could gain respect and power in a society that despised them and had consigned them to a permanent underclass. Politics didn't care if you'd been born in a filthy hovel without the means to put food on the table and clothes on your back; it cared only for ambition and sheer bloody-mindedness. This the Irish understood completely. They also understood the path to such political power was not necessarily paved with roses. If the price to be paid was in the currency of bribes, chicanery, extortion, blackmail and intimidation, well then, at least the process wasn't boring. The Yankee ethic of fair play and gentlemanly conduct during an election was brushed aside and the Irish took to the political stage with drama and flair. By December of 1884, the City of Boston elected its first Irish born, Catholic mayor. For the Irish community there was no looking back. Political maturity would come in the twentieth century when the name of Kennedy made magic right across the country.

The Irish-Americans, even as they began to climb the ladder of political ascendancy and to gain, if not the riches of fabled America, at least then a certain respectability, didn't forget what and where they'd come from. Ireland and her interests were never far from their hearts. Clann na Gael was formed in 1858 and became, to some extent, the American wing of the Irish Republican Brotherhood. The Clann would fund the 1916 Easter Rising and, through Eamon de Valera, would supply the money to start *The Irish Press*. They would use their influence with politicians and powerbrokers to further the cause of Irish emancipation. The pull of the mother country would eventually lessen but Ireland would not be forgotten.

By the 1960s, Clann na Gael would be a somewhat spent force, having splintered into ineffectuality, but the memory of an immigrant, even two generations removed from degradation and poverty, could still be stirred to a longing for the homeland never seen.

Which was how Casey found himself sitting in the office of Lovett Hagerty, a man who held within his considerable fist the far-flung strings of Boston's Irish population. Rumor had it that the Irish were on the way out in the corridors of Boston power. No one, it seemed had thought to inform Lovett Hagerty of this fact, however. In his plush, tilted leather chair, with the fumes of a fifty dollar cigar coiling about his head, he seemed blissfully unaware of it.

Lovett Hagerty, some said, was the last of the old time political bosses who had once ruled all of Irish Boston. He still understood that the key to political power was the listening ear and attentive eye. He was the product of an unlikely marriage, one between a mother who came from an old Yankee family and had Brahmin sensibilities oozing from her finely pored skin and a tough, enterprising first generation Irish-American lad. Despite predictions of doom and gloom and being disowned on the maternal side of the family, the marriage had prospered and was now in its fifty-third year. Lovett Hagerty was the oldest son of five children. He'd been named Lovett after his great-grandfather on his mother's side and though he'd taken his fair share of teasing over the moniker he'd turned it to his advantage during his first run for alderman using the tag-line; 'Lov-ett or Leave It—Vote for Lovett Hagerty.' Whether or not it contributed to his remarkable win or not was moot, Lovett understood the nature of the political beast and it understood him. He was that rarest of creatures, a Boston hybrid, combining Irish drama and oratory with good old-fashioned Yankee shrewdness and know-how. He could do a backroom deal securing himself five hundred union dockworker's votes and then take tea on the hill with Mrs. Cabot-Lodge and not turn a hair in the process. He was America's child, with all the immigrant's ambition and the inherent American belief in limitless possibility. He also had an unaccountable and deep-running belief in lost causes, hopeless fights and a fondness for the underdog, which to this point hadn't hurt his political career though it hadn't helped it in any discernible way either. Love, as his cronies and fans called him, studied the man in front of him and wondered if that wasn't all about to change.

"How much money exactly are we talking about here?" he asked, noting that the man's face remained impassive, clearly he understood something about backroom dealings himself.

"Several thousand in seed money, enough for a decent first haul of arms and an introduction to the head of what's left of Clann na Gael over here."

Love nodded. A nervy demand but he liked that. The man knew he was likely to try to deal him down.

"And you think I can provide such an introduction?"

"So I've heard."

"I think you may be misinformed."

"I don't think I am."

Love sighed, he wasn't going to be able to wiggle away from this.

"Listen Mr. Riordan, it's been a long day and I'm hungry, can I interest you in joining me in a bloody steak and a good bottle of whiskey?"

"Now yer talkin'."

An hour later the two men sat back easy in their chairs, dinner, as bloody as promised, had been consumed and they were halfway down the contents of a bottle of Bushmills whiskey. A contented glow had set itself up at the table and promised to last as long as the whiskey did. They chatted easily about Irish affairs both in Ireland and in America, about the gilded, glory days of Honey Fitzgerald and P.J. Kennedy in Boston politics and then about more personal matters, the son in college who showed no ambition, the daughter who was consorting with an Italian of questionable character and how the Mrs. wanted a new house with a conservatory in it, even though no one played the piano or any other instrument for that matter.

"And yourself, is there a wife at home?" Lovett asked as he lit one of his infamous cigars and handed a fresh one to Casey.

"No, not a wife, at least not yet," he laid the cigar politely to the side of his plate.

"You've the look of a man doomed to find himself at the altar in the near future. I'd bet money on it."

"Do I? What else might ye be inclined to bet money on, Mr. Hagerty?"

Lovett sighed, the man was incorrigible.

"Do you have a few days? I'll need at least two to sniff out the situation and see what sort of funds can be funneled through discreet channels. I'll need to know what's in this for my colleagues and myself."

"The freedom of a small nation," Casey said and swallowed the remainder of his whiskey with one quick movement.

"You're serious aren't you?" Lovett drained his own glass and took a long, speculative puff on his cigar. "You busy for the next three days?"

"Nothing to do but await your answer like a moony suitor," Casey said easily.

"Good, I'd like to show you around the city, give you a feel for the place. Introduce you to some people who could be useful in the future."

"And how will we explain me?" Casey raised his eyebrows in amusement.

"My long lost seven times removed cousin from the old sod ought to suffice."

"Here in search of my American roots?"

"Amongst other things Mr. Riordan, amongst other things."

Casey leaned across the table and Love got a sense of how intimidating the man could be if he so chose. "I think if we're goin' to get into the revolutionary bed together ye'd best call me Casey."

"Casey, I like the cut of your jib," said Lovett Hagerty and shook hands with the boy from across the water, upon whom he'd just bestowed the most Yankee blessing of all. The irony of it was lost on neither of them.

🗱   🗱   🗱

AMERICA WAS A REVELATION TO CASEY, or at least the bit of it controlled and owned by Lovett Hagerty. Love seemed to have the ability to be in ten places at once, to shake hands, kiss babies and listen intently to the woes of a plumber whose wife had just left him for a mechanic and whose business was going under. The man never seemed to tire or grow irritable with the endless demands his various constituents placed upon him.

"People need help and I'm here to give it to them, that's what got their vote in the first place and that's what will keep it. As soon as I forget that I'll be drummed out of office and deservedly so."

The pace of his life was hectic and yet as smoothly organized as a well-oiled machine and through it all Love's black-haired, blue-eyed Irish charm stayed firmly buttoned in place. There were deals, calls and last minute saves all done with lightning-quick reflexes and maneuvering worthy of a snake charmer. And at night, there was the family to be attended to, the pert blonde mistress installed in a pretty little apartment in a smart section of the city, and the deals done over cards in backrooms into the wee hours of the morning and still he'd be at his desk by eight o'clock the next day.

On the morning of Casey's third day, Love broke from his morning meeting early and told his secretary to take messages; he'd be back the next day.

"Come on, there's something I want to show you," he said to Casey, taking the stairs down from his office at a jaunting pace that belied the scant two hours of sleep he'd managed to fit in the night before.

His car took them to Beacon Hill, once bastion and sanctuary of Boston's merchant princes. Beacon Street, Oliver Wendell Holmes had once said, 'was the sunny street of the sifted few.' It still seemed so with its gently curving streets, the great spreading hardwood trees shading its pavements, the terraced lawns and elaborately arched entrances. It was a neighborhood of wealth and privilege, of gold-edged lives lived out in oak-paneled libraries and brilliantly lit ballrooms.

"It's something ain't it?" Lovett said, gesturing for his driver to stop. "They say old John Fitzgerald used to sell papers up here as a boy and dream of the life that went on inside those pretty walls. I used to walk up here myself as a boy, I'd wait until twilight when all the families would be in having their evening meal and the light would spill out across the lawns and I could watch them unobserved. Let's walk, shall we?"

They left the car and strolled along the wide avenue lined with overarching elms, dark and heavy with mist on this winter morning.

"See this house up here?" he pointed to a mansion set upon a knoll, its side turned to the street, so that it would not have to observe the comings and goings of the street. Snow covered the grounds thickly but Casey knew in the summer there would be long swathes of velvety lawn, sweeps of flowers and the buzzing of bees fat on such prolific nectar. The house itself was elegant, pillared in the Greco-Roman fashion, colored a soft umber, its mullioned windows reflecting back the snow as it softly dropped from the twisted trunks and branches of oaks, elms and maples.

"It's a beautiful house," Casey said, feeling some response was required.

"Isn't it though? Takes a lot of people to keep a place like that running. Footmen, valets, cooks, housemaids, parlormaids, ladies maids, governess'. Of course, that was in the glory days when ladies took tea each day and presented one another with calling cards, and the rooms were lit with the soft glow of gas lamps, and the governess' wore starched and ruffled white and young ladies went to dancing school and were presented at cotillions. My Daddy used to deliver groceries to the back door here and I used to come up here in the dark and stare through the windows, the poor little mucker in the snow."

"Whose house is this?"

"My grandfather's of course," Lovett Hagerty said with a smile that contained a rueful sadness. "I worked up the courage to go to the door once, took every ounce of daring I had. They wouldn't let me in to see the old man, said I'd no right to come to the front door but he came out to see what all the kerfuffle was about and I announced myself as though I'd every right to be there. Said, 'I'm Lovett Joseph Hagerty and you are my grandfather'. I couldn't have weighed ninety pounds soaking wet and stood five feet three inches in a thick-soled pair of shoes but I was determined to make him acknowledge me. He looked at me with those icy blue eyes of his and said, 'Aren't you the little ruffian who stares in my windows, I ought to call the police on you.' And I said 'I am your grandson,' again, not quite understanding what was going on. And he looks me up and down and there was no emotion in his face, other than maybe contempt and he says 'I have no grandson and even if I did he wouldn't be a filthy little Paddy half-breed like you.' Then he had me lifted by the collar and thrown out of the house, through the back door mind you, not the front. He couldn't even give me the dignity of that. The butler was instructed to offer me a hundred dollars if I'd promise to stay away. It was somehow the worst thing about the whole ordeal, that he'd offer me money, knowing that I'd never seen that much in my whole life. It was like the devil tempting me."

"Did ye take it?" Casey asked, catching a drifting snowflake on his hand and watching it melt, the way the privileged time on this hill had once melted away.

"I did, it was the start of my fortune believe it or not. I invested it in a paper kiosk and the rest, as they say, is history."

"An' the moral of this story?"

"Is that a mick is a mick is a mick, I suppose. Regardless of how you dress us up, put us in the best schools, educate us in the arts, give us ten forks to eat with, at the core, on some level we still know we're just a bunch of goddamn paddies. Well, Mr. Riordan," Lovett turned away from the sight of his grandfather's home, "if you want your money you can have it. I may just be a mucker in fancy dress and good shoes but never let it be said I wouldn't help another Irishman when it really mattered."

"Thank ye man, I hope ye'll not have cause to regret yer decision."

"Casey, we Irishmen may have had to leave Ireland but we never forgot her. She's in here," he touched his hand over his heart, "and always will be. Though I'm not saying I wouldn't rather keep you here," he gave Casey a shrewd look, "I've got room in my organization for a man such as yourself. If you ever consider a move across the sea, I'd be more than happy to assist in any way that I can. You could still serve the cause over here, in ways you may not even be able to imagine at present."

"Yer offer is more than generous Mr. Hagerty but Ireland is my home."

"Then I'll say no more on the subject, but you keep my offer in mind."

"I will."

They walked back slowly to the car and Love Hagerty paused to give his ancestral home a last, lingering glance.

"Does yer grandfather still live there?"

"Yes he does, he had a stroke some years back now and can't walk, or talk but the old buzzard keeps on breathing day after day. He doesn't own it anymore though, he went broke in the fifties, took a dive in the market that no one could have foreseen."

"Who owns it then?" Casey asked, though he knew the answer.

"I do of course," Love Hagerty said.

"After he kicked ye out an' all, ye let him stay?"

"Don't give me too much credit; part of me wanted vengeance when I bought it. He was already ill when he lost his money; he never even knew he lost it. Still thinks the house is his though so he can go to his grave hating me without any conflict." Lovett shrugged, "What can I tell you; he's an old man and he's never lived elsewhere and, like I said, I'm an Irishman, believing in lost causes is in our blood. Maybe when he dies I'll tear the damn place down and set his ghost to rolling in the grave."

"Be a shame to tear a pretty house like that down," Casey said, watching as the fog dithered and curled and settled in the dripping elm branches, wrapping protectively around the house.

"It would be a shame, a great shame indeed. Come on man I need a whiskey."

For a second Casey thought he saw a face at the window, an old face, once proud, now twisted and a hand palsied with age and illness touch the inside of the glass. He shivered and turned back towards the car.

"What will you an' yer partners be expectin' in return for yer assistance?" Casey asked as the car rolled down the avenue, warm and snug, in contrast to the chill gray outside.

"There's an old Gypsy saying Casey, perhaps you've heard it, that says 'bury me standing, I've been on my knees all my life.' I think the Irish have been on their knees for several lifetimes, you do what you can to change that and we'll consider it money well spent."

Chapter Twenty
Exit Unicorns

DUNCAN MACGREGOR HAD SERIOUS MISGIVINGS about the day right from the very start of it. But as the train had run on time, the day had been fine and Bernie had seemed, at least to begin with, in an amiable enough frame of mind, he had shrugged off his feelings of impending doom and enjoyed the football game they'd traveled up from Belfast to see.

That had been the first half of the game. In the second half, their team was soundly thrashed, the sky opened up and poured buckets and Bernie's temper, as it was wont to do, had turned ugly as the weather. A few years earlier, Duncan would have known what it meant, a brawl in a pub or vandalism of some sort. Smashing glass and looting had ceased satisfying Bernie's appetite for trouble some time back. However, Bernie had moved onto bigger venues, Bernie had joined the police force. Two months ago he'd been culled from the ranks of the Special Constabulary and had been on active service ever since.

Duncan only saw Bernie occasionally now, and even at that it was only out of misplaced childhood sentimentalism. They'd grown up in the same neighborhood, played in the same streets and attended the same church. That was where the similarities ended. The truth was Bernie scared the hell out of him even on his good days now. There were rumors floating around the old neighborhood about the company Bernie kept and they weren't talking about the regular crew he took up to Derry on Sunday jaunts. He'd heard the words 'Ulster Volunteer Force' whispered with appropriate terror upon more than one occasion. The UVF was the Loyalist answer to the IRA. A bloodthirsty, radical crew who seemed less motivated by politics than by a sheer orgiastic love of violence, equaled in measure only by their hatred of Catholics. Being neither particularly Loyalist nor particularly fanatical, Duncan had a pacifist's disdain for radical military factions. Bernie on the other hand, being both virulently Loyalist and fanatical, saw such organizations in a very different light. Every July 12, from the time he'd been old enough to walk, Bernie had marched and beat the drums in tribal fervor, in hatred and ignorance. Bernie was a believer.

Duncan had tried to see it from both sides, being blessed or cursed (however one saw it) with liberal parents who had preached tolerance from the cradle along with a healthy dose of learning to think for oneself. Thinking was not, on the other hand, a virtue cherished in the household of Bernie McKoughpsie, beating one's wife and children every day of the week excepting Sunday, religious zealotry and hatred honed to razor-like sharpness were the lessons well and thoroughly taught.

More disturbing of late was Bernie's worship of the rankly unendearing Reverend Ian Paisley. Reverend Paisley, zealot of the old and narrow faith, whose sermons veered along the edge of militancy but never outright sank into recommendations of violence. Paisley, who saw the IRA as nothing more than the minions of the Pope, Paisley to whom Catholics were aliens, whose paranoid rhetoric was thickly imbued with the idea of the savage Celt ready at any moment to burst out into barbarism. Duncan, having heard him speak, thought him purely demented and more surely dangerous than an entire squad of the IRA let loose in a building full of Loyalist hard-liners.

Despite Duncan's deep distrust of the man, even he had to admit that Dr. Paisley could not be blamed for some of Bernie's more radical ideas. The word segregation had come off his lips several times.

"We ought to do like the Americans done with the niggers an' keep them separate." Duncan thought it wisest not to mention that the Americans had reversed their policies and all to the better. He had had the great privilege of hearing Dr. Martin Luther King speak only months before in Atlanta and had been filled with humility at the greatness of the man. When Dr. King had been slaughtered by blind bigotry, Duncan had wept. The 'them' of Bernie's hate were of course the Catholics, Catholic of any sort, political affiliations not required. Bernie seemed to be looking for a way to smash and annihilate anything he could not understand, anything that had an element of goodness, peace or beauty. The pinched, bruised faces of his wife and children were proof of that.

After an afternoon of Bernie's company and Bernie's vile temper, Duncan had been relieved to get on the train, thinking only of parting company with the degenerate crowd with whom Bernie surrounded himself. Duncan had thought the train car was empty at first, hadn't seen the couple in the end seats. But when he did see them, his relief quickly evaporated into panic. Especially when he realized that Bernie had already spotted them.

Bernie could, he supposed, be forgiven for that. A man would have to be blind not to notice the girl and Bernie, unfortunately, was not blind. It was the way Bernie looked at her that frightened Duncan, though, like she was prey, as if he wished to devour that which was most precious about her and leave the blood to run down his chin.

The events of the next few moments and the many, many moments that

followed would be imprinted on Duncan's memory for eternity, a silent
horror film, where one is not allowed to leave the theater. It seemed to happen in slow motion, the girl turning her head, laughing at something her
dark-haired companion said, or did he ask a question? For she had answered,
'truly, madly, deeply,' and then tossed her ponytail over her right shoulder.
Had he asked, 'do you love me?' Duncan was to wonder later, for there had
been a look of sweet happiness on the boy's face. But as his gaze lowered, he
saw with a wrench of fear in his bowels what it was that had so transfixed
Bernie. For the girl's muffler was green with white stripes, the colors of the
team that had just so soundly beaten their own, a team made up of Catholic
boys. And over her muffler, swaying to the rhythm of the train was a delicate,
pale-gold crucifix. 'Symbol of our Lord's suffering' thought Duncan wildly
and about to become the cause of much more pain.

Bernie had gone deathly still and in accordance so, like rats smelling rot,
had his three other companions.

The girl turned feeling, no doubt, burning eyes upon her and met them
with a clear, undaunted green gaze. The boy had gone very still, a mask of
nothingness pulled down over his face, his body ready in every limb and
cell for movement. Even if the train were not moving, Duncan had a feeling
these two would not run. The still and silence held for several more moments
and though he could hardly breathe through the tension, a ragged hope was
beginning to form within Duncan that the fraught atmosphere would gel
and stay until they reached their separate destinations. It wasn't to happen.

At a lurch from the train an empty lager can rolled across the dirty floor
and the noise from the rattling can was enough to break whatever uneasy
truce had existed a second before.

"What's yer name beauty?" asked Bernie sounding no more harmful than
the average drunken lout, Duncan thought uneasily, wondering what game
he was about to play. The girl, eyes now held steadily to the floor, didn't
answer. Bernie rose and crossed the car, coming to a stop only a foot away
from where the two were seated. The boy's arm was around the girl now,
offering what scant assurance it could.

"I asked yer name princess," Bernie said in a too congenial tone. Duncan
began to shake.

Her head came up slowly, steadily and she met Bernie's stare head-on.

"I don't see that my name is any concern of yours," she said firmly. Duncan's heart dropped down into the vicinity of his knees.

"The princess doesn't want to tell her name," Bernie said over his shoulder
to his cohorts who had sauntered up behind him. "How's about we guess?
D'ye know any good Catholic names for a good Catholic girl?"

"Maude, Molly, Colleen," came the slurred and sneering replies. Duncan
began to make his way slowly across the car, not trusting his trembling legs,

uncertain of how closer proximity was going to alter the fate of these two young people.

"I'm tellin' ye boys, ye've missed the most obvious, a good Catholic girl is named after the queen of the virgins, this here is Princess Mary."

Bernie put a booted foot up on her seat, the polished steel toe insinuating itself brutally between her pale, naked knees.

"Are ye named after the queen of virgins, Princess Mary? Are ye?" Bernie's foot advanced, touching now the hem of her short plaid skirt. Duncan saw her fine-boned hand lay itself on the boy's arm like tensile steel. She was warning him.

"Are ye a virgin then Princess? Or is this little boy yer lover?" Bernie poked the boy in the shoulder and got a half-rise out of him before the girl pulled him down sharply and said, "Don't he's not worth it." She faced Bernie, unblinking and slowly but firmly pushed his foot off her seat. "Please leave us alone."

"O-ho lads the princess said please. Do ye say please in bed princess? Please an' thank you an hail Mary an' all the rest. Do ye kiss a picture of the Pope before ye spread yer legs fer yer little papist boy here?"

"Shut yer fockin' mouth," said the boy tightly, his face taut with fury.

"What did ye say boy? I wasn't talkin' to ye, I was talkin' to the princess here, wasn't I princess?" Bernie reached down and caressed the collar of the navy pea coat she wore.

"Ye get yer fockin' filthy hands off her ye bastard, or I'll break every bone in them for ye." The boy rose from his seat, shaking off the girl's frantic hand.

"Break my fockin' filthy hands, will ye?" Bernie said drawing the words out pleasurably.

"We've done nothing to you, will you please just leave us alone?" the girl said her voice no longer calm, her face gone dead white.

"Ye've done nothin' to me then have ye? Well," Bernie bent down so his face was even with hers, "I wouldn't say that's quite true," he tilted his head until a long, puckered scar was visible just above the top of his collar, "now would ye, Jewel?"

The girl gasped and Bernie reached down with one blunt, callused hand and pulled her up by her ponytail. "But I won't hold that against ye. I think we should reacquaint ourselves though an' let yer little loverboy here watch, maybe he'll learn somethin'."

The boy lunged forward just as Duncan said, "Bernie don't be such a bastard," and smashed a rock solid left punch into Bernie's face. Bernie's face seemed to explode into a roar of crimson spray. It took all three of Bernie's accomplices to grab the boy and throw him down to the floor, where Bernie, after wiping a torrent of blood off his face, kicked him hard in the stomach five, six, seven times. He turned back to the girl then, who stood paralyzed with fear against the wall of the train.

"Come on then, Jewel, let's have a little fun, you an' me."

"No," she said defiantly, her fists clenched hard by her sides, eyes wide with fear, the proverbial deer caught in the headlights.

"No," Bernie echoed and turned, drawing one booted foot back and delivering a kick to the boy that made him retch blood onto the dirty floor.

"That's what 'no' will get ye princess. I make the rules, d'ye understand? Ye do as I say an' I spare yer little man the worst beatin' ye can imagine. Understand?" She stood mute, defiance leaking out of her as she realized the trap was set on all sides.

Bernie kicked the boy again and Duncan heard the sound of ribs splintering.

"I think it'd be in yer friend's best interest if ye answered," Bernie said happily.

"Yes."

Bernie kicked the boy again, this time with a steel point to the chin that sent his head snapping back, where it smashed hard into the steel frame of the seat. Duncan began to fear that Bernie intended to kill him.

"Yes what Princess?"

"Yes, I understand. Now please, please don't hurt him."

"Good. I see we have a meeting of the minds here, now I'd like the introduce ye to the rest of myself."

Duncan reached out a hand and grabbed Bernie's shoulder.

"Don't do this Bernie, ye stop now an' we'll get off the train in Belfast an' no more will be said about it. Otherwise I'll turn you in to the police."

"Ye'll go to the police?" Bernie laughed, "Who the hell do ye think yer talkin' to? The police in this country understand about lookin' the other way. The police are on my side, Duncan."

He took a deep breath, trying to find some courage in the stale air. "You stop now, Bernie."

A backhanded fist caught him across the face and sent him flying to the floor.

"Ye go to the police Duncan an' ye'll fockin' go home to yer family in a body bag." Bernie smiled and Duncan suddenly understood that he was a psychopath who was using his position of authority as a convenient excuse for mindless violence. Bernie could kill him here and now and feel no regret for it in the morning.

"Take yer clothes off," Bernie redirected his comments to the girl who looked with terror on her companion, who was facedown on the floor, firmly pinned with his arms twisted brutally up to his shoulder blades, squinting through a haze of pain.

She hesitated for a second and Bernie kicked her friend in the face, the crunch of bone followed by a rush of blood down his face.

"When I issue a command, ye obey it instantly, understood?"

She nodded frantically, shrugging off her coat and beginning, with shaking hands, to undo the buttons on her white blouse.

"Too slow," Bernie shook his head and kicked the boy hard in the stomach again, then reached over and tore the girl's blouse down the front and off of her.

"Now take the rest off an' do it quick or there's more of the same for him," Bernie prodded the boy in the ribs roughly, eliciting a low moan from the prostrate form.

Duncan, seized by desperation, grabbed Bernie's leg and tried to upend him. He barely managed to make him stumble and for his efforts received a brutal blow to the face. The rest of the events unfolded through a miasma of pain and nausea.

The girl had taken her bra off and stood barebreasted before them, shaking hands futilely yanking at the zipper on her skirt.

"Too slow again Princess," said Bernie merrily and nodded at one of his accomplices, "break his arm."

Duncan heard the sickening crack of bone and a grunt of pain that belied the agony the boy must be in. Bernie pulled the girl's skirt off and then pushed her down on her knees in front of him. Duncan closed his eyes when Bernie pulled down his zipper and only heard the rest of it. There was a small choking sound and then the boy yelled, "Don't Pamela, don't, I don't care if they kill me, just don't."

Another crack, a small cry of pain and the girl's voice ragged and angry. "Shutup, just shutup."

Duncan squeezed his eyes shut as tightly as he could, the way he had as a child when darkness had frightened him, as if by not seeing it he could make the evil go away. But he could not stop his ears from hearing the pain and violation, nor his nose from smelling the blood or other smells he fought hard to put no name to.

He dared to slit an eye some moments later, only to see one of Bernie's friends on top of the girl, who lay now facedown in the dirt and blood of the train. Her eyes were open, focused with an inner resource, on the bottom of his own shoe. 'They are taking my body but they are not having my mind' her grim stare seemed to be saying, but then she looked up at his face and her eyes met his own for a minute and he saw something so fragile and broken in her face that he felt as though he were witnessing the murder of a child. Then she looked away again, staring once more at his shoe. Duncan turned his head slowly away, an agony of pain shooting up his neck and into his jaw. The boy, Pat, she'd called him, was watching the girl, his eyes not wavering, though tears ran in endless streams, commingling with the drying blood to ghastly effect. He'd likely be better off if Bernie did kill him, poor bastard.

When the third of Bernie's friends got on top of the girl and another took his place over top of her head, Duncan rolled over and threw up. The rest he mercifully blocked out. The sounds had degenerated from those of humans to mere animals taking their pleasure. From the boy and girl there was no sound.

An eternity later, the train came to the end of its journey. The doors opened and there was the sound of men fleeing into the night. Then he heard Bernie's voice, a chill hiss, "I don't forget either you dumb bastard, you might want to remember that next time you brutalize a policeman." Duncan felt the air charge and stir in front of him. "Open yer eyes ye damn coward."

He obeyed, one lid at a time, gingerly, carefully, terrified to the roots of his being of what he might find. The sharp point of a knife nicked at the base of his throat, Bernie's breath was hot on his face, his hazel eyes electric with triumph. "No police, d'ye understand Duncan, I know where ye live, an' I know where yer mam an' dad are. Accidents can happen in all sorts of ways, don't forget that Duncan if ye should go gettin' any crazy ideas." He stood, flicked his knife back into its casing and began to whistle a buoyant tune as he walked off the train and into the night.

Duncan took a shaky breath, the silence pressing in on his head painfully. A minute passed, then two and he heard a small scratching noise, a scraping, flesh on floor and a mute cry that filled the air, that seemed to rent it and rip into his skin.

"Stop it," he begged, "stop making that noise."

"No one's making any noise and your friends are well shot of here so you can quit crouching in the corner."

He turned to face her, she was kneeling, bloody, bruised and half-naked, but at least she was upright. The boy was not. His eyes were closed, his skin tinged a macabre blue under all the red and black, a stream of fresh blood trickling from a cut across his neck.

"Jesus God," he breathed in horror, "did he cut his throat?"

"No, I believe he left his signature," she said wearily and crawled across to the boy, clutching her torn and filthy shirt to her chest with one hand. She put two fingers to the side of his neck

"He needs help, you've got to go and get help for him, I can't leave him like this, you need to go now." Duncan winced from the harsh light of the train that backlit the girl, making her seem like some avenging angel, blood-streaked, bruised and ivory-skinned.

"Me?" Duncan managed to squeak out through his bruised throat.

"Yes you, I cannot leave him alone, he might—he could," she faltered, a long hard tremor shaking her body, the way a dog might a bone, and then with a visible effort to hang on to some shred of sanity she continued. "We haven't much time, I can't move him and it's only a matter of minutes before someone finds us. That cannot happen, do you understand, it cannot. You must call the number I give you and ask for James Kirkpatrick, you cannot talk to anyone but him. Tell him Pat's hurt very bad and that Pamela asked that he should come as quickly as possible. We'll meet him under the bridge by the shipyards, can you remember all that?"

"Yes, yes I can, but do you think it's wise to move him?"

"No, but we cannot stay here, if we stay here and someone finds us, it could go very badly for all of us, do you understand what I'm saying?"

"Noooo," Duncan said slowly, though it was terrifyingly clear what she meant. She told him the number then, slowly and twice over and made him repeat it twice back to her.

"Here," he said as he rose to go, "You'd best take my coat, it's cold."

She nodded, not looking up, her hand streaked and sticky with blood pressed hard into the boy's neck.

It took five minutes, though it felt like five hours, to locate a phone, to assure the barman he was neither dying nor about to make a long distance call to foreign relations. He dialed the number slowly, reciting the numbers off as though they were a child's nursery rhyme.

The voice that answered, on the fifth ring, was tired, annoyed and in no mood, Duncan suspected, to be running out into the night at the behest of a total stranger. "I'd like to speak to James Kirkpatrick," he said trying for a strong and commanding tone.

"This is he," came back the curt reply.

"My name is Duncan MacGregor an' I'm callin' fer Pamela or rather on behalf of her, I was to tell you that Pat is badly hurt, an' I can vouch for that an' that yer to meet us under the shipyard bridge, she said ye'd know where an' that I wasn't to tell anyone else, I was only to talk to yourself."

There was a long pause at the other end of the line. "Have you quite finished then?" asked the voice, still curt, but now with an underlying note of urgency.

"I have," Duncan replied meekly.

"Is she hurt?"

"Yes, in a manner of speaking, you could say she's pretty bad off."

"You go back, you help her in any way you can and you tell her I'm coming." The phone went down then with a sharp click and Duncan swallowed a lump of nausea in his throat. This was not a man to cross; however, Duncan also sensed this was a man that could handle the travesty of this evening.

It was three minutes hard run back to the train, where he saw to his dismay that the train had been moved off the tracks for the night and was shuttered in darkness. Dear God, were they locked in for the night? If so, there was hardly any way to get them out without raising one hell of a lot of unwanted attention. He glanced about wildly, half-blind with desperation and saw a dim flash of white. Beyond the lights of the train yard, in the phosphorescent blue of late night he saw her and, slumped, in her arms was the boy, still unconscious. He ran for them, head pounding, throat constricted.

"He's coming," he gasped out, stopping abruptly some two feet away from her.

"Do you know where the bridge is?" she asked desperation written clearly across her face.

Duncan nodded.

"You have to go and get him, bring him here, I cannot move Pat, I had to take him off the train and I'm afraid of what that may have done. Bring Jamie to me, please." Her voice was pleading, her eyes bright with tears and he wanted to tell her that she needn't beg, he would fly to the ends of the earth for her at this moment, he would run as far and fast as need be in order to flee from the images on the train. In order to grasp back something that he had lost irrevocably on the train, something inside of him that had turned its face in disgust and pain as he saw men become beasts and take far more from a girl than her body could offer.

It was a hard ten minutes to the bridge and when he arrived there he couldn't speak, his bruised throat clutching for air, his legs feeling like jelly underneath of him. There was a man waiting beside a somber gray car, a man who stepped forward sharply and grabbed a heaving, winded Duncan.

"Where is she?"

Duncan gasped and flailed in the general direction from which he'd flown. He was thrust unceremoniously into the car and asked directions in a brutally direct voice. Duncan gestured and croaked and prayed with half his mind that they would make it there in one piece. However fast the man drove though was more than equaled by his precision. They were on the edge of the trainyard within minutes.

She was collapsed on the ground, still bare from the waist up, her coat gone to cover the boy, who lay frightfully still and inert on the ground. She gleamed there under the moonlight, blue, black, ivory, like some glowing, too fine jewel. The man went to her first, ripping his jacket off, covering her and then turned his immediate attention on the boy. He felt down his body, pressed his thumb into the boy's wrist and then turned to Duncan,

"Give me your shirt." Duncan obeyed without question, shivering as the night air hit his body. The man stripped down as well, tied the clothing together into a crude, makeshift stretcher, then said,

"Duncan, you'll have to help me, Pamela roll Pat up on his side, the right side, put one hand on his hip and one on his shoulder, we need to avoid his ribs at all costs, Duncan we'll put the stretcher under him, then ease him back onto it. Gently and slowly."

Duncan gratefully followed his commands, making each step and move as he was instructed until the boy, Pat, was lying on the back seat of the big gray car. The girl huddled in the front and Duncan was about to back away, head for home or the hills he cared not which, when the man's voice stopped him cold.

"Get in the car. Until I know exactly what happened tonight and who did it, no one goes anywhere."

It didn't even occur to Duncan to make a run for it. There was that much authority in the man's voice.

He sat in the front, the girl wedged between himself and the man, from the back there was no sound, not even that of breathing.

When they stopped at long last, Duncan gazed out in stupefaction, realizing quite suddenly what shock had hid from him previously. His father had shown him the house and told him the tales of it more than once. Kirkpatrick's Folly. He'd never thought to be on the inside of it though and had he ever had such small daydreams, they certainly never included this sort of dire circumstance.

"I'll need you to help me get Pat inside," the man said and the knowledge of exactly who this man was, shook Duncan's staid soul to the core.

For the next half hour, he followed orders precisely and without hesitation or thought. The boy (he tried desperately not to think of him as Pat, somehow him having a name made the situation that much worse) was moved inside, to a downstairs room obviously prepared for him. There was a small, gray-haired man present, whom Duncan realized shortly was a doctor. Only this house on the hill could exert the summons that would bring a doctor on a housecall.

He lost track of the girl (it was even harder to think of her without a name, but he was grimly determined not to, just the same) in that first half hour and sat finally when it seemed everyone had disappeared, waiting until the man (Lord Kirkpatrick, god help him) told him he could go. If he hadn't been entirely certain that he would be hunted to the ends of the earth like a dog, he'd have run for it at the first chance.

He was completely disoriented and frightened by the whispering voices he heard upon waking some time later. It came back to him in bits, the events of the night and he had to hold his head in his hands for some moments to control the nausea that surged through him. He stood then, trying to locate the voices, realizing that they weren't whispering, but just distant from him.

He walked down the thickly carpeted hall, towards the sound, individual words forming out of the up and down cadences of agitated speech. 'Boy, stranger, not certain, multiple breaks,' these words made themselves clear and then hesitating by a set of oak double doors, Duncan heard the conversation of the two people inside.

"Honestly James he should be moved to a hospital, he's going to require surgery, who on earth is he? Even the pope goes to hospital."

There was a murmured reply that Duncan could not make out and then a sharp intake of breath from the doctor and "well yes I can see the difficulties presented there, however we could make up a feasible story, it's possible to the inexperienced eye that this could seem like the result of a car accident. We'll take him in under an assumed name, I have to be certain that there's no internal bleeding and that arm will need pins, it's broken in at least five places that I can discern, heaven knows what will show up on x-ray."

"And the girl," came the other voice, hard and flat.

The doctor sighed before replying, "Less physical damage but Lord only knows what happened, she's not saying much. She was raped multiple times though, I can tell you that. There are cuts in her mouth that would indicate—" Duncan plugged his ears and slumped against the wall. He didn't need to hear what the doctor was saying, he would never forget what had happened to that girl on the train, that girl who had been laughing, green eyes shining at her friend and then only moments later had been kneeling on the dirty floor of the train, naked, mouth forcibly opened by the blunt, brutal hands of Bernie, opened to receive him in terror and disgust. Duncan felt the nausea sweep him again and unstopped his ears. "...left her with some antibiotics to deal with any secondary infection, stitched the tear in her vaginal wall—took four stitches that. She'll have to be checked again on a fairly regular basis, god knows what sort of venereal diseases those animals might have and of course there's always the possibility of pregnancy. She'll need help, Jamie."

"She'll have it," was the terse reply.

"Fine, be certain she takes the antibiotics. I want to see her again in a week, here if that's better for all concerned but now I have to arrange to get that young fellow to hospital."

"We'll follow later," the man named Jamie said.

"Not to hurry, he'll be unconscious for quite some time," there was a deep breath, whether the doctor's or Jamie's, Duncan could not tell, and then, "this is really a police matter, if it should somehow get out of my hands at the hospital..."

"Don't allow it to," came the reply, "the RUC are hardly likely to look with sympathy on her case once they realize who she is or rather who she lives with. Regardless, she refuses and I tend to agree, this system would only re-victimize her and if her," he paused and coughed, "husband were to find out there would be hell of a kind you can't quite imagine to pay."

Duncan raised his head at that. Husband? The girl had a husband? This was getting messier by the minute. He stood and looked around in bewilderment for an exit and finally decided on the door off to his far right when a cool voice said, "Duncan, I'd appreciate it if you'd stop eavesdropping and come in."

Duncan meekly did as he was told.

The eyes, green as jade, held no mercy, no compassion. Nor did the face, hard and composed against its bones, betraying nothing, unrevealing of what stakes this man held in tonight's events.

"Sit," said the man, whom Duncan had seen only in magazines and on the television where he constantly seemed to be evading the camera, even while facing it directly.

Duncan sat and found a glass of whiskey placed in his hands.

"Drink it, you'll need it before you see an end to this night."

Duncan drank it, eyes filling with tears from the strength of it.

"Now you will tell me what happened tonight."

"I didn't—I couldn't—" Duncan began, tripping over his tongue in his nervousness.

"For some things Duncan," the voice was mild, though it held the sting of poisoned honey, "excuses may be applied; in this situation they are not acceptable."

"Yes, sir," Duncan replied, free hand bunching the cloth of his trouser leg.

The story came out then, from start to finish—the game, Bernie's resulting mood, the couple on the train, the brimstone smell of hatred and danger in the air and his knowledge of what was about to take place from the instant Bernie set eyes on the girl. What had been done to the boy, what had been done to the girl in its detail and grotesqueness. He did not spare himself even the tale of his own cowardice. Through it all the man who sat in front of him uttered not a word, not a sound, nothing to indicate that the story touched him in the slightest. Finally, to his own relief he burbled to an end and was grateful for the silence that followed. A paper and pen were placed in his hands a moment later.

"The names of the boys, first and last, middle if you know it. Where they live, where they wander, what they eat and to whom they pray, no detail is to be considered too small."

"I—but—" Duncan began to protest but the words quickly wilted on the vine as he looked up and met the unemotional gaze and ungiving mouth of his host. Here, he thought, was someone far more frightening than Bernie. Excuses did not apply and would be less than welcome. He would have to take his chances with Bernie. He wrote the names and across from them all the habits he understood if not of the individual boys, than of their neighborhood, of their race, the dark haunts, the appetites bred in some by poverty and ignorance, in others by some vicious twist of nature itself.

"Thank you," said Lord James Kirkpatrick when Duncan handed him the paper, trembling, that could signify a swift and ugly end to his young life.

"What now? I mean shouldn't the police be called?" Duncan asked desperation spilling out and ahead of his words.

Folding the paper in half and laying it with a light hand beside him, James Kirkpatrick said, "I think you will find this entire situation simplified Duncan if you abandon pretense."

"No police then."

"No police."

"What do I do, where do I go?" Duncan asked with the anger of one who knows home is not an option.

"Perhaps a university overseas, in a place where the pearls of democracy float toward the shore rather than away and men," the green eyes, lightless and dense, met his own like the thrust of a sword to a soft vulnerability, "still have the ability to dream."

Duncan took the point as he was indeed meant to. "But how, I don't know anyone or anything—" he faltered, aware that he was treading on ground not of his own making.

"Duncan you will find life considerably less confusing if you realize that all things can be arranged piecemeal to become a, if not familiar, at least livable structure. Do you understand?"

Duncan, for not the first time in his abbreviated history, thought miserably that he did.

In the time it took to mount the stairs, traverse the hallway and enter his own bedroom, Jamie had sorted, sifted and refined his emotions for the task that lay ahead of him. He opened the door to the room and closed another within his mind, recently cracked to light and hope. He turned to the paler declivities of the brain, ones without emotion and frailty and put the hasp firmly to its lodging and slid the bolt home. There was no place for weakness here, he must tonight and for possibly a great deal longer be the flesh to blunt the knifepoint, the beebalm upon the thistle, the sponge to sop the venom from wounds unseen. He put away from him, as the man in the psalm once had, the things that could or might have been.

She was no more than a huddle of wool and linen on the bed, the bedside lamp providing only a small halo of light that puckered in folds and hollows.

"Pamela?" he whispered, but to his ears overly alert and sensitive, it seemed a shout.

"Can I have a bath now?" she asked, voice small but steady. "Now that the doctor is done."

"Of course," he said, grateful to have a task, however small, with which to occupy his hands.

He started the bath, adjusted the water and then rummaged through the cupboards to find some scent, to take from her nose, at least, the memory of the train. At the far back of one shelf, pushed carefully there after his wife had left, were rows of small dark bottles, stoppered with old, cloudy glass. Oils from flowers and fruit, from herbs and trees, elixirs to bind thought and fear, for Colleen had been very desperate to believe that anything might help, even the bitter scent of dead blossom. He picked up the one closest and read the carefully lettered label in Colleen's small, precise hand. '*Betony- For Purification and Protection against evil.*' A bit late for that he thought but dropped a small stream of it into the water. '*Heather- to guard against violence and aid in the conjuring of ghosts,*' read the next. Again too late, he returned the bottle to its place and chose another. '*Fragaria Vesca- Strawberry- For Love and Luck.*' The irony of that for before tonight she had seemed imbued with an uncanny amount of both. Jamie unstopped the bottle and scent wavered out, rising on the steam like berries crushed between pale hands. He added it to the bath. The last bottle he chose lay on its side, the color of rubies with an amethyst stopper. He remembered finding it in an antique store in London, how the day had been full of rain and heavy gray clouds and the bottle had glowed from amidst a clutter of glass. How it had seemed a bit of magic in a bad time when so many things were fading to black and white. Colleen had loved it, as she always loved pretty, abandoned things. It had become the talisman of her collection, the *genus loci* that would keep and contain the magic, turning mere liquid into medicine that would make whole all the parts of their lives. Fairy nonsense and as history had borne out it had not worked. Happiness could not, it seemed, be found, much less bottled.

He turned the vial carefully in his hands, the label worn and smudged and the glass cold where it had once possessed an unnatural warmth. '*Balm of Gilead- To Mend a Broken Heart.*' Jamie emptied the entirety of it into the bath.

He sensed her in the doorway behind him and closed his eyes in a hasty and wordless prayer before assembling his mask and turning to give what he might and restrain what he could not.

"Do you need my help?" he asked, no trace of anything but a careful gentleness in his words.

"I can't seem to stop shaking enough to get the buttons on the shirt," she gave a short bark of laughter that was dark and strangled in its infancy.

She wore an old nightshirt, all Dickensian white cotton and pleated creases that Colleen had given him as a joke one Christmas. The buttons, tight and flat, were numerous and a challenge to even the steadiest of hands. He unbuttoned them slowly, hands light and mind averted. He pulled it over her head and laid it aside, then gave her his arm to lean on and assist herself into the bath. Once she was settled, soap, shampoo and cloths at hand he turned to leave the bath.

"Please stay, I don't want to be left alone," she said.

He stayed and helped, for her hands, comprehending what her mind had yet to, would not cease to shake and she, holding them clasped tightly in front of her, seemed afraid to let them go.

He washed her tenderly, as one does an infant, with concern and care. He noted the blood—black, blue, violet and crimson that had dried on the skin of her thighs, the bruises and scrapes on her back and front, the welt rising on her jaw, the raw split on her lower lip, the swelling on the upper one and knew what it signified. These things he witnessed and put aside one by one, saving the anger for later, knowing it had no place here and now. It would serve neither of them this night.

After he had washed and rinsed from her what physical traces as could be removed with soap and water, he wrapped her in a large towel, patting her hair down with another.

"Would you like to lie down again?" he asked handing her the nightgown.

She shook her head slowly but firmly, "No I've got to go to the hospital, I have to be there for Pat, I have to be there if..." her voice faltered, her eyes came up and met his for the first time that night, "he can't be alone, Jamie."

"Of course," he replied quietly, leaving unspoken the words both of them felt with utter clarity. Pat must not be alone, for no man, even if it is meant, should die alone.

"HE WON'T DIE, BUT HE'LL WISH HE HAD FOR A WEEK OR TWO," the doctor said acerbically. "The internal bleeding wasn't as bad as I'd originally feared and the bones seem to have set up nicely. He's young and he'll mend well. But," he sighed and gave the two faces before him a weary regard, "the arm is broken very badly, in five places and it may never function fully again. The breaks weren't entirely clean and the bone was near mashed in some spots. I'm keeping him in for at least two days," he gave them both a stern look, "for observation and to be certain the internal bleeding is fully stopped. After that he'll need constant supervision and help and someone to administer pain medication on a regular basis."

"He can stay with me," Jamie said firmly, "we'll hire a round the clock nurse if that's what's needed."

"I can do for him," Pamela said, voice low with determination.

"That will be something for the two of you to work out," the doctor raised his eyebrows at them.

"Can I see him?" Pamela looked up at the doctor with dry, burning eyes and Jamie wanted to say 'no' there on the spot.

"Yes, but only to rest his mind that you are safe and sound, a few minutes at most."

"Thank you," she said as if the doctor had just granted her a reprieve from the gates of purgatory.

"Nurse," the doctor stopped a long-nosed fearsome looking woman on her way past. "Nurse Browning will take you to your friend."

Pamela, with a small smile of gratitude, followed the nurse, who after quickly and circumspectly taking stock of her visible bruises and cuts, indicated with a gentle nod of the head that Pamela should come with her.

"Do you think it's wise to allow her to see him?" Jamie asked as soon as Pamela was out of earshot.

"Yes, the both of them need to ease their minds a bit, he woke up just before he was anesthetized and tried to get off the operating table, he was shouting for her, certain that she'd been taken off the train by those bastards who beat him. I tried to reassure him but he was certain I was lying and I can't say I blame him after the night he's just had."

"But he will be alright?"

"Physically yes, his mental and emotional rehabilitation will rest a great deal on how the girl recovers from all of this. If anything is to halt his healing it will be the guilt he feels over not being able to prevent what happened to her."

"He couldn't have done anything."

"No, but that won't stop him from raking himself over the coals for it. It looks as if he put up a damn good fight as it was; I've never seen a more savage, sadistic beating in my life. But still as I say, if she manages to come through it I suspect he will as well."

"She'll come through it," Jamie said grimly.

The doctor patted him on the shoulder, "Seems as if she'll hardly be able to help it with so many stubborn men in her corner."

"Aye well, one can only hope, can't one?"

The man who had attended to all the ills of the Kirkpatrick family for two generations, who had been present at all tragedies replied,

"Hope is half the battle, Jamie."

PAT SLEPT FOR A VERY LONG TIME AND PAMELA REFUSED TO LEAVE his side until he awoke and knew she was safe. Jamie, having assured himself that each would survive until his return, informed Pamela that he would be gone a short space and that if she could supply him with a key he would pick up a few odds and ends in the way of clothes and toiletries for her. She had handed him the key without speaking, merely fishing it from the pocket of an old cashmere coat that had belonged to Colleen.

He conducted what little business he had to in his office and, supplying a few terse orders, memos and instructions to his secretary, he made his way back through the clog of Belfast afternoon traffic. It was near two o'clock when he walked up the crumbling path to the red door. He could think of any number of events or occasions that might have at one time or another, for one reason or another, brought him to the other side of this door but this one had not ever occurred to him. He had failed and miserably so to keep an eye out for her, miscalculating the danger that lay in wait for anyone, regardless of reason, who ventured behind this door.

It was, on the other side, neat and clean, smelling faintly of lemon polish and bleach. The furniture was sparse but worn and comfortable looking. An ancient radio that sat on a equally ancient table, was, other than the remains of a broken lamp, the only adornment in the living room. The kitchen was clean as well, its table made by hand and used, he guessed from the style, by several generations. The entire place had the feel of a small, hardworking bunch of people making the best of dismal surroundings. At least there was, he thought wearily, even in its emptiness, some sense of lives being lived, not merely ghosts scratching at the windowpane.

Pat's room, the first he poked his head into, was spare as a monk's cell, the bed neatly made, a small cross hanging above it, the cheap blue beads of a rosary that was the domain of every Catholic child hanging over the bedpost and, on the wall opposite, a poster of Jim Morrison holding out his hands in supplication, the sixties version of prayer to a higher power no one could admit to needing or believing in. Beside the bed, a small stack of books, two on Eastern philosophy, loans from his own library, a copy of *Ulysses* and one of Jack Kerouac's Beat classic *On the Road* and two volumes of the poetry of Jack Stuart. Jamie smiled at that, Jack Stuart seemed to have become the demi-god of the young Republican movement and one could not speak to any of them without being liberally quoted at and to from the small body of his work. Jamie moved on to the next room, beginning to feel rather like Goldilocks stumbling about the bears' home.

It was Casey's. No mistaking the smell of cigarette smoke, blanketed as it was under the smell of cleaning fluid and a whiff of varnish. Small carvings lined a shelf nailed to the wall, songbirds in a variety of incarnations, some with breast and beak stained cherry and gold, some with feathers just emerging from the wood. The wood indicated a fine and painstaking touch, the work of a man who had once had a great deal of time to concentrate on detail. His eyes avoided the bed, her scent was here and he didn't need any tracery of hair on a pillow to confirm her presence. The sheets he knew would smell ripely of strawberries with only the smallest bitter undernote of that plant's greenness.

A small window looked out into a patch of backyard the size of a man's handkerchief. Someone had tried to brighten the scenery with a ruffle of material printed in pink and red cabbage roses, but it only served to further delineate the particular bleakness of the view.

He found a suitcase that must have survived from Victorian times so battered and otherworldly did it seem. In it he packed what he, as a man unused to the details and rituals of everyday female life, thought was necessary, which is to say he packed everything he saw. Sweaters, skirts, jeans, underwear which refused to stay folded and slipped and slid about as if it had a life of its own. The suitcase was bulging before he was even half-done and, unable to find any other sort of container, he had to take an armload of slippery sweet-smelling things out and dump them in his car. This earned him a very odd and narrow look from the woman next door who was just shuffling up her lane, a bag of food under one arm and a wailing baby under the other.

On the second trip, he grabbed some of Pat's things, torn denims, neatly mended socks and thoroughly disreputable looking t-shirts and jerseys. Neither of them would be coming back here for at least several days. Just as he was giving a last shove to this variety of items it struck him that he ought to take a few of Pamela's personal articles that she'd used to brighten up her room, something that might give her a touch of comfort in the days to come.

He chose a flask of scent called '*Wine of Angels*', made by a very exclusive parfumier in London that he had visited once himself and wondered how she had come across it in her own travels or who, perhaps, had given it to her? Waterhouse's print of *The Lady of Shallot*, the one he'd given her himself at Christmas, he took down from its place above the bed. Finally, he turned to her shelf of books, knowing that she, like him, derived comfort from the printed page. He chose a volume of Yeats, one of Byron, a dime store paperback that had a marker in it, sighed at the omnipresent collection of Jack Stuart's latest work, skipped over it and took as his last selection a much thumbed, shiny with wear book. It slipped from his hand as he turned, an onion skinned flyleaf floating out like a translucent butterfly on a ruffle of summer breeze. He picked it up, opened the front cover of the book and froze at the sight of his own handwriting there before him.

'*To island summers, broken ankles and youth that is far too fleeting*' and below it a snippet of Wordsworth he'd always liked, then his signature and the date. The summer of 1962. He flipped the cover back, *Les Miserables*. He shook his head, remembering why he had come here, what circumstances had precipitated this visit and that he still had a long trip back to the hospital to make. He replaced the copy of *Les Miserables* on the shelf and headed for the bedroom door, then with sigh, turned back and tucked the book under his arm.

PAT'S FIRST WORD, GRITTY AND GRAINED WITH BLOOD AND ANESTHETIC, was her name. The mere sound of it filled her eyes with tears and stuck in her throat so painfully that it was several seconds before she could answer him.

"I'm here," she managed to whisper, fearing he would panic if he couldn't ascertain her presence at once.

He squeezed her hand with his own good one. She had placed hers in it so that he would know, even in unconsciousness, at some level that he was not alone. He then commenced a fit of coughing that sounded like his lungs were being shredded.

She turned, intending to go and find a nurse, but Pat's grip on her hand was tight.

"Please don't," he said around the last gasping coughs, "I'm alright now." His voice was little more than a whisper. "I'm sorry, I'm so sorry—" he broke on the words, a lone tear leaking out around the bandaging on his face.

"Don't you dare, Pat Riordan," she said, gritting her teeth in an effort not to join him in his tears. "Don't you take the blame for what happened, there wasn't a damn thing either of us could do. They almost killed you as it was. I won't let you take the blame for this."

She stroked the back of his hand gently, "The only thing either one of us have to worry about now is somehow keeping this from your brother."

"How can we do that?"

"I don't know," she said fiercely, "but we have to find a way, because this would kill him Pat and then he'd go out and do something crazy, you know he would. And how would that help any of this, it would only make it all worse. I won't have him going back to prison or worse because of this. I won't. I'll look after it, you don't worry about it, I'll handle everything. We're going to be okay, Pat, I swear to you we will. We just have to stick together."

She lifted her hand from his own and gently cupped the side of his bandaged face, "You need to sleep now. Your only job is to get better, because that's one thing I couldn't bear Pat, is if you weren't alright."

She laid her forehead against the bed. "I'm just going to sit here and think, you go to sleep and I'll be right here when you wake up."

There was a long spell of quiet and she thought he'd drifted off when he said, "Pamela?"

"Yes, are you in pain, should I ring for the nurse?"

"No I'm kind of numb still, it's just—have ye ever been to California?"

"Yes I've been to California."

"Lots of times?"

"Four times."

"Could ye describe it to me? The nice bits, I think it would help me stop thinkin' about—about—"

"Of course I can describe it to you, do you need water or anything first?"

"No," he coughed slightly, wincing as the movement caught him in the ribs, "just tell me what the Pacific Ocean looks like."

"It's blue as you ever dreamed and then just a bit bluer and the waves that come in are a surfer's dream. I used to go down to the shore in the morning and watch the surfers. It's a religion with them you know, riding the waves, always in search of that one perfect crest, the wave that will take them to the limit into that ultimate place where everything is the moment and all of life makes sense and there's no thought, only feeling. And the sand, the sand feels like silk under your feet and everyone has honey-blonde hair and treacle-brown skin and looks as if they could do toothpaste adverts in their spare time. The palm trees line the streets even in the big cities like Los Angeles and everybody looks as if they could be a movie star. I saw Cary Grant once you know and his voice was just the way it was in the movies he said 'hello there, little girl' and I couldn't even say anything back I was so stunned just looking at him."

"Go on," Pat said groggily, "tell me more about how blue the ocean is."

"It's blue forever," she said, "forever and ever and ever. Like violets and indigo nights and blue the way God is in your dreams. Someday we'll go there together and you'll see how perfect it all is. I'll take you horseback riding at dawn on the beach and we'll rent a little cottage and have fires at night and..." her voice wove on, intermingling with Pat's breath which came easier and deeper with every word, until finally when she was absolutely certain he was asleep, she laid her head on the coarse white hospital sheet and let the tears fall unchecked.

JAMIE WATCHED THE MOON SET AND THE STARS SLOWLY ROTATE across the sky through the glass walls of his study. His mind sought order from the chaos of the day, picking out the constellations, naming them in Arabic, filing them by distance and magnitude. It was an old game, making the brain use logic, facts and mathematical equations to stoke its linear paths and force it to run on a smoother, straighter road. Most nights he sought comfort in words, but tonight he could not have borne poetry. Only the great aching void of night offered any solace.

"Trouble sleeping?" said a quiet voice behind him.

"Haven't tried yet," he replied mildly. She moved across the floor and came around his chair, her robed figure solid against the ephemeral sky of night. "Why aren't *you* sleeping, didn't the pills work?"

"I didn't take them."

"You really ought—"

"I'm not ready for oblivion yet," she said sharply and then in an altogether different tone, "I'm sorry Jamie, I didn't mean to snap. I know you're only trying to help."

"You may snap as much as you please, you may yell and scream at me if you think it'll help, you can even hit me if it gives you some relief."

"It's alright Jamie, I'm not angry, at least not on my own behalf, but I could murder them for what they did to Pat."

"What do you feel on your own behalf?" he asked quietly.

She shook her head. "Casey said to me once that he'd never met a woman who didn't have shame about her body, that didn't feel that nakedness was somehow wrong. It was something he liked about me, I think, that I didn't feel any shame."

"Liked?" he prodded gently.

"My body was always just this living thing, mine, a part of me, something that gave me pleasure and sometimes pain but just intimately mine to give if I so chose. But yesterday, those men made me feel shame and now I don't know if my body will ever be mine again. Does that make any sense?"

"Yes. When my sons died, there wasn't a damned thing I could have done to save them and yet I've never stopped feeling guilty. It was never the sense of the thing only that I'd failed them before I'd even been given a chance."

"I knew you'd understand," she said, the smallest bit of relief in her words. The quiet of night held them for a time after that, the moon, softly white, drifting and spinning, the stars spiraling in the nebulae, the gossamer arms of the Milky Way turning, spilling, whirling. Circles revolving within circles in the great primordial dance and dealings of stardust.

"Jamie," she said after a long while.

"Yes?"

"Maybe you can't hold me in your heart, but could you see your way to holding me in your hands just for a little while? Until daybreak?"

He stood and took her in his arms, wanting for the first time since he'd laid baby Stuart in his coffin, to stop and still the world, to throw away the clock and make time cease its run.

Above her head, silky soft and smelling of heartbreak, the moon was fading, its pearls ground to powder and he knew with a terrible certainty that he was never going to be able to find unicorns on it again.

Chapter Twenty-one
Dead Man Running

BERNIE MCKOUGHPSIE WAS A MAN RUNNING SCARED. Three of his mates had gone missing and it wasn't likely they'd taken a notion for a holiday and gone off without telling anyone. People who disappeared in this neighborhood disappeared for good and all. Then this morning he'd been called and told that Danny was dead and if he was interested, he might find the body in an abandoned house just beyond the limits of the city. He'd taken a knife, hidden under his pant leg and a gun, newly acquired, with the profits of his latest job. The gun he left just visible enough for anyone who was interested to notice.

Things had been going so well, 'the job' as he called it, paid well and required his services only sporadically. He'd bought new clothes, a leather jacket that made him look like a real swank and even gotten a car, a long shining symbol of blood-red status. There could be no doubt about it, Bernie McKoughpsie was somebody in his neighborhood, the men knew it as they gave his car a wide berth, the women knew it as they hung on his arms and every word he spoke. Cheap tarts the lot of them, but in quantity a man could not complain. He'd never actually known who he was working for but he was paid not to wonder too much. The job on the train had been worth five hundred quid to him and had been a pure pleasure. A man couldn't keep a rat's ass comfortable on the pittance the RUC paid. But now he was scared, everyone on the train that night was either missing or dead and he was extremely nervous about who was directing the scenes in this particular puppet show. He'd not heard anything about the boy they'd beaten on the train and there'd been no report of the rape. He supposed they were too scared or maybe the boy was even dead.

It was really Duncan who disturbed him the most. He'd not seen him and Duncan's mother, when questioned in a way Bernie felt was charming and subtle, claimed to have seen neither hide nor hair of him since that night.

There were marginal factions, even in West Belfast, a community that was no stranger to desperation and failure, to bitterness and anger, which housed and sheltered the true misfits of society. The losers and vigilantes, the drifters and hard-core career criminals. Bernie wondered, not realizing that he was as marginal as they come, if it was upon the toes of one of these small but deadly organizations that he had unwittingly trod. If so, it wouldn't be long before they came hunting him. He would be ready however, he thought smiling to himself and caressing the gray metal of the gun under the buttery leather of his coat.

The house, isolated and empty, was not so hard to find. Bernie, having footed the last three miles because none of the rare cars that had happened past had been either brave or foolhardy enough to pick him up, was sweating from more than just fear.

He approached the house cautiously; aware that there could be eyes at all angles training crosshairs on his silky, shining head. But with the cunning of all rodents, Bernie had a talent for smelling danger in the air and didn't sense it here. Danny was in the kitchen of the deserted house, facedown, one shot to the back of the head, very tidy, minimum of fuss, get the job done and it was then Bernie began to feel the beads of sweat escape his hairline and trickle like ice down his face. It was classic IRA this, a death for a death, nothing personal, just a little note, economical in its lines that said, quite politely, 'you are a dead man.'

He fled the house then, taking no care in his panic to conceal himself in shadow. It was only hours later, curled like a snake in the corner of a dark pub, his hand cramped around his gun, that he wondered if he'd been working for the IRA all along. He knew what happened to informers, heard about British informants who, after they'd outworked their usefulness were thrown to the IRA as bargaining chips. He knew where men who walked both sides of the street in this neighborhood ended up. Whoever was pulling the strings on this job was likely to throw him back on the mercies of his compatriots, of which there would be none.

He was, he knew, no more than a rat in a cage now, with no safe corners to burrow down into. They would toy with him until they saw fit to do as they'd done to Danny. They'd come faceless and voiceless and he'd never know whose dirty work he'd done.

He stayed in the pub, nursing one drink, until near closing and then when the bartender's back was turned, took with all the subtlety he could muster up, his escape through the back entrance. So intent was he on his own fear that he didn't notice the man who'd sat with his back to him all night, drinking more slowly even than Bernie himself, get quietly off his stool and follow, just as quietly, the smell of Bernie's fear out the door.

Chapter Twenty-two

Losing Maude

I WOULD HAVE CALLED HER MAUDE,' she said at the end of the week, at the end of a week during which they pretended that everything was just the way it had to be. 'I would have called her Maude.' Six words to sum up a lifetime that wasn't to be and to put a point on the blood, fear and grief of the entire week. It began in his office, with a fistful of pound notes and ended on a bench in a dark gray and dripping Hyde Park. 'I would have called her Maude.' Called her Maude if she had been the product of love and fecund dealings in a warm bed. Called her Maude if she had a father to whom a name could be put and an emotion assigned other than fear and loathing. Called her Maude if she'd been meant to see the light of day and breathe her first stinging breaths. But she hadn't and so she became someone who would have been called Maude.

It was a week earlier then, on a perversely sunny day when the world seemed to be slowly asserting itself once more onto an even keel, at least from Jamie's perspective. A week earlier and Shannon, his red-haired, green-eyed walking travel advertisement of a secretary, had called into his office that there was a girl, without an appointment, that was most insistent upon seeing him. He had barely had time to look bemusedly up from the unending stock reports covering his desk, when Pamela, white-faced and in no mood to deal with cute secretaries shoved her way through the door.

He'd merely nodded to Shannon who melted out of his office in the quiet way she'd perfected.

Pamela, characteristically, wasted no time in coming to the point.

"I need to get an abortion and I need your help to find a doctor who will do it."

"Not here in Ireland," he'd said.

"Of course not, in England."

"Are you certain?"

"I wouldn't ask otherwise."

It was nearly all there was to the conversation, a sterile conjunction of various vowels and consonants, as if they'd transacted business and set up the terms by which it would be conducted.

'*I would have called her Maude.*'

He dreamed of Stuart that night as he'd known he would and avoided sleep for long hours in anticipation of it, dreamed so vividly of his red-haired boy that he could smell him on his hands when he awoke—the smell of milk and angels. After, there were the phonecalls and favors pulled in, the finest doctor found, his services procured, a very discreet man, all the foibles of the toffee-nosed set were handled there. The man had actually said *handled* as if it were an action, just a bit of business to be settled. Inevitable that he would dream of Stuart.

'*I would have called her Maude.*'

A plane, a train and an automobile, all private, all *discreet.* That had become his verb, as if discreet were a viable action. And while he was perfecting the act of being discreet, Pamela was grimly silent, offering a smile now and then that pulled the skin of her face so tight against its bones that it seemed one must break and tear the other. Discreet and silent, a pretty pair.

The clinic, a cream and beige affair on Harley Street, was also discreet and silent. Hushed became the adjective of choice. Hushed with the smell of antiseptic and chemicals, hushed with the quiet of death and regret. Hushed with the silent white mist of anesthesia, hushed with the effort of not thinking about what was actually being done, being committed under the rose-tinted oil based ceiling. Hushed with the feel of clean sterilized cotton sliding up his arms and the smell of harsh detergent in his nose.

'Most irregular,' the doctor had said, looking down over his beaky nose, when Pamela had refused to go in without Jamie.

'I thought irregularities were your stock in trade,' Jamie had said smoothly, voice almost friendly, almost, but never quite. The doctor had blinked three times and nodded his assent.

'*I would have called her Maude.*'

Called the blood and bone and cartilage Maude. Called the silent scream that radiated in her eyes the entire time, called the knees in stirrups, the invasive instruments that rooted and pulled at the very base of her womanhood, called the pads of cotton gauze packed against the torrent of blood and tissue, called the small, jelly-like lump that was spine and heart and beginning lung and primal brain, Maude.

She bled quite badly, more than was normal the doctor had said sounding somewhat put-out about it, as if her near hemorrhaging was a personal affront to him. If she wouldn't stay over in the clinic then at the very least he must insist that they stay over in London for a night or until the bleeding subsided.

He couldn't take her to the good hotels, he was too recognizable in any number of them. So it was a middling one, where the landlady was a suspicious sort who looked at them as if she knew exactly what they'd get up to the minute the doors were closed. The truth, Jamie thought grimly, was actually more hair-raising than any fantasy she might have tricked out in her mind.

He helped Pamela to the bed, covered her up and then made tea on the tiny hotplate the hotel provided. He closed the curtains on the dark drizzle of a rainy London afternoon and sat in the lumpy, stained armchair beside the bed waiting for Pamela to sleep or wake or say one word and break the horrible white silence that had gripped them both.

The rest of the day and the following night passed in this fashion. Jamie went out into the drizzle that had become a downpour in the afternoon and got them some food, simple things they could eat without fuss, fruit and pastries. Light things to tempt the appetite Pamela did not have. He gazed longingly through the doors of an off-license but in the end passed on by.

Pamela was asleep when he returned so he ate a little but found the food only nauseated him. He knew too well what it was his body craved, what his mind demanded as due for what it had witnessed today.

He formed a makeshift bed out of the chair, a tatty footstool and his suit jacket balled up for a pillow. He dozed fitfully, whorling slowly down into dreams of his sons, Stuart small enough to fit into the cup of his hand, wrapped in baby Irish lace. Stuart luminous as a pearl backlit by the moon, bones shimmering softly under his skin like phosphorescent light on the surface of a primordial ocean. Alexander, tiny wrinkled body like warm slubbed silk, covered in pale golden down, looked like his mother only they never knew what color his eyes were because he'd never opened them. Michael, a celestial being, with the eyes of an old man, as if he'd been there many, many times before and was just too tired to make the journey again. Pretty, pretty boys, underwater angels. And he, Daddy, caught fast in the pain like a star stabbed hard and tight against the deluge of night.

He awoke to the sound of muffled crying, emerging from sleep with a pounding heart and dry throat.

She had tried not to wake him; all that was visible of her was her hair, a spreading black mist over the faintly grubby pillows and sheets.

He was beside the bed on his knees, hand on her shaking shoulder before he even took a breath.

"Are you alright, are you in pain? Pamela," he said desperately, "you have to tell me what's wrong."

"I—I—didn't know it would hurt so much," she said, teeth chattering around her tears.

"You're in pain then? Is the bleeding very bad?" he tried to assert calm into his words through visions of blood transfusions and emergency surgery and endless prying questions that neither he nor she could afford to answer.

"No, it's not so much worse than period cramps and the aspirin took the edge off. No I mean I didn't know that it would bother me so much." She turned her face from the crush of linens and he saw that it was washed clean, faintly pink like a well-scrubbed child, her scar silvery white, with only the faintest traceries of angry red visible. "I don't even know who her father was, Jamie," she said.

He reached out a hand and pushed the damp hair away from her face, smoothing it down over her ear.

"Her?" he asked softly.

She smiled weakly; a tear caught trembling on the cusp of her lip, "Just a feeling. I can't stop thinking, who was she? Which of those boys on the train put her there inside me? Was it the one who smelled of his own urine? Or the one who backhanded me across the face, or the one who broke Pat's arm—" her voice caught up on a sob and she rubbed her face miserably, "and why Jamie, why does it have to be her fault? The rest of us will live, those bastards on the train and me, me I'll go on and on with a little ghost inside, oh Christ, Jamie," she punched the pillow, "I can still feel that thing the doctor put up inside me, it was so big and cold. Why do they need something so big to get rid of something so tiny? Do you think," her fingers curled tightly into the pillow until her knuckles were white and sharp against the skin, "she felt it?"

Jamie wanted to lie, to tell her half-truths prettily cloaked in scientific supposition and emotionless words but found he simply couldn't under the penetration of her eyes. "I don't know sweetheart, I just don't know."

"Will you do something for me?" she asked.

He nodded, "You know I will."

"Just lie down beside me, it's not as if I'm in any condition to seduce you," she said, weakly attempting a joke.

"Alright," he replied.

He lay down on his back, quite suddenly longing for sleep and she covered the space between them, leaving him only with the crush of damp cotton and warm flesh against his side. He took a deep breath, the smell of strawberries climbing up the cells of his nasal passage, the scent accompanied disturbingly by an undernote of iron and salt. It was a smell he knew from his dreams and his own humanity, the smell of blood.

"What is it?" he asked some time later, when his breathing had established regular patterns and sleep was knocking softly with its white fist. She'd curled the tips of two fingers, the index and middle of her left hand, into the hollow at the base of his throat.

"I just like to feel your heart beat," she said.

He slept then and did not dream.

HE AWOKE TO A ROOM GRAY AND MORE DISMAL than it had seemed the night before and to the absence of warmth, the bed beside him smoothed with light hands, a tiny spot of blood bruising its unrippled surface.

He found her outside in the cramped back garden, its meager space full of bare black branches and sodden brown foliage. She was standing, eyes closed, face held up to the rain.

"I just wanted to come out," she smiled, deepening the purple hollows beneath her eyes, "so that when I am a very old woman I can say that I felt London rain on my face."

"It's hardly a world away and as the rain here is fairly incessant, I'm sure you'll feel it again," Jamie said, relief making his voice sharper than he'd intended.

She shook her head. "I don't think that I'll ever come to this city again, Jamie. So take me to Hyde Park will you? So I can stroll through it once and pretend I'm a character in a Henry James novel."

He took her to Hyde Park, green and empty in the chill winter air and they strolled until the light deepened into a winter afternoon. It was there, sitting on a bench a bag of uneaten roasted chestnuts between them, that she said,

"I would have called her Maude. Maude Gonne you know, never here, never will be, never was. I think it's right that I should at least give her a name. Don't you?"

"I do," he said.

She slipped her hand into his and he could not tell if it was the rain or tears slipping down her face, runnelling into the collar of her navy coat.

"It's time to go home, Jamie."

He closed his eyes, tasted the memory of scotch on his tongue and knew he would pay for these days in the long months to come.

"Time to go home," he echoed and thought quite uselessly that last night in a hovel of a hotel room that smelled insistently of fish and strawberries and blood he had felt more at home than he had ever felt in his beautiful, gilded albatross high upon its hill.

"Home then," he said and they stood, hands still clasped and left London behind, taking their ghosts with them.

Lullabies never sung,
Moon and stars never hung.
Kisses not brought to bear
Upon a cheek never there.
Losing Maude.

Fairytales never spun,
Sugar beaches never run.

Dimpled hand never held,
Tiny troubles never quelled.
Losing Maude.

Frilly dress never worn,
Crayon drawing never torn.
Dancing steps never turned,
All the bridges never burned.
Losing Maude.

Fancy's fever never fed,
Closet monsters never fled.
Morning sun never seen,
Mama's baby never been.
Losing Maude.

Chapter Twenty-three
The Scent of Violets

WELL, WHAT DO YE THINK?" CASEY ASKED EAGERLY.

"I hardly know what to think," Pamela replied honestly eyeing the oddity before her.

"Do ye like it, then?"

"Like seems a rather weak word," Pamela said rather weakly herself.

"So ye do like it then?"

"Does it hold water?"

"It does," Casey said with some satisfaction.

"Then I love it," she replied firmly.

In West Belfast in 1969 tubs were somewhat of a rarity, a luxury with which only the newer homes came equipped. Families made do with handbasins and washtubs screened modestly behind a makeshift sheet on Saturday nights. Pamela, used to the opulent facilities at Jamie's house, had found it a bit of a hardship, but hadn't complained. Casey however, wanting to provide her with such small luxuries as he could afford, thought it a stroke of divine intervention when he stumbled across the particular treasure that lay before them now.

"Wherever did you find it?"

"In a heap of scrap metal, if ye can believe it."

"I can hardly imagine," she said faintly.

"Of course," he continued proudly, "it didn't look the way it does now. 'Twas just an old corroded tub someone had tossed out. I've a friend that used to work in a porcelain factory though an' he knows a bit about restoration. He's also a bit in the way of bein' an artist as ye may have noticed."

Pamela, eyeing the naked cherubs lasciviously munching grapes that adorned the tub, was inclined to ask if the friend had apprenticed at a French brothel, but bit back the temptation.

The tub in question was a remnant of the Victorian era, an enameled, rolltop, cast iron, ball and claw footed wonder. Its arrival had occasioned quite a stir in the neighborhood, particularly since it had taken an hour to squeeze, push and cajole the monstrous thing through the door. Word of its arrival spread and by the time Casey and the poor man who'd delivered it had it halfway through the door, the street was full of curious onlookers. Its decoration had raised eyebrows, with some mothers clapping their hands over the tender eyes of their children.

It sat now in state in the center of their small front room, overwhelming the modest furniture like a peacock squatting down amongst a flock of scabby sparrows.

"We can't leave it here," Pamela said, wondering if she'd only imagined the half-naked imp, drawn sitting on top of one leg, winking at her.

"We'll have to," Casey said, "a big old cast iron tub like this full of water weighs a ton, it'd crash through the bedroom floor."

"We'll not be able to sit in here, our knees would bump up against the tub," she said practically.

"We don't sit in here anyhow," Casey replied even more practically. "Besides," he grinned, "there's room for the both of us in there if we've a wish to sit in the parlor. Shall we christen it?"

"Now?"

"No time like the present," he said cheerfully, "I'll go get the bucket an' fill it."

He disappeared into the kitchen and she could hear him humming happily to himself, the creak of protest as the water came bubbling up through the tap and the clank of a bucket into the sink.

She wished vehemently that Pat would come home and by his presence put a halt to the proceedings. But Pat, since the night on the train, had made an art out of avoiding her. He couldn't, even when pressed, meet her eyes. He'd made a brief appearance when Casey came home and between the two of them, they'd managed to concoct a feasible story about the car accident that had supposedly broken Pat's arm. Casey, beyond a small lecture on driving too fast in other people's cars and expressing relief that Pat had not killed himself, said little. However, he watched the both of them carefully as they spun their lies. Pat had left shortly after that, arm still inert in a sling, saying he'd things to do. Where he slept, what he did with all the hours of his day, she didn't know. Part of her was glad, his guilt, so thick and palpable, sat between the two of them, making it hard to breathe. She was afraid it would betray them both and bring down the fragile house of cards they'd built in Casey's absence. It angered her as well that he by his guilt might ruin all she'd done to protect his brother.

Casey had been home five days now and had, not unexpectedly, expressed a desire to make love to her. She'd managed to avoid it by claiming she had her period, hoping he didn't remember the pattern of her cycle from before he'd left. He'd accepted it though and contented himself with holding her in their bed at night.

The doctor had warned her that while physically her body was ready for normal adult relations again, mentally and emotionally it could take a far longer time. Time that she did not have. Time that she could not beg, borrow nor steal.

Several buckets of water and a scoopful of bath salts later and she knew the last grain in her hourglass had dropped down.

"Ah, this is bliss," Casey said with a sigh, breathing in a great lungful of rose-scented air. "If the boys on A-wing could see me now. Are ye certain ye won't join me?" he asked in a wheedling tone.

"In a minute, let me do your hair and back for you first," she said, clenching and unclenching her fists behind her back in an effort to still their shaking.

"Before I forget there's a wee package for ye on the table, it was tucked away in the pocket of my bag an' I'd missed it durin' my unpackin'," he said, taking the soap she handed him. A hard white cake of hand milled French soap out of a basket of things Love Hagerty had sent her with his compliments.

The wee package bound in plain brown paper turned out to be a faded, gilt-lettered copy of 'The Great Gatsby'.

"Thank you," she said, oddly touched by the tiny volume in a way a grander gift would not have done.

"I remembered ye sayin' it was yer favorite an' ye didn't seem to have a copy anymore. I found it in a rack of books on a sidewalk in Boston." He soaped his arms and throat, wrinkling his nose at the strong floral scent. "Have we got any of that brown peppermint stuff ye buy at the chemist?"

She fetched the soap and kneeling behind the tub, lathered the breadth of his shoulders slowly, reacquainting herself with the contours of his body.

"I read the book on the plane comin' home," he said, leaning forward to scrub vigorously between his toes with a soapy cloth.

"Did you like it?" she asked, trailing one finger over the nodules of his spine.

"He'd a pretty way with words yer Fitzgerald did," he put a hand over his shoulder for the soap and she placed the pungent brown cake in his palm.

"He was a very sad man," she said softly, thinking of poor, bruised Fitzgerald and his mad wife, his alcoholic pen twisted into silence by bitterness at the end.

"I tend to like an' endin' with more resolution," he continued, swishing his feet about in the water to rinse them and then laying back, propped them up on the end of the tub where they dripped extravagantly onto the floor.

"Death," she paused to drizzle some of Love Hagerty's expensive shampoo onto her hands and apply it to Casey's wet curls, "is about as resolute as it's likely to get."

"Aye," he sighed happily as she worked the soap into his scalp, "ye've a point but Gatsby didn't accomplish anything he'd set out to do, he just kept hangin' about Daisy waitin' for something to happen."

"It wasn't really Daisy he was trying to capture, it was the past. A past," she paused to push a strand of hair behind her ear, "that only existed in his mind."

"I wondered," he took one of her hands and rubbed his cheek against it, "if ye were so fond of the book because it reminded ye of him?"

"Him?"

"Jamie."

"Jamie's nothing like Gatsby," she said sharply, her hand stiff and still in his. Casey cracked one dark eye open, blowing a soap bubble away from his lips. "Ye don't think so?"

"Gatsby was an impostor."

"Aye, an' Jamie's the real thing, is he?" the pressure on her fingers increased, trapping her hand. "An' I wondered if there wasn't somethin' of Daisy in ye, somethin' cryin' out for a decision."

"If Jamie's Gatsby and I'm Daisy, I suppose you think that makes you Tom. Is that how you see me, some empty-headed female who couldn't have the man she wanted so took the first fool who wandered past?"

He let go of her hand, dunking his head under water to rinse his hair and emerged spluttering.

"Here," she said dropping it directly into the water, "is your towel."

"Thanks," he replied with no little sarcasm and stood, water cascading down the length of his body, droplets of it trapped here and there in thickets of hair. He gleamed in the dim light of the small room, its confinement making him seem all the larger. Not a body meant for small rooms, she thought, slightly dizzy in spite of her nerves. Pure, male animal, made more potent by the incongruity of his surroundings. A body that could commit violence and tenderness with equal ease.

"Could I have a dry towel, then?" he asked shortly.

"Of course," she said and went to get another from the freshly laundered stack on the stairs.

He took the towel from her wordlessly, drying himself down with an abrupt economy of movement.

"Is that how you see us, like characters in a sad novel?" she asked quietly as he stepped from the tub, skin steaming with rose-scented vapor.

"I don't know," he replied, "I don't know what I see. I've been gone over a month though an' I missed ye every minute of every hour, dreamed about ye at night, ached for ye 'til I thought I'd go mad from it an' then I come home an' find ye can't meet my eyes an' ye can't bring yerself to our bed with honesty. Aye," he replied to her startled look, "I know ye don't have yer monthlies."

"How do you know that?" she asked.

He flushed slightly, "Because ye smell a bit different when ye do, a bit less like strawberries an' a bit more like the ground they grew in. Earthier somehow."

"Oh," she said faintly.

"If ye don't want to have me in yer bed ye only have to say so, ye needn't lie about it. I," he said, briskly toweling his hair, "can manage."

"Can you?" she asked, for his body despite his protestations seemed to have its own views on the subject.

He took in the direction of her gaze and primly wrapped the towel about his hips.

"Aye, I've desire, I'm flesh an' blood after all an' it takes little more than ye walkin' past me to stir it but I've scruples as well an' I've no wish to take a woman to my bed who's longin' for another man. Mayhap ye like that damn silly book because yer like Gatsby, standin' on a dock waitin' for a dawn that isn't comin'."

"Casey," she said, trying to ignore the panic percolating in her veins, "I think—" she hesitated and felt something unfold slightly that had been wrapped tightly since the night on the train.

"Ye think what?" he said impatiently, bending over the tub with the bucket half-full of rose-scummed water.

"I think perhaps you'd best," she cleared her throat nervously, "take me to bed."

His eyes met hers and he quirked his eyebrows slightly, "Reassert my claim so to speak?"

She flushed and the folded thing inside of her opened a little more, "Something like that."

He seemed to consider her proposal for a moment, then holding out a broad callused hand to her, he said, "Aye, perhaps that's best."

Her hand, no longer trembling, joined his and she followed in his wake up the stairs and into the bed.

IT CAME TO HER IN ODD MOMENTS. She could be sipping tea in the morning and suddenly he'd be there, present as flesh, solid as bone. Her own personal demon.

She'd expected Casey's presence to lessen his somehow, to take away the power of his grip on her thoughts. But he hadn't.

For a moment, when Casey had first come through the door she'd thought it would work, that his solidity would chase away the ghosts. But then he'd kissed her and she'd tasted violets on his tongue and had to fight nausea.

"Just these hideous wee candies I've grown a strange taste for," Casey said when she'd asked him what the scent was and handed her an old-fashioned oval tin half-full of candied French violets. The scent sickened her, made her want to crawl into a corner somewhere and hide.

He had been the only one to kiss her, the rest had not. And somehow the touch of his tongue on hers had a brutal intimacy the others had not been able to scar her with. His mouth had tasted strongly of flowers, clean and cloying. His words scented with violets as he whispered them in her ear, whispered all the things he was going to do to her and then did them. The scent of violets, once merely the pretty smell of woodsy flowers, had now become a trigger for nightmares.

Beside her in the bed, Casey turned, mumbled softly and settled again, breath coming in a rumble like that of a contented bee.

It had not been so bad. He had been very, very tender, as though he sensed her fear. She had been surprised when her body responded, softened and yielded, under his hands and mouth. Surprised and relieved. It would be all right now, they would manage.

She watched his face in the strange waxy light of the bedroom and beyond him the curling roses of the wallpaper. And beyond that still a shifting, watery light. The pale green light of Gatsby's hope.

She believed in the light of dawn and if its promise eluded her today, well then tomorrow, like Gatsby, she would run faster and reach farther until it was secure within her hands.

> *...I have promises to keep,*
> *And miles to go before I sleep,*

She whispered and then closed her eyes to the night and its demons.

Chapter Twenty-four
A Brief History of Time

THE SIGN ABOVE THE DOOR READ, *'Herr Blumfeld, Amateur Horologist, Repeating, Musical and Plain Clock and Watchmaker, Etitivator and Collector of Esoterica. Enquire within.'*
The tiny shop was buried at the end of a narrow close and had been difficult to find. As she pushed the door in, a set of bells began to play an orderly and precise rendition of one of Bach's minor fugues. Inside was a veritable cacophony as she'd the misfortune to enter on the precise stroke of four when all the clocks were chiming, singing, ringing, clanging, rolling, hooting and grinding about on their gears. She put her hands over her ears, eyes flickering about the shop in search of the proprietor.

She saw clocks of every variety and description, clocks without hands and clocks with seemingly too many, clocks that appeared to be constructed inside out, clocks with pendulums ticking away the seconds in stately precision. There were clocks with tiny people shuttling in and out of doors upon the quarter, half and full hour, ball clocks that looked like looping labyrinths and in the midst of it all an elf-like creature who emerged amid a cloud of dust, sneezing into a grayish colored rag.

"*Gesundheit,*" she said automatically.

When he smiled, which he did with face crinkling thoroughness, he looked much more like a gnome than an elf.

"Welcome Fräulein, how can I be of service?" he asked, inclining his head slightly down and to one side.

"I am looking for a man who can translate from the Arabic," she said.

The smile disappeared like dew upon the desert. The little man gave her a sharp look and going to the door of the shop, locked it and turned the sign in the window to read 'Closed.'

"Where did you hear of such a man?" he asked sharply, face no longer amiable or gnome-like.

"It's my understanding that Arabic is a close cousin of the Hebrew language and that you are an expert in these languages," she said as coolly as she could.

Herr Blumfeld laid a speculative finger alongside his nose, tapping the bridge of it three times. She could feel the cogs of his mind turning over with a precision equal to the clocks that surrounded him.

"In Hebrew I am classically trained," he said quietly, "I can write and understand the three periods of it, Old Testament, Postbiblical and Modern. The language of Zion is my own, with Arabic," he shrugged slightly, "I am somewhat less steady on my feet, though it is true there are many similarities. If not blood brothers, then the languages are at least kissing cousins. You have something, I believe, for me to look at?" He nodded, indicating the manila folder she carried.

"Yes," she said and handed him the onion-skinned contents of the folder. He cast a quick glance to the street outside and then carefully unfolded the sheets. He gave them a cursory glance, mumbling a little to himself. There was a gleam of something near to delight in his brown eyes.

"Come Fräulein, we will sit and have tea."

She followed him towards the back of the shop, past curio cupboards choc-a-bloc with clocks, dusty old books, strange twisted scraps of furniture, delicate bits of crystal and china, as well as many oddly shaped curiosities that defied description.

"Do you know Fräulein, how the dictionary defines esoteric? Anything with a private or secret meaning that is understood only by those who have the necessary instruction or training or more simply as something that is difficult to understand. I am a collector of the oddities of this world, of things that are difficult to understand," Herr Blumfeld said over his shoulder as he swept aside a curtain, opening the way into a cramped, dark sitting room. "When one is Jewish, one comes to feel esoteric oneself and so I am comfortable with things that do not fit, objects that others have discarded and forgotten. Please, you will sit?" He indicated, with one small, dark hand, a large wing-backed chair swathed in grimy looking brown corduroy.

"Surely clocks are not so difficult to understand?" she asked, settling herself on the chair, discreetly stifling a cough as a cloud of dust rose around her.

"When one," Herr Blumfeld put an ancient kettle on a gas burner, "collects clocks, one also collects time, which is no simple thing. For how to collect something that is only an idea, agreed upon by the majority of the human race granted, but nonetheless an idea."

"I thought you only repaired clocks."

"I do, but one must love the thing one fixes or else one cannot do the job properly. A good doctor will love the mechanisms of the body; he will even love that which is flawed in it. A psychiatrist will be enamored of the processes of the brain and heart. I love the instruments that keep time and yet allow it also to escape. You think it is a mistake, Fräulein, that the part of the clock that allows us to read the time are called hands? It is our attempt to grasp and hold that which cannot be caught." During this small monologue, he had shuffled about stacking mismatched pieces of china on a silver tray, filling a teapot and then placing the tray on a low spindly table between the two of them, discommoding an assortment of clock workings laid meticulously on an oily cloth.

"You will excuse my untidiness, I am not used to having company and it hardly seems worth it to clean for myself. I had a lady who came and did such things but," he handed her a cup of tea with a delicate almond cookie balanced precariously on its saucer, "she developed romantic ambitions and I'm afraid I had to let her go."

"Why time Herr Blumfeld?"

His eyes narrowed slightly and he seemed to give her question due consideration before answering. "The practical answer, Fräulein, is that my father, and his father before him, going back many generations, were clockmakers. It is what I was born to, it is what I knew from the cradle and will take to the grave."

"And the impractical answer?"

He smiled and nodded, "A romantic I see. The impractical answer is that time is what divides this earthly duration from eternity, the finite from the infinite. Without time there is a void, an unimaginable emptiness that would eat the very sun from the sky. Perhaps you are too young to know this Fräulein, but there is a comfort to be found in numbers, in mathematical equations, an ease not found in less rigorous disciplines."

"And yet," she said setting her empty teacup down carefully amidst the miniature pendulums and pinions, "it is mathematics that opened the door to the universe and, some would say, there is not a great deal of comfort to be found in the heavens."

"There is often a conundrum at the heart of life's great pleasures Fräulein and even you are not too young to know that. Come, we will speak of less weighty matters. I will show you my clocks."

He stood and shuffled to a cabinet behind her, unlocking its doors with a key that hung on a string about his neck. She turned about and peered over the top of the chair, trying to ignore the benign stare of a spider descending from the ceiling on a filament of web.

"All clocks must have two basic components, Fräulein. The first is a regular, constant or repetitive process or action to mark off equal increments of time. The ancients used the movement of the sun across the sky, candles marked off in precise measurements, oil lamps with marked reservoirs, sandglasses and in the Orient incense that would burn at a certain pace. Our year came into being because of the movement of the star Sirius which rises next to our sun every three hundred and sixty-five days. The second component is a means of keeping track of time's passage by the use of clock hands. Of course, hands are a more recent addition. The earliest clocks depended on more natural mechanisms. Take this for instance."

He reached into the cupboard and withdrew a small bowl with sloping sides and a tiny hole near its base.

"It is what the Greeks called a 'water thief', a much smaller version granted than the working models, but accurate nonetheless. In the morning it would be filled with water and throughout the day the water would drip out at a nearly constant rate, when the bowl was empty it was night. Simple but effective. The Greeks and Romans elaborated on this humble timepiece and made mechanized water clocks that rang bells and gongs or opened doors and windows to display little people or moved dials or tiny models of the universe. Water however," he placed the tiny bowl back in the cupboard, "is a contrary element, its flow is difficult to control with the precision needed by timekeepers."

The next item he withdrew was a series of four wasp-waisted glass vials, graduated from large to small in a heavy base of iron scrollwork.

"Renaissance sand glass," he said, "though more accurately the largest marks the hour, the next the three quarter, the third the half hour and the smallest the quarter hour. The problem of the hourglass is the problem one might say of life itself. The sand, much like time itself slips through the narrow funnel and wears it down, so that as time goes on it slips faster and faster through the neck thus outwearing its usefulness with the advancing of years."

"And this one?" she asked pointing to an elaborately carved clock set in three tiers topped by a brass dome with an open lotus on the base of the second tier.

"Ah Fräulein you have an eye for the luxurious. It is said this clock was one of the six hundred that used to keep time in the hall of China's Imperial Palace. I will show you its secret." He took one finger and moved the long hand slowly across the face of the clock until it stood upon the hour. A tinny, mechanized melody began to play as the dome slowly opened into four quarters to reveal a perfect lotus unfolding its petals, while the lotus on the front of the clock curled its petals inward until it became a tightly packed bud. In the base a series of glass rods turned giving the impression of a tumbling waterfall.

"It does the reverse upon the half hour," Herr Blumfeld said, closing the glass door over the clock's face, "as if to tell us that only one flower will be open at a time, as night must have day as its opposition, and joy must have pain, love hate and so forth."

He went on to show her clocks that depended on weights and pulleys, spring-powered clocks, clocks driven by the electric field of quartz, French bell clocks, the blue-by-blue Nuremburg clock with the pale color representing day and the dark representing night. Clocks based upon the canonical hours with chimes to call the faithful to prayer. And finally, a small wooden clock in the Swiss fashion with a cock who crowed and flapped his wings upon the hour.

"This I call the traitor's clock," Herr Blumfeld said as the tiny rooster flapped his wings for the third and final time before disappearing back into the clock.

"The traitor's clock?"

"Yes. You will perhaps know Fräulein the origin of this mechanism? It was used in many early clocks. It derived from Christ's warning to Peter that he should deny him thrice before the dawn, it is a reminder to all traitors that there will come an hour of reckoning." He closed the cupboard abruptly and locked it as if somehow the little rooster had disturbed him. He seemed suddenly very weary.

"My apologies Fräulein but I am an old man and it has been a long day, if you will leave an address with me I will see what may be done with your papers and return them to you in the mail. If it is not," he coughed delicately, "inconvenient for you to have me do so. I will of course take care to disguise it in some way."

"That will be fine," she said, feeling a sudden and profound sadness for the small man who lived his life out amongst dust and lifeless mechanisms.

She collected her coat and bag, feeling somewhat relieved to be leaving the dark, dim shop. But in the doorway, light and fresh air but a knob's turn away, she hesitated and turned back.

"Herr Blumfeld, if I may ask a question?"

"Of course," he replied politely, already seated with a sharp, fine instrument in hand over the open back panel of a watch.

"If I may say so Ireland seems a rather odd place for a German Jew to end up."

The old man blinked, considering this.

"Perhaps it would seem so. But to me it seems that here all are Jews—Catholic Jews, Protestant Jews, but Jews nonetheless. The Irish understand persecution without reason. And Fräulein there is enough sorrow in the air here for an old Jew such as myself to breathe comfortably."

"But before," she said softly, "you spoke the word Zion as if it were sacred. You might have gone to Israel after the war, mightn't you?"

Herr Blumfeld was still bent intently over his work but his shoulders stiffened perceptibly at her words. A long silence stretched itself between them and she was about to apologize and take her leave of him when his words, hollow and toneless, broke the quiet.

"Fräulein the Torah tells us that Israel is denied to those who are unclean. A man who touches a corpse is unclean for seven days and can only be cleansed by purifying waters. In my time Fräulein I have touched too many corpses.

I worked on the burial detail at Belsen throughout the war, on some days we put a thousand bodies under the earth. Seven days times countless dead is more than the days of my life. Israel is forever denied to me."

"I am sorry," she said.

"Do not waste pity on the old; they have had their choices as well. Even under the Nazis, Fräulein there were choices."

"What other option could you have possibly had?"

"I could have chosen my own death, but I did not. I live with the consequences of that."

In the narrow close outside the shop fog was crowding in, scuttling with silent feet into crooks and crannies, filling up the air and blotting out the light but before her she saw, instead of yellow creeping fog, a wrist, finely boned with the strongly etched tendons of one who works with their hand in precise, small movements. Upon it written a set of numbers, black and crude, an equation for sorrow and guilt and madness. And above it an extra number, two digits that identified him as someone set apart from even his own people. A traitor to his tribe.

There were some numbers, Pamela thought, that regardless of order were not designed to give comfort. She walked away into the fog, contemplating the pleasures that awaited her at home, warm food, a warm bed and a warm body to keep out the horrors of the night. While behind her, in the dusty shop, an old man laid his head down and held his breath while a small, wooden rooster called out the hour.

Chapter Twenty-five

My Brother

S O ALTOGETHER YE'D SAY IT WAS A SUCCESSFUL TRIP?" Seamus asked, watching Casey pore over bank documents and customs regulations in an effort to make some head or tail of the situation in which they found themselves.

"Aye," Casey said distractedly, "though it'll take longer than I'd like for the money to come through the appropriate channels, we can only let it in a trickle at a time, so we'll have to bide. Havin' someone run back an' forth from Switzerland on a regular basis is goin' to get suspicions roused right quick. As for the weapons, well how I'm to get eight crates of guns through customs is above an' beyond my powers of imagination."

"What's it to be labeled as?"

"Stoneware from Germany. They'll weight the guns appropriately against the number of settings on the claims form an' hope to heaven that no one has a hankering to view German china patterns. Do ye remember the story about Brendan O'Boyle an' the time he'd nine cases of ammo comin' in at Cobh, but he only picked up eight an' the other case took a round the world voyage before comin' back to Ireland an' then when he went to pick it up his usual customs agent wasn't on duty. I tell ye I've nightmares about that sort of scenario happenin' to me."

He rustled through more papers, yawning and absently scratching his head.

"An' everythin' here?"

"Went smooth," Seamus said quickly and looked swiftly towards the window.

"How smooth?" Casey asked, alerted by Seamus' deliberately casual tone.

"Ye know there's been nothin' goin' on about here. Will ye look at that wee bird on the window ledge, looks like an Australian kookaburra, imagine that." He rose from his chair and went over to the window peering with apparent fascination at the bird sitting on the sill.

"Seamus, would ye quit fakin' an interest in ornithology. That's a perfectly ordinary sparrow an' ye know it. Now I think ye'd best tell me what went on here."

"Well on the business side it all went quiet as I've said, but on the personal side..." he trailed off, not liking at all the look that had come over Casey's face.

"What do ye mean? Did Pat do somethin'? What sort of trouble has the little bugger gotten himself into now? Was there more to the car accident than he let on?"

"It's not Pat," Seamus said quietly, "it's the girl."

"What about her?" Casey said in a flat, hard tone that warned Seamus to tread lightly.

"Casey," Seamus swallowed over the sick feeling in his stomach, "we have to talk."

ON THE TABLE THERE WAS A SMALL PARCEL, addressed to her in a careful, painstaking hand, wrapped in crumpled brown paper. She untied the string on her way up the stairs and the paper fell away to reveal a small book, lilac hued, that bore the eyebrow-lifting title of *'Confessions of a Bodleian Boy, A Tale in Two Parts Concerning many Erotic Adventures' by Archibald Swansea, Esq.* Her eyes flicked hastily upwards to the top left-hand corner—there was no return address.

She shut the bedroom door behind her, heart beating a little harder than it had only a moment before. She sat down on the foot of the bed, laid the book in her lap and opened the front cover. At first glance, it seemed an ordinary book, though the paper it was printed on was of a weight and quality that wasn't generally used for erotica. She thumbed the pages over, one at a time and then thumbed them back, finally fanning them upside down in an effort to reveal their secret. Other than releasing the slightly moldy smell of old paper they gave out nothing. She then tried reading it, eliminating every other word, then every fifth word, then every other letter. From this endeavor she gleaned no useful information, unless one counted the sensual adventures of a Victorian libertine as useful contents in the storehouse of one's knowledge.

She turned back to the beginning and with a sigh of frustration began reading from the opening line.

'In which we meet our hero of tender years and accompany him on the first of many am'rous dalliances and are treated to Philosophick digressions upon the Fickle Nature of Love.'

'A September day, if you will, and myself in the tenderness of youth that allows for a certain innocence, or what the French call—' It was at this point in the proceedings that the door flew open in an explosion of air and light, causing her to jump in shock, the book tumbling to the floor. She blinked rapidly, the sudden infusion of light from the landing effectively blinding her.

"Casey?" she asked, sensing him by mere presence and size, even in the taking up of space there was no mistaking him for his brother.

"Aye, it's me."

The three simple words were enough to make her stiffen and to cause her heart to skip a beat or two. Her hands, traitorously shaken, clutched at her blouse which she'd absentmindedly unbuttoned during her reading.

"Modesty is a bit late in coming, I'd say," his voice was rough, sharp and without preamble.

"What?" she asked blankly, fighting off the mindtwirling combination of surprise and the huge surge of adrenaline pumping through her body.

"Don't play with me Pamela, I'm hardly in the mood fer it. I want ye out of here."

Her eyes adjusted suddenly to the influx of light and she saw that he was not as she had thought, drunk, but instead terribly angry and very, very sober.

"I don't understand," she said, though she was afraid she did.

"It's simple, ye pack yer things, ye get out an' we with luck fergit ye ever were here."

"Why?" she cried, "why are you doing this?" For he had entered the room and begun throwing things out of the drawers, with the obvious intent of banishing her with as much haste as possible.

"Ye know why," he replied coldly.

"Casey," she laid a hand on his forearm, trying through her touch to infuse some calm into the situation. He flung her hand off as though he'd just been hit with scalding water.

"Do not," he said coldly, "make the mistake of touchin' me again."

"Where am I to go?" she asked quietly, questioning herself more than seeking any answer from Casey.

"I don't care, go ask yer lover, he's the money te put ye up in style somewhere."

Relief crashed in on her, replaced just as quickly with an icy trickle that told her in order to correct this misunderstanding she would have to break her own solemn vow and set in motion all the forces of destruction she'd so carefully dodged these last weeks.

"Casey, you don't understand—" she began but then stopped short as he turned and looked at her, what afterall was she going to say? The truth was an impossibility and he would smell a lie for exactly what it was.

"What is it that I don't understand? Hm—uneducated as I am, I know a whore when I see one."

She flinched visibly from the word as though he had struck her full across the face. It was a confirmation of her own fears, that somehow the hours that had passed on that train had made her something less, something dark and ugly and twisted that deserved this.

"Casey, please, I..." she held her hands up in a helpless gesture, her whole body beginning to shake violently in the effort not to lose control and scream out to him all the darkness harnessed within her.

He kept on, throwing out clothes onto the bed, the floor, all her scant personal items becoming spills, reams of talc, a smashed bottle of scent no more than an acrid burn up her nostrils, a gag to her lungs. He reached then onto the bookshelf Pat had built her, reached for the fine soft pages that Jamie had given her and she screamed then, screamed with all the force of the sickness within her.

It was enough to halt him, enough to make him stop and stare at her as she wailed in a high, keening assault on the air. They stood thus for endless moments, he staring in fascination at the spectacle she created, half-naked and insane with howling, until when it seemed she would vomit from the pain and the throbbing behind her eyes, someone began to pound on the outside door.

He clapped a hand over her mouth then and shoved her down on the bed. "Enough," he said sharply.

She bled down to whimperings within seconds and slowly the knocking on the door subsided and the person outside went away.

He was sitting on top of her, still uncertain, she could see, of whether she would go crazy on him again. It was half-light on the border between night and day, a soft, rosy glow bathing the room, purifying his face, making it saintly in its rage. It took a moment for another piece of knowledge to trickle down into her consciousness, but it was there nibbling on the outer edges and she did not push it away. She wanted him and he most assuredly wanted her even in this most unlikely of moments.

She reached up, wanting to stroke his face, to meld his features into tenderness and desire. "Love is like the Lion's tooth," she whispered.

He caught her wrist in an iron grip.

"Don't mistake lust for something else," he said harshly. "Is that poetry from one of his fine books yer quoting, did he read it to ye in bed, did ye whisper all the sweetnesses in his ears that ye did in mine?" His grip loosened a fraction and his free hand rubbed hard across his face. "Oh Christ help me that I should still want ye at a time like this, what sort of a man is that? What have ye made of me, woman?" He rolled away from her then and she knew she'd lost, that there was no way out of this now save telling him the truth and that she could not do.

"I've a question," he said wearily, sitting on the edge of the bed.

"Yes," she said throat aching with all the words she couldn't utter.

"Why?" he asked, his hands fisted on his knees, breath still coming in uneven, ragged measures. "Why, when ye knew what it cost me to trust? I accepted ye with yer divided heart an' all. I never asked where ye came from, because I figured ye were runnin' away from yer past an' I understood that. I knew what it was to have things ye couldn't say anymore, things that had no words, pieces of me that were just gone but somehow with you I felt whole. I believed ye felt the same. Christ there is no fool like a fool in love, is there? Ye must have been havin' a good laugh the whole time." The line of his shoulders, broad and strong, trembled visibly and she had to restrain herself forcibly not to touch him.

She shook her head mutely, but he merely snorted in derision.

"I didn't want to love ye, ye know, but I just fell, dropped right onto my damn knees, couldn't stop myself even though I knew I was hurtin' Pat. Maybe I deserved what I got."

He stood and took a long, shaking breath and then leaned down slowly, his eyes narrowed. "What the hell is this?" he asked.

She peered over the side of the bed and saw to her consternation that the entire floor was elegantly carpeted in sheets and sheets of what looked like the composition for Viennese nocturnes but which upon more intent perusal, contained long scrolling swatches of Arabic.

"What the hell are these?" Casey repeated, grabbing a corner of one sheet and holding it up in front of his face, where the last of the sun shone pinkly through it, revealing what a first glance had not—small, blocked letters of English, done in a very pale pencil.

She made an abbreviated noise.

"Never mind," he said, "I don't even want to know."

"Casey please I—I—" she faltered for she had been about to say she could explain and knew, watching the sheet of decoded Arabic drift gently back to the floor, that there was far too much she could not say. Things had rapidly accelerated past the point of explanations.

"Get out," he said grittily, "please get out."

She sat stiffly on the bed as he walked away, desperate to stop him, powerless to do so and whispered, "I love you," to the slamming of the door.

When Pat came home, some hours later, it was to a house gleaming and overwhelming with the scent of bleach. Pamela, when he looked through the open doorway of her bedroom, was piling clothes into a suitcase, the same battered, rose-patterned one she'd been clutching when she wandered into his life.

"What's happened?" he asked quietly

"Your brother has asked me to leave."

"Why?"

"Because he thinks I'm sleeping with Jamie," she answered in a tight voice.

"He what?" Pat said in confusion.

"He found out about the abortion and that Jamie took me to England for it and he's put two and two together and come up with a very tidy four."

"An' ye didn't tell him otherwise?" he asked in outright bewilderment.

"No and nor will you, you know the consequences of the truth in this matter are worse even than what's happened here today."

"Where are ye' goin'?"

She turned and he felt as if he'd been struck, so bald was the pain on her face. "Yes well, that's the rub, isn't it? I don't know where to go, you and Casey are all the family I have in this world, aren't you?"

"Yes, we are," Pat agreed firmly, "an' yer not goin' anywhere."

"Pat you can't, you swore—"

"Are ye sayin' that it's better to just walk out of here an' never look back? He'll not forgive this. He needs to know the truth. No," he raised a hand to stall the protests he saw forming on her face. "All my life I've done what someone else told me was right, an' tonight this one time, I'm doin' what I know to be right." He strode to the door, closing his ears to the frantic pleas behind him.

Casey was where Pat had known he would be, only it was the fifth pub he checked not the first and he was intent on imbibing half the contents of the place and seducing two, not one, girls.

Pat wasted no time on conversational preambles and was in fact gripped by a rage so red and consuming he'd the sense of standing firmly outside of himself and watching it happen from a safe distance.

"Outside ye damn bastard," he said.

Casey narrowly missed choking on his Guinness and only just managed to sputter out, "What?"

"I said outside, now," Pat repeated grimly, steadily ignoring the stares they were beginning to draw.

Casey laughed. "My little brother callin' me out, never thought I'd live to see the day, don't twist yerself up boy I know what this is about an' I'd rather ye didn't waste yer time, nor mine." Casey turned his attention back to the blonde seated snugly beside him, coyly rubbing his thigh with her rough, red-nailed hand.

"I'm not jokin' an' I'm not here as yer little brother, goddamn ye. Outside, I said," he could feel his anger rising higher, starting a strange buzz in his head and making his feet feel as though they were nowhere near the floor.

"Ladies," Casey said with exaggerated charm, "excuse me fer a moment, my brother an' I need to straighten a little matter out between us." He stood and took Pat firmly by the arm.

"I'm in company here an' I've no wish to discuss her with ye at present."

"How can ye allow that girl to touch ye, when ye've an angel cryin' her soul out at home?"

"An angel, is it? An angel that's been screwin' Lord James Kirkpatrick fer the last year? An angel is it, that takes herself off to England with her lover to abort a baby? Ye don't seem terrifically surprised by all this Pat, perhaps then ye'll tell me, did she know was it his Lordship's bastard or was the blighted thing mine?" Pat felt the first twinge of something other than fury at his brother. This was ripping Casey apart inside.

"'Twas neither," he answered quietly.

"What?" Casey asked in a low, deadly tone. Pat knew the tone all too well, had seen his brother use it when severely tested to the limits of his monumental patience, had heard it as one hears the hiss of the cobra before it makes its fatal strike. He had never dreamed to have it directed at himself.

"Was it yers then?" Casey asked, a dark mask coming down and closing over his face. "Did ye lie with her as well, are ye only another of a long line that took his pleasure from her?"

"I'll say one thing for ye Casey, ye've a helluva nerve," Pat said quite calmly before pulling back his left hand and letting fly a punch that sent his brother sprawling onto the floor, Guinness flying in great, lovely amber arcs to drop like bits of jewel amidst the shattered glass.

"Have ye completely done yer fockin' nut?" Casey yelled at him, still prone on the floor as Pat walked out of the bar, a small pulse of satisfaction thrumming through him in beat with the throbbing in his knuckles.

There was a bruising rain pelting down outside, warm and full of wind though, a clean rain. He walked into it gratefully.

"Stop!" He heard the yell behind him but kept on into the rain, blinded by night and as sensitive as a water rat in a subterranean tunnel. He could feel his brother before the hand even touched his shoulder and whirled fists at the ready, rage still pumping its purifying fires through his veins.

"Jaysus, will ye put yer fists down, my head's still reelin' from the last blow." Casey was, even in the dim light, already sporting a fat lip and a badly bruised cheek. Pat put down his fists warily, still ready in the balls of his feet to knock his brother into the pavement.

"What the hell was that for?"

"I never slept with her," Pat said in a low, gritty voice.

"Alright, that was the wrong thing to say an' I'm sorry but Pat ye come in there callin' her an angel and actin' like a wronged husband, ye don't know what she is man, ye don't know how dangerous she is. The things I've told her, the things she knows an' she's been sleepin' with that king on the hill himself an' feedin' 'im God knows what from my lips to his goddamn ear."

Pat shook his head sadly, "Ye goddamn, dumb-arsed bastard ye can't see the fockin' forest fer the trees can ye? How can ye lie with her in yer arms an' not know even the slightest bit of her?"

"I know what ye think, an' she had me fooled too, couldna' see beyond the length of my cock as Da' used to say, but I'm seein' clear now an' it's a very ugly picture that's shapin' up."

"'Twasn't Jamie's baby, twasn't yers, twasn't mine," he said quietly.

"Yer not makin' a damn bit of sense man," Casey said in frustration.

"She was raped man, raped an' raped in every fockin' way ye can think of that an animal can take a woman, she was taken. Raped by men who spit on her an' stripped her naked on a train an' made her do things that could drive a man mad just to think of it," he hit out blindly at Casey's chest and felt the thunk of flesh under his fist, "an' if it drives a man mad to think of it, to remember the degradation an' the smells an' the sounds an' the pure agony of her silence, if that can drive a man mad what the fock do ye suppose it does to the wee lass it happened to? What the fock do ye suppose my brother?" He lashed out again, a solid left that knocked Casey's breath out. Casey fell to his knees, more from blow of words than his brother's fist, Pat knew.

"How Pat?" he asked in a flat tone.

"On the night train back to Belfast, we'd been to a game an' there was only us an' the four of them in the car—"

"Four?" Casey asked, some mute appeal in his words but Pat would not, could not spare him now.

"Aye, four an' they all took turns."

"An' what did they do to ye, brother?" Casey asked, in that same flatly disturbing tone.

"Made me watch, an' broke a bone or two every time she didn't do exactly as she was told, nearly killed me or so the doctor said, wish to Christ they had," he finished softly.

"So there was no car accident?" Casey asked.

"No."

"Why didn't ye tell me?"

"I wanted to but she made us swear not to, if ye could have seen her, all bloody an' bruised an' all that mattered to her is that ye were not told. She was desperate to protect ye, said ye'd go mad from the knowing an' she wouldn't have that."

"So Jamie knows about this as well?"

"Aye, 'twas him that came an' picked up the pieces after, got the doctor an' likely saved my life an' very likely Pamela's sanity. She made him promise too, though he thought ye should know."

"An' the pregnancy?"

"Ye'd been away fer a month after an' she said ye'd taken," Pat faltered, eyes sliding away from his brother's, "precautions to prevent such things," he took a deep breath, "she was certain that it wasn't yers."

"Oh Mary mother of God, all this time an' she never let on, an' the things I said to her Pat, I called her a whore an' wiped her touch off as if she were poison. All this time an' she's come to my bed without turnin' a hair when it must have been killin' her inside, oh Christ what have I done?"

"I don't know my brother, I don't know," Pat said softly. "I think now though, ye should go home to her."

"Pat?" It was a question, more painful in its quiet tone than had the words been shouted.

"No, ye go to her alone. I can't come with ye."

"Yer not comin' back, are ye?"

"No, I can't man an' ye know the reasons why."

"Aye, I suppose I do," Casey said tiredly, rubbing a mud-smeared hand across his face. "Patrick I want ye to know, I hold no blame against ye for this."

"I'd rather have ye kill me than forgive me right now," Pat said wearily. "I cannot bear forgiveness just yet."

"Paddy—"

"Don't use that name on me," Pat hissed, "it's a child's name an' I'm not a child anymore."

"No," Casey said quietly, "I don't suppose ye are."

"Aye, well," Pat replied and had one of those flashes of insight that tells you this moment will be yours forever, the sight of your brother kneeling in the rain, the relief of confession your own and the knowledge that you have burned your bridge to home and will never find a way to rebuild it. The knowledge was gone as fast as it had come and left him feeling only weary and old.

"Get up off yer knees man an' go home to her, she needs ye," Pat said softly and then walked away into the night and the cleansing rain.

"I STAYED TO BE CERTAIN PAT WAS ALRIGHT," was all she said when he came home. She could have been at that moment, any one of a million women, stiffened by pain, shorn of innocence and ready to walk out into the dark arms of the world rather than be hurt one more time by someone she loved.

She shouldered her bag defiantly and stood, a slim soldier, ready to do battle.

"Darlin' don't," Casey began, barely above a whisper, coming face to face with how badly he'd treated her only hours ago. That he had said their love was merely of the physical and how she might have interpreted that sickened him now. Something hot and malignant began to grow in his chest right then, something that choked off all the repentant words he had been about to speak, all the things that would redeem the dark, sweet hours spent in silence, wordless and gripping. How had he dared to believe that he could restore sanctity to those acts? How could he have been so blind as to not see the strain in her face, how she was thin with a tension that was unnatural. The ivory, the opals, the roses gone from her skin, leaving only those burning, aching eyes, no longer like emeralds but rather a sea of calm, a deceptive terrible calm that waited for the next drowning, the next suffocation.

"Darlin' I—" he began weakly, but stopped as she shook her head.

"Please don't," she said, "I only stayed to be certain that you and Pat hadn't come to blows, which," she looked pointedly at his bruised and swollen face, "obviously you did."

"But darlin' I didn't know," he said feeling a terrible weakness in his knees that threatened to poleax him where he stood.

"I know, but now you do and I can't change that, I can't keep things safe and tied up ever so neatly anymore."

"Ye should never have tried," he said softly, fighting the desire to touch her hair, to smooth it back from her face, to comfort her with the caresses of childhood, comfort that could not touch her where she stood now.

" It was what I had left Casey, it was the only thing, what else was there to do?" she asked and sighing let her bag slip to the floor.

"Ye don't have to protect me from my ownself darlin'," he said hoping that the bag on the floor meant what he thought it did.

"Don't I?" she asked with a grim little smile and then she put her hand to her face and said, "If you'll excuse me," and bolted for the sink.

He held her hair back as she vomited, dampened a cloth and wiped down her face and neck, then rubbed her back as she retched over the chipped enamel for what seemed like a small eternity. When she was done, he sat her down on a chair while he rinsed the sink and found warm clean clothing for her. She resisted no more than a new baby might as he changed her damp and soiled clothes, brushed back her hair with sure, quick strokes and tied it with a bit of ribbon he'd found discarded in their room. Then he made a pot of tea and sat finally when it was ready, across from her, the aromatic fumes of the brew rising between them. He sighed and ran his hands roughly through his own hair.

"Christ, a fockin' pot of tea, I don't know what possessed me to even make it."

"It's what we do then, isn't it? When there's nothing else to be done and all else has failed, you make a fockin' pot of tea." She was smiling at him, a weary smile, but a smile nonetheless. "And actually I could do with a cup."

He poured some, willing his hands to remain steady, watched as she took a sip and then closing her eyes sighed and said, "well it won't cure all the ills of the world, but it's something."

"It's not the ills of the world we're dealin' with here Pamela, it's—"

"Don't," she cut him off abruptly, "I can't talk yet about it, I don't have the words for it."

He nodded and a moment or two of silence followed where he could hear the ticking of the clock and the small sounds of her breathing as though they'd been magnified a thousand times.

"Will ye allow me to take ye away?" He could feel her stiffen slightly even across the distance between them. "Not away from that," he said, "but perhaps away from this, just for a few days or so." He indicated the walls around them, though he meant the city as well. He waited long minutes, each a mute agony of loud, angry ticking on the clock.

Just when his despair had mounted to the place where he thought he'd have to say something, anything to break the silence, her hand, palm up, impossibly white and fragile, laid itself upon the table, giving her answer.

"Aye then, we'll go," he said roughly and put his own hand, dark and hard, large enough to cradle the head of a baby or to break a man's neck, into hers and then wept as though his heart would never cease to break.

Chapter Twenty-six
Casey Riordan, Will You...?

L IKE A DITHERING SERPENT WINDING FAR ABOVE THE SEA and far below the sky, the Lonely Road wound through the rocks and rills and improbable greens of Kerry. Kerry, lost to the Atlantic more surely than any other county, was a place of magic, a land that time had forgotten, a place where the forgetting came easier, as if the gentility of the land itself absorbed the sting of memory. It was for this last reason that Casey brought Pamela to a tiny cottage that stood so precariously upon a cliff that it seemed half inclined to tip into the sea.

The cottage, hidden from the road by a steep hill that cut sharply away from the narrow road, was submerged in ivy. Its small front windows looked seaward, its back sheltered by a half-crescent of salt-blasted pine. It had belonged to Casey's grandfather Brendan once upon a time and now was in the possession of the local priest.

"I've my Daddy's key," Casey explained, "Father Terry has never used the cottage anyhow; he only keeps it out of some sort of respect for my family. I'll go down an' clear it with him in the mornin'," he added to her uncertain look.

But in the morning, they were locked in by one of those dark, heavy spring storms the Atlantic is infamous for. All day the rain pounded down and they were kept occupied by the appearance of a number of leaks. By evening, the floor was littered with an array of pots and buckets, tins and cups and a steady plinking informed them that the storm had no intention of receding. Casey, never comfortable for long in small spaces, announced his intention of going for a short walk after supper and Pamela, bidding him a drowsy farewell, settled by the fire with a copy of Dickens's *Old Curiosity Shop.*

She awoke some time later, with the odd sense of having slept for a very long time, though a glance at the clock assured her that only two hours had passed since she'd nodded off. The steady plink of dropping water had subsided into an occasional and irregular splatter.

As it was Casey's habit to disappear for long periods of time, Pamela did not worry about him until an hour after full dark had descended. He was, after all, not used to wandering the cliffs and rocks in this area. The thought of him smashed to bits on the rocks where the tide relentlessly surged was enough to drive her out of the half-doze she was lost in by the fire.

The storm had abated and the wind had died down to a soft thrum instead of the banshee wail it had assumed earlier in the day.

She called his name twice trying to push back the small thump of panic that began to uncoil in her stomach. She had, in the last few days, allowed herself to depend on him totally, he had become the calm in the center of her own personal storm. Even his movements had an economy, a fineness, a perfect control that said he would do nothing, say nothing and allow nothing to frighten her.

"Over here, darlin'," he stepped out of the shadows of a huge rock, twice as high as himself and three times as wide. She had to resist the urge to run to him, she didn't want the worry in his eyes to become any deeper.

"What were you doing?" she asked when she was safe within the circle of his arms, the beat of his heart sounding out a rhythm of comfort and security.

"Havin' a bit of a smoke an' watchin' the stars fall down."

"The stars fall down?" She peeked over the rough wool of his sweater, inhaling the smell of male sweat, cigarette smoke and peat, all like mother's milk to her now, all facets of him in his myriad parts that made up a most satisfying whole.

"Aye, here look," he turned her in his arms and with a forearm snugged around her used the other arm to point out into the dome of night, "it's a bit odd, the really good meteor showers come in August, there generally aren't too many to be seen this time of year, we're on the wrong side of the sun, so to speak. But there've been three or four spectacular ones in the bit of time I've been out here, ah there did ye see that?" His arm swung in a smooth arc towards the northeastern sky and she bent her face into the night the last drops of the storm, carried in off the sea, touching her hair and running down her skin. The sky was shot with long streaks of silver and gold, splitting and spilling into the basin of the ocean, the whole horizon breaking and tremoring before them, light tearing from zenith to ground and then fading as if it had never been.

"It's like the sky is bleeding itself," she said wonderingly, wishing that she could catch stardust in her hands and hold forever the image of the faint white lines that crisscrossed each other in the sky.

"Tis hard to believe that they," Casey indicated the last flicker of light drowning far out in the Atlantic, "are made of the same thing as this," he rubbed her hand softly along the worn surface of the rock. "The sun is anvil, the stars are forge and earth the cauldron beneath. My Daddy told me that once an' I could never believe that I was made of the same things as that amazin' fire in the sky, but I can believe it now."

He rubbed one finger down the side of her neck and kissed her as softly as a bumblebee pulling nectar from a flower. She shivered, anticipation running quietly through her veins. "When I look at ye, Jewel, when I touch ye an' ye are so fine as not to be believed, then I know that ye are made of stardust an' I'm afraid I'll wake up an' ye'll be no more real than those falling stars. An' I know," his voice lowered to a smoky whisper, "there's nothin' ye could ever ask of me that I could refuse." His face was buried in the hair at the nape of her neck and he moved restlessly, inhaling and absorbing as would a blind man.

She let her head fall back on the stem of her neck, like a half-broken flower defenseless and crying for water in the midst of some primordial desert. His hands stroked the length of her back in one complete motion, up from the soft swell of buttock until his hands were on either side of her head her hair raining through the hard strength of his fingers. She swayed slightly, feeling as insubstantial as if she stood on the edge of a cliff and the ocean below waited to embrace her. She almost fell when he released her and she felt as if someone had dashed her with freezing water.

"Oh, Christ, Pamela, I'm sorry, I just—I almost," he ran one big hand through his hair in frustration, "I wanted so badly to have ye just then, I could see myself takin' ye down on the ground an' makin' love to ye until neither of us could think anymore an' neither of us could see what—" he stopped suddenly at the look she could not prevent from flooding her face.

"Oh darlin' don't, I didn't mean..." he trailed off and shook his head like a dog flinging water off its back, as if in the violence of movement itself he could forget and shake loose all the memories that did not even have the dignity of being his own.

"So neither of us could see what happened on the train," she said, "It's alright, you can say it, we can't spend forever avoiding it. But you didn't see what happened on the train and I'm grateful as hell that you didn't, though I'm wondering if you'd be better to know instead of imagining in your head. Perhaps if you knew the truth of it, you could let it die. I'm not some damned piece of china, Casey, yet you approach as if I'll splinter and cut you to pieces. Now, man, tell me are you not touching me for my own sake or are you not touching me because you cannot bear to?" She felt all the anger swamping her that she'd avoided since the wretched night on the train and found it was quite a relief. "Because let me tell you if you're doing it for my sake, don't." She put her hands up to her face and rubbed it hard, feeling less numb by the minute, the rain had begun to fall again and it coursed in hard needling streams down her skin, soaking the heavy cotton of her blouse.

"I don't know what ye want, I don't know how to treat ye, I'm afraid that ye'll never enjoy my touch again," he said despairingly.

"Do you think I lied to you all that time in your bed? Do you think I felt nothing? I'm not made of stone boy, but I'll not break and bleed when you touch me."

"Tell me then," he said hoarsely, "tell me what to do, tell me an' I'll do it."

"Will you? I don't think so. You see, all I can think is that I want you to push me down on the ground and take me with no more emotion than a beast in the field, I want you to do everything to me that they did as hard and rough as it was then so that I can erase them in my mind, I want you to lay claim to every inch of me and touch me everywhere, every bit of skin and hair and help me scour them off." She was breathing hard as if she'd run miles, "Now do you think you can do that for me, Casey Riordan? Do you think you can hear every word they said and know every way they used my body and repeat it so that I'm yours. Even if it makes no sense to you, even if it disgusts you in the very marrow of your bones can you do it for me? Can you love me that much? Because that is what I ask of you Casey, that you love me more than your own darkest fears, than your worst imaginings of what happened that night. Can you do it?" She pulled awkwardly at the buttons on her shirt, finally yanking at them in frustration, sending buttons in all directions and then pulling her shirt off and tossing it in a sodden heap on the ground, then she dropped to her knees in front of him and fumbled just as angrily with his belt, resisting his attempts to pull her to her feet.

The rain had begun again, a swift sweep of it coming in hard off the sea.

"It's the first thing he did to me Casey, does it help to know?" She yelled against the rain that tore and spit and ripped at her skin. "Will it make you able to touch me again, if you know this?"

"Jaysus woman have ye gone mad?" he stumbled backwards and yelped as he fell to the ground but she followed remorselessly.

"Pamela, stop, this isn't—"

"Isn't what," she said tugging at the zip on his trousers, "isn't what you had in mind? Well that night on the train wasn't what I had in mind either."

"Yer not in yer right mind, an that's to be expected," he said managing to struggle back in the mud far enough to elude her hands and holding up his own in protest as if he were dealing with a mad creature of some sort.

"Not in my right mind is it? Perhaps not. But," she smiled in a sly sort of way, a sudden shaft of moonlight biting through a gap in the rain clouds and providing just enough light for him to see her, "Jamie knows all of this and seems able to bear it."

"Damn ye," Casey roared, "if this is what ye want then this is what ye'll get." He pulled his sweater off in one quick motion and was over and above her in a movement so fast there was no time to react. He looked positively mad, glowering like some pagan beast, water dripping from his hair into her face, one knee shoved brutally between her own.

"Do ye want me to continue then? Do ye want to tell me all they did? How they took from ye? How they hurt ye an' made my brother watch so that he'll never be a whole man, if that's what ye need to heal, then I'll do it. Damn ye woman I'll do it!"

"Then do it," she said and reaching up bit him sharply on his bottom lip, he let out a muffled yell and ground his mouth into her own. It was nothing like a kiss, it was power and rage and hurt. She could taste his blood running into her mouth along with the rain, cold and pure, mixed with the hot iron and salt of the blood and let it drain into her throat, welcoming it as part of the sacrifice he was making. She pulled his hair and slapped his face when it seemed that he might succumb to the gentleness that was his instinct with her, goaded him with hissed insults mixed well with the things she'd heard herself on the train, face pushed down in the dirt, then tilted up into the cheap hard lighting, like some poor, dumb creature.

But the rain ceased and suddenly the quiet made too loud their gasps, grunts and curses and Casey collapsed on her, his need still burning through him like fire, scorching his skin, evaporating the rain off her own.

"Pamela, I can't, I'm sorry darlin' I just cannot take ye without feelin'. Even if ye think ye need it, I cannot."

His head lay on her breast, water dripping from his curls where it ran to form a small, silent pool in the hollow at the base of her throat.

"Aye man, I know," she whispered, lifting a scraped and stinging hand to stroke his head and back, "but I love you for trying."

It was an exhausted silence that held them after that, as the wind wound down from a howl to a mild flirtation with grass and sedge. The sky deepened and softened, the moon rode in and out upon wispy clouds and then the world lightened and it felt as if the earth stretched a bit, yawned beneath them and slumbered for just a few minutes more. From the east, riding in the waves of faintly stealing gray, came the haunting and lonely cry of the curlew, come early and alone, to his northern home. And just before the sun, faint and misty, glimmered above the horizon, a last star fell to its silver death.

"My Daddy told me that falling stars were the tears of God," she said quietly, not wanting to disrupt the gentle hum of his breathing.

"Mm," he mumbled sleepily.

"I like to think that someone up there cries for us sometimes," she said and taking a deep breath added, "Casey, when you said that I could ask nothing that you could refuse, did you mean it?"

"Aye, I did," he said on the rise of a yawn, "why do ye ask?"

"Because," she shivered slightly, the warmth of his expelled breath touching the pebbled surface of her breast just as the sun pinked the sky, "because well—" she hesitated and he rolled his head up until his chin rested on her breastbone and she could see him, eyes dark in the morning light, dark but full of gentleness again, like ever deepening pools, circles within circles, warmth within heat, heat within fire.

"Aye, what's the question?"

She pulled a bit of grass from his hair releasing a shower of dried mud and smiled with conviction for the first time in months.

"Will you marry me, Casey Riordan?" She asked as the sun, throwing off its watery robe, stepped above the horizon and turned the world into a glowing ball of crimson.

He pushed himself up off the ground with his arms, separating their skin and letting the morning air, chill and sweet, run the length of their bodies.

"D'ye know, as mad as ye are woman," he replied "I think I just might."

Chapter Twenty-seven
The Past Come Back

FATHER TERENCE MCGINTY, OPENING THE DOORS TO HIS CHURCH for Lauds, (which would be attended only by old half-mad Mag Ruffey in her bare feet and heavily shawled head, but nevertheless, being a servant of God, he would give the service and intone the prayers) saw for the first time in twenty odd years, smoke rising from the Riordan cottage. He crossed himself reflexively and muttered, "Strange bit of business that," before sighting Mag Ruffey huffing down the hill, feet blue with chilblains, hands already fingering her rosary in anticipation. Mad as a bloody hatter this one and she'd have to be attended to, gently and patiently, as he had done for ten years now. He made a mental note to discuss the advantages of footwear with her and looked longingly over at the blue-gray smoke spiraling lazily out onto the morning breeze. It would have to wait, he thought impatiently and smiling greeted Mag with his expected morning salutation, "Ah, it'll be a terrible old beast of a mornin' then won't it Miss Ruffey?"

AN HOUR LATER AND SOME SMALL DISTANCE FARTHER UP THE LANE, Margaret MacBride rose from her bed and, out of long and painful habit, glanced out the north window of her kitchen. This morning though, she did not glance away as she normally would. Instead, she set the kettle down with a thump, spilling water in a small pool across the floor. She didn't notice it (and wouldn't until she stepped in it much later in the day) but instead gazed transfixed at the long thin column of smoke that unfurled in a long curling ribbon against a fiercely blue sky.

"Jaysus, Mary, Joseph an' the little green men,' she said loudly to the china goose above her sink, "whatever can it mean?"

BY NOON FATHER TERENCE, unable to bear his own nosiness any longer, fairly hustled Mag Ruffey out the door of the tiny church kitchen, shoving a thermos of hot cocoa and a sack of sandwiches into her arms and swinging the door shut with such alacrity behind her that Mag muttered, "Strange doin's 'bout here this mornin'," and stared at the inoffensive white door suspiciously for some moments before setting off for home.

Father Terry meanwhile, uttering a rather unholy prayer that no needy parishioner would come along and detain him, flew through his humble abode, out the front door and down the lane with a speed that belied his seventy years. He made himself halt some yards away from the little drive that led up to the Riordan cottage and compose himself. He took a deep breath and seeing that smoke still rose steadily from the chimney, folded his hands into the recesses of his old wool cardigan and realized to his horror that he hadn't changed out of his rather ratty soutane.

"Can I help ye, Father," said a distinctly polite yet quite unfriendly voice from the vicinity of the overhanging yew hedge directly in front of him. Then a figure stepped out into the roadway and Father Terence McGinty—who prided himself on the one hundred sit-ups he did each morning and night, and the yoga he had practiced without fail for the last four decades of his life, taught to him by a wizened old Indian on a Tibetan hilltop as many decades ago—thought his heart had taken an attack. A ribald limerick flitted through his head instead of the prayers he'd thought would come at this moment. It was through a haze that he felt strong hands grab him and seat him gently on the grass.

"Are ye alright then, man?" the apparition in front of him asked.

He nodded, not trusting himself to look again at the too familiar features.

"It's just that, well," he smiled weakly, "'tis nothin' lad."

"I imagine it's just that I look a wee bit too much like my grandda'," the boy said with some amusement.

"Aye, ye could say that," Father Terry agreed responding to the smile.

"Father Terry?" the boy asked, but the question was only slight, the answer already quite certain in the boy's mind.

"Casey?"

"Aye."

"How—how—" he stuttered weakly.

"I'd know ye if I'd run into ye on the streets of Calcutta, my daddy's descriptions were that strong. An' I've my own memories."

"An' yer daddy?" he asked hoping the boy did not hear the hope that trembled in his words.

"Six years gone now," Casey said, eyes gentle.

"I didn't know," he felt a spectacular old fool, collapsed in the lane and receiving such news as this. But then there was never a great deal of dignity to be found in grief. Brian, his Brian, gone.

Terry took a long, shaky breath, willing his heart to slow, taking from memory the picture of a child, a dark-eyed boy full of bumps and bruises, rushing from one scrape to the next. There were no traces now in the face above him of the mischievous, burr-ridden child, who'd galloped pell-mell into everything. It was Brendan with minor alterations. There was the same ruthlessness in the face despite the charming smile and the same brute strength, reined in barely by force of intelligence and a will of iron.

"Aye, ye'll have given me the helluva shock," Terry said putting a trembling hand up to his face and searching for a calming breath.

"Will ye come in an' have a cup of tea with us?"

"Us?" Terry asked accepting the lift up off the ground the boy offered.

"Aye, us," was Casey's unenlightening reply.

Terry usually visited the Riordan cottage twice a year, in the spring to open the windows and air it out and at the onset of winter to batten down the hatches. He never lingered, afraid always that if he so much as sat down for a moment the memories would swamp him. It was a comfort to be in it now though, with a fire crackling merrily in the hearth, tea on the boil and Brian's son moving within it with grace and expediency. He was so like Brendan that Terry had to squelch the desire to sit him down and catch him up on the last thirty years. Much as he had to squelch the desire to ask for a whiskey in place of the tea that steeped in a little blue and white teapot in front of him. He needed the courage it provided, false or not, before he could ask what had happened to Brian.

Casey, in a way that was typical of the Riordans, saved him the trouble.

"I'm sorry I didn't get hold of ye when Daddy died but I was feelin' so badly for myself that I didn't spare a thought for anyone else. An' then I went to prison an' I just couldn't write. But Pat found this some time ago goin' through Daddy's things an' I brought it down for ye." He slid a crumpled bag across the table.

Terry opened it and withdrew a letter, still sealed, yellowing a bit with age and a small carving of a boat, the gray-hulled curragh they used to spend many quiet hours in. So Brian had remembered and had tried in this small way to apologize. "I think," he said, not quite able yet to meet Casey's eyes, "I'll read it later."

"It was quick an' he likely never knew what hit him," Casey said, pouring out the tea.

"Pardon me?" Father Terry said.

"Daddy's death, it was a bomb."

"That transparent, am I?" Terry gave a half-hearted smile that did not make the journey to his eyes.

"No," Casey replied quietly, "it's only I knew ye'd be wonderin'."

"Thank you," Terry said just as the door swung open and amidst the skirl of cold air stepped a girl. Us, eh? He smiled broadly; the Riordans had the damnedest luck with women.

"Pamela, this'll be Father Terence McGinty, he was my Grandda's best friend an' an honorary member of the Riordan family, what there is left of it," he smiled ruefully and the girl stepped forward, rain beading in tiny crystals in her hair, face flushed with the cold and damp.

"Pleased to meet you," she said, dropping a bouquet of pine boughs, pungent and sharp with rain, onto the floor by the peat shod. Product of the seedlings Brendan had brought back from the States forty years ago, now grown to adulthood and outlasting Brendan by many years.

"'Tis my pleasure surely," Terry said and extended his hand. She returned his grip firmly, meeting his eyes squarely. He blushed under such a frank gaze; here was him seventy years and then some, still knocked sideways by a girl's beauty. There was some nonsense, he supposed, that a man never outgrew.

"I was thinkin' perhaps, darlin'," Casey began with a careful glance at Terry, "that we could ask Father Terry to marry us?"

There was no mistaking the surprise in her face. "Now you mean?"

"Not this exact instant but in the next few days if possible." He turned to Terry, "Would it be possible?"

"If ye have a license, I suppose I don't see why not. 'Tis a bit unorthodox but then yer family isn't exactly notorious for stickin' to tradition. A few days to tell yer relations an' anyone else ye might want to witness the nuptials—"

"There isn't anyone," the girl said quietly, meeting Casey's eyes in a look of pained understanding then smiling softly, almost shyly, "there's just the two of us.

THE WINDOWS IN TERRY'S HOUSE WERE NOT LIT and Peg, knowing this could mean only one thing, hesitated to go in. Though they had supper together every Tuesday night, she knew tonight was different. It was the wind that finally goaded her to the door; it came off the sea in great sheaves, tearing the breath from her lungs. At her age, it was no longer romantic to get soaked and catch your death, as generally it was too literal to do so.

Terry didn't answer her knock, so she let herself in, took off her wet things and stepped into the kitchen. It was silent as the grave and twice as dark. She cursed mildly as her good foot hit the corner of a coatstand and tipped it over with a great roaring crash.

"Turn a light on before ye bring the roof down on us both," came a dry voice from the midst of the darkness.

"Bloody old fool, sittin' in the dark," she grumbled, waving her hand to and fro above the sink in a vain attempt to locate the pull for the light.

"Little higher," said Terry's voice seeming to move up and down in the darkness.

"Well if ye can see it, ye damned old scarecrow, then turn it on yerself."

The light came on a moment later and Peg expected to find Terry giving her the odd stare he always did when she failed to accomplish simple things. Instead, he just looked old and very tired.

"Well I hardly need ask, do I? Ye've been down to the cottage then?"

"Aye, I've been down," he replied and sat down heavily on a chair.

"Well then, who was it?" she asked her throat suddenly tight and dry.

"Wasn't the ghost of himself come back to haunt us, though I must admit it did seem so for a minute."

"Did it?" She sat as heavily as he had, wanting to scream at him to hurry and say what he had to tell and on the other hand wishing she still had the legs to fly out the door and into the wind.

Terry stroked the old, satiny top of the table under his hand, the long-boned fingers swooping in perfect rhythm, back and forth, back and forth. It was oddly soothing and yet Peg, having known this man all but ten years of his life, knew that it was not comfort he was deriving from it.

"What is it, Terry?"

He closed his eyes so she could not read the strange irises as she'd become so accustomed to during their long chats.

"Brian's dead," he said finally, "I never even guessed, all those summers that passed an' still I was waitin' for him te come an' gaze at the stars with me, te fish on fine days an' te tell me that his boys had long ago left this country. We'd of had a fine time of it over that then wouldn't we of?"

"Oh God, Terry, I'm so sorry, I didn't know." She reached across the surface of the worn table between them and patted his hand awkwardly, in all the years she had known him it was only the second time she'd touched him in comfort and the last time had been for her own, not his.

He looked her bluntly in the eyes. "Aye well why would ye have known? He was only Marie's son to ye an' nothin' more."

"Aye, well perhaps I should leave ye to yer grief," she said quietly, gathering up her strength to stand and head for the door."

"Dear God Peg, I'm sorry, I'd no right to say such things to ye, please don't go off, I don't think I can be alone just yet."

"It's alright ye old fool, I've said worse things to ye durin' the passin' of the day. I'll fix us a bite then, a man yer age can't be runnin' on tears an' the drink alone, don't look at me that way Terence McGinty, I'm not such a teetotaler that I don't know the smell of whiskey anymore. Sit, 'twon't be much but it'll fill the hole," she said getting to her feet and hopping rather nimbly over to the sink. Fifteen minutes later, her dress covered in a white apron, she was up to her elbows in potato and carrot peelings, water boiling merrily on the Aga, bread sliced and piled on an old Wedgewood saucer and cold roast from Terry's Sunday dinner cut to papery thin slices.

When everything was on the table, butter running clear down the mashed potatoes, baby carrots from his greenhouse steaming, and tea steeping on the sideboard she said, "Perhaps I deserved what ye said Terry but I am sorry, no I did not know Brian but I didn't have a right to then, did I? The fact remains that he was Brendan's only surviving son an' if ye think that doesn't hit me in the chest like a knife, ye are more a fool than I've always believed ye to be. Ye've not said so much but I can occasionally read between the lines an' I know that he was more son to ye than if ye'd had yer own blood. Now man ye've got to eat somethin'."

He did manage a bit in the end and two cups of tea to wash it all down.

"Who's in the cottage then?" Peg managed to ask mildly enough, but he saw that the hand she stirred lemon into her tea with shook like it was palsied.

"Brian's oldest son Casey an' a girl."

"A girl," she said almost managing to fake a noncommittal interest.

"Aye, a girl, one that makes a man mourn his lost youth, but then the Riordans always did have a taste in women that'd make the angels writhe with jealousy."

She could not suppress some small smile of pleasure at that. So her vanity had not completely deserted her as yet.

"Aye well beauty is fleeting an' so is love, as we've both cause to know Terence McGinty," she got to her feet slowly and cleared the table all too aware that she was confirming the truth of her statement with every step.

"They want me to marry them," he said and she could feel his eyes on her back, watching for a reaction.

"Do they, then? Well are ye goin' to do it?" she asked clanking dishes in a rough fashion.

"Well I thought perhaps it was time. I've buried a lot of Riordans but I've never married one. I'd like to be present at a happy ceremony for a change. So I've said yes. I thought perhaps ye'd come along as a witness."

"Did ye? Kind of ye to presume," Peg said sharply, banging a pot with unnecessary force onto the counter. She stopped and fought for a deep breath, hands stilled in hot, soapy water. "Is he so very much like him then, Terry?"

"Aye, he is, as near as one man can get to another, in ways big an' small."

"I don't know if I can bear it," she whispered, but Terry with ears like a bat heard her.

"Well that will be your burden Peg."

'Aye, it will be mine,' she replied, but only to herself.

They cleaned up the remnants of dinner in silence, Terry retreating to his sitting room after she'd refused his offer to walk her home. Undoubtedly, the old fool would sit and watch the stars all night to keep communion with the son he'd never had.

Peg left for home, lifting her face to the wind and inhaling the salt, sea and smell of winter that the air was lashed about with.

If wishes were fishes
And tears swam like rain
Dropping into rivers
Of memory
Then I would bid my grief
Goodbye
And watch him walk
Over white waterfall
Without a backward glance.

She'd read that in a little book of poems recently and liked it. She would have dearly loved to leave her grief behind as well. Even, sometimes she had thought, if it meant having Brendan erased entirely from her memory. Now though as old age sat upon her shoulders squarely and unforgivingly she thought perhaps the memories were worth the price of grief and that whoever had written that poem was still very young indeed. Grief, she thought to use a term that was being bandied about all too frequently these days, was about as real as the human experience ever got. Unlike joy, grief was pure. Joy came with the taint of a small demon whispering in your ear of the black clouds coming to mar the blue sky. Joy was a state of superstition, grief was absolute. If she didn't know much else in this world, she knew that absolutely and purely.

Chapter Twenty-eight
Macushla

IT TOOK TWO DAYS TO MAKE ALL THE ARRANGEMENTS, which consisted only of a license and finding two witnesses. Father Terry had given his congratulations without reservation and yet Pamela had sensed a certain sadness about him, a resignation almost since the announcement of their intent to marry. She knew why and was determined to pointedly ignore the doubts about the wisdom of this venture. If love could fix the ills of the world then surely it could stop Casey from walking the road to destruction that he was currently on. That love had not indeed cured many ills, and that her own corner of the world had been bent on self-immolation for the last eight hundred years was not something she cared to look at too closely, if at all.

On the evening before the wedding, a strange figure came thumping up their path. Casey had nipped into the village to fill a last minute list and, Pamela suspected, to see if he couldn't procure a good bottle of whiskey. Pamela therefore, eyeing the scarlet coat, the purple skirt, the green shoes, the fiery red hair and the formidable black oak cane that the woman was adorned with, opened the door with some trepidation.

"I would be Peg," the apparition announced very matter of factly, "will ye be standin' there with yer mouth hangin' open or could I hope for the hospitality of a cup o' tay?"

"Of—of course," Pamela stammered and stood aside as Peg came in bearing her cane as though it were a royal scepter and the tatty green of her skirts the finest silks in a sultan's harem.

"P'raps the Father will have told ye I'm to witness yer nuptials tomorrow, and I thought I'd like to acquaint meself with the bride an' groom first."

"Of course," Pamela replied wishing she could stop staring at her odd guest and yet finding herself unable to.

"Have a look then, I don't mind, Jaysus but I ought to be used to it. When I was but a slip of a girl, like yerself, I was the prettiest girl in all of Connemara, the min stared plenty then I tell ye. And now I'm the village oddity, old one leg Peg they calls me, fergitting and in the main not knowing that in me day I was Margaret MacBride, fairest in the land. Lost me leg in a train accident, too damned drunk to git off the tracks if the truth be known but I let them's that wants to, think I'm a figure of tragedy, gives me a certain stature that alcoholism wouldn't."

"Indeed, " Pamela said feeling precisely as if Peg had whacked her upside the head with the beautiful black oak cane.

"Not much in the way of a talker are ye, girl? Well I suppose with a face like that the min don't much care if ye can talk or not. No matter, I can talk plenty an' then some for the both of us, jist ask Father Terry and he'll tell ye so. Many's the hour I've near taken the ear right off the man, though to be sure it's his own fault for listenin' so well, a rare talent, that is listenin', not so many people do it nowadays. But that's enough about me. I've come to give ye marital advice and seeing as tomorrow is fast on its feet I'd best get on with it. Ah," she sighed and actually stopped to sip the steaming cup of tea Pamela placed before her "yer tongue may not be energetic but ye've a rare hand with a cup o' tay, that's something to be certain. Now where was I?" She drummed one scarlet nailed hand on her forehead as if she would beat forth the thoughts that eluded her.

"Advice," Pamela said meekly.

"Advice?" Peg asked and looked at her as if she'd no idea what on earth Pamela was getting at. "Well I'm not sure why ye'd ask the likes of me fer advice but here's a piece I've always held with, redheads should never wear pink. But thin ye've 'air as black as coal so it hardly seems a matter for ye to worry about."

"I'll bear that in mind," Pamela replied, deciding that she'd never met anyone so instantly delightful as Miss Margaret MacBride.

"Ye'll be wearin' white I hope, it seems not so much the fashion these days, what with all the free love an' blue jeans, though I do be thinkin' I've missed out on something this decade here. Me body may be too old fer the wild sex unfortunately me mind hasn't quite come to the same conclusion." She sighed and Pamela found she was holding her breath waiting for the next thing to come out of One Leg Peg's mouth. But Peg had ceased speaking and looked out the window, apparently without the slightest bit of discomfort.

"Would you like to see my dress?" she asked, feeling the need suddenly in the absence of a mother to share this last night before her marriage with an older woman.

Peg nodded and Pamela retrieved the pale cotton dress from the closet, it was blue and scattered with tiny cornflowers and daisies. It was the best she had and the only thing that came near to being appropriate.

"Well," said Peg digging out an ancient monocle from the bosom of her red coat and clapping it firmly over one bright blue eye, "I'll not deny it 's pretty but it simply will not do, blue girl, blue on a wedding day, well yer just askin' fer trouble child."

"I am?" Pamela asked, never having heard of blue carrying any particularly ill omens.

"Blue, my child, is the color of sorrow, of tears and loss, no it simply will not do, ye must be married in white." Peg said it firmly and with a small thump of her cane as if indeed there were no other way round this matter.

"But I don't have a white dress," Pamela said feeling that, indeed, to be married in blue would be the worst possible start a marriage could have.

"An' did I say that ye did?" Peg asked impatiently. "Ye'll wear mine, I niver had the daughters I saved it for, an' sure it's so fine it deserves to be worn more than the once."

"I—" Pamela began, feeling she should protest before she found herself standing in the back garden in ostrich feathers and sequins.

"Ah" Peg waved one scarlet-tipped hand airily, "ye need not be thankin' me, it'll be a treat to see someone as lovely as yerself wear it. An' don't worry" she grinned impishly "it's a respectable bit of a dress; ye won't be gussied up like a Vegas showgirl. Now I suppose we'd best be getting on to my place and see how it fits, not a great deal of time to be makin' alterations. Ye've not much meat on yer bones an' I was four months pregnant on my weddin' day so we may need to nip it in a bit."

"Four months pregnant," Pamela echoed before she could think, then she blushed and stammered "heavens, I'm sorry, it's none of my business."

"Nay matter girl, I'd not have told ye if it wasn't yer business. Hard to imagine that crazy old Peg was someone's mother once, but indeed I was. And someone's wife and someone's daughter, near every woman can't get through life without bein' those three things, though it'd be a sight better for some of us if we could manage it." She sighed again and seemed to slip off into some place that had existed many years ago.

The door opened and Casey stepped in, filling and taking up the room as he always seemed to do no matter the size or grandeur of the setting.

"I got all your bits and pieces though why ye'll be needin' one extra large, round carpet needle at this point is beyond me, I'm only hopin' it's nothin' to do with tomorrow night—ah beggin' yer pardon, I'd no idea we had company."

"An' you I expect would be the groom?" Peg asked in a quiet voice that for all her strangeness seemed especially strained. Pamela turned to look and saw that Peg's demeanor had indeed changed and she was staring fixedly at Casey, shadows filtering slowly across her face as if she had glimpsed something irretrievably lost and then lost it again only to bring the pain afresh.

"I see ye'll have met our Mrs. MacBride," said Father Terry slipping in the door, in the strangely silent way he had, behind Casey. "I've asked her to witness the marriage tomorrow, with Bertie Small from down the road that makes the requisite two witnesses. That is if yer still certain about not wantin' any family there?" He looked from Pamela to Casey and sighed, "I see ye've the Riordan stubbornness firmly in place. Well then," he stepped into the breach between Peg and Casey. "Mrs. MacBride, this would be Casey Riordan and I see ye've already made yerself known to Pamela, she'd be an O'Flaherty."

"Call me Peg," a soft reflective look came into her eyes and she crossed the room slowly to where Casey stood, " a Riordan are ye? I'd not need the name to know ye for who ye are. Ah those eyes, burnin' black and the hair," Peg lifted her hand and gently stroked the back of it across Casey's cheek, "Ye'd be Brendan's grandson, an' Brian's son, no?"

"I would be both of those things," Casey replied with unaccustomed gentleness taking Peg's hand within his own and kissing the back of it.

"I'm sorry," Peg said "that yer grandfather died before ye could know him, he was a fine man. I cried fer three weeks when he died, didn't even cry that long for Arthur, who was me own husband and father to my son. It's a rare man to deserve that many of a woman's tears."

"May I be deservin' of half as many when my own end comes," Casey replied, as Pamela stifled a groan.

"May ye not follow in the footsteps of yer Daddy an' his and she will have no need of tears," Peg said with a nod toward Pamela.

"I intend only to make her smile."

"Mmph," was Peg's only reply, as if she doubted the ability of any man to make a woman smile for too long.

"Well then I suppose that's all then, we're ready for tomorrow." Father Terry said obviously intent on stopping Peg before she said anything more. " Mrs. MacBride will I be givin' ye a lift home?"

Peg gave the priest an odd look and said, "Just what in the hell is this Mrs. MacBride stuff, call me Peg as ye always have, or inny of the other dozen or so indecent things ye used to call me when we were younger than these two children here, but fer the love of Old Scratch don't be after callin' me Mrs. MacBride, Terence Donovan McGinty!" With that she began her regal procession out, cane tapping its slow dance. She reached the doorway before she turned and said, "I'll be takin' the girl home with me, she can't be spendin' the last night before her weddin' with the groom, 'tisn't fittin'." She swept down the steps then, stopping in the yard where she waited for Pamela to follow and had herself, from the looks of things, a most rousing conversation with the rhododendrons.

Pamela hastily gathered the things she would need for the morning and giving Casey a brief kiss, whispered, "I love you."

Casey nodded and brushed her forehead with his lips. "Until tomorrow then."

"Tomorrow," she agreed meeting his look with one of her own that answered the soft heat in his eyes.

"Well ladies, if ye'll just step into the Lady Beatrice there," Father Terry said, indicating his wee rust heap of a car, "then we'll be off."

"No Terry, I believe we'll be walkin', it's a fine evening and we've a bit of talkin' to do, things that are none of the business of ye men, so p'raps ye'd do better to stay and keep the lad company, a man should never have too much time to think before he marries."

"Terry could be talkin' shoe leather to death," she added in a none too quiet aside to Pamela, "yer fiancé there'll be asleep before he knows what hit him." She tucked her free arm neatly into the curve of Pamela's right elbow and said loudly, "We're off then gentlemen. Casey don't be letting Father Terry get into that whiskey ye've hidden under your coat, he's a scrinty mean drunk." She laughed, a lovely silvery sound that floated on the cool spring evening, a sound that seemed an omen of good things to come.

She tugged Pamela's arm, "Let's be off darlin' ye've a dress to try on and a good sleep to put in as I doubt ye'll be gettin' much rest tomorrow night. Which brings me to my bit of marital advice, havin' seen your man, I remember what it was."

"Yes," Pamela said biting her lip in an effort not to laugh.

"Keep that one happy in the bedroom an' the rest will hardly matter to him. Holds true for most men, ye know." She waved back over her shoulder to Father Terry and Casey who still stood in the doorway, Casey laughing and Father Terry shaking his head in exasperation, as if even after all these years he could still not believe the outrageousness of Mrs. Margaret MacBride.

"A dangerous woman that one," Father Terry said as the two women disappeared down the heavy leafed lane.

"Dangerous?" Casey asked, "Honest certainly, but dangerous?"

"Ah lad, ye'll be too young to know this but a woman who doesn't know how to lie is a dangerous woman indeed. Now then," he smiled, "about that bottle of whiskey ye have in yer coat, shall we be toastin' the bride?"

BY THE TIME THEY REACHED PEG'S LITTLE GREEN COTTAGE tucked back in its bower of rose cane and honeysuckle vine, Pamela felt as if she'd known Peg forever.

"I know the paint's in great need of a face-lift," Peg said, indicating the faded green and peeling white, "but it suits me so. And would ye believe I'm such a sentimental auld sot that I keep it so 'cause Arthur painted it an' somehow I just never wanted to cover over the last thing his hands did."

Inside it was just as enchanted as it had appeared from the road, half caught, it seemed, in a Victorian time warp. Like light trapped inside an empty perfume bottle, it held the charm and fragrance of times long past.

"Put yer things in the lavender bedroom, I don't stand on ceremony here, so just flop yerself down where ye please an' I'll fix us a wee bite an' I'm thinkin' a nice hot drink of tea wouldna' be amiss." So saying, Peg abandoned her scarlet coat to the embrace of a deep rose velvet armchair only to reveal a bright yellow blouse that contrasted even more brutally with the virulent green of her skirt.

Pamela did as she'd been instructed and put her things away in the lavender bedroom, which was not at all lavender, but considering what she thus far knew of Peg this did not surprise her.

The parlor, located at the front of the house, was a miniature symphony in color and comfort. Victorian in its romance, without the stuffiness or grandiose darkness of the era. Here each element graced and made way for the next. The rag rose rug with spiraling velvet blossoms spilling out from its center, traveling from the great bursting notes of crimson down to the soft windblown of pale pink. The opposing echoes found in the striped emerald and ivory silk of the sofa, the faded and crushed blooms of an ancient and well-loved wing chair, the purple pansies of the ottoman, the slivered white surface of a sideboard reflecting the delicate blushes of myriad wafer-thin tea cups.

Three walls were lilac-hued, glimpses of them afforded between a vast array of cloudy, pewter-framed photographs. Different faces peered out from sepia-toned paper in groups and singly but amongst almost all was a slight girl with pale skin and big, laughing eyes. An astonishingly beautiful girl who seemed not at all in keeping with the poker-faced men and women that invariably surrounded her.

The fourth wall was papered in William Morris' fantastical and unlikely birds. On this wall was a painting alone. A girl, caught on the cusp of running, her eyes half-curious, half shy, the luminous eyes of a gazelle, trembling at the brink of womanhood. Flame-haired, orchid skinned, veiled in the filmy sort of fabric the Pre-Rapaelites had once painted to such perfection. She was, just there, as delicate and perfect as an apricot before the bruising.

"Told you I was a grand beauty in me day," said Peg's amused voice behind her "an' don't think I didn't know it, I was fool enough to think 'twas all that mattered, me shiny red hair an' me blue eyes, an' Lord I had ankles that'd make men weep for the fineness of them. Silly, little fool I was," Peg said fondly and picked up a picture of her hanging on the arm of a big, fair-haired man with a rather stern look on his face. "Sure an' it didn't bring me much but heartache in the end. Didn't give me any talents, just made me a flighty thing that thought if she fluttered her lashes enough men would forgive her regardless of her sins."

Pamela thought she saw a tear sparkle briefly in Peg's eye but then quick as a wink she smiled, "Well then we'd best get you into this dress, come have a look an' pray the moths havena eaten the thing."

She bid Pamela to follow her into the back bedroom, a lush little gem of a room, striped and flowered, chintzed and satined, powder-puffed and befrilled. It ought to have been obscene with all the color and pattern but somehow it wasn't. It was like a cozy harem, if such a thing was feasible, thought Pamela.

Peg dragged out a three-legged stool and said "If ye wouldn't mind, I'm not so handy as I used to be at hoisting meself up on things. It's in that big purple box, an' while yer in there best grab the green one too."

Pamela fetched them down and handed them to Peg who laid them on the bed with reverence.

Peg opened the purple box and gently pushing aside the yellowed tissue, carefully pulled the dress out. Pamela had hardly known what to expect having only a limited view of what Peg might consider tasteful, but this, this bit of perfection, of stardust and wild, white flowers, this dress that would surely make even the plainest of women look like a resplendent rose, had not figured in any of her imaginings.

Peg held it up against Pamela and sighed with satisfaction, "Sure an' it looks as if it were made for ye, much as I hate to admit it, it suits ye even better than it did me. Ye'll have his head dinnilin' fer weeks after he sees ye in this. Perhaps it was fate, me takin' it into me windy auld head to come an' see the wee bride tonight, what with ye marryin' a Riordan an all."

Pamela slipped into the dress and felt the worn velvet and French lace fall into place on her as if indeed she'd been meant to wear it.

"Come an' have a look in the mirror, darlin'," Peg said and Pamela walked to the full-length mirror that sat amidst artfully hung paisley silks. "Ah, would ye look at ye child, the skin on ye like roses wid the dew still clingin' on 'em, an then me like an old raisin in the sun too long, age is some bitch, is she not?" Peg asked in a voice that held no question.

"We'll do your hair up wid the flowers from Terry's hothouse, white on that black hair of yers, I'm thinkin'," Peg said taking a handful of Pamela's dark curls and furrowing her brow at them.

"How did you know Casey's grandfather?" Pamela asked softly as Peg artfully twisted her hair this way and that, mumbling inaudibly to herself.

"Well now that's a long story an' best told on a full stomach, come and have a bite an' then if the mood strikes me I may tell ye of me own Riordan."

Peg had made a simple dinner of sandwiches, watercress and smoked salmon.

"Don't mind me high falutin' san'wiches here, I niver did be gettin' the hang of good, plain cookin'. Arthur spoiled me too much, I suppose, only knew how to make wee, feckless meals like me ownself. I can still see him standin' next to the stove in his business suit an' a frilly white apron some fool'd given me when we married, peeling taties and fryin' eggs while I sat keepin' me little hands soft and unsullied by the likes of dirty potatoes. 'Course then I've an Irishwoman's natural aversion to potatoes an' Arthur bein' English did not." She drifted again, giving one of her splendid sighs and then turned, a strange half-wild look in her heretofore merry blue eyes. "If yer bent on marryin' a Riordan, child, there do be a few things ye ought to know. Come take yer tea an' let's retire to the parlor."

It was some moments before Peg began her story. Instead she gazed into the bowl of an antique lamp. How many worlds and bygones existed in that glass bowl for Peg, Pamela could only guess and so she waited quietly, comfily ensconced in the rump-sprung, fern-patterned armchair.

"I was born lovin' Brendan Riordan," Peg began in a voice that was low but fierce with a memory that time had apparently done nothing to dim. "Or at least it seemed that way, though to be certain he was a grand lad of ten when I came screeling me way into this world. The Riordans ye mind, were Connemara men, farmers to begin wid, wid heads as hard as the rocks in their fields. Brendan's sons were the only boys not born to the land. Though each fool man in the family had his own personal purgatory, Brendan found his in Derry. He was only nineteen when he went there an' found himself a whole group of fools to play the pied piper to. It's a talent the Riordans have girl, convincin' themselves and everyone else that anything is possible. Here," she leaned forward and pulled open a drawer on the sideboard. She withdrew a picture, one worn from many handlings, one gazed upon with regret and other emotions, Pamela suspected, that only Peg would ever know.

"Yer Casey has the look of his grandfather about him, same bold eyes, same silver tongue, divils to the man are the Riordans, an' sure there's nothin' more irresistible to a woman."

Pamela took the picture carefully and was shocked to see Casey's face with a few minor alterations looking back at her. He obviously took far more after his grandfather, while Pat was leaner and quieter looking like their own father.

"He's near the spit of him, isn't he?" Peg asked and Pamela nodded though she knew no answer was needed.

"I was damn determined to be his wife though for many years he saw me only as a child, a wee brat he'd dandled on his knee and amused with bits of string an' paper. I was only nine when he left for Derry an' when he came back the man had replaced the boy. He was a full-fledged member of the Brotherhood by then and it had taken things from him that no woman could give back, particularly a very silly sixteen-year old. It took me three more years after that to convince him that I was no longer a child, though I think he never did rightly believe we'd make a go of it, I just sort of wore him down. No small feat with a Riordan, but then it's likely ye'll be having had a taste of that yerself." Peg took the picture back and gazed at it for some moments, the soft light filtering through her hair and erasing the lines of her skin. She stroked the picture softly as if she could still feel the heat of the man captured there in his image. "Ah ye were a fine one Brendan an' ye broke me heart fer life, did ye know that man?" Pamela knew that she did not imagine the tears that glinted in Peg's eyes this time.

"Ye'll not tame him ye know." Peg said with a sudden fierceness, leaning forward and glaring Pamela in the face. "He'll never be there when ye need him an' ye'll always be second to his real love, this country, this whore we call Ireland. She's not flesh and blood so ye cannot compete, an' she's got wiles that're thousands of years old that even presentin' him with a son cannot compare to. An' lass," Peg's voice softened and her face seemed once again to fall into the lines of its age, "ye'll never get him to leave. The Riordans never run from a fight, even if the fight takes their years and in the end their life, which it will, darlin'. The shadow hangs heavy over them from the day they're born, it's only a matter of how and when, bullet or blanket and for one or two of them, it's been the hangman's noose."

"Why did you never marry?" Pamela asked.

Peg shook her head and sighed.

"Because he up and went back to Derry and married a girl there. I like to think he left because he loved me enough to know that living with him would have broke me like a butterfly caught in a fan. But perhaps he loved her more an' sure Marie was suited to his way of life, she was part of the movement herself, politicized, while I was still worried about dancing and havin' meself a fine time." Peg smiled tiredly. "Sentimental old fool I am seein' his grandson tonight only made me think that he might have been my grandson as well but then p'raps it's best he isn't."

"And the man you did marry?"

"I'm thinkin' that the story of Arthur is best saved fer another time, it seems wrong to me to think of him and Brendan at the same time. Most men seem a bit washed out after a Riordan an' I'll not do Arthur the disservice in death that I did him in life of comparin' him to Brendan." She tapped her cane lightly on the floor, "We'd best be gettin' some sleep, havin' bedded down with a Riordan meself I'm knowin' that sleep'll be a rare commodity in yer life fer awhile."

Peg stood and thumped her way down the hall then, without so much as a backwards glance, leaving Pamela almost sorry that she'd asked about Brendan.

She went herself only moments later to the lavender bedroom and undressed, washed in the small basin Peg had provided and then feeling anything but tired slid between worn white linen sheets. She was surprised to hear a soft knock at her door and bid a quiet 'come in' to Peg.

"I'm sorry to disturb ye child but I'd forgotten I meant to give ye this as well," she handed Pamela the green box that had come down with the wedding dress from the top of her closet. "Brendan gave it to me, he'd been in Paris on Brotherhood business, an' he saw this in a shop window, said it was the loveliest thing he'd ever seen an' he knew I had to have it. I niver got a chance to wear it; Brendan left me shortly after. Seems only fittin' somehow that you should wear it for his grandson. "

"Oh," was all Pamela could manage, tears having gained a chokehold on her throat for all this woman had lost and missed in her life. "It's breathtaking." She lifted it out of the box and yards of pink silk fluttered out pale as pearls, sinuous as a waterfall, a garment intended purely for seduction. "But redheads I thought are not supposed to wear pink," Pamela said smiling through her tears.

"Ah well," Peg lifted a corner of the material, "sometimes it's not so much the color as the cut of the cloth, if ye'll be mindin' what I mean."

Pamela rubbed the silk against her face, fine as swansdown, empty of the memories it should have held within its weft and thought that God had not made man to understand the heart of a woman.

"I'm sorry, Peg." she impulsively took the woman's hand and pressed it to her face.

"Ah darlin' child don't shed tears for me, havin' the love of Brendan for a bit was better than niver havin' it at all." She stroked Pamela's hair gently, "Ye'd best sleep now an' shed no more tears, it's ill to do so on the eve of yer weddin'." She bent down to kiss Pamela's forehead gently, a benediction a mother might have placed upon her daughter the night before her wedding and then turned to go. It seemed to Pamela suddenly that there was nothing very outrageous or crazy about this woman but rather just a personage worn and washed old with years of pain and regret. But still the story was not done and Pamela for one hated loose ends.

"What happened to him, Casey's grandfather, what was his end?" she asked half afraid of knowing, for what if Casey truly did carry some sort of family curse?

Peg turned back and leaned tiredly in the doorsill.

"He was the head of the IRA for some years, me darlin' and like all Riordans he did his bit in the Republican university of choice, his own bein' Portlaoise Jail. He and a number of others went on the blanket, refusin' to be treated as common criminals. It was a very bad time they say. The men could hardly go to mass naked an' they were not allowed books or conversation even. They sat out the war and time beyond in solitary confinement wid the lights switched on an' burnin' in their faces twenty-four hours a day. Once a week they were allowed out to bathe, barely more than animals were they treated as, truly it was a wonder they didn't go mad, though one might suppose the Riordans are born in that particular condition anyway and hardly need help maintainin' their madness.

"He went on hunger strike to protest their treatment and received a terrible beating as a result. It did little to him though; the Riordans count beatings and floggings merely as a matter of course. Fifteen days into his fast three of his men broke him out, rumor was that one of the guards inside had come under the spell of Brendan's charm and helped to free him. Was hardly worth the effort in the end though," Peg closed her eyes and Pamela knew she was seeing the events of forty some years ago as if they unfurled frame by agonized frame on a screen in front of her. "Wasn't so many years later that he was shot in the street in front of his house, four times in the heart. They'd killed his sons too, the two younger, Brian was the oldest an' survived only by not bein' present at the time. He was just only eighteen. Marie, thank the Virgin, was down in Dublin visitin' her sick mother, otherwise, Lord knows what they might of done to her.

"Brendan never intended that Brian should be part of the family legacy, Brian was quiet, a scholar, a man perhaps meant to lead through thought and word not violence but after havin' his father and brothers slaughtered, he'd little choice on what path to follow. But then it seems the Riordans never do, theirs is a long and bloody story, goin' back to the time of the O'Neills and goin' forward in chapters yet unwritten. Likely the best thing ye can do girl is never bear Casey a son." She slumped tiredly on her cane, "If I thought ye'd pay me any mind I'd tell ye to run like the very devil was chasing ye with his pitchfork, but I see the looks ye two shared and know there is no sense that will intrude upon such feelins'," she smiled wryly, "that much I do understand. Now sleep girl, I've spoken too long and freely but as Arthur said I niver did know how to be still an' that surely went twice over for me tongue."

Pamela to her own surprise did sleep eventually but not until long after the image of Casey bright with blood and cool with death faded from her mind.

"YE'D NOT BELIEVE THAT KANDINSKY ONCE ASKED TO PAINT ME, would ye?" Peg asked throwing a baleful look over Pamela's shoulder into the mirror as she carefully arranged pale waxen white roses in amongst Pamela's bath damp curls. "Me hair, he said, was the color of Russian earth, red with the blood of her people. He was rather given to melodrama, but in the end he didna' paint me for Madame, his wife forbid it. Ah well, 'twould have been nice to have seen me mug in the hand of a Master and all me other bits as well but Arthur was a bit in the way of bein' a painter and daubed me down in oils and water more than once. 'Twas the village scandal I tell ye, me posin' in the altogether, five months gone with Siddy, but Arthur insisted the light was right in the garden by the poppies an' I did so love stirrin' things up. There now," she said giving Pamela's hair a final pat, " it's like an angel that could lure a man to his death that yer lookin'. Though it's a rare man I'm thinkin' that wouldn't view it as a fine way to go."

Peg herself was looking resplendent on this morning in violet taffeta with a silk gardenia tucked amidst the violent and glimmering red of her hair.

Peg gave her a few moments alone as she went to collect her wrap and Pamela took the time to say farewell to the woman, young though she may be, who today was taking an irrevocable step forward into a future that held anything but certainty. She was afraid. She supposed she'd be a fool not to be, but she also knew she wanted this, to be Casey's wife, to be a part of another and not alone in the wilderness of her own self. That in itself was infinitesimally more frightening that the prospect of pledging her life to Casey's.

Peg returned with her wrap and rubber boots in hand and Pamela was confronted with the unromantic proposition of having to wear black Wellingtons under her beautiful gown.

"Tis' hardly the most delicate of accessories but it's the only practical one, we had a hard rain last night an' the ground is a bit on the squadgy side."

They set out, in velvet and silk, black Wellies and green Macintoshes, skirts rucked up most indelicately above the knees, looking rather like two exotic and very misplaced birds from a distance thought Father Terry as he came up behind with a surrey and horse. Pamela and Peg gratefully clambered aboard with his help and the procession continued to where Casey stood smoking in the garden, with a small weather-beaten soul who turned out to be Bertie Small, the all-important second witness. Casey'd scarce time to crush the cigarette under his heel and send a thin column of blue smoke wafting up from amongst the winter jonquils when Peg let out a screech that Father Terry was certain pierced the heart of the gannets far out on little Skellig.

"Turn yer face man, ye musn't see the bride!" Casey accordingly did so and Peg alit with relief from the brown surrey. "Well then that was a bit too close of a shave for my likin', skedaddle yer rear end into the house before the sky falls in on us," she directed Pamela who wasted no time in obeying her.

The sky however did not fall in, the sun that had been making himself rather scarce that morning did indeed deign to show his face and the bride, having discovered she'd no fit shoes, found her way barefooted to the dark-eyed man who awaited her.

"Nervous boyo?" Father Terry whispered as Pamela, perfectly, wildly beautiful as the soul of Ireland herself came into view.

"As a three-legged, blind mouse in a cat house, " Casey replied without his usual jocularity.

And then it was easy somehow as their hands fitted together and Father Terry, clearing his throat, began the ceremony. Peg sniffed occasionally from her position as matron of honor and a seagull wheeled overhead screeling its heart out. The vows old and time-honored were repeated, the silver bands exchanged and then before the kiss that sealed all that had been said, Casey and Pamela exchanged their own words.

Pamela began, her voice trembling with the emotion this man stirred within her, "For even as night comes to ease the weariness of day, so shall I come unto you."

And then Casey took up the ribbon and spoke clearly and certainly, "I will be the candle flame that guides you forth from your darkness."

And then Pamela again, "I will be water to your earth, food to your hunger, shore to your sea."

Casey winked at her his black eyes twinkling. "I shall be the salt on yer potatoes." They all laughed then and Father Terry said the groom could go ahead and kiss the woman for after all she was his wife. Peg wept openly with a smile on her face that would have brought the sun out had he not already obliged, Bertie Small nodded in approval, and Casey delivered a kiss that left his bride blushing and the good Father applauding.

Then there were congratulations all round and Peg hugged them both wishing them enough happiness for ten lifetimes and Father Terry, with a grin, produced a bottle of champagne that had a duck on the label. Lunch was a simple affair, though the bride, being fed by her new husband hardly noticed the taste of anything so submerged was she in the perfection of the day. It was in general and in detail, in ways large and small, a dream of a day.

Father Terry told stories, strange and amusing, Casey was induced to sing and Peg watched it all with a tenderness in her blue eyes that seemed to pour a blanket of warmth and light over the entire day. It would remain so in Pamela's memory always, a day filled with golden light, distilled by time, scented with roses and threaded through with the wildness of her first love and so she danced with light and joyful feet when it turned out that Father Terry could play a fiddle like Old Scratch himself, as Peg astutely said. Danced with a pure abandon that sent rose petals tumbling and catching down the cascade of her hair, danced until Father Terry found he had to look away for the pain of seeing such beauty, danced until her husband caught her up in his arms and she tumbled dizzy with cheap champagne and unfettered love into his lap. His eyes caught her own and she trembled to see the burning there, the absolute searing heat that was reserved for her and her alone.

Father Terry, Bertie and Peg bid them quiet good-byes and set off in the little brown cart, feeling suddenly old and too far distanced from the passion of youth.

And then it was only the two of them, husband and wife, strangely nervous. Casey took her hand and led her into the cottage where a peat fire he'd slipped off to build warmed the smoke smudged walls and gave off a glow that was comforting. He poured them each a finger of whiskey though he showed no inclination to drink his own but rather sat on the bed and loosened his collar, undoing the top two buttons. His jacket, having been long ago abandoned was now followed by shoes and socks, cufflinks and suspenders.

He looked suddenly more largely and ferally male than Pamela could ever remember him being, she gulped her whiskey nervously, gasping as it tore a raw strip down to her belly.

"That's poteen, darlin'," Casey said with a smile "it hardly bears sippin' much less tossin' the whole thing back." He took her hand and pulled her over to him, placing her between his knees and putting his large hands on her hips firmly. "There's nothin' to be afraid of, 'tis only you an' I, we've many nights ahead of us, if it's too soon for you then we'll just hold each other, there's time."

"You would give me that—time?" she asked looking down into his face and brushing an errant curl from the tangle of his lashes.

"Forever and then a bit more darlin', as long as there's breath in my body and blood in my veins it's yers for the askin'."

"I want you now," she said, "tonight I want you to do all the things your eyes have been saying all day. I want you to make me your wife in the flesh as well as the word." She felt her soul rise and break and begin again on the words and knew her body would have no fear this night or any of the nights and slow, sweet dawns to follow.

He raised a hand and trembling traced the contours of her face, her neck and then laid his fingers to rest briefly in the hollow of her collarbone where the blood of her heart pulsed deeply.

"No one is ever going to make ye fear again," he said and she couldn't tell if it was the reflection of firelight or tears that glistened in his eyes. "*Macushla,*" he whispered. Beloved.

The dress he took from her with reverence, his eyes never once breaking the faith they held with hers. Then he took her chemise and underwear 'til she stood bare to him, outlined by fire, shivering with want.

He drank her in inch by inch with his eyes as though a hunger lay there in the dark of them that would never be satisfied.

"Ah darlin'," he said at last, "even if I'd slept a thousand years I'd not of had a dream as fine an' lovely as the reality of you."

He made love to her that night that sang his soul into her own, as if all the poetry that he professed not to understand lay there within his own body, expressed more eloquently and with a depth the carving of ink could never attain. Beloved, he whispered with his hands, beloved he sang with his skin as it brushed her own, beloved with lips and tongue, until all the whispers built within her blood and became a high, humming threnody that invaded all the corners dark and ugly, that burned the fear with the whiteness of its heat and sank the ashes with this water of retribution he fed her with every touch. Until finally she cried his name over and over like litany, a private prayer that was the final blessing on the day.

"LORD I FEEL GRAND," CASEY SAID SOMETIME LATER blowing frowzy edged smoke rings into the air above their heads. Father Terry had procured from some unknown source a true Cuban cigar and Casey had saved it for what he perceived as the perfect moment.

"I forgot Peg's fancy French lingerie," Pamela said feeling bone-meltingly satiated and in no way inclined to be dressed from her cozy nest of rumpled sheets and the long warm expanse of her husband's body. "I feel a bit guilty really, your grandfather gave it to her and she never got the chance to wear it. She thought at least one Riordan ought to have the pleasure of it."

"Pleasure I've had," said Casey "an' sure it had little to do with what you were wearin'. She loved him, then?" he asked.

"I think she mourns him still or mourns what she thinks might have been. She meant no disrespect to your grandmother, I hope you know that."

Casey nodded, "Aye Father Terry told me a bit about it. My Da' always said his parents had a love that was about endurin' all the bad that life had handed them, perhaps my Granda' knew that was not the life for Margaret MacBride. A man can't live with divided loyalties, my father used to tell Pat and I and yet he did every day of his own life and so it would seem did his father before him."

"And his son after him?" she asked not really knowing if she cared for him to answer.

He rolled to his side and turned her face up to his own, " I never intended to marry that's true, I was born with my destiny there inside," he touched his hand over her heart, "there was never any real doubt what path I would eventually follow and my Da's death only hastened my journey, but then I never planned on you and I could no more stop the inevitability of loving you than I could stop a train with my bare hands. Life hands ye gifts when ye least expect it an' sometimes there's no choice but to simply take it with both hands and be thankful for it. I think my father and grandfather would both understand that."

"Doesn't it ever frighten you, the sheer weight of all that history bearing down on you from the moment you're born?"

"I'd be a fool if it didn't but, darlin', haven't ye learned yet that there is not much more we Irish have to pass on to the next generation, our history, our resistance to oppression, the fight to live free as a man should be born, to call our land our own, to make the rules and have the freedom to break them and make better ones from the foundations of the old. Sometimes it's as simple as wantin' the dignity of a job and the ability to provide for one's own family. It isn't just about me and my Da' and Grandda an' all the Riordans that came before him, it's for Pat and any number of Pats that I will never know, so that they might have somethin' better and not have to leave their own land to do so."

"And would you pay for the freedom of strangers with your own life?" she asked, trying and failing to keep the anger from skewing her voice.

He looked long into her eyes with a tenderness and sadness melding there that bewildered and frightened her.

"Aye I would," he answered simply. And she knew then with a finality that her youth could hardly bear that in those three simple words was an enormity of belief and despair that she could never hope to fight. Eight hundred years of weight and blood filled those words, his very DNA twisted into strands that marked him out for this, this intangible thing, and forced him to live in a world where hope was a luxury and a word could kill a man. Yet to use his own words she could no more stop the loving of him than she could halt a train with her bare hands. And for now he lay within her own sights and this night was for their making alone, the world outside with all its cries of need and pain could go hang.

She turned to him this time making her need known with a ferocity she had never before displayed and he responded in kind as though if this baptism were fiery enough and shed enough heat and light it would keep them safe and warm even if only for this one night.

Chapter Twenty-nine

Peg

MARGARET MACBRIDE, MORE COMMONLY KNOWN AS PEG, was having the very devil of a time trying to sleep and had, after tossing and turning and cursing at sheets, bed, room and finally in utter frustration, the moon, had given up and rose from her tangle of abused linen to make herself a cup of chocolate. It was hardly a guaranteed sleep aid but it was pleasant and passed the time. Waiting for dawn to come had ceased to be an exercise in angst years ago and had quite simply, she supposed, now become the affliction of the old, a simple inability to sleep.

In the tiny kitchen with its north and west-facing windows, she had not bothered to turn the lights on, but boiled the kettle and mixed the chocolate and cream by the fitful light of the moon. There wasn't much gumption left in the wind anymore, it'd be a soft day of it tomorrow. She hoped the sun would make its appearance again, the chill, mist-laden days that had once seemed like so much manna to her romantic soul now seeped insidiously into her bones and stiffened her joints and there was simply nothing romantic about that. It rather reminded one far too sharply of one's age, she thought, taking her chocolate and walking painfully into the sunporch she'd had built, (in some fit of lunacy as the sun was rather a rare player in these climes) five years ago. Arthur had left her a great deal of money though, rather a shocking amount really for a man who had lived such a simple, uncomplicated life, and she'd really nothing to spend it on. Siddy and his uptight wife, Clarice, had been well shot of her years ago and hardly needed her assistance in matters financial. So when she had taken a hankering for a posh car, she'd had a second hand Bentley shipped over from England and when she'd wanted to see Paris once more she had simply put cash on the barrelhead and gone and when she had, one particularly glittery day, thought a sunporch would be just the thing she had called the contractor the next day and two months later there had been her sunporch. She'd felt a bit foolish about it at first, but then Terry had declared it perfectly grand and they'd taken to having their tea in it and she to sitting in it on sleepless nights, like tonight.

Overhead there was a great tangled snarl of stars, like the string of a child's kite caught hopelessly in the branches of an unforgiving tree. The night sky was comforting at times and at others so remote as to seem Godless. It took a moment or two to settle herself in her chair; an act that had once seemed so perfunctory now took a merciless toll on her body. But at last she was settled, if not comfortably, then at least bearably. One learned to live with what small graces life extended and was thankful for them. She sniffed the dark perfume of her chocolate and enjoyed the warmth the steam of it provided for the tip of her nose. She took a large swallow and sighed gratefully as the heat spread outward from her stomach to the extremities of her anatomy. Then she sighed again and set the chocolate on the small table beside her. This sigh contained no satisfaction and certainly no relief to the heavy weight straddling her chest. She had lied to Terry, Terry who just happened to have another life as a priest. She could not altogether shed the trappings of her Catholic childhood and supposed this would require attendance at mass at least twice and a substantial offering to the poorbox. Would that all sins, she thought wearily, be cast off so easily. Some sins were unforgivable though and she had lived long enough to know it for truth. And she had committed hers long ago, though she still could not feel a true regret for it. Perhaps regret would come when she felt the fires of hell at her feet but she had burned on earth, burned for fifty years for a man who'd turned to dust more than thirty years ago. Perhaps that would count, that earthly torture or perhaps, and this was not a new thought to her, maybe this was hell, right here, and humans just didn't know it.

She *had* known Brian, for a brief time granted, but he'd never been 'just Marie's son' to her though it was hardly something she could tell Terry. Brian had come to see her in England, a long time past now, must have been '37 just before war broke across Europe. He had been sitting on her front stairs one morning when she arrived home from doing the marketing. He'd risen up in one long fluid line, the grace of his father present in his movement and taken her bags from her wordlessly.

'Ye'll know who I am then?" he asked quietly as she fumbled with the key.

'Aye, I'll know," she replied finding her Irish slipping back into her speech, thick and clotting, a sure sign of nervousness. "Though what yer doin' here is something I'll be less certain about."

He didn't answer at once but brought her bags into the house and set them down in the kitchen. She offered him tea but he replied that a cool glass of water would do him just fine. She settled for the same and then faced him across the kitchen.

"Well Brian, what have ye come for?" She nervously lit herself a cigarette and offered him one, which he politely declined.

"Don't usually indulge myself," she said, "Arthur doesn't like the smell of it *about."*

Brian nodded and she could see him appraising her across the cheery, sunlit room, the shadow of a willow rippling and rustling on the floor.

She knew she was still a fine looking woman, men's eyes being the mirror of affirmation. Closing in on forty-five and the wrinkles only just beginning. Her waist still no more than a large man's handspan, her hair, with help from a hairdresser in London, still fiery red, deepening into auburn glints. Arthur, she knew, still had his moments of disbelief that she had ever agreed to be his wife. Poor Arthur. Yes, still a woman who could turn heads in the street, but how, she wondered, did she look to this boy sitting in her kitchen? Old, most likely, old and ridiculous and hardly the flame-haired temptress that had lured his father away from his marital bed.

"I just wanted to see ye," Brian said, "I wanted to see the woman my Da' spent years agonizin' over. I wanted to know what it was that pulled him like a madman to ye."

"Bit disappointed, aren't ye?" she said angrily and ground her cigarette out in the sink. She busied herself with the groceries then, tossing things into cupboards willy-nilly, so that she'd find apples in the potato bin and nutmeg in the fridge the next day.

"No," he said, "yer fine as any woman I've ever seen, but if my Daddy loved ye it had little to do with what he saw on the outside."

"I'm sorry," she said and collapsed into a chair. "What is it that ye want from me then?"

Brian didn't answer for a moment, he looked down at his hands loosely clasped on the table in front of him and when he replied his answer was so quiet she had to lean forward to hear.

"I want te know my Daddy, all of him an' Terry always leaves out the bits about ye. I want to know my father through yer eyes."

There was a long silence then, during which Peg studied Brian's hands, long and broad and blunted at the ends with a strength that was formidable. His father's hands, his father's gentleness and his own quiet need to rebuild the past brick by brick until the wall gave him the protection he sought.

"Are ye certain that ye want to know it all," she asked in a much softer tone of voice, "d'ye know what it is ye're askin'?"

"Aye, I know," he replied simply.

He left shortly after that but he'd come back, seeming to know instinctually when Arthur was home, when Siddy was likely to drift in and out. Though Arthur, to be certain, wasn't hard to pin down. Arthur was as constant and as regular as the sun, up in the morning, down in the evening, wore a tie Monday to Friday and short sleeves on the weekend. You could set your clock by him or your life and never be late or off balance. It was what she loved and hated about him. Arthur was the quintessential English country barrister. Whitfield, Grey and Whitfield,

Arthur being the Grey in the middle. Arthur who had loved her with the devotion of an old and blind dog and she supposed she had treated him as such for years, like a beloved pet, faithful and dependable. Banishing him to other rooms, houses and women when his need became too distinct. She hadn't understood, even in the beginning, what it was that so attracted him to her. She'd been half dead with grief and certainly not in the market for an eligible, if somewhat stodgy, young British lawyer. But Arthur, like the proverbial dog with a bone, had not let go and eventually his persistence had worn her down. His proposal had been like the rest of their life, not quite what it should have been.

"I'll never love ye the way a wife should," she'd said bluntly, "and I'll never be the sort of wife a man like you should have."

"I can love enough for two, Margaret," he'd replied in that soft, yet solid way he had, "and as for the rest, we'll manage."

But they hadn't, not really. Certainly Arthur had made partner in the firm at a very young age, but even at fifty it seemed that he had never ceased to be the junior partner. She hadn't wanted children, but had found herself quite miserably pregnant in the second year of their relationship. Arthur, strangely triumphant, had declared marriage unavoidable then. Tired, heartsick and uncaring, she'd agreed. Siddy had been a carbon copy of his father, it was as if he'd known her rejection of him and refused her genes, had not wanted any part of his mother. His wild Irish mammy, as Arthur used to call her with affection and a certain unquenched longing in his eyes that turned her cold. Siddy had been bothered by her wildness and particularly her Irishness from a very young age. In Siddy's little, gray soul the only longing that persisted was to be a proper British gentleman and an Irish mother who said and did outrageous things didn't have a place in that picture. He'd retained a solemn tolerant fondness for her though until the spring that Brian came into her life, then she had committed an outrageousness that no one could forgive.

Brian had been her secret for months, a sweet half-boy, half-man who made the past a little more livable and brought back the joy of it instead of the horror and pain. They met quite often in the mornings and he'd help her with the marketing, doing various chores and bringing small delights that he thought she might enjoy. It was for the first time in many years truly spring for her, spring in her own soul, where she'd thought nothing would ever grow again. And on their various journeys, she would tell him about his father, a bit here, a story there, an adventure they'd had, a conversation shared and remembered like diamonds mined.

She changed her hair, bought new clothes, listened again to music that had been too painful to even contemplate before, when nothing could be allowed to thaw or even chip at the ice she'd hidden behind in her heart. She drank wine and laughed and one evening as dusk fell and she felt an utterly terrifying restlessness seize her, Arthur said, "I like the way you are wearing your hair these days, it suits you." It had been that simple. But with Arthur, you learned to hear the words behind those actually uttered. It meant he had noticed, he had noticed and knew that the balance of their lives, always precarious and dependent on her grief, had shifted and would not be regained.

"I needed a change," she said but shook with the enormous lie of the words. Brian was the change.

It was the dress that would prove to be her undoing. She wondered, later, if she'd known that as she picked it out. It was the color of first spring lilacs, pale and silken lavender. It was a color that Brendan had loved on her and she had not worn it since his death. She should have known better than to ever wear it again. It hung in her closet for several weeks and each time she saw it there she felt like an old fool. But one evening when she was alone and far more restless than was good for her, she succumbed to the temptation of putting it on. It slid like pure water over her body and its swish as it settled about her hips felt like the caress of a young man's hands. Giddiness seized her and she had run down to the kitchen to pour herself a glass of pale gold wine. Back in her bedroom, she had surveyed herself in the mirror and seen reflected back a woman who looked and suddenly felt far younger than her years. It was twilight, that hour that is much kinder to women of a certain age and she turned and twirled and flirted with her reflection until she was dizzy and laughing. Then she'd stopped abruptly, her heart pounding and head whirling. In the shadows stood a man, a tall man with such a very sad face, for one brief moment she thought it was Brendan, or rather Brendan's ghost but it was only Arthur, her middle-aged eyes and the failing light had deceived her into seeing the desired phantom.

"Have you met someone?" he asked, dispelling, like so many smoke-hurled stars, the illusion of youth.

"No," she replied too quickly, too crossly.

That had been all he said at the time, but he wanted to make love that night and her guilt had stopped her from turning away, she merely closed her eyes and conjured a ghost the way she had a thousand times before, but this time it was not the spectral touch of Brendan she felt, it was his son.

His son, whom she asked to dinner a week later, when Arthur went up to London on overnight business. She understood what his business was and had never objected; she'd never had a right to and hadn't ever really cared.

Brian was going back to Ireland in a few days and she wanted to take him somewhere nice, telling herself it was a bit like a proud mother wanting to dine with her son. She knew it for a lie even as she spoke it to herself.

She had worn the dress, with pearls in her ears and at her throat, warmed and wrapped with the scent of her favorite perfume, not the English country garden scent that Arthur preferred but the million roses and one jasmine note of 'Joy' that she used to comb through her hair even, in the days of abandon and excess that were her youth. Because that was what she had felt with Brendan, pure joy and terror, and fury and love so tender that it seemed a breath might break it in *half and yet she'd known not even an ocean could move it.*

She took him to a very expensive restaurant with a lush decor, and even there in a roomful of excessively groomed, bored rich women she stood out like a jewel on white velvet. She drank too much wine and laughed too much and told him things about herself that made him smile and even blush a little. She was completely reckless with the awareness of how soon he was to exit her life. Not much else, she was to later think, could explain the scene in the garden.

But before that, at the end of their meal, she'd presented him with a little blue-bound book.

'*Leaves of Grass, it was—*' *he began*

'*Your father's favorite, I know, he gave it to me,*" *she'd finished.* "*He could recite* '*Song of Myself' you know, from the first word to the last. I remember once,*" *she laughed,* "*after we'd made love, he stood by an open window, naked and—*" *she flushed scarlet as she realized what she'd said.* "*Oh Jaysus, Brian I'm sorry, my tongue's gotten ahead of my brain as usual.*"

He looked at her for a long moment, such a strange look that she had found it hard to breathe. Then he'd said—

> "*Hands I have taken, face I have kiss'd,*
> *mortal I have ever touched, it shall be you.*"

"*I suppose he would have said that to you at some point, only he didn't mean it for himself as Whitman did, he meant it for you, didn't he? Everything in his life he meant for you.*"

She shook her head, uncaring that tears were gathering in her eyes with the force of an impending storm. "*If that were true Brian, we wouldn't be here together now, would we? It was all meant for Ireland,*" *she said and even twenty years after Brendan's death the bitterness tasted like poison on her tongue,* "*oh yes all meant for a goddamn country that loved him enough to kill him like a dog in the street. All meant for Ireland and not a drop left over for you and me, Brian. Not a drop, parched and dying from thirst but not a goddamn drop.*" *Other diners were staring as her voice rose and the maitre'd looked slightly horrified, but Brian merely gave a cool glance around the room and people turned back to their meals shamefaced and without appetite.*

"*I'll take you home, Peg,*" *he said and had sounded so much like his father that she'd wanted to slap him, call him a faithless bastard and take him to bed all in one go. Instead she followed quietly, tears slipping silently down her face, destroying the meticulous maquillage of a forty-five year old woman.*

He took her home, but he didn't leave her the way she had been certain he would. They sat in the garden and he talked to her in such a low and gentle voice that she thought she would go mad if he didn't touch her. Touch her as a man, not a boy. He told her his story about the man he'd known, the father he'd loved and at times hated for his strength and his death, which Brian had struggled not to see as deliberate on Brendan's part.

She was later to think how funny it was that gardens often played a part in the downfall of man, or woman as the case may be. How five minutes of madness in a lilac drenched patch could forever alter the constructs of a life.

Before the madness struck, he took her hands in one of his and wiped her face gently with a cloth in his other.

"I must look a dreadful sight," she said, profoundly and wearily meaning it, not looking for pretty denials as she would have years ago.

"No, no you don't," he said and the look on his face had been enough to make her move away from him to stand under the overarching lilac branches, heavy and swollen from a sudden rain. He followed, as she must have known he would.

"I'm not my father," he said simply and she whispered, "I know Brian, I know too well." And then of course, he kissed her, softly, achingly, arching her back into it. Her body, so long dormant, leaped like a tightly strung bow to his touch. She felt on fire at once and responded like a woman whose death sentence has just been removed. She never knew later, or perhaps she just didn't want to know, who removed whose clothing, she would remember only the touch of his hands sure and hard on her breasts and how she breathed in sharply at the sight of his body half-bared to her. It was madness, but an irresistible insanity, that made her laugh as his hands, his fine, young hands slid down over her hips, lifted her, settled her so that her back would have scratches and long bloody scrapes for weeks after from the rough bark of Arthur's much loved lilac trees. And then just as suddenly she knew Brendan was there, that his hands touched her as they had in so many painful dreams, painful for the waking, not for the dreaming. It was Brendan whose breath came hard upon her neck, Brendan's hands cupping her hips, Brendan's teeth and tongue upon her breasts, Brendan inside of her and the knowledge, longed for, hungered and ached and tossed and turned for through endless agonies of nights, the knowledge left her cold. She pushed him away and saw him in the moonlight, stunned and hollow-eyed before she covered her face with her hands and began to weep in a way that had nothing to do with tears.

"I—oh Christ—I—for a minute I thought..." he trailed off as he saw her face and she knew that he had felt it too, had felt his father enter his body, his blood and push him aside to have the woman he'd burned for in life and it would seem, even in death.

She felt sickened and ashamed and leaned down to pick up her dress, crumpled and sodden with dew, a dress that, even if it hadn't been ruined, she would never have worn again. As she straightened up, she caught a flicker of gray in the corner of her eye and stood to see Arthur standing at the entrance to the garden, his face ashen behind a mist of filmy apricot roses. Brian turned then, sensing a watcher behind him, and gave Arthur the small dignity of looking him in the eyes, before bending to retrieve his own fallen attire and shrugging into its drenched shell.

She didn't know how long she might have stood there watching Arthur turn to dust, watching him fall and crumple and die though he never moved an inch, perhaps forever if there hadn't suddenly been a vicious rush across the space that separated them and the whirling eddy of adolescent fists flailing at her naked body and a voice, shrill with betrayal and blood-hate, screaming 'filthy Irish whore' at her. Her son, calling her a whore, while his father stood like a statue by the gate and she welcoming the blows that rained down and bruised her in ways that would never show on her skin. It was Brian who stopped him, Brian who pinned his arms at his sides and bodily moved him over to his father and then gently told Arthur that it would be best to take the boy inside and that Peg would be in shortly.

Arthur seemed almost grateful to be instructed what to do. He nodded at Brian and without a backwards glance herded Siddy into the house. Siddy, who followed quietly enough after spitting in Brian's face.

Brian calmly wiped his face and then came to Peg, helped her into her clothes and gently kissed her on the forehead.

"I'm sorry," he said simply and she was grateful that no embarrassment tinged his words. He looked so young standing there in the moonlight and yet a full man, apologizing for nearly making love to his father's old mistress. It struck her as ludicrous and she began to laugh, hysterically, nauseated with misery, and acutely pained by the thought that she could never so much as lay eyes on this man again. When it seemed that she might never stop, Brian took her head hard in his hands and said 'no more' sharply. She stopped.

"Will it be better if I stay or go?" he asked and she was touched by his youthful bravado.

"Go," she whispered, "Arthur has been hurt enough tonight; I can't make him stand under his own roof with you. Go Brian. Go home. He won't hurt me," she added, seeing that he was uncertain of leaving her to cope alone. And if he does, she thought silently to herself, it'll be much less than I deserve.

He had gone, into the night. Without promises, without any more words and she had been old enough to be grateful for it.

Siddy had barricaded himself in his room and would not come out and she was too weary to try very long to persuade him. She went to the kitchen and saw that Arthur had put the roses he'd brought her into a vase, carefully filled with warm water. It was very like him, even in moments of great pain, not to punish an innocent flower for its mere presence. She stayed in the kitchen for awhile, cleaned the already gleaming sink and counters, then rinsed the wine glass she'd used before taking Brian out and carefully folded it in a linen napkin, then went into the downstairs bath and removed her makeup, changed into a velvet, apricot robe Arthur had given her on her last birthday and balled up the stockings, underpants, brassiere and dress she'd worn and tucking them under one arm took them out through the kitchen where she collected the wineglass and then took the lot of it to the outside trash bin, which she then lugged to the street. They would come and take it away in the morning. It would be too late but at least she would *never have to look at the damn dress again.*

Arthur was in their bedroom, carefully folding his clothes into a suitcase.

"I'm not leaving," he said calmly, "I won't give you the satisfaction. However, I do think it best if I take Sidney away from here for a few days. It's likely to be unpleasant around here for a bit and he doesn't deserve to be a part of that."

"No, no he doesn't," she found herself calmly agreeing. She was relieved actually; cowardice or not she really couldn't bear Siddy's self-righteous anger at present. "Where will you take him?" she asked, as if inquiring about a seaside jaunt.

"To Scotland, Laura will be happy enough to take him; he can finish out the term there. I've already called and she'll make up the spare room for him."

"He'll hate it," Peg said softly, "you know what he thinks of the state school system."

Arthur took a deep breath and she noticed how tightly he gripped the sides of the suitcase, "At present, Margaret, I can't say I much care about the wishes of a spoiled, pompous little boy. Perhaps his cousins will knock some of it out of him. It'd do him no end of good."

She'd given a sharp gasp of laughter more from shock than amusement and he looked at her wearily as though she were just one more disobedient, headstrong child that he had to deal with.

He was gone four days, time enough to settle Siddy in with his wild pack of Scottish cousins and register him at the local school. He arrived home on the evening of the fifth day, obviously exhausted.

"What did you tell Laura?" Peg asked as he poured himself his regulation two fingers of scotch and then looked disconsolately at the glass and poured two more.

"That you didn't feel well," he said and took his scotch and went upstairs to have a bath. She made him a light meal, the only sort of cooking she'd ever developed skill at and he ate it quietly while thumbing through the day's paper. He was acting so perfectly normal, so perfectly Arthur that she wanted to scream at him to hit her, break the dishes or walk out the door. But then, to be fair, what had she expected? A madman to come flying back from the north, ready to rant and rave and drag her about by the hair? It was inconceivable and simply not in his nature regardless of the depth of his pain. He was, in the finest and most out-of-date manner, a true gentleman.

After full dark, when the air cooled and the scent of the lilacs seemed to pour through the windows and steal across carpets and rooms, she went upstairs to find him gathering his things, pyjamas, toiletries, pillow, suits, socks, underwear and removing them to the downstairs bedroom.

"Arthur you don't have to do this," she said, a tearing loss within her that she'd never thought this man could make her feel.

"I don't really see any other possibility Peg, I cannot share this room," he looked sadly around, "nor this lie of a marriage bed."

"I'll go," she said desperately, "I'll move downstairs or out completely if that's

what you want."

He shook his head, *"No, I'd still smell your perfume on the air and feel your absence in that bed. If you want to move out Peg that's your choice, it always has been."*

"Do you want me to leave?" she asked, fear squeezing her heart so tightly she thought surely it would stop.

"No, Peg, fool that I am, I do not want you to leave, I'll never want that regardless of how much you grow to hate me."

"I don't hate you, Arthur," she said but he did not reply. It had taken several trips to remove all his things from the bedroom, when he was done it seemed lopsided in the room, lopsided and very empty. On the last trip, as he gathered small mementos, he stopped and sat down on the bed and finally looked at her standing helplessly in the middle of the pretty Persian carpet they'd ludicrously overpaid for in a bazaar in Turkey.

"Who was he, Peg? Who was he, this man that has lived with us all these years but never shown his face, dear God Peggy, who was he?"

She took a long moment to answer, afraid suddenly of conjuring the very ghost she'd sought to raise for years.

"His name was Brendan," she whispered and felt her own words come back and echo tinnily about the empty room.

"I know his name, Peg," Arthur said, *"you've cried it often enough in your sleep. I want to know who he was and why you've never been able to live without him."*

"Maybe if he'd lived I could have," she said, *"maybe if he'd lived I'd have been a good wife to you or maybe I wasn't ever going to be good for anyone whether he'd been on this earth or not. Who's to say?"* She felt very exhausted suddenly and went to sit on the bed beside Arthur. *"He was everything and when he died I was nothing and that's what you got in me Arthur, nothing."*

Arthur sighed, his hands lying flat on the bed's white coverlet, a bit of stray light catching and sparking off of his worn wedding band.

"The first time I saw you Margaret, the first time I thought I'd die just from the sheer shock of how beautiful you were. I loved you right then, I'd never known I was capable of that sort of feeling and I thought you were my moment of wonderful on this planet. I believed that I could love enough for two and that eventually my patience would win you over. Every once in awhile I was fool enough to think that it had. I remember everything about that first day, how you looked and how the light hit your face, how completely and utterly lost you seemed. I thought I could save you from yourself but I couldn't."

"The time for my redemption is long passed Arthur," she said and believed it.

"I know you've never really loved me Peg, but what about Siddy, did you ever really care for him?"

She winced; it had been a very direct blow he'd dealt her.

"Aye, I loved him in spite of my best efforts not to. I will always love him but

I'll never be the right mother for him."

"I was disappointed when he was born, you know," Arthur said and Peg felt herself go still with shock, Arthur had been both mother and father to Siddy for the first few months of his life, due to a black depression on her own part. He had never expressed anything but delight in him, delight, approval and unswerving love.

"I never knew," she said, "why?"

"Because I wanted a little girl," Arthur said, "I wanted a little you, a little redheaded wild girl that I could love and spoil shamelessly. When you were pregnant, I'd imagine her lying there inside your body and she grew for me from this tiny, silent water creature, glowing like a pearl, to a young woman who looked like flame when she moved and all the dreams I invented in between, the parties and the horse I'd give her on her seventh birthday, the schools and dresses and when the boys started coming around I'd disapprove of them all until I found one that would treat her like the queen that she was. And then Siddy was born and suddenly all those dreams turned to ashes and he was so much like me, I couldn't help but be disappointed. I even had a name for her you know."

She touched his shoulder and felt him shudder at the contact of her hand on his flesh. "What was it?"

"Julia," he replied and sounded like a very old man.

"I'm sorry Arthur, I really am. I wish I could have given you your daughter."

He nodded but she couldn't see whether he believed her or not.

"I think maybe, Margaret, that I just wanted to see love and approval coming out of a pair of eyes that were just like yours." He stood and faced her in the unforgiving light that spilled in from the hallway, "I always knew when we made love that you imagined I was someone else and after the first months of our marriage I even knew his name. And I knew it was the only way you could find any fulfillment in my arms. Did you have to pretend with that boy in the garden Peg? Or was he enough all by himself?"

"Don't Arthur, it was the only time and I—I hardly know what happened."

"Nice looking young man," Arthur said his voice brittle and dry as old bones, "does he look like your Brendan, does he remind you?"

She lifted her face up to him, knowing her age had settled upon her tonight with a vengeance, "He is his son."

"I see," he said and turned his back on her to make his way slowly downstairs. In the seven years which were all that was left of his life, he would never enter their bedroom again. He would never touch her body again, except for one dark night when he could not bear to be alone with his pain any longer.

In the morning he chopped down the lilac bushes and burned them, and when it was done he came in, had his tea and went into the office. He never said another word to her about what he'd seen that night in his garden.

For a man that had lived such a well-ordered and tidy existence Arthur had a very messy death. Messy, long and dreadfully painful. Two Aprils after the one *when he ceased to be her husband, he was diagnosed with cancer. It took five years to kill him. And in those five years Peg had been nurse, mother, sister and best friend to him. They'd finally had a marriage, one that she managed to find fulfillment and love in. They occupied the bottom floor of the house together, Arthur unable to climb the stairs after the third year of his illness and she having no desire to roam the empty rooms upstairs like a ghost. Siddy had never come home again, he'd finished out his schooling in Scotland and then matriculated up to Cambridge. Arthur went to see him at vacation time and after a few thwarted attempts, he'd not mentioned Siddy's mother to him again. Peg knew that in the world Siddy inhabited she no longer existed and thought that perhaps it was for the best. He came to see his father in his illness but only when Peg was out doing the few errands that she did.*

Arthur died in April and there was a certain poetic irony in that, which she could not miss. For she knew she'd killed him seven years before on an April night in a lilac-drenched, moon-ridden garden. He died with her by his side in the depths of the night. He'd asked her to open the windows and let the breeze in only an hour before and the room had filled at once with the perfume of the neighbor's flowers and he, generous to the bitter end, turned slowly, agonizingly and looking her full in the eyes said, 'You were my moment of wonderful, Margaret, you really were.' She had cried after that, cried in her husband's arms as she should have years before and Arthur died that way, trying to comfort a woman who had only lately become his wife.

Siddy avoided her at the funeral and sat in stony silence at the reading of the will. His father's estate was meticulously ordered and surprisingly large. Both his wife and son were well taken care of.

Peg stayed on in England for a few more months, tidied up various affairs, gave away or sold off the assorted odds and ends of a lifetime. The house brought in a very nice profit, which she put into a trust fund for any children Siddy might one day have. Trust Arthur to purchase a house whose value, through good and bad economic times, never decreased. Trust Arthur, she thought as she stood in the doorway of the home she'd shared with him for twenty-one years, yes trust Arthur. She had always trusted him, with her life really, a thing she had never known with Brendan. She hoped Arthur knew, in whatever sort of place he'd gone on to, that trust was a form of love so rare, it seemed infinitely precious now. She walked out the door to the taxi that waited on the street for her. Six hours later, she was in Spain and it would be many years before she went home to Ireland.

Peg sighed, the sun was beginning to crack the sky in the east and, facing morning, she felt quite tired. She supposed she could go and sleep for a bit, there was none to complain when she didn't rise, there was none to complain if she never got up again, come to that.

She stood, groaning at the pain in her hips, she ought to have known better than to stay in one position for so long.

She would have to forgive herself the lie to Terry, it wouldn't be right, not ever, to tell him about Brian. It would change his love for the boy, put a taint upon his memories. She had known Brian was dead; the copy of *Leaves of Grass* had come to her one summer day, when she was holidaying in Greece. Brian had asked that it be sent on to her. She had burned it in some symbolic madness of grief and tossed the ashes to the Aegean winds. She had loved him, loved him merely for being the son of Brendan, a millstone, she knew that he'd likely carried in many ways all his life. Loved him for being a boy who saw her as a woman one night in a garden.

In the north, a quarter mile up the road, smoke, soft and faintly brown, rose already from a stone chimney. She rested her face against the glass of the window, wondering why no one ever saw fit to prepare you for age, to tell you that the emotions would still be young, that the heart would still hurt, that the soul would long to flee the aging bones and skin and that *that* would be the damnation of age, unable to escape the prison of traitorous flesh. Unable to quit yearning for that which was no longer possible.

The sky was a drowsy pink as she settled herself into her bed and she smiled softly at the bit of world she could see from her bedroom window and then closed her eyes and slept the sleep of the old and unredeemed.

Part Three

Between the
Dark and Dawn

Chapter Thirty
The Brotherhood

"I MUST SAY YE DON'T SEEM TERRIBLY SURPRISED," Casey said somewhat indignantly to the man who occupied the seat across the round table from him. Seamus smiled and shook his head.

"Ye fergit I've seen ye with her, I didn't hold out a great deal of hope fer ye after Kevin's weddin'." His expression sobered and he drummed a pencil nervously against the table. "I'm sorry I didn't watch their backs better an' I'm sorry I jumped to conclusions about the nature—"

Casey held up a hand and shook his head, eyes opaque and steely. "I'm married to her now an' that's an' end to it, we'll not talk of it again."

"I wish ye happiness, man," Seamus said, "ye deserve it an' I've faith that ye can keep yer marriage separate from yer profession."

"Profession," Casey sighed and shook his head at the papers arrayed before him, "'tis a bit of a grand name fer an organization that is in the possession of five handguns, some," he bent his head to look at the papers again, "that seem to have come home with their owners from the Boer War. Can this be it?"

"'Tis," Seamus replied easily, as a man who senses the tide about to shift.

"And as fer this," Casey waved his hand over a small leather-bound green book, "who the hell can we even trust anymore."

"Yer lookin' at him," Seamus said "an' beyond that the feelers are out an' we'll have to see what that brings back in."

"I don't want a bunch of reckless kids, it's time we got back to runnin' this army like it wasn't some playground exercise."

"So are we clear then, ye've reviewed the material an' ye know where ye stand, are ye in with us or not?"

Casey looked hard at Seamus, "I was never out to my own knowledge, now if ye've heard somethin' to the contrary ye'd best tell me."

"Do ye understand what we're askin' ye here, man? There aren't many of us but we are agreed on one thing, young as ye are, yer the man to take us forward an' pull us out of the muck we've been sleepin' in these past ten years. If ye want to step down at this point, no one would blame ye. Ye've a beautiful wife an' yer young, yer future does not have to lie here. But if ye step up now there is no comin' back down those stairs man, not ever."

"Ye think I'm not aware of that, do ye remember who ye're talkin' to here? I may be the son of yer oldest friend Seamus, but if yer askin' me to do this then ye must fergit ye ever knew me as a child; I have not been one for a very long time. There can be no insubordination or second guessin' me."

Seamus nodded, silenced for a moment by the unflinching hardness in Casey's eyes. The boy was right, in his mind Casey was still Brian's hotheaded son and someone he could give fatherly advice to. There would be none of that now, it would alter their relationship in ways that neither of them was going to enjoy or feel entirely comfortable with, ever.

"Alright then, I apologize man, I meant no disrespect to ye."

Casey nodded, "Well then if that's clear ye can call the rest of them in an' we'll get on with this."

Seamus nodded and stood, "Dacy, ye'll tell the rest of them to come in."

A terse 'aye' sounded from the doorway and in a moment, the twelve chairs arranged around the wooden round table were filled with men who ranged in age from twenty through to sixty. They came from various walks of life, most were from a working-class Catholic background and had a pretty fair idea of exactly what they were fighting for and against. One or two could be accused of being idealists and though it was perhaps less clear what they were fighting for their commitment was no less. There were two representatives of the old guard, men who had known Casey's father and respected both the man and the vision he had presented to them once a long time ago. They only hoped the son had the balls and the brain to continue what his father had begun. There were a couple of new recruits, fresh-faced and full of fire, they would either have to be gently but firmly removed from the organization or tested beyond the limits of human endurance to prove their loyalty. Casey smiled slightly, altogether not a bad group. None were informants and none could be lured by the promise of money, they'd all been tested on that scale, discreetly and without many of them even suspecting what was up.

They were eyeing him up as well, trying to take his measure he knew. He laid his hands palm down on the table and took a deep breath, "Well then gentlemen shall we get down to it?"

There were a few nervous 'ayes', some coughing, a sigh from his right and then a slight commotion by the door.

"What is it, Dacy?" Seamus said as twelve bodies tensed and likely reconsidered the wisdom of being part of an illegal military body.

"'Tis Jimmy Mack, is he to be let in?"

Seamus missed only a beat before looking at Casey.

"Aye," said Casey, feeling a strange shiver root at the base of his spine.

Jimmy Mack sat, taking the thirteenth chair which had to be wedged between the two idealists and looking neither right nor left, stared directly at Casey. Casey met the challenge and there was a long silence, in which there was a great deal of withheld breath and then finally Jimmy Mack let his eyes slide sideways around the table.

"Ye'll perhaps be used to a different sort of organization," Casey said, "ye'll not be late again."

Jimmy barely inclined his head in a semblance of a nod.

"Well, on that note, perhaps we'd best begin with our personal code an' what is expected of each of ye, there will be no exceptions from this code an' I will follow it to the letter myself. First, there is to be no drinkin' on our time."

There was a collective gasp from around the table and a few pairs of raised eyebrows, then a low rumble of discontent.

Casey held up one hand, "Talk induced by the drink is a dangerous situation in any organization, in a military organization it is suicide. We cannot afford to have clouded minds or loose tongues, which brings me to my second point. Pillow talk is temptin' an' bein' recently married myself I can understand the need to unburden yerself. Don't do it. Yer wives, sweethearts, children, parents, ye name them, they are not te hear one word from ye on this subject. Is that understood?"

There was a chorus of 'ayes' and 'mmphms' from around the table.

"Thirdly, I will not tolerate disobedience in any form, this ramshackle little outfit will become professional if I have te drag ye all kickin' an' screamin'. That means no lateness," he looked pointedly at Jimmy Mack, who stared insolently back, "no talkin' amongst yerselves. If ye have a problem with me, then ye are te take it up with me immediately, I want no dissension amongst the ranks. Ye'll be paid a small salary when ye are on Army business, when yer not yer on yer own. Now I trust gentlemen that ye can be grownup an' mind yer manners. Ye'll be workin' by yerselves fer the most part an' there will be no fraternizin' amongst the lot of ye off the job. It's too much of a risk, if one of us is caught we do what we can to help but if it means revealin' ourselves then I'm afraid if yer apprehended yer on yer own." He took a deep breath, "Now I'm about to move onto exactly what our plans are an' how we are going to implement them, so any man here who's got so much as a nigglin' doubt in the back of his head should go, any man who's not willin' to stand his life fer this country an' our objectives, any man who's afraid of sittin' behind bars must in all good conscience leave this room now." Several minutes elapsed during which there was a great deal of throat clearing, bums shifting to and fro on chairs and deep breaths drawn, however not one man left the room or showed the slightest inclination that he wished to do so.

"Now as plans go, mine is fairly simple, it consists of three points," Casey held up three fingers to underscore his words, "One, defense, two, retaliation, an' three, offense. These three principles of warfare are put into action at the time I deem ready. Overall it's a five-year plan. Now during this first year we set up our defenses, we make our connections within the community, we establish no-go zones for the British army, the UVF an' the RUC. It is vital, an' I cannot stress this enough, that we establish our links with the community. If we do not get back the support of our own people then we have lost this little war before it has even begun. To this end, I want relationships established with the People's Democracy, the civil rights movement, an' as much as some of us might like to we cannot ever underestimate the power of the Church, any priests with Republican leanings can be an invaluable resource for us. They know the people an' how the politics of each neighborhood works. An' in this business it never hurts to have someone who's got an in with God."

He looked around the table meeting each set of eyes individually and finding no questioning of his authority there, until he met the cold blue eyes of Jimmy Mack and felt without question they had let a maniac into their midst. Maniacs, he knew, had their uses; they just had to be handled with great delicacy.

"I think there can be no question that the state of our weaponry has gone far beyond pitiful an' is teetering on the nonexistent. We are at present awaitin' a shipment from America, the details of which have yet to be fully worked out."

"An' where is the money comin' from for these guns?" asked one of the older men, a hard-line Republican Casey remembered from his childhood.

"There's money comin' from the States. American businessmen who still have a certain fondness for the ancestral sod, have been fairly generous towards our cause. It has to be strained through a variety of channels before we can lay hands on it however. An' it'll have to be split in several directions once we do. We'll need it, not only for weaponry, but to bribe an' cajole, an' a good bit of it will go to keep various mouths shut an' eyes blind. As to how an' where the weapons will be transferred, that will be only the concern of the men directly involved in the transaction. All of ye," his gaze swept the table again, "will be on a strictly need-to-know basis. If it isn't vital to yer own piece of ground, ye will not need to know.

"Point two is retaliation, they strike we strike back twice as hard, force is met with force. For every man we lose, they lose two. We show them in no uncertain terms that we mean business, that the new IRA is not to be taken for some harmless bunch of old men reliving their glory days in pubs and backrooms. Now, I hope none of us is fool enough to believe that once the British are out, our problems will be solved; however it is the first step. We do not, an' I repeat this as it's a very important point, we do not take any initiative in striking first, there's other priorities that for now must come to the fore."

"What makes ye so certain that ye can accomplish with some simple three pronged plan what we've not been able to accomplish in the last eight hundred years?"

Casey turned his head slowly in the direction of the speaker, a man who though young, was likely a few years older than himself.

"I am not here," he began slowly, "to fill yer heads with illusion an' dreams, that is how we differ from the Dublin boys; I know we may not revolutionize the country, but that isn't our job. Our job is to support an' make way for the people who will. Ye may not have noticed, lads," and his voice was heavy with sarcasm, "but the earth is tremblin' out there for some people, for thousands of them walkin' arm an' arm down the streets there is a smell of change in the air. What I am suggestin' is that we give them the means, clear the road of all obstacles so to speak an' they will find a way to make the real revolution."

Heads nodded around the table, men who had seen the stunted promise of the fifties come to naught but were not so disillusioned as to not see that this time it was different. This decade held within it some burning promise of hope, people believed that the time and the place had come since it had not come nor been since 1916.

"Are ye sayin' I have to wait fer the fockin' bastards to run a gun up me before I'm allowed to give them the time of day?" Jimmy Mack asked a lazy insolence tainting his voice.

"I'm sayin'," Casey said turning a hard face on the man he already wished he'd never laid eyes on, "that ye can take yer unthinkin' arse out of here unless ye've somethin' useful to contribute to the conversation."

Jimmy muttered something under his breath that sounded distinctly uncomplimentary.

"What did ye say?" Casey asked, voice deceptively calm.

"I said that I'd heard ye were married an' that marriage can make a man soft," Jimmy Mack drawled, his blue eyes never flinching from Casey's dark, hard stare.

"If that's what ye think lad, then yer goin' about it all wrong," Seamus said, desperately trying to inject some humor and defuse the situation before it exploded in all their faces.

"You," Casey said sitting back in his chair, "may get the fock out of here before I break yer neck with my own two hands." There was no anger in his voice, no levity to indicate that he was anything other than completely and deadly serious.

Jimmy, in his first smart move of the night, elected to leave before Casey made good on a threat that did not seem idle, even to his slow moving brain.

"Have the rest of ye anything to say?" Casey asked after Jimmy Mack's form was hastened in its exit by the none too gentle hand of Dacy. His question was met with silence.

"Aye then, we'll continue, the third an' final point I wish to present is offense. To that end I suggest we take the war onto British soil, when our situation is stable enough here to warrant it." He was met by mild shock on all the faces surrounding the table. "The truth of the matter is that we Irishmen can kill each other 'til there's not a one of us standing an' it won't matter a great deal to the powers that be in England, but when the blood an' terror is affectin' their own people it will be a different matter altogether. I don't want civilians hit but we'll discuss strategy when the time comes an' I don't see that happenin' for a couple of years. To that end," he produced from his side twelve books bound in green cloth, "ye will study this like it's the bible. Ye will know it like ye know the color of the sky an' grass an' then ye will burn it. Commit it to memory an' then set it to fire.

"Gentlemen, I've said my piece an' now it's yer turn." Casey laid his hands on the table in front of him, broad and capable hands and Seamus eyed them with a settled feeling. The boy had the back for it and the brain whereas his father had one but not the other. This one was built in the mold of his legendary grandfather and for a moment, it made Seamus pity him.

Discussion buzzed and swirled about the table, some men cautious, some caught up in the excitement of having found the man to lead them. Seamus sat quiet, an old soldier who understood that some wars are never won but must be fought regardless. In the faces and voices around him he saw the required elements, commitment beyond reason, a dogged persistence in the face of insanity, some uneducated and ill-read, the backs upon which revolution has always been built. He wondered tiredly as the meeting began to break up, how many would be dead and how many behind bars come ten years hence. Then he decided as he looked at Casey shrugging into his coat, making the shift already from commander to infatuated husband, that he really didn't want an answer to that particular question.

THE BELFAST THAT CASEY RETURNED TO IN 1968 was not the Belfast he'd left in 1962. Even Ireland, lost like a jewel on the Atlantic, could not ignore the seismic quakes that were shaking the world out of a long slumber induced by the horror and exhaustion of two world wars. The times, in the words of a folksinger he'd heard, truly were 'achangin'. He'd felt it first in the waters of nationalism, so long tepid to the touch, now hot and ready to boil over and take a nation with it. In the waning days of the sixties, it seemed that anything was possible. Not in America anymore, there the revolution was beginning to wane, the conflict in Vietnam tearing it asunder and leaving a generation bereft and disillusioned. Ireland, slower to change, was only now beginning the slow grinding shift on its axis.

Casey knew he would have to be a fool not to anticipate change, even in Ireland where the Church had held back progress for hundreds of years. But even he, with a shrewd intellect and a capacity to embrace change without actually succumbing to it, was surprised by the feeling that had gripped Belfast. The city was the flashpoint for a nation more than ready to catch fire. For the government, the old policy of standing on the necks of the oppressed, which had served them so well in the past, now no longer held the power of intimidation. Television was in great part to blame or praise for this, depending on which side of the coin you were looking at. Coverage of riots begat more riots which in turn begat more coverage and so the wheel of protest turned ever more quickly. Thousands of bodies shouting 'We shall overcome,' could turn a man's head, could make a man believe that all roads now ran downhill to a glorious future. But Casey was not a man easily turned and so watched with caution and yet could not quite squelch a yearning that rose up and ached inside him as he saw the great tidal surge of youth cresting across a nation some had thought irreversibly sunk in old age and half-baked myths. They were not quite his generation though and he could not hope in the way that pure youth finds so easy. It was simpler, though perhaps wiser to be cynical in a system where a march for peace was disrupted by police, and an Orangeman's parade, long a symbol of oppression, blood and bigotry was led by the future Prime Minister and guarded by six hundred armed police and complimented by dogs and armored cars. The right to oppress would be protected, served and cosseted by the fearful and the right to be free and live as man was born to would surely be crushed and violated by the same.

Casey understood these things but knew that not to fight, even in the face of such odds, was to lay down and beg for a beating. He saw, as well, that the Celtic Twilight that Yeats once dreamed of was actually a possibility. The era of 'the Big House' epitomized by the huge Anglo-Irish estates was over and the men that came from that world were no longer fit nor needed to lead.

Regardless of the rhetoric that was always applied to revolution despite the largeness or smallness of it, Casey knew that in his own particular country it came down to two very simple things, jobs and housing and the ability to achieve the skills that were necessary to acquire either of these things. In a system, though, where one-third of the vote managed to get two-thirds of the seats in parliament even such basic fundamentals seemed far beyond reach. Such a system bred hopelessness deep within the bone and to turn apathy, which was fairly disguised as a realistic view, was no easy task. Protestants hired Protestants and they liked it that way. They felt their superiority was a given, something they were born with and like any group in such a tenuous position they would hang on with tooth and nail before they'd give an inch.

Catholics did not get a fair crack at the vote, therefore did not get the jobs and therefore did not get the housing. It was an ugly cycle that no one could see a way out of. He was the first to grant there were no simple solutions and that anything less than actually ripping the country apart and waiting for the blood and smoke to clear was not going to achieve much of anything.

So, if indeed the dogs of war must be let slip, then he was the man to untie the leashes. He came from a long line of men who did what needed to be done and didn't make a fuss about it. The speeches and glorying of ideals were best left to other men, but if something needed to be done, if someone needed to strike the first blow in order to crack the long, insular column of Northern Ireland tradition, then he certainly knew how to wield the hammer.

Unrest was brewing, and the head of militancy was rising from its dreamless slumber. Across the north were disparate people, like pearls waiting to be strung together to form a long unbroken chain, that would not, this time, be broken by those who felt themselves the rulers by divine right. The time for the old ways was gone and those who grasped these things to their chest, like children in a sandbox, were going to have to learn to let go or get the hell out of the way. The back of British supremacy, be it of the Loyalist persuasion or the Conservative Party mold, had long needed to be broken and if someone died and there was blood upon the hands of others—well no sacrifice came without its price, being a Riordan he understood that all too well. It was long past time for Ireland to emerge from the shadows of eight hundred years oppression, time to become a real nation and not just a sentimental dream of green hills and fairy stories in the eyes of the world. Ireland, lovely and wistful, but easily forgotten, even by those who should know better than to forget.

No longer, he had promised himself, on the night he'd returned to his own country and seen the lights of the city he'd been born to shining before him. No longer, he'd sworn when he'd seen his brother ablaze with student slogans and the pure fire of youthful ideal. No longer, he'd said to himself on the day that he married the girl of his dreams, dreams he'd never thought he'd a right to. No longer to the bruises of oppression, the degradation and despair of unemployment, the hopelessness of living in a gerrymandered system where your vote meant no more than in a dictatorship. No longer to peace without justice, which really wasn't peace at all, only a mock-up for the powerful to hide behind in their comfortable homes and schools and jobs. No longer would he accept being treated as less than a man, as less than free.

No longer.

Chapter Thirty-one
Divorce Me, Darling

S PRING HAD ARRIVED ON THE HILL. A cold, wet, damp spring filled with the scent of beginnings. First feathers, greening grass, burgeoning tendrils of vine and leaf. She would miss all of this, Pamela thought, as she opened the footgate. Miss the cypresses with sun sifting down through their ancient branches, miss the isolation, the swift smell of the pines, the wind that never seemed to descend into the valley and the city below. She'd miss the books and the chats and the quiet evenings with only the crackle of a fire and the sound of Jamie slowly turning the pages of a book. She'd miss the stars and the lilt of his voice telling her the stories of the sky. But, she stopped and gazed at the house, its long windows bathed in light, the cream lines of it softened as winter's chill gave way to spring's soft aura, she would miss him most of all.

She found him in the study, as she had supposed she might. There was no fire in the hearth, only ashes, dark and cold. Jamie sat beside the empty fireplace, a near empty bottle of whiskey at hand. He rose as she entered the room, a gentleman first and foremost.

"You'll have to forgive me; I wasn't expecting to see anyone today. I'd left instructions—"

"That you weren't to be disturbed, I know. Maggie thought perhaps I might be the one exception to the rule," she said and sat opposite him, arranging the delicate folds of her dress around her.

"How well pale colors become you," he said, "such contrast, I suppose."

"Compared to what?" she asked, "The shade of my soul?"

Humor, she quickly realized, was a mistake.

"Are you quite certain you want to drag the state of your conscience into this?" he asked, a dark, refracting fire simmering low in his eyes.

"Am I to take it that you think I'm suffering from pangs of guilt?"

"Inconvenient damned things, emotions, but nevertheless it would seem rather inescapable. Of course one has to wonder just where the guilt is directed."

"And why would I feel guilty?"

"Because dear girl, men are really rather conventional creatures and prefer the woman they marry to be in love with them, solely."

"I do love my husband," she said stiffly, "I don't know why you'd presume otherwise."

Light, filtered through the willows outside the walls, played fretfully across the bindings of books behind Jamie's head and slanted, dappled and rippling across his face, alternating in shadow and stippled gold.

"Because it's not so tidy as all that, is it?" he said and she began to fear the strange glittering in his eyes, the fire in the air that signified an abundance of drink. "Because we don't love who we're supposed to, do we? I mean look at our own small circle, would you? My wife has decided to love Jesus, to devote her life to an idea, the embodiment of madness that is swiftly going out of fashion. My wife who loved marriage, or at least some spent idea of it and all its darker accoutrements, she embraced those and she embraced me, in times," he saluted her with a bitter rise of his scotch, "less golden than these."

It was more than mere drunkenness she knew fueling his bitterness, the spite in which his words were well-bathed.

"Jamie, I think perhaps," she made to leave her chair, "I should go now."

"I think," he imitated her words and tone with prim exaggeration, "you won't. I think perhaps," the green eyes blinked slowly and menacingly, "you will allow me the dignity of saying my piece, you will grant me the favor," his voice lowered to a chill hiss, "of your listening ears. I think perhaps," his voice spun the words like sugar through vitriolic acid, "you owe me that little thing."

She slid back into her chair, wishing the opulent, buttery wings of it would allow her to disappear into some altogether more comfortable world.

"Fine," she said tightly, "speak your piece."

Jamie raised one fine golden eyebrow at her. "Thanks for the permission slip but I don't actually need it. I'm not certain what you expected here today, that I should say congratulations warmly, isn't it lovely that you've married a terrorist, what's your household in need of, guns or rounds of ammunition?"

"I didn't expect," her voice was grating on the edge of tears, "a damned thing."

"Didn't you?" he smiled. "Don't lie Pamela, you don't do it half so well as the rest of us."

"I came to tell you I was married and to say that circumstances made it such that I cannot come back here to work."

He tapped his hands together lightly, "Applause if you're wondering," he said to her confused stare, " for your pretty words, which mean exactly nothing. Smoke and mirrors are my stock in trade, dear girl, I'm not likely to be fooled by terse little rehearsed lines."

"Jamie, please will you just say what it is you wanted to say?"

"Why the hurry," he asked giving her a look that trod the border between cold and fury, "can't wait for the last word to be uttered so you can run home to hubby? But please take a moment and define circumstances for me, would you?" He balanced his glass on the palm of one hand as condensation pearled and gelled and rolled down to form a rivulet of water that dripped from his hand.

"Just that Casey and I feel that it would be best if I no longer worked here."

"Casey and I, or just Casey?" he asked tossing the words into the air lightly and letting them all fall, as intended, into her court.

"Casey and I," she said keeping her eyes fixed on the water that dropped steadily from his hand now.

"Very loyal of you," he said bitingly, "but you'll need it, the loyalty, blind and otherwise, it'll be most important in the years to come, won't it? Loyalty will keep you warm when he doesn't come home at night, it'll keep you snug and secure when he can't look you in the eye and won't answer your questions. And even you, my curious darling, even you will learn not to ask those questions. And what of the night when he just doesn't come home ever again, what then, what will loyalty have bought you, other than early widowhood?"

"What would you have had me do, Jamie?" she asked in a level tone, "Wait for you to quit anguishing over your sons and lost wife until you felt capable of loving someone again? What if that never happens? Is a life of waiting in vain better than making the best of the situation you are in? Have you found it to be so yourself?"

"Did you marry him to spite me?" Jamie asked his tone a little less malevolent.

"No more than I would marry any man to spite you, but I love him a great deal, more than I think you give credit for. Jamie." She sighed, "What is the point of this? I've lived with him for months now, you had to see this was inevitable, this is where I've been headed with him from the start."

"The point," Jamie said leaning towards her so that she could smell the whiskey on his breath, "the point is I've gotten a divorce and I'm not finding it as liberating as I'd hoped."

"Divorce? I thought your marriage had been annulled," she said in confusion.

"It was. The annulment was enough for a long time, there was never, shall we say, any impetus to make it more formal, to sever the ties in a way that I felt was irrevocable."

"I don't understand, Jamie."

"Don't you? Or do you just not want to understand?" His eyes had turned an unnerving shade of deep, hard green, the hand that gripped the glass strained to the point of shattering the crystal it held.

"You told me to go away Jamie. You said you could not love me and that I was not to love you. I thought you meant it."

"And I thought your feelings were genuine."

"You're drunk," she said angrily.

"Yes," he smiled, a poisonous show of teeth and parted lip. "Yes, I am. I'm drunk and I'm being honest. It's a change for me, I've gotten so used to lying I can hardly recognize the appearance of truth much less the actuality of it."

"What is it you are trying to say, Jamie?" She made an effort to gentle her voice, perhaps to undermine some of his hostility.

"Don't try to handle me Pamela, I'm better at that particular game than anyone you've ever known."

"I'm going," she said rising quickly from the chair and knocking his drink flying from his hand in her haste.

"I'm sorry. I'll get something, a cloth."

"Don't." Jamie's voice was ragged, exhaustion breaking through the sharp edges.

"It'll ruin the rug; it'll only take a minute."

"I said don't, I don't give a good goddamn about the carpet at present."

"Alright," she replied quietly, standing still in the pooling, sinking whiskey.

"Do you know what it is I'm trying to tell you?" Jamie asked, willing her to look up and meet his eyes.

"I know what you think you want to say, but it's maybe just the whiskey talking."

"Will you please look at me, Pamela?" his voice had softened, drifting down around the edges beyond anger and spite.

She looked up as he'd requested and he almost wished she hadn't such was the misery in her face.

"Do you think I don't know my own feelings?" he asked, standing, crossing to her and taking her arms in the grip of his hands.

"No I don't," she said firmly, two white spots blazing along her cheekbones. "I think you're panicking because I've distracted you these last few months and now I'm leaving and you'll have to face yourself again. It scares you."

"I love you," he said, standing very, very still as if constrained by the air itself. "Don't you understand?"

"What I understand, Jamie, is that you couldn't feel that, nor certainly say it until you knew there was no possibility of my being able to accept and return those feelings equally. And that's not love, that's fear."

"I divorced my wife Pamela before I knew you were married, before any of this seemed impossible."

"Your wife, listen to yourself Jamie, you still call her your wife, not ex nor quite former. You are still a married man in your heart and no amount of legal papers is going to change that."

"Now who's afraid?" Jamie asked bitingly.

"I asked you once," she said softly, tears gathering in the corner of her eyes, "not to hold me in your hands if you couldn't hold me in your heart. Now I'm asking you not to hold me in your heart because you can't hold me in your hands any longer."

"And if I find I can't let go?"

"You can," she said and gently disengaged her arms from his fingers.

"Do you love him?"

"Do you really want me to answer that?"

"No, I don't suppose I do."

Through the canted windows of the study came a sighing breeze, fluttering the pages of an open book, turning it on to the next chapter without the allowance of finishing the present one. A breath of lilacs, white and heady, accompanied it.

"You came with the spring, perhaps it is fitting that you leave with it as well." His hands dropped to his sides, the long, graceful fingers unfolding and releasing. He drew a ragged breath and then continued in a voice so tired and low she had to strain to hear. "I apologize for my behavior; the whiskey can hardly take the blame for such a display. From knight errant to court fool in one move, how swiftly the fates canter across our little stage."

The telephone rang and he cursed softly.

"Answer it, it may be important," she said, welcoming the momentary respite.

The conversation heard only from her end was terse, accomplished mostly in one word sentences.

"Excuse the interruption," he said only a minute later. "It seems my bid to cast myself into the political ring has been accepted."

She gasped and looked at him in shock.

"The look on your face isn't terribly flattering. Though perhaps you have to be forgiven for supposing I would let the fair Reverend have his way with my father's old district. I had, however, planned to get off the fence in all manner of ways today. I suppose though, considering recent developments, this will have to suffice."

"Congratulations," she said, through a throat that felt suddenly tight.

"Congratulations to you as well," he said, "and I mean that. I hope, if this is what you want it will make you happy."

She nodded, "Are we saying goodbye then, Jamie?"

A long moment stretched between them, sundered by sunlight and dancing dust motes, before Jamie replied quietly and in a tone of voice she was accustomed to, "I rather think we must, don't you?"

She reached up quickly, touched the side of his face and said, "God go with you wherever the journey may lead."

She fled the room and was gone before she could hear him say, in perfect and unfettered Arabic, "And also with you, my love."

From under his desk, where he'd lain in atypical good behavior throughout the whole miserable interview, Montmorency emerged. He padded over to Jamie and laid his head against his leg, wagging his tail in commiseration. Jamie reached down and patted his piebald head.

"Well Monty, we have the consolation of trying. And trying, as they say, at least requires action."

In answer, Montmorency walked slowly over to the study door, lay down, put his muzzle upon his brindled paws and sighed a thoroughly heartfelt, heartbroken canine sigh.

"My thoughts exactly," Jamie said.

Chapter Thirty-two
Sinking Ships

FOR A MAN WHO'D NO GREAT FONDNESS FOR WATER Casey Riordan seemed to be spending an inordinate amount of time in it. Submerged up to his neck, the hour somewhere on the wrong side of midnight and not a damn boat in sight.

"Where in Christ is he?" he asked through clenched teeth and blue lips.

"Do I," Seamus spit a duck feather out of his mouth, "look as if I have any fockin' idea?"

"Rhetorical question," Casey muttered and hugged himself tighter against the frigid water.

"Five more minutes?" Seamus asked hopefully.

"Ten," Casey amended, "we can't afford to miss this shipment."

"Christ I'm like to freeze my balls off in eight," Seamus sniffed for emphasis.

"Think warm thoughts," Casey said unsympathetically.

Silence reigned for the next two minutes, during which time Casey thought many dark things about the absent boat and its absent skipper and Seamus stifled an overwhelming desire to sneeze.

"How's the wife?" he asked *sotto voce*.

"The wife," Casey said, "is fine."

"Are ye happy then?"

Casey turned and threw a black look in Seamus' general direction, "What the hell is this, highschool confession time?"

"Just tryin' to make conversation," Seamus said with an injured sniff, "yer mighty touchy these days."

"Mighty touchy? I'm up to my damn neck in freezin' cold water, a boatload of guns is late an' if it doesn't show up in the next five minutes it's likely the both of us will be spendin' the next twenty years in prison."

"Shh—" Seamus grabbed his arm suddenly, "someone's watchin' us."

"What, where?" Casey instinctively dropped lower, until there was only a hair between his nose and the water.

"I don't know, it's only a feelin', the back of my neck is creepin' like a caveman's with a sabertooth tiger behind him."

Casey, ignoring his own discomfort, focused on the back of his own neck and felt the small hairs rising. Seamus was right, someone and not too distant, was watching them.

"Yer right, I can feel it too."

"We're trapped," Seamus said with a grim finality.

"No we're not, I'd rather die than go back to jail," Casey replied just as grimly.

"What do ye suggest we do?"

"We turn around slowly, *very* slowly an' then we assess the situation before we do anything."

"Right," Seamus sounded less than convinced of the genius of this particular plan but took a deep breath and began to turn with Casey. The feeling of being watched intensified with each second that passed. Were there guns trained on them? Would they open fire first and ask questions later? Casey closed his eyes as he made the last step that turned him a full one hundred and eighty degrees. He then opened them and had to fight the desire to laugh. In front of him, floating serenely, heads cocked in curiosity was a three-man flotilla of ducks.

"Ducks," Casey said just as Seamus sneezed.

"I'm allergic, just the thought of them damn feathers is enough to set me off," Seamus said and sneezed again, a strange gurgling noise as he'd lowered his head into the water.

"Stop that would ye? We'll get caught for certain."

"I can't help it," Seamus said, "I've always been allergic, my Auntie Kate," *sneeze,* "who lived in Canada," *sneeze,* "sent us a down quilt," *sneeze,* "when I was a boy," *sneeze,* "an' we all shared the same bed," *sneeze,* "the four of us, head to toe," *sneeze,* "It was the height of luxury," *sneeze,* "an' the thought of sleepin' under it," *sneeze,* "was like heaven itself had floated," *sneeze,* "down onto our bed," *sneeze.* "I almost died under the," *sneeze,* "damned thing. Nearly squeezed my lungs shut."

"Bless ye," Casey said darkly, fluttering the water near the ducks in an effort to shoo them off. They merely cocked their heads in the other direction and happily rode the waves he caused with his hands.

"Move."

Both he and Seamus sidled away from the ducks, trying not to leave the cover of the overhanging willows whose branches trailed along the water's surface. The ducks followed. By now, Seamus had dissolved into a flurry of sneezes, one following so close upon the last that he sounded as if he were alternatively choking and drowning.

"Hold yer breath," Casey said.

"For what?" Seamus managed to gasp out between paroxysms.

"For this," Casey replied and placing a large hand on Seamus' head shoved him under water. After a last gasping wheeze, Seamus subsided under Casey's hand.

He listened carefully to the night around him, the ducks were silent behind him but he'd heard something under Seamus' sneezes or perhaps he'd felt it. It came again just as Seamus emerged from the water, took a breath and plunged under once more.

Casey stilled himself, forcing his heartbeat to slow and his breath to become even. There was a definite throb in the water, a gentle susurration that was too rhythmic to be made by nature. It was the feel of an engine slicing through water. He filled his lungs with air and bent his knees down until only his eyes were above water, with measured and agonizingly slow movement he walked forward through the screen of branches.

He could see at once that something was strange because the boat moved all wrong. Erratically and too fast, pushing with great speed toward them. He stepped back through the water, reached down and grabbed Seamus by the hair and moving as fast as the water would allow, ran for shore.

They hit ground on their knees. Seamus, understanding only that something had gone awry, bolted to his feet and ran with Casey.

Behind them the boat struck the shore and halted with a grinding crunch, then there was only time for a heartbeat and thunder split the air forcefully with a great cracking boom followed by a flash of light that temporarily blinded the two of them.

Casey turned back to see long flames cleaving into the darkness, burning deep in violet and blue tongues.

"Oh Jesus," he whispered, "Jesus—the guns."

"The guns?" Seamus said incredulously, "Someone just tried to kill us. An' what about the pilot of the boat."

"Already dead," Casey said harshly, "saw him tied on deck, couldn't see clearly but it looked as if his throat were slit."

"We've got to get out of here," Seamus was still low to the ground, his head bobbing around in an effort to scan the area.

"We don't move just yet," Casey whispered, "they may think we're dead in the water right now but if we start movin' they'll know for certain we're not."

Seamus nodded his agreement. They'd hung onto some small luck and landed in a hollow of land, bumped and ridged around them, unpredictable enough to make them seem no more than another knobbly bit of grass and rock. Or so they hoped. Behind them a large hill rose, close enough to provide them some cover and not allow anyone to sneak up on their backs.

A chill wind played across the valley, drying clothes stiff and icy, forming bits of ice in hair. They each lay on their bellies, flat to the ground, hands parting tufts of dry and brittle grass so they could see the lake and the flames that still shot twenty feet high into the night.

Hell must be like this, Casey thought to himself, ignoring the cramping in his legs and the numbness in his fingers, able to see the fire but unable to partake of its warmth. In his mind's eye he could see the guns, gone now, money the Brotherhood didn't have and certainly couldn't afford, drifting down in the form of carbolic ash. A haul of fifty AK-47's, Kalashnikov rifles named for the Soviet who'd designed them. Two hundred pounds of ammunition, sharp-nosed 7.62 mm bullets, designed for the dark barrel in single shots or fully automatic spray. Simple to operate, easy to maintain, the Arab who'd sold it to him, had said. The weapon of choice in North Vietnam at present. Inferior only to the M-16 which had proved too pricey and far too risky to obtain. Gone, if indeed they'd ever been loaded onto the boat in the first place. And a man dead, one he'd never met, paid well for his averted eyes but not, in the light of events, well enough.

How long they lay in the grass Casey never knew, he was only aware of an iron-edged cold creeping up into his bones, and a terrible lassitude falling through him that warned of impending hypothermia. Seamus, thankfully, had stopped sneezing and lay silently beside him eyelids fluttering closed every now and again. Casey would reach over and jostle him before sleep actually set in. Casey didn't see morning come, didn't see it creep, chill-fingered and softly frosted over the hills, tumbling slowly down into the valley and putting a heavy breath over the lake. He only woke up when he felt himself being eyed so intently that the hairs at the base of his neck rose up. It took a moment to place his bearings, to focus and find himself staring eye to eye with one of their feathered friends from the previous night.

"G'morning," Casey said blearily. The duck ruffled its feathers and quacked.

Seamus was nowhere to be seen. Casey shot a quick look over the surroundings. A fine, scudding smoke still rose off the boat here and there, parts of it already sunk and gone. The area was still, a faint light soft as talc drifting down between the bare branches of the trees, the grass crystallized and brittle. Spring's early promise had been premature. He tried to get up on his knees and found his shirt had frozen to the ground and was now unwilling to part with it. His mind was sharply clear and from this he knew the dreaded nibbling fog of hypothermia hadn't settled in.

"Seamus," he hissed, loudly as he dared.

"Present an' accounted for," came a voice behind him, startling him into rearing back and half tearing the buttons off his shirt.

"Christ, are ye tryin' to give me a heart attack," Casey said irritably, moving his fingers to see if the cold had done permanent damage.

"Yer too young an' fit for a heart attack," Seamus replied dryly tossing Casey a warm bun and then passing over a steaming cup of tea.

"Why the hell did ye let me fall asleep, I could've died of hypothermia," he accepted the stream of liquid into his tea that Seamus poured from a small hip flask.

"Ye've been asleep for an entire fifteen minutes."

"Where'd ye get the food?"

"Shop ten minutes trot back that way, noticed it on our way in yesterday."

"An' no one mentioned the explosion?"

"Not a word, I think the hills kept the sound localized."

"Well it'll be discovered soon enough, we've got to get clear of here."

"Ye think it's safe now?"

"As safe as it's goin' to get. I still can't believe ye left me there freezin' to death."

"Ye were puttin' out heat like hell's own kitchen, yer daddy was the same, warmth to spare."

They ate their buns and drank their tea quickly, grateful for the small glow of warmth the brandied tea provided, however temporary.

Casey polished off the last of his drink and rose, stamping his feet to put some feeling back into them.

"Ready?"

"Aye."

He set off downslope towards the lake, morning mist picking at his clothes and settling on his skin in clammy sheaves.

"Wrong way, man," Seamus said uneasily.

"Not leavin' here without checkin' for the guns."

"They'll not have survived the explosion." Casey continued down into the water, ankle deep in it in the frigid morning.

"Daft bugger," Seamus muttered and then followed.

Little remained. Charred hunks of wood, the steering shaft, melted and twisted into grotesque sculpture had been thrown to shore along with a piece of rope liquefied until it resembled a blob of plastic.

Seamus saw that Casey had removed his shoes, socks and pants and left them on dry ground, he was stripping his shirt off now, tossing it back where it floated down like a blue cotton cloud onto the shoes.

"What the hell are ye doin'?" Seamus demanded, the small heat the brandy had given fading already.

"Humor me man, this'll only take a minute." Casey dove under the water, leaving only a faint ripple in his wake. He was under a long time and Seamus could feel his nerves begin to jump in protest. Twice Casey's head emerged and twice it went back down again. Minutes ticked by and Seamus felt the prickle of imaginary eyes on his back. On the third dive Casey stayed down so long Seamus began to think he'd have to go in after him. However just as he was taking his shoes off Casey emerged, streaming and blue with cold, skin marbled in the gray morning light.

"Well?" Seamus' voice was tight around chattering teeth.

"Well nothin', which is what I thought."

"What the hell do ye mean?"

"Nothin', no goddamn guns to be found. There weren't any on the boat to begin with."

"How can ye be certain of that? The explosion an' the fire could have melted them down."

Casey eyed him with a bemused look. "Ye must think me a rank amateur. I gave very specific instructions that the guns were to be crated in a box that was to be built into the boat, so that should something unforeseen happen," he paused to yank his pants up over goosebump stippled legs, "the guns would stand a chance of survivin' or not bein' discovered. The box is there alright, but it's empty an' always was."

"Christ," Seamus said in a whisper that sounded like the last of the air hissing from a balloon. "All that money."

"Money's fine," Casey said giving his shoelace a vicious yank, "it's in place with a middleman who wasn't to move with it until I gave the go ahead. We've got bigger problems than that now. The gentlemen who sold us the guns will be expectin' the money for goods delivered, regardless of who has the weapons in their possession."

"Do ye mean to say—" Seamus stopped, horrified suddenly at the scenarios that seemed to be presenting themselves.

"Aye, the question we need to answer is who has those guns, how did they find out we were expectin' delivery on them an' why exactly did they want to kill us?"

"Christ," Seamus said again, the full ramifications of the situation threatening to drop him to his knees where he stood.

"Aye," Casey did up the last buttons on his shirt, "ye'd best say all the prayers ye know Seamus, because we need any help we can get. Now let's get the hell out of here."

They followed a rift between two hills whose tops were shrouded in mist. Seamus cast a glance over his shoulder to where the fog still rose in vertical lines off the face of the water, for a moment it seemed as if some of it clung to the air, took form and drifted towards them, shifting, shaping, warning. He shivered, a convulsion of nerve-endings that had nothing to do with the cold. But when he looked back again, it was only fog.

Chapter Thirty-three
Well but Not Wisely

SEDITION, JAMIE HAD LONG AGO DECIDED, WAS A MOST EXHAUSTING BUSINESS and the complexities of it were best followed by a glass of whiskey, a volume of Keats and a stretch out on the sofa by the fire. He was barely thus employed when the long and annoying peal of the doorbell rang through the house. The staff was off for the night and he himself expecting no one. He resolutely closed his eyes, intent on unconsciousness but the bell continued to toll. He glanced irritably at the clock, just the wrong side of midnight, hardly the hour for innocent doings, which only made it the more likely that the business that lay on the far side of the door was of a nature he most devoutly wished to avoid.

At length the bell ceased its plaintive chorus and Jamie, with a sigh of relief, sank deeper towards oblivion allowing the day's events and oddities to scroll off into the whiskey's fog like ticker tape unfurling across an empty floor. A moment later, when disjointed lines of poetry were beginning to replace columns of numbers and myriad pages of convoluted code in his mind, he was jolted upright by a sharp knock on the window some six feet from the sofa. Uttering a few carefully chosen and none too poetic words he made his way over to the window and slit the curtain slowly, then seeing what was on the other side, blinked in surprise and motioned towards the door. The apparition shook its head and jabbed one large hand in indication towards the window. Jamie merely raised his eyebrows and unhasped the lock.

Muttering curses that even Jamie found impressive, the apparition heaved itself over the sill to stand dripping on a 12,000 pound Persian rug, loomed by hundreds of dark-eyed women who knew far drier climes.

"And what the fock," said the apparition flinging off rain like a waterlogged St. Bernard, "if I may be so bold as to ask is a summons at this unholy hour all about?"

"I might ask you the same," Jamie said dryly "if indeed I had any bloody idea what exactly this is all about."

"Ye sent me a note," the apparition said exasperatedly, "said it was urgent that we meet, here, tonight. Now granted it's hardly subtle summoning me like the friggin' lord of the manor but then I figured if the shoe fits, a man is likely to wear it. "

"If I may be spared your profundities for a moment," Jamie said "I will repeat for the benefit of all listeners that I've no idea what you're talking about."

The apparition looked at him suspiciously, sniffed and then said rather succinctly, Jamie thought, considering the pickle they now found themselves in, "Shit."

"Indeed it would seem we are up to our hipwaders in said substance," Jamie replied without a trace of amusement to leaven his voice.

"How much time do ye think we've got?" asked the apparition, looking hopefully over his shoulder at the still open window.

"Not enough I imagine," Jamie replied and barely got the words out before feeling the gust of air that preceded a great walloping thump on his head. As he sank to the carpet, he found to his surprise that he really wasn't very surprised at all.

"Finished yer nap, then?" said a voice, disembodied and floating somewhere above his head. Not God this time, unless of course God was Belfast Irish, working class with just a hint of west country underneath.

Two fingers, without the gentleness one could have expected of God or even one of His lesser minions, pried open an eye that Jamie really would have preferred to keep shut.

"Ow," he said as slowly his vision began to clear and he realized that hell suddenly seemed an attractive option. The figure before him certainly bore no resemblance to any harp playing angel and the devil was likely, Jamie thought closing his eye again, to have a much better wardrobe.

"Come on it's time to wake up." There came a sharp tap to the side of his face and then another sharper still. "We haven't got a lot of time and I could use some help here." This last was said with no little sarcasm, Jamie noted before slowly and painfully opening his eyes. The world, for an endless moment, looped off its axis, did a pirouette and seemingly leaped over the moon before settling somewhat blearily down into the shape of large, freezing cold room made of some strange bubbling material, which in another moment reconstituted itself into large gray stones. A barn, deserted and likely miles from any sort of help, he thought slowly raising himself up off the floor until he was in a sitting position and swallowing back the nausea, found himself inches from a glowering countenance.

"I think after the fiasco of the last hour we rank in the top five stupidest people in the world," said a voice, that instead of floating up near the rafters, was only a foot or two away from its owner whose face slowly pulled itself together until it became the nose, mouth, eyes and ears of Casey Riordan.

"Don't blame yourself," Jamie said muzzily, awkwardly patting at Casey's face.

"Blame myself," Casey snorted, "it's not likely I would man as it's yer own tender hide they were after. I was in the way of a bonus, I believe."

"Me?" Jamie echoed in disbelief, "I'm not the one with the lifetime subscription to Republican Weekly now am I? What on earth would those men want with me?"

"That," Casey said, "is the exact same question I've been asking meself these last two hours." He gave him a burning look that did nothing for the state of Jamie's head.

"Well it's a question that will have to remain unanswered because I've no idea what the answer is," Jamie said a trifle too calmly.

"Don't try yer Oxford airs on me man. My da was a man of some learnin' ye know,"

"Indeed," Jamie replied as Casey took a long, and in view of the situation they currently found themselves in, very relaxed pull on his cigarette. "I'm very happy for your father I'm certain but exactly how it pertains to our present condition I'm rather more mystified by."

"Sarcasm, ye must be feelin' yerself again. Well it's not very hospitable of ye to not take the time to hear a man's story, an' as this one is short an' fairly to the point I think ye'll find it interestin'." He smiled then in a way that would have been quite disarming if there wasn't such a great deal of menace behind it.

"Please, do tell," said Jamie feeling his head gingerly for open wounds.

"I've looked ye over, ye'll not die any time soon, or if ye do, it won't be from a head wound." Jamie taking the none-too-fine point glared at Casey, who genially raised his eyebrows in return, then sighed and said, "Ye'll not be the most appreciative audience I can tell but fer lack of a better ye'll have to do. My Da', may he rest in peace, loved a good story, Pat gets his love of readin' from him, told us every Irish legend there was to know. Finn Mac-Cool, The Cycles of the Tain, an' of Ulster. All the true stories of every rebel an' patriot. It's what all we Riordans are raised on, stories of blood sacrifice. 'Twas those stories I liked the best, the ones where men did what they must, but our Pat was always of a more fanciful bent, ye may have noticed the lad has his head in the clouds moren' is good for anyone. An' Da', god rest him, was of the same mind, they liked their stories well embroidered with fairies an' flowers an' pretty words. There was one in particular though that caught myself as well. Had a pretty woman in the center of it an' I've a weakness there as sure as any man."

Jamie, whose stomach had only begun to settle suppressed another surge of nausea and considered that he didn't quite like the direction this one-sided conversation was taking.

"Perhaps ye'll have read it yerself, 'twas a romantic little tale called 'The Scarlet Pimpernel'.

Jamie felt himself start involuntarily and saw the responding smile on Casey's face.

"Well then, hit a nerve have I, yer Lordship?" Casey lit another cigarette off the butt of his still smoldering one and took a long and Jamie could not help but notice, satisfied puff on it.

"And if you had, what exactly would be the point?" Jamie asked warily, feeling like a bemused gazelle being circled by the hungry lion.

Casey rubbed the red-hot ashes of his cigarette carefully into the stone floor. "No particular point, it's only that a man in my line of work often finds it useful to know exactly who he's dealin' with."

"And you think you know now?" Jamie asked, blinking slowly in an effort to keep his head clear.

"Not exactly, let's just say that it certainly makes the fix we're currently in somewhat more interestin'."

"Death with a spin on the tale is still only death," Jamie said bitingly.

"Aye, I suppose ye've a point but as I've no intention of dying here tonight it's only a point." Casey stubbed out his cigarette and sighed, the boldness of a moment ago gone.

"Where's my brother?" he asked in a lightning turn of subject that somewhat relieved Jamie.

"You ask like a man who knows the answer," Jamie said.

"I'm not here te play verbal word games with ye man, there's really no time fer that. In case the bastards that col'cocked us are more efficient than I suspect them to be, I'd like to go on my last sleep knowin' that he's safe."

"Knowing that he's safe?" Jamie echoed, "He's of the rather certain opinion that you really didn't care whether he died in a gutter somewhere."

"Oh Christ," Casey rubbed a large hand roughly over his face. "Did ye never have yer moments when ye wished with everything ye were that ye could take words, an' erase them from time altogether, that ye could just wash the air clean of them and say what ye really meant."

"You haven't seen him since, I think perhaps he interprets that as you being unable to stand the sight of him," Jamie said less harshly.

"It was him that didn't want forgiveness," Casey said stubbornly.

"Did you ever think that he didn't want it because he knew you were incapable of giving it?"

Casey raised his head and Jamie was appalled to see the grim desperation there. "Ye'll not know just how desperate that night was, to learn what I did an' that he'd hidden it from me. Pamela had from shame, but Pat, why couldn't he be honest with me, he ought to have told me."

"She made him swear not to, it was the only thing she asked of anyone that whole wretched night, that you not be told. Don't blame her for loving you more than her own pain."

"I don't blame her, at least not now, alright maybe there was a bit of me that wondered why she couldn't tell me, but she could lay every burden at your feet an' give ye the gift of her trust."

"You know why she did that," Jamie replied quietly, "and you know what it cost your brother, you weren't the only one hurt in all this. Pat's life will never be the same; in some ways it scarred him more than it did her."

"I know that," Casey said angrily, "do ye think I don't know what it did to my own brother? Do ye think I don't know that he'll never be the man he should have been? Do ye think I'm blind?"

"Are you?" Jamie asked in a level tone.

Casey pushed himself up and paced the floor in agitation.

"It's all turned into some fockin' Greek tragedy then, hasn't it? I can't bear the sight of my own brother because he reminds me of what I couldn't prevent, I see my own weakness mirrored in his face. My brother that I swore on my father's grave I'd protect with my last breath."

"Then why can't you forgive him?"

Casey paused in his violent path and looked Jamie full in the eyes, one bleeding man to another. "Because he loves her, doesn't he? My own brother loves my wife and I couldn't stand it, I couldn't bear the pain of watchin' him kill himself over somethin' that is not his for the takin'."

"Only yours," Jamie said in anger before he could stop himself.

"She is my wife, she lies in my bed an' even then I am not fool enough to tell myself that I'm not sharin' her with you."

The silence that ensued was blisteringly uncomfortable. Jamie cleared his throat several times and then said, "Would you feel better if you punched me?"

"Aye," there was just the ghost of a smile playing about Casey's mouth. "Aye, I think I would."

Jamie stood, avoiding a glance at Casey's broad and all too capable hands and said, "Well then have at it."

As he lay on the floor a second later, clutching his nose, he wasn't sure what surprised him more, that Casey had taken him up on his offer so promptly or that it hurt more profoundly than he had expected it to.

"It's broke," he said in a muffled tone before spitting out blood onto the floor.

"Aye, I apologize for that, I didn't mean to hit ye quite so hard."

"Forgive me if I find that particular pill a little hard to swallow," Jamie retorted taking the hand that Casey proffered to him.

"I realize it'll be of small consolation but I do feel better."

"You're right, it's of small consolation," Jamie replied.

"Now will ye tell me man, where my brother is an' if he's safe."

"He's at my house, catching up on all the schoolwork he's neglected and working at a printer's shop in the evenings. He's safe enough for the time being and he's as happy as could be expected at this point."

"Mmphm," Casey mumbled looking with great interest at the laces of his boots, "well then I suppose I owe ye a debt of thanks."

"You're welcome," Jamie said dryly.

"I'm glad he's gone," Casey said so quietly that Jamie wasn't certain he'd heard the words right. "Maybe he'll stay away, maybe he can do what no other man in my family has done an' live a long an' full life."

"Maybe you could do that yourself."

Casey gave Jamie a long look and shook his head, "Tisn't my road to follow."

"That's rather fatalistic for a fine upstanding revolutionary, aren't you supposed to believe all things are possible?"

"I'm not so much a revolutionary as a realist, this business makes ye become one after awhile, I know what's likely to be the outcome of another generation of fighting."

Jamie felt himself growing angry.

"Then why bother? If you can't change it, if you don't believe there's a chance for peace, for the freedom you espouse and the murders you excuse in its name, then tell me what is the point?"

"This country is the point, it's that simple. We have the right to live as free men in our own land, the right to jobs where yer qualifications are the decidin' factor an' not the church ye go to on Sunday. We deserve to vote with some hope. People should not have to leave this country to get a fair crack at life but that's not the reality, is it? My wife should have been safe on that train, but she wasn't."

"Women are raped everyday in all parts of the world, that's hardly something you can chalk up to the bloody politics in this land."

"Jamie she was not raped for who she was but for what she was an' I'm not talkin' about the fact that she's a woman. Some would say I should just thank my lucky stars that she and Pat are even alive. Some, as ye well know, have not been so lucky. Though I'm inclined to believe that night on the train was no random act."

"What?" Jamie sat up, his head clearing with a violent swiftness.

"Ye heard me, an' don't tell me the thought hasn't occurred to ye, I'll grant yer inquiries have been discreet but as our questions have been leadin' us down the same path 'twas inevitable that we'd cross at some point. You an' I have asked the same question one too many times, it's why we're here. Though to be certain if we'd been on the right track I believe we'd both be dead by now."

"I suppose being smacked over the head is somewhat more subtle than a swift and brutal death," Jamie mused acidly, his pulse quickening as he considered the possibilities that lay on the other side of the door.

"Aye, more subtle an' infinitely more dangerous," Casey said rising to his feet once more and vainly glancing about for an opening of any sort.

"Are we being sent a message then?"

Casey nodded, dark eyes traveling over every inch of stone and wood.

"The rape, my brother's beating that was intended for me, tonight they were speaking directly to you."

"Redhand militants?" Jamie inquired mildly.

"No," Casey replied, "the rape an' beating that was their style, blunt, brutal, violent an' if they'd killed Pat an' Pamela I'd of thought it was them. Would suit their 'take-no-prisoners' style. No, there's something far more involved goin' on here, I just haven't been able to wrap my mind round the right answer yet. The boys on that train were lackeys, the question is whose?"

"So you're saying that by looking into the rape, by trying to find the bastards that did it we're moving too close to something far bigger?"

"Aye, got it in one," there was a strange look forming on Casey's face, strange and slightly jubilant. "Well I'll be damned," he said the look becoming an outright grin.

"Would you mind sharing what's making you grin like an idiot," Jamie said, the lump on his head beginning to throb again.

"Bird shit," Casey said, the grin becoming wider and more annoying by the minute.

"Bird shit," Jamie echoed, eyebrows raised at this latest turn in the conversation.

"Aye, bird shit," Casey replied merrily, pointing up the very limits of the stone walls.

He had to squint to see it, pale, runnelling streaks on the walls nearly indiscernible in the dim light, but there. And where there was bird shit, there was most certainly—"Birds," Casey said triumphantly. "An' where there's birds there's a hole somewhere to get the hell out of here.

Jamie looked doubtfully at the smooth, stone walls that rose thirty feet into the air and thought that if they, like the aforementioned birds, could fly, they'd be out of here in no time at all.

"I don't quite see," he began then stopped abruptly as he realized that Casey hovered some five feet off the floor already, clinging to the wall like an oversized, genial spider. "What the hell are you doing?" he finished.

"Getting the fock out of here," Casey replied calmly, "as I suggest ye do if yer as overfond of breathin' as I am."

It was a long, bruising climb and it took over an hour to accomplish, by which time both men were soaked with sweat, shaking with fatigue and gasping for air. Twice Jamie had slipped, once at around ten feet and then again when he was within a hand's breadth of reaching Casey, who was by then precariously balanced on a blackened and ancient beam. It had only been Casey's agility and lightning reflexes that had saved him from the long fall that would have resulted in certain death. He wasn't entirely certain how comfortable he was with Casey saving his life, but thought now was hardly the time to worry about it.

There was indeed a hole, though it was hardly a wonder that the bastards who'd sealed them up in here had missed it as it was barely large enough for a man's fist to pass through.

"Now what?" Jamie asked feebly, his lungs seared with the effort of climbing and clinging like a flea on a dog to the greasy beam.

"Don't know," Casey said peering through the fetid blackness at the small hole of resurrection that lay only three feet in front of him. It might as well have been a mile, Jamie thought dejectedly, hoping rather morbidly, that one died of fear before actually smashing to bits at the end of a long fall. "Well there's nothing for it but to try," Casey mumbled and proceeded to do a slow turn until he laid flat on his back on the beam, a four inch wide piece of wood, slick and slippery as a greased pig, then levered himself inch by inch towards the wall, looming up in the dark like an impenetrable medieval fortress. After several fraught moments of grunting, groaning and a sharp gasp, with Jamie peering like a mole up for his first daylight in months, Casey reached the wall with his feet and bent his knees back to his chest.

Jamie could stand it no longer and began to shimmy slowly up the beam, eyes focused on the white expanse of Casey's shoulders, the only bit of light in the gloom.

"Brace yer feet on either side of my neck man an' hold on damn tight," Jamie did what he was told without question, not even uttering a peep when he bit into his tongue in the effort to get his feet firmly entrenched on Casey.

There was a small, scraping sound, a muffled oath and the words, over-familiar to Jamie as he'd been chanting them in his head for the last hour, "*Mary, Mother of God, blessed art thou amongst women*' and then a few more lines, condensed and edited for the benefit of their situation and then a strain of muscles in all concerned and a great cracking, crumbling and tumbling. Jamie overbalanced and surprised found himself hanging upside down and grappling for dear life with the beam and stone that seemingly turned to dust each time he thought he had a handhold.

"Casey," he gasped and upon breathing in a cloud of dust, began a fit of coughing that threatened to dislodge and kill him.

"Aye," a head liberally coated in mortar dust popped up through the opening, now the size of a large man's shoulders, "though just barely, I said brace yer damn feet not shoot me out to kingdom come. Here give me a hand, I've a hold out here now," Jamie gave the hand and was pulled out onto the other side with what was rather more ferocity than was strictly necessary.

"Don't look down," was Casey's sage advice after Jamie, having looked down, turned a pale green under his mask of white. "It's maybe twenty feet down to that tree and if ye can get a grip on to it, we're home free. Now," he twitched his head slightly the right, "we're on a bit of a lip here so we might as well use it as long as we can, it's forty steps near as I can figure to yer right and then a straight drop down to the tree, though ye'll have to find a substantial branch to land on."

"You don't say," Jamie hissed through clenched teeth, sweat beading on his forehead and wet limestone stinging his eyes like the devil.

Forty steps to the right, he counted them out carefully, measuring each one so that it was as close in length to the one before it as possible, he'd no desire to look down again so he'd just have to risk the possibility of missing the tree altogether. In between each number, he chanted its Latin counterpart to himself in order to keep a desperate grasp on his rapidly building panic. Jamie Kirkpatrick, calm in the face of many dangers, was not very fond, it could be fairly said, of heights. Even his hands had begun to perspire and mix with the limestone dust to form a thin coating of slick mud.

It was Casey however, cool and calm as Sunday tea, above him that lost his footing just as Jamie found a branch he trusted to be sufficient to his weight. He slid down the wall in a shot before somehow finding a hold with one hand and there he hung precariously, fingers of his left hand dug in with a grip that was astonishing to a bare inch of protruding gray stone.

"Jesus Christ Almighty," Jamie whispered and intended no disrespect to the gentleman whose name he uttered.

"If ye could put aside cursin' me for the moment an' get me the hell off this wall," there was a muffled groan, "I'd appreciate it."

"Right," Jamie said and inched back out along the branch, looking for another solid one beneath him to brace himself and take the weight of the man above him, without sending them down to the ground which was still far away enough that although death would not be certain, great pain and disfigurement would be.

"Alright then," he said a moment later, having found what he thought was the best of a very dismal set of options and set himself precariously upon it. "I don't see any toeholds beneath you so," he took a bracing breath, "throw yourself back and I'll catch you."

"I see strategy would not be yer strongpoint," Casey said with a rather biting wit, Jamie thought, considering his current predicament.

Casey pulled his feet up slightly and then asked in a fairly meek voice, "Are ye ready man?"

"Ready," Jamie replied grimly.

He came down with the graceful ease of a big tree falling or at least it seemed so to Jamie's horrified eyes and Jamie, much to his own surprise, managed to get a handhold on him before a cacophonous pop split the air and launched them towards the ground at breakneck speed.

Jamie, knocked momentarily unconscious by a branch he hit headfirst on the way down, awoke to the feeling of hellfire and the forks of a thousand imps whose only duty was to stab him mercilessly on every inch of skin he possessed. It took a moment to regain some sense of bearing and when he did realized he'd fallen into a thick and wondrously thorny bed of roses.

It took several minutes and the manufacture of long, bloody scratches on his hands, arms and face before he would extricate himself from the wickedly painful embrace of the roses. He was relieved to find that other than assorted bruises and bumps, he'd sustained no breaks.

He limped across the grass, graying with the arrival of morning and heavy with dew. Casey was laid out on a flat bit of ground, too silent for anything but unconsciousness or death. Jamie hoped fervently for the former but was, he found, to be disappointed when he reached Casey's prone form.

"I've broke my fockin' arm," Casey said disgustedly.

"Better than your neck," Jamie ventured only to receive a look of frustrated disgust.

"We've got to cover some ground an' quickly, we've got maybe an hour before full light an' we'd best be well hidden by then," Casey was all authority but still made no move to get up off the ground.

"Do you need my help?" Jamie asked.

Casey sighed and said, "Aye, I've dislocated my shoulder as well an' I'm afraid if I sit up now I'll vomit from the pain."

"Is anything else broken?" Jamie asked politely.

"No," came the answer.

Jamie allowed no room for hesitation and grabbed Casey by his good arm and pulled him up quickly. Casey, by way of thanks, threw up on his shoes.

After helping Casey rather more gently to his feet, Jamie went and wiped his shoes on the grass. When he turned back Casey, the color of old bed sheets, was scanning the horizon.

"Which way?" Jamie asked.

"There," Casey pointed off to the southwest, down a long slope of loping green hills. "There'll be a barn somewhere over that rise an' though I'd prefer to get much further away, it'll have to do."

It took an hour, freezing, soaked with dew and beginning to throb and sting all over, Jamie was distinctly relieved to see a barn over, as Casey had predicted, the first rise.

With no time, nor really much care for subtlety, they walked right through the doors, which were ajar. The animals were only beginning to stir and barely lifted an eyelid in response to the appearance of two bedraggled and bloodied humans in their midst.

They made their way up to the loft, large and filled with sweet-smelling fresh hay. Casey went up first and Jamie pushed from below. They had barely settled in when they heard the cows begin to rustle below.

"Milking time, man'll be out any minute," Casey whispered and then collapsed, gray and sweating in the hay. Jamie followed suit and then moved not a muscle for the eternity it took the man below, whistling and chatting amiably to his herd, to do the milking. His neck muscles were protesting vehemently when at last, with a final, 'Aye there, Bessie, there's a gude girl an' a pretty one too, not as fine as my Nora mind but fine as a cow's likely to be,' they could hear the sound of feed being poured into buckets, water splashing into a trough and then the farmer departed back to the house.

Jamie sat up, blowing bits of straw out of his face and turned to look at Casey. Even in the dim light filtering through the rafters of the barn, the man did not look well. It would have been a mercy if he'd passed out but he was all too conscious, teeth clenched together, sweat running in streams from his forehead.

"We'll have to do something about the pain," Jamie muttered, half to himself.

"I don't doubt it'd appeal to ye to knock me out cold but have a check in the rain barrel first would ye, man? If there's nothin' to be had ye're more than welcome to hit me over the head." The rain barrel which oddly enough was situated in the farthest, darkest corner of the barn, where it wasn't likely to catch even the most adventurous drop, did, when Jamie sunk his arm up to the shoulder, in its murky depths, offer up manna directly from heaven. Four bottles, filled with peaty brown liquid, guaranteed to relieve a man of his pain as well as the rest of his faculties. He tucked them under his right arm and was back up the ladder in a shot.

"How did you know I'd find this?" he asked uncapping a bottle and helping Casey to tilt up his head and take a long draught off the bottle.

"Didn't, good guess is all. I hide my own in a hatbox at home."

Jamie helped Casey to drink half the bottle, in long steady swallows, before lowering him back into the straw.

"Pamela tells me that ye've a bit of medical knowledge," Casey said and Jamie didn't like at all the way the man looked at him.

"An ill-considered two months floundering in the sciences hardly constitutes a sound base for a medical career."

"Do ye know that ye use too many words when yer nervous?" Casey asked. "Now I'll need a minute or two for the alcohol to take away my nerves an' then ye'll put my arm back in for me."

"I will?"

"Aye," Casey gave him a black look, "ye will."

Jamie took the allowed minute or two to cast back in his mind to his brief flirtation with medicine. If Casey had been bleeding profusely Jamie would have known exactly what was required, however upon reflection it seemed to him that he'd never quite made it to the chapter on the realignment of joints. He looked over at Casey's deathly pale countenance and thought perhaps now was not the best time to mention it.

He kneeled down in the hay beside Casey's prostrate form and felt gingerly along the forearm, from what little his uneducated hands could tell him it was a clean break about halfway up the radius, the swelling seemed minimal and it wasn't hot. These were all good things, or at least he hoped they were.

"Ye need to get my elbow in close to my body an' then ye whip it up fast an' that should rotate the joint back in. Normally the wrist should be up but I don't know if I can manage that with the break," Casey gritted his teeth and pulled his wrist up onto his chest.

"We'll wrap the break," Jamie said feeling at last some modicum of ease settle in, "make it as stable as possible and then we'll get the joint back in."

He took his shirt off and tore two even strips out of the back where the shirt remained the cleanest. He wrapped the break tightly down the length of the forearm and then hooked the ends around Casey's thumb and back to the wrist to give him some small amount of leverage. He then tore what was left of Casey's shirt up to the shoulder, which was hot and swollen to the touch. They'd allowed too much time to elapse and the muscles had swelled and knotted, making the task ahead of Jamie that much more difficult.

"I think it'd be best if I sat on your chest and attempted this," Jamie said grimly.

"Aye," Casey said weakly, rather less enthused by events than he had been a minute ago.

Jamie straddled his chest and took the beleaguered arm in hand, the elbow resting snugly in his palm, his other hand grasping the offended shoulder and taking a deep breath counted to three and whipped the arm up, hearing with immense relief the crunch of a maligned joint falling into place.

"Jaysus Christ," Casey let out an explosive breath and closed his eyes in relief, a small measure of color already beginning to tinge the edges of his face. "Give me another swallow of that whiskey, will ye?"

Jamie helped him to another substantial slug and took one himself for good measure.

It was only then, adrenaline dropping from a roar to a hum in his ears that he realized they were not alone. Peering above the stairs, looking for all the world like a silver-whiskered badger was the none-too-pleased face of a man he could only presume was the owner of this establishment.

"Hello," he said a trifle giddily, causing Casey to open his eyes and shift over to his side with a startling swiftness.

"Hello yerself," came the unamused reply and then face moved upwards and was joined by a body, cradling a rifle in the crook of one arm, "my wife has sent me out te see if ye lads would like some breakfast and if ye'd need of her medical box."

It took Jamie a moment to gather his faculties at this astonishing turn of events but Casey said easily, "Aye, we'd be grateful for a bite an' if yer wife has any medical knowledge we're in sore need of it."

"She nursed durin' the border campaign an' has like seen the helluva lot worse than the two of yez. Right then, I'll be back."

True to his word, he was back in minutes with a minute woman with an equally lined face and jolly blue eyes behind him. Jamie and Casey had made it to the floor of the barn, Casey rather precariously as he was experiencing dizziness and another bout of nausea.

"Christ, I've seen the hind end of mules that looked a sight better than the two of you," said the woman with uncharitable succinctness. "Broke is it?" she asked Casey, nodding curtly towards the arm he held to his chest. "Ye'd best sit, yer the shade of old bathwater. Jacob get the milking stool an' fetch me two splints, yea long," she gestured with her small brown hands, "an' be sure they are thin an' straight as ye can find them. Now lad," she fixed her gaze on Casey, "let's have a look then shall we?"

She unwrapped Jamie's bandaging, her touch deft and light and Casey seemed as though he hardly minded even when she felt with precision along the break itself, her brow furrowing in concentration. "Mm, it's a clean one an' will mend nicely, swelling's minimal." She then prodded his shoulder pushing here and there for long minutes. "Twill help to unknot the muscles," she said to Jamie's questioning look, "it's best to relieve the tension in the muscles, an' though an opiate best serves there, knowin' where an' how to touch never hurts either." She laid Casey's hand gently across his lap and with a brisk no nonsense air, laid out the things she needed to set his arm.

"Your husband said you had nursed during the border campaign," Jamie said venturing at small talk.

"Indeed I did," she answered swabbing Casey's arm with some fragrant smelling concoction. "'Twas mostly men on the run, stray bullets that didn't quite hit as close to the mark as was intended and some that did. I'll need yer help here, the arm'll have to be pulled taut, so's not to risk trappin' any nerves. Here," she guided Jamie's hands to a firm yet not untender grip just above Casey's wrist. Jacob returned with the splints and a cloth covered bucket which held within it piping hot tea, a bit of sugar and fresh cream. He then unloaded what appeared to be a fuel box and from it arose the heady aromas of ham, fried a crispy, sweet brown, eggs done in butter and fresh bread. Jamie's stomach rumbled loudly.

"Eat while it's hot, lad," she nodded toward the food as she tidily wrapped long lengths of plaster soaked gauze around Casey's arm, "yer friend here'll only be a minute an' then he can tuck in as well."

Jamie, abandoning all vestiges of his polite upbringing, dove into the food with the relish of the famished. Casey joined him only minutes later and attacked his food with only slightly less vigor.

When Jamie had devoured two eggs, three slices of ham and mopped it up with two slices of bread, then washed it down with two cups of hot tea, the woman looked at him with what seemed great relish and said, "It's your turn laddy."

"My turn," Jamie said blankly trying to ignore the grin on Casey's face.

"Come sit," she authoritatively patted the stool upon which Casey had recently been enthroned. "Let's have a look at that nose and ye've a score of thorns that need pulling an' disinfectin'."

He had to swallow an undignified scream as she pushed the bridge of his nose between her two thumbs. "Aye, 'tis broke, must have been the helluva blow."

"You could say that," Jamie muttered shooting a black look at Casey's shaking back.

"Well there's not so much to be done for a broken nose, though I don't think it'll heal too badly on its own, 'tis a pity though it looks to be a fine specimen of a nose but I'd need to put ye under te set it, an' if I'm not mistaken ye lads don't have that sort of time."

"No, we don't." Jamie agreed wincing as she poured a clear colorless liquid onto his chest that stung like the fires of hell.

"Ye look like ye've had a tussle with a bramble bush man," she said beginning to extract thorns and the myriad splinters of them from Jamie's flesh. "Ye'll have to stay low 'til full dark, there's been men about askin' if anyone has seen two men on the run, possibly injured."

Jamie stiffened perceptibly and she patted his shoulder gently, "Not to worry man, our sympathies lie on the right side of the blanket, ye've nothin' to fear here. We'll go about doin' our daily bit an' if anyone is watchin' they'll be none the wiser."

"Thank you," Jamie said gratefully, aware suddenly in every part of himself just how tired he was now that his belly was full.

"They'll have noticed yer husband's gun," Casey said quietly.

"He keeps it inside the barn an' is hardly fool enough to trot across the yard with it," the woman replied shortly. Minutes later, she washed Jamie's back down with the same burning liquid and set to work on it.

"*Iarr thu aithnich an amhran o amhran?*" Casey asked softly his eyes dark and opaque, fixed with a curious intensity on the woman. Jamie could feel a strange tension fill the space between the woman behind him and the man seated only feet in front of him.

O gradh tha an crocanach ni
an sin tha nicorp eolach gu leoir,
Do faigh a muigh uile a is an e.

She replied saying the words in a rusted voice that indicated it had been a very long time since she'd spoken Gaelic. Something in the words seemed to satisfy Casey however and he sighed expansively rubbing one hand over his stubbled face.

"If ye'll be so kind as to excuse me, I think I'll hit the hay, so to speak."

"Sleep well, boy," the woman said her voice softened by the odd exchange of a minute ago.

Jamie watched Casey make his way up the ladder and heard him rustle about like a dog and then there was complete silence.

The woman had moved to his hands, bathing them with a cloth then applying the clear liquid and beginning the arduous task of extracting the endless array of thorns from his fingers and palms.

"Ye've the hands of an idealist boy," she said pushing down on the fleshy pad of Jamie's thumb, "are ye new to all this then?"

"I suppose you could say that," Jamie replied carefully.

She moved on to his index finger and Jamie drew in a sharp breath as she pulled out a deeply imbedded thorn. "It doesn't sit on ye so well," she said quietly as if she didn't wish Casey, drowned in sleep, to hear.

"It doesn't?"

"No, there's somethin' about ye, it's as if yer a bit too fine for it."

"It?" Jamie queried his voice automatically lowering to her own level.

"Aye, it. 'Tis hardly a glamorous existence now, is it? Bein' shot at, never certain if ye'll live to see another dawn an' many don't ye know," she eyed him sharply and then bent her head over his torn fingers again. "My first husband was in the Brotherhood, but it was in his people's ways an' mine as well, if yer born to it ye don't think so much about it. I've seen a lot of men come an' go, some dreamers, some saints, some plain murderers, an' some who just didn't fit. That's you laddy, ye don't seem to fit." She sighed and straightened her back and reached for a dark, stoppered bottle, uncorked it and poured a little of it into his palm. It had a pungent smell, not unpleasant, and it took away the sting of the tiny holes in his hand. She smoothed it in with long, even strokes, running her stubby, work battled fingers down the tops and sides of his own fine, long-boned ones. She then turned to the palm, beginning at the center and working her way out in a sunburst motion.

"Ye've a strong life-line an' a very deep heart one, ye know how to love that's plain," Jamie, who had begun to doze, started a little. She peered intently at his palm, tracing lines with the tops of her own fingers.

"Does that mean I'll live a long and happy life?" Jamie asked, his tone rather more serious than he'd intended.

"I said ye knew how to love not that ye were wise about it," she replied tartly, dabbing a dark-green foul smelling ointment on the worst of his cuts. "Yer destiny though, it's entwined with his," she indicated with a quirk of her head where Casey lay, soft snores floating down to them now.

"How can you tell that?" Jamie asked intrigued in spite of the exhaustion that was threatening to pull him to the floor any minute.

"Ye see enough hands ye learn where one person's life line shows another, you an' himself are important to each other somehow, linked through another person." She laid cool strips of gauze across his palms. "A woman mayhap?" her blue eyes looked up under gray eyebrows.

"Mayhap," Jamie replied with a small smile.

"I'm Nora," she said and returned his smile with all the wisdom of a woman who has seen many years of life.

"I'm Jamie."

"'Tis a nice name," she said, "soft an' yet a man's name, it suits ye." She turned and poured some hot water out of a pot, added drops from three small brown bottles and then put a pad of cotton in to soak. A heady aroma soon filled the air and Jamie found himself floating rather dreamily on the fumes. She wrung the cloth out a moment later and put it to the bump on his head, "'tis only a bit of lavender, geranium an' rosemary, 'twill help the swelling an' draw out the bruise. The lavender will give ye a good sleep as well. It's handy in a love potion too, though it's said when lavender is mixed with rosemary it works te preserve a woman's chastity an' that hardly helps yer love problems. Anyhow, ye'd best have yerself a sleep an' Jacob'll wake ye shortly before dark."

"Thank you again, for everything,' Jamie said softly, amazed at the ease with which this couple had taken them in hand, treated their wounds, fed them and all it would seem without so much as a blink of the eye.

She fixed a bright blue eye on him, "Yer welcome lad."

Jamie was halfway up the ladder when he turned and looking down asked, "Your husband, the first one, what happened to him?"

She looked up, startled, from where she had been carefully placing her oils and salves back into their case. "He died in the Border campaign, 'twas one of those stray bullets ye know, it lodged near his spine an' there was nothin' I could do for him." She returned to sorting her things and Jamie made his way at last into the straw, easing himself into the sunshine smelling hay.

He was in a heavy doze, helped along by the buzz of a bee droning in lazy whorls somewhere far above him and Casey's snores, when Casey and Nora's cryptic words came back to him.

"*Will ye know the song of songs?*" Casey had asked, and Nora had replied in that tongue rusty with disuse:

> *O love is the crooked thing*
> *There is nobody wise enough*
> *To find out all that is in it.*

He recognized it of course, it was the Yeats poem 'Brown Penny', what significance it held for Casey and Nora though he could only hazard a guess at. Some sort of code he supposed, but it had obviously relaxed Casey enough to feel they could safely sleep here.

A few lines from the poem swirled softly in his head before slipping like flotsam down the dark river of unconsciousness.

> *Go and love, go and love, young man,*
> *If the lady be young and fair.*
> *Ah, penny, brown penny, brown penny,*
> *I am looped in the loops of her hair.*

Somewhere in the dark slipstream of first sleep he dreamed Pamela rising and falling, her hair coiling down over his hands, his body and he smiled. Nora's words echoed far away, '*I said ye knew how to love not that ye were wise about it.*'

And then all consciousness slipped away to the shores of the dark river and he slept.

Jamie awoke to a sky bruised with twilight, a head that felt extremely light and the comforting smell of burning tobacco wafting about him. Casey was already awake, sitting up and looking far healthier than he had some hours previous.

"Feeling better?" Jamie inquired sitting up on the breath of an expansive yawn.

"Much," Casey said briefly, tapping his cigarette out carefully and folding the remainder of it up in a bit of cloth and tucking it in the pocket of his torn shirt.

He sat quite relaxed, on the head of an upturned barrel, watching the first, small stars, through gaps in the barn roof, as they began to blink in the sky.

"'Twill be a couple of hours before we can safely leave, Jacob's been out an' said supper'll be along in a few minutes, after we eat ye might want to catch a bit more shut-eye, I can't guarantee that ye'll be able to get much in the next few days."

"If they've already proved their point, whoever the hell they are," Jamie said grumpily, "then why do we have to lurk about the country trying to elude them?"

"Because I'm not entirely certain they have proved their point or if this is just the opening gambit. Besides, I need to get back into Belfast without anyone knowing."

"Why?"

Casey eyed him blackly, distrust still playing about his face, then he sighed and seemed to momentarily capitulate.

"In case it's someone from our side that's set us up."

"Our side?" Jamie said raising his eyebrows and wincing as the cut across one of them opened up. "Your side you mean, I don't even pretend to have a stake in this particular game."

"Have it yer way," Casey said cheerfully, "but yer part of it now whether ye were before or not."

Jamie was about to deliver some stinging denial, which wouldn't have convinced Casey in the slightest but would have gone a long way towards relieving his own overburdened conscience, he was stopped short however by the savory smell of supper entering the barn.

"Come on down lads," Nora's cheery voice said from directly below them. They navigated the ladder each in his own turn and sat down to a rough table of a board across two overturned buckets. The food was far from rough though. There was roast mutton, done tenderly in thyme and rosemary, potatoes mashed creamy and rich, carrots, peas and more of the bread, this batch still warm from the oven.

"I've packed yez lunches," Nora said briskly pouring them out each a mugful of milk, "tisn't much, just bread an' cheese an such. Jacob says yer to take a bottle of the whiskey each," she gave them both a look that turned their faces red, "an' I've put a little jar of something each in yer bags. Yers will ease the pain an' leave ye clearheaded," she nodded towards Casey, "an' yers," she set a steaming bowl of pudding down by Jamie's plate, "is to be taken externally only, it'll keep the cuts an' such from infection."

Casey stopped briefly from forking food into his mouth to say, "We're much obliged fer yer hospitality ma'am, an' if there's anythin' we can do in return ye only have to say."

She looked at Casey a long time as if memorizing something about his face then reached out and patted his hand, "Well then lad there's not so much I wouldn't do fer the grandson of Brendan Riordan, 'tis an honor really."

Casey almost choked on a swallow of milk.

"Did ye take me fer sheer daft then boy, yer the mirror image of yer grandda' an' there's not so many people that knew that particular phrase ye threw at me before, did ye think I'd not know ye fer who ye are?"

"I guess not," Casey stammered.

"My first husband worked with yer Grandda' an' near worshipped the ground he walked on but then so did anyone who called themselves Republican back in those days. Would take a big man to fill Brendan Riordan's shoes," she looked rather pointedly at Casey who returned her gaze quite mildly. "Mmphm," she said, "well we'll have to see then won't we lad." It was more statement than question and Casey did not answer. It was a question that would take years to answer, years and monumental sacrifice from a man who was still young and relatively untried. Destiny, Jamie reflected, could be a damned inconvenient thing.

Nora and Jacob took their evening tea with them, Nora putting out a plate filled with rich, dark fruitcake, saved no doubt for special occasions, Jamie thought guiltily, knowing it was likely these people had provided their best for them and would eat scantily for the rest of the week to make up for it. He would have to send the man a case of his best whiskey when he got home, any other gift was likely to insult the generosity of these people; their pride was hard-won and all the more valuable to them because of it.

"Why don't ye read the lad's tea leaves?" Jacob suggested to Nora, "Ye read his grandda's, 'twould be fittin' to do his as well."

Jamie saw a look of anger or dismay cross her face but it was gone in a flash.

"What did ye see in my grandda's cup?" Casey asked his voice soft but with an undernote of tension.

"Och, 'twill be a long time ago lad an' my memory is not so good as it once was, 'tis no more than a game really, here give me your cup," she grabbed Jamie's before Casey could hold out his. He felt ludicrously nervous. She stared for a long time at what had seemed to Jamie no more than black muck at the bottom of his cup, then she closed her eyes and breathed deeply. "There is much pain in this cup, pain that has passed, pain still to come but in the end there is happiness hard-won an' well-deserved." Jamie shivered and had to squelch the desire to rip the cup out of her hand. Her voice was strange not the rough, tart tone of before, but something that sounded as ominous as the tolling of medieval bells. She handed the cup back slowly, and Jamie was shocked to see how old she suddenly appeared, "There are still children waiting," she said as she released the handle.

"Do mine then," Casey held his out to her and she took it with what seemed great reluctance. Jamie knew with one of those long, primal quivers of the spine that he did not want to hear what she saw in Casey's cup. Nor apparently did Nora for she blinked and rubbed her eyes, then sighing said, "I'm sorry lad but I'm tired an' my eyes tend to blur on me after a long day, I can't make head nor tail of the leaves."

"'Tis alright," Casey said quietly, accepting back the cup and refraining from pointing out that she'd read Jamie's cup only a minute before. But there was a look of quenched hope on his face that chilled Jamie to the core. He, quite suddenly, wanted to run from this place and this man and not have to see the future, to feel it unfold in long arcs in front of them here in this dark barn and know that there was no hiding, no ground upon which to seek purchase from the fears he'd sought some small comfort from.

Nora bid them both farewell and a safe end to their journeys but it was Jamie she came to and touching his face with a rough hand said, "Have patience man, it will come, if ye'll only have patience." Jamie had remained silent knowing she expected no words, only that he should carry her own with him and remember them when necessary.

They slipped off through the fields, chasing in the wake of shadows, hiding from the revelation of light. Casey leading, Jamie following wondering when he'd put his faith in this rather hostile stranger.

They traveled a good part of the night, stopping only for short breaks to catch their breath and wet their tongues. Casey's conversation consisted of tersely whispered commands about which way to turn and when to stop and still in the darkness.

They took shelter for the day in a narrow, thickly wooded ravine, shadowed and whispering with the talk of leaves that fretted to and fro to the wind's tune above their heads in the light. Sleep, made so by bone-deep weariness, was just possible. By noon, Jamie was awake, silently cursing all the bugs who'd had a piece of him while he slept and generally speaking, feeling quite out of sorts with the entire world. He stared peevishly at the blissfully slumbering Casey until the object of his annoyance opened one eye and said, "Could ye look at somethin' else, yer disturbin' my rest." So he contemplated the undersides of the trees for a few minutes, then decided to explore a bit beyond the fringes of their tiny hole. He crawled some ten feet on his belly, upsetting several small grubby creatures, ripping a sizable hole in his pants and stifling a yelp when some unknown (and best left that way) object plummeted out of the trees above and landed with a sickening *kechunk* on his head. Finally, he was rewarded with the find of a small patch of wild strawberries, from which he plucked the main course of their sparse lunch.

When he wiggled his way back, with what he thought was great stealth, to their hiding spot, Casey pulled him one-handed out of the bushes.

"It's me," Jamie said tersely closing his eyes to avoid a flailing branch.

"I know," Casey said, "I didn't think anyone tryin' to sneak up on me would make as much noise as ten drunken miners."

"I did not," Jamie said indignantly, fishing a rather crushed handkerchief full of berries out of his pocket. He thumped them down with wounded dignity in front of Casey, who grinned as they rolled in delicate disarray before him.

A repast of strawberries, bread and cheese, followed by a dessert of whiskey did a great deal to restore their humor.

Casey passing the bottle over to Jamie, burped extravagantly and then leaning back in apparent loose-limbed relaxation, gave voice to the question that had hung over them since the entire fiasco had begun.

"So why is it ye've become of such interest, that we've men chasin' us about with the apparent wish to see us dead?"

"I've no idea," Jamie said, loftily intent on retrieving a strawberry seed firmly wedged between two molars.

"I've an idea or two that ye may find rather interesting," Casey said tone still indolently jovial.

"Mmghmmph," Jamie replied, still trying to remove the pesky seed.

Casey spoke two words then, a name that charged the air with accusation halved with sincere admiration.

Jamie denied rapidly, calmly and with, as Casey had recently pointed out, far too many words. Casey merely smiled in a most annoying manner and Jamie thought if he'd been Carroll's Alice, he might have choked the Cheshire Cat to death.

There was a long silence inhabited by the twitterings of birds, the buzzing of flies and the quiet of two men who have, most unexpectedly, come to feel comfortable in one another's presence.

"I'm sorry about yer Da'," Casey said quietly, "it'll never be an easy thing to lose a father."

"Thank you."

"My da' died makin' explosives," Casey said, studying with deliberate nonchalance the cuff of his sweater.

"My father killed himself," Jamie rejoined quietly, surprised at how easy it was to say it after such a long and hideous silence.

Casey met his eyes without provocation, but merely and for perhaps the first time, with honesty. "It'll be the same difference, then."

Jamie nodded, understanding now the twin burdens they carried as sons. "Aye, it'll be the same." He was silent for a moment, taking a swallow of whiskey, feeling with gratitude its golden burn. "Your daddy, it will have been no accident, then?"

"No," Casey shook his head, "no, the man knew his way around explosives, had since he was a boy. He wanted it that way I suppose, so that we could think it an accident an' live easier with the grief."

"I'm sorry," Jamie said and meant it.

"'Tis alright," Casey said rolling the whiskey bottle back and forth between his hands. "My Daddy was never quite right with the world, if ye know what I mean?"

"Nor was mine," Jamie said.

"He was a bit too sensitive, I suppose for the sort of work bein' a Riordan meant. I don't think my Grandda' ever wanted him to be part of the family legacy, but when all the other boys died an' so did his Da' there wasn't much of anything else for daddy to do but to pick up the reins an' continue."

"Do you ever wish he hadn't?"

"Aye, I'll admit that there are times that I do. I'm more built for it though, Da' was like Pat, things bit him too deeply an' he could never stop the bleedin' from it."

"You believe you can keep Pat from it?" Jamie asked, looking out from under eyebrows that were becoming increasingly numb.

The answer was a blunt and unequivocal "aye".

"Yer Daddy, why did he do it?"

"The black dog," Jamie said with great gravity, peering with one eye through the wavy glass lines of a rapidly emptying bottle.

"I take it we are not talkin' about four legs, fur an' a waggin' tail here," Casey said trying, with little success, to balance a stalk of clover on his nose.

"It's what Winston Churchill called it," Jamie sighed, and drained the remainder of the whiskey. "Depression that is, my father always had it but sometimes it will get worse as a person gets older and it had got to the place with him where there were many more bad days and not so many good."

"Ye have it yerself?" Casey queried, seeming to Jamie's increasingly bleary vision to be having some trouble focusing himself.

"More good days, not so many bad," Jamie replied, feeling, at the moment, that there was very little wrong with the world that a pint or two of Black Bush could not cure. "What happened to your mother?"

"Ran off, if ye can believe it," Casey said with great and martyred seriousness, "with an Indian an' runs a curry takeaway somewhere in Londontown."

"You don't see her anymore," Jamie asked, finding his lips slipping fuzzily about any word of more than one syllable.

"The Belfast Queen?" Casey snorted, "It's not likely I would then is it? Gone for near to eighteen years an' not so much as a phone call on Pat's birthday, nor a card for him at Christmas. It didn't matter to me if she remembered myself but I can't forgive her for forgettin' Pat, because it did matter to him. His wee face on holidays was always full of hope thinkin' Santa Claus could bring her, an' the disappointment in his eyes when she never came would break yer heart."

"Should we be this drunk?" Jamie asked, realizing in some dim way that it was far past time for such a serious question.

"No," was Casey's blunt answer.

Lack of judgment, prompted by the excessive alcoholic goodwill coursing through his veins, could be the only thing that led him to ask the next question.

"Why did you marry her?"

The same boozy love of mankind was likely the only thing that stopped Casey from beating him senseless. "Why didn't ye?" Though preferable to being punched was rather too close to the point for even drunken comfort.

Jamie looking across the rustling and shadow-laden space thought with a twinge of panic that Casey didn't look near as sodden as he had a moment ago.

"It's a fair question," Casey said the lush harmonies of a few sentences ago altogether stripped from his speech.

A breeze, rippling and sweet, stole speech for a moment and allowed Jamie to gather what senses were left and construct from them some answer.

"Aside from the obvious, my age, her age, my drinking and the fact that I'm already married, I'm not entirely certain why I wouldn't marry her," he said and found the words much less invested with sarcasm than he'd intended.

"Yer married," Casey sat up a little straighter, finding this morsel of information of great interest.

"Aye," Jamie replied grimly, wondering if the man understood the concept of small talk. "More from a lack of effort at getting a divorce—until recently that is—than any other entanglements you might be imagining."

"Where is she?" Casey asked looking really quite happy.

"In a convent."

Casey laughed and then ceased abruptly looking at Jamie's humorless face. "Christ yer serious, aren't ye?"

"Yes," Jamie said and seeing the next question forming on Casey's lips, added "she's a nun."

Casey plunked back against the tree, the better to ponder this surprising revelation, Jamie supposed and then said quite genuinely, "I'm sorry man."

"Don't be, she's very happy or at least a good approximation of that particular emotion," Jamie replied dryly, ardently missing the drunken jollity of minutes past. "We lost three sons to a nasty little disease with a name ten miles long, that kills before life begins. My wife," he said and closed his eyes so he couldn't feel the words quite so sharply, "my wife found a way to deal with the pain. God granted her some sort of reprieve and so she's devoted her life to him."

"An' did he grant ye one, a reprieve?" Casey said dark eyes mild in the clear afternoon light.

"No," Jamie said, feeling there wasn't a great deal of room for polite lies in this narrow ravine.

"I married her," Casey said looping the conversation back on the intake of a deep breath, "because I had to. Not for the usual reasons that make people marry, ye know, the fear of loneliness an' gettin' old with no one to care if ye breathe from one day to the next. Or to have children, or reasons of economy or even sheer desperation. I married her because I love her, it's simple, so simple that I can't ever explain it properly, not even to myself."

"It's not a terribly sensible reason but it's a good one," Jamie said smiling.

"Aye well there's not so much sensible about love is there?" Casey said rising from the ground in one restless motion and studying the light, counting the hours Jamie knew until they could make their escape into darkness.

"If you're talking about real sense, about the sort of sense that actually makes or breaks a life, then I think love is about as sensible as it gets."

Casey turned in the soft green-gold air of the day and nodded, "Aye I suppose yer right. Ye'd best catch some sleep if ye can find it," he said, filching a cigarette out of his battered pack and tossing one to Jamie. "We go at full dark, we should get back to Belfast in the small hours."

"And then what?" Jamie asked taking a heady drag on the cigarette and wondering if he'd revived another destructive habit.

"Oh," Casey turned and grinned, "I've an idea or two."

Chapter Thirty-four
Not Peter's Brother

IT WAS RATHER WELL KNOWN IN CERTAIN LESS-THAN-ELEGANT CIRCLES that many a Republican and wanted man, though not necessarily in this particular order, could be found of a Saturday night tipping his elbow at the Sniffy Liffey. It was a comfortable establishment with the required dark corners for the faces and whispers that wished to remain unnoticed.

The Sniffy never had a set of regulars except for the two old men who sat at the bar and talked to Mike the publican and proprietor, their claims to glory harking back to back Easter 1916, where one claimed to have stood shoulder to shoulder with Padraig Pearse and to have heard his last words before he was carted off to be shot. The story was told several times a day to any stranger that passed through and generally assured the man of his five daily pints. The second, a wee gray man who went by the name of Eamonn, claimed to have been part of the entourage that was guarding Michael Collins on his ill-fated trip through his home county of Cork. Which to be certain was nothing to be after bragging about said Mike the proprietor, for sure hadn't the Big Fellow been slaughtered right by his car in the middle of the road, without a body to protect him? To which, old Eamonn would hang his head and say with a great sigh 'tis true, 'tis true, but it might have been worse.' How it might have been worse, Mike wisely did not inquire and other than the occasional eye roll he let them ramble on to various and sundry clientele. They were harmless enough and a welcome distraction to men who did not wish themselves to be noticed, who avoided direct eye contact and straight answers.

On this particular Saturday night things were a bit quiet-like, there was a nervy looking group over in the corner and one or two loners. Eamon and Matty were at the bar, stools shaped with years of use to their backsides. Then through the door came the oddest looking pair Mike had ever seen outside a circus tent.

The taller of the two, a big man by any standards, wore a gently bemused expression and seemed to float rather than walk. His hair was dark but streaked with powdery white whorls, his eyes, barely discernible behind thick glasses, were decidedly myopic. He wore a robe of sorts, unbleached cotton with 'Gunderson's Best Baking Flour' stamped at random across it. Around his neck was a monstrous rosary, crude wooden beads interspersed with what, given the dim light, looked to be garlic. Certainly the smell that wafted ahead of the man was enough to attest to it. At the tip of it, hanging halfway down his chest, was the largest cross Mike had ever seen strung about a human neck.

As odd as this first apparition was however, it was the second man who elicited the most gape-mouthed observation from the men at the bar. He had red hair that curled and sprang from his head and was saved from outright riot only by the grubby elastic that held it together and from which it spilled in abundant abandon down his back. Each ear held four earrings apiece and he'd a three-day growth of brightly red beard. On his head was a hat, one of those floppy hippie things, on which 'Jesus Loves You Man' was harshly emblazoned. The arms of his t-shirt were cropped off and across his chest was the message, 'Bikers for Jesus—Ride the Righteous Winds.' His long legs were encased in a dusty faded pair of denims and on his feet he wore a pair of shiny snakeskin boots.

The first man sat at a table close to the bar, still wearing a benignly confused look and the second made his way over to Mike.

"Guinness, two," he said with a smile that split his dark face into amiability.

"Travelin' through?" Mike asked. He prided himself on being able to spot foreigners at a glance.

"Yez might say dat, da good Fadder and oy'ze jist come home from Sout America. E's a bit by way of bein' a celebrity over dere."

"Really, he's—he's a priest then," Mike asked looking dubiously over at the flour sacked gentleman in question.

"A praste man, e's da fookin' eighth wonder of da world, yer lookin' at the right reverent holy of holies, dat's de Father Joseph Jesus Bunrattey, have ye never 'eard of 'im then?" The red-headed man looked at him as if he could not believe anyone would not have heard of Father Joseph Jesus Bunrattey.

"I can't say that I have," replied Mike calmly.

"Weel, that jist fookin' beats it then don't it? We comes 'ere at the re-quest of de pope 'imself an' find dere's been no advance notice." He leaned across the counter in one sudden snakelike movement and poked Mike with a grubby forefinger.

"Yer lookin' at a fookin' natural wonder, 'is mudder named 'im after da holy family an' e's been performin' miracles since 'e was three years old. Can make light dance on da ends of his fookin' fingers an' water pour up instead av down. 'E saved me life an' blinded me in the left eye the first time I laid me eyes upon 'im." The man elaborately crossed himself and kissed the tips of his fingers, "Da virgin bless an' preserve him." He leaned even closer to Mike and smiled evilly, one eye rolled back in his head exposing a pale bluish white. Mike who had seen all sorts of freakish flotsam and jetsam took an involuntary step back. "It's glass, 'isself says 'e'd never gazed upon sich wickedness short of a daymon. 'is purity it burned me eye clear fookin' troo, can ya beat it? I've been followin' 'im ever since."

"And who might you be?" Mike asked with a slight stutter.

The man sighed elaborately and leaned back into a stool.

"Lutie O'Toole and no I ain't Peter's brudder before ye ask." He pointed to his chest, "Biker for Jaysus, rode me Harley clear crost Sout America, takin' Fadder Joseph Jesus to minister to the sick an' unholy, dere's a powerful lot of unholies in dis world man."

Mike slid the dark frothing Guinness across the bar and darted a look at the priest who was fingering his rosary and mumbling incoherently, his face a picture of beatific holiness.

Lutie leaned close again and said in a whisper, "Could ye help me out an' tell 'im dere's like a three drink limit or sumfin' coz fer all his religiosity de Fadder 'as a powerful keen likin' fer da drink." He looked about himself suddenly as if every ear in the place were trained on him, which indeed most were, "if e's 'ad too much ta drink 'e'll start channeling' da Virgin 'erself. Oy've seen 'im do it meself," Lutie shuddered dramatically and recrossed himself, "'an it's not a sight I'd wish on de Scratchman 'isself, it can go on fer hours, 'til ye fair tink yer ears are goin' ta bleed if 'e don't stop. Mind now dere's no one I'd radder have on me side in a fight, 'e's de former Golden Gloves champeen of Brazil an' Paraguay, 'e knocked an ape out colder dan a witch's tit one time." Lutie smiled reminiscently and took a slug on his Guinness. "Fookin' amazin' it was. I'd best git 'im 'is drink now, e's a mightly thirst on, 'e always does after da bleedin' though."

"The bleedin'?" Mike said, swallowing as a chill raced down his normally implacable backbone.

"Aye, da bleedin'. It's only rare an' 'e gets no warnin' as to when it's comin'." Lutie lowered his voice even further and darted his eyes from side to side, rolling the glass one round in an arc that did terrible things to the pit of Mike's stomach. "E's got da stigmata on 'is 'ands, like the very man 'imself," he hissed directly in the barman's face, letting fly a warm Guinness impaled spray of saliva, "da peoples in Sout America, dey tougt 'e was da Messiah."

"An' is he?" asked Mike recovering some of his composure.

"Weel, I'll not say 'e is an' I'll not say 'e isn't, but oy've seen 'im do some powerful strange tings." Lutie grabbed the two drinks and made his way over to Father Bunrattey, who was becoming progressively more pained looking at each 'fook' out of Lutie's mouth.

Mike was rather taken aback when the priest took his Guinness and in one fluid motion drained the glass, then leaned across the table and grabbed

Lutie less than gently and said something rather urgently into his face. He would have been even more surprised had he heard the conversation that was taking place in low hissing tones.

"Channelin' the Virgin fer Chrissake that's layin' it on a wee bit thicker than I'd like," said Father Bunrattey, "I only said to create a distraction not put on a fockin' sideshow."

"Indeed," said Lutie in a well clipped, Oxford honed voice, "well I'm thinking on my feet here and not used to being the lure for some murderous lout, you'll simply have to follow my lead."

The Father, his myopic eyes shooting black flame through his heavy lenses was about to retort when a voice above them broke into their cozy tête-à-tête.

"Would ye be the self-same Father Joseph Jesus Bunrattey that saw the face of Jesus in his ma's kitchen curtains when he was but an infant?"

Father Joseph Jesus looked startled then suddenly jumped up in his seat and upon regaining his perch shot a murderous glance across the table.

"Weel 'e would be if yer talkin' about da very same Joseph Jaysus Mary Bunrattey that was born in a caul an' could speak in the tongues of angels from da time he was six months old," said Lutie O'Toole rising rather menacingly out of his seat. "An' indeed 'e would be if yer talkin' about da man who was struck dumb for ten long years, 'an 'e certainly would be if 'e's da man dat sat on a mountain top in Tibet fer forty days an' nights widout da benefit of food nor drink an' lived to bear witness to it. Would dis be da self-same Father Joseph Jesus Mary Bunrattey dat ye speak of wid yer sinful tongue, an' furdermore," said Lutie puncturing the air with his index finger," who da fook would you be ta ask about the likes of dis holy an' righteous man?"

Father Joseph Jesus was rather desperately trying to wave the incensed Lutie back into his seat as a sizable crowd began to gather around their table. Even Matty and Eamonn who once seated had never been known to move until closing time had wobbled their way over to get a closer look at the growing spectacle.

"I would be Ben Hanrahan an' I think yer both fakes."

At the pronouncement of the man's name, Lutie and Father Joseph Jesus exchanged a quick glance.

"Ah, it's a sad old world when dere do be unbelievers in every fookin' crowd, why just last month I wuz sayin' to da pope, Pope sez I—"

"I was not talkin' to ye, ye loudmouth huckster, I wuz talkin' to the father here or is Jaysus still holdin' his voice for 'im?"

"Why ya impertinent, filthy-tongued, fookin' eejit," Lutie rose to his full height and cocked back one fist, "it's lucky ye are that the good Fadder don't be usin' 'is fists to spread the light of his Lord anymore, but I believe I can make yer teeth part of yer ballocks in short order, stand back men, stand back—"

Father Joseph Jesus Mary Bunrattey rose then and the crowd backed away a foot or two. He was a man of impressive stature and half of them believed the story about the cold-cocked ape.

"Lutie my child I know ye mean only to protect me but put down yer fists, if it's proof these gentlemen want then it's proof they'll get. Though to my way of viewing things the world has come to a pretty fix when a man can't even have a drink in peace." The Priest's voice was a bit shaky but nonetheless it held an authority that tolled as loudly as the angelus bell. He sighed and rolled his head about three times on his shoulders, cracked his knuckles and then seizing his head with his good hand, gave it a vicious yank in either direction. His head fell back on his shoulders then and his mouth gaped open, his right arm slowly rose until it was at chest height and straight out from his body.

"Leekin, spleekin, rom and nod, bookay, throm ud feddum—" intoned Father Joseph Jesus in sonorous chant.

"Jayse, what language do he be speakin'?" asked old Matty in a tremulous whisper.

"It do be da tongues," replied Lutie "Jayse but it do be givin' me the shivers when 'e does this."

"Michael Collins did occasionally be speakin' in the tongues, now there was an angel of a man," said Eamonn with a sigh.

"Jaysus but will ye shut up ye old windbag Michael Collins no more spoke in tongues than I am after speakin' Greek an' Latin to me old mother at tea on Sundays," this said by a man who looked like an old wizened turkey.

"I'll thank you to remember Mister that ye was still pissin' in yer nappies when the Big Fellow was shot so don't be tellin' me what he did an' did not do." Eamon said indignantly his watery blue eyes near popping from his head in consternation.

"I would be thankin' ye all to shut the feck up," said Ben Hanrahan shaking one beefy fist in the general direction of Eamonn, Matty and the turkey-wattled man.

Father Joseph Jesus meanwhile had worked up a fine sheen of sweat across his face and was still chanting melodically on, "Swinkum, blinkum, sorgum and roo," while the crowd began to get dangerously antsy.

"Back off men, back off, da good Fadder do be needin' some room ta do 'is miracles properly," Lutie said waving his hands about as if to flap off chickens.

Joseph Jesus' head snapped up and he stared off into the distance above the heads of the men who surrounded him, "Alright then, if you insist," he said into the vacant air.

"Oo's 'e talkin's to now," whispered Matty squinting into the air as if he expected something to materialize.

"Ah, no," sighed Lutie and pressed his heavily tattooed hands into his face, wagging his head back and forth in what appeared to be great distress, "ye've fookin' done it now, wud wid da bleedin' only hours ago an' now da stress of havin' yez call 'im a fake, ooh no," Lutie shook visibly.

"What the hell are ye goin' on about?" asked Ben Hanrahan, a slight edge on his voice that hadn't been discernible before.

"It's well ye might ask," said Lutie rocking back on the heels of his iridescent boots, "as ye wud be da fooker dat brought dis on. But ye'll be excusin' me language, as we're about ta be blessed wid da presence of da Lady of ladies 'erself, da Virgin Mary."

"That's—" began Matty but was smartly stopped by Lutie's hand across his mouth.

"Not anudder word fer da sake of Christ, it's more dan we're all wort if she comes out mad. Oy've seen dat before an' it's a very bad scene ta be in." With that pronouncement, Lutie shut his own mouth, which Matty commented, in a quiet aside to Eamonn, was sure miracle enough for him.

In a moment however, they were all struck speechless for Father Joseph Jesus, a man of seemingly few words, became, without warning, a woman of many.

It started simply enough with a delicate and airy rendering of the song "How Do You Solve a Problem Like Maria?" sung in a high and sweet soprano that a man of such size could not possibly possess. But seemingly did. He wove through each verse flawlessly, the ribbon of song coming off his tongue effortlessly, mincingly, causing Lutie to shed a tear or two into the great bush of his beard and shake his head as if to say he certainly needed no more convincing. At the end of the song, which had trilled up into a show-offy aria, he abruptly stopped and fixed his eyes upon Ben Hanrahan, who was looking a little green about the ears.

"Benjamin Louise Hanrahan, ye wee snivellin' doubter, 'tis yer Auntie Mary come to call an' here ye stand blasphemin' a man of God, it's sore disappointed I am lad." Father Bunrattey said still in the hugely disturbing, sweetly feminine voice.

"His Auntie Mary?"

"Benjamin Louise?" said Eamonn and Matty in querulous unison.

Benjamin Louise turned, scarlet of face and made a less than polite gesture in their direction.

"I was named after me Auntie Louise who died on the very day I was born, 'twas me mother's idea an' sure I've never forgiven her for it." He turned once more in Father Bunrattey's direction his voice taking on a distinctly unpleasant edge. "How the hell did ye know, it's been a dead secret for years."

Father Bunrattey sighed and shook his head, "Are ye deaf then lad, I said it's yer Auntie Mary. Have ye lost yer mind so soon, yerself it was took me to see 'The Sound of Music' fourteen times. Ah lads," Father Bunrattey looked about with a melting smile, "an' didn't he weep like a babe each of those fourteen times."

"I did no such thing," said Ben Hanrahan rather weakly.

Father Bunrattey clucked his tongue several times in high disapproval.

"Here is me, scarce cold in me grave havin' made the long an' uncomfort-able journey te see ye an' ye stand here wid de lies pourin' off yer tongue smooth as the crame on milk," there was a pause filled with several more tsks, "tis' a sad an' sorry sight I see before me lads, a sad an' sorry one indeed."

"Sure an' it's not da Virgin but his own Auntie Mary, da Lord bless an' preserve her," breathed Lutie O'Toole in a stagey whisper.

"The Big Fellow had a sister Mary, thought she was a saint he did," said Eamonn sadly to no one in particular.

"Yer not my Auntie Mary an' I'll thank ye not to defile her memory, ye whorin' son of a—"

Father Bunrattey stepped forward swiftly and lightly took Ben Hanrahan by his shirtfront.

"Now I really wish ye hadna said that for I did not want to do this but ye've forced me to it lad truly ye have. Do ye be rememberin' the time ye got sick on me shoes at the Dublin tea house, an' me jist havin' bought the things a fortnight before, or p'raps ye'd like for me to tell the story of yerself an' yer Uncle Jimmy's poor wee sheep or the time ye had to say a hundred an' fifty Hail Mary's for thievin' from the collection plate or how ye got drunk on the communion wine an' threw up on Father O'Neill's white soutane right in the middle of mass, he did be after havin' the weak stomach on 'im lads," said 'Auntie Mary' by way of explanation.

"Ah Michael Collins did be havin' the same affliction wid his intestines," Eamonn said nodding in grave understanding.

Ben Hanrahan sat in the nearest chair his florid face almost pitiful in its childlike confusion. He cocked his head as a dog might when it cannot comprehend something and said "Auntie Mary," in a weak little boy's voice.

Father Bunrattey patted his head comfortingly, "There now lad, I'd no desire to embarrass ye but I had to convince ye. I've come here for an alto-gether different purpose, an' as long as I'm here I might as well tell ye that I'd always meant for ye te have me own bit of the shroud of Turin, but yer Auntie Rose did be sneakin' in to me room before I was even finished wid this world an' stole it, 'twas sadly enough the last thing I was to see this side of the veil."

"I knew ye'd meant for me to have it Auntie, I knew it," Ben said his voice truculent as a child denied its sweets.

"Well tis' of small matter now Benjamin, for I've come to tell ye somethin' of much greater import—" 'Auntie Mary' stopped in mid-stream and Father Bunrattey looked around suddenly as if he'd no idea where he was or how he'd gotten there. "Lutie?" he said his voice deep and strong as it had been when he'd entered the premises.

"Auntie come back, auntie ye said ye had something to tell me?" Ben Hanrahan leaned towards Father Bunrattey, his face shiny with eager rapture, "Auntie ye musn't go now."

"Tis no good now man e's lost 'er, it 'appens sometimes, could be de first time she's channeled, it's not like that she'll come back," Lutie said placing himself between Father Bunrattey and Ben Hanrahan's beseeching, out-stretched hands.

"Tis alright Lutie, she's left a bit runnin' about in me head, she said yer to look behind the picture of Joseph Plunkett that hangs in the hall of her house. Now will someone be standin' me to a pint, for I've a large thirst upon me."

"I will," said Eamonn unexpectedly, for in all his years as a resident of the Sniffy Liffey he had not been known to open his wallet for any man. "Michael did always be standin' a pint to many a man less fortunate than he an' I'd be a spot on his memory if I did any less."

"Shut up would ye," Turkey Wattles bellowed unexpectedly, "torty-four years ye've been comin' te dis same bar an' sittin' on the same goddamn stool an' tellin' de same goddamn lies. Ye no more knew Michael Collins than I did be dancin' wid Finn Mac Cool at the crownin' of the high kings at Tara. Jaysus but I am sick of it. Lies and feckin' fairytales, 'tis all this country can manufacture, 'tis what we live on, 'tis what we eat, breathe an' shit an' it all comes an' goes on de wind leavin' nothing behind but a bunch of dried up old liars like yerself," he pointed a palsied and spindly old finger in Eamonn's direction.

Even Ben Hanrahan's attention had turned away from summoning back his Auntie Mary and was fixed silently as was everyone's on Eamonn.

Eamonn sat there for a moment, a shrunken old man; who suddenly looked very tired and frail, his hand poised over his wallet, his pale blue eyes looking down at his hand as if he could not remember what he'd been in the process of doing. After two interminable minutes, he stood and shuffled his way over to the bar and quietly bid Mike to pour the Father a pint and not too much froth mind you. Then he shuffled back and placed the dark liquid quietly in front of Father Bunrattey.

"Thank ye man, 'tis kind of ye," said the Father nodding to Eamonn and offering him a near-sighted smile. Eamonn merely nodded in reply and silently made his way back to his stool.

"Coward," muttered Turkey Wattles, hunching like a greedy buzzard over his Guinness. Eamonn remained with his back to the crowd though there was a visible shake in his shoulders as he sat staring down into his drink. Men slowly turned back to their own drinks and looked to Lutie and Father Bunrattey for further entertainment. Lutie had just embarked on a rather titillating tale about a young and buxom South American lady who'd abandoned her wicked ways to become a devout follower of Father Bunrattey's when a sharp crack filled and split the air above his head.

"Beggin' yer pardon Mister O'Toole, ye've a fine way with a tale but if ye don't mind I'll be takin' possession of the floor fer a moment," said Eamonn who stood now on the shiny oak of the bar a large and ancient pistol swaying uncertainly in his hand.

"Even if oy wuz inclined ta disagree wid ye sir I'm not so much a fool as ta fight wid de autority of a bullet," Lutie replied.

Eamonn took a second to wipe his nose on the sleeve of his coat, a garment that from the looks of it had seen many such disreputable acts.

"I know that most of yez think I'm a daft old bugger that tells lies to be able to live with the unimportance of his own life but I did know Michael Collins, an' I loved the man like he was father and brother to me an' there were days that I hated him. I niver had a wife nor children because I served Mick an' there was no room for anything outside of him. Every day for ten years I got up an' took my orders from the Big Fellow, I did as I was told, without question. 'Eamonn,' he'd say, 'there's a fellow that's talkin' we'll be needin' to silence, ye'll know the house, tis yellow wid red trim three doors down from yer old mother.' An' I would go widout question an' shoot the poor bugger in his own bed. Eamonn, Mick would say to me the next day, I've a hankering for a roast beef sandwich go find me one, an' I'd go, such was my way. 'Eamonn' he says to me on the last day of his life, 'someday people will not believe ye ever knew me, because then my name will be bigger an' more filled with smoke an' illusion than I ever was, for such is the Irish way but ye'll remember me Eamonn, ye'll remember me true just flesh wid bones like any other man, ye'll know the truth Eamonn an' it will be enough.'" Tears ran and caught in the rivulets of his face, sunk and seeped away into his parchment fine skin. "But the sad thing is, tisn't enough in the end, is it?" The pistol wobbled uncertainly and then rose, alarmingly, to a level even with his head. "Because in the end it all comes to ashes, doesn't it? All the people we loved and the ideals we thought we were fightin' for an' the men who seemed like giants are after all just as dead as any other man is when the breath leaves him." His mouth quivered visibly now and his frame, frail to begin with, seemed to shrink in tighter upon the brittle bones of old age with each word he spoke. "An' his blood when it pours into yer hands as red an' warm as any other," his voice cracked and he pushed the pistol in tight to his ear, cocking back the ancient and rusty hammer with a creak that reverberated throughout the low ceilinged room.

"Eamonn man don't be daft,' said Mike the bartender, "sure an' wouldn't that stool be sore lonely without yer bony old arse to keep it warm."

Lutie, unnoticed, had slowly risen to his feet and sidled his way around the crowd until he stood now an arm's length away from Eamonn, unmoving but poised as a snake about to strike. The pistol swung in his direction and was pointed right between his eyes.

"We'll have no heroics here this evenin', Mr. O'Toole, 'tis me own life, an' should I wish to end it I will," Eamonn's voice was calmer now but somehow this only sent a chill throughout the room that was felt by all.

"'Twas very dark on the road that night, we couldna see a goddamn inch in front of our faces, but Mike insisted that we make Bael na mBlath," he shook his head and drew in a long and trembling breath, "an' we were drunk, I am here to tell you. We had the safekeeping an' life of the Big Fellow in our hands an' we were drunk to a man. 'Twas a fine day, folks turnin' out to wave an' cheer him on an' I felt like I was in a feckin' parade. But he felt somethin' different in the air, I knew 'cause he picked up his rifle before we got to Bael na mBlath an' I said to him, 'Mike we should stop fer the night, sleep off the drink, resume our course in the mornin', said I." Eamonn paused in his story and rubbed futilely at the tears that still fell and wobbled at the end of his chin and thin-bladed nose, never once taking the bead off Lutie's forehead. "An' Mike he turns to me an' he says, 'Eamonn a man must go where the road takes him,' jist like that he says it calm as if he were discussin' the weather or the wee flowers at the side of the road, 'a man must go where the road takes him." Eamonn had begun to sway slightly to and fro in his agony and Lutie edged an imperceptible bit closer to him. "An' then the light faded an' the sky fell in on us. The road was narrow, no moren' the span of a large man's arms an' there was a donkey jist grazin' there at the side of it, we had to skid into a ditch to avoid killin' the damn thing. 'Twas then the shootin' started. Mike was never one fer keepin' his head down an' some of the finest shots in the country were out there tryin' to kill him, stupid bastard. There we were takin' cover behind the car an' there's a wee lull in the firin' an' he gets out to see what's happenin'. His last words to me were 'keep yer stupid feckin' head down Eamonn,' an' then he walks out fer all the world to see, right into the middle of the road an' they get him, right through his skull." Eamonn looked round about at the faces frozen below him, his old eyes burning with all they had seen and could never forget. "An' the giant was felled, gone like some ancient oak that has withstood the tests of time an' weather until someday someone feels 'tis their right to chop it down. 'Twas all a bit blurry after that, draggin' him to cover an' the race to make it somewhere that he could get medical attention. But I knew it was too late. I laid his head against me, an' I could feel the blood seeping an' the life that drained away wid it. 'Twas much later that night when he'd been taken away to Shanakiel hospital that I looked at me own hands, frightful stiff they were, caked wid his blood an' some gray stuff that I knew was his brains. There are nights I still wake an' can feel the blood dryin' in me hands an' the gray matter like it was that day, knowin' that I was holdin' the death of Ireland's hope in this," he held up one hand, a shriveled claw bent harshly by the rheumatism that plagued it. "There are no giants anymore, not a single one." The arm that held the gun slumped in defeat and he said in a weary voice, "Ye may have my pistol now Mr. O'Toole, fer I've done with the wars."

Lutie took the pistol and handed it carefully to Mike who tucked it behind the bar and then did something he had not done in twenty years of owning the establishment; he poured two fingers of whiskey and neatly shot it down. Eamonn stood still rocking back and forth, a broken and tragic old figure. Lutie helped him down and to his chair where he slumped.

"I lights a candle fer his soul an' me own each Sunday," he said looking at Lutie as though for absolution, "may God forgive us both fer all the wrongs we committed in the name of freedom, though I am inclined to believe," he smiled weakly and without humor, "that God does not so much pay attention to the troubles of man."

Matty laid his hand on his old friends shoulder.

"There now man 'tis over, ye've told yer tale as it should be told, widout the rose-colored glasses, 'tis well past time ye should have let Mick lay to rest, sure an' he would not wish ye grievin' this long. There is a giant or two left in this land after all ye know, 'tis only the vinegar of old age makin' ye think otherwise." Matty turned and smiled gently at the drained faces around him, "Drink up lads, ye look as if ye've all been visited by a ghost. Men in this country have always made revolution, some with the gun like Eamonn an' meself an' some wid their pens an' it seems to me that the men who breathe the fire of change through their pens are the more powerful. Jack Stuart is such a man," he said quietly fishing out a slim green volume from the inside of his brown coat. On it stenciled in pale gold lettering were the words 'The Last Revolutionary- A Volume of Verse by Jack Stuart'. He opened it reverently and putting a pair of battered glasses on his nose, began to read in a soft and melodic voice.

Old Mad Meg stood by the sea
A thousand years stood she
Her memory deep, her anger long
A cunning lass was she

The lives of women
Held in her hand
The lives of men
Beneath her feet.

Old Mad Meg danced by the sea
A thousand years danced she

Her skin flame, her touch burn
A threnody sang she

The fates she wove
With crimson thread
Her laughter cruel
Flew free.

Old Mad Meg died by the sea
A thousand years died she
Her youth fled, her body scorned
A lullaby heard she.

Her eyes were blind
Her voice was silenced
Her pagan heart
No longer given beat.

Old Mad Meg birthed by the sea
A thousand years birthed she
She came in blood, she came in pain
And her pagan heart sings free.

Matty closed the book as carefully as he had opened it and said, "He speaks revolution an' he speaks it for the people, in a language that flows in their blood, so man do not tell me there are no giants left in this land. For as long as Jack Stuart holds a pen there is one left among us."

"Aye, perhaps there is," said Eamonn in a whisper.

"Well gentlemen," said Lutie with a regret filled sigh, "as lovely as it has been ta be in the presence of sich as yerselves, de Fadder an' meself must be shovin' off, we've an airly mornin' meetin' wid da Cardinal hisself, 'e's hopin' da Fadder here can cure his hemorrhoids fer dey've resisted da ministrations of da medicinal community for torty an' five years. Ye've all been most 'ospitable, our tanks to yez. Fadder Bunrattey," he nodded deferentially at the Father who smiled benevolently at all and sundry before making an airy and not completely accurate cross in the air above their heads. They moved towards the door then, this strange couple, Father Bunrattey with 'Making the U.K.'s bread rise higher for twenty years,' stamped in red and blue across the width of his backside and Lutie's back bearing the not altogether comforting message 'Jesus was a Beatnik.'

"Feckin' pair of nuts," was Matty's unromantic assessment as the men of the Sniffey Liffey resumed their drinking. All excepting Ben Hanrahan who reaching into his pocket to pay his tab, found nothing within, roared a few uncomplimentary things about the recently departed pair and then lumbered as quickly as a man of his size might out the door.

"Well then lads,' Mike said genially as he took a swipe at the bar with a rag, "it's been a rare evenin' altogether then hasn't it?"

Lutie O'Toole readjusted his wig and sat down to catch his breath, while Father Joseph Jesus Mary Bunrattey lit a badly needed cigarette.

"I see ye managed to shed yer reservations about our little act quite quickly," Casey said, eyes watering as he let out the first lungful of smoke.

"Give me one of those," Jamie said putting up a hand to catch the pack of cigarettes Casey threw at him. "How much time have we got?"

"I give the bastard a few minutes to realize he's missin' his wallet an' then another fifteen to figure out where we've gone an' then ten more for his lack of speed. So altogether we've about half an hour on him."

"He didn't seem altogether brilliant," Jamie said, wiping a hand across his forehead, leaving a swatch of white in its path, rimmed by bronze foundation. "How the hell did you know so much about the man?"

"Went to school with him, was thick as the day is long then an' it would appear nothin's changed. Thought he was my best friend, followed me all about the schoolyard, nearly ruined my reputation. Was a bit surprised to see him there, truth be told."

"Are you certain he's our link?" Jamie asked, pulling one earring at a time off his tender ears.

"Not entirely, but he'd have the connections, he'd never much backbone it's possible he could be someone's flunky." Casey looked about, eyes narrowed against the dark.

They were sitting in a back lane that stunk virulently of stale food and urine, both animal and human. It was as far, Jamie thought, as he could possibly get from his Belfast, if not in distance then certainly in atmosphere. It was also a brisk twenty-minute walk to Casey's home. A place Casey seemed in no great hurry to reach.

"She'll kill me," he'd said in reply to Jamie's question of why he didn't go home first. Jamie thought he'd personally risk it for a hot shower.

In twenty minutes, they readjusted their disguises and waited. Ben Hanrahan while not, as Jamie had pointed out, terribly brilliant, had a certain cunning and an ability to follow a trail like a bloodhound. It was who trailed him that was of interest to them however, not Ben himself.

Neither was prepared for the sight of Jimmy Mack, who came into the alley with no more warning than the glowing tip of his cigarette.

"Gentlemen," he said and Jamie could hear Casey's sharp intake of breath beside him, "I believe ye have something that belongs to my friend here."

"Do we?" Casey said, stepping out so that he stood in the dim light over the back entrance of a shop. He pulled his glasses off with slow deliberation and then stepped out of the makeshift cassock and faced his opponent squarely. "An' what is it ye have that is mine, Jimmy?"

Jamie could see the man raise his eyebrows and tip his head to the side, lighting a second cigarette off the butt of the first one. He took the time for a casual puff on it before replying. "Yer so far over yer fockin' head on this one Casey Riordan, so far over that ye can't see worth shit."

"I've a fairly good idea that's what I'm lookin' at now. Where the fock are my guns Jimmy?"

"Why," Jimmy walked further into the alleyway, "don't ye ask yer friend there? I daresay he knows a thing or two about it, don't ye Lord Muck?" his voice floated like viscous oil through the heavy, stagnant air, ripe with decay.

Casey did not so much as turn an inch in Jamie's direction.

"I want to know where ye hid them Jimmy, they'll do ye no good, ye've burned yer bridges with the army an' ye know it."

"Maybe I know where the guns are an' maybe I don't an' maybe," Jimmy blew smoke into Casey's face, "I've information more interestin' than a boatload of guns."

"Aye?" Casey said harshly, "I'm listenin'."

"Ye've been searchin' for a particular set of men, four to be exact, four names that no one will tell ye."

"Aye, go on," Casey said and Jamie could feel a slight shift in the air that indicated Jimmy Mack now had the upper hand.

"I can give ye what ye want man, if yer willin' to give somethin' in return?"

"What might that be?" Casey asked, tone carefully neutral.

"Only a set of blind eyes on yer part. They tell me yer tryin' to clean up the streets a bit, usin' the strong-arm tactics of the army to make people watch their step. They say every crime, no matter how small, gets reported back to ye. I've a little organization of my own that has operated with the blessin' of yer predecessors for some time now an' I'd like to keep it that way."

"Are ye sellin' drugs?" Casey asked, voice deadly quiet.

"Things to cure an' things to kill, dependin' what ails ye. I sell hope in liquid form. I've a good solid client base; I don't need to make new customers. All ye have to do is pretend we never had this conversation an' I'll tell ye who raped yer wife an' beat yer brother to a pulp."

Jamie could see Casey struggle visibly to keep his hands from Jimmy Mack's neck.

"Ye've a nerve ye bastard, ye expect me to lead my own people to the slaughter like lambs?"

"I thought that was the specialty of the IRA," Jimmy replied smoothly, "slaughterin' that is."

"I cannot deal in these terms," Casey said and Jamie noticed a slight movement in the shadows behind Jimmy Mack.

"Aye well," Jimmy crushed the butt of his cigarette out in the palm of his hand, "then I suppose ye'll never know will ye? They tell me the lad quite enjoyed his dalliance with yer wife, it's a pity then ye'll never meet. There's only the one left ye know, the other three have mysteriously disappeared. It's almost as if someone is takin' care of yer business for ye Casey, ye might want to ask yerself why someone would be inclined to do so. Of course ye could simply ask yer friend there."

There was a great splintering that severed the air and Jamie only had time to see a surprised looking Jimmy Mack sink quietly to the pavement, before Casey grabbed his arm and said, "Run."

Jamie, seeing the wisdom of the suggestion, did as he was bid. Ran through blind alleys and deserted streets, tripping over a keg left outside a pub, only to have Casey haul him mercilessly to his feet and tell him to keep going. Ran until his lungs were seared and burning, with only the occasional landmark leaping out at him to remind him that this was the city he lived in. Stopping quite suddenly as Casey came to a dead halt ahead of him and bent over cursing volubly.

"Jaysus H. bloody Christ!"

"What," Jamie just managed to squeak out, watching in mystification as Casey did a rather undignified dance in the dark alleyway they'd stopped in.

"I've been shot in the arse, that's what an' it hurts like bleedin' bloody hell."

"Shot?" Jamie echoed stupidly, wondering how he'd missed the transpiring of a second bullet.

"That's what I said isn't it," Casey replied, voice biting despite his ragged breathing. "Must have passed right through the bastard an' caught me as I was turnin'. Did ye happen to get a look at the man who fired the gun?"

"Not enough," Jamie said, noting with trepidation the dark stain that was flowering out across the back of Casey's trousers. "Did you?"

"No," Casey expelled a long shaky breath, "though somethin' about him seemed familiar, I couldn't get a fix on him though he was too far in the shadows an' I'll warrant wasn't too eager to have his face seen."

"You think you know him then?"

"Maybe," Casey grimaced as he tried to stand upright, "maybe I only want to think that I do. I'll tell ye Jimmy Mack came as a bit of a shock."

Jamie looked about the street, slick and glistening in the dark. The air was heavy and swollen with the promise of rain and he was as exhausted as he could ever remember being.

"Do you think it's safe to go home now?" he asked.

"As safe as anywhere else, unless ye count havin' to face my wife," Casey said a decided amount of resignation in his words. "Ye'll come with me then," he asked, "it's only that I'm bleedin' like the proverbial pig here an' feelin' a bit faint."

"Aye," Jamie replied longing for the comfort of his own bed, "I'll come with you."

Ten minutes later they were standing outside the familiar red door, Casey looking rather green about the gills and Jamie not entirely eager to face the music that lay on the other side. It was Jamie who finally knocked, three precise polite taps on the door.

"She may be sleepin', " Casey said hopefully.

The door swung inward with a violent swish. "She," said the figure in the doorway, "has not slept in four damn days."

"Now darlin'—" Casey began.

"Get in off the street," she said sharply and they meekly obeyed.

She flicked on a light and they flinched from the merciless onslaught of brightness.

"Oh so you've brought a friend then have you?" she asked, glaring at Jamie with such ferocity that he moved closer to Casey.

"I see you're both alive and not in any present danger of dying."

"No but if ye'd just hear us out—" Casey began in a wheedling tone.

She silenced him with a glare that would have evaporated a lesser man.

"Not another word Casey Riordan, so help you God, not another word." She looked down at the floor and turned quite suddenly white. "What is that?"

"Blood," Casey replied matter-of-factly, "I've been shot in the rear end. Now darlin' don't look like that 'tis only a flesh wound, I just won't be sittin' comfortably for a week or two. An' I will," he smiled sheepishly, "need some help gettin' the bullet out."

"Will you?" Jamie could swear she almost smiled. "Well I believe your compatriot here can help you with that. You," she turned to Jamie, "had best wash your hands; you look like something the cat dragged in."

Sooner than he would have liked, Jamie was confronted with a bare, white buttock that looked as if it had been bitten by a large-toothed dog.

"Disinfectant?" he asked weakly.

"I believe you'll find it in the hatbox," she said sweetly and left him to confront the bullet alone while she went to the kitchen to make tea.

"'Tis only relief that's makin' her so sharp," Casey said amiably as Jamie rummaged about in the infamous hatbox.

"Grab the poteen, it's the highest alcohol content, it's in the little brown bottle."

Jamie accordingly did so.

"Let's get it over with then," Casey said with grim determination, injured buttock clenching despite his show of bravado.

"Right then," Jamie took a deep breath and poured the clear liquid onto the wound. He had to credit Casey; he only let out one small yelp before fainting.

Pamela came into the room, holding a pair of tweezers and a razor blade. "Boiled," she said and laid them down beside Casey's still form.

"He's passed out," Jamie said helplessly.

"Best under the circumstances I'd think, wouldn't you? Now shouldn't we get the bullet out before he comes around again?"

Sensible if not welcome advice, Jamie thought and set about his task, fingers slippery with perspiration and nerves. Casey mercifully did not wake up until the bullet, small and blunt headed, lay on the table beside the bed where he lay face down, buttock neatly gauzed and taped.

Pamela sat on the bed beside him, silent. Casey reached with his good hand and groped about until she placed one of her own in it.

"Tis alright darlin' it'll take moren' a bullet in the arse to knock me down."

"That's precisely what I'm afraid of, you great big silly bastard," she said and burst into tears. Jamie, surgical skills no longer needed, quietly left the room and shut the door.

He took a drink of water and was half out the door when Pamela's voice stopped him.

"Where the hell do you suppose you are going?"

"Home?" he said.

"Not until the two of you have sat down and told me where the hell you've been the last four days and why it occurred to neither of you to pick up a phone. And seeing as Casey's in no shape to talk about anything tonight it'll have to be done in the morning. Besides you've no car," she added sensibly as Jamie turned back into the entryway.

In the uncompromising light of the kitchen, she looked frail and exhausted.

"I thought you were both dead, Jamie," she said voice drained with fear.

"I'm sorry."

She nodded and bit her lip to stop a fresh batch of tears from welling up.

"If you just point the way to the spare room," he said awkwardly, longing to take her in his arms.

"I'm sleeping in Pat's room," she said, a flicker of what almost seemed amusement in her face. "You are bunking in with Casey, my side of the bed is free. There's fresh towels in the bath and a spare blanket on the foot of the bed. If you need anything else just ask Casey, he can tell you where it is." She paused in the doorway and looked back over her shoulder, "Oh you might want to watch yourself as Casey's hands tend to roam in his sleep." With that, she shut the door with a firm click behind her leaving Jamie open-mouthed as a beached fish.

He stood there until he heard Casey's voice groggily call him.

"Yes?" he poked his head into the bedroom.

"Ye may as well come lie down man, she means it."

"I can sleep on the couch," Jamie said.

"It's like sleepin' on the Cliffs of Moher," Casey yawned one long-lashed eye looking blearily at him, "dangerous an' none too comfortable. There's room enough, I shared a bed with Pat half my life, I won't even notice yer there."

After a wash in hot water and scrubbing his teeth, with a toothbrush laid out for him, until his gums were raw, Jamie found himself stretched out next to the deeply asleep and snoring form of Casey.

Surprisingly he slept well and woke only once in the middle of the night when Casey left the bed and limped down the hall. He could hear the sound of a brief conversation and then Casey was back in the bed.

"She meant it then?" Jamie asked.

Casey sighed, "Aye she meant it, though ye can't blame a man for tryin'. She said someone in my condition ought to be more careful. I'm thinkin'," he grunted as he shifted from his back to his stomach in the bed, "it's goin' to be a long an' cold week in this house. She had a message for the both of us as well."

"Hm?" Jamie could feel himself slipping again into sleep's luxurious tunnel.

"She said the two of us are not allowed to play together anymore." Casey laughed, "an' I think she was only half-jokin'."

"Casey?"

"Hmm?" came the semi-conscious answer.

"What that man said about the guns, I don't know where they are. But why didn't you ask me?"

"Mm," Casey rumbled sleepily, "a man is entitled to his secrets Jamie an' I trust ye with whatever they are."

Jamie was grateful for the darkness that touched his face and hid his eyes.

Chapter Thirty-five

Lover, Make Me Forget

SHE WAS HOME LONG AFTER DARK HAD FALLEN and Belfast lay under fog, heavy and impenetrable, with only the odd sulfurous orange light finding its way through. The Ardoyne was even more depressing than usual, dark buildings thick with condensation streaming in dirty rivulets down their sides. Her feet ached and her throat was stretched tight with the prickle of unshed tears. It had been a long day. Since leaving Jamie's employ, she'd worked at a meat-packing plant, on her feet for eight solid hours a day. It was back-breaking, mind-numbing work and she suspected that her hands would smell of blood all the rest of her days.

The house was wedged in darkness, complete and silent, yet still a ripple of unease fluttered its way up her backbone as she let herself in the door and put down her bag. She took a deep breath, slowly letting it out, trying to ease the knot in her chest without actually opening the floodgates. Though she could have a good cry, she supposed, and there was none to question her. Casey, gone on yet another trip the details of which seemed to be shrouded in mystery, was not due back until late tomorrow afternoon.

She put the kettle on the stove to boil and made her way up the bedroom, dropping her skirt to the floor, unbinding her hair from its knot and rubbing her scalp in an effort to relieve the prickly tension. She was just reaching for the wooden chair where she'd thrown her worn jeans the night before when she heard a sound like the sibilant hiss of a snake uncoiling. She froze there, her hand halfway in the air, poised like a petrified dancer. There was a suffocating lack of light in the room, the fog outside shrouding even the faintest bit of outside light.

"Who's there?" she said, hearing her voice treble out and falter.

"Where've ye been, darlin'?" Came the reply, calmly, smoothly, oil untinged by the water of emotion.

The voice was disembodied, but a second later there was form as a flame struck out, ghostly wisps of smoke dissipating into the air, reaching with boneless fingers to curl their tendrils, deceptively tender, through her hair and into her skin.

"Casey," she croaked. She reached for the light, but then hesitated. There was no move from the other side of the room and she knew suddenly that were she to pull the string on the light it would illuminate nothing. The words spoken would be uttered in the anonymity of darkness.

"Where've ye been?" came the words again, terrifyingly calm.

"At work. Betty's been feeling poorly and so I worked the last half of her shift as well as my own. My feet are killing me and I've left the kettle on the boil so—" she broke off suddenly feeling the resounding silence swallowing her words whole before they could be heard or felt at the other side of the room.

"Well then I suppose a woman who's walked half of Belfast in a day deserves to have sore feet."

"Pardon me?" she squeaked out indignantly.

"Well forgive me but I believe it was you I saw standin' on the doorstep of Jamie Kirkpatrick's house not an hour ago, lookin' like a dog who doesn't know whether or not to wag its tail. Tell me I'm mistaken, that it was all a trick of the fog an' my eyes, darlin' an' I'll believe ye."

"Even if you know me to be a liar?" She asked, exhausted by subterfuge and half-truths.

"Even then," came the reply.

"It was me as you well know."

"Do ye visit him on a daily basis or only when yer husband is out of town?"

"Only today and if you'd stayed to see, you'd know that I never so much as rang the bell."

"So why were ye there?" There was something remorseless in his voice that insinuated without the slightest effort. He would be a brutal interrogator, she suspected, feeling once again the tightness grab and claw at her throat.

"I needed someone to talk to," she said quietly finding that it was easier somehow to tell the truth here in the dark.

"About what?"

"You."

There was a deep breath expelled in the corner and then his voice, tired, somehow defeated, "I think we'd best turn the lights on, don't you?"

She felt him move, the air stirring the very slightest bit, no more disturbed than by a cricket's passing. Had he known how to do this his entire life, been born with the ability to move in silence like a ghost, so one was never entirely certain if he'd passed or not. The light came on seconds later and she forced herself to look at him, frightened as she was of meeting his eyes. There could be no hope for lies now.

He was exhausted, that was at once apparent. There were rings under his eyes, a beard that made him look like a cross between a pirate and the devil and a great, overwhelming emanation of fatigue that said he had not slept in days.

"Why would ye go to Jamie to talk about me?" he asked, no anger in his face only a need, a desperation that was matched by her own to be held, to find oblivion.

"I couldn't think of anyone else."

"An' why now, why this sudden urgency to talk about me?" His voice was flat, gentle and she almost gave in then to her desire, to be taken in his arms and told soft and tumbled lies that would hold the day at the door, until she saw, with a flash, what was happening. Inside her something curled itself tighter, refusing light.

"When did you get back to Belfast, Casey? Or did you ever actually leave?" she asked fighting hard not to tremble, not to fly across the room and strike his face.

He gave her a hard look for a moment and then something crumbled and she could see he had made the decision to tell her the truth.

"I was in Derry for the first two days an' then an emergency came up an' I've been back in Belfast since."

"You've been back in Belfast for two days and you saw no need to come home," she said quietly.

"No one was to know that I was back."

"Am I on the list of those not to be trusted now?" she asked angrily. She turned trying to find her jeans through the red mist that clouded her vision. The bastard, how dare he! Then suddenly cold realization gripped her and she turned back to find him watching her carefully. "Where did you stay all that time?"

"With Seamus," was the reply.

" I went to see Seamus today," she said uneasily.

"I know ye did," he said, looking down at his hands which lay flat against his thighs.

"Were you there listening?"

"No, I was gone on business."

"But he told you, didn't he?" she asked, tears of frustration boiling up into her eyes.

Casey nodded looking half-apologetic. "He'd no choice but to darlin'."

"No, of course he didn't, you men never do, do you?"

"He gave me the gist of it but said he'd leave it to ye to fill in the holes."

The kettle was screaming now, the sound rising higher and higher, like someone trying to burst their own heart with agony. She went down the narrow staircase into the kitchen, each step precise and careful as if to release any of the control she had on herself would guarantee permanent madness. She shut the flame off, removed the kettle and then taking an envelope out of her bag, walked back up the stairs to the bedroom.

"There," she said shoving the innocuous white gummed paper under his nose. "Did he tell you that as well?"

Casey opened it slowly and after glancing at the contents held the envelope out to her. "Ye do as ye wish with it, run as far as it will take ye."

He held the envelope towards her still, a glaring accusation between the two of them. Then finally when she would not take it, he let it fall and spill onto the floor, and she watched silently as their freedom scattered a hundred different ways.

"I asked him to order you to leave, to throw you out of the damn country if need be and he said he would if he could but that it wasn't his place anymore. Just what," she looked up from the thousands of pound notes that carpeted their bedroom, " the hell did he mean by that?"

He rubbed his forehead wearily and closed his eyes for a minute before answering. "He can't order me, darlin'."

"Why is that Casey?" her voice was steeled, its persistence needle sharp.

His face was unguarded as he met her eyes and she saw with a sudden terrible clarity how he would appear as an old man and knew just as certainly that he would never survive to be that old man.

"It's because he takes his orders from you, isn't it?" she asked in a bare whisper. "Doesn't he?" her voice began to escalate and she felt her carefully constructed control shatter and fall to the floor where it waited to cut her and leave her to bleed slowly to death. Her next words came out wearily; so far away from her it seemed that she could barely hear them. "Doesn't he?"

Casey's very posture gave her the answer she sought. Her knees buckled under her and she collapsed to the floor, pound notes crinkling and rising, sticking to her skin, suffocating her nose and mouth. It stank, the curious way money always does, metallic and sulfurous, leaving its stench on anything it touches. It smelled, she thought dimly, like old blood, the kind you tried to wash out but it just wouldn't leave, the stain somehow just getting darker and bigger. She could hardly breathe for its smell sticking in her nostrils, but this did not, strangely enough, panic her. She heard things as though from a great distance. People did these sorts of things when they were in shock, didn't they? She could feel the air move back and forth above her and someone saying 'Oh Christ, nononono...' and knew it was herself. The thing inside was curling tighter and tighter, refusing the light and knowing that it could not run far or fast enough now. The truth that she'd so ignorantly thought she needed, could not survive without, was here, out on the table the way she'd demanded and she could hardly stand the sight of it. She turned her face slowly, feeling the filth of the money coat her skin and knowing that somehow she would never be clean of it again.

"Were you ever going to tell me that I was married to the head of the IRA?" she asked rather calmly, all things considered.

"I'm tellin' ye now."

"Yes, I suppose you are," she said feeling a strange desire to laugh hysterically, laugh until she was unconscious, unfeeling, uneverything. Shock again, she supposed.

She heard Casey get up and leave the room, heard various rustlings and clatterings in the kitchen and then his firm step around her prone form and the scent of tea and something far stronger.

"Come on darlin' sit up; ye can keep yer eyes shut fer the rest of yer life 'twon't change a damned thing."

"Fucking prosaic Irishman," she muttered and pushed her way onto her knees, as exhausted as she would have been from a twenty-four hour shift at the plant. The steaming cup he put into her hands was short on tea and long on brandy. Two stiff swallows put a little strength back into her muscles and loosened the knot in her chest slightly.

"Better then," he said softly, hunkering down amidst the crumpled piles of money beside her.

"Better," she agreed without enthusiasm, as the brandy poured its balm through her veins. She shifted, the money filling the air with its accusing crackles, uncomfortably aware of Casey's proximity, aware that he was waiting for some sign, some word from her, to allow him the knowledge of what his first step should be. She'd be damned if she'd give him the pleasure. Instead, she fixed him with a hard, unblinking green stare, to which he replied in kind with a hard, unblinking black stare. For the first time he faltered before she did, eyes dropping down to stare sightlessly at the heavy calluses on his hands.

"I don't know what to say, darlin', it's what I am, it's what was expected of me, there was never another road to be traveled." He looked at her with a kind of resignation in his face that she had never seen there before and, for the first time, she saw that it was true, even if only for him, there had never been any other way. Within his prison, she was beginning to catch a glimpse of her own.

"Are you saying that your father expected this of you?" she asked and wondered for a moment if she'd pushed too far as anger flared in his face and was quickly suppressed. Then he sighed and wearily scratched at his beard with one hand.

"No, I am not sayin' that but I've told ye again an' again, I am not like my father."

"No, you're like your damned grandfather," she said angrily "and we all know what a glorious end he came to, don't we?"

He sat down heavily and leaning against the bed let his head fall back onto its surface. "Pamela, I'm too tired to argue. I'm not my Da' an' I'm not my Grandfather. I'm me, an' I'm doin' the only thing I know how to do an' that is to fight. I understand better than anyone what the costs of that are or could be. Ye've known who I was an' what that meant from the first. An' perhaps the picture I've painted of my Da' was more for Pat's sake then my own. Da' was just plain frustrated with this 'new' IRA, said to me that all the societies, papers an' lectures in the world weren't goin' to make a damn bit of difference. Sure an' the only war he'd known was the border campaign an' ye'll know that was no grand success, but he believed that this new reformed army was only stalling because they were too afraid to step forward, to grasp the future by the throat an' give it a good shake. Ye've got to understand that the Belfast chapter was a shambles then an' is almost nonexistent now. Dublin was never real conscientious about keepin' the Belfast contingent abreast of their doin's. Ye see," his gaze was locked solidly with hers now, his eyes burning with frustrations near to a thousand years old, "those Dublin boys with all their lofty notions don't understand the Belfast soldier," his voice echoed all the bitter resentment of the front-line man for those tucked cozily away at headquarters. He breathed out heavily, the dark circles under his eyes seeming to deepen perceptibly as he did. "But then, for what's left of the Belfast army, Republicanism has become a social event, a series of dates on the calendar to celebrate the births and deaths of heroes they never knew."

"They," Pamela echoed, "why do you say they, Casey, you're their leader are you not, don't you consider yourself one of them?"

"No, darlin' I do not." It was said quietly but emphatically and she did not miss the current that slid blackly, insidiously between the spoken words.

"And Seamus?" she asked fighting back a nameless panic.

"Nor does he," he replied watching her face carefully for a reaction.

"How many of you are there?" she whispered bleakly, horror washing through her in tiny rippling waves, building far-out, threatening to drown that thing inside her that even now shriveled in the breeze that warned of the impending storm.

"Our numbers aren't large, yet."

It was the yet that felt like a stinging slap in the face and thrust her into the harsh light of the room, this room that she had one day believed to be delivered from into the marble arms of milk and honey America. But that had been before she realized her husband was splitting a terrorist organization in two in order to force peace in the only way the Irish had ever understood, violence. Born to the gun, Jamie had said of Casey, and she had had the arrogance to deny it, she had listened to the poetry-fed idealism of Pat and believed that it could be the same for his brother and now knew that it could not. She remembered the night they had first made love and wondered if they hadn't cursed themselves, somehow, there under the scorching light of the moon, lying on those black rocks, trying through passion to deny the finiteness of life. Lying on the names of dead men scored unflinchingly into eternity.

"If ye want to go," Casey said his voice purposefully flat, "the money is yers, Seamus saw to that. I would not begrudge ye the life ye deserve darlin'."

"And is that what I deserve Casey, to live without you? How am I to go, if you won't? Did you think of that, you bastard, when you stuck this blood money in a goddamn envelope?" She crumpled the incriminating piece of white paper up and threw it at him. It skimmed his ear and landed impotently on the bed behind. "Did you forget my ticket to Disneyland, for this little fairytale I'm supposed to want to live?"

"It's not blood money," Casey said in a low voice, "d'ye think I'm so daft as to do that to ye? It's me own money, an' now it's yers."

"It's your money," she said, tilting her head at him in mystification. "What the hell do you mean? Casey there's thousands of dollars here."

He sighed, "Aye, there is an' it's mine to give or to burn as I see fit."

"You told me the Riordans hadn't so much as a pot to piss in for the last fifty years."

"The money was meant for the cause, each generation has put aside what they could. When Ireland was liberated it was to be used to help pull her up out of the muck that civil war was likely to leave behind."

Pamela sat down hard, completely dumbfounded.

"And the money was not to be used for anything else, no matter how desperate the situation, was it?" she asked, the knowledge of the answer making her feel far older than her years.

"No it wasn't." he replied so quietly she had to strain to hear the words.

"But you were willing to give every last cent to me?"

"Aye, I was." He met her eyes, his gone dark and sad, the merciless light of the room seeming to pull the bones up to the surface of his skin, to create shadow and the multiplications of pain the years will bring.

"Sweet Jesus, why would you do that, Casey?"

"Love," he replied, "it'll be a strange an' desperate thing at times, won't it. Ye'll do things ye'd never have imagined yerself doin' an' it'll seem like the only road open to ye."

"You'd do this for me? You'd pay for my freedom with your ancestor's dreams?"

"Aye, I would. I've chosen a certain way of life; it doesn't mean that ye have to live it as well. I want yer happiness Jewel, an' if this money will give it to ye then yer welcome to it."

"But the money was never meant for this sort of end."

"No, but darlin' Ireland is never goin' te see the sort of freedom my family dreamed of. I think my Da' was beginnin' to see that near the end of his life. Maybe someday there will be peace an' some sort of unity but it's not likely to be the sort the Riordans have fought for."

"Then why pursue this madness, if you don't even believe it's possible, why stay?"

He smiled sadly. "To give Ireland the best sort of freedom that can be provided under whatever circumstances are existing when an' if that freedom should come."

She shook her head hopelessly and smudged angrily at the tears, hot and futile, that welled up and poured down her face.

"You make me so sad man, do you know that? You make me so damn sad."

"I told ye I would," he said and then pushed himself wearily onto his knees and across the breadth of the tiny room, so close she could feel the heat of his skin.

"Ye've forgiven me my sins in the past an' ye'll have so many to forgive in the future darlin', there are no chains bound around ye, when ye decide ye cannot take another day, another moment of this, I'll let ye go."

She watched him for a moment. Such a big man to humble himself so. Such a small man compared to the cross he'd been designated to bear. Her own man, in all the ways that mattered.

"I need ye to touch me, Jewel, I cannot touch ye first, not tonight."

Damn him, she thought wearily, closing her eyes, taking the only refuge available to her at present. He knew what it was for her to be close to him, that his mere presence would begin the craving in her fingertips, the purely sensate bliss of skin, how soft the unsullied ivory of his shoulders was compared to the roughness of the black whorls of hair that ran the width of his chest. The scars and bumps and ridges she could trace with perfect precision in the dark, what it was to have him tremble and shake in her arms, all that power in the daylight, all that need in the dark.

She touched him, stroked her hands firmly up the contours of his face, felt beard on the cusp of rough to silky, then the baby-fine edges of his shorn hair. Smelled the smoke of close, dark meetings, the whiskey of their aftermath, the iron of sweat, the blood of fear, the bitter wine of despair. Touched his mouth with her own, lightly, the fragility of forgiveness, hard, the anger of loneliness. Heard him moan and smiled, just a little, to herself. There was a place, a cocoon she could create for him, a refuge bound in rough cotton sheets and silhouetted by sulfurous streetlights, that he would never be able to find elsewhere, even if he should try.

She opened her eyes, found dark eyes invading her, saw what his self-control was costing him and what it was saying. Make love to me, the words were silent but no less forceful in their muteness. Make love to me and make me forget, forget with skin and hair and teeth and tongue, with dance and drum and bone and blood, make me forget that I found you seeking solace with another man. A stranger to this room, this bed, this sacrament of two. Lover, make me forget.

And forget he did, as she took away his clothes and with them his fatigue, with the shedding of her own she pushed away any world beyond the bed and her touch. She shut out the light, brought darkness down and then on the bed, body to body, she became a map for his fingers, Braille for the blindness of emotion. On the collarbone, read vulnerability, on the swelling upslope of breast, read succor and rest. Down then to the swift glide of ribcage, the smooth upthrust of hip and belly, in these read the foreshadowing of the next chapter, bound in gold leaf and roses, in salt and dark, damp earth, in the parting of the thighs find velvet, fecund and warm. Upon entry into the body, find oblivion, red and swaddling. Know the final chapter is about the road home, the finding of peace, the communion of one under God's loving eye. Lover, make me forget.

The afterword, the aria, the female's song that is sung for herself is reassurance, to lie in the lover's arms and be soothed, to be the child as he was only moments ago. To believe for a fragile space, that those arms that curve protectively around her can hold the world at bay, that God loves lovers and will not tear them apart. To believe with eyes closed that love is all sweetness, that bodies are all fire, that life is more than a coursing of blood through too precarious veins. Talk, if small, is possible then.

"Casey, what's to become of us?" she asked quietly.

"We fight an' we win where we can," he answered sleepily, the words his last bit of consciousness before the death-like slumber of true exhaustion found him.

"And if we lose?" she asked the empty air around her, relieved that Casey could not answer her.

Chapter Thirty-six
May the Lord in His Mercy Be Kind to Belfast

FOR THE BRITISH THE HISTORY OF THE IRISH HAD MELTED rather conveniently into the Celtic mist after the civil war of 1921. Ireland had been put back in her place and quite soundly so. The Irish memory, however, was much longer and less forgiving. Fifty years were as nothing to the Irish memory. They had learned the first commandment of history the hard way; it had happened before and thus it could happen again.

The summer of 1969 opened with unease in Belfast. Protestants and Catholics who lived on the edge of tribal boundaries quietly packed up and began the retreat from the undeclared frontlines. If the government couldn't admit that trouble, real trouble, was coming, then the people whom it affected most deeply wouldn't be so foolish. In Belfast, the threat of violence was very real, with its tens of thousands of working class people, many unemployed and with the prejudices and old hatreds that straddled both sides of the divide. A small scuffle could easily turn into a pogrom as it had done before in the city of blood and steel. And so, in the stifling summer air, tension reigned supreme, waiting for only a sign, some small skirmish, to break the entire city open.

Since January's long march, the country had been priming itself for a blowout. The People's Democracy had staged a series of protests, against unemployment rates, which in the Catholic population always ranked as some of the highest in the western world, against discriminatory housing practices, against iron clad electoral boundaries and against the oppression of a people who were too angered to be kept down any longer. In the streets of Derry, the Catholic youth were ripe for a fight, the marches and demonstrations that had channeled their frustrations were now banned, and so their rage simmered and bided its time.

On the Orange side unease was brewing as well, from the well-heeled Unionists of Stormont to the hard-liner on the streets, there was a sense that the tide, with two hundred and fifty years of history to their advantage, had turned and was about to run against them.

In March and April of that year there were several explosions that destroyed an electricity substation and a reservoir in the Mourne Mountains that fed the water pipes going into Belfast. Orange extremists blamed the IRA and everyone else blamed the Orange extremists. *The Protestant Telegraph*, an organ of extremist propaganda said the bombings were proof of a reactivated IRA and were an ominous warning of what lay in wait for Ulster under the aegis of a shadow army reborn from the ashes of rage and blood.

On April 22nd though, a much larger bomb was dropped in the form of the election to Westminster of Bernadette Devlin, one of the founders and leading lights of the People's Democracy, a miniskirted, raucous-voiced force of nature that turned the Mother of all Parliaments on its bewigged ear with one of the most electrifying maiden speeches the rarefied walls of Westminster had ever heard. The second shock of the day, rather appropriately, was the announcement by Prime Minister Terence O'Neill that the one man, one vote issue would be put into law. The next day his cabinet began to resign in protest, feeling that he was opening the gates of their world to the rabble of angry Catholics. More bombings of water mains took place and on the 28th of April, O'Neill resigned, figuratively and literally bombed out of office by the very people who'd once supported him. He had failed his own people, had never had the support of the Catholics, and had now angered Britain who'd expected him to toe the old line and keep Ulster's contentious house in order.

Lured by the scent of chaos that was slowly building and leaking its way through the streets, activists and student protesters began to fly in from around the world, as if the coming conflagration were some sort of social event, a stamp on the passport of professional protest.

April in Derry saw fierce rioting after the police banned a march from Burntollet Bridge to Derry and, in the ensuing fight, the police rushed a house, mistakenly believing that stone-throwing youth were sheltering there and batoned the innocent occupants. Samuel Devenney, a forty-two year old taxi driver, died from internal injuries caused by the batons. Through the oracle glass of hindsight, he would be claimed as the first death of the Troubles. But then under a sweltering summer sky, the troubles were not yet spelled with a capital T and people had no way of knowing that a middle-aged man's death was only the first of many.

Summer brought the marching season and with it the torch of sectarian hatred and Belfast, with eight hundred years of rage, was more than ready to burn.

FATHER TERENCE MCGINTY HAD NOT BEEN TO THE CITY by the lough for many years. And though much was familiar, much had also changed.

There were always the inevitable landmarks, the things innate to a city that even a visitor would recognize. The long velvet sweep of the grounds at Stormont, the Romanesque pillars of city hall, the greening gates of Queen's University. And then there were the things that one who has gone and come back will know. The crowded streets, the dingy brick lines of the rowhouses, sprouting the ubiquitous two, three and four potted chimneys, the well-scrubbed pavement stones outside the homes, the open doors, the neighbor-hood pubs where only the locals drank, the shops run by three generations of the same family, the people who had left and those that had stayed.

And what had changed? The tension in the streets was not entirely new but it was of proportions he'd never known before. People hurried about their business, didn't linger over back gates and in laneways chatting and there was a feeling in the air of dread expectation that made it hard to breathe. Belfast was a city in waiting.

He'd arrived on a mid-August afternoon, with the intent of staying with his old friend Father Joe Swinney in the monastery of the Resurrectionist Church. The red brick colossus stood like an ancient guardian over the dividing line between what was unofficially acknowledged as the Catholic and Protestant areas. Over one wall was Sandy Row, an area that was famous for Protestant militancy and behind it stretched the predominantly Catholic enclaves of the Lower Falls and the Clonard district, both Republican strongholds. The Resurrectionist Church had provided refuge and succor for people of both faiths and during the second world war when German bombs rained down with impunity upon Belfast, people of each denomination had huddled in its shelter.

Father Terry arrived in time for afternoon tea, a worn carpetbag tucked under one arm and a burly oak walking stick at the end of the other.

Father Joe, as he was fondly known to his parishioners, greeted him affectionately, kissing him on both cheeks, a habit he'd picked up during his years in Rome and never dropped. He was a short, rotund man with a rosy beaming face, twinkly blue eyes and a balding head, fringed now with faded blond hair. Father Terry had always thought he looked exactly as one might imagine Friar Tuck to look.

"I've got the kettle on; we'll sit and take a break then. Are you tired from your trip? No, well that's probably best as we'll need all the hands we can get soon enough."

"Why?" Terry asked mildly, watching as the cherubic priest took down the familiar green box of Lyons tea and shook a few crumbly digestive biscuits out onto a plate.

"Because this city is a stick of dynamite and the fuse has already been lit, we're all just awaiting the explosion now. Did you hear the news out of Derry?"

"Could hardly avoid it," Terry took a sip of his steaming tea and a bite of stale biscuit. Monday night in Derry, 'Roaring Meg', a siege gun used by the Protestant defenders in 1689 against the Catholic forces of James II, had bellowed out over the city signaling the beginning of the Apprentice Boys Day March. On that same evening, the RUC had been given permission to gas the Bogside just before midnight. Derry was a city under siege. The defenders wrapped their faces in wet rags, built the barricades even higher, pried up streets for stones to throw and took to the top of Rossville flats, where they were above the choking gas and could rain their fuselage down on the police below.

"There's talk of the British Army being called in," Father Joe said and sat down heavily. He paused to put sugar in his tea and take two biscuits before continuing. "There's been attacks on the RUC stations here and there's barricades going up. Stormont has lost control and knows it; calling in the British Army is throwing in the white towel. Bit ironic isn't it, a police state that doesn't have enough police? Have another biscuit, will you, you're still thin as a sideways rake."

"The church is in a rather vulnerable position here," Terry said waving away a third biscuit.

"We are," Father Joe agreed, "but I try to look at it from the angle that we're in the best position to help any and all when the trouble breaks."

"An' ye believe it's inevitable that it will?"

"Terry my old friend, you've seen some trouble in this old country over the years, have you ever felt the tension the way it is now?"

"No," Terry agreed quietly, "ye'll have to forgive my naïveté Joe, it comes from having seen it all come to naught before. I can't countenance blood on the streets again an' see it make no difference."

"You still grieve Brendan, don't you?"

"Aye an' Brian. I don't particularly want to outlive Brendan's grandsons."

"And how are the boys?" Father Joe asked, absentmindedly taking a fifth biscuit, the crumbs of the previous four speckling the front of his cassock.

"Good, the oldest got married a few months back an' the youngest is doin' quite well at university."

"Married?" Father Joe sighed, "I remember baptizin' him, roared like a banshee when the water hit his head and then peed down the front of my soutane."

"Well ye know the Riordans never did feel kindly about water."

"True enough. Well then, Terry, are you ready to roll up your sleeves and get to work? I was just itemizing the contents of the medical cabinet when you came."

"Aye," Terry sighed and pushing back his chair, stood, "let it never be said that in Ireland we aren't prepared when the blood starts to spill."

CONTRARY TO FATHER TERRY'S WORDS, Casey was not, at present, faring very well at all.

"We cannot," he said for the third time, "put armed men out on the streets, we'll have an all out bloodbath if we do." A semi-circle of hostile, stubborn faces looked back at him. "Be reasonable boys, ye know the state of our arsenal is extremely limited we've had every old Republican an' his mother out diggin' up weapon caches from the fifties an' we still are only lookin' at a handful of guns an' ammunition. They have automatic weapons, armored vehicles and an unending supply of bullets."

"But we can't stand back an' leave our own people to fend for themselves," protested a fair-haired boy named Sean.

"I never suggested that we should. There's us an' every old republican who can still stand an' the lot of us'll be out in the streets in force. We have to keep the peace as best as we can though. We're not equipped to go to war, we don't have the numbers an' we don't have the weapons an' that is final. Any aggression on our part is goin' to provoke a backlash against our own neighborhoods an' families that the RUC will only be too happy to provide."

Just then, Dacy came running around the corner and stopped sharply in front of them, breathless and winded.

"There was a—demonstration—up at Divis Flats. RUC attacked the marchers—an' they've pulled back into the Falls," he gasped for air, "an' there's barricades goin' up. Word on the street is they're goin' to call out the B-Specials."

"The time is upon us I'd say."

Casey took a deep breath, "Right, well, everyone with so much as a trickle of Republicanism in them has been mobilized. We'll have to take special care of the areas that are mixed with or right on the border of the Protestant neighborhoods. Seamus an' I'll take the Lower Falls, Sean you an' Dacy are in the Ardoyne, Kevin an' Mack take the end of the Shankill by Unity Flats. John checked in with me before an' he's got Clonard an' the top end of Springfield Road covered. Worst comes to worst, encourage people to retreat into Andersontown an' the Murph."

The men split off quickly, going their separate directions, none really knowing what to expect or what they might return to in their own homes and neighborhoods when the night was over.

Old rubbish, broken down furniture, vegetable crates and cardboard had been collected earlier for the traditional August 15th bonfires. Here and there they'd been set ablaze already, crimson crackles heady in the twilight.

"D'ye smell that Seamus?" Casey asked, drawing in a lungful of smoky air.

"Smell what?" Seamus asked, noting with alarm the number of people milling about the barricades.

"The smell of change."

"Oh aye, if change smells like we're approachin' the gates of hell, then I smell it."

HELL IN A VERY SMALL PLACE WOULD BEAR AN UNCANNY RESEMBLANCE to Belfast tonight, Pat thought grimly as he passed yet another barricade burning, with a goodly supply of youth bent on a long, ugly night of it, illuminated behind it. His own band of rebels had been meant to be protesting up in front of Divis Flats, but he'd been overwhelmed by a sense of futility. Protest in the face of tanks seemed too much like casting pearls before swine, with the pearls being crushed into conformity by the uncaring hooves of the swine. He longed for a different sort of action, to mend rather than wound.

Ahead of him loomed the Church of the Resurrection, windows ablaze with light, small beacons of sanctuary for those who would fall tonight. It was his destination, this is where the wounded and the frightened would come, and he would be here to do what he could.

He rapped on the faded door of the service entrance and then rang the bell beside it. He waited patiently for the minutes it took before a hurrying set of footsteps answered his call.

"Yes?" A tall scarecrow of a priest stood before him, sandy hair, peppered with age, hanging across his forehead, the lace-trimmed edge of his alb sagging below the bottom of his cassock.

"I—I came to help," Pat said, uncertain now that he was here what to say.

"Then ye'd best come in," the priest said.

Pat stepped into the light of an entryway just off a kitchen that smelled incongruously of gingerbread and antiseptic. On the table lay piles of gauze, splints and tape. Bottles of iodine were lined up precisely like small brown bowling pins. Kettles boiled on the huge stove and a round, amply-fleshed woman bustled about the floor.

"Maggie?" he said disbelievingly.

The woman turned from the cake she'd just extracted from the oven and gave him a shrewd glance. Then her eyes twinkled out from the folds of flesh. "Pat, is it yerself? We'll not have seen ye the last few nights on the hill."

"Pat?" the old priest echoed, though no one paid attention.

"What are ye doin' here in a monastery Maggie?" Pat asked, some vestige of his Catholic boyhood feeling shock at seeing a woman where none had been seen before.

"The same as yerself laddie I imagine, came to help. I'm not much good for sewin' up cuts an' such, nor providin' spiritual help but the stomach prevails through emergencies of all sorts an' I was thinkin' people comin' here may need a bit of tea an' comfort an' that I most assuredly can provide. The rest," Maggie turned her cake out and patted its well-risen top with satisfaction, "I'll leave to the good Lord an' yerselves."

"Pat?" the priest echoed again and this time Pat turned and said, "Yes?"

The old man stared at him a long moment. Pat noticed that he'd one blue eye and one brown, which gave his stare a concentrated energy it wouldn't have possessed otherwise.

"Yes?" Pat said again, beginning to feel distinctly uncomfortable.

"Ye'll not remember me," the old man said softly, "ye were just a wain last time I saw ye, barely crawlin' about though that didn't stop ye from eatin' my potted asphodel down to the roots an' vomitin' the results of it up on the cat."

"Father Terry?" Pat said in wonderment.

"Yer brother said ye'd the look of yer daddy about ye, an' I see he's right."

"I ate a potted asphodel?" Pat said.

"Oh aye, had to have yer wee stomach pumped out fer it too. Threw up in the car on yer dad an' yer brother, threw up on the nuns at the hospital. Terrified the lot of us I can tell ye. But two hours after yer tummy was emptied, ye were right as rain. Didn't stop the nuns from tearin' a terrific strip off yer dad an' myself. Tellin' us the Good Lord hadn't equipped men for the proper Christian upbringing of a child. We tended to agree with them in principle if not in practice at the time."

"I've come to help." Pat said blankly not knowing if Father Terry expected any response to his story.

"Aye, well that's good, we'll need all hands on deck this night. We've already had some poor miscreant come in with his hands burned from tryin' to make a Molotov cocktail. Told the wee fool it might have helped if he'd thrown the silly thing after he'd lit it."

Just then, there was a terrific pounding at the door.

"Merciful heavens what'll it be now?" Maggie muttered, dusting floury hands on her apron and waddling for the door.

A white face popped itself in seconds later, "Father, Father ye must come quick, they've set the school on fire!"

The school, situated in close proximity to the monastery was indeed ablaze. Fire licked up one side and across the shingled roof in a merry dance. Smoke rolled in heavy coils into the night, choking in its density.

"Right then," Father Terry said briskly, "we'll go get the extinguishers from the monastery an' put it out."

Father Terry might have been oversimplifying the whole thing, Pat thought moments later as he fought to put out burning desks, books, and shelves amidst the zing and crack of bullets. Outside the mob who'd put match to the school had opened fire and the men inside the school were ducking and dashing trying to quench the fire's voracious appetite and avoid the bullets that tore through the shattered glass of the windows.

Outside, the fire had roared like a great deep belly laugh at its own greed. Inside it whispered, a harsh hiss as it licked at fragile papers, caught on to ink, burning words and maps, thoughts and feelings. Pat could feel blisters rising on the back of his hands. It was like being in the heart of an inferno. He saw in the pandemonium Father Terry dash past him numberless times, stamping out spot fires, pulling desks into the center of the room, piling vulnerable books on top of them. He seemed to have the strength and fortitude of a much younger man.

Twenty minutes later, it was a sorry bunch of men who stumbled out of the school, burned, soot-smeared, blistered, lungs seared with smoke. The fire was out, but whether the effort had been worth it was debatable. One wall of the school was burned away, the roof was on the verge of collapse and all the windows had exploded out in the heat. It appeared the gun-wielding mob had moved on in search of fresh victims, for no more bullets harried the night.

"Ye alright lad?" Father Terry laid a filthy hand on Pat's shoulder.

"Aye. Yerself?"

"Been worse." The priest surveyed the bedraggled bunch around him, "At least no one was hit by a bullet. I suppose that's somethin' we can be grateful for. Aye, what is it lad?" For a small hand was plucking insistently at his sleeve.

"Father ye must help, I can't find Father Joe an' there's a boy lyin' in the street."

Pat turned toward the street and saw in the ashy light a very still form lying under a street lamp.

Father Terry was already halfway there before Pat could take a step. He was kneeling, one hand on the prone figure's head when Pat caught up to him.

"Ye musn't be afraid, yer goin' to be fine," he looked swiftly at Pat and Pat read in his eyes that the boy wasn't going to be fine at all. "Call for an ambulance an' then stay put in the church." Pat ran to do as bid and then, against orders, ran right back.

"The ambulance will be here soon as it can," he said trying to infuse a reassurance that he did not feel into his voice.

"Ye see there's nothin' to fret about then, we'll get ye to the hospital an' they'll fix ye up." Father Terry had torn off the bottom of his alb and balled it up to place under the boy's head. "This here is Finn," he said to Pat as if he were introducing them under perfectly sociable conditions.

Finn, Pat noted, was no more than sixteen from the looks of him. He'd a round, snub-nosed face that wore an expression of extreme terror at present, fine blonde hair and a hole in his stomach where a bullet had punched through it.

"I must confess, Father," the boy named Finn managed to gasp out.

"Confess what lad?"

"My sins, I—" Finn grimaced and tried to put a hand down to his stomach, which Father Terry gently took before he could reach the wound.

"If it'll make ye rest easy, then tell me yer sins laddie."

"I—I stole petrol," Finn's eyelids fluttered and then opened again, though his eyes seemed a bit more hazy than before, Pat noted. "I stole it for the petrol bombs, I'm sorry," he sobbed then gasped, his body spasming with pain. "I'm sorry Father, will ye tell God I'm sorry?"

"Did ye take more petrol than was necessary for the makin' of the bombs?" Father Terry asked, smoothing the boy's sweat-soaked hair away from his forehead.

"N—oo," Finn gasped out.

"Then if ye only took what ye needed for yer purposes it isn't a sin. Ye are absolved, Finn. Now is there anything yer mammy used to sing to ye when ye were small, or a bedtime story that ye liked in particular? It'll help to pass the time until the ambulance comes."

Finn blinked slowly and Pat noticed that it took him longer each time to open his eyes again.

"Mam always sang *The Black Velvet Band* when I was small," his eyes fluttered slowly, "'twas the only thing that would put me to sleep." The hand in Father Terry's, pale and small against the priest's, was beginning to slacken a little.

"That's one of the more unusual lullabies I've come across," Father Terry said and then began to sing in an off-key croak that sounded like a crow with a severe head cold.

> *In a neat little town they call Belfast*
> *Apprenticed to trade I was bound*
> *And many's the hour of happiness*
> *I spent in that sweet little town.*

Pat didn't possess Casey's melting tenor tones but he did have a decent, soft voice that joined Father Terry's—

> *Til a sad misfortune came o'er me,*
> *That forced me to flee from the land*
> *Far away from my friends and relations*
> *Betrayed by a black velvet band.*

Pat realized suddenly that he was singing alone, for Father Terry spoke in low, softly cadenced Latin, his free hand making a cross on Finn's smooth forehead.

> *Her eyes they shone like the diamonds*
> *I thought her the queen of the land*

And her hair hung over her shoulder
Tied back with a black velvet band.

Pat had known the words since childhood and knew they would be with him always now. Finn smiled softly, his eyes closed, lashes like cornsilk against his child's cheek.

"Sing me on to sleep mam," he whispered and then his hand slid from Father Terry's to lay limply across his chest and so Pat sang on, while around them the pall of smoke grew thicker and bullets cracked and thundered and the world as they knew it burned away.

REVOLUTIONS MAY HAVE BEEN STARTED ON SO SMALL AN ARSENAL, but Casey was quite certain not a one had ever been won in such a manner. A Thompson, a .303 rifle and four pistols. Hardly an arsenal to be reckoned with. His own weapon an ancient pistol whose barrel had to be turned manually after each round.

He was crouched down under a window on the first floor of St. Colum's grammar school. Around him lay the shattered remnants of glass where the window had been blown out. Behind him, the four men he'd holed up with inside a classroom. Liam Miller knocked out cold against the far wall, a huge bruise flowering across his face where a rifle had kicked back and rendered him unconscious. Above Casey, visible against the dark night, long red tracers split and opened the sky, flowing and flowering in a display of deadly fireworks. In the street, the mob surged back and forth and the police were nowhere to be seen. It had been a solid forty minutes of holding the howling crowd back, denying them entrance any further into the Divis Street area.

Seamus stood and cocked an eye out to the street, "Do these bastards not know when to call it a day?" he asked and, taking aim, fired out into the night. The answer to his question was a sustained barrage of bullets whizzing above his ear.

"Shit," he said and sat down with a decided thump.

"Are ye hit?" Casey asked urgently, crawling across the paper-strewn floor to him.

"No, but the damn thing near took my ear off an' I've sat on some little bugger's compass, aagh, oh— Jayse—there I've got the damn thing out."

Casey stood, scanned the scene outside, aimed above the head of the crowd and squeezed off a bullet. He crouched back down quickly, smelling the thick tang of cordite heavy in the air.

"We can't keep this up much longer, there's maybe five rounds apiece left an' then we're done for. Seamus?"

Seamus didn't answer; he was leaning against the wall illuminated by a burst of fire from outside, the reflection of flame licking up his face like a gruesome, shifting deathmask.

"The bullet," he whispered, "the one that missed me..." he pointed, words failing.

Casey's eyes followed the direction of Seamus' finger reluctantly, as if by not looking he could change what had happened.

In the strange, dancing light he saw Liam Miller, still unconscious, mouth slack. Casey blinked, no, not unconscious afterall. A neat round hole, black about the edges, sat where Liam's throat had once been.

"Oh Christ," he breathed, crawling across the floor between the rows of desks.

He'd seen dead men before, in prison it wasn't a rare occurrence and so he recognized the form of it. The look of startlement, if death had come hard or fast, the rictus of terror for the ones who had met their end with violence, the peaceful aspect of those who'd gone willingly. But Liam merely seemed asleep, neither profoundly peaceful nor afraid of the departure he'd just taken. Casey took his hand; the skin was already cooling, stiffening with the absence of life. He knew what he would see if the light were stronger. The misted blue that began about the lips and spread slowly across the surface of the body, as if, as the ancients had believed, the soul was breathed out through the mouth at the end.

He passed his palm gently over the eyelids to be certain the eyes were closed. He then dipped the pad of his thumb in the dark stream of blood that chilled and congealed even now beneath Liam's throat. He raised his thumb and tried to recall what he knew about Liam Miller. He'd only met him twice before today. He was an old republican, part of his father's generation, one of the old guard who'd come out today to defend their neighborhoods and their honor.

"Seamus, do ye know anything about him?" Casey asked.

"What do ye mean?"

"What was special about him?"

Seamus shook his head, rubbing a thumb speculatively across his chin.

"He grew roses," he said at last. "Loved 'em, was the pride an' joy of his life. Took first place in a flower show once with some hybrid he'd created himself. Was so damn happy about it he bought everyone at the pub a drink that night."

Casey nodded. His thumb pressed into the cool forehead, slid down to the scarred bridge of the nose, rose and glided across the bony ridge above the eye sockets. "May ye grow roses in God's garden for all eternity," he whispered. He took Liam's hands and folded them gently one over top the other and then, grabbing his pistol moved quickly back across the floor to his position by the window.

He fired off two more rounds over the heads of the frenzied mob, pausing to crank the barrel over each time. The mob outside was quieter now and in the distance there was a steady hum like the sound of a large, lumbering insect moving across dry ground. There was something disturbingly familiar about the noise and he tried to separate it out from the explosions and sharp cracks of gunfire that surrounded it. His ear was distracted however by a scuffle at the door behind him.

"State yer name an' business," he heard the old man guarding the door say gruffly.

"Casey are ye in there? It's Dacy. I've just come from the Ardoyne."

"Let him in," Casey said tersely, his hands suddenly shaky around the gun. "What the hell do ye mean by leavin' yer station?"

Dacy took a minute to breathe, his hands on his legs in an effort to steady himself. "They're burnin' out the Ardoyne, there's nothin' left to defend. We're out of ammo an' Sean took a hit in the arm, he was bleedin' somethin' awful. I got him to the Church an' then I came here."

"What do ye mean they're burnin' the Ardoyne out?" Dacy flinched visibly as Casey grabbed his arms and shook him.

"Mobs of Loyalists, pullin' people out of their homes an' then settin' fire to the houses. They're destroyin' everything."

"An' the police?"

"Are lettin' them do it. Sean said he even saw a few police in civilian overcoats millin' around with the crowds. They've brought in tanks, fockin' Shorlands, an' they've got machine guns shootin' right through the walls of houses. Was an old lady cryin' in the street said they killed her grandson, only nine an' layin' in his bed, goddamn bullet went right through the wall an' into his head."

"Did ye go to my home?" Casey asked and Dacy looked into his face and saw an awful and terrible stillness in the man's eyes.

"Aye. 'Twas on fire Casey."

"My wife?" Casey asked, his voice low and trembling.

Dacy wanted nothing more than to look away from the man, but found himself paralyzed by the dark unflinching eyes.

"I don't know Casey; the fire was out of control I couldn't get near to the door."

"Was the door open?"

"No 'twas closed. Casey if she'd been inside—" He hissed involuntarily as the hands on his arms clenched harder.

"Don't ye say it Dacy, don't ye goddamn say it."

"Casey, I asked the neighbors an' they saw no one come out or go in."

The hands on his arms released and pulled back. Then Dacy felt the smooth heft of a gun placed into his hand.

"Ye'll need the gun," he said as Casey stood and walked toward the door, "it's pure madness out there."

Casey turned in the doorway, "I am goin' to find my wife, an' if I find her hurt or worse I shall find the bastards who did it an' kill them with my bare hands an' then," his voice faltered for a moment and resumed in a softer tone, "an' then I really don't care much what happens to me. Either way I've no more need of the gun this night." He nodded and moved out into the darkness beyond the door.

"D'ye think we should stop him?" Dacy asked Seamus.

"Wouldn't do any good to try," Seamus sighed, reaching in his pocket for his last three bullets, "either way he'll have to see for himself."

Dacy looked down at the gun in his hand, "Where's the bullets for this thing?"

Seamus eyed him mildly in the flickering light, "Ye've only the one shot left."

"One bullet?" Dacy said disbelievingly.

"Aye," Seamus nodded, "best make it count, boy."

THE WORST OF THE FIGHTING, WHICH HAD BROKEN ACROSS BELFAST like a wave, was over near morning. Here and there fires still raged, parked cars small infernos on the roadside, a great thick pall of smoke hanging over the city, cloaking it off from the sky.

Dawn filtered down over a scene of absolute devastation. Gutted houses, torched vehicles, entire streets laid to waste. The small enclosed communities gone, forever. A way of life for hundreds of years vanished in a puff of smoke. Lives, memories, moments, now hardly more than rubble in the streets.

Dawn drifted into morning and people began to pick their way through the ashes, sifting through the rubble for any bit of familiarity, something solid to rebuild their lives upon. An old photograph miraculously untouched, a necklace, a saucepan, anything that might serve as a reminder of their life before.

The Falls and the Ardoyne were the areas hardest hit. One hundred and fifty houses had burned down and people, homeless and set adrift on a sea of misfortune, wandered blankly through streets they'd known all their lives and saw nothing they could recognize. And some unfortunate few found their dead and carried them unseeing out into the gray morning light. Five Catholics and one Protestant had not survived the streets of Belfast that night.

Casey found his own home roofless, half collapsed but with the red door strangely unmarred and closed firmly. The brass knob was still hot to the touch when he put his hand around it. He stood against the door for a moment, the knob slowly turning in his hand, a quarter turn, a half-turn and he without the courage to face what lay inside. Three-quarters and he turned his face up to the sky, asking a God he no longer trusted to give him the strength to do what he must. A full turn and the door fell away into ashes.

Everything gone, kitchen table burnt to cinders, the tub half melted, its enamel stripped away. The wallpaper no more than curling wisps in the air, ashes of forgotten roses. Shards of pottery on the ground, splintering as he walked across them.

The staircase stood in a void, some steps entirely gone and he had a sudden vision of her walking up them ahead of him, a white nightgown billowing out around her and a glance over her shoulder, her eyes soft in the dim light, her hair a spill of furled black ribbon against the white of her nightgown. He wanted more than anything to follow her up those stairs. Two nights ago, an eternity now.

Some stairs held but others gave under his weight. There was a two-foot gap at the top before the floor resumed itself. Pat's old room now nothing more than smoking blackened brick and a view of the ravaged street. He turned right, made his way across half-crumbled beams and boards to the door of their bedroom.

It was open, smoke still drifting across it in the quiet morning air.

The bed was intact, the sheets starkly white against the black smoldering interior of the room. And it was there that he found his dead. Three steps to cross the room, not caring now if the floor held. Three steps to look down upon a still figure, sheared by fire of all its distinguishing features. He reached out a trembling hand and the flesh felt like leather under his fingers, hard, yet it gave and fell away with a soft sigh down between bones that shone like polished ivory in the gray light.

Black and white, bone and flesh that flaked away at the slightest stir. The wrists held tightly together, the ankles as well, as if she'd sought shelter within her own frame at the end.

An arm under knees, a hand under neck. He lifted her, the heat of her body making him gasp and he thought for a moment that he could feel the silken sweep of her hair fall down across his arm. He felt oddly weightless now, as if he had no more substance than the smoke, as if all the world were suspended, holding its breath.

Down the stairs then, carefully, one foot after the next. He didn't want to stumble, didn't want to jar her in the least. It was the last gift he could give her, the one of dignity.

Out through the door, over the threshold, the same one she'd walked over so trustingly as a girl, as a lover, as a wife.

On the paving stones, his face stark against its bones in the strange smoky twilight of morning, stood Jamie.

He opened his mouth as if to speak, saw the bundle in Casey's arms and closed it again.

Casey took a step, felt a terrible weakness take him in the legs just as a knife blade of pain caught him hard in the stomach.

He stumbled and sank to his knees, the sky above him blossoming a soft, warm red and knew with a hazy relief that he'd been shot. He passed his dead up into the arms of Jamie just before hitting the ground on his face.

The last thing he was aware of was the taste of ashes in his mouth.

Chapter Thirty-seven
Except Thou Bless Me

AND SO AS YOU CAN SEE," PAMELA SAID from over the top of a currant scone, "the rumors of my death have been greatly exaggerated."

"What did Casey say when he saw ye?" Pat asked from across the scrubbed oak table, sopping up the remains of his eggs with a bit of toast.

"He opened his eyes for all of two seconds, looked up at me, smiled and said 'it's good to see we both made it to the other side, darlin'' though he seemed a little confused that he wasn't in purgatory. And then he went right back to sleep."

"Poor laddy's still drugged up. I tell you it's a miracle he's with us this morning, if that bullet had been even another millimeter to the left..." Father Joe left the thought hanging in the air as he helped himself to a third of Maggie's delectable scones.

"He might still be here," Jamie put in dryly, "but he'd not be fathering any children."

"Take some more tea, James," Father Joe said, pouring himself a cup, "there's brandy on the sideboard if you need extra fortification. And how," he turned his genial countenance on Pamela, still in her nightgown and reeking of smoke, "is your head m'dear?"

"A bit sore, but considering the alternative I'm not complaining."

"Indeed, that's the spirit child," Father Joe said. Everyone was silent for a moment, considering the alternative. It was a little too firmly imprinted on their collective consciousness just what the alternative was. The alternative was at present wrapped in a sheet and lying in an unused monk's cell. Just who was the recipient of Pamela's intended fate wasn't yet quite clear. And if anyone knew, they weren't telling. It had been the least of their worries in the early morning when first Jamie had shown up dragging a bleeding and incoherent Casey and then, only moments later, Pamela had appeared on the doorstep wrapped in a blanket, a large bump on her head with no idea of how she'd gotten there. And then Pat had run in after an absence of several hours, soot smeared and frantic, having been unable to locate either his brother or Pamela. In the hours since, everyone had had their hands full, for the church had been filled with milling anxious people, fleeing fire, guns and the wrath of angry mobs.

Father Terry, who'd anointed five heads the previous night and held countless hands, thought that he could very well do with a shot of Father Joe's medicinal brandy himself. He surveyed the faces around the table and silently thanked God for the small mercies He'd seen fit to extend over the last twenty-four hours.

The kitchen was a scene of cozy domesticity, smelling vaguely of the bleach Maggie had scrubbed it down with that morning, pleasantly overlaid with bacon and freshly baked scones. Maggie stood at the stove, stirring a vast pot of porridge with one hand while cracking eggs into smoking hot bacon fat with the other. The stomach did indeed prevail through emergencies of all sorts.

The talk at the table had been deliberately careful, though inevitably the events of last night had been hashed and re-hashed. No one had been particularly forthcoming about their individual adventures though and therein lay rather a lot of mystery and many questions no one was asking.

Pat, now polishing off a glass of milk like any perfectly ordinary boy, had been vague about the hours he'd been gone. From three o'clock until six o'clock he'd been unaccounted for and had said, upon returning, that he'd gone to the Ardoyne, found the house burned and had combed the streets after that looking for his brother and Pamela. Father Terry had merely bandaged his burned hands, applied salve to the blisters on one side of his face and said nothing.

Pamela said the last thing she remembered was the tanks coming up the street, the smell of smoke and then being hit over the head with something large and heavy. For her Father Terry had avoided looking too long at the long, thin cut on her neck that wasn't deep enough to warrant special attention and again, said nothing.

Terry's eyes moved from the disheveled form of Pamela to the man at her right elbow. Even in the strange ashy light of the day, the man seemed lit by full sun. His face, after a sleepless, anxious night was perfectly attuned to his bones, revealing nothing. Occasionally he would cast a shrewd look at Pamela, or eye Pat speculatively, as if he suspected, much as Terry himself did, that each of them held pieces to the puzzle of last night, that for some reason they wouldn't or perhaps couldn't reveal.

Terry had recognized him, even in the confusion of Casey being brought in and having to dig a bullet out of the boy's thigh, even in the shock of the man then calmly going out and bringing in a wrapped body and saying that though he'd no idea of the identity of the corpse, it would seem that Casey was thoroughly convinced that it was Pamela. However, the man had been so cool and businesslike that Terry saw at once he'd no such fears himself.

So he'd known the girl was safe. For him Terry had merely poured a glass of whiskey and left him alone with his secrets. He'd an uneasy feeling that all three of his suspects were perfectly aware of the identity of the heap of bone and charred flesh that reposed in its cell.

Late breakfast concluded, Father Joe announced he must get ready for mass, today would require a special one, for the comfort and sustenance of an entire neighborhood, which was at present shattered and bleeding in both body and mind.

Pamela declared her intention of finding a tub and soaking in it. Pat was off out the door to check on the situation in the neighborhoods, see who needed help finding safe houses as a stopgap and generally to avoid the questioning stares at the table. Maggie was humming to herself while setting a batch of bread to rise, which left only Jamie and Father Terry at the table.

"The British Army moved into Derry last night," Terry said by way of conversational preamble.

"They'll be in the streets of Belfast by tonight," Jamie replied.

"How do ye know that?" Terry asked, stirring the tepid depths of his tea with a fork handle.

"Hardly takes foresight to leap to an obvious conclusion. There's no choice really, someone has to restore order on the streets."

"And you think the British are the ones to do it?"

"There isn't anyone else, is there?" The green eyes met his own, clear and unblinking. "The United Nations won't send anyone, the Taoiseach already opened up that call and no one answered. The Republic has no money to lend, no army to deploy and no friends in London. Stormont's already declared Lynch a traitor." He took a last drink of tea and stood up from the table, "Neglected patriotism is a bitter cup and one can hardly blame the South if they don't wish to drink from it. We are another country here, a world apart from the Republic, we just won't admit to it."

"So the Irish question has been re-opened with the British has it?"

"It would seem so," Jamie flexed his long fingers against the table and politely stifled a yawn, "and God help the man who tries to find the answer to it."

"I tend to hope that God does help the man who tries to find an answer to peace," Father Terry said quietly, his eyes holding the other man's.

Nothing moved in the room, even Maggie was still, her back to them. Green flame sparked lightly in Jamie's eyes, simmered and died within the second.

"You'll forgive me Father but I tend to think God has rather convenient hearing. And now, if you'll excuse me, I must leave. Will you tell them I'll be back later? My home," he said with a charming smile, "has many empty rooms and they will, I believe, need a place to stay."

"And many locked doors, I suspect," Terry muttered to himself as Jamie turned and after a quick word with Maggie, left the room.

A bowl of porridge, thick with cream and sprinkled with brown sugar was placed with a thump beneath his nose.

"I've always said that thin men ask too many questions." Terry looked up and met the ferocious gaze of Maggie, who reminded him of a mother bear whose cub has just been threatened. She cocked her head and pointed at the bowl, "An' as I've never seen one so thin as yerself, I'd advise ye to eat."

Terry, with the wisdom of a man who'd grown up under the tutelage of five older sisters, ate his porridge and kept his questions to himself.

SOMEONE HAD LIT CANDLES IN THE ROOM, a bit of flame and warmth to light and ease the way through the darkness of death. Ironic that the man's last stop before the road to eternity should be in the sanctuary of the Roman Catholic Church.

He still lay wrapped in the sheet, folded carefully now, ends tucked in snugly as if to prevent the soul from escape. Was he beyond the flames now, the burning, the hatred? Or had he, by his actions, condemned himself to an eternity of those very things? She wasn't certain which she would prefer.

She touched a cool hand to her throat and felt it constrict under her fingers, tensing as it had under the knife. She could still feel the searing heat of the fire, even if he was now beyond it. She closed her eyes and took a deep breath, stepping back from the bed, where the miasma of charred flesh cluttered her senses. Behind her eyes, she could still see the fire—long, grasping fingers of it. She could hear the pandemonium in the streets, the sound of tanks and people screaming...

Sleep had been unthinkable that night. She was jumpy, nerve-ridden, the ringing crack of gunshot like an electric shock laid on bare nerves. Near frantic with worry. Casey had promised to come home before nightfall, but dark had come without the reassuring sound of his footstep over the threshold.

She'd known trouble was inevitable, the streets had smelled of it for days. A sharp, rank scent like an animal soaked in its own fear. She'd stayed inside, door locked, wanting to burrow away from the trouble, to put her head down and keep it down until it was over. She ought to have known better, from past experience if nothing else, trouble didn't care whether you looked it straight in the face or not, it just kept on coming.

Just before midnight, she'd smelled smoke, heavy and invasive, and then heard a hard banging on the wall between their home and that of their only neighbor. Mr. Delaney, a widower on his own, partially crippled and confined to his tiny home, its four tiny rooms the entire expanse of his world. He was a quiet man, bothering no one, passing the time of day with her as he leaned out his window to water the window box geraniums that were a bright spot in the dingy street. He must be in trouble or he wouldn't bang.

She girded up her courage, unlatched the back door and run across the meager patch of dew-soaked grass they shared with him. His back door was unlocked thankfully and she'd stepped into Mr. Delaney's tiny kitchen, the smoke choking her instantly. It was everywhere, obscuring vision, disorienting her. She dropped to her knees, crawled to where the sink should be and bumped her head hard into the table and then remembered that everything in his house would be backwards to their own and crawled back in the other direction. She'd found the cupboard, felt her way up and turned the tap on by feel alone. A shriveled rag lay to the side of the sink and she wet it thoroughly under the stream of water and clapped it quickly over her mouth and nose. The smell of sour milk almost made her throw up, but she'd swallowed over the nausea and forced herself to breathe through the filthy rag.

She crawled the length of the narrow hall and found the foot of the staircase by smashing her knee painfully into it. To her immediate left lay the tiny front parlor, and here smoke was flame. The heat of it so intense that she could feel the fine hair on her arms shrivel up against the tightening skin. She'd pressed herself tight to the right wall that ran beside the staircase and crawled up the stairs, one at a time, her knees feeling like bruised rubber by the time she reached the top. Right or left? She didn't know and couldn't see anything in the heavy, shifting cloud of smoke. In a flutter of panic, she remembered being told that it was rarely fire that killed people, it was smoke. But then she'd heard a weak thump coming from the right and had crawled as quickly as she could toward it.

Mr. Delaney was lying in the hall outside his bedroom door, having dragged himself that far before succumbing to the smoke. He was barely conscious, eyes opening and shutting over milky cataracts. She forced herself to push down the panic and review her choices. She could stand, try to get him upright and shoulder his weight down the stairs. The problem with this simple plan being that the man weighed about two hundred pounds. Or she could try to drag him down the stairs, while crawling down backwards. Neither plan seemed to have an advantage over the other, so she'd crouched, tied the rancid smelling rag around her head and placing her hands firmly under his armpits, began to drag him towards the stairs. It was a long, hard process and her muscles protested at once, the sweat evaporating as soon as it hit the surface of her skin.

When she reached the head of the stairs, she'd laid him down for a second trying to steady her quivering arms. The fire had reached the bottom of the stairs, was rolling small, avaricious tongues up the peeling wallpaper and igniting in happy little bursts. At most she had a minute, maybe two. In desperation, she yanked on the inert man, nearly toppling them both down the stairs. He was unconscious and she was grateful for it.

By the time she'd made it halfway down, the fire had spread across the bottom *of the staircase and begun to rise in a hissing sheet from the floor. It was a good three feet high and she might, alone and unencumbered, have a chance at clearing it with one good jump off the stairs but there was no way she could drag the old man through it.*

The smoke had infiltrated her senses; it seemed to be stealing her hope, laying a heavy blanket over reason. She fought an impulse to sit down on the stairs and simply give herself over to the heat. And then salvation had appeared through the inferno, a bright blond head and hazel eyes at the foot of the stairs, terrifyingly familiar. She'd darted instinctively away from him, up the stairs. But he'd merely run up the stairs, grabbed the old man and heaving him over his back gone back down through the fire.

Having little choice in the matter she'd followed. In the street all was chaos, broken glass littering the pavement, shattered petrol bombs, fire roaring up into the night, casting a hellish red glow over everything. The packed rowhouses were like kindling bundled tightly together, one match would take out the whole neighborhood. People were running heedlessly, some still laying dazed in the street where the mobs had pulled them from their homes. And in the wake of the mob traveled the looters and firebugs, stealing anything of worth, destroying what they couldn't carry and then torching the remains.

She didn't see that bright yellow head anywhere, though she'd spotted Mr. Delaney, being attended to by a man and a woman. She saw an ambulance up head of the street, beyond the clog of the burning barricade. Mr. Delaney would be alright.

She glanced at the door of her own home, saw it was cracked open and knew she'd left it closed and locked. She picked her way across broken glass and then, looking back to be certain no one was watching, darted in. The fire hadn't made it through their walls yet and there was an odd silence, as if the house were waiting for something, the sounds outside muffled. She went through the rooms quickly, whoever had been was gone it seemed and she turned for the door, knowing it was only a matter of minutes before the fire would breach the thin walls.

When her hand was on the door she noticed it was bare, the ring finger pale and naked. Her wedding ring was upstairs; she hesitated for a moment and then ran for the stairs. Casey had worked extra shifts at a job he loathed to put that band on her finger and she'd be damned if she'd leave it for the looters.

In their bedroom, the fire was starting to curl out from the joint of the ceiling and wall, slithering overhead like a luminous serpent. The ring wasn't on the little bedside table where she'd left it; she turned in a circle, her mind frantically trying to recall where else she might have put it.

He was standing next to the door, having hidden behind it while he waited for her to come up the stairs as he must have known she would.

"Looking for this?" he asked and took a step across the room towards her, a circlet of silver lying against his palm. "Women are oddly predictable."

She snatched at it without thinking but he'd closed his fist over it quickly. The bait had given him what he wanted though, brought her close enough to grab around the neck. He pulled her face tight to his and she had one of those strange, surreal moments when all the senses are heightened, all details clarified. She could see the flecks of color in his eyes—gold, green, amber, smell the sour whiskey on his breath and his sweat, rancid with terror. His fear gave her a strange calm.

"Where's that bastard husband of yours now? Off fighting silly battles while I'm here with you." He leaned his forehead against hers, their noses touching and his hand hard as tempered steel across the back of her head. "He'll miss you, won't he? He'll grieve you for the rest of his days. I doubt my pitiful wife will even shed a tear, but it doesn't matter, does it? Her tears can't comfort me in hell. Besides," *he breathed out harshly and she clenched her mouth against it, "I'll have you for company, won't I?"*

She tried to bring her knee up, but his body, so close to hers, anticipated the move and he brought his free hand up and shoved her hard away from him. She stumbled and fell back onto the bed, her head grazing the post on the way down.

"Do you know how most men would like to leave this world, if they had their choice?" He loomed above her, an open switchblade in one hand and the other hand on the buckle of his belt.

He put one knee to her stomach and leaned over her, his hair a nimbus of rose-gold as the fire spread across the entire ceiling, crawling down the walls, as if just yet it could not bear to part from the thing that fed it. Horribly beautiful in all its shifting, kaleidoscoping color. Red, orange, violet, green and blue, soft and mesmerizing at its very center. She felt herself begin to slide from consciousness, grateful that she wouldn't be present at her last moments.

A sharp stinging on her neck brought her back around. The knifeblade was pressed against her throat.

"I've marked you," he said triumphantly, "even in hell they'll know you're mine. It'll be like a string connecting the two of us."

She tried to swallow the hot bile that had risen in her mouth, but her throat couldn't move under the blade of the knife. She was going to die here in this bed, with a man who wanted her last moments to be filled with horror and he would make certain she was awake for every last minute of it.

"Don't close your eyes," he whispered, spittle spraying in her face, "for I'll cut you every time you do. I'll see to it that you suffer the way I have for months. Being chased like a rabbit down every hole. D'you know," he said almost conversationally, "I dream about that bastard now, he follows me even in sleep. I've wondered why he didn't just kill me outright and be done with it. He's everywhere, can't escape from him, can't sleep," his eyes narrowed, only a breath away from her own, "but now it's him who'll suffer, him who'll never be at peace again, 'cause he'll know he killed you as surely as he's been trying to kill me. I may be a dead man, but I won't go alone." He dropped his head against her chin, as if exhausted, but his hand never relaxed the grip it held on the knife.

Cindy Brandner

There was very little air left in her lungs and black spots had begun to dance amongst the flame like tiny sprites, their feet snared in violet tongues. And then out of the gathering haze, something moved. She blinked, fought to clear her vision, to pull air into her bursting lungs.

He emerged in flame, like Lucifer just after the fall, one finger held to his lips. In a daze she watched his hands rise into the light, stretch toward the flame, a glint of sliced moonlight in them, saw bemusedly the hands arc down, clasped together as if in prayer.

And then a comforting veil of darkness, warm and familiar, easy as going to sleep after a long and hard day.

She shivered. Her hair was still wet from the bath and the tiny cell was far off from the warmth of the main body of the church. Against her will she approached the bed, reached down and untucked the folded cloth from about the head. She had to see for herself.

Bones tell their own story, the flesh may lie but the bones do not. She'd reason to know his body intimately and though she had tried to bury the memory of it, she'd been unable to. He'd shown her the dark underbelly of something Casey had only given her in love and tenderness. And in the process he had become a third to their two. Her own demon made flesh. In the night, while Casey slept, the shade of him would rise and she could smell, feel and see him. The bright, silky hair, the hard, clean flesh, smelling of flowers. The scent of violets still made hot acid flood her mouth.

The contours of his body were there, as present and real as Casey's. The map made up of muscle, bone, flesh and the intricately entwined experience of the three. When death comes it takes the flesh quickly, freezing the muscle instantly. But the bone will linger, like the final fading notes of the symphony that is life. Providing, through their fretwork, the tale of a fleeting passage through time. In age they will calcify, begin to disintegrate, preparing for the dust of the grave. In youth they are soft, uncertain, tender, pillowed with cartilage.

Bone is a living organism, regenerating constantly. In middle years, it is stronger than reinforced concrete, yet more pliable and much, much lighter. Breaks, fractures, stresses, leave little more than faint lines of calcification. But if a bone is wounded from within, if germs invade and multiply within its tender marrow, then the bone will retain the visible trace of memory.

She lifted the sheet, shuddering a bit as the air swirled in tiny eddies, the smell of burning thick upon the cloth.

He lay on his side, curled inward as a sleeping child. As once he had been a child, a creature of innocence and inexperience. Perhaps even someone's beloved son. Perhaps not.

The left femur glowed dully in the light, rippled with striations of myriad color. Dark, glistening brown—earth. Pale, polished silver—water. Delicate bubbles of transparent lilac, amber and ochre—air. Streaks of red, umber and indigo—fire. All the four elements here within a single few square scorched inches. She touched one of the outcroppings of vestigial bone and marrow, matrix and mineral shattering beneath her touch like a bubble bursting. The honeycombed insides as frail as the milk-washed innards of a shell.

A fever to begin with? Not so uncommon in a child. Favoring the leg, complaining of discomfort, not so uncommon either. But left untreated until too late it had become a much more serious illness.

His flesh, scarred by surgical knives beyond healing, had been the cover of the book. The bones, now bared, the open pages. Scored, pitted, bubbled, they spoke of a lifetime of infection raging in the blood, returning again and again to the weakened site. As if the poison he contained had been so virulent and abundant that it had needed to be physically drained. As if his own hatred had laid him waste. And identified him positively for her now.

"The constable," said a quiet voice behind her, "had very fine bones for a man. They say a person educated in such things can see the small differences and know by the bones if it is a man or woman. But to the uneducated eye, they appear much the same."

He crossed the floor silently, resting a hand gently on her shoulder, "Your husband is awake and being forcibly restrained in his bed. I think perhaps you'd best go prove that the rumors of your death were indeed—"

"Greatly exaggerated," she finished softly for him. "Did you see who shot him, Jamie?"

"No," he shook his head, "but I imagine it was someone who meant to miss."

"A warning then," she said grimly.

"Yes, but next time it won't be."

"What will happen to him now, Jamie?" she asked, nodding toward the skeleton. "He has a wife that will be missing him soon."

"He'll disappear, his wife is agreeable with such measures and questions can be answered in any number of ways."

She turned sharply, dislodging his hand from her shoulder. "You've spoken to her?"

Green eyes met their like across flickering air and then disappeared under the constraint of lid and lash.

"Indirectly," he said and for a second an emotion spasmed across his face, giving her some small notion of what the night had cost him. "Leave the dead, won't you? The living await."

He steered her toward the doorway, but she hesitated looking back in uncertainty.

"What is it?" he asked.

"Do you lay a demon to rest with a blessing or a curse?" she asked, feeling a chill spread itself in her marrow with a ghostly hand.

"Bless him for what he might have been, curse him for what he was," Jamie replied, face impassive once again, "that ought to take care of all possible outcomes."

She blinked, startled at how closely his words mirrored her own thoughts of only moments ago. She crossed the floor again, and stood over the bones, hands spread, mind searching for the words that would break the ties. And found them in the cries of Jacob.

'And I said, Let me go, for the day breaketh. And he said, I will not let thee go, except thou bless me.' She whispered it and his own words came back to her, spoken only hours ago. *'Say my name, say it, speak it to me and I won't cut you. Say it soft.'*

"Bernard," she said softly into the shrinking light.

Jamie, joining her beside the dead, took care of the curse.

'Depart from me, ye cursed, into everlasting fire, prepared for the devil and his angels.'

It was only later she would think to wonder how he'd known, with such certainty, the identity of the bones.

THE BRITISH CAME TO BELFAST THAT DAY. They came in armored trucks, with rifles strapped to their shoulders. Came with wariness, for the Irish were an unpredictable lot.

In Derry they were greeted with tea and relief. In Belfast, disbelief and outrage in some quarters and an exhausted resignation in others. The police could no longer hold the line in Ulster. Six thousand British troops were sent in to keep the peace or, as some thought, to keep the natives securely behind the barricades. The RUC, past history considered, had acted with admirable restraint in most areas. As with any organization composed of large numbers some policemen reacted to the riots with savagery and others with heroism.

The British Army was brought to guard the precipice in the gorge of which lurked the specter of civil war. For one mad moment, the province had trembled on the brink of open warfare in the streets of a city in the United Kingdom. It had been heady for some and horrifying for others. Either way there was no turning back the clock for Northern Ireland, the future was here with guns and tanks, bombs and bayonets.

Under the Special Powers Act, twenty-four Republicans were interned for suspected activities. Paranoia was rife in the city, with men being lifted from their beds and women and children in the streets behind them, uncertain if they'd be returning.

In the Protestant neighborhoods, within the ranks of the police force and even in the corridors of Stormont, the rumors of a reborn IRA became fantastical. Their numbers were huge, it was claimed, a force no one could have imagined. It was the only way to explain the Catholics holding out as well as they had.

In the Catholic neighborhoods, the truth was known—the IRA was more theory than actual flesh and blood men at present. Still people were bitter that *their* army, *their* protectors had not materialized during the fiery night. IRA—'I Ran Away' was graffittied onto the sides of buildings and ill feeling towards the mythical army ran high. Others knew another truth: that a small band of men, dispersed in tiny pockets, armed with ancient, malfunctioning weapons had done what they could to protect the neighborhoods, without starting a bloody war they weren't equipped to finish. The army from the South had not come. GHQ in Dublin had issued communiqués but no arms and no foot soldiers for the cause. The Republicans in the North, as they'd always suspected, were on their own.

No-go zones were established rapidly in both Belfast and Derry and woe betide any RUC officer or British army personnel who dared put a foot over those lines. The Bogside of Derry would be forever after known as Free Derry, its gritty streets home to a risen people.

Walking the streets, Pat saw a city torn to its foundations both physically and spiritually. What ghosts, he wondered, would rise from the ashes?

It had been a long day of it. He'd gone from neighborhood to neighborhood, street to street, stopped by barricades, halted at makeshift checkpoints as people rallied round and hurriedly formed defense committees manned by locals, rotating in shifts. Relief committees set up at local schools provided temporary shelter, warmth and food for those who'd lost their homes to fire. Others opened their homes, gave up their own blankets, food and even beds to those less fortunate. Transportation into Nationalist Belfast had been suspended and the logistics of getting food through the barricades looked to become a large problem. But a structure was already arising from the rubble, the people, as they always had, would look after their own.

He found his last name provided him with an easy currency, which he wasn't entirely comfortable using. If they didn't know him directly, they knew Casey or they remembered his father with some fondness and the association, however tenuous, got him past checkpoints and through doors which were heavily guarded. Three times during the day he'd run into Jamie, a bright, elegant point in the midst of a clutch of women, on his knees in the street handing out food to children. Listening to accounts of the previous night's horrors, making promises for relief and spreading in his wake a feeling of reassurance that things would be taken care of. At one point, finding themselves side by side in a church basement, they had a cup of tea together.

"It's good of you to come down here," Pat said.

Jamie raised an eyebrow and smiled, "Haven't you managed to sprout some cynicism yet Patrick? This is the politically expedient thing to do. Perhaps I'm merely oiling the electoral waters."

"Ye don't fool me," Pat replied dryly, which ended the conversation.

It was late by the time he dragged himself back to the shelter of the Resurrectionist Church, the morning's large breakfast a vague memory. His stomach rumbled loudly and he was disappointed to see that the kitchen was empty, lit only by the small glow emanating from the stove. He'd half-hoped that Maggie had left him a bite tucked away as she did at Jamie's. Considering the number of mouths she'd fed over the last couple of days, he supposed that was asking a bit much.

"Yer dinner's been left to warm in the oven," said a voice from the vicinity of the table. "And Maggie said to tell you she hid a piece of pie behind the cream crock for ye and that I was to be certain ye drank at least two glasses of milk with it all as she doesn't like how thin yer lookin'."

"Sylvie?" he said, heart thumping madly.

"Aye, it's me." She stepped out of the dark, her hair a soft halo of light.

"How on earth—why—what were—?" he stuttered overcome suddenly by an emotion he couldn't fathom.

She stuck three fingers up where he could see them and ticking them off individually said, "How—by car with a Protestant friend of mine, which made it easier to get out of Derry. Though we still had to drive through a few fields to get here. Why—because I couldn't stand being stuck there while you were down here an' not knowin' if ye were hurt or tired or hungry. An' as for what I'm doin' here, the fact of the matter is I've run away from home, suitcase an' all an' any further answers to that question depend quite a lot on you."

"On me?" he said in stupefaction.

"Maybe ye'd best eat yer supper while I explain." She pointed to a chair and he sat while she retrieved his dinner, put a kettle on the boil and brought a bottle of milk to the table. Despite the savoriness of Maggie's stew Pat didn't taste a bite. He ate it quickly when he realized Sylvie wasn't going to talk until he'd done so and then shoved the bowl aside. He met Sylvie's eyes, dark and soft, above the milk bottle and thought he didn't care if she didn't explain a damn thing, he was just happy to see her.

"I saw yer brother today," she said, "I'm glad he wasn't seriously wounded."

"Aye, I'm glad of it as well."

She held her hands in lap, took a deep breath and with an apologetic smile said,

"I've moved here."

"To Belfast? Now?"

"Aye, things are no better in Derry."

"But where will ye stay?"

"Yer friend Mr. Kirkpatrick said I could put up at his house with the rest of ye until I find more suitable accommodations. An' as for work, he said if I could type an' answer a phone, I could work for him. Said he lost his assistant some time back and hasn't been able to replace her."

"Ye said ye'd run away from home. Does yer mam know?"

"Aye she knows. Though the truth is I'm not so much running away as running to something."

"Running to?" he repeated stupidly, dazed by the smell of lemon verbena and lilac.

"Do ye plan to act obtuse all night, Pat Riordan?" she asked, a flicker of annoyance puckering her brow.

"I imagine I will unless ye flat out say what yer meanin' to say."

"I'm running towards you, eejit," she said, face flushed even in the dim light.

"I see."

"Is that all ye have to say? I see? See what—a girl throwin' herself at yer feet that ye've no wish to take on? Is that it?" She stood and snatched his bowl, smacking it hard against the milk bottle and tipping it over.

"No, I think I've one other thing to say," Pat said as cold milk first poured, then trickled in a steady stream onto his lap.

"An' what might that be?"

"It's more of a request actually."

"Aye," she sniffed, face still a deep pink, milk bottle spinning down on the table between them.

"Well it's only that I've had a question to ask since the first I saw ye but there never seemed a right time to ask it."

She looked at him warily.

"See the thing is—"

"Will ye give over an' kiss the girl before the two of ye are old enough to have grandchildren," said an exasperated voice, issuing out of the pantry.

Pat jumped out of his chair in startlement, sending the milk bottle flying onto the stone floor where it bounced twice before settling unbroken.

"Jaysus," he yelped as he stubbed his toe on the solid oak table, "what on earth do ye mean steppin' out of the closet like the angel of death, Casey?"

"I've been stuck in there the last half hour while ye tried to get around to askin' Miss Larkin if ye could kiss her."

"What the hell were ye doin' in there in the first place?" Pat asked angrily, toe throbbing and milk running in rivulets down his legs as his brother emerged on crutches from the tiny pantry.

"Eatin' yer pie would be my guess," Casey said, holding an empty plate awkwardly in one hand while trying to balance a wobbly crutch. "Then I could hear the gist of yer conversation an' it seemed," he smiled charmingly at Sylvie, "an indelicate moment to come out. But ye were takin' so long to kiss the girl, I thought I'd best see if I could speed the situation along a bit as I didn't think I could stand much longer without collapsin'." He grinned, turning his attention to Sylvie, "He's a slow starter but he gets there eventually."

Pat was saved from committing fratricide by the appearance of Pamela in the kitchen, barefoot and fuming.

"So that's where you got to, harassing poor spooning couples in the kitchen."

"Spooning?" Pat squeaked indignantly, the situation having progressed rapidly from romance to farce.

Pamela ignored his protests and putting her hands on hips ordered Casey in no uncertain terms back to bed. Casey with an aggrieved air hobbled out of the kitchen behind her. He hesitated though in the doorway, looking back, his expression tentative.

"It'll be good to see ye. Patrick," he said, voice slightly husky.

"Aye, an yerself as well my brother," Pat replied without hesitation and saw the look of gratitude that spread across his brother's face before he turned to follow his wife down the hall. Pat could hear their voices echo off the stone walls until they turned off the main corridor that linked the main body of the church to the private quarters.

"And if you think you'll get any sympathy from me Casey Riordan..."

"It was only a tiny bit of pie..."

"...and furthermore you know what the doctor said..."

"...feel perfectly fine..."

"...not that fine, it's a monastery for heavens sake, keep your hands..."

There was a sound of muffled laughter, the thud of a heavy door closing and then silence.

"I apologize for that," he said, his own face flushed now.

"Was he right?" Sylvie asked.

"Right?"

She sighed, "Were ye goin' to ask to kiss me?"

Pat stepped towards her and put his hands gently on her shoulders. This close, his senses swam with her scent, her hair resting on the backs of his fingers like the brush of down. "He's a right pain in the arse my brother, but he's the annoyin' habit of bein' right almost all the time."

He leaned down and kissed her softly, briefly, feeling all the trouble outside the door recede at the touch of her lips.

They parted awkwardly, Pat bumping his nose against her forehead and apologizing profusely for it.

At their feet, the milk bottle had finally stopped spinning, its stubby neck pointing away from them. Sylvie stuck out a slippered foot and toed it around until it pointed directly at Pat's sopping wet feet.

"My turn," she said.

THE DUKE OF DUNGARVON'S TOWN RESIDENCE, located within the manicured and hushed confines of a huddle of mansions called Knockdrum Park, seemed light years away (rather than the few miles that it actually was) from the smoky center of Belfast. Here the light, rather than grasping its way through smoke, filtered down through stately rows of beech trees.

The drawing room, being filled with this particular brand of expensive light, felt a bit like an underwater cavern, all shifting gloom with the occasional watery ripple of sunlight.

But, as the Duke's guest knew, it had the advantage of secrecy, being at the back of the house with only dense thickets of trees for a view.

"Lemon or milk?" The Duke asked, heavily beringed hand poised above a delicate Spode teacup.

"Neither," said his guest politely.

"Well it seems we have achieved what we set out to do," the Duke, his own tea in hand, leaned back heavily in his chair.

"Did we? It seems you have dropped many of the key points of the original plot as we set it out."

"One thing at a time my friend, one thing at a time. Leastwise we've got my dear James where we want him."

"Do we?" his guest took a delicate sip of tea. "He's poised to take over half of Belfast. When you have the working stiff on the streets in your hand you hold the city's soul within your grasp."

"It's what we wanted," the Duke toyed idly with a filigreed drawer handle.

"Is it? If you think he'll listen to you, or be fooled by your manipulations, you've underestimated the man severely. If I've learned anything these last months, it's that the man trusts no one, not even, it seems, himself."

"He's brilliant as a sharpened diamond, I'll give him that, but he carries the family curse and an illness of the mind like that handicaps him quite badly," said the Duke feeling casually in his pocket for the small vial he'd palmed there only minutes ago. Reassured by its liquid heft, he continued in a mellow tone, "Besides you're overdramatizing things. When in doubt James always goes with his conscience, it's his greatest weakness, this streak of goodness that he can't shed. His father was the same, bottom line, they always make the choice that will allow them to sleep at night."

"Is that why you murdered him?" his guest asked without so much as the flicker of an eyelash.

The Duke, long schooled in such matters, retained a calm exterior.

"Utter foolishness to suggest such a thing, you know perfectly well that the man committed suicide." An idea, uneasy in its brewing, bubbled up from his subconscious. "Is that why you had that absurd article placed in the paper, to throw suspicion out into the open? Have you been trying to sabotage this from the first?"

"How easily your mind leaps to such distrustful conclusions Percy, I wonder why that might be?" The occupant of the chair opposite him, leaned forward and placed the teacup on the desk. The Duke squirmed slightly, the cup was still full. "Do you ever wonder why all the breadcrumb trails we've followed lead off in such obscure directions and yet always give us a whiff of something that might be the truth, or might not?"

"Are you suggesting that he knows and is deliberately leading us astray?"

"You may not have noticed, Percy, but the body count has been climbing steadily and not just by our own hand."

The Duke swallowed, the muscles of his throat contracting painfully. He took a drink of tea to try and ease them.

"Are you saying you didn't kill our friend the constable?"

The slender set of shoulders across from him shrugged. "It's neither here nor there is it whose hand killed him? He's gone, as you requested."

"He was becoming a liability, completely out of control and crazed."

"Yes," his guest said with a disdainful sniff, "he did have a rather fanatical way about him."

"Did you or did you not kill him?" The Duke leaned across the desk he sat behind, lines of perspiration gathering under his hairline, worry beads his wife called them.

"Are you going to become dogmatic? How boring." His guest glanced at one pale, delicate wrist and yawned. "I must go Percy, places to go, people to see as they say."

"You're leaving?" The Duke's face was red with fury, "We've not concluded our business here, not by a long shot." He fought for a breath as his throat constricted involuntarily again. He wondered briefly if he was having a heart attack for he felt suddenly as if a large fist was squeezing his heart between clenched fingers.

His guest, face calm, rose with delicate ease from the chair.

"Oh I'd say our business is concluded, wouldn't you? Percy, are you familiar with the structure of Shakespeare's *Hamlet*?"

"Of course," he wheezed, groping around in the pocket of his coat for his heart pills, "Though why you always ask such confoundedly inane questions I'll never know."

"It's just that the play is layered rather cunningly, a play within a play, where the imaginary world overlaps the real one, so that one cannot distinguish between reality and illusion."

The Duke looked in sudden horror at his teacup, his throat so tight now not even a whisper of air was getting through to his starved lungs.

"Cyanide," his guest now even with him, whispered, "has such a distinctive scent, bitter almonds, quite strong against the background of the tea, wouldn't you say? It's a rare talent you know, the ability to smell it, how unfortunate for you that I'm one of the select few. I prefer subtler poisons, something that takes more time, don't you Percy? Cat got your tongue? Pity. I really wanted to hear your response to what I'm about to tell you." His guest leaned closer and whispered a message, brief and to the point, that caused the Duke's eyes to bulge out of his head.

"Thought you'd enjoy that, well I'd best go, wouldn't do to get caught here with your corpse would it? Besides, I've eight crates of guns awaiting my attention. Oh yes, I've got the weapons Percy, had them all along. And the IRA paid for them, there's a very sweet irony in that wouldn't you say? For the revolution is coming and I," the Reverend smiled, "am prepared for it."

The Duke, eyes now closing, felt the stir of a passing breeze from an open window and knew his guest had departed. It was his last conscious thought.

Chapter Thirty-eight
Betwixt the Ice and the Fire

FOR THE GOOD OF ONE'S SOUL, he'd been taught as a child, one ought not to have all one desires. Now as far as the the drink and consumption of food went, Casey could see the merits in such advice, in fact he believed his Grandma Murphy had been the one to say it to him when he'd reached his hand across the table for his fourth jam bun in fifteen minutes. She'd rapped his knuckles sharply and when her back was turned, he'd grabbed it and ran outside to eat it. He'd had a godawful tummy ache later and she'd been full of sage 'I told you so's.' However, he didn't think such doctrine extended itself to the act of love with one's own wife.

The difficulty lay not in the element of desire but rather in the environment. He could not, regardless of his body's enthusiastic signals to the contrary, make love to his wife under Jamie Kirkpatrick's roof. And the woman hadn't made the situation any easier. She'd insisted that a man so recently wounded, particularly in such a delicate area, ought to proceed with exceeding caution. The dainty nature of his wound notwithstanding, and being a man of somewhat stubborn nature, Casey had tried in a variety of ways to convince Pamela otherwise. However, the humiliation of being caught by Maggie in the back hall with his hand up his wife's shirt, had the effect of dampening his ardor somewhat. Maggie, being Maggie, had merely cocked her eyebrow and said,

"Ye might want to find a door to do that behind."

A door was not what he had in mind however. A blanket and a bit of grass uncluttered by people would suit him fine.

He waited until the house was quiet, until the very night itself seemed to breathe in and out with the darkness. He nudged her awake, and she grumbled a bit then squinted at him through a tangle of hair.

"The night is fine, will ye come for a walk with me?" he asked.

She closed her eyes and then opening them again, nodded.

Outside the world was suspended in silver blue, like a miniature in a glass ball held by a trembling hand. The dew beneath their feet was chill, the sky above swiftly turning its cheek toward autumn, the air hushed and clear with cold.

Hand in hand they ran down the hill, breathless and laughing like two children without permission to be out in the dark. Against the sky, the pines stood like dark sentinels their scent sharp amber and heady as wine. Inside the stand of pine, the light was fainter, ribbons of it running in and out of the trees against a star-strained sky.

"Here," Casey said, stopping in a small ring of trees, the ground underneath springy and fragrant with needles. He lay the blanket he'd brought with him down over the bed of needles then faced her in the moonlit space and cleared his throat, suddenly nervous.

"A walk, you said," she smiled, her words accompanied by a slipstream of frosted air.

"If ye don't mind, I'd like to make love to ye," he said with the air of a man who has made up his mind and intends to follow it.

"And if I do mind?" her voice trembled with either cold or suppressed laughter.

"Then ye'll have to close yer eyes an' think of England or whatever it is good wives do, because yer lookin' at a desperate man here."

"Well," she said, "we can't have that, can we?" In one fluid motion, she pulled her sweater up over her head and tossed it to the ground, then unbuttoned her jeans and shimmied out of them. In the dark she stood out like blue-dipped ivory, her edges outlined by the distant hand of the moon.

"Touch me, Casey," she whispered.

He leaned in and their fingertips met in tryst, her mouth warm and sweet under his own. He ran his hands down her back, felt her shiver and the skin that rose in goosebumps under the wake of his fingers. He lowered her to the ground then, safe within the soft couch of pine needles below and the hard shelter of his body above.

"Are you certain you're up for this?" she asked, one hand running lightly along the stitches in his upper thigh.

Casey, with the proof that he was indeed up for it rather plentifully in evidence, merely put his mouth over hers.

His fingers traveled down her ribcage, bumping along the road of tender flesh and shivering bone, carried light above a whirlpool of blood and then there was the sweet press of rude, blind muscle, a sighing parting of swollen tissues and he was home and gone. Creating madness from movement, a dilation of the senses that was all exquisite agony.

"I have pitch in my hair," she said drowsily some time later.

"Sorry about the roughness of the surroundins'," he murmured, "but a bit of oil will take it out."

"An Thou beside me singing in the wilderness

And wilderness is Paradise enow." She replied rather cryptically.

"Ye want me to sing?" Casey said, cracking open an eye to the night.

"No," she laughed softly, "I'm just saying any surroundings are home when I'm with you."

"I hope to provide ye with better than stars for a roof an' leaves for a pillow someday."

"You're my shelter Casey, don't you know that yet? I don't need walls and ceilings and pots and pans, I just need you."

"Aye, ye say that now but wait 'til it snows."

"You're a terribly practical man," she said.

"I feel anything but practical when ye touch me like that," he gasped as she took him firmly in hand. "Talk about ice an' fire, yer hands are frozen."

"Isn't there a poem about that by Dante, something about beyond the ice and the fire?"

"Mmmnn," he said, "not Dante, Jack Stuart an' it's *'between heaven an' hell, betwixt the ice and the fire, you an' I shall drown in the well of desire.'*"

"That man," said Pamela, "does have a way with words."

THEY AWOKE TO SEE VEGA DECLINING INTO THE WESTERN SKY, its blue-white fire making the journey down to where summer skies slept.

"Do you know the story of the Lyre?" Pamela asked, knowing where his gaze had fallen.

"My Daddy told me long ago, but I can't remember," he replied, "will ye tell it to me?"

"Well it's said that after Orpheus' wife died he grieved terribly. He wandered about lost, unable to play his music any longer, denied the one solace he might have found. The Thracian maids saw him and wanted him, desired his beauty for themselves and tried to lure him with their charms. He rejected them, though, and this made them very angry, they shrieked and howled abuse and threw their weapons at him. But Orpheus had found his music again and their weapons were as dust before the sweetness of it. This enraged the maidens further so that their howling increased and rose and rose until the darkness of it drowned out even Orpheus' music and the weapons mortally wounded him. The maidens dragged him back to their lair and tore him limb from limb, casting his head and his lyre into the river. Orpheus, torn apart, floated down, down the river until the muses gathered all the parts of him together and buried him at Libertra. And Jupiter, sorely grieved, took the lyre and knowing it was Orpheus' soul cast it into the face of heaven, where it could shine forever."

"Bit of a bloodthirsty tale, isn't it?"

"I think what it's really about," she said, sitting up and hugging her knees to her, "is eternity."

"Eternity?" Casey said, running a leaf idly down the groove of her spine, "I'm not certain I see that, hell hath no fury like a woman scorned an' all that, but eternity?"

"Think about it. No matter what happens to us, the tragedy, the pain, the uglinesses of life, when that all falls away we're left with what's true and beautiful, even after we're gone."

"That sounds like somethin' my father would have said, he'd have thought ye a wise woman ye know. Vega was his star. When I was in Parkhurst, I'd try to find it through the bars of my window at night an' when I could I'd pretend it was him watchin' over me. An' I knew I could survive another day because he'd watch my back for me. In the winter I felt so alone because without his star he was gone for another season."

"What do you remember of your mother?" she asked softly and turned to look at him. His eyes shied away from her, down to the leaf he held between his fingers.

"Not so much really; she wasn't like the other mums, I suppose that's the one thing I knew clearly even then. She didn't bake bread or make chat about the menfolk while scrubbin' down the pavin' stones, she didn't leave the door open to the rest of the street the way everyone else did. She was quiet an' pretty, dark-eyed an' fine skinned. Ye'd never know Devlin was her brother to look at the two of them. She'd grown up soft compared to my Da', there was only her an' Dev. Her parents had money, they weren't rich, but they always had a car an' holidays in the summer. I remember that she smelled good, like somethin' expensive. An'when she left, there was a hole in my Daddy an' he never learned how to fill it. Pat an' I tried to putty it up the way children will, 'cause ye don't know any better." He took a deep breath, "We couldn't know that a woman leaves a loneliness behind that nothin' cures." He sat up beside her, "But I understand that now." He took her hand, turned it palm up and kissed it. "Because ye hold my soul right there in the palm of yer little white hand."

"I'm not leaving though."

"A day could come when ye might see it as the only sensible option."

"Never," she said vehemently.

"When I thought ye'd died in the fire," he said quietly, "I wanted to walk into it myself, to be consumed by flame an' have my ashes join yer own. Nothin' seemed to matter then for how was I to care about anythin' properly again without ye there. An' I remembered somethin' a wee wise man in a bar had said, he said 'a man must go where the road takes him,' an' it seems to me now that perhaps my road has changed, without my fully knowin' it."

"And where does this new road lead?"

"I don't entirely know," he said ruefully, "I only know I'm standin' at a crossroads an' the sign isn't clear just yet. My Daddy used to say that the decisions ye made at the forks in the road were the ones that defined ye as a man an' ye had to weigh yer options carefully in such moments so as not to regret the choice later."

"Well as long as you take me along with you when you decide which way you're turning," she said and shivered, reaching for her sweater.

"Don't," Casey said, "not yet. I just want to see ye so for a few more minutes."

"But I'm freezing," she protested.

"Then I'll warm ye," he put his arms around her from behind, wrapping the blanket about the both of them. "Better then?"

"Better," she agreed relaxing back into his warmth, feeling the rasp of his whiskers against her neck.

"If I ask ye a question will ye answer me honestly?"

"Is that why you wanted me naked? Because it's harder to lie when you're naked?"

"Is it? Never thought of it but come to that I see yer point. No I'd other plans for your nakedness but if it makes ye unable to lie, I'll consider it a bonus of sorts. I want to know, no I need to know, the man who died in the fire, was he the man who raped ye?"

She started and knew his body felt the answer before she even voiced it.

"It was him, wasn't it?" he said in a low and deadly voice, as if the man stood before him now.

"It was."

"An' who was he, Pamela?"

She shook her head and pushed away from his body. "He's dead and gone, it doesn't matter anymore."

"It matters to me. Was it the policeman, the one whose neck I cut? Was he the man who raped ye?"

"And what if it was him, what does it matter? He's dead and it's over now."

"Did Pat kill him?"

"No," she said wearily and knew he didn't believe her.

"Then it is my fault," he said and she turned in surprise.

"Your fault? How the hell is any of this your fault?"

"I threatened him, didn't I? I made him angry an' he took his vengeance out on yerself an' Pat. Ye weren't protectin' me from him were ye, ye were protectin' me from knowin' that I'd done all this? Weren't ye?"

"And what if I was?" she said angrily, "Would that be so awful?"

"Aye," he said the anger in his words matching her own, "it would be. D'ye think me such a coward that I cannot face up to my own failures, d'ye think me so small in soul that I couldn't be a man for ye?"

"You stupid bastard," she said and hit him hard in the chest, knocking him into the tree behind him, "how dare you! This is not about your stupid pigheaded pride. It wasn't even about keeping you from running out bent on vengeance."

"Then what was it about?" he asked, rubbing the back of his head where it had hit the tree behind him.

"Love."

"Love," he echoed stupidly, fingers stuck by pitch to his hair.

"Do you know how I love you Casey, do you have any idea?"

"Nooo," he said slowly, looking at her warily as if he expected her to hit him again.

"I love you for everything you ever were and all the things you'll become and even the things you won't ever be and I love you now just for this moment and for all the moments to come, even the ones we won't have together."

"Why didn't ye say so to begin with?" he said and reaching out pulled her back to him before she could evade his hands.

"Don't," she said sharply, pushing a knee into his belly, "don't make light of this."

He grabbed her leg and in one fast move was over and above her. "I'm not makin' fun of ye, lie still will ye? It's only—" he heaved a sigh of frustration and moved his body away from her own, reaching for his shirt and pants.

"It's only what?" she asked, "Leave your clothes off; I don't want you to lie to me either."

"Jewel," he rubbed his hands over his face, "bare-arsed or not I don't seem to be able to lie to ye."

"It's only what?"

"Yer a pushy woman ye know that?" He gave her a half-hearted smile and then capitulated. "It'll only be that no one's ever loved me for all the bits that are missin' as well as for all the bits that are present. It'll be a bit frightenin' to be loved like that."

"Don't you love me that way?"

"Ye know I do," he said softly, "but I'm a working-class boy from the streets of Belfast and you, you're someone who ought to have known better than to get involved with the likes of me. I see ye wanderin' the cliffs in the mornin' an' I see ye lookin' out to sea as if yer heart is breakin'. An' I wonder what it is I can't give ye, what it is ye see when ye stare out at the water?"

"When I was a little girl I used to play a game," she said looking down at her hands, "I'd spin the globe and let my finger ride over it to see where I'd live one day. I didn't really have a home you know until I came here, I never felt safe and I never felt that I really mattered to the fibers of someone else's life. But then I found you and in you, my home. But I'm afraid that you'll take that away from me with your own destructiveness. And so when I look out over the sea I'm looking into all those spinning globes of what might or might not be."

"Do ye want to go back?"

She looked at him, puzzled, "Go back where?"

"To America, d'ye think ye could keep us safe there?"

"I don't know," she shrugged her shoulders, "maybe that's what I do believe. Foolish as it sounds."

He rolled his fingers slowly over the pine needles, releasing their clear scent sharply.

"If ye had that globe now, Jewel, where would yer finger land?"

She weighed her answer for a moment, not entirely certain of the truth herself. Was it superstition to believe that safety lay across the ocean, that she could keep him alive and whole in another land? He had waited so long to come home, did she—did anyone have the right to take the joy of that away from him now?

"Here and now, this is where I'd stop the world. This is where I'd stay forever if I could," she said, "with you."

"Come here to me," he extended a hand in truce, drawing her along his length until they lay skin to skin, bone to bone, hardness to softness. He reached up and cupped her face between his hands, holding her eyes softly with the force of his own. "This is where I'd stop it, here, with ye next to my heart, safe an' warm."

Beyond them, the horizon tremored softly like a blind eye opening in the dark. The smell of pine overridden suddenly by the heavy exotic brush of cinnamon mixed to dubious advantage with the scent of frying ham.

"Maggie's making breakfast," she said yawning against the broad expanse of his chest.

"I'm of the certain opinion that woman," Casey sighed, "is tryin' to fatten me up for the fall slaughterin'."

"You don't know how happy it makes her to feed a man who can eat in such volume."

"Aye well, I'm glad to be of service but I'll start lookin' like one of her honeyed hams if I have to eat much more."

"We'd best head back," she said rolling off him and reaching for her clothes.

"One last bit of truth before ye get dressed, darlin'," Casey said.

"Hm," she eyed him over the top of the sweater which she'd yanked up both arms.

His face was relaxed with exhaustion, stubble a deep shadow, but the line of his body and the directness of his gaze implied an urgency that unsettled her.

"If ye need me to take ye home, ye only have to say it darlin' an I'll take ye."

She shrugged into the sweater, her hair a tousled mass of static electricity, rising like a cloud in the air.

"Have you heard nothing I've said in the last half hour?"

"Aye, I heard ye, I only want ye to know—"

She cut him off with a finger to his lips, laying her other hand on his chest.

"I do know Casey," her hand pressed firmly over his heart, fingertips reassured by its steady thrum, "but here, now, I am home," she smiled, "safe and warm."

Chapter Thirty-nine

In the Light of the Stars

HE WATCHED HER SLEEP, SWEETLY AT PEACE. It did his heart good to see her so; she was so rarely peaceful in her waking hours now. And who could blame her? Since January, it had all become a nightmare that there was no waking from.

He kissed her softly in the hollow of her shoulder, where the pale light from the garden paths pooled, stilled and became glowing ivory. He found his clothes, donning them as quietly as he could then making his way out, closing the door with a barely audible click.

His feet knew the path he meant to take before he even became consciously aware of it. They'd taken it often enough in childhood. Every Sunday in fact, his daddy had insisted on it. "Can't prevent ye from bein' a heathen every other day of the week but ye'll behave and get some goodness into ye on Sundays," he used to say.

He hadn't been inside a church since his father's funeral, had long ago stopped finding comfort in the rules and regulations of organized religion. He'd been bitter about the Church, angry at God for not saving his Daddy's life.

He dipped his fingers in the font, genuflecting automatically, bowing his head as he'd been taught since he was old enough to obey commands. He remembered the Christmas masses of his childhood, the gleaming altars cloaked in white, the ring of small white candles surrounding the larger central one that symbolized Christ, the Light of the World. Thronged in greenery and scarlet flowers, it had been pure poetry, the kind that touched you on a level deeper than words ever could.

He knelt before the altar rail and lit a candle, borrowing the flame from another and wondered whose memory, whose pain he was taking from. Here flame and memory were one, divine and prescient, burning you with their truths when you least expected it.

In his childhood, God had been a permanent fixture, a tree with long roots and innumerable rings, solid, there, always. Now He seemed more distant, a spark of fire in the heart of a storm. When his child's heart had begun to grow and ask for deeper answers to the great unknowns his father had tried to give him an answer that would quiet the fever, even if only for a little while. He'd taken his wedding ring off and placed it in Casey's palm.

'What do ye see?' he asked.
'A ring.' Casey replied, going for the obvious.
'Deeper than that, what do ye see?'
He thought for a moment, furrowing his brow in concentration.
'Yer overthinkin' it, don't think just tell me what it is.'
'A circle.'
'Aye, and a circle is?'
He began to get a glimpse of what his father was trying to say.
'Unending.'
'In every ending there is a beginning an' in every beginning the shadow of an ending. All of life is a circle. D'ye think it's a mistake that the universe is constructed in circles? That in all creatures there is such symmetry? Look at the perfection in a bird's wing; it's a feat of engineering that's pure genius. Every artist leaves his signature somewhere in his work, even if it's not at once apparent. God's signature is in a bird's wing or a baby's tiny fingers. It's everywhere if ye'll only have the sight to see it.'
'An' if I need more Daddy?'
His father had clasped the back of his neck, hugged him in the awkward manner of two grown men and said,
'Then look up son, an' see His face. It's there in the light of the stars.'

He put his hands together, bowed his head onto them and began to pray, "Our Father who art in Heaven, Hallow'ed be thy name..." he sighed, it was no good, he couldn't feel the words anywhere other than in his throat. "Ye'll excuse me God, but it's my own Daddy I want to talk to an' this seems as good a place as any other to do it in." He cleared his throat feeling oddly nervous, "Well, Daddy, I hardly know where to begin. It's been an eventful few months, aye? Makes it a little hard for a man to think clearly. We always thought when the revolution came it would be glorious, but it isn't, it's just confusin' as hell. The house burned down an' I thought I'd lost my wife in the fire, an' for the hours I believed her dead nothin' mattered anymore, nothin' I'd ever believed true, not even freedom. There's a man dead an' I wished him so, I committed murder in my heart a thousand times an' then it happened an' I was relieved, though I felt cheated because I wanted to do it myself. What does that make me, Daddy? I don't know what's wrong an' what's right anymore. An' I miss ye, there isn't a day that goes by that I don't wish I could come to ye an' have ye tell me what to do. I still don't understand why ye had to leave, Daddy, 'cause ye never said ye know, ye took our burdens but ye never shared yers. I wanted to know ye as a man, I wanted to see ye eye to eye an' watch ye hold yer first grandchild, I wanted to make ye proud. I wish ye could know my wife, ye'd like her, she's lovely in so many ways, she's like a dream I never want to wake from. An' she's afraid an' unhappy an' she wants to leave Ireland, but I don't know if I can Da', I just don't know if I can. Who am I away from here?"

He waited in the silence, felt the flickering heat of the candles waver under his breath and opened his eyes to the flame. "It makes no sense Da', for he's a grown man but how do I leave Pat here? How can I keep an eye on him from across an ocean? But how do I stay an' watch my wife become a shadow of herself? Why can't ye be here to answer my questions? Why? Oh please," his clasped hands had become clenched fists against the altar rail, "please can ye answer me."

He could hear the soft hiss and bubble of wax as it succumbed to fire, could feel his heart slow itself as if it too awaited something, sensed the silence and the weight of expectation held in it. He looked into the candle flame, right down to the blue heart of it and wondered if it would serve his memory always and if it would bring back seasons and holidays, people and moments. For even without him spring would come, fine and misted on the heels of winter. The bogs would open in furrowed cuts and bleed black under the tender sun and the ground would yield up its must, a sighing breath of ages to the sweet blue above. And if he were not here to see it? To smell and feel the itch of it in his hands and feet. Would his memories survive, pocketed and sealed like a young grape? Or when he opened them carefully in chosen hours, would they give only a bitter wine, scented with dust and disuse? And who would remember him? Would he just become another boy who went over there and never came back?

And then the memory came, quiet, light-footed, his father and himself on a lonely, moonlit path, walking, talking. A summer night, a ribbon of road, the smell of hawthorn, soapy and sharp, the sound of the sea in the distance murmuring soft, summer things to the moon, full-bellied and tinged slightly gold with autumn's approach. He'd reached the same height as his father early in the summer and showed signs in his large hands and feet of becoming larger and broader. It had been odd and not entirely comfortable at first to find himself looking directly at his Daddy and not up into his face. Uncomfortable and frightening. But that night he'd felt comfort in his father's voice, in the warm smell of him. They'd gone fishing, the three of them and after Pat had fallen asleep, facedown in a book, they'd left their places by the fire and walked, a man and his son as they would never walk again. And Casey had found, in the quiet of the night and the burn of moonlight the courage to ask his father about his mother.

"Do ye miss her?" he asked abruptly, blurting it out without any parameters for his father to fix upon. But Brian understood, he always did.

"Do you?" he answered back.

"No," Casey said quickly, too quickly.

"Well, I do," his father had said, "or at least the part of me that was once eighteen an' mad about her does."

"You still love her?" Casey asked in disbelief.

"Casey, she gave me two sons that I'd die for, of course I still love her. The part of me that was once a young man married to her is still a part of me and will always belong to that time, doesn't mean I'm going to rush over to England an' beg her to come back."

"Did ye love her always?"

"From the first time I saw her I knew it was different an' when I held her it was like the first time I had good whiskey in a crystal glass. I knew the difference then between something consumed merely to warm my belly an' something to be savored for its depth an' quality. The first woman ye love, an' I don't mean calf-love, but love down to the marrow of yer bones, divides time. She's a defining moment, everything else in yer life came before or after her. She's sacred in an' of herself."

"I don't want to love someone like that," he said vehemently.

"Someday ye will laddy an' it'll have little to do with what ye do or do not want. Ah look," Brian turned his face up into the night, "there's the Pleiades, that means Orion is down just below the horizon, waitin' for the dawn."

Casey looked up at the cluster of stars that were the Pleiades, fuzzy with luminosity. Orion was the blind giant of the winter skies, cursed to stumble alone and unaided across the vast ocean of night, but on the cusp of the seasons the seven sisters of the Pleiades, soft-skinned, waited to guide him home.

"Only when ye go to the edge of all the light ye possess an' enter into darkness can ye truly begin to see son."

"An' what do ye suppose Orion found in the dark woods?" Casey asked softly.

"His soul an' the courage to turn his face to the sun in the dawn. Even a warrior needs to know when to lay down his sword an' head for home."

The candle flame flickered, as though it had been brushed gently by a passing breeze, threatened to gutter out and then steadied itself around its clear blue heart.

"Thank you, Daddy," Casey whispered into the fire.

"Are ye ready?"

"I am," she said, trembling, uncertain what outcome she was hoping for.

"Right then," he took a deep breath and looking her full in the eyes, flicked his thumb upwards. The penny flew, an arc of sunshot copper, tumbling, toppling, tipping on the ascent, hanging for a hair, a half-breath of eternity and then plunging heart shot into descent, stumbling, lurching, pitching, tilting, sprawling and then impact, mineral to flesh, conductor to vessel, electricity to heat.

"What does it say?" her voice was strangled, caught between what was and what might be, on an edge place where the spinning planes were dizzy with regret and hope. "Well," she prodded, impatience and irritation making her palms slick and her teeth chatter.

He looked at the penny for a long time, a bright circle against fragile flesh. In its circumference lay the answer to what? Happiness? Happiness could be found and lost and found again regardless of what streets they called home. Or could it?

Casey looked up but she couldn't read what his eyes said, couldn't even hazard a guess from the leaves and shades and intonations of iris, pupil and cornea. His eyes were merely dark and deep as night and like night kept their secrets close.

Will ye go lassie go?

he began, voice soft, yet oddly flat.

O the summer time is coming
And the trees are sweetly blooming
And the wild mountain thyme
Grows around the mountain heather.

His voice picked up in strength, a rich shiver piercing his throat, his eyes still dark as night, but a night of soft breezes and stolen kisses.

Will ye go lassie go?

"Where am I to go, man?" she asked, moving into the circle of his arms. "Why to Boston lassie."

"Yes," she said and shivered as his lips moved across her face, "I'll go."

"An' will ye take me with ye?" His lips were on her ear now, soft with demand.

"Always, Casey Riordan," she said body arching towards his, "I'll always take you with me."

And heard the penny drop to the floor and roll away so that she never was to know if it had really come up heads at all.

Chapter Forty

I Shall Call You Hope

D AMN," SAID DANNYBOY KILMORGAN, stubbing his toe for the third time in as many minutes, "it's as black as the underskirt of a nun's habit up here."

"There's a clearing ahead, just over this last set of rocks, that's our destination."

"Will ye not tell a man why yer after draggin' his ancient arse up hills in the pitch dark?" The question, asked for the third time, was becoming less polite with each uttering. From the man in front there was no reply.

Ahead of him, the trees thinned and he saw a bare suggestion of light, shifting and small but there. Above, night's cauldron had spilled an uneasy brew of roiling, dark cloud, piling up over the sea in heavy banks. Dannyboy shivered.

The clearing sat above the treeline, arcing out over the sea, a small naturally ringed area, with trees blocking off the long steep hill, boulders cutting it off at the sides and a long perpendicular fall into the sea effectively sealing off the fourth side. At present, the area was lit with torches rammed between rock and into ground. It looked, Dannyboy thought, like the scene was set for some pagan sacrifice. But the man who stepped lightly into the ring of fire was not pagan, though Dannyboy would have preferred a naked, howling savage, all things considered.

"What the hell are ye doin' here?" he snarled.

"It's alright, Dannyboy," Jamie said, "the Reverend is here at my invitation." Jamie turned his attention to the man who stood unmoving, lit by brimstone's light.

"Mr. Kilmorgan," Jamie continued politely, "is here in his capacity as referee and to ensure," he smiled charmingly, "that I don't kill you."

"Your ambition," replied Reverend Broughton, "is admirable, though I wouldn't count me out just yet."

"There are gloves if you're afraid of bruising your manicure," Jamie drawled, "but I prefer bare knuckles."

"As you wish, Lord Kirkpatrick," Lucien replied genially, his eyes like two chips of ice. "And what are the rules by which this little match is to be governed?"

"Mr. Kilmorgan as our referee will cite the rules, so as to be fair," Jamie said unbuttoning his shirt in a leisurely manner.

"Alright," Dannyboy said uneasily, "are ye quite certain about this, Jamie?"

"Oh very certain," Jamie said.

"Well then we'll go with the basic rules, ye'll both be familiar with them." He picked up a stick and drew a square in the middle of the clearing. "Ye'll start here an' return to face one another after every fall. Ye've thirty seconds after each fall to return to the square, otherwise yer beat. No hittin' a man who's down an' that includes," he gave them both a sharp look, "bein' on yer knees an' no hittin' below the belt," Dannyboy took a deep breath, "To yer separate corners gentlemen."

Dannyboy followed Jamie to his own corner, a junction of two large boulders and said in a strained whisper, "Are ye daft? Have ye seen the man fight? He knocked Gilly unconscious."

"You wanted me to get off the fence," Jamie said coolly, "I'm getting off. If you don't like the manner I've chosen to do it in, don't watch."

Both men entered the staked out center a moment later, one white, one gold, both lean, Jamie the taller of the two.

"Jaysus, Mary an' Joseph," Dannyboy muttered, swiftly crossing himself, "help the lad get through this. Right then on the count of three gentlemen we'll commence. One," he said, his own battered hands curling instinctively into fists, "two," the two men took up their stance, fists held at face level, knees slightly bent, left shoulders canted inwards, "an' three," Dannyboy said on an explosive breath.

Lucien launched his attack immediately, coming out in a flurry of hard right jabs aimed directly at Jamie's head. Jamie parried them easily, with a forearm that was no more than a blur of up and down, inside, outside movement. Dannyboy was relieved to see that the boy had kept his form. Jamie had always been a graceful, quick fighter with lightning reflexes. However, Lucien was as quick and fast and Dannyboy had witnessed his devastating left hook in his fight with Gillybear.

Jamie's face, in the ripple and flicker of firelight, was impassive. He was taking the other man's measure and gauging his own stamina, while he made light annoying taps to the sides of Lucien's head.

Lucien, on the other hand, had pure, no-holds-barred, aggression in his corner. And was the possessor of a cunning Jamie just didn't have.

"You seem a little tense, Lord Kirkpatrick," Lucien said aiming a hard right into Jamie's solar plexus, "forget to take your dram of hemlock today, did you?"

Jamie parried the right effortlessly, "I do hope you found my medical records pleasant reading." And then sent a short and deadly jab into Lucien's chin, causing the Reverend's head to snap back sharply.

"Ready to fight now are you?" Lucien said, shaking his head a little and then dancing away. "Then let's fight," and so saying feinted with his right and brought his left around from the inside. It caught Jamie a glancing blow just below his temple and Dannyboy hissed sharply. Jamie didn't miss a beat, he danced away, buying a precious few seconds to clear his head and find his feet.

"Did you enjoy your time away?" Lucien asked amiably, bouncing lightly on the balls of his feet. "The accommodations were a little severe to be certain, but it was the best I could do on short notice."

"I'm not overfond," Jamie replied, "of rooms without windows," and shot a blow that landed with a *whomp* in the Reverend's midsection.

Dannyboy had to credit the man, he only buckled slightly, but when he came back there was a sheen of perspiration on his forehead and an annoyed light in his eyes that hadn't been there before.

"I should think, Lord Kirkpatrick, that a man with so many secrets to keep," Lucien's voice was slightly thicker than a moment before, "would be uneasy with too many windows."

"For you, my life is as an open book," Jamie said and caught a crunching straight right aimed at his head on his left shoulder, Lucien followed it with a left cobra strike to Jamie's face, splitting the skin above his right eye and effectively blinding Jamie on that side as blood poured out of the cut. He then pressed his advantage with a cascade of rights to Jamie's ribs. Jamie reeled slightly then danced back out of the reach of the Reverend's blows. Lucien had taken the offense and had the upper hand, Jamie on the defense was fighting at a disadvantage, too much of his energy would be consumed by fending off blows, rather than delivering them. Dannyboy felt slightly sick.

"Feeling unsteady, Lord Kirkpatrick?" Lucien asked breathing lightly through his mouth, "Perhaps it's because the air up here is so very thin."

"As I," Jamie said, wiping away a black stream of blood, "am the only one breathing it I don't seem to notice."

"Ah yes, that's right," Lucien said in a mocking sympathetic tone, "your paramour left you for that big Fenian lout, didn't she? Strange creatures, women, there's no accounting for their taste. You should have bedded her while you had the chance, it'd hardly have been a difficult task, her morals being what they are."

Jamie's response was a right hook that Lucien caught with his left wrist and countered with a right jab that whanged home into Jamie's jaw. Jamie wobbled slightly and shook his head as though dazed. Dannyboy felt as if his breath were stuck hard under his ribs.

"They tell me she didn't cry on the train," Lucien said with a thin smile, "that she asked for no quarter after they had begun. It made them treat her much worse, you know. But one has to admire such stoicism, doesn't one?"

Jamie, eyes shooting green fire through a sheet of blood, threw out a reeling punch that Lucien stepped neatly out of the line of before retorting with a breathtaking punch that slammed into Jamie's throat. Jamie buckled in two, gasping for air and Lucien took the opportunity to rabbit punch him hard in the kidneys and rain repeated blows about his face and head.

Dannyboy stepped in and pulled them apart. "That's an illegal blow an' ye know it," he said furiously, "ye agreed to fight fair, now back off, or I'll disqualify ye."

Lucien backed away with a creamy smile, breathing rapidly, pulse fluttering visibly in his neck. Dannyboy realized with a sickening lurch in his stomach that the man was excited, excited in such a way that only a woman should inspire in a man. He'd seen it before, fighters who were stimulated by pain, who enjoyed the bloodlust, who got an erotic thrill from another's agony. It had always disgusted him but even he had never seen it in quite the degree that shone from the Reverend's eyes and glowed in his whiter than white skin.

Dannyboy, keeping a wary eye out for Lucien, led Jamie back to his corner.

"What the hell do ye suppose ye are doin' out there?" he asked in an enraged whisper. "Yer givin' him every opportunity to pummel ye. The man intends to kill ye, are ye goin' to stand back an' let him do it?"

"I have," Jamie said in a slightly slurred drawl, "no such intentions at all."

"Lord above," Dannyboy exclaimed having got a whiff of Jamie's breath, "yer drunk. Ye must be mad," he huffed in exasperation, "I want no part of this. Do ye want the man to kill ye because it seems that ye must. I'm callin' this off now," he turned and began to walk into the scuffed circle but was stopped by a steely voice at his back.

"You'll do no such thing Dannyboy, this is my fight and it will be over when I deem it over."

"It'll be over when yer lyin' with half yer blood on the ground an' yerself well-prepared to go six feet under it," Dannyboy said angrily.

"Then so be it," Jamie said with a weary finality, "but regardless of what happens you're to let the fight go on, even if you think he's going to kill me."

"Jamie lad," Dannyboy began pleadingly but Jamie just shook his head and repeated stubbornly,

"It's my fight and I have to end it here and now regardless of the outcome." Dannyboy took in Jamie's bleeding face, a welter of bruises and crusting blood and looked up into the green eyes which seemed much more sharply focused than they had a few minutes previous.

"Aye, it's yer fight then," he said and stepped away reluctantly.

Lucien came out solid and refreshed, dancing again, Jamie lurched unsteadily from his own corner and the fight was on again.

After five minutes Dannyboy didn't think Lucien was trying to kill Jamie, he *knew* he was. Jamie was visibly exhausted, breathing heavily, gleaming with sweat, while Lucien, still high on adrenaline, thrashed him with blow after blow after blow until finally Jamie dropped to his knees and toppled over into the cold embrace of the ground.

Lucien, standing over him radiating a thrumming satisfaction, looked expectantly at Dannyboy.

"I believe, Mr. Kilmorgan," he said, voice thick with satisfaction, "it's customary to count at this time."

Dannyboy reluctantly began to count. The first ten beats passed without so much as a stir from Jamie's bloody form, another five and still nothing. He reached twenty before there was a small groan and Jamie's head came up, slowly and stiffly, but up. Five more counts and the boy was on his knees, rising out of the dirt in a superhuman effort that had him on his feet only a half-count before thirty. Looking at him, Dannyboy fervently wished he'd stayed down.

Jamie stumbled back to the center, sinking slightly, knees trembling visibly in an effort to keep him upright. His right eye was swollen shut and crusted tight with drying blood, his ribs densely bruised and a huge welt was rising out of his jaw. He was breathing heavily and Dannyboy, long experienced in such things, heard the sound of air being drawn through blood.

If Lucien had been a fair man with an ounce of compassion he'd have offered a draw, but it seemed that the Reverend was far from finished with Jamie. He smashed a right and left punch into Jamie's face, re-opening the partially sealed cut above his eye and mashing his knuckles into the other. Jamie stumbled backwards and managed, though just barely, to keep on his feet. He then lurched forward and fell into the Reverend's arms. Lucien held his swaying body and said in a low voice,

"The girl is alive because it suits me to have her so at present. It won't always suit me," he pushed Jamie away with a vicious thrust, causing him to fall backwards and crash into one of the large boulders, "but for now she's the only pawn of worth in our little game so it amuses me to keep her alive."

Jamie rolled over onto his knees and Lucien kneeled down beside him, his voice silky and intimate, "But when I do kill her I shall do it slowly and I shall watch her die. What the boys on that train did to her shall be nothing compared to the lessons she'll learn at my hand and then I shall tell you all about it, detail by painful detail." He stood, trodding upon one of Jamie's long, fine-boned fingers and turned his back on the man who knelt in the dust at his feet. It was his second mistake of the night; the first had been to forget what sort of mind he was dealing with. Dannyboy had forgotten as well.

From the dust he rose, fluid grace in firm place of the drunken stumbling of only seconds before. Through the bruises, the blood and the gore Dannyboy glimpsed something that looked very much like a murderous smile.

And realized with a sudden shock that the boy had meant for this to happen, he'd meant to take a beating that would almost kill him in order to wear his opponent out and then, then it would be his turn.

"Reverend," Jamie only uttered the one word, but it came with such chill and sober menace that Lucien whirled about at once.

Jamie stood just slightly away from the center of the improvised ring, flame throwing a hellish light over his bloodied form, a concentration in his eyes that seemed to still the atmosphere itself, as if the ground he stood upon were fixed solid in the universe while all else swirled about him. He lifted his chin slightly, easily, as a cat will scent the wind before moving in for the kill.

But Jamie did not move, he stood still, his gold bloody but undimmed. Like the mythical Peris, he seemed descended from fallen angels and cast forever out of Paradise. And he made, through sheer will, the Reverend come to him. Lucien came across the space quickly and Jamie held up his arms as if inviting him, demanding of him that he hit him.

Dannyboy held his breath wondering what the boy had planned and then saw it clearly. Jamie, a southpaw, had led with his right all night and saved his left for this moment.

He parried Lucien's blows easily with his right forearm and brought around his left in a crippling hook that hit the side of Lucien Broughton's head like the sound of a thousand trumpeting angels. Dannyboy grinned, he ought to have known better, the boy always saved something for the end.

Jamie did not just beat Lucien, he dissected him, took him apiece part by part, calmly, surely. He broke him down mentally and physically until the Reverend lay gasping in the dust, his head rising up slowly like a drowning man searching for a desperate breath. Dannyboy counted the seconds with joy, whooping when he came to thirty and the Reverend still lay on the ground, eyes glazed, uttering an occasional small sound, like that of a wounded rodent.

"Reverend," Jamie said, putting the point of his foot under the man's chin and forcing him to look up into his face, "I thought perhaps you'd like to know that at this moment eight crates of guns are being removed from a small island and they'll be dumped in the ocean, in an unknown location."

Lucien made a strangled noise, blood trickling in a steady line from the corner of his mouth. From far below came the sound of a vehicle stopping and voices speaking. Jamie leaned over, his voice like a razor blade running the length of the Reverend's spine, "And if you ever touch a hair on her head I'll see you in hell." He straightened, body slightly stiff, knuckles cut and running with blood.

"There are men coming for him," Jamie said to Dannyboy. "They'll take him away. Can you manage him for a few minutes?"

"Ye just try me boy," Dannyboy replied with relish and then in a softer tone he added, "don't drown out there; ye took a fair few hits to the head."

"How do you know where I'm going?" Jamie asked, a light smile on his lips.

"Because I know ye lad, an' if ye could go to the woman an' find yer comfort there ye would but ye can't, so ye'll go to yer other mistress an' let her do what she can to heal ye. Go on," Dannyboy nodded out towards the cliff where rock fell and bowed before the wrath of water, "let the sea do its work."

Jamie went, the sound of the waves crashing in his ears, the scent of it in his nose, swirling heavy in his veins. The path he took was an old one and his feet remembered every rock of it, every twist and turn and blade of grass.

He hit the water running, dove in and glided through the icy currents. He let it carry him for a ways after that, held sure in its embrace and felt the blood sluice off his skin as it returned from whence it had come.

Later, much later, he lay near the shore, head pillowed by kelp as the frothing fingers of the sea danced up and down his body, easing the ache, dousing the fires of pain.

Above him, the cauldron of night had tipped back taking its spill of clouds and leaving the heavens open in all their glory. In the east where all things begin, sat a small but steady star, nascent with beginnings, glowing with the gold, green and roses of the nebulae, fresh from the cradle of infant stars.

"Shall I name you?" Jamie asked the star, as saltwater lapped at his skin.

The star sparkled in reply.

Jamie laughed aloud and felt something within him stir and break free.

"I shall call you Hope," Jamie said to the star and the night and the sea and perhaps even to God.

Myth teaches us that when a star falls a soul dies but when a star comes new to the sky, as if God had opened his fist and rolled it gently into the heavens, it means a soul has been reborn.

Dearest Jamie,

I'm sitting here in your study and you, for once, it would seem, are asleep. Oblivious and safe upstairs. In two hours, we leave. Gone to Boston and, one hopes, a new life. Somewhere that Casey can manage to avoid a bullet for more than a month at a time.

I had planned to slip away without a word, but find here at the last, I cannot do that. For what you have been to me, I owe you more than that. I owe you the truth.

I came to you deliberately, put myself on your doorstep like an unwanted alien. I imagine you may know this already, but what you don't perhaps know is that I had help in placing me there.

My father, you knew him once and I can only guess what you may have observed or learned, was part of Clann na Gael, what was left of it in those years at least. It was an accepted part of my life and republicanism was in my blood. I am more similar to Pat and Casey than I can ever tell you. After my father was gone, an old friend of his approached me from the New York chapter. To make a long story short, I did occasional work for them. Young, pretty girls are asked a lot fewer questions at customs. I never asked what I couriered, never really cared. The cause was not necessarily mine but it was something I could do for my father, I know that makes no sense but when do the dealings of blood make any sense? I guessed a month or two into the game that I really had no idea who I was working for and suspect, if I was to find out, that I wouldn't like the answer very much.

I suppose you may have guessed the next part? I was placed as a spy in your home. They suspected you of dealings with the British government. I was to find a way into your life. You made it rather too simple for me and I, I repaid your generosity with betrayal. Though you never really left much of a trail for me to follow, did you? I wondered about that, did you know not to trust me?(The erotic Arabic poetry in rhyming quatrains was a nice touch; Herr Blumfeld is probably still blushing). You were right from the beginning, I lied, a set of obvious lies to smokescreen the more complicated ones. And it was complicated.

I didn't set out to harm you. That may be hard to believe but I didn't. Once I saw you again, I only wanted to save you from whatever demons you couldn't outrun. And now I'm saving you from myself.

I didn't always lie Jamie. That day last summer when I told you I'd give you everything, I meant it. It wouldn't have been hard, you've held my soul in your hands from the first moment I saw you. You opened your hands that day though and let me go. Know that some of me remains behind and always will.

Remember Maude for me, will you? I entrust my memories, the joy and the pain of them, to your safekeeping.

And so to business. I think the Duke was up to his eyeballs in bad dealings, I think it's why he's dead. I've got no proof to back that up but it's a feeling, female intuition if you will. As for Lucien Broughton, well, recent events have cast a strange light onto him. That night in the fire—well I still can't say with any certainty what exactly happened but when the constable attacked me there was someone standing over his shoulder in the flames. I was knocked unconscious and when I came to, as you know, was safe and sound on the doorstep of the Church. The face I saw in the flames was his, Jamie, an unlikely hero I know, but there you have it. Of course as we both know, guardian angels come in all sorts of shapes and guises. Don't they?

To end I leave you my talisman, the one you gave me so long ago, for love and luck you said and so I return it to you, hoping it will always give you these gifts in abundance.

May God go with you wherever the journey may lead.

Pamela.

Morning had come while he sat reading her letter and a chance ray of sun had stolen through the fog, entering the object he held in his hand in one smooth beam and leaving it in a hundred splintered rainbows. A blue crystal angel, given long ago and now returned to the giver.

Jamie stood, placed the tiny angel on top of a sheet of paper that held unfinished lines of verse and walked over to the study doors. He grasped the handles and turning them, pushed the doors slowly outward. A morning breeze, earthy with the scent of rotting leaves and woodsmoke, drifted and sighed about his senses. He bowed his head knowing he only imagined the greening scent that underlay it, the promise of spring, the beginning in the ending. Then raising his head, he opened his eyes to morning and to light.

About the Author

Cindy Brandner lives in the interior of British Columbia with her husband and three children, as well as a plethora of pets. She is currently working on the continuation of the Exit Unicorns series.

CPSIA information can be obtained at www.ICGtesting.com
Printed in the USA
BVOW02s1339020114

340719BV00004B/234/P